The Unholy Consult

Also by R. Scott Bakker

THE PRINCE OF NOTHING SERIES

The Darkness That Comes Before, Book One

The Warrior-Prophet, Book Two

The Thousandfold Thought, Book Three

THE ASPECT-EMPEROR SERIES

The Judging Eye, Book One

The White-Luck Warrior, Book Two

The Great Ordeal, Book Three

WRITING AS SCOTT BAKKER

Neuropath

Disciple of the Dog

THE UNHOLY CONSULT

THE ASPECT-EMPEROR
BOOK FOUR

R. SCOTT BAKKER

The Overlook Press
New York, NY

This edition first published in hardcover in the United States in 2017 by
The Overlook Press, Peter Mayer Publishers, Inc.
141 Wooster Street
New York, NY 10012
www.overlookpress.com
For bulk and special sales, please contact sales@overlookny.com
or write to us at the above address.

Cataloging-in-Publication Data is available from the Library of Congress

Type formatting by Bernard Schleifer
Manufactured in the United States of America
FIRST EDITION
1 3 5 7 9 8 6 4 2
ISBN 978-1-4683-1486-1

To Chris Lotts
For floating from the same string

Contents

Appendices

Fictional seduction,
On a black snow sky.
Sadness kills the superman,
Even fathers cry.

Black Sabbath, "Spiral Architect"

Have you ever in your life commanded the morning, And
caused the dawn to know its place, That it might take hold
of the ends of the earth, And the wicked be shaken out of it?

Job 38:12-3

What Has Come Before . . .

THE PRINCE OF NOTHING

Wars, as a rule, fall within the compass of history. They mark the pitch of competing powers, the end of some and the ascendancy of others, the ebb and flow of dominance across the ages. But there is a war that Men have waged for so long they have forgotten the languages they first used to describe it. A war that makes mere skirmishes out of the destruction of tribes and nations.

There is no name for this war; Men cannot reference what leaps the short interval of their comprehension. It began when they were little more than savages roaming the wilds, in an age before script or bronze. An Ark, vast and golden, toppled from the void, scorching the horizon, throwing up a ring of mountains with the violence of its descent. And from it crawled the dread and monstrous Inchoroi, a race who had come to seal the World against the Heavens, and so save the obscenities they called their souls.

The Nonmen held sway in those ancient days, a people that surpassed Men not only in beauty and intellect, but in wrath and jealousy as well. Their Ishroi heroes and Quya mages defended the World, fought titanic battles and stood vigilant during epochal truces. They endured the Inchoroi weapons of light, watched their enemy wilt before their own. They survived the treachery of the Aporetics, who provided the Inchoroi with thousands of sorcery-killing Chorae. They overcame the horrors their enemy crafted: the Sranc, the Bashrag, and most fearsome of all, the Wracu. But their avarice at last betrayed them. After centuries of war, they made peace with the invaders in return for ageless immortality—a gift that was in fact a fell weapon, the Plague of Wombs.

Thus it became a war between doomed species, the one beauteous, the other vile. In the end, the Nonmen hunted the Inchoroi to the brink of annihilation. Their surviving Quya mages sealed the Ark, which they had come to call Min-Uroikas, and hid it from the world with devious glamours.

Exhausted, bereft of hope or purpose, they retired to their underworld mansions to mourn the loss of their wives, their daughters, and the future of their once-glorious race.

As much as nature, history abhors vacuums. From the eastern mountains, the first tribes of Men began claiming the lands the Nonmen had abandoned—Men who had never known the yoke of slavery. Of the surviving Ishroi Kings, some fought, only to be dragged under by the tide of numbers, while others simply left their great gates unguarded, bared their necks to the licentious fury of a lesser race.

So began the Second Age, the Age of Men. Perhaps the Nameless War would have ended with the fading of its principals, but the Ark itself remained intact, and Men ever lusted for knowledge. Centuries passed, and the mantle of human civilization crept along the great river basins of Eärwa and outward, bringing bronze where there had been flint, cloth where there had been skins, and writing where there had been recital. Great cities rose to teeming life. The wilds gave way to cultivated horizons.

Nowhere were Men more bold in their works, or more overweening in their pride, than in the North, where commerce with the Nonmen had allowed them to outstrip their more swarthy cousins to the South. In the legendary city of Sauglish, those who could discern the joints of existence founded the first sorcerous Schools. As their learning and power waxed, a reckless few turned to the rumours they had heard whispered by their Nonman teachers—rumours of the great golden Ark. The wise were quick to see the peril, and the Schoolmen of Mangaecca, who coveted secrets above all else, were censured, and finally outlawed.

But it was too late. Min-Uroikas was found—occupied.

The fools discovered and awakened the last two surviving Inchoroi, Aurax and Aurang, who had concealed themselves in the labyrinthine recesses of the Ark. At their hoary knees the outlaw Schoolmen learned that damnation, the burden that all sorcerers bore, need not be inevitable. They learned that the world could be shut against the judgment of Heaven. So they forged a common purpose with the twin abominations, a Consult, and bent their cunning to the aborted designs of the Inchoroi.

The Mangaecca relearned the principles of the material—the Tekne. They mastered the manipulations of the flesh. And after generations of study and searching, after filling the pits of Min-Uroikas with innumerable corpses, they realized the most catastrophic of the Inchoroi's untold depravities: Mog-Pharau, the No-God.

They made themselves slaves to better destroy the world.

And so the Nameless War raged anew. What has come to be called the First Apocalypse destroyed the great Norsirai nations of the North, laying ruin to the greatest glories of Men. But for Seswatha, the Grandmaster of the Gnostic School of Sohonc, the entire world would have been lost. At his urging, Anasûrimbor Celmomas, the High King of the North's mightiest nation, Kûniüri, called on his tributaries and allies to join him in a holy war against Min-Uroikas, which Men now called Golgotterath. But his Ordeal foundered, and the might of the Norsirai perished. Seswatha fled south to the Ketyai nations of the Three Seas, bearing the greatest of the legendary Inchoroi weapons, the Heron Spear. With Anaxophus, the High King of Kyraneas, he met the No-God on the Plains of Mengedda, and by dint of valor and providence, overcame the dread Whirlwind.

The No-God was dead, but his slaves and his stronghold remained. Golgotterath had not fallen, and the Consult, blasted by ages of unnatural life, continued to plot salvation.

The years passed, centuries became millennia, and the Men of the Three Seas forgot the horrors endured by their fathers. Empires rose and empires fell. The Latter Prophet, Inri Sejenus, reinterpreted the Tusk, and over the course of centuries the faith of Inrithism—organized and administered by the Thousand Temples and its spiritual leader, the Shriah—came to dominate the entire Three Seas. The great Anagogic Schools arose in response to the Inrithi persecution of sorcery. Using Chorae, the Inrithi warred against them, attempting to silence their blasphemies.

Then Fane, the upstart Prophet of the so-called Solitary God, united the Kianene, the desert peoples of the Great Carathay, and declared war against the Tusk and the Thousand Temples. After centuries of jihad, the Fanim and their eyeless sorcerer-priests, the Cishaurim, conquered nearly all the western Three Seas, including the holy city of Shimeh, the birthplace of Inri Sejenus. Only the moribund remnants of the Nansur Empire continued to resist them.

War and strife ruled the South. The two great faiths of Inrithism and Fanimry skirmished, though trade and pilgrimage were tolerated when commercially convenient. The great families and nations vied for military and mercantile dominance. The minor and major Schools squabbled and plotted. And the Thousand Temples pursued earthly ambitions under the leadership of corrupt and ineffectual Shriahs.

The First Apocalypse had become little more than legend by this time. The Consult and the No-God had dwindled into myth, something old wives tell small children. After two thousand years, only the Schoolmen of the Mandate, who relived the Apocalypse each night through the eyes of Seswatha, could recall the horror of Mog-Pharau. Though the mighty and the learned considered them fools, the Mandate's possession of the sorcery of the Ancient North, the Gnosis, commanded respect and mortal envy. Driven by nightmares, they wandered the labyrinths of power, scouring the Three Seas for signs of their ancient and implacable foe: the Consult.

And as always, they found nothing. Some argued that the Consult had finally succumbed to the toll of ages. Others, that they had turned inward, seeking less arduous means to forestall their damnation. But since the Sranc had multiplied across the northern wilds, no expedition could be sent to Golgotterath to settle the matter. The Mandate alone knew of the Nameless War. They alone stood guard, but they were both blind and a laughingstock.

Thus was the World when Maithanet was elected Shriah of the Thousand Temples and called the First Holy War, a great expedition to wrest Holy Shimeh from the Fanim. Word of his challenge spread across the Three Seas and beyond. Faithful from all the great Inrithi nations—Galeoth, Thunyerus, Ce Tydonn, Conriya, High Ainon and their tributaries—travelled to the city of Momemn, the capital of the Nansurium, to commend their strength and treasure to Inri Sejenus. To become Men of the Tusk.

Internal feuds plagued the First Holy War from the outset, for there was no shortage of those who would bend the campaign to their selfish ends. The Inrithi host marched victorious nonetheless, winning two great victories over the heretic Fanim at Mengedda and Anwurat. Only with the Second Siege of Caraskand and the Circumfixion of one of their own would the Men of the Tusk find common purpose. Only when they discovered a living prophet in their midst—a man who could see into the hearts of Men. A man like a god.

Anasûrimbor Kellhus.

Far to the north, in the very shadow of Golgotterath, a group of ascetics called the Dûnyain had concealed themselves in Ishuäl, the secret redoubt of the Kûniüric High Kings ere their destruction in the First Apocalypse. For two thousand years the Dûnyain had pursued their sacred study, breeding for reflex and intellect, training in the ways of limb, thought, and face—all for the sake of reason, the Logos. They had dedicated their entire existence to mastering the irrationalities of history, custom, and passion—all those things that determine human thought. In this way, they believed, they would eventually grasp what they called the Absolute, and so become true self-moving souls.

Some thirty years previous, Kellhus's father, Anasûrimbor Moënghus, had fled Ishuäl. His reappearance in the dreams of the brethren fairly upended the order, given the Dûnyain repudiation of sorcery. Knowing only that Moënghus dwelt in a distant city called Shimeh, the elders dispatched Kellhus on an arduous journey through lands long abandoned by Men—to kill his apostate father.

But Moënghus knew the world in ways his cloistered brethren could not. He knew well the revelations that awaited his son, for they had been his revelations thirty years previous. He knew that Kellhus would discover sorcery, whose existence the forefathers of the Dûnyain had suppressed. He knew that given his abilities, Men would be little more than children to him, that Kellhus would see their thoughts in the nuances of their expression, and that with mere words he would be able to exact any devotion, any sacrifice. He knew, moreover, that eventually Kellhus would encounter the Consult, who hid behind faces that only Dûnyain eyes could see—that he would come to see what Men with their blinkered souls could not: the Nameless War.

The Consult had not been idle. For centuries they had eluded their old foe, the School of Mandate, using doppelgängers—spies who could take on any face, any voice, without resorting to sorcery and its telltale Mark. By capturing and torturing these abominations, Moënghus learned that the Consult had not abandoned their ancient plot to shut the world against Heaven, that within a score of years they would be able to resurrect the No-God and bring about a new war against Men, a Second Apocalypse. For years Moënghus walked the innumerable paths of the Probability Trance, plotting future after future, searching for the thread of act and consequence that would save the world. For years he crafted his Thousandfold Thought.

Moënghus had prepared the way for his Dûnyain-born son, Kellhus. He sent out his world-born son, Maithanet, to seize the Thousand Temples from within, so that he might craft the First Holy War, the weapon Kellhus would need to seize absolute power, and so unite the Three Seas against the doom that was their future. What he did not know, could not know, was that Kell-hus would see further than him, think beyond his Thousandfold Thought ...

That he would go mad.

Little more than an impoverished wayfarer when he first joined the Holy War, Kellhus used his bearing, intellect, and insight to convince ever more Men of the Tusk that he was the Warrior-Prophet, come to save mankind. He understood that Men would render anything to him, so long as they believed he could save their souls. He also befriended the Schoolman the Mandate had dispatched to observe the Holy War, Drusas Achamian, knowing that the Gnosis, the sorcery of the Ancient North, would provide him with inestimable power. And he seduced Achamian's lover, Esmenet, knowing that her intellect made her the ideal vessel for his seed—for sons strong enough to bear the onerous burden of Dûnyain blood.

By the time the battle-hardened remnants of the First Holy War laid siege to Shimeh, Kellhus had achieved absolute authority. The Men of the Tusk had become his Zaudunyani, his Tribe of Truth. While the Holy War assailed the city's walls, he confronted his father, Moënghus, mortally wounding him, explaining that only his death could realize the Thousandfold Thought. Days later Anasûrimbor Kellhus was proclaimed Holy Aspect-Emperor—the first in a millennium—by none other than the Shriah of the Thousand Temples, his half-brother, Maithanet. Even the School of Mandate, who saw his coming as the fulfillment of their most hallowed prophecies, knelt and kissed his knee.

But Kellhus had made a mistake. Before reaching the Three Seas and the Holy War, his passage across Eärwa had delivered him to the lands of the Utemot, a Scylvendi tribe renowned for warlike cruelty. Here he had struck a murderous compact with the tribe's chieftain, Cnaiür urs Skiötha. Moënghus had also fallen into the hands of the Utemot some thirty years prior, and had used the then adolescent Cnaiür to murder his chieftain father and effect his escape. The youth had spent tormented decades pondering what had happened and had come to guess the inhuman truth of the Dûnyain. So it was that Cnaiür and Cnaiür alone knew the dark secret of Anasûrimbor Kellhus. Before his disappearance, the barbarian revealed these truths to none other than Drusas Achamian, who had long harboured heartbreaking suspicions of his own. At the coronation, before the eyes of the entire Holy War, Achamian repudiated Kellhus, whom he had worshipped; Esmenet, whom he had loved; and the Mandate masters he had served. Then he fled into the wilderness, becoming the world's only sorcerer without a school. A Wizard.

Now, after twenty years of war, conversion, and butchery, Anasûrimbor Kellhus prepares to realize the ultimate stage of his father's Thousandfold Thought. His New Empire spans the entirety of the Three Seas, from the legendary fortress of Auvangshei on the frontiers of Zeum to the shrouded headwaters of the River Sayut, from the sweltering coasts of Kutnarmu to the wild rim of the Osthwai Mountains—all the lands that had once been Fanim or Inrithi. It was easily the equal of the old Ceneian Empire in terms of geographical extent, and far more populous. A hundred great cities, and almost as many languages. A dozen proud nations. Thousands of years of mangled history.

And the Nameless War is nameless no longer. Men call it the Great Ordeal.

THE ASPECT-EMPEROR

In the Year-of-the-Tusk, 4132, the Second Holy War crosses the Imperial frontier and besieges Sakarpus, the ancient vault of the Chorae Hoard. In twenty years, Anasûrimbor Kellhus has rebalanced the whole of the Three Seas upon the axis of his Great Ordeal, bent the labour of millions to forge this, the earthly spearhead of the Thousandfold Thought. History has never seen such a host, more than 300,000 souls drawn from the far-flung reaches of the New Empire. The finest warriors of every nation comprise it, led by their Kings and Princes and Heroes. All the Major Schools accompany it, the greatest mustering of sorcerous might ever witnessed.

Sakarpus falls and Sorweel, the grieving son of the slain King Harweel, becomes a hostage of the Holy Aspect-Emperor. But he is nowhere near so helpless as he believes. To play Prophet is to risk the wrath of the Gods: Yatwer herself, the Dread Mother of Birth, has taken umbrage with Anasûrimbor Kellhus, loosing the White-Luck upon him, the vengeance of the oppressed against the oppressor. And Sorweel discovers himself central to her design. A priest posing as a slave rubs Her spit into his cheeks, shielding him from the all-seeing Anasûrimbor, convincing Kellhus and his children, Serwa and Kayûtas, that Sorweel stands among the Empire's most ardent Believer-Kings. She also provides a murder weapon: a pouch that conceals sorcery-killing Chorae from sorcerous eyes.

But the youth is conflicted, for evidence of the Aspect-Emperor's cause encircles him, and he finds himself torn between the demands of Heaven and the testimony of his heart. The Goddess compels him. His father's blood demands vengeance. Even his friend, Zsoronga, Prince of Zeum, counsels murder. And still he cannot but ask why ... If the Unholy Consult were simply a fiction, why forge something so stupendous as the Great Ordeal?

Nonmen emissaries intercept the Host in transit, offering an alliance in return for three hostages. The Aspect-Emperor promptly sends Sorweel along with his daughter, Serwa, and his adoptive son, Moënghus—not realizing that Nil'giccas, the Nonman King, has fled the Mountain, and that Ishterebinth has fallen to the Consult.

The three youths are seized and interrogated upon their arrival, but when the Nonmen discover that Sorweel has been doomed to destroy the Aspect-Emperor, they release him to Oinaral Lastborn, who seeks to save his Mansion. At long last, the youth learns the wicked truth of Golgotterath, not simply from Oinaral, but from the Amiolas, a sorcerous artifact that allows Men to understand Nonman language via the trapped soul of Immiriccas. The youth need only remember the losses suffered by the long-dead Ishroi to understand the depravity of the Aspect-Emperor's foe, and therefore the righteousness of his cause, the Great Ordeal.

At long last he embraces the faith of his Enemy. With Oinaral, he embarks on a quest to the very bowel of the Weeping Mountain to find the Lastborn's hero father, Oirunas, intent on overthrowing Nin'ciljiras, the Consult pretender to Nil'giccas's throne.

The Great Ordeal, meanwhile, continues crawling north toward the ever-withdrawing, ever-growing Sranc Horde. The desolation of the Istyuli gradually gives way to the knuckled landscape of ancient Sheneor, and the Ordealmen rejoice for finally reaching the outskirts of scripture. But if the Ordealmen find their conviction renewed, their Exalt-General, Proyas, finds his faith in his Aspect-Emperor challenged as it has never been challenged before—and by Kellhus himself, no less.

Supplies become ever more tentative, and the Sranc grow ever more desperate, ever more bold. Disaster strikes the westernmost contingent of the Host at Irsûlor, and the Great Ordeal loses a full quarter of their contingent, as well as the Vokalati, a Major School. At Swaranûl, the Holy Aspect-Emperor reveals the catastrophic truth: they have scarce travelled halfway and already they were out of food. Henceforth, he informs his astounded followers, the Men of the Circumfix will subsist upon their raving foe.

And so the Host of Hosts advances across the eastern shoulder of the Misty Sea, the Horde a roiling, retreating tide before them. The Ordealmen gorge upon their foe, feast about fires of Sranc carcasses. A darkness grows within them, consuming more and more of what comes before. Kellhus reveals the truth to Proyas in stages, first dismantling his certitude, then his faith, and finally, so it seems, his dignity and his heart.

At the derelict fortress of Dagliash, the Horde is cornered, and the might of the Great Ordeal is unleashed whole. But within the fortress itself, a Tekne artifact detonates and the very earth is Scalded. Thousands die, among them Saubon, who finds himself cast into the Hells.

Gazing upon the foul toadstool of smoke boiling above them, Kellhus tells Proyas that he must leave, that it is up to him to deliver the Great Ordeal to Golgotterath alone.

On the wild fringe of the Three Seas, meanwhile, Drusas Achamian has spent twenty years exploring his Dreams of the First Apocalypse. If he can find Ishuäl, he believes, he can answer the question that burns so bright in so many learned souls ...

Who is the Aspect-Emperor?

Anasûrimbor Mimara, the step-daughter of his foe, arrives demanding he teach her sorcery. Her resemblance to her mother, Esmenet—who has become Empress of the Three Seas—returns the old Wizard to all the pains he sought to escape. Desperate to win his tutelage, Mimara seduces him.

This event casts a shadow over all that ensues, for not only does Mimara become quick with child, the Judging Eye—the ability to see the goodness and evil of things—fully awakens within her. Only in the shameful aftermath does she tell the old Wizard that Kellhus has already embarked on his quest to destroy the Consult and so save the world from a Second Apocalypse.

The old Wizard does not know where Ishuäl is, but thanks to his dreams, he knows the whereabouts of a map marking its location: in the famed Library of Sauglish, deep in the northern wilds. He contracts a company of Scalpers, hard men who make their living selling Sranc scalps to their Holy Aspect-Emperor, to accompany him on the quest: the Skin-eaters, renowned as much for their ruthless Captain, Lord Kosoter, as for his sorcerous companion, a Nonman Erratic known as Cleric. The outcast expedition sets out for the

Library of Sauglish, fraught with grudge and rivalry from the beginning. The Judging Eye turns their trek into a march of the damned for Mimara, simply because not a soul among the company is saved—apart from her own. They pass through the ruined Nonman mansion of Cil-Aujas, and would have died there, were it not for Mimara and her cryptic use of her Chorae.

The journey across the Sranc-infested North harrows both the old Wizard and the Princess-Imperial alike, for they have come to increasingly depend on the Nonman, Cleric, and his dispensations of Qirri, the soul-quickening ashes of the legendary Cû'jara Cinmoi. After months of toiling, the expedition arrives at Sauglish maddened for both the drug and the deprivations it has enabled them to endure. Cleric is revealed as Nil'giccas, the Last Nonman King, bent on finding memory in betrayal and tragedy. The Skin-Eaters turn upon one another, and all are destroyed save Achamian and Mimara.

Together, they find the ancient map described in Achamian's dreams, the map to Ishuäl—the hidden stronghold of the Dûnyain, the birthplace of the Holy Aspect-Emperor. They gather the ashes of Nil'giccas to replenish their supply of Qirri, then set out on the final leg of their journey. They persevere, gain the Demua Mountains, and surmount the glacier overlooking the vale of the Dûnyain. At long last, they see it, Ishuäl ... ruined.

Beneath the toppled walls, they wander through the blasted galleries of the Thousand-Thousand Halls, across floors gravelled with the bones of Sranc. In the room of the Whale-mothers, the Judging-Eye opens and Mimara sees the dizzying evil of the Dûnyain. But does this mean Kellhus is evil? They realize their quest is not over until Mimara apprehends Kellhus with the Judging Eye.

They also find two survivors, the son and grandson of Kellhus himself, the former scarred beyond recognition. Mere days into their journey, he kills himself upon imbibing the Qirri, seeking the Absolute in annihilation. They glimpse the Scalding of Dagliash over the horizon, wonder at the pillar of ash. As they cross out of the mountains hying north, they are seized by Scylvendi outriders, and find themselves dragged before the insane regard of Cnaiür urs Skiötha, the King-of-Tribes ...

The People of War shadow the Great Ordeal.

Far to the south in Momemn, the capital of the New Empire, Esmenet struggles to rule in her husband's absence. With Kellhus and the bulk of his armed might faraway, the embers of insurrection have begun to ignite across the Three Seas. The Imperial Court regards her with condescension. Fanayal ab Kascamandri, the Padirajah of what had been the heathen Kianene Empire before the First Holy War, grows ever more bold on the fringes of the Great Carathay Desert. Psatma Nannaferi, the outlawed Mother-Supreme of the Cult of Yatwer, prophecies the coming of the White-Luck Warrior, the godsent assassin who will murder the Aspect-Emperor and his progeny. Even the Gods, it seems, plot against the Anasûrimbor Dynasty. Esmenet turns to her brother-in-law, Maithanet, the Shriah of the Thousand Temples, for his strength and clarity of vision, yet she wonders why her husband would leave the Mantle in her incapable hands, when his brother is Dûnyain like himself.

Even as the first rumours of this sedition reach his mother in Momemn, young Kelmomas continues his own devious insurrection. Where before he had driven Mimara away, now he engineers the death of his idiot twin, Samarmas, knowing that grief will make his mother even more desperate for his love. He secretly murders Sharacinth, High Priestess of the Yatwerians, an act that incites riots across the Three Seas. When he fears that his uncle, Maithanet, is beginning to suspect his double-game, he plots with his mad older brother, Inrilatas, to murder him as well, but the attempt goes awry, and Maithanet ends up killing Inrilatas instead.

War breaks out between Empress and Shriah. Grief-stricken and paranoid, Esmenet contracts a Narindar, a priest of the Four-Horned Brother, to murder her brother-in-law, not knowing that she parlays with the White-Luck Warrior. But Maithanet strikes first, storming and seizing the Andiamine Heights during her absence, and so Esmenet finds herself a fugitive in the very Empire she ruled, trapped with Naree, a prostitute living much as she had before marrying Kellhus and mothering his inhuman progeny. When she is finally captured and dragged in chains before Maithanet, he looks into her soul and sees the truth of the conflict between them. But before he can name Kelmomas, the White-Luck Warrior strikes him from the one place overlooked. As the sole remaining connection to her husband, she finds herself acclaimed as Holy Empress once again, even as Fanayal and his bandit army besiege the walls about Momemn.

She hastens to organize the city, showing the will her ailing subjects so desperately need to see. She invites the White-Luck Warrior, whom she still thinks is a mere Cultic assassin, to live with her and her surviving family in the Andiamine Heights. As much as his mother's newfound strength dismays him, Kelmomas is more fascinated by the White-Luck Warrior, whom he sees as proof that Ajokli, the evil Four-Horned Brother, has chosen to be his protector. This conviction is confirmed when he watches the man bring about the death of his sister Theliopa—for she, after Maithanet, had been his greatest threat. But this triumph is instantly transformed into disaster when his mother, wild with grief, spies him *celebrating* his sister's death.

A powerful earthquake strikes Momemn, laying low her walls and exposing her inhabitants to the desert fury of Fanayal and his Kianene. Psatma Nannaferi mocks the Padirajah as he readies himself for the assault, watched by an apprehensive Malowebi, the Emissary of the Zeumi Satakhan. Though the Mother-Supreme is Fanayal's captive, the Goddess Yatwer has assured her mastery of the man. Without warning, *Kellhus steps into their midst*, killing both Fanayal and the Mother-Supreme. He overpowers Malowebi and *severs his head*, which he transforms into one of the Decapitants bound to his hip.

Aftershocks hammer the Imperial Capital. Kelmomas follows the White-Luck Warrior through the collapsing palace into the throne room, still thinking him a servant of Ajokli. But when he glimpses his *father* standing with his mother upon the dais, he realizes that the assassin hunts no less than the Aspect-Emperor—and at his mother's behest. The little boy gains the assassin's attention, hoping to assist, but the man gazes at him as though dumbstruck, as if a completely different soul has awakened behind his once implacable eyes.

The ceilings give way, and the boy learns that what is ruined can become more ruined still.

CHAPTER ONE

The Western Three Seas

There's a rumour they say,
that lures our husbands away,
from field and pillow,
and babe and willow,
to the Ark, to the Ark, to the Ark,
to the dark, to the dark, to the dark,
to the Idol more fearsome than its God.
—ancient Kûniüric Harvest Song

Mid-Autumn, 20 New Imperial Year (4132, Year-of-the-Tusk), Momemn.

His father sang into the tumbling world—a Metagnostic Cant of Translocation, Kelmomas realized. Sorcery scooped him whole, then cast him as
grains across the face of nowhere. Light lanced through the sound of clacking thunder. Crashing, crushing darkness became the miracle of sky.

The Prince Imperial curled about convulsions. His ears roared for misery
and cacophony both, but he could still hear his mother keen. Grit scored
his cheek. Vomit clotted his hair. His fabled home shrugged and fissured
in the distance, collapse dragging down collapse, all the taken-for-granted
spaces clamped into ruin, the *Andiamine Heights* vanishing into mountainous, ashen billow. He spit and heaved, wondered that he had stood *within*
those stone shells but heartbeats before ...

Watching Ajokli murder his father.

How? How could this be happening? Theliopa was *dead*—was that not proof of the Four-Horned Brother's will? Kelmomas *had seen him*, concealed in the cracks where no eyes strayed, preparing to strike his father the way he had struck his uncle—to murder the last soul that could sound him, threaten him. *Mother would have been his*! At long last, truly, utterly his! *His*!

Not fair. *Not* fair.

Maithanet dead. Theliopa dead—her bitch skull hammered into a sack! And then when it came to his father—*the only one that mattered*—the Narindar had crashed from the Unerring Grace—and after glimpsing *him* no less! That was the mockery, wasn't it? The Godspit, as the Shigeki slaves called it! Or like dramas written by slaves, where the heroes always perish by their own hand. But why? *Why*? Why would the Four Horned Brother give such a gift only to take everything away?

Cheat! *Deceiver*! He had committed everything! Gambled his very—

We're dead! his inner brother wailed, for *he* towered above them both, their *father*, Anasûrimbor Kellhus, the Holy Aspect-Emperor. *Abase yourself*! Samarmas demanded. *Grovel*! But all Kelmomas could do was cramp about his nausea, expel the honeyed pork and onion he had last eaten. He glimpsed his mother kneeling on the far side of his father, gagging on her own misery.

They stood upon one of Momemn's walls, near the Girgallic Gate. The city smoked below, levelled in places, reduced to shattered shells in others. Only ancient Xothei stood untouched, rising through the haze of ruin, a monumental miracle in fields of raked charcoal. Thousands streamed about, over and between the wreckage, crawling like bugs over their losses. Thousands wailed.

"Momas is not finished," the Holy Aspect-Emperor called over the roar. "The Sea comes."

The eye balked at the sight, the Meneanor rising such that the city *whole* seemed to drop down. The River Phayus *swelled* along its length, drowning first the piers and then the banks, pulsing monstrous through the canals, slipping black and shining into the alleyways and streets, clotting into muck with accumulated wreckage, engulfing bug after racing bug ...

His nausea subsided in the wake of his wonder.

The boy glanced to his mother, who looked only to the calamity that was his father, her face raised in anguish, cheeks silver beneath black-smeared eyes. It was an image the little Prince-Imperial had seen many times before, either hewn from panels of wood or stone, or daubed in paint across plaster walls, the *desolate mother*, the soul who had given only to be ransacked. And there was joy even here, he realized. There was beauty.

Some losses could not be fathomed.

"*The-Thel-Thel—*" she stuttered, clenching bumbling hands together.

Thousands drowned below them, mother and sons pinned beneath the ruin, gagging, jerking, drowning. The water climbed the stages of the massive city, making a great sty of its lower environs. The Sea even broke across the eastern walls, rendering the heap that had been the Andiamine Heights an island.

"*She's dead!*" his mother barked, her eyes pinched in anguish. She shook like something ancient and palsied, even as the violence of her grief made her seem young.

The little boy watched from across his father's booted stance, possessed of a terror greater than any he had ever known. He watched her eyes pop open, fasten upon *him* in lunatic fury, pin him as certainly as a shipwright's nail. The lips thinned into a venomous line.

"*You.*"

His father gathered her in the crook of his right arm, then hoisted Kelmomas by the scruff, bundled him under his left. Language summoned light, and *reality* was passed from tongue to lip—and the little boy was pitched once again, cast headlong into pricking grasses. His gut balled his limbs into a wretched fist. He glimpsed Momemn even farther away, wrecked heights smoking.

His mother wept, shrieked, lamentations that continued leap after wrenching leap.

———— ❦ ————

That night, he stared at the two of them through skeins of grass, Mother obscuring the firelight, rocking and keening as sorrow after incredulous sorrow kicked through her slight frame, Father sitting as an idol full in the twining flame, his hair and plaited beard striate with pulsing gold, his eyes flashing like blind jewels. Though Kelmomas lay with his ears pricked to their merest breath, he found he could not follow what was said, as if his soul had wandered too far from his ears to hear what had been heard.

"*Y-you came back ...*"

"*For yo—*"

"*For your Empire!*" she barked.

Why did he still live? Why would they cling to him so, even when they understood the necessity of his destruction? What did it mean, parenthood, bags of meat birthing meat? He was the prodigal Viper the priests prattled about in Temple—Ku'kumammu, from the Tusk! The accursed Babe-with-teeth!

"*The Empire has served its purpose. Only the Great Ordeal matters now.*"

"No ... No!"

"*Yes, Esmi. I returned for you.*"

Why not murder him! Or drive him away!

"And ... and ... Kelmomas ..."

What source cares for its consequence? What sane soul weighs doom on the scales of love?

"*He is the same as Inrilatas.*"

"*But* Maithanet *murdered him!*"

"*Only to save himself from our sons.*"

"But Kel ... K-Kel ... he ... he ..."

"*Even I was fooled, Esmi.* No one *could have known.*"

Her head hunched into the line of her shoulders, which bounced to the rhythm of her sobbing. His father watched, impassive and golden. And it seemed to the youngest Prince-Imperial that he was truly dead, that he had been cast from a cloud or a star to land upon this very spot, where he adhered shattered. A patch of warmth was all that remained of him. Dwindling warmth.

"*He murdered all of them,*" Father was saying. "*Samarmas and Sharacinth by his own hand. Inrilatas through Maithanet, and Maithanet through ...*"

"*Through* me? Me?"

"Yes."

"No!" she screeched. "*Noooo! Not him! Not* him!" She swiped at her husband's face, fingers drawn into claws. Blood welled across his cheek, spilled into his flaxen beard. "You!" she raged, her eyes wide with horror at what she had done—at what he had permitted her to do. "*You're the monster! The accursed deceiver! Akka saw it! Akka knew all along!*"

The Holy Aspect-Emperor closed his eyes then opened them.

"*You're right, Esmi. I am a monster ... The monster this World needs. Our son*—"

"*Shut up! Shut up!*"

"*Our son is a different kind of abomination.*"

And his mother's wail rose as something high and lilting against the silence of the night. Something beloved. Something true to the honed edge of hope.

The little boy lay broken, watching, breathing.

Willing his mother to break.

Exhaustion claimed Mother first, leaving only his father sitting upright before the dwindling flame. Anasûrimbor Kellhus, Holy Aspect-Emperor of the Three Seas. He had carried them bodily across more than a dozen horizons since Momemn, two sacks, each bearing their portion of terror, fury, and grief. Now he sat cross-legged, his silk gown taut between his knees, bloodstains mapping random islands and continents. The fire made shining hooks of the creases about his shoulders and elbows. One of the Decapitants lay akimbo across the other, so that its black-paper scrutiny repeated the implacable regard of his father, who stared directly at *him*, knowing full well the boy only pretended to sleep.

"You lay defeated," his father said, his voice neither tender nor harsh, "not because you are defeated, but because victory consists in appearing so when necessity demands. You feign a paralysis you think commensurate with your age and the disaster you have suffered ..."

He's going to kill us! Flee!

The little boy lay as immobile as he had when spying upon the Narindar. Everything was as eggshells in the callused grip of Anasûrimbor Kellhus, be it cities or souls or lastborn sons. One need not fathom his designs to understand the mortal consequences of obstructing them.

"There is no flight from one such as me," his Father said. Twin conflagrations glittered from his eyes, reflecting the fury that should have shook his voice.

"Are you going kill me?" Kelmomas finally asked. He could speak anything here, he understood, so long as it was to the point.

"No."

He lies! Lies!

"Why?" Kelmomas croaked, a burning about his lips and eyes. "Why spare me?"

"Because it would kill your mother."

Theliopa's answer—and mistake.

"Mother wants me dead."

The Aspect-Emperor shook his head. "*I* want you dead. Your mother ... she wants me dead. I'm the one she blames for what you have done."

See! See! I told you!

"Because she knows I truly lov—!"

"No," his father said, swatting aside his son's voice without any perceptible increase in volume or intensity. "She sees the surface of you, merely, and confuses this for love and innocence."

Rage flexed the Prince-Imperial bodily, hoisted him upright.

"I *do* love her! I do! *I do!*"

His father did not so much as blink at the display.

"Some souls are broken in such a way as to think themselves whole," he said. "The more they are flawed, the more they presume their own perfection."

"And I'm so broken?"

Though he had not so much as moved, his father had come to seem something titanic, a leviathan coiled into the limbs and heart of a mortal man.

"You are the most flawed of my children."

The boy trembled for suppressing his scream.

"So what will you do with me?" he finally managed to ask.

"As your mother wishes."

The boy's eyes darted to the Empress curled in the grasses to the left of his father, pathetic for the delicacy of her finery ... Why? Why would a man such as his father pin his life to such a feeble soul?

"Should I be afraid?"

The fire sputtered, becoming scarce more than a pile of golden coals. The featureless tracts of the Cepalor gained colourless substance, scarcely more than the corpse of a world beneath the Nail-of-Heaven.

"Fear," his dread father said, "has never been among the things you control."

Kelmomas lowered himself back to the prick and weave of prairie grasses, his thoughts a clamour, his accursed brother shrieking within, demanding he slip away in the deep of night, live among more bestial, more trustworthy things, an animal among animals, free from the sublime terror of his father, the idiot tyranny of his mother.

Flee! Run-run-run away!

But the Holy Aspect-Emperor watched over all, a gaze that paced horizons, *worlds*. The numbness eclipsed any the eight-year-old had ever experienced, until he seemed as inert as the chill earth beneath, little more than another mound of clay.

Afterward he would recognize it as despair.

Each leap had delivered them to a more tousled world, from skin-smooth plains to gnarled foothills to rutted mountains. Father deposited them beneath a mountain that, from a distance, had appeared bent about a broken arm, bones jutting from voluminous gowns of granite. The extent of the overhang only became visible after the Cant delivered them into its shadow. It no longer resembled anything in the mossy gloom; it merely loomed, vast heights hanging out and *over*—shelter from the rain gowning the foothills, as well as a source of nagging worry. One could raise a hundred ziggurats from the bulbous stone affixed above, a *thousand*. Kelmomas could feel the torsions emanating from the concavity, it seemed, the elemental need to slough and plummet, to fall as a million hammers.

No ground could hang such for long.

Father muttered for a time to his mother, explaining the need to secure provisions and clothes as quickly as possible. The boy watched with fascination, then dismay, as he unbound the Decapitants from his waist and set them upon an oyster-shaped stone. He curled the hair of each into a black nest then laid the desiccated things like sentinels surveying different directions. Mother peppered him with demands as he did so, insisting they go to Sumna to take command of the forces she had mustered there. She did not realize they raced *for* the Great Ordeal far more than they fled from the Empire. Rescuing them had come at a cost, the boy understood, one Father was now keen to recover as quickly as he could ...

Was the Holy Host of Hosts nearing *Golgotterath?*

The Empress aborted her protest at her husband's first sorcerous word, and stood watching dismayed as lines of brilliance ravelled about him, then cinched him into blinking absence. Kelmomas fairly trembled for the *hatred* he glimpsed in her eyes.

Father was right, Samarmas whispered.

The youngest living son of Anasûrimbor Kellhus very nearly wept, such was his relief. Only his *hope* kept his face blank. He feigned distraction just to be safe, gazing up at the cleft ceilings, peering out across the rain-shrouded foothills.

It was just the two of them ... finally. Wonder. Joy. Horror.

"How?" his mother said, her gaze dead for losses. She sat upon heaped wrack some five paces below him, huddled in the ceremonial absurdity of her station, attire that made her seem a flower in winter. Tears flowed down her famous cheeks.

It was just the two of them ... and the Decapitants.

"Because ..." he said, feigning something he could neither express nor fathom. "I love you."

He had hoped she would flinch; he had imagined that her gaze would flutter and her hands would fist.

She closed her eyes instead. The long blink of horror confirmed.

She believes! Samarmas cried.

Father had said as much: his life hung from a hair strung about *her* heart. Were it not for Mother, he would already be dead. The Holy Aspect-Emperor would not squander the Strength on cracked bowls. Only the intransigence of motherhood, the impossibility of his mother hating a soul hatched from her womb, vouchsafed his survival. Even now, her *flesh* angled to redeem him—he could see it in her!—even as her soul balked at the instincts his presence summoned.

She forbade his execution because she wanted him alive, because in some deranged fashion *his life was more precious than her own.* Mummy!

The only real mystery was why *Father* would care ... or why he would bother returning to Momemn at all. For love?

"*Madness!*" his mother bawled, her voice so raw as to burn in his own throat.

The Decapitants lay akimbo to her left, the one husk leaning against the other. The mouth of the nearest gaped like a dreaming fish.

Were they watching? Could they see?

"I-I ..." he began. He could almost feel the faux pang that broke his voice. "*What?*" she nearly screamed. "*What?*"

"I didn't want to share," he said blankly. "I could not abide the portion you had allotted."

And he wondered why it seemed all the same, lies and confession.

"I am my father's son."

Nothing to see. Nothing to hear or taste or smell or even touch. But he could recollect all these things, enough to ache for their absence.

Malowebi could remember.

The Holy Aspect-Emperor shining before him. A whirlwind roaring about them, a ruinous blur that had been Fanayal's pavilion. His head *tipping from his shoulders*. His body still standing, spouting blood, voiding bowel. Anasûrimbor Kellhus singing, eyes like blown-upon coals, smoking with meaning as he chanted the terror of the Daimos ...

The Daimos!

And though Malowebi had no voice, he screamed, thought crushed into thought, heartbeat fluttering into steam, a thread of anguished heat waving in the embalming cold, bottomless deep. Pursed! He had been pursed in the manner of Zeumi sailors sentenced to execution at sea, and now he drowned, sewn into a sack woven of oblivion, absolute insensitivity.

No limbs to kick.

Void for wind.

Glimpsing shadows of his suffering, merely.

And then, inexplicably, *his eyes were open.*

There was *light* in the dark, feeling. Cold pressed his cheek, but his body remained utterly insensate otherwise. He tried to draw breath, to cry out—for elation or for horror he did not know—but he could not feel any tongue, let alone taste any breath ...

Something was *wrong*.

Malowebi saw milky firelight. He could make out heaped and hanging stone, twigs broken into insect-leg tangles ... Where were his limbs? For that matter, *where was his breathing?*

His *skin?*

Something disastrous had happened!

Sparks twirled in skirts of smoke climbing to vanish against unfamiliar constellations. He heard voices—a man and a woman arguing some lament. The cherubic face of a young Norsirai boy bobbed into existence from the nocturnal verge ...

Bearing a stick.

———— ⊗∞⊗ ————

To be desolate is to be of a piece with things inanimate, to *belong* in a manner the joyful can never know. The little boy could feel the sum of the World in his embrace, that endless, rolling ache. His mother and father bickered about firelight several paces distant. He breathed like other little boys he had heard sleeping, the rhythm of rocks cooling in evening shadow. No matter how his thoughts raced, his heart beat slowly, like a thing made of mud.

And even still, his father said, "He is not asleep."

His mother made a noise.

"I care nothing for what he is."

"Then let me do what needs to be done."

Mother hesitated. "No ..."

"The boy needs to be *destroyed*, Esmi."

"Destroyed. You make him sound like a sick dog. You do tha—"

"I do that because he is *not* a little boy."

"No," she said, her assurance absolute for exhaustion. "You do that to change the words from those belonging to a *son* to those belonging to an animal."

Father said nothing. A dead peashrub branch jutted from the intervening ground, forks dividing the orange image of his father not so much into pieces as possibilities. Kelmomas had marvelled at the Narindar, envied him his Unerring Grace, all the while forgetting the Grace belonging to his father, the unconquerable Anasûrimbor Kellhus I. He *was the Shortest Path*, a wave of inevitability flapped through the fabric of blind fortune. Not even the Gods could touch him! Not Ajokli, the wicked Four-Horned Brother. Not even Earth-cracking Momas!

Father had survived them ...

"But why even care what I say?" Mother was saying. "If he's so dangerous, why not simply grab him and snap his neck?"

His brother could not stop keening, *Mummeee! Mummeee!*

Father was implacable. "Why come back to save you?"

She held two fingers to her lips and mimed spitting to her side: a gesture she had learned from the dockmen in Sumna, Kelmomas knew.

"You came to save your accursed Empire!"

"And yet, here I am with *you* ... fleeing the Empire."

Her glare faltered, but only for an instant. "Because you know there's no holding it, not after Momas has struck down Momemn—his very name-sake!—*trying to kill you and yours*. Empire! Pfah! Do you know how much blood runs in the streets, Kellhus? The Three Seas burns! Your Judges! Your Princes and your Believer-Kings! The mob feasts upon them all!"

"Then mourn them if you must, Esmi. The Empire was but a ladder, a way to reach Golgotterath. It collapses in all incarnations of the Thousand-fold Thought."

The little boy did not need to see his mother's look, so loud was the silence.

"And that's ... that's why you ... left it with me? Because it was doomed?"

"Sin is *real*, Esmi. Damnation is *real*. I know because I have seen it. I bear those two grisly trophies to overawe, certainly, but to serve as a constant reminder as well. Knowledge is responsibility, and ignorance—though you and so many others abhor it—truly is *innocence*."

Mother glared in disbelief. "So you deceive me, keep me ignorant, to *save me from sin?*"

"You ... and all mankind."

The little boy thought of his father bearing the weight of every malicious act committed in his name, shuddered for the thought of damnations piled upon damnations.

Something insane rolled through the Blessed Empress's look.

"The weight of sin is found in *premeditation*, Esmi, in the wilful use of oth-ers as *tools*." His gaze clicked to the flames. "I have made this World my tool."

"To destroy Golgotterath," she said, as if naming the solitary point of agreement.

"Yes," her divine husband replied.

"Then *why are you here*? Why leave your precious Great Ordeal?"

The little boy gasped for the sheer beauty of it ... the effortlessness of his mastery.

"To save you."

Her ferocity dissolved, only to be reborn as something more violent and shrill. "*Lies!* Another to add to your pestilent heap—tall enough to shame Ajokli!"

Father looked from the fire to her, his gaze both forthright and yielding, always promising forgiveness, space for the heart to recover. "And this," he said, "is why you enlisted the Narindar to kill me?"

The little boy watched the Blessed Empress catch her breath at the fact of the question, then choke for the fact of the answer. Her eyes grew oily with grief. Her entire body seemed to *wobble*. The firelight painted her anguish in filaments, pulsing orange and crimson and rose shadow, beautiful as all things fundamental.

"Why, Kellhus?" she called across the interval between them. "Why ... persist ..." Her eyes had grown wide as her voice had grown small. "Why ... forgive?"

"I know not," Kellhus said, shifting his position. "You are my only darkness, wife." He wrapped her within greater arms, pulled her into the warm blanket of his embrace.

"The only place I can hide."

Kelmomas clung to the cold beneath, the World rolling beneath the Void, willing his flesh to become earth, his bones to become twig and bramble, his eyes wet stones. His brother shrieked and wailed, knowing his mother could deny his father nothing, and his father wanted them dead.

CHAPTER TWO

Ishterebinth

One topples from events mighty and great
as from clouds and not mountains.

—TSILARCUS, *The Sumptitudes*

Early Autumn, 20 New Imperial Year (4132, Year-of-the-Tusk), Ishterebinth.

"The Anasûrimbor is almost certainly your Saviour ..."

There was serenity in confusion when it was profound, a peace that comes from fathoming so few distinctions as to grasp contradictory things as one. Sorweel was a Man. He was a prince, and a Believer-King. He was an orphan. He was the instrument of Yatwer, the Dread Mother of Birth. He was a Son of Sakarpus, scarcely a man. He was Immiriccas, great among the Injori Ishroi, older than the ages.

He was stretched between life and damnation.

He was in love.

He lay panting as the world resolved into sensible form. The Weeping Mountain loomed, but more as a papyrus cutout than anything substantial. His face pricked for being naked, bald. Clots of Emwama raced through fog, frantic, running as fast as their stunted frames would allow. Memories came flooding back, images indistinguishable from panic. Descending through screeching halls. Oinaral dying in the Holy Deep. The *Amiolas*—

Sorweel clawed his cheeks, fingers hooked in dimpled skin. He was free! Free of the accursed thing!

And halved.

He remembered the swine-larded Haul, the descent down the Ingressus. He remembered Oinaral's father, Oirûnas, the monstrous Lord of the Watch.

He remembered Serwa bound and gagged, reaching out, even as his eyes found her in the mayhem, standing wrapped in a bolt of black that lay like paint across her skin—Injori silk. Wind thrashed the gold from her hair. Ishterebinth climbed beyond her, obstructing all creation with recombinant imagery and ruin. Smoke issued from points across its immensity.

Sorweel made to call out, only to be choked silent by misapprehension. Did she know? Had the Ghouls told her of the Dread Mother? Did she know what he was?

What he was supposed to do?

With consciousness comes place. They lay upon the Cirrû-nol, he realized, the great mall before Ishterebinth's shattered gates. He pressed himself from the stone, drew up one knee.

"Wha-what happens?" he croaked over the uproar.

She turned to him as if jolted from some disturbing reverie. Her left eye was a violet grin for swelling, but her right fixed him with characteristic clarity. His breath caught in joyous certainty that she knew as little of *his part* in what had happened as he knew of hers.

Even then, he began rehearsing his lies.

"The Last Mansion dies," she called. "The Intact war one against the other."

"*Good!*" a voice barked from behind Sorweel. The young Believer-King turned on a start, saw Moënghus sitting upon debris as though upon a latrine, slouched, great arms slung across his knees, black-mane obscuring his face. He, like his sister, was clothed only in a bolt of silk, black like hers, only embroidered with a crimson horse motif, and bound into a kilt about his waist. Blood dribbled from the fingers of his right hand.

"*Good?*" Serwa asked. "What could be *good* about such a thing?"

The Prince-Imperial did not look up. The wailing of the Emwama sounded like bleating sheep.

"I *heard* you, Sister ..."

Blood continued to bead and drip from his fingertips.

"Between my screams ... I heard you ... *sing* ..."

———⚬⚬⚬———

"*Pain too has its sorcery,*" the Ghoul-most-hated had said.

They climbed the footings of the Weeping Mountain, as much fleeing those who fled the Soggomantic Gate as anything. Serwa led them into the graven heights, following the joints that welded the eastward ramparts to the greater bulk of Ishterebinth. The ways were guttered with shattered masonry, the slough from the faces and forms stamping the heights above. Smoke spewed from the countless shafts the Ghouls used to ventilate their obscene Mansion, streamers of grey and black, even white gilled with odious yellow. All of them had suffered, but Moënghus need only glance to know that his had been the greatest trial. They did not stumble and sway as he did, one thousand muscles warring over one hundred bones, a slouching motley of passions, grimacing about sobs, shuddering about breaths that stabbed for the ruin that inhaled them. They moved as singular souls possessing but one lever for their actions. They looked to the horizon, while he could only boggle at his naked feet. They had been *tested*, and their temper had rung *true*.

He had been sacrificed.

Mocked. Tortured. Possessed. Raped.

And now this ... *weeping*?

No matter how far the High Floor dwindled behind and beneath them, the air nipped and nauseated for corruption. All of them blinked, periodically pestled their eyes with their thumbs for the sting. But only *he* sobbed. Only he shook for terrors buried a league below.

Who? Who was this little black-haired boy? Who was this child who drew the smirking eye of gossips wherever he pattered? "Imperial Bastard," they had called him, a name he had even dared relish, for a time. Wear a thing long enough, and you will think it something earned.

Like the name Anasûrimbor.

The Weeping Mountain reeled about him, a vertical landscape of ghouls chiselled enormous and small, their poses unnatural, dead-eyed. Serwa found him huddling between great thighs of granite, somehow crouched, somehow muttering. Her beauty terrified him for but an instant.

"Podi! Brother! We must make haste!"

She loomed above him, upon the higher step as always, garbed only in depraved Nonmen silk. The purple cleft that was her eye did not so much obscure her beauty as shout her complicity. Graven heights and noxious plumes piled above.

"*Yooooou!*" he heard himself roar, a sound all the more titanic for the tremulous keen that had preceded it. His throat ripped about it. For the first time he could remember, he saw his sister recoil in shock.

A single blink occasioned her recovery.

"Harapior is dead," she said with matching sibling fury. "*You* are still alive! How long you lay upon his unholy rack is something only you can decide."

It made her all the more accursed and inhuman, spearing matters to the pith with but a single breath.

He cast his eyes from her aspect, spat for the taste of damnation. The sun. Even smothered in clouds, it was too bright.

<hr />

To be human was to be bound, aye, to suffer *what one was*, always, no matter what the debility or perversity. To be human was to flinch from the raised hand, to conspire against the indignity, to shrink from the torment, run and run from the horror. And Moënghus was human—he had no doubt of that now. The notion that he might be more had been murdered in the black bowels of the Weeping Mountain ... along with countless other things.

So they fled Ishterebinth, which had once been Ishoriol, possessing such might and glory as to be extolled to the ends of the World. So they fled the Nonmen's last, guttering light. He climbed as they climbed, scrambling across the breakneck slopes, but where they fattened the distance behind them, he accrued only more emptiness. He could no more escape the Thresholds than he could carve his bones from his frame. He was *human* ...

Unlike his accursed sister.

The bulk of the Mountain now lay between them and the sun, softening the contrast between the graven figures and the recesses they stared from. What had been intricate in bald sunlight now seemed dissolved for millennial neglect. Noses no more than pinched clay, mouths reduced to lines, eyes little more than holes between brows and cheeks. Moënghus started for realizing he and the others stood upon a great palm, the base of the thumb rising like the flank of a dying horse, fingers shorn so long ago as to be little more than nubs.

"Sing to me!" he heard himself cry. "Sing that song to me once again, Little Sister!"

Serwa regarded him with her infamous pity. "Podi ..."

"*Vas sillja ...*" he cooed in sneering mockery, hearing her voice wend dulcet through his flailing screams. "Do you remember? *Vas sillja enil'cu va loinirja ...*"

"We have no time for th—!"

"*Tell me!*" he roared. "Tell me what it means!"

For a heartbeat, it seemed she might almost stammer. "No good can come of it."

"Good?" he heard himself cackle. "I fear the damage has been done. I look for no good from you, Little Sister, not anymore. I seek only *truth* ... Or has that also fled you?"

She watched him with a pensive sorrow he knew no Anasûrimbor could suffer, not truly. "'Your lips,'" she began, tears welling, her voice splinted with false regret. "'Only your lips can balm my weal ...'"

Her voice trailed into the ghostly roar emanating from the Mountain.

"And what is the song?" he barked. "What is it called?"

He so wanted to believe the slack eyes, the tremulous lips.

"The Lay of Linqiru," she said.

And it dropped from him, then, the ability to feel.

"The Incest Song?"

The first of many falls.

"*It burdens you*," Harapior had said. "*That name.*"

Everything we say to one another, we also say to souls absent. We continually speak to the speech that comes after our voice, forever *prepare* those who would listen. No truth spoken is true simply because *words have consequences*, because voices move souls and souls move voices, a great radiation. This is why we so readily admit to corpses what we dare not confess to the living. This why only the executioner can speak without care of consequence. Our speech finds freedom only when the speaker is at an end.

This was how Harapior spoke to him: as to a dead man.

Honestly.

"No one can see us, here, manling, not even the Gods. This room is the *darkest place*. You can speak without fear of your father in the Thresholds."

His courage had been that of the idiot. "I do not fear my father."

"But you do, Son of Summer. You fear your father because you know your father is Dûnyain."

"Enough of this madness!"

"And your brothers and sisters ... Do they likewise fear him?"

"No more than I!" he cried. Few facts are more tragic than the ease with which outrage bends about terror, how we will betray anyone with our meaning so long as we are conceded the look and tone of defiance.

"Yes ..." the ghoul said, once more hearing words other than those spoken. "Of course. For them, solving the riddle of their father solves the riddle of themselves. Not so you. Your riddle lies elsewhere."

"I have no riddle."

"Oh, but you do, Son of Summer—you do. Any mortal soul raised in such monstrous company must."

"They're not monsters!"

"Then you do not know what it *means* to be Dûnyain."

"I know well enough!"

Harapior laughed the way he always laughed—without sound. "I will show you ..." he said, gesturing to figures in the black beyond him.

And so he found himself chained before his younger sister, and he had wept, understanding the trap they had lain. He was to be her goad, as she was to be his. The ghouls would draw the knife that is sheathed in all love, and they would cut what they could. Harapior and his understudies smashed him against her, made a bludgeon of his suffering, and she remained ... imperturbable.

When they exhausted what mundane atrocities they could commit, they turned to sorcery. In the dark, their heads had smoldered red, a muddy glow about blue-white precision. They were creatures of blood, no different than Men. Pain had its miracles, and chained beneath his nude sister, Moënghus learned the obscenity of each. He screamed, not so much for the sum of his torment as for its *division*, like a thousand thousand wicked little jaws with wicked little teeth affixed to his every vessel, his every sinew, chewing, savaging ...

He screamed and gagged. He voided his bowel, bladder, stomach and dignity.

And more than anything *he had begged.*

Sister! Sister!

Show them! I beg you please!

Show them our Father's portion.

And she gazed through him and ... *sang* ... words he could not under-stand, in Ihrimsû, the accursed tongue of the Ghouls ... words that flexed and resonated, that coiled serpentine through the blackness surrounding ... a wandering knife's edge. She sang her *love*—of all things in creation, *love!*—but not to him, the one she had professed to love many times, to *them*, the abominations ... the *Ghouls!*

He could scarce remember details. Endless convulsions. Hanging entirely intact and utterly mangled ... skinned and shredded. Harapior whispering mock profundities, revelations ...

"Think of Hell, child. This is but a scintillant drop in that ocean, what you suffer ..."

And his divine sister, Anasûrimbor Serwa, celebrated and dreaded across the Three Seas, the one soul who could speak her father's miracles ... who could rescue her broken brother if she wished ... If she wished!

Singing ancient lays ... goading the ghouls to ever greater acts of deprav-ity, the recitation of Torture Cants unknown to any Gnostic sorcerer, in-flicting agonies unknown to this, the bleeding side of life. With the patience of fat wolves, they tore pain from pain, despair from despair, horror from horror, separated his ever quivering thread, so they might weave tapestries of sublime misery.

The *physical* indignities they had merely smeared upon him as butter. Like all artists, they were loathe to forego all visible sign of their labours.

"A drop ..."

The Lord Torturer had stayed with him in the blackness afterward, watching him drip.

"I know because I have seen."

———— ❦ ————

I know.

Who was he, the wolf-eyed child upon the Aspect-Emperor's knee?

The truth, Moënghus would later realize, had always lurked in *Esmenet's* embrace, the absence of instinctive desperation, the way a decision of some kind always lay behind it ... He loved her, more fiercely than any of his siblings could love, but he always knew, somehow. Anasûrimbor Esmenet, the Blessed Empress of the Three Seas, never *captured* him in her arms, never clutched and clung, at least not the way she did the others.

But as obvious as it was, the question of his parentage had never occurred to him—likely because she had hair as black as his. He had mooned over her, marvelled as little boys are prone to marvel at their mothers, adored the way his pallid siblings made her dark beauty wax bright. And he assumed that he merely stood halfway *between* his parents, possessing her jet hair and his alabaster skin. If anything, he had been *proud* of his distinction.

Then Kayûtas told him that mothers provide no more than the soil for a father's seed.

Even after Theliopa and the others were born, Esmenet would come to cuddle "her bigger boys" together before bedtime, so one night he asked her if she were his real mother.

Her hesitation alarmed him—he would always remember that much. The pity would be forgotten.

"No, sweetling ... I'm your *adoptive* mother. Just as Kellhus is your adoptive father."

"Seeeee?" Kayûtas had said, nestled against her right side. "That's why your hair is black, while ours is blon—"

"*White*, more like," Esmenet chirruped, poking the boy for his impertinence. "Only slaves live in the sun—you do realize this!"

To dwell with and to not know *is to trust*; belonging is ever a matter of insensitivity to what divides. And what ignorance can no longer serve, only *indifference* can provide. Perhaps this was why the Blessed Empress had elected to make light what had buried him alive.

"So then who are my *real* mother and father?"

This time her hesitation terrified.

"I am your father's second wife. His first wife was Serwë."

He spent several heartbeats digesting these words. "The woman from the Circumfix? *She's* my mother?"

"Yes ..."

Absurd facts are often the easiest to bear, if only because of the way impossibility mimes abstraction. Things grasped with a shrug are generally things easily released.

"And my father ... Who is he?"

The Blessed Empress of the Three Seas breathed deep, swallowed.

"Your mother's ... first husband. The man who delivered our Holy Aspect-Emperor to the Three Seas."

"You mean the ... the *Scylvendi?*"

And suddenly it became so obvious, the turquoise gaze regarding him in the mirror.

Scylvendi eyes!

"You are *my child*, my son, Moënghus—never forget that! But you are also the child of legends, *martyrs*. Short your mother and your father, none of this would be, and the very World would be doomed."

She spoke in the rush to make reparation, to recast things lost as things gained. But the heart knows catastrophe as well as the mouth knows the tongue and its propensity to lie. Either way, there was very little she could say that would long survive the ruthless scrutiny of his brothers and sisters.

They would decide what he thought and how he felt about the matter. They always had ...

At least until Ishterebinth.

———— ⊗ ————

They passed back into the forests of Giolal, walked beneath the dead boughs in shambling file, each too emptied to speak. They dared a fire, supped on sorrel, wild apples, and an ailing wolf they found limping through a ravine. Moënghus could scarcely feign sleep, let alone surrender to it. His sister and the Sakarpi youth had fairly collapsed into slumber, and he found comfort in the sight of them about the dying flames, or the memory of it. They fretted for him, he knew.

The Nail of Heaven glared as high on the horizon as he had ever seen, hoisted upon the shoulders of constellations he did not know—alien stars. The night air kissed what injury he had bared, and for a moment, he could almost breathe ...

But when he blinked he could only see the masticating light, the mouths of the ghouls singing what was unthinkable. Whatever hopeful gloaming his relief found, he need only blink to tatter it, squint to blow it away.

His shoulders hitched in silent laughter—or was it sobbing?

"Brother?" he heard his sister call. She watched him intently from her side, her face a mask of pulsing orange. "Brother ... I fear y—"

"No," he barked. "You ... you do not get to speak to me."

"Yes," Serwa replied. "Yes, I do. Pestering is the right of little sisters."

"And you are *not* my sister."

"Then what am I?"

He graced her with a sneer. "You are your father's daughter. Anasûrimbor..." He leaned forward to cast a thigh-bone of wood into the fire. "Dûnyain."

The Sakarpi youth was awake and watching now.

"Kindly tip your head, Brother," Serwa said. "Pour out Harapior's foul concoction."

"*Harapior's* poison?" he replied in mock surprise.

Animated by some self-annihilating will, he proceeded to tell the flames how she and Kayûtas had toyed with him from the beginning, playing upon habits so profound as to rule without existing. He had always been the one known, the one counselled, the plaything of capering abominations. Where other fathers gave their children dogs so they might learn how to make a thing—a thing with teeth—*love* them, Anasûrimbor Kellhus had given his children *Moënghus*. He was *their pet*, an animal they could train to trust, to defend, even to kill. He could feel his voice constricting, his eyes widening for the lunatic dimension of what he apprehended. He was their human diversion, their puzzle-box, their chest filled with games.

"Enough!" the Sakarpi youth cried. "What madne—?"

"Truth!" Moënghus snapped. His smile seemed to crack the fired clay of his face. It seemed he could feel the inner slop ooze. "They are *always at war*, Horse-King. Even when they pretend to sleep."

Sorweel lingered upon his gaze, swallowed. The fire snapped violently, and he disguised his start by turning to Serwa.

"Is that true?"

She regarded the boy for one heartbeat too long.

"Yes."

Sorweel awoke just before dawn. He ached in arcane ways, pangs rooted in muscle and tendon, yet following paths outward, forming joints where none should be. He blinked against images from his dreams, Nonmen on chariots, loosing flaming arrows across fields of sorghum, laughing for the starvation sure to follow. Serwa lay opposite the dead firepit, curled for warmth, still sleeping. She had taken her left arm as her pillow, squashing her cheek against her mouth and nose, but she seemed no more vulnerable for laying so placid, so insensitive to her wicked surroundings. His memories of their escape from the Weeping Mountain were hazy, fragmentary where at all clear. He need only close his eyes, it seemed, to see her hanging in the Ilculcû Rift, naked between brilliant panes and shining geometries, fending the booming song of the Last Quya ... And here she lay unconscious across leaves become dirt, clutching a bolt of Injori silk, and she seemed no less magnificent, no less invincible.

Whatever the merit of her brother's case, there could be no doubting *the Anasûrimbor did not break.* The Quya themselves had crumbled about her! As had her brother ...

As had he.

Even now, he could feel it, buzzing proof of what he could not bring himself to countenance the previous day. *He could feel his own decapitation—* or evisceration, or whatever one called violent amputations of the soul. He could feel the absence of *Immiriccas*, a nagging, a scratching at what was missing, a groping for sources that had been torn away with the Amiolas. He could feel his *halving* as surely as he could feel his desire for the miraculous woman slumbering beside him, too far to reach.

He loved this Anasûrimbor before him. Where Ishterebinth had sundered Moënghus from his sister, it had welded Sorweel to her and her cause. And how could it not, when *he could remember Min-Uroikas?* He had seen the Copper Tree of Siol fall on the Black Furnace Plain! With his own eyes he had witnessed the horror of the Inchoroi and their wicked Ark! How could he serve the Dread Mother knowing that *She could not,* that She was blind, as Oinaral had said, to the possibility of Her impossibility?

The No-God was real.

Many questions remained, of course—countless complications. Sorweel was newborn thanks to the Amiolas. His future lay blank before him, utterly inscrutable outside the fact of his conversion. And his past had yet to be rewritten, the history of hating and, yes, even plotting against the Aspect-Emperor, this man who dared the Gods in the name of Men.

The fact of her open eyes spared him this labour. She batted her unswollen eye, slurped drool the way any human soul would. "How, Sorweel?" she asked, her voice gentle, so as to not spook the sunrise. "How could you still love me so?"

He still lay as he had slept, his head resting in the crook of his arm. He swallowed, focussed upon a small spider scuttling along a barked branch on the forest floor between them, then found her eyes once again.

"You have never loved, have you?"

Something unfathomable gleamed in her eyes.

"I am as my brother says," she replied. "I am Dûnyain."

Sorweel's smile felt crooked for crawling out from his arm. His heart hammered in his ears. The sound of Moënghus hacking and spitting snuffed any possibility of reply.

They collected themselves from the forest floor with an air of incredulity. They lived. They were safe. No one had possessed the heart to discuss anything yesterday, let alone what happened next. But sleep had sealed the interval between them and the Mountain, whose blue hulk yet obscured the southwestern horizon. Yesterday they had fled; today, they resumed a journey they had thought doomed.

"Father is almost certainly in Dagliash by now," Serwa declared. "He needs to know what happened here."

"So do we leap?" Sorweel asked, both alarmed and thrilled by the sorcerous prospect. The ghost of her lithe form tingled along the inside of his arm.

She shook her head. "Not yet. We're too deep in the wood."

"She fears the Mountain polluted her," Moënghus grunted, spitting blood. If there was malice in his observation, Sorweel could not hear it.

"What are you saying?"

The Prince-Imperial twitched as if jabbed by a fork. He looked even more a ruin in the infant light. He held his face down, as though preparing to retch, but his white-blue eyes glared up from beneath his brow, peering through crabbed locks of hair. "The Cant of Translocation. Meaning turns on being, does it not, Little Sister? It's Metagnostic ... at the very limit of her abilities. If the Mountain has remade her, then it has unmade those abilities ..."

The Swayali Grandmistress ignored him. "We go that way," she said, pointing to the bald outline of a hill rising to their immediate north.

"But I'm guessing," Moënghus continued, "that she has escaped un-scathed ..." He regarded her grinning as if he too had been untouched. "Eh, Little Sister?"

Serwa graced him with a blank look. "We're too deep in the wood."

And so they struck out beneath the lifeless canopies of Giolal, great boughs winding as pumice tusks, forking into branches worn into thorns. Sunlight showered through, grilling the ground with shadow. Sorweel ac-companied Serwa, while Moënghus trailed various distances behind. No one spoke. Heat thickened the spare chill of the early morning air. Move-ment lubricated aching limbs.

"*Oirûnas* brought you the Hanging Citadels ..." she finally said.

Sorweel told himself to not look stupid. "Yes."

He could remember so little of what had happened after Oinaral had died in the Holy Deep.

"How does a boy fall in with a legendary Nonman Hero?"

Sorweel shrugged. "The Hero's *son* takes him on a mad journey through his mad mansion, all the way down to the Deepest Deep, where his father dwells ..."

"You mean Oinaral?"

His heart winced for her knowledge of him. "Yes."

I saw the Whirlwind walk ...

"Oinaral took you to his father ... His *Erratic* father. But why?"

"To let his father know that the Consult ruled Ishterebinth."

She was peering at him now. "But why take *you?*"

He prayed the Spit-of-Yatwer that Porsparian had rubbed into his cheeks wouldn't falter for his apostasy. What madness, depending on the dispen-sations of the very Goddess he now sought to deceive!

"I th-think because I could remember."

And it seemed the greatest wonder and beauty he had ever seen, her blue-eyed belief.

"What happened when you found Oirûnas?"

The Believer-King of Sakarpus trudged onward, now watching the slow scroll of barren forest floor, despairing the perversity of his straits.

"Oinaral provoked him ... intentionally, I think ..." He drew a shudder-ing breath. "And in a fit of antique rage, Oirûnas killed him ... murdered his own son."

His friend. Oinaral Lastborn. The second brother the World had offered him after Zsoronga.

"And then?"

The youth shrugged. "It was like he ... Oirûnas ... came to his senses. And I knelt there ... trembling upon the Deepest Deep, and I told him what Oinaral had instructed me to tell him ... that the Vile had taken Ishterebinth."

She paced him in silence for quite some time. The grade had tipped upward in stages, so that they now climbed as much as walked. Bare white sky could be glimpsed through scrambled growth ahead, revealing the bare line of the summit.

"I have some experience with the Amiolas," she said without prompt or warning. "Seswatha wore it thrice, more than any other man. Each time, he was changed irrevocably—because of Immiriccas, the Goad. Why Emilidis would use such a vengeful proxy for his artifact has always been a matter of fierce debate. Immiriccas was a stubborn, ferocious soul. Seswatha believed it was Nil'giccas's doing, that the Nonman King compelled the Artisan to use him, hoping to instill the Goad's hatred in every Man who donned the Amiolas."

Sorweel expelled a reservoir of anxious air. Blinking, he glimpsed his lover, Mu'miorn, in the Entresol, so filthy and malnourished. He shook the image away.

"Yes," he said more raggedly than he would have liked. "Stubborn."

They clambered up slopes of bare sandstone, rock that twinkled on different angles of sunlight and observation. The sky seemed to shrink from all things terrestrial, featureless and starving. Moënghus had fallen behind—an alarming distance, Sorweel thought, but Serwa did not seem concerned in the least. Together they tottered to the pinnacle of the scalp, watching the distances rise to greet their will to circumvent them, hills folded into ramps, piling into the crisp blue of the Demua mountains.

Their first leap was going to be mighty.

He turned to Serwa in abrupt concern, recalling what Moënghus had said earlier. She was already watching him—waiting. His breath caught for her beauty, how the Injori silk managed to at once conceal and expose her nudity.

"There's something I must tell you before my brother comes," she said. A gust caught her flaxen hair, lashed it about her face.

The youth cast a glance down to Moënghus labouring up the slope, then looked back to her squinting. "What?"

"The love you bear for me ..."

It was too windy to breathe, he decided.

"Yes."

"I have never seen anything like it."

"Because it's *my* love," he lied. "And you have never seen the likes of me."

She smiled at that, and he almost whooped for wonder.

"I thought I had," she said, still peering at him. "I thought you callow, wrecked by hatred and sorrow ... But that was before ..."

The Believer-King of Sakarpus swallowed.

"*Sorweel* ... What you did in the Mountain ... And what I see in your face! So ... divine ..."

A dark, masculine corner of his soul realized that for all her worldly knowledge and power, Anasûrimbor Serwa, Grandmistress of the Swayali, *was still a child.*

And what did lies matter so long as love was real?

"*Ware yourself!*" Moënghus barked, now scaling the bald stone immediately below. He climbed into their midst, chest heaving, looming, scowling.

"Their words are never soft, Horse-King ... only too sharp too feel."

———— ⬦ ————

Serwa had no difficulty with the Metagnostic Cant. Sorweel found that leap and the one following exhilarating in ways he could not articulate. Where before he had been thrown, now he *strode* from place to place, bringing horizons to heel with a single planted foot. He found it hard to concentrate, what with his every other thought reaching for a soul that was no longer his own, knowledge assumed yet missing, desire kindled yet bereft of fuel. He knew he was broken, that the Amiolas had rendered him a perpetual fragment, but whether dealing with Moënghus or Serwa, he found this made him more impervious, more thoughtlessly assured.

Her brother's aggrieved humour forced them to segregate, and so the young Believer-King found himself, impossibly, *alone* with the Aspect-Emperor's daughter upon the flank of Shaugiriol, or "Eaglehorn" as she called it, the northernmost peak of the Demua. Finding some place to comfortably sleep was no easy task on a mountainside. Moënghus claimed the first, meagre horizontal shelf they encountered, forcing him and Serwa to scale a diagonal cleft to a lolling tongue of granite some twenty cubits above.

Sorweel's hands seemed to float and his boots seemed leaden. He dared not look up, lest some opportune glimpse of her nethers strike him numb. He feared for his life as it was, such was his vertigo, the sense of sideways gravity drawing him *outward*. But he clung and he climbed, the stone close enough to his face to smell. His breath a shallow pang, he followed her out to the edge of the outcropping, joined her sitting, gazing. He silently thanked the Hunter for the preternatural absence of wind.

The Nail of Heaven flared high and white directly to the north, frosting the nocturnal tracts below, and he listened as she explained the vast stage before them—the Leash, and Agongorea, and the soaring Yimaleti—enthralled not so much by her knowledge as by her proximity, her heat in such high, clean air, and he wondered how *it could possibly be*, wooing the daughter of an incarnate God with weapons provided by one without time or place.

"And *Golgotterath*," she said, "lies in that direction."

If she had said "Min-Uroikas," his bones would have bolted in their flesh. Instead he turned, heart thrumming, to kiss her bare shoulder. She clasped him by his soft-furred cheeks, drank deeply from his lips. He lay back, drawing her down upon him. Taking the stars as her mantle, she straddled him, whispered, "*I am not what you think I am*," as she lowered her fire upon his.

"Nor am I," he replied.

"I can see through you ..."

"Nooo," he groaned. "You cannot."

And so they made love, perched high on the Eaglehorn, the mountain from which so many ancient invasions had been spied. They moved slowly, gasped rather than cried, and yet the violence of their coupling, the desperation, would leave them sapped of all difference, wrapped one about the other, slicked in the same sweat, breathing as a single human being.

He awoke for a need to urinate. Eaglehorn's stone was harder than it had seemed in the fog of carnal undertaking: the ground gnawed with grit and cold. Serwa lay nestled against him, buttocks to thighs; he rolled away, lest his rising lust disturb her. Far more than he or Moënghus, she required sleep. So he lay breathless and throbbing, his manhood aching in open air.

He gazed northward, searching for distraction. Golgotterath lay out there

... somewhere. He looked for some glimpse of its fabled glimmer, but found himself peering after a flicker of movement instead, something hanging high in the great gulf between mountains. He squinted, even raised a hand to shield the Nail's glare.

Horror climbed as a foam through him, crawling from his innards to his extremities ...

A *stork* strung the dark void, buoyant upon the gusts, edges bleating.

The whole mountain seemed to turn on a wheel moving too slowly to see but still quickly enough to dizzy.

The *Dread Mother* was watching.

She had not forgotten her apostate assassin.

She *knew*.

His thoughts roiled. How did the Old Gods punish his brand of treachery? Damnation?

Would he burn for loving Anasûrimbor Serwa?

For seeing what Holy Yatwer could not?

He lay motionless, his body pressed against the space between him and the woman that had so bewitched him. A sob cracked the chill air, and he started a second time, afflicted by the mad certainty that *he* had authored the noise. But it was Moënghus, he realized, weeping upon his shelf below. Bull-chested gasps punctuated high-hooking moans, so obviously the issue of someone mighty, but belonging to a child all the same, the little black-haired boy who had been raised among the Dûnyain.

And so the Believer-King drifted back to sleep believing sleep would be denied him.

Mu'miorn held him pinned to the pillows, grunting in time with his thrusts. Unpared nails left threads of pink and violet across milk white skin.

And then Serwa was crying out to him, and he found himself shivering upon the lip of oblivion. "We are in peril, Son of Harweel! Up! *Up!*"

He blinked against the dawn glare, the impossible bright, rolled to his fours groaning, immediately realized that what he had thought soil upon their roost was in fact the aggregate of bird droppings. He pressed himself to his feet, only to be felled by the yawing spaces, the plummet of what seemed all things ...

Serwa was crouched at the edge, staring down. "Do you see them, Brother?" she was calling. "Approaching from the east!"

Sorweel steadied himself upon one knee, squinted at the Grandmistress, dumbfounded as much for her beauty as for the dregs of unwanted dreams. His breath bubbled about the fact that they had lain as man and wife—*man and wife*! And now ...

The Dread Mother?

"Sranc?" he asked on croak.

Just then an arrow rifled the air just to the right of his face, struck the scarps behind and above. He ducked low, nerves aflame.

"No," she said, her tone clipped. "*Men.*" She leaned forward to call down once again. "Do you *see* them, Brother?"

Sorweel pawed at his eyes, stared blearily eastward, saw nothing. "Men?" he asked, crawling to a better vantage. "*Ordealmen?*"

"No ..." An arrow zipped high over the tumbling slopes, chipped from an invisible plane about the exposed Grandmistress, then fell away, clattering. "Scylvendi ..."

Scylvendi?

Another arrow threaded a different path, this one *passing through* the sorcerous Ward that had deflected the previous bolt. But Serwa was already leaning back, reaching out ... It seemed natural watching it happen, and stupendous, even miraculous, afterward, how the neck of the shaft simply appeared in her hand. She held the bulb of the Chorae away, salt sparking like frost across her knuckles and forearm, then cast the thing out over the abyss.

"*Podi!*" she cried.

Peering with greater caution, Sorweel began picking their assailants out, one by one, a thin cloud of helmed heads and armoured shoulders ascending the ramped stages almost immediately below. Two more shafts whistled into Serwa's defenses.

"So what ... forty-five of them?"

"Sixty-eight," she said.

"Skirmishers ..." Moënghus called on a grunt, hoisting himself through the cleft they had climbed the night previous. Even still he made a point of only looking at Sorweel. "They likely saw our arrival last night."

"Come," Serwa said, gesturing for the two of them to join her.

Sorweel retreated from the edge, and keeping low, withdrew to her side.

The vista leapt about him, dizzying for the endless miles of depth.

Moënghus grinned, scowling, standing hunched in a manner the ledge did not require, as if his ligaments were being wound and released unevenly. A shaft cracked the stone above and behind his head. He did not flinch.

"*Come*," his sister implored on an outstretched hand. "I can see deep into Agongorea from here."

Something wild bucked through her brother's glare. Another shaft skittered from her Ward, bruising the air with a blue glow flattened like paper.

Already clasped in her left arm, Sorweel followed the Prince-Imperial's gaze to her abdomen, saw the dimpled residue of his seed across the Injori silk.

"*Brother!*"

Moënghus lowered his turquoise gaze. After a congealed heartbeat, he ducked into her embrace much the same as Sorweel had, his frame dwarfing both of them. A small barrage of arrows peppered Serwa's arcane defenses, drumming light from empty air. The morning sun burnt across the back of the east.

Her spine arched the familiar way, and she dug the knuckle of her thumb in his flank in the way Sorweel had decided was involuntary. She leaned her head back, and answering to her inaugural sorcerous cry, pearl incandescence spilled from her mouth, her eyes, so bright as to utterly occlude her beauty.

Her song loosed a thousand spiders across opposite sides of his skin, scuttling in perfect time together, inside and out. Mist climbed about them, somehow untouched by turbulence, shot through with spiraling white. The dawn-stark landscape flattened into something more stark still. He clenched teeth across an omnidirectional outward heave, the sense of bloating across all dimensions ... and then the *drop*, the instant imploding into cracks in reality, inhaled as smoke ... Moënghus was screaming, roaring. He felt the man's arm yanked nerveless, glimpsed him toppling onto Eaglehorn's grudging ledge, then over—

Lashing brilliance, then a lurching *coming to be*, as if he were a babe tugged clear his mother's womb.

They both fell gasping upon lifeless dirt.

CHAPTER THREE

Agongorea

*Only those Principles finding no warrant in other Principles can serve
as the warrant of warrants, or the immovable Ground. Absent such
Principles, the Ground is merely something that happens when we run ...*
　　　　　　　　　—The Third Analytic of Men, AJENCIS

Early Autumn, 20 New Imperial Year (4132, Year-of-the-Tusk), Golgotterath.

The Meat be praised.

Proyas never discovered who first shouted this phrase, but the uproar it
had occasioned among the others convinced him to make it his own. That
it was insane mattered not at all.

Rain baffled the horizon, bathed the land's wounds and mired its gutters. The Ordealmen toiled through the mudded pasture north of the
Urokkas, great rivers of them dragging supplies, gazing to the blackened
slopes and gorges, the heights wreathed in charred Sranc. The skies showered down upon them, flattening hair, hunching shoulders, and rinsing the
filth and blood from their arms and armour, the purple that so quickly
dried into cracking black. In their tens of thousands they trudged across
the rain-sizzling flats, stunned for what they had witnessed, frightened for
what they had heard. Clean of skin, soiled of heart. Far enough from home
to be struck breathless for reckoning the distance.

They struck camp on the banks of the River Sursa, at the legendary Wair Chirsaul, the Mandible Ford, leagues to the north of Antareg. The call was sent out, and Believer-Kings, Generals, and Magi descended on the Umbilicus from all quarters of the encampment, bridling with questions and unnatural vitality. The need to escape the contagion had prevented any kind of accounting the previous night, meaning these Men had gnawed on rumour alone for a full day and night. They were hungry for explanations, famished, even. Twice Proyas bid them to await the arrival of their brothers. "Our Lord-and-Prophet lives!" he cried on the second occasion, seeking to allay what he supposed was the question that burned brightest. "He has taken leave only because our victory was so complete!"

A good number of the assembled had donned their white penitentials to honour the souls taken from them. But if the Lords of the Ordeal mourned in sooth, they showed little sign beyond their garb. Bearded faces bellowed joy and greeting. Eyebrows leapt and eyes twinkled at the exchange of ribaldries. Several coarse jokes regarding Sranc sent gales of laughter across the crowd, left kings and princes knuckling tears of hilarity from their eyes, daubing cheeks with funeral garb. "Just nibble their sardine a little," Coithus Narnol brayed, "and it'll put hair on your *wife's* chest!"

"Well that explains my wife's mother!"

Men dressed for dirge and prayer stamped feet for derision. Lord Grimmel roared from high on the back tiers, beating his chest, frothing his mustaches in spittle. Proyas had already decided the man was among those most sensitive to whatever was happening, the least able to *hold their Meat.*

"Grimmel bears watching ..." Kayûtas murmured from his side.

The flood of new arrivals had slowed to a trickle. Fairly every eye in the Umbilicus noted where they stood, that they spoke, but for the moment at least, the chatter boomed as before. "What's *happening* to us, Kayu?"

The Prince-Imperial shot him an intent look, one not entirely devoid of malice.

"We *eat Sranc,* Uncle."

The rumble dropped through the earthen floor, and Proyas found himself standing before the Lords of the Ordeal, the singular object of their manic regard. There was no mistaking the thinning of their numbers. But there was a ferocious aura to them, the apprehension of storms advancing—it seemed that lightning should vein the shadowy heights above and behind them! They were foul and ragged and dark, their eyes as bright and avid as their dress was soiled and tattered. It seemed he should have been frightened, but King Nersei Proyas of Conriya was not. He raised his hands and cried what had to be cried, invoked the only goad he possessed ...

"*The Meeeat!*" he thundered, matching Grimmel's savagery. "*The Meat be praised!*"

The Men of the Three Seas stamped and roared.

Two dozen Pillarians barged through the entrance bearing three Sranc roasted whole into the heart of the Eleven-Pole Chamber. The Lords of the Ordeal howled their approval, fell upon the fare with ravenous enthusiasm. Rather than wire the creatures into poses reminiscent of pig or lamb, the cooks had served them laying on their backs, each in the attitude of charred and blistered slumber, so that between blinks they seemed fire-roasted Men. Proyas at once watched abhorred, and participated. He salivated for the smell, so like burnt mutton, and shuddered for the *savour*, the bloom of heat and salt and exquisite grease. Here and there, one after another, different souls caught his eye and called out their approval. Proyas smiled and nodded to each, acting the serene commander he needed to be, wondering when had desecration become something he could *taste*?

The Lords of the Ordeal hunched as dogs over their repast, sawing and wrenching at the bodies, baring bone with bared teeth, chewing only to better bolt down. A glutinous racket squatted in the air, the clamour of mouths masticating. He looked to Kayûtas, wondering if the youth had noticed. Mere moments ago, these Men had begged him for tidings of their Master ... and now?

Anasûrimbor Kellhus had been forgotten by his followers.

Proyas smiled in reply to Baron Nomiyal of Mols, who had sparked a small cheer praising him, thinking, *We stray!*

We have wandered from His Path!

There was no pointing to it, but it lay in plain view nonetheless. Something dull and evil and ferocious possessed these once-noble Men, something scarcely bridled, something that gluttony and gluttony alone could assuage. Obwë Gûswuran, illustrious Grandmaster or no, began scavenging the rinds of skin and fatty white disdained by others, slurping them in strings. Lord Gora'jirau, a surviving Invitic Knight, made sport with one of the heads, tearing away the blistered lips and cheeks, his manhood arched against his tattered linen kilt.

Proyas watched as grisly feast became lurid demonstration. He stood where he always stood during Council, to the right of the vacant place belonging to the Holy Aspect-Emperor. The panels of the Ekkinû undulated according to their own, ethereal rhythms. He had directed Saccarees to stand on his left, knowing the water his presence would draw among the Schoolmen. Even more importantly, he had instructed Kayûtas to stand on his right: no argument for authority carried more weight than blood. As Kellhus had told him on many occasions, the appearance of continuity *was* continuity for Men.

"Gird yourself, Uncle," the Prince-Imperial muttered, his beard as wetted for grease as any other. "More and more they will be as crocodiles ... beasts that must be sated to be assuaged."

Unnatural as it had become, their appetite still possessed limits. Groaning aloud for distension, belching and loosening belts, the caste-nobles retired from their monstrous repast and formed conspiratorial clusters on the tiers surrounding. Mutters quickly piled into patriarchal thunder. Individuals once again called out for answers and explanations, faces slicked for grease, beards flecked with debris.

Their surviving Exalt-General raised a hand to command silence, took the attitude of appraisal, regarding them as the final voices were hounded into silence. His gaze flinched from the gutted carcasses that lay on the tables between him and these Men he must lead. A skull lay tipped in the wreckage, its face half eaten. Proyas clenched his teeth for the heat fondling his loins.

"Anasûrimbor Kellhus ..." Nersei Proyas finally declared, paused out of some bardic instinct. "Our Most Holy Aspect-Emperor has charged *me* with leading the final march upon Golgotterath."

One heartbeat passed, then the assembly leapt to the limit of stature and voice, howling incredulity, shouting dismay. Frenzy had seized them *whole*, soldered them into a singular beast.

Or nearly so, for Prince Nurbanu Ze barged quite alone to the floor, bellowing, "Nooo!" among the burst carcasses. "The Scald consumed Him! My men saw this!"

The uproar crashed into silence.

"Even as the Scald struck them blind, *they saw this!*"

Proyas squinted, then scowled, but Kayûtas was already in *motion*, leaping the nearest trestle with his broadsword drawn, Proyas stammered something he would never remember. The Prince-Imperial's blade hooked white—*cutting* white ... Nurbanu Ze stood stupefied, his expression clogged for incredulity. Blood jetted hot and crimson across the greying scraps and gelling grease ...

Death came swirling down.

And for the merest heartbeat they all saw it, flaring as luminous as flame in a nocturnal cavern, the miracle of the Father in the Son. No mere Man could have done what he had done. No human.

The Jekki Prince pitched backward, flopped across the soiled carpets. Proyas glanced up and out, saw the Lords of the Ordeal laughing, roaring in lunatic *approval*—exultation. And his gaze caught upon the blood-slicked joints and lobes. Drool crowded the corners of his mouth.

He raised his arms high, as though bathing in the elation. He thrust the arch of his manhood against the cheek of their raucous image. Couras Nantilla howled in seizures, mucous threading the black hole of his mouth. Grimmel had dared go so far as clasp his manhood through his kilt.

Kayûtas stood above Nurbanu Ze, strangely stooped and blinking, as if not quite comprehending what he had done. The dead man's bleeding had wetted more than dinner scraps: his dying had pitched poppy red across the Prince-Imperial's nimil hauberk as well—a pattern like a Wracu's crest ...

Few things had seemed so beautiful. Enticing.

Kayûtas caught his gaze, and as if recalling some crisp routine from the blurry edge of stupor, he turned to Proyas stiffly, thrust his hand high in salute, his frame trembling for something more profound than exultation.

Even the *Son* had succumbed, Proyas realized with dim horror—succumbed to the swollen tyranny of the Meat.

What of the Father?

The Lords of the Ordeal redoubled their thunderous acclaim. Hell itself had cast open its gates before them. Tens of thousands had fallen beneath the Scald of Dagliash. Tens of thousands more languished dying for contamination. Their Holy Aspect-Emperor had abandoned them for no reason ...

And yet they *rejoiced*, understanding, at long last, that *murder was glory*.

The air was already filled with orisons when the Interval tolled the following morning, the encampment's myriad thoroughfares and alleyways already brimming with believers. Today Men would cross the Wair Chirsaul—the famed "Mandible Ford" that figured so prominently in the *Holy Sagas*— and begin the final march on Golgotterath. But even though genuine passion cracked their voices, animated their demonstrations as much as ever, something impeded their manner, muddied eyes that should have been clear, blurring hope into hunger, gratitude into gloating.

The weather aggravated matters. Rain fell as cold pellets that stung up-turned cheeks, but sparse enough to make a percussive clatter of canvas and ground alike. It was a drizzle that relentlessly promised downpour, that augured some violent tempest that never came. Blackness lay in the direction of Dagliash, but for ash and smoke, fires that could not be doused by waters, heavenly or terrestrial.

The River Sursa had quickened, taking on the dull grey of the barrens beyond. The shallows of Wair Chirsaul had slowly travelled north over the intervening centuries—a fact attested to by the league or so separating them from the ruins of the Wairing Wall, which had defended the crossing in Far Antiquity. Despite this remarkable pilgrimage, they remained much as the ancient authors had described: a field of rushing waters, cracked and combed into white by the stone beneath, here kicked into roostering geysers, there sucked into swift, ink-black channels. Only the famed bone-fields so eulogized in ancient days were missing; the fords appeared every bit as treacherous as described, otherwise.

A lassitude possessed the Ordealmen, the void of heart and manner that so often follows revels gone mad. The Great Scald had made plain the catastrophic beam of their Enemy's power, and now their Lord-and-Prophet, their Holy Aspect-Emperor, *had abandoned them*. Word of his Will as declared by their Exalt-General had spread as wildfire through the encampment; they knew *what they had to do*, but they knew not how they should *feel*. And so they awoke, frightened by the dark and wanton turbulence kindled in their souls, by the rumours that *they were becoming Sranc*, and for the first time they realized how very far they had wandered from home.

For this was the great secret of faith, the making near of distant things, the making *home* in what was vast with cruelty and indifference. Had the Gods not existed, Men would have almost certainly *made them up*, if only to people what was endless and empty, to trust in what was inscrutable. With Anasûrimbor Kellhus leading them, they had marched the sacred way of Salvation, followed the *Shortest Path*. With King Nersei Proyas, a man like themselves, it seemed they walked as any man walked, naked to untold danger and temptation ...

Only now in the absence of their Master could they fathom how utterly they were exposed. The leagues between them and their homes leaned heavy against their heart and for a time, at least, smothered the embers kindling there.

The Judges saw this apprehension, and so walked among the mucked tracks crying out their exhortations over the droning priests. "Rouse! Rouse! Rejoice, Brothers! For our trial draws to holy conclusion! *Golgotterath*—the very Blight!—lays upon the yonder!" Those they deemed mutinous they seized on charges of impiety as they always did. Only the number of charges laid and the severity of the penalties levied distinguished this morning from any other. Twenty-three Men of the Ordeal, including Baron Orsuwick of Low Kalt, would be staked to the lash, and another seven would be hung from the limbs of the monstrous willow that stood as an unlikely and arthritic sentinel overlooking the Wair. Three would vanish altogether, spawning rumours of ecclesiastic murder and cannibalism.

Were it not for the seven strung from the willow, these events might have vanished in the mass toil of the Crossing. The Exalt-General was not consulted (even though the Aspect-Emperor almost certainly would have been). The Judge who ordered the display, a Galeoth caste-noble named Chassain, had been too ingenious devising his admonition. The nude bodies were lashed to the great boughs not by the arms or torsos, *but by the shins*, so that the miscreants hung upside-down, their arms dangling in tireless supplication, *exactly the way Sranc were hung to bleed*. Thousands of Ordealmen either passed beneath or near them, a great fraction of those who had camped to the north of Wair Chirsaul. Not a soul failed to hear of them. And even though very few made the connection between their dead brothers and their butchered foe, the image roused no less conflict in their hearts. They denied harbouring any such worries, of course, made as they always did when confronted with the grim handiwork of the Ministrate. They played scoundrels, speculating on the offences committed, the punishments meted, and thought themselves holy for scorning dead sinners.

They named the tree the Blood Weeper, and its gloomy image would trouble them all in the wee hours of the following nights, beckoning as a whore might, warding as a leper must—the last tree they would ever see.

The Crossing required two full days. Five lines were strung across the wairing, each bound at intervals to iron poles that had been driven into the water-kicking rock; five tenuous threads that transformed the wairing into the neck of a wrecked lute, strings knotted by labouring, struggling forms, legs braced, steps infirm for the blast of waters, backs heaped with armour and supplies. Many bore the butchered arms and legs of Sranc, meat scavenged from the fields to the south. The limbs were bound at the wrists or ankles to short segments of rope that could be slung over shoulders or across necks, conspiring to create what, from a certain distance at least, appeared a most ghastly apparel, a swinging mantle of what seemed the arms and legs of *women and children*, given the creature's lithe and pallid hairlessness. Those who fell from the upstream lines would often spin into others, creating a flailing avalanche, dozens of Men reaching out from wagging blooms of severed, Sranc limbs.

No fewer than three hundred and sixty-eight souls perished for mishap. Few names of note were lost, among them Mud Waigwa, a monstrous Holca thane who attempted to drag ten Sranc carcasses across the wairing with him; and Lord Urbommû Hamazrel, one of Nurbanû Soter's martial advisors, who simply stumbled, let slip the rope, and was ripped away.

As the Ordealmen gained the mire of the far shore, their brothers pulled them gasping from the collapsed embankments. Still sodden, they were funnelled into packed avenues, hounded by shouts to keep moving, always keep moving. So they stumbled onward, wringing hair and beard, pawing brow and eyes. A more amorphous congregation engulfed them, an immense gyre of souls likewise lurching, sorting between backs and shoulders, calling out to unseen kinsmen. The lifeless ground beneath their feet would be all they could see of the legendary Field Appalling. And it seemed more carnival than invasion, at least until the bristling masses thinned and parted, yielding space to cast aside their grisly encumbrances and find breast-heaving respite either leaning against or dropping to their knees. To a soul they peered into the west, across the vacancy that was Agongorea seen from Agongorea.

Distances piled upon distances as with any other vista, but the land was so scalloped as to possess an *edge*, to scrape as an oyster shell against the habits of the eye. Men are but one more fruit of the earth, at least apart from the divinity that animates them. To gaze upon land, any land, is to gaze upon *what can sustain Men*. But to peer across the Field Appalling was to look upon a land that suffered no life whatsoever, that rebuked, not simply Men, but their very foundation. "No ants," the Southron Men would say, disguising their unease by pretending to marvel. "The land has no ants." And they shuddered for the premonition of poison.

The sun lay as a crimson bulb upon the horizon by time the final contingents, Shigeki and Nansur for the most part, had "leapt the Knife," as the Ordealmen called the act of crossing the wair. The Lords of the Ordeal raised greasy bowls in slicked fingers to toast their Exalt-General in the Umbilicus that night. "Steersman," they called him, a blessed name, for despite the grievous toll, despite the losses of countrymen, even friends, it seemed a miraculous thing to deliver souls so numerous and unruly across the honed edge of the Sursa. If anything, the eulogy given for the Palatine of Kisht-ni-Secharib occasioned more relish than solemnity among those gathered. Rumour said that Urbommû Adokarsa, Lord Hamazrel's younger brother and nominal successor could not stop *grinning* as he related the events that saw his brother drown.

Nersei Proyas called on the pits to be fired, the carcasses to be hoisted, so they might plot their glorious final march sated, their hearts clear of hunger. But such never happened. Called on to plan nothing less than *Salvation*, the Lords of the Ordeal traded morsels and howls instead. They lingered deep into the wiles of night, recounting stories of mishaps witnessed, drownings rumoured or seen. And Meat or no Meat, how could they not roar in exultation? How could they not set aside their care, if only for a span, and glory in the cruelties they had survived and inflicted?

The Horde was destroyed. They stood upon the fabled shores of *Agongorea*, the limit of the great Field Appalling. Soon they would spy the very *Horns of Golgotterath*! Soon they would *overthrow* them! Deliver the God's own fury to the Unholy Consult.

And so they set aside their care and *rejoiced*, indulged acts that would have seen them shamed and murdered, stricken from the ancestor lists of their progeny ...

Were they back home.

Faces were always more real. This was why they appeared scowling or grinning in so many things, from the mottle of fired bricks or the staining of
sodden plasters, to the deformities of trees and the grace of clouds. *All
things possessed a face*; one need only coax or coerce it from hiding. And
as much as faces betrayed the kinship between Men and the World, it betokened their kinship to one another far more. The face both regarded
and *was* regarded, bold before foes and downcast before lovers. Bodies
were but impressions, glimpses stretched to cover the whole. Ever did Men
turn face to face.

And it was *this* that Proyas saw leaning into the small heap of flame, *faces*
... faces bleached in his combusting vision, beards larded, cheeks lacquered,
sockets housing twin incendiary glitters ... faces exulting, grinning beneath
a dark look, about a famished bite, at the daring malice of some brother ...
grimacing, shrieking, whipping in mammalian extremis ... faces thrown like
rags against balled fists ... faces cracking, folding into cloth and mud an

"*That is not for you to do, Uncle.*"

Proyas yanked back from the Seeing-Flame, marvelled as always that he
could feel its heat only as he leaned away. He pawed his own mien to convince incredulous fingers that he had not blistered then turned. A warlike
figure stood at the threshold to the Aspect-Emperor's spare chamber, otherworldly for the thousands of dancing tangerine lines the firelight cast
across his Ishroi arms and armour. The leather-panelled imagery hung as
shadowy apparitions about him, more history and scripture, lost to the
mummery of the immediate.

"You should leave the Hearth be."

"Your father ..." Proyas gasped, staring wide at the flame-etched phantom
that was Anasûrimbor Kayûtas ... his Prophet's son, the boy he had all but
raised. "He wanted me to see."

The air became thick with the unthinkable.

"We are *exempt*, Uncle, can you not see?"

The figure neared ... so like *him*, only cold with nimil, alien with ghoulish
insignia, afire with mirrored splinters. The lips beckoned from the corn-
silk mat that was his beard.

"What misdeed," Kayûtas said, his voice lowered to a growl, "can be committed in the shadow of such a foe? What wickedness? The license to do
evil—this has ever been the great prize of the righteous!"

The young man closed a callused hand about his aching handle, bore him up to the brink.

"What did Father tell you?"

The Exalt General stood riven, bent crooked to some essential asymmetry, like a broken bow fiercely drawn. His eyes fluttered. He sneered about drool. And it seemed that he cared not what happened ... so long as there was *blood*.

"That—" Proyas began only to pause on a thick swallow. "That the Men must ... must *eat* ..."

The Prince-Imperial smiled in impish triumph.

"See?" the hand said, for that was all that existed now—mouths and hands.

"What does it matter, *becoming Sranc*," cruel fingers cooed ...

So long as we save the World.

Did you hear? More shrieking.

I love the crack of those fat teeth in the fire—the sound of something precious heeled.

It burns ... burns as a beacon within you.

But where char meets the fat ... that is what quickens!

Your hatred. Your will to tear down, destroy.

Sweet, yet with the salts of fired life!

It comes as a clawing, I know ... A wolven panic.

The fat seething about the crisping skin ... Yes!—it lies in the juice of the beast.

The Meat is *obscuring us*—can't you see? Like a cataract of the inner eye.

And that beard of sizzling froth!

Scratching us into something ... too scrawny for human fetters—too quick!

The way it hangs like spit.

The residue of strife lay strewn across the lifeless plain.

King Iswolor rested out there, his bones as old as Ûmerau. So too did those belonging to the legendary Tynwur, the Bull of Sauglish, sent to his death for the jealously of King Carû-Ignaini of Trysë. His skeletal remains also lay exposed in eternal indignity, blunt and elephantine in a ring of layered Sranc helter ...

No bones found burial in this land.

No bones found burial *because nothing grew.* No thistles. No amaranth. No lichens graced the rare bare stone. Black stumps yet stubbled the outermost swath of the landscape, pilings of rotted obsidian, remnants of the arboreal forest blotted by the arrival of the Incû-Holoinas. Lying in the lee of the cataclysm, the plain had been mortared in ash, a powder as fine as pumice but toxic to all life, and perpetually sodden, like the earth about waters. One could clench it in his fist, cast it skyward, but it would not blow. The wind whisked and whistled across the bleak horizons as though over a vast shield of metal.

The keen-eyed swore that gold flecked the unholy humus. And indeed on certain angles of sunlight, it *gleamed* in the corners of one's eye.

The Men of Kûniûri had called it Agongorea, which the scribes of the Three Seas, ever slaves to their manuals, translated as 'the Fields-of-Woe.' But Agongorea was itself a translation of the Ihrimsû name the Far Antique Norsirai had learned from their Siqu teachers: Vishrûnûl, the Nonmen called it—the Field Appalling. Their whiter bones lay beneath the wrack of Men, the splintered and charred residuum of their millennial war against the Inchoroi: the nocturnal slaughter following the disaster of Imogirion; the bitter glory of Isal'imial, the battle that cast the last of the Inchoroi and their bestial hordes upon Min-Uroikas for the final time; and much more, enough to transform the flats and the valleys into a vast crypt floor.

The rain had stopped. Dawn bullied the last of the clouds from the sky, and the Interval tolled sonorous through the stone-combed wash of the River Sursa. The Ordealman stirred from their uneasy slumber, rose to join those already gazing and blinking at the sunlit revelation. Many peered, turned to their fellows with anxious queries. The distance, once uniform in its cadaverous pallor, was now sheeted with smashed pottery, grey embroidered in great columns and arcs and rings of human gravel.

The dead, they were told. The dead cobbled their way. "*We march into a tomb ...*" the impious muttered, though under their breaths, lest the Judges hear.

None spoke of the debauched night. They skirted the corpses and the flotsam of brutality, avid to move on. Men squared their kits, gorged on the remnants of the feast. Within a watch, the clarion horns of the Three Seas sounded, and with hymns to their Aspect-Emperor kindled in innumerable hoarse throats, the Holy Host of Hosts embarked. The dead were left as daybreak had found them. There was no question of counting them, for they, like the crimes that had maimed and murdered them, charged a toll too high to be permitted to exist.

The Great Ordeal passed as a migratory cloud into the vacancy of Agongorea. That night they camped across what the ancient Norsirai had named Creärwi, or the Bald. For the first time, the Holy Host of Hosts trod upon the *very same earth* as had the ancient Ordeal assembled by Anasûrimbor Celmomas. The Judges passed as wild hermits among the Ordealmen, vestments soiled, eyes overbright, exhorting them to rejoice for reaching the very Bald named in scripture! They bid them *feast*, for never had salvation lain so near! "The *Horns*!" they cried. "Soon the Horns of Golgotterath shall prick the horizon!"

And so once again was wickedness transmuted into worship, atrocity into praise. Night fell as dishevelled hair, a fraught reprieve from the sun's tyranny. The Nail of Heaven hung as a bared knife pending judgment, and the sprawling desolation of Agongorea gleamed as though alloyed with diamonds. The errant Sons of the Three Seas gorged upon their cherished foe. Pavilions became fuel, and sizzling shanks were held out upon spears over the fires. The singularity of the night consumed them, a darkness and an appetite out of joint with the passing of the days, a welling up from oblivion. Orgiastic excess, priapic violence, shrieks and gales of vicious hilarity—these blew through them, licentious gusts that commanded fists, mouths, and hands. Compelled crimes—both of the meat and for the meat. Only the exhaustion of their supply bridled the evil intensity of the bacchanal. For this was the night they consumed the last of the Meat and began slaughtering the first of the remaining ponies.

The morning saw the Ordealmen anxious for hunger. A strange rictus seized the faces of those few who, either for wretched luck or station, had gone entirely without, a grin that spoke of toothless hate and death in the desert sun.

Proyas looked out from the fires of the hallowed Tribe of Truth and despite his revulsion, exulted in the countless sins he saw.

Images slick and hard and labile, fixing him, whipping his heart with tantrums, meat pummelling meat, bone breaking bone, sweet with visions of stink, shining with exertion, excreta. It was the *meat* that winced, the *meat* that battled then struggled then twitched and curled.

Nothing could be more deep.

And yet Men chose *breath* over meat in all things fundamental. Everywhere, they hung what was holy upon the ephemeral and the fleeting, things too thin to age, too numb to suffer, or too quick to need flee. They would sooner celebrate their own exhalation than submit to the bottomless fact of their meat.

Fey fools! What was the soul if not a veil drawn by Men to spare themselves the indignities of their stink? A gown always unmudded for being always unseen!

Crouched naked in his Lord's chamber, the Exalt-General rocked and cackled and screamed.

"Yes!" he cried. "*That's* it! *With the knife!*"

The God was inhuman ... A spider.

Of nothing and for no one.

While the Meat, of its own accord, grew dark and swollen for beauty.

The Interval did not sound the following morning.

The sun found the encampment strewn across the vast bleak, the capital of a savage and refugee nation.

They rose one by one, lurched from their tents and shelters, more the artifice of potters than Men. Not a soul had dreamed. A breathlessness stubbed their hearts for glimpsing the wages their fellows had paid for their bliss. But a void dwelt where the clamour of trauma and unspeakable transgression should have been, a reflexive blindness to what they had become ...

Were becoming.

"*Our Prophet has fled us ...*" some dared whisper to their brothers.

And so too had the Meat.

With infirm haste, the Ordealmen made ready, toiled to expense the fund of horror within them. But it was the prospect of the days ahead, not the insanity of the nights passed, that moved them. *The Meat had been exhausted!* And now they marched *away* from fields where the carcasses lay heaped. What did the count of days matter, when rot simply made skinnies taste sweet? To simply think this was to be stricken to the pit. Skin flushed moist. Scalps pricked. Everywhere one looked, Men could be seen *swallowing*, endlessly chasing the mirage of charred and larded morsels from their tongues. And they hurried, lest sloth further license their wistful imaginings ... make incarnate what could not bear the shaming sun. There is a way that Men *lean* against the hungers that wrack them, an angle that leverages their greater nature. Ever are Men raised upright by what twists their soul. There is a fanaticism that radiates in proportion to the monstrosities concealed.

The Holy Host of Hosts set out without order or cohesion, rancid flocks moving as though condensed in the same oil, drifting in runnels and clots across the pubis of the land. Bones cracked beneath innumerable heels. The sky claimed the stunning emptiness that makes for sharp autumnal days, a wintry premonition. The air forever seemed too thin to feed the fire creeping about their limbs. Not a voice was raised in conversation, let alone song or psalter. The march, rather, became one of reflection and private re-monstrance, an occasion to enumerate all the accursed errors that had de-livered them to such disaster ...

What would they eat?

The Ordealmen wandered across the horizon-spanning exhumation. Souls teemed across every vista, Tydonni with their beards cast over their left shoulder, Ainoni dragging their shields like harrows, Nansur Colum-naries with their packs teetering on their heads. Despite their unkempt ap-pearance, they toiled with hale vigour, an alacrity rendered fearsome for their expressions.

The remaining horsemen roped ahead of the migration. They stared across what seemed a more elemental earth, a landscape flayed and whittled, *peeled*, a ground skinned to the *foundation*, so that for some, it seemed they wandered the very Floor of Creation. Even the clouds, spare as they had become, seemed to whisper for reverence. Bones and dirt extended ad in-finitum about them, radiating into a plate that raced the sky. Many found solace in the desolation, hallucinating evidence of design in its simplicity. Never, it seemed, had they been less *embroiled*. Their shadows leaned in their saddles, peering. To cross Agongorea was to autopsy all landscapes, to cut down to the essential, to be stranded with implacable emptiness ... and the life required to conquer it.

Men began praying aloud for sign of Sranc.

"Who?" they began asking. "Who will feed us now?"

Behind them, the smear blackening the skies above Dagliash had become the last visual relic of the old World. Mouths watered at the sight, despite the halo of poisonous ochre.

By midafternoon, guarded looks had become bold unto reckless. Eyes began roaming ... Anyone who faltered for any reason was noted by a parade of passing glances; those who vomited, especially, or betrayed lesions, or shed locks of hair. For some unfathomable reason, the victims never seemed to know ... or to care ... even as they scrutinized those about them for the selfsame signs. No one fled. Not one soul so much as curried favour, let alone resorted to unmanly acts of ingratiation. Aside from a dark and scintillant play of looks, everyone acted as though night would never come.

Had any soul reflected, it would have noted how *everything*, in fact, had taken on the lean glamour of pretense, how all the old actions, all the old words, everything impeccant habit rendered effortless and automatic, had somehow become *besides the point* ...

How all the old realities had decayed into matters of the Meat.

Simply hearing the once-accursed name, *Sranc*, pricked the ears, alerted the heart to the possibility that somewhere, somehow, *more Meat had been found*. Dolour was roused into clamour. And as so often happens, anonymity offered up the very tales that want and suspicion demanded. Stranded with their households in the thick of the masses, several Believer-Kings went so far as to whip their horses to the fore of the Host, chasing this or that rumour of contact with their foe. "Secure our portion!" their kin and countrymen cried. An eagerness was kindled within the breast of thousands, a need to *see for oneself* what lay beyond the obscuring humanity. A corresponding dread voided the souls of thousands of others, an abrupt certainty they would be *denied their due*, robbed of their portion. Individual shouts cascaded into a general outcry, which served to provoke haste from thousands more. Men began running where they could. Some cast down their weapons and shields. Others tripped into chasms between their fellows, bellowed, first in incredulity, then in suffocated terror, infecting the roiling plains with even more fear, more abandon ...

Death came swirling down. The first of the Schoolmen abandoned their baggage-trains to the chaos and took to the sky singing. The thousands about them cried out, and the crowds convulsed with even greater violence, convinced the sorcerers acted on word of Sranc ...

Soon hundreds of witches and sorcerers hung pinned over the riotous plain.

And so, after conquering thousands of leagues, surviving the cleavers of a million Sranc, the Great Ordeal *was put to route* by its own dark humours. Men chased for bald sight of chasing, nothing more—bodies echoing bodies in panic. What had been a great mass trudging westward suddenly blew outward, thinning across the plain. Since nonexistent Meat had no direction, the Ordealmen apparently chased all directions.

Those Lords who stood firm could only marvel, stupefied. The Exalt-General, the Conriyan chronicler Mirathais would write, grew as ashen as the ground vacated around him. "Smoke," he allegedly said. "For want of meat, we have become smoke."

Then it happened.

The Ordeal had shattered upon its own depravity, a collective end dissolving into more than a hundred thousand grains of evil desperation, which then ... miraculously, *found themselves caught.*

Heads turned to the charcoal line of the west, where the afternoon orb of the sun hung ringed with sundogs, brilliant in a manner that darkened rather than illuminated what lay below. Not a soul could fail to see them: two shining threads, like golden wire poked through the horizon's reptilian hide ...

Something like a moan passed through the Holy Host. Trumpets wailed from points across the plain. The Men of the Circumfix began falling to their knees, fields drawing down fields, though for worship or wonder or dumb relief, none would ever know ...

The dread Horns ... *The Horns of Golgotterath* had finally pricked the horizon, a shining beacon of all that was wicked, all that was obscene and unholy.

For the nonce, the Meat was forgotten.

The Exalt-General wept, Mirathais would write in his journal, "as a father who finds a vanished child."

CHAPTER FOUR

The Demua Mountains

A fetish is a belief that a fist might hold.
—"Rejoinders," Pseudo-Protathis

Early Autumn, 20 New Imperial Year (4132, Year-of-the-Tusk), Far Wuor.

Daylight fell upon the dead land, warmed the clay and the canopy alike. The virtues once extolled by the Bardic Priests of yore thrummed with the grasshoppers that exploded from their feet, warbled with the birdsong that resounded above their heads. Resurgent earth. Air quick with flies and lazy with bees. From the Mountains all the way to the mighty River Aumris the land was thus, temperate, fertile. Wuor it had been called, a name that came to mean "plenty" to the Sons of ancient Ûmerau.

But then came the reoccupation of Min-Uroikas and with it the infiltration of Sranc across the narrows of the Leash. Despite the oaths made and the redoubts raised, the northwest became perilous to the point where only the forts remained, and the region was eventually abandoned. Wuor shrank, becoming a more limited province on the shoulder of the Aumris. The new frontier came to be called Anûnuarcû, a march that would be famed for the Knights-Chieftain it sired. The land conceded to the Foe, the land Achamian and Mimara now travelled, would come to be known as Far Wuor.

It had been long forsaken, a victim of Golgotterath centuries before the First Apocalypse had blighted the Sons of the Norsirai entirely. His chest ached for simply walking ... for crossing Far Wuor as Seswatha had. Henceforth, the old Wizard realized, it would always be thus, always be a matter of travelling into ever more accursed land. They were drawing near—insanely near! Soon they would set eyes upon *them*, the shining horrors on the horizon, the golden tusks climbing to the height of mountain peaks, goring all that is true ...

Just thinking about it winded him, set his limbs upon bubbles of terror.

"You're muttering again ..." Mimara piped from his side.

"What?" Achamian barked, affecting indignant surprise.

Given all they had endured, it was mad to think they could still be such cowards when it came to each other. But such was love, in the end, forever fearing the testimony of the other.

Mimara was the lesser coward, of course, always the first to discover her fortitude, and so always the first to plague and harry.

"Who's *Nautzera?*" she pressed, her attention pointed and immovable.

He flinched, walked with a more hooded manner.

"Spare me your vinegar, woman. My cuts sting quite well unassisted ..."

Achamian had suffered too much to possess a generous, or even an honest, soul. To be put upon is to rehearse grudges, to ruminate upon welts and switches, the marks left and the instruments responsible. Writing his banned history of the First Holy War amounted to writing the *history* of his degradation. Ink affords all souls the luxury of innocence. To write is to be quick where all else is still, to bully facts with words until they begin weeping. And so the old Wizard drew up lists of offenders and summaries of their crimes. Unlike other embittered souls, he knew the particulars of his victimization with a scholar's self-serving precision, and he had long ago determined that Nautzera was the greatest of the criminals.

Even after all these years, he could still hear the wretch's voice creaking through the gloom of Atyersus. "*Ah yes ... I forgot you numbered yourself among the skeptics ...*"

Were it not for Nautzera, he would not be here now, freighted by losses beyond numbering. Were it not for Nautzera, *Inrau* would still be alive.

"*I guess, then, you would say a possibility, that we are witnessing the first days of the No-God's return, is outweighed by an actuality, the life of a defector ...*"

Inrau!

"*That rolling the dice of apocalypse is worth the pulse of a fool ...*"

"Nautzera is from the old days, isn't he?" Mimara persisted. "The First Holy War."

He ignored her, fuming in the disjoint way Men are prone when unaware of their fear or anger. Mumbling! When he had he started mumbling?

Together they followed what had been the bed of an ancient road across the many-cloven feet of the Demua. The stonework had been pulverized for the weight of emptiness and weather long ago, leaving only an overgrown dike that roped high and low, continuous save for the countless creeks and streams that had cracked its nethers asunder long, long ago. To their left, the world piled upward, conifers spearing dark from the climbing canopies. What might have been turrets flanged the nearest scarps, stone skinned in lichen where not otherwise flayed and pitted. The mountains reared massive and snow-capped beyond. But to their right, the world fell away, knitted the very horizon with arboreal crowns—birches, maples, larches and more— great and full and summer-weary.

And ahead of them ... to the north ... It was at once the direction he walked, and the direction he could not see.

"It terrifies you ..." Mimara said from his side.

"I *know* what awaits us," he replied, spooked for her penetration, speaking more from the ache in his chest than his throat.

He trailed to a stop at the summit of the rise, watched Mimara stroll ahead, hands pressed to the back of her hips, her abdomen making a bulb of her golden hauberk. The pregnant woman snapped a birch branch obscuring their view, left it hanging like a lamed bird wing. The Demua buckled the horizon beyond her, backed everything into indeterminate haze, one too cold to be called violet. And it seemed *he could feel it out there*, Golgotterath, like a bruise hidden for shame, like a stitch in the throat that could not be swallowed away. There was nothing to see save a vibrant land unfurling from cloud-wricking knuckles of stone, but he could feel it all the same ...

Waiting?

"Nautzera is an old rival of mine in the Mandate," he admitted. "The soul that set me upon the very path we trod now ... The one I most blame, I suppose ... aside from Kellhus."

Mimara had unstopped her waterskin to take a swig. "Why so?"

The old Wizard waved away her offer to drink. "He's the one who sent me to Sumna, to suborn a former student of mine to spy on your uncle,

the Holy Shriah. He feared Maithanet might have something to do with
the Consult—even though no one had uncovered any sign of them in centuries, at that point ..."

"And what happened?"

"My student died."

She peered at him. "Maithanet had him killed?"

"No ... The Consult assassinated him."

She frowned. "So the mission was a success."

"*Success?*" the old Wizard cried. "I lost Inrau!"

"Yes, well ... Lives must always be thrown with the sticks when you command. Surely your student knew as much. Nautzera as well."

"No one knew anything back then!"

She graced him with an insouciant shrug—one of many little relics of
jnan she had carried away from Carythusal.

"So you don't think uncovering the Consult was worth *one* life?"

"Of course it was!"

"So then Nautzera merely demanded *what had to be done* ..."

Achamian sputtered, tried to communicate his fury through his glare,
knowing he betrayed something quite different.

"What? What are you saying?"

She gazed at him, devoid of expression for a long moment.

Every human act has its season, its effortless stage, even determinations
of the heart. *Nothing* guarantees judgments made in one age will be appli-
cable in the next, that piety and justice will remain pious and just *come
what may*. We all understand this, somehow. We all possess the joints required to bend this way and that, to be what our circumstances sometimes
gently, sometimes violently, demand. If hatred renders us inflexible it's because, like love, it commits us to *others*. To hate is to *sin against* ... What
soul was so execrable as to wish evil on the *innocent*? Or worse yet, the *heroic*.

Nautzera *had to be criminal*, lest Achamian himself stand charged.

"Your student ..." Mimara said, picking her words as if fearing what she
saw in his mien. "Inrau ... You do understand that he perished for a *reason*,
Akka ... that his life had more meaning than he could possibly fathom."

"*Of course!*" he cried out, his ears buzzing.

It was happening! The Second Apocalypse was happening!

Which meant that *Nautzera had been right all along* ...

The Wizard hung breathing, every pinch of his being a tingle, a sting.

Nautzera had been right all along. Inrau's pulse had proven a *bargain*.

Achamian turned from her, the mother of his unborn child, lest she see him weep. He plunged down the spine of the ancient road, into the wilds of Far Wuor ...

Some two thousand years after the light of Men had been extinguished in this corner of the World.

They had taken to snorting the Qirri the way the Survivor had before leaping to his death. Neither of them made mention of this, though both of them understood it with the clarity of monumental inscription. Instead, they told each other that the *Scylvendi* pursued them, that *Cnaiür urs Skiötha* peered into the horizon, seeking some glimpse of their furtive forms. More than wisdom or even hope, Qirri was *necessity*. After all, the *People of War* galloped in their wake ...

So they raced through the night, trotting through wooded galleries, wading across rushing, roaring, moon-silvered streams. Mimara fell picking her way across one particularly evil tributary. She lost her footing on the mossed lip of a boulder, swung about in an attempt to recover, then simply vanished into the gushing blast. For a heartbeat, Achamian could scarcely breathe, let alone call out or leap into sorcerous action. By time he recovered his wits, she was already hauling herself onto the far shore some twenty lengths away, hacking water. He rushed to her side, fussed in the speechless way of one who ministers to disasters of their own making.

"What of the pouch?" he finally managed to ask.

She swatted through her sodden pelts, her eyes wide, but quickly found the rune-embroidered thing flattened against the purse she used to hold her two Chorae. They crouched upon a moonlit rock, hunched to inspect the contents, with their nostrils if not their eyes. She looked beautiful for the way the damp flattened her hair into jet—so very much like her mother. He could do no more than glance at her gold-scaled belly.

"Why?" the Scylvendi barbarian raved in his soul's eye. "*Why have you come, Drusas Achamian? Why have you dragged your bitch across a thousand screaming, rutting leagues? Tell me, what moves a man to cast number-sticks across his woman's womb?*"

Though Mimara was the one sodden, Achamian would be the one wracked with chills when they resumed.

So they crossed Far Wuor in fits and sprints. Mosquitos plagued them during certain watches, hung so thick as to form scribbling haloes around the moon and the Nail-of-Heaven, and left them almost entirely unmolested during others. Walking had ceased taxing them at some point, becoming something far nearer sleep—or at least something less wakeful, more automatic, more effortless. Achamian did not so much own or experience his strides as he *floated* on them, like an indolent Ketyai prince borne upon the litter of his own body. He found himself wandering at right angles to the world, both walking, negotiating pitched ground and rugged terrain, and dreaming in a peculiar, frenetic sense, hearing a voice that he recognized as his own voice, and suffering desires more obstinate than his own.

"No!" he heard himself cry. "*What you say ...*"

He found himself walking *into* the Scylvendi's apparition, the wraith of Cnaiür glaring into his eyes, grating in the voice of floods and landslides, the *heat* of him, the *stink*, promising at once murder and congress.

"*Twenty winters have thawed, and now you find yourself in my tent, sorcerer, every bit as lost, as baffled and dismayed! Every bit as blind to the darkness that comes before!*"

He wandered far from his walking.

The Qirri was there, of course, a prop for the canvas ceilings of his heart and soul. It alone cleared the spaces within and about him, made it possible for his body to march where his will could not hope to follow. It was *always* there, not so much lurking as mooning about, sulking for being bound within a sack, desiccate, inert. A nagging in the background. *Free me! Give me life!*

And for all the madness, nothing, it seemed, could be more proper. If they consumed Nil'giccas, then Nil'giccas imbibed them, the residue of one soul blown across the coals of another, flickering into a brighter flame. Consuming Qirri, the old Wizard realized, was a form of *giving*, not taking, a way to resurrect the Last Nonman King—Cleric!—to bear his being upon the back of their own living life.

He caught himself shouting aloud at one point, crying, "*What choice? What choice?*" The Qirri was the only reason they had found Sauglish, the only reason they had survived Ishuäl, the only reason they trod the skirts of Golgotterath. *They had no choice.* So why was he arguing? Because it was evil? Because it amounted to cannibalism, *eating* another sentient soul? Because it was slowly twisting their sensibilities in ways they could scarce conceive? Because it was beginning, ever so slowly, to own their thoughts, let alone their passions?

What did any of this matter to someone damned always already?

This was his death march, his long and anguished climb to the Golden Room. His Dreams even augured as much! This!—*this was his death*, his doom and damnation!

To die the death allotted to Seswatha.

"No," Mimara was gasping, from somewhere—behind? The whole world was walking now, angular shadows massed into scissoring forests. "No, Akka, no!" Had he been speaking aloud? All that distinguished them was their *direction*, how they walked *toward* what all Creation fled.

"We march for *life*!" she cried, her tone as absolute as prophecy. "For hope!"

He would remember nothing else until dawn gilded the wild rim of the East, save laughing at her declaration.

The vista seemed colder than he had remembered—in his Dreams at least.

No matter how carefully wrought, maps always misled. So on surviving maps of the Ancient North in the Three Seas, the estuary Achamian and Mimara peered across was invariably called the "Straits of Aögus," a title befitting the dignity of the names surrounding. But outside those schooled in the cartographic traditions of Sauglish, no High Norsirai of Seswatha's day had called the waters thus. They called it, rather, Ogni, a Condic slang term for "Leash."

The great estuary heaved chill and black before them, crashed into foam along the stunted shore. Gulls, terns, and a great many other birds seemed to have gone mad for the waters, some hanging upon unseen sheets of breeze, others buzzing the surface, descending in constellations, spooking in flurries. Scavenging cries harrowed the wind, pricked the autumnal emptiness ever deeper as Mimara and the old Wizard laboured near, becoming a shrill racket.

Scalloped for exhaustion, the companions wondered at the avian horde without any will to puzzle or resolve. Wind runnelled the grasses about them, flapped scrub and sumac like blankets.

Achamian was the first to cry out, for once his eye registered them, *he saw them everywhere*, congesting the straits. Sranc. Innumerable carcasses tangled the shallows, putrid rafts bending about swells, larding the waters with corruption. On and on the mass extended, out across the deeps, drawn into eddies the size of cities, monstrous wheels of sodden and blasted meat.

The old Wizard tripped back onto his rump, eyes fluttering. Mimara was slow to kneel at his side. Even hovering over him, her gaze lingered upon the spectacle. An errant cloud smothered the sun, and a sudden translucence revealed the tattered face of the drowning, as well as the rare *Men* bobbing among the fish-white masses, their limbs clothed, their jaws bearded.

Achamian gawked at the girl, stammering, "Kellhus ... he ... he *found a way* ... a way to destroy the Horde." He combed his scalp, his eyes darting. "At-at Dagliash ... Yes-yes! Remember that black cloud we spied on the horizon leaving Ishuäl? That could have been Dagliash ... the *cause* of this."

She blinked, finally focussing. "I don't understand."

The old cogitations came to him quickly. "The River Sursa empties on the north shore of the Misty Sea ... It would catch the Sranc as the Ordeal marched on Dagliash. Kellhus would have no choice but to grapple with the Horde in its entirety ... to somehow overcome it!"

Mimara looked back to the carrion expanse. At some point she had started clicking the scales of her Sheära hauberk with her fingertips when rubbing her belly.

"So this is the Horde ..."

"What else could it be?"

She regarded him more narrowly than he liked.

"So my stepfather already marches on Golgotterath."

Teeth set, he nodded. They needed Qirri, he thought. Haste.

The World was ending.

"I can carry you across ..." he said with the tentative air of broaching old and unresolved feuds. He could weep for the sight of her, gowned in rotted hides and cloth, her cropped hair matted, her eyes shining mad from the stained oval of her face ...

Immense with child—*his child!*

"But you must relinquish your accursed Trinkets."

The injury these words occasioned shocked him.

"They only appear such," she said, "because *you* are accursed."

CHAPTER FIVE

Agongorea

Men are ever the edge of Men, the plummet most near, and the fall most fatal.
Rhetoric consists in the artful use of ropes and ladders.
—The First Analytic of Men, AJENCIS

As flint they fracture,
As flint they sharpen,
Men only cut for breaking.

—Scalper shanty

Early Autumn, 20 New Imperial Year (4132, Year-of-the-Tusk), Golgotterath.

Four hundred horses were butchered, many of them cruelly, so that for watch after watch, equine screams lacerated the night. Many Men danced besotted, mimicked the screams in grotesque parody, especially those that had sacrificed their own steed. Sorcerous fire alone burned that night, for even as fratricide passed unmentioned, the burning of belongings had been forbidden. The Judges stamped through their midst, demanding worship, urging celebration. *The Horns lay on the horizon*, an evil Nail bent and jutting into Eärwa's scarred bosom, the thorn infecting the whole of history and legend—and what they themselves must draw. But for all their fanatic ardour, the Judges themselves seemed half-hearted—even false. The horseflesh provided no sustenance, tasted cold even when sizzling, and swallowed like clay. Stomachs cramped for outrage. Throughout the night thousands arose to vomit their repast, all in terror of those who observed.

But few would be assaulted that night. Though the dark hungers of the Ordealmen had waxed more keenly if anything, they had become more difficult to *aim*. Even as the watches dwindled, so their yearning to *consume* came to blot the greater host of wicked desire. The recitals and ceremonial rites crumbled as bread, dissolved as sand. Sickened for horseflesh, the greater number of Ordealmen retired rather than pursue congress, huddled riven in the black, oppressed by growling, rending thoughts of the Meat, reliving the ecstasy, the horror ...

The Nail of Heaven gleamed in the clarion void above them, wetting their ruined tents and pavilions with luminance, a gloaming across the endless crypt that was the Field Appalling.

The Horns flashed mercurial on the darkling horizon, the hook upon which all lines converged.

Shimmered as an earthbound twin.

"Can't you see, Uncle? This hunger *is naught but the Shortest Path* ..."

The Exalt-General stared up at Kayûtas, stunned. The scriptural panels hung indistinct in the shadows about the man, a congregation of spies. When had the gardened, sanctuary air of his Lord-and-Prophet succumb to the reek and lather of a catamite lair?

"Why do we trade gods as we trade spices?" the Prince-Imperial pressed. "Why do philosophers endlessly dispute the abstract? The *flesh*, Uncle"— he spanked his bare thigh—"*meat* anchors our every measure. The bliss that indulges versus the bliss that denies—*both reside within the flesh!* Don't you see? The hermit is naught but an insane libertine, a soul that has confused war for empire, and so must twist its way to dominion."

The *things* ... the things he had witnessed, the bloody harems, strung in grinding tangles throughout the encampment, blood-slicked beauty convulsing in the pit of each.

He had fractured at some point, become someone who watched *without touching* as the Greater Proyas seethed unbridled ... romped unchecked. It had occurred to him that perhaps he held his face pressed into some *higher flame*, that he merely watched in a manner *more profound*, more entrenched—

that life was nothing more than grovelling in flame. Either way, the moments where he watched and lived *as one* were becoming progressively more rare ...

And unendurable.

"Enough!" he erupted. "What are you saying?"

He was missing something. There was more to this ...

"What you already know, Uncle."

"And what is that?"

The Prince-Imperial loomed pale and flaxen and carnivorous.

"That *something must be eaten.*"

The artful general, Triamis the Great famously wrote, must keep slack looped within a cruel fist.

"*Sweet God of Gods, who walks among us,*" the caste-noble chorus intoned, voices deep with majesty, clipped with harried inattention, a need to dispense with mere ceremonial mummery ...

"*Innumerable are your holy names ...*"

To be commanded, Men must always *feel* the constraint of their commander, the firm hand that perpetually *threatened* to choke each warrior *individually*. Individuals could be culled, whipped or even executed. So long as there was reason in it, the ranks conceded this to their commanders. A disciplined host was a victorious host, and the punishment of malcontents was preferable to slaughter on the field. But if there was no reason or proportion to the punishment meted, or if the crimes punished were collectively viewed as *spoils*—as due exchange for grievous sacrifices made, say—then woe to the general who dared yank the leash too hard. Great generals, Triamis believed, had to be as much *augur* as orator and tactician; among all the traits and abilities that conspired to create battlefield brilliance, none was so crucial as the ability to *read the ranks*, to look into the amorphous rumble and see when the leash need be jerked, slackened, or even altogether *released*.

The simple fact of the matter, after all, was that armies *went where they willed*. By divining that destination, the general could command what had already been decreed, dispense the inevitable as wages, and so transform mutiny into adulation. The great general always *owned* the acts of his army.

No matter how depraved or criminal.

Proyas—who had first read the famed *Journals and Dialogues* when he was eleven, who had presided over as many victories as Triamis himself!—knew this lesson as well as any soul breathing.

He must own what was happening ...

He must bid his Men *eat* ... lest he be consumed.

He stood panting at his place to the right of his Lord-and-Prophet's vacant bench. The Lords of the Ordeal stacked the tiers before him, intoning the Prayer, each a feral slick of pollution—the new Unclean. Once meticulous beards now hung loose and slovenly, strung into rat-tails for negligence and grease. Once polished armour now reflected nothing more than shape and shadow. Once groomed hair now lay matted or leapt crazed ...

> *"May your bread silence our daily hunger ..."*

But nothing attested to their transformation so much as their *eyes*, too bright and over-wide, the one point where their savagery lay raw, exposed to the open air. Proyas could feel them paw at his surfaces, simmering gazes, peering with the hostile incredulity of those who *know* they hunger too much to warrant feeding.

> *"Judge us not by our trespasses*
> *but according to our tempta—"*

"We should go back!" someone erupted from the gloom of the far tiers—Lord Grimmel. Cries of hoarse assent followed, a cascade that tumbled into thunder. As Kayûtas had predicted, the Temple Prayer crashed into ruin at the feet of their impatience. They lacked the will to sustain even this.

"Back to the skinny fields!" Lord Ettwë Cundulkas cried, eyes fairly rolling.

Yes! the Greater Proyas whispered. *Yes ... We should return to Dagliash!*

Others joined the chorus, an upswell that terrified for its fury as much as its unanimity.

"*There is no returning!*" Proyas screamed, cutting into the uproar as decisively as he could.

"Our *Lord-and-Prophet* commands this ... Not me."

It seemed miraculous that invoking Him yet possessed any weight whatsoever, so profoundly had the scales been overthrown. He need only look at them, his brother Believer-Kings, to apprehend the throttling truth. What had once been an assembly of glory had become a council of *fiends*.

Madness ruled the Great Ordeal.

But not one was so demented as to contradict their Holy Aspect-Emperor—at least not yet. The Eleven-Pole Chamber rumbled with indecision. It was almost comical watching them digest the paradox, how they hung as beasts on the very limit of their Lord-and-Prophet's leash, trembling for the equipoise of lust and terror. One by one, a wariness stole over their looks, the scoffing manner of those frightened by what they had revealed. To eat your enemy was to *need* him. And to eat Sranc, they were now learning, *was to be enslaved.*

The Believer-Prince of Erras, Halas Siroyon, would be the first to crack the stone silence.

"No one has seen so much as a track," he said, his tone plain. "The earth is dead in this accursed country. Dead all the way down."

The meaning was clear. They had all assumed, given the *Holy Sagas*, that Agongorea would be teeming with Sranc—with sustenance. "More rotted hide than earth," the *Book of Generals* famously described it, "a mire of baying mouths." Perhaps this had been the case in Far Antiquity, when the High Norsirai had kept the creatures penned to the west of the River Sursa. It was not the case now.

"Siroyon speaks true!" Lord Grimmel cried, his face hot with blood, his jugular a skinned cord on his neck. "There's nary a scrap to be found on this accursed table!"

"He's *starving!*" Lord Ikkorl cried, stabbing the Earl's image with a thick finger. "Look! You can even see his rib through his breeches!"

The Umbilicus at once chortled and raged. Proyas glanced to Kayûtas, who stood upon his immediate right, the youthful image of the ghost that somehow yet commanded them. Nimil did not sully easily and tarnished not at all, so his Ishroi armour gleamed with rivulets of light and pools of concentrated image. He had managed to maintain his appearances otherwise, braiding his golden beard, combing oil and order into his flowing hair. As a result, he stood before the assembly as a visual rebuke, an unwanted measure of how far their debauchery had cast them from grace.

"Impertinent Holca dog!" Lord Grimmel roared, fumbling for his sword.

"Dagliash!" Nuharlal Shukla, the normally reserved Grandee of Saw'a-jowat screeched. "We mus—!"

"Yes!" Prince Charapatha bellowed in affirmation. "We must return to Dag—!"

"But they rot! How ca—?"

"If we flay them! Stretch them out! Dry them out! Turn them into *rations!*"

"Yes! Yes! We can gnaw on it, suckle the salty swee—!"

"*Enough!*" their Exalt-General boomed. "Where's your Reason? Where's your *Faith!*"

Kellhus had been preparing him all along—Proyas could see that now. The Holy Aspect-Emperor had known from the very beginning that He would have to abandon the Great Ordeal, that *someone else* would have to navigate the shoals of Golgotterath ...

That he would need a Steersman.

"Reason lies at Dagliash!" Shukla barked in reply. "And we have fled from it!"

Proyas did not need to see it, for he could *feel* it, the way hunger warped souls *to the very frame*, so that what was crooked appeared true, and what was mad determined what was sane. And so it was the *God of Gods* who required they withdraw from Agongorea, who wanted them to sit on polluted plains and grow fat and lecherous on the rotting carcasses of Sranc. What else could be more obvious? More true?

Even he trembled at the prospect ... it was so ... so ... *delicious.*

"Death lies at Dagliash!" he bellowed, throwing himself against what seemed a thousand needles of inclination. "Death! Disease! And *damnation!*"

This was why Anasûrimbor Kellhus had broken his heart, why he had *broken Proyas in two*: so that he might stand apart from the seditious conspiracies within *his own soul*, and so call them out when uttered by others. To be confident was to be at one with what was believed, to resort to the thoughtless axioms of dogma to solve all things. To be confident was to embrace the blindness that Men called their *heart*.

The very faith, the very belief that had delivered the Lords of the Ordeal to the Field Appalling, was about to visit them with destruction.

"Any man!" Kayûtas ranted from his side. "No matter what his station! Any man who deserts the Holy Host of Hosts *shall be offered up as spoils to the others!*"

Kellhus had foreseen this dilemma—of this much, at least, Proyas could be certain. The Holy Aspect-Emperor had known the perils of the Meat, and more importantly, he had known the hash it would make of a *believer's* arrogant soul. And so he set about razing the very convictions he had manufactured in his two Exalt-Generals, tearing their certitude to the ground, knowing that it was the weak soul, the *heart set against itself*, that would prove strongest crossing this contradictory ground.

His Steersman had to be an Unbeliever.

The Exalt-General wept for the realization.

This *was* Conditioned Ground. His Lord was here ...

In him.

The Southron Men roiled in fiendish consternation. Nuharlal Shukla had become the object of sudden, openly predatory attention, and he shrunk back to his place on the tiers, scowling for all the looks that fondled him. An air of communal sorting had fallen across bowled assembly, men rehearsing carnal whims that were no longer notional, counting out those they deemed the most treacherous among them.

As easily as their hunger had united them, it now divided.

"Enough!" Proyas cried with paternal disgust. "Turn aside your foul longing! *Turn your gaze forward*, to the Horns that daily creep upon the horizon!"

This was Conditioned Ground. Kellhus had chosen *him* because, unlike Saubon, he possessed a conviction that could be obliterated. And Kayûtas, as His son, Dûnyain, was simply too strong to be weak, to succumb the way the Shortest Path demanded.

"This is the Slog of Slogs, my brothers!"

He stabbed a warrior's forefinger in the direction of Golgotterath beyond the mottled black walls of the Umbilicus.

"And the skinnies await us *there! There!*"

Fresh. Alive. Hot with violet blood.

The Lords of the Ordeal erupted, baying as much as cheering. The gloom buzzed.

Only *he* could do this. Only Proyas ... the boy who had never abandoned Achamian's knee—not wholly.

Only he could feed them.

"Golgotterath is now our granary!"

Riots broke out across the encampment that night. Gangs of men had formed, and with threats and beatings, managed to pursue hundreds of "deserters" into the bone-scattered wastes. The inevitable reprisals devolved into pitched battles—and even more blood for the Judges to celebrate. Screams climbed beauteous beneath the infinite vault of the night, the fluting of distressed life ... thrashing meat.

The mutiny itself did not begin until the following morning, soon after the toll of the Interval. Before prayers had even concluded, an Ingraulish knight by the name of Vûgalharsa threw down his great shield and began bellowing the only thing that mattered, the only thing he *deserved* given the mad deprivations he had endured. "*Mich!*" he began bellowing. "*Mich-mich-mich!*"

Meat.

An estimable if not mighty warrior, the Tydonni thane cudgelled the first Judge to seize him, a diminutive Nroni by the curious name of Epithiros. By all accounts, Vûgalharsa and his kinsman began to *eat* the unfortunate priest, who apparently lived long enough to kindle the lust of thousands, so piercing and effeminate were his screams on the wind. The mutiny proper began when his fellow Ingrauls closed ranks against the company of eighty-three Judges dispatched to recover Epithiros: Men who were likewise murdered, desecrated, and in the case of three, partially consumed.

A contingent of Ainoni—Kishyati for the most part—lay camped adjacent to the Ingraulish mutineers. One could scare imagine a greater gulf between races, and yet the madness leapt between camps with ease. Like the Ingrauls, the swarthy sons of the River Sayut chased away their caste-noble commanders and fell upon the Ministrati encamped among them. They gathered in unruly mobs, their outraged cries falling in and out of unison. The dead they passed across the tips of their spears, exulting in the blood looping across their cheeks and lips.

Souls had become desiccate tinder, and words sparks. Throughout the Great Ordeal, Men threw aside all restraint, and swarmed down the thoroughfares of the encampment, screaming for Meat, and murdering all those who would restrain them. Baron Kemrates Danidas, whose father Shanipal governed Conriya in the Exalt-General's stead, found himself crossing a camp of Auglishman, a barbaric people hailing from the coasts of Thunyerus, when the mutiny struck. Despite the protestations of his younger brothers (who counselled flight), he attempted to restore order, and so doomed all of Lord Shanipal's sons. General Inrilil ab Cinganjehoi, another celebrated son of another celebrated warrior from the days of the First Holy War, actually managed to forestall the mutiny among his own

Men, only to watch that order dissolve for no reason short the steepening angle of the sun. The General would survive, but only because he, like most other Lords of the Ordeal, refused to raise more than his voice against the growing riot.

Within a watch, the Judges ceased to exist. The manner of their death would soil the heart for hearing.

Despite the profundity of the crisis, the Exalt General's martial instincts and acumen did not fail him. Even before word of the Kishyati uprising arrived, he understood the mutiny was about to crash about them all and that *the Judges would have to be sacrificed.* His first decision would be the most crucial: to surrender the bulk of the encampment to the roiling mobs, while rallying those he knew he could most depend upon—the Schoolmen and the caste-nobility. He commanded his retinue—the motley of souls, mostly Pillarians, who happened to be in the vicinity—to lash his family's standard, the Black Eagle on White, to a second pole so that it might be plainly seen, then led them galloping to the perimeter of the encampment, not because he feared for his safety (the Umbilicus, as it turned out, became a sanctuary for those few Judges who survived) but because he knew this was where the sane were always driven in times of madness—to the margins.

Kayûtas, leading hundreds of his crimson-skirted Kidruhil, added the Horse-and-Circumfix standard to his own. Others joined in sporadic succession, all those who had neither perished nor joined in the rampage, and Proyas eventually found himself with the bulk of the remaining horsemen. Together they watched as the Great Ordeal convulsed about its own members, excised instances of *itself* from within. That so few Lords of the Ordeal had joined their countrymen was perhaps no surprise. Many had dwelt in the presence of their Lord-and-Prophet for *decades*, let alone years, and all of them—as vessels of his authority—had been whelmed as Judges. Even maddened by the Meat, even drooling for the reek of fired flesh and possessions, even aching for glimpses of unholy congress, the Lords of the Ordeal remained true to their Most Holy Aspect-Emperor.

Like a wolf about a trapper's fire, they paced the outskirts of the encampment, a bolus of thousands drawn the length of a mile. They leaned upon their pommels agog, aspiration and appetite waging open warfare across their look and manner. Some gasped for ardour, or the throttling shame that followed. Some wept softly. Others aired their lament—for none could deny that the end was upon them. Far quarters smoked. Near quarters shivered for scenes of carnage, appalled for glimpses of porcine obscenity. Castle-noble blood lay trammelled. The Judges shrieked for torments and degradations that at once stoked and battered souls. Thousands grunted and roared, smeared their faces and armour with the blood and filth of their victims.

"How many?" the Grandmaster of the Shrial Knights, Lord Sampë Ussiliar, was overheard crying. "Sweet-sweet Seju! *How many are damned this day?*"

Living, breathing Men were hammered into mewling worms, things that twisted in slicks of blood. They thought of wives, children, caught a lifetime of worry into a single anguished pang. They sputtered about smashed teeth, perpetually tried to clamber free of the serial assaults but only managed to inflame them. The Agmundrmen took to hoisting mutilated Judges upon Circumfix standards, binding them upside down in grisly mockery of the symbol that had once made them weep. The Massentian Columnaries were nowhere near so generous, stashing their victims away in pavilions that could be easily identified for the mobs crowing and cheering about them. A company of Moserothi scavenged a great sheet of canvas from some pavilion (that belonging to Sirpal Onyarapû, their Lord Palatine, it would turn out), which they used to toss carcasses high into the air.

The multitudes roared and danced, arm clasping arm, throat joining throat, legs leaping for the purity of their transgressions, the beauteous *simplicity* that is the wage of atrocity. The Ordealmen *gloried* in their excision, cast their seed across the fell earth of Agongorea. The near-dead lay like sacks of quivering burlap, bald skin scored with crimson, so moist, so vulnerable as to burn as beacons, wanton as Temple whores. *Judgment* had been cut from the heart of the Holy Host of Hosts.

No sign could be seen of the Schoolmen, who had evidently recused themselves from the matter. Their canvas enclaves remained aloof, shadowy pools of calm in thrashing waters—even that of Swayali, who had been the lodestone of so many base and lascivious desires. They had no stake in mundane grudges, and for all their reckless abandon, the mutineers took care not to cede them any.

The Lords of the Ordeal urged their Exalt-General to call on the Schools to end the riots, and none with such violence as Lord Grimmel, the Tydonni Earl of Cuärweth. "Command them to strike!" he snarled. "Let them burn the sin from these sinners. Let *fire* be their redemption!"

The Exalt-General was outraged. "So you would blot those who act upon *your own* obscene hungers?" he cried in retort. "Why? To better set yourself apart in the eyes of your fellows? I know of no other soul, Grimmel, whose eyes are so reddened for leering—whose lips are so cracked for licking!"

"Then burn me *with them!*" the Earl cried, his voice cracking for passion ... for *admission.*

"And what of the Ordeal?" Proyas snapped. "What of *Golgotterath?*"

The caste-noble could do no more than sputter in the rabid gaze of his fellows.

"Fool!" Proyas continued. "Our Lord-and-Prophet *foresaw this event* ..."

Some witnesses report that he paused to survey the shock these words occasioned in the Lords of the Ordeal. Others claim that he paused not all, that it only seemed such for the shadow of a cloud that encompassed the blasted plains. A handful would claim to have seen a *halo* about his wild, Ketyai-black mane.

"Aye, my brothers ... He told me this would happen."

At Proyas's behest, Anasûrimbor Kayûtas commanded the Kidruhil to dismount and strip their ponies. The half-starved mounts were gathered on the western perimeter, some five hundred of them, chins pitching, heads ducking to shake manes, before being whipped into the encampment, into the once rampaging, but now eerily quiet, belly of the mutiny. The outcome was not so miraculous as it seemed: all mutinies outran their occasions, stranding those who had merely aped their brothers' outrage with the cold ashes of fury, searching for excuses, eager to appease their betters. Save for those most responsible, the Ordealmen required only some excuse to set aside their grievances and resume the charade of pious resolve they had been so quick to overthrow mere watches previous. Wary, the Lords of the Ordeal dispersed through the camp in the wake of the Kidruhil horses, each making their way to their own nations and tribes. Equine screams serrated the air about them, compounding into an eerie, unnerving chorus that slipped as oil across the plains. The horses themselves were not so much butchered, as their capacity to suffer was dissected, sorted into strings the most cruel among them might play as a lute. For all their declarations of hunger, the Ordealmen were all but indifferent to horseflesh. Only *transgression*, it seemed, could replace the Meat, the vicious glee that belonged to wickedness. Only torment could nourish them ...

Sin.

That evening, innumerable thousands gathered to watch the execution of those accused of inciting the mutiny—some twenty men, who, apart from Vûgalharsa, had been picked more or less randomly. Proyas had prepared for more trouble, to the point of deploying the Schools about the accused. As much as he feared the prospect of martyrs, he feared the perception of impotence even more. *Someone* had to die—if only to reignite the communal fear that all authority requires.

In accordance with the Law, the "leaders" of the mutiny were flayed in public, their skin shaved from them a thumb's breadth at a time. Between shrieks the wretches called out to their kinsmen, either urging them to rise up, or begging them to set an arrow in their hearts. But far from inciting outrage at some common oppressor, they provoked only paralysis and terror or ridicule and uproarious merriment—the laughter of crazed fools. Most howled and pointed, scooped tears with thumbs and clutched cramping ribs, cheered the tortured shrieks of those they had celebrated, raised upon their shoulders, mere watches before. But others gazed without expression, their eyes as wide as their lips were narrow, like souls incredulous of the horror that awakened them. And the Exalt-General watched, compelled. He could not but ponder the possibility that this demonstration, which was meant to instill as much terror as respect, was far more a *reward* than a punishment ...

That out of some blind, bestial instinct the Ordeal had begun volunteering portions of itself *to feed itself*.

Of the four hundred and thirty-eight dead Judges recovered, nearly four hundred of them had been *partially consumed*. According to the mathematician Tusullian, the Lords of the Ordeal could assume that at least ten thousand of their Zaudunyani brothers had engaged in some form of cannibalism ...

In addition to whatever other obscenities they had committed.

———— ✦ ————

Proyas bid the Pillarians set his chair upon a knoll just beyond the southern limit of the encampment, and there he sat in full battle-dress, his posture more that of a Seto-Annarian Emperor than a Conriyan King. Kayûtas stood to his right, gazing as he gazed. "We will ponder Golgotterath together," he had told his nephew, "from a place all souls can see."

So they peered out across Agongorea's pewter desolation, the barrens inked in the strokes and curls of deep evening shadow, and meditated upon the image of the Horns rising from a chapped rim. *Anochirwa*, the ancient Kûniüri had called them, particularly when viewed from this distance, "Horns Reaching." Sitting high across the cadaverous plain, the gleam resembled nothing more than a whore's golden piercing, the fetish of some unlawful Cult threading a corpse's puckered skin ...

The Incü-Holoinas.

Golgotterath.

Horror pricked his innards.

His mouth watered.

Years ago Kellhus had bid him to imagine this moment, spying Golgotterath from the Field Appalling, and Proyas could remember his throat tightening at the fancy, the presentiment of standing upon *this very spot*, only upright, brimming with both fury *and humility* ... to have been delivered so far ... to come so near *Salvation*.

And now here he sat *bent*, a deformed angle of himself, a shadow thrown across accursed ground.

He was the Steersman!

The one chosen above all others, not for the strength or purity of his conviction, but for the *loss* of these things—for the bloody socket where the limb of his heart had been.

The sun slipped behind a crimson veil, and slivers of the Horns blazed like uncanny torches, like beacons, either beckoning or warning away, unnerving for the premonition of raw *immensity* they conveyed—to stand so tall as to bathe in a younger day, a brighter sun.

"Will it be enough?" he heard himself ask Kayûtas.

The Prince-Imperial gazed at him for a long moment, as if willing away urges as fundamental as his own. The crimson upon the Horns limned his cheek and temple in rose, flecked his pupils. "No," he eventually said, turning back to Anochirwa.

"So how does a general pilot insanity?"

It horrified him, the way the Horns continued to smolder bright after the purple extinction of the sun.

"I fear that power is reserved for prophets, Uncle."

"Aren't you *afraid* of the Hells?" Proyas had once asked Achamian as a child.

It was the kind of brusque query young boys were prone to make, particularly when they found themselves alone with those physically or spiritually deformed, questions inappropriate to the degree they were honest. And how *keenly* he had wanted to know what it was like to wield such miraculous power in the shadow of damnation.

Achamian's eyebrows alone registered any shock he might have felt. "Why should I be punished?"

"Because you're a *sorcerer*. The Gods *hate* sorcerers."

Always the laughing wariness in his look. "And you? Do *you* think I should be punished?"

The previous week his older cousin had begun responding to all his questions by asking him the same question back—a tactic that had flummoxed Proyas enough to warrant adopting.

"The question is, Do *you* think you should be punished?"

The portly Mandate Schoolman had chuckled and frowned all at once, scratched his beard in that way that would forever make Proyas think of philosophers.

"Of course I do," Achamian said, his voice on the sly side of lighthearted.

"You *do?*"

"Of course. I would be punished for saying otherwise!"

"Only if I were to tell anyone!"

His tutor smiled wide.

"Perhaps it is *you* I should fear then."

Something must be eaten ...

Something stronger than hope.

That night Proyas roamed the encampment the way some general out of legend might, either seeking clues to the tenor of their men or answers to some turmoil lurking in his own heart. The sky could have belonged to the

Carathay, the night was so clear. The moon shone from the southeast, bleaching the wreckage white, and inking the shadows. Thrice Proyas found himself surrounded by panting gangs, and without fail they hesitated upon recognizing his station, and he had *seized* that wonder, that heartbeat of roiling indecision, gesturing to the leering wretch that most obviously hung upon the sufferance of the others, the one they had *already* raped and defiled in the twilight carcass of their souls, and saying, "The God offers *this one* in my place."

It was not so much madness rendering them one of their own to eat, because occasion was all any of them sought, the pretext of *being one among others* punishing an evil unto bliss. The screams subsequent to his departure cast a wicked glamour upon the night, for they were no different than the cries of his wife, Miramis, naked, shaking, pitching for the bliss of *him*.

The madness of this troubled him not at all.

The Great Ordeal was his hole to fill, his stomach to feed.

His Horde.

It gaped within him, his hunger, transformed him into a living hole.

Proyas ransacked the Holy Aspect-Emperor's baggage, pretending to be seeking evidence of his merciless Will. He found nothing that was not ornamental, nothing that expressed any truth of *Him*.

He absconded from the stores with only a ceremonial shield squared about a curve in the Columnary manner. When leaned properly in a leather-panelled corner, it shattered his reflection across dozens of etched and stamped circumfixes, yet conserved his ghostly aspect all the same, transforming him into a being of luminous threads. He savoured the illusion.

He alone had been divided against himself.

Not Saubon. Not Kayûtas ...

He alone was weak enough to be strong, at this time, upon this ground, the Field Appalling.

He alone could see the *Sranc* standing in his own skin. Pale. Dog-hunched. Porcelain and perfect ...

Lecherous for blood.

Proyas was relatively certain that no soul in history had killed so many as

Anasûrimbor Kellhus. The cities razed. The captives massacred. The sons and husbands stolen in the gullet of night. The heretics burned en masse. Every atrocity, no matter how miserable or spectacular, was but a wheel in the greatest argument of all: *that the World should be saved ...*

The Holy Thousandfold Thought.

Now morning had come, and he stood flushed and panting before an ocean of *faces*, the assembled Great Ordeal of Anasûrimbor Kellhus, and the potency of it leapt through him, the primeval knowledge, the surging, stag-stamping vitality, and he knew, for all the ache of demonic expression, that what he did was what must be done, that the finality of what was holy redeemed the madness he was about to commit. He stood upon the summit of all that was wicked, *and yet he was holy*, steeped in sacred inner light!

"Do you *feel* it, my brothers? Do you ride your own heart as an unbroken steed?"

The Men of the Great Ordeal danced for righteous frenzy, their arms and faces black for sun. They were the wicked, the low and the base. By eating Sranc they had become Sranc. They were the monsters they had eaten. And now that he knew as much, he understood what was required to lead them, to bend them to Kellhus and his Great Argument ...

Victims. That had been the lesson of the Mutiny: if he failed to provide the Ordeal with victims, it would simply take them.

It would begin feeding upon itself.

"Let us *show our Foe!* Let us *demonstrate* the compass of our strength! Our murderous lust! Let him cower, tremble for knowing He will be *eaten!*" He howled this last in a drawn sing-song that sent vicious gales warbling through the uproar. Even now, staring out across the heaving distances, he could see Ordealmen throwing *severed heads*.

"Let us garland our arrival in might and horror!"

The Horns gleamed in the clear morning sun behind him, baffling the eyes the way they loomed *above* the smashed teeth of the Ring Mountains, the famed Occlusion, despite lying miles beyond them—despite being things *manufactured*.

"Now let them gaze upon us! Let them witness the bottomless extent of our resolve!"

One final repast was all they required.

"*Let!*"

"*Them!*"

"*Fear!*"

He stared across the threshing expanse of madmen. His every glance revealed some depraved vignette: Men shaking, their eyes rolled to white; Men cutting their own limbs, making war-paint of their own blood; Men rutting like dogs, strangling and pummelling, smearing seed upon themselves and their brothers ...

"*We! We* are the *Chosen!*"

And he could feel *It*, the Spider that was the God ...

"*We! We* are the *Exempt!*"

Seizing his voice with tempest lungs, blowing *truth* as a howling roar.

"The *Wicked-that-are-Holy!*"

It seemed so obvious ... so true ...

"And we shall pick of the *lowest* bough!"

As if his heart had become an unconquerable fist.

"And we shall eat—*eat!*—of the fruit that He—*He!*—hath given!"

Hands outstretched over the ravenous multitudes ...

"We shall eat what *Hell* hath cooked for us!" he screamed.

And so led them all into irrevocable damnation.

———⊗———

Hunger had drawn them as a bow. A single word loosed them ...

His word.

———⊗———

His pony galloped for the promise of expanse, of fleeing without obstruction from cruel spurs, and for the first time it seemed Proyas could breathe the *pallor* of the air, the odour of land without pungent life, soil that had been rotted to the mineral nub.

The smell of absolute ground.

———⊗———

He had loved Achamian, the Divided Man. Whatever animus he had borne against him, he had borne out of terror of this love. Out of his own divisions.

As Kellhus had said.

———⊗———

The Scalded shambled across Agongorea, a leprous swarm, their heads hung low, their skin hanging from bodies become wounds. They drank of such rivers that braided the bone-strewn plains. They did not eat. They suffered as few had suffered, rotting while they still lived, becoming putrescent in macabre stages. They lost their hair, their skin, their teeth. They vomited blood upon ancient Ishroi bones.

Went blind.

They had not so much marched *from* the banks of the River Sursa as stretched themselves across Agongorea, for not a moment passed without another ghastly soul slumping to the ground, sometimes inert, sometimes curling upon final breaths. Lord Sibawûl te Nurwul lurched upon their forward edge, though his stride never slowed and his gaze never sagged from the line of the horizon, the fell image of the Horns. What had happened at Wreoleth still smouldered within him somehow, so that he seemed to *char* as much as decompose, cook about some infernal, interior fire. In their thousands they followed in his footsteps, trusting the constancy of his image, warring with the misery of their undoing, a wet and wheezing avalanche of leprous humanity. A Leper's Ordeal.

Not a soul knew what they did, let alone why they did it.

Indeed, *this was their revelation.*

Not a penitent among them questioned the apparition, or even cared to regard it when it appeared on the northern horizon. Those who thought were those who died. Sibawûl Vaka did not so much as glance across a sodden shoulder. He, like all those who followed him, had found a line that ran diagonal to the lines pursued by the living. So he laboured as before toward the golden Horns, not so much oblivious to the twining Horde descending upon them as utterly indifferent.

The Great Ordeal resolved as a vast, marauding mass on the north, dark and seething, winking as though powdered with diamonds. No shouts, no howls carried on the wind, only the susurrus of thousands trotting across the tomb floor that was Agongorea. The Scalded pilgrims shambled onward heedless, drawn as filings toward the golden terror. The interval dwindled, and those at the fore of the unpoisoned masses broke into a sprint, their countless faces pained amalgams of joy and exertion. Suddenly Men were running, fields of them whooping for exultation, cackling for the festival madness, for the promise of vicious transgression.

Few among the Scalded so much as turned to regard their charging kin and countrymen.

And so did the pure fall upon the defiled. The surging boundaries of the Great Ordeal tumbled through the spare fringe of the leprous train. Wails and shrieks joined the triumph that rifled the starving sky, a chorus that grew in volume and density as the Holy Host of Hosts consumed more and more of the wretched column. The last remaining horsemen had hooked about the westward barrens to corral those Lepers attempting to flee, but the rotted mobs simply stood insensate as the bestial multitudes engulfed them. The air rang human and shrill.

Some few of the rotted drew weapons on the hale, and if they were fortunate, they managed to die for being dangerous.

Otherwise, the night would be unending ...

When darkness finally wedded abomination on the Field Appalling.

If Nersei Proyas, Believer-King of Conriya, Exalt-General of the Great Ordeal, rode at the fore, he did not lead. It was just him perched upon a gallop, the parallax grinding the dead earth into immobility with distance. Agongorea clutched the whole of what could be seen, save the Horns pricking the horizon. The Great Ordeal loomed unseen behind him, a dread rumble that fell like hair about his neck and shoulders.

The first figures shocked him, so abhorrent was their appearance, so indifferent was their gait, slouching to Golgotterath, falling forward, catching themselves step by wretched step.

The Scalded.

Hairless wraiths, stripped, each flayed to the degree they were diseased, plagued by flies, scribbling shadows. Proyas hurtled as something armoured and merciless among them, riding for the head of the wretched mob. He laughed for piteous looks that accompanied his passage.

He found Sibawûl te Nurwul standing alone upon a knoll that reared like a capping wave, scarcely recognizable save for his antique cuirass and fur-rimmed boots. The man faced west, his gaze fixed on the twin golden nails that pinned the horizon.

Proyas leapt from his horse, savoured the sudden immovability of the earth beneath his feet. His groin ached, buzzed in a manner that set his whole being afire. The rotting Chieftain-Prince turned to him, a vision so horrific he polluted all breath for simply breathing. He was hairless, save for errant blond wires. Ulcers did not so much adorn as *clothe* him, a raiment of septic flesh, here mottled and woolen, there slicked with effluent, shining like greased silk. His ears were missing, leaving only muddy holes. But for some reason, his eyes and the skin about them had been spared, so that he seemed to wear himself as a mask, the edges red with inflammation, curled like burnt papyrus, running high upon his cheeks across the bridge of his nose, and pinned to blond brows.

Words should have been exchanged.

Proyas strode into him fists balled, hammered the putrid horror to his knees. The arch of him thrashed for violent bliss. He clasped the Chieftain-Prince's pestilent cheeks, licked the ulcerations across his forehead.

The taste of soil and salt and bitter. The sum of his sweetness lay in his infection.

Sibawûl Vaka's gaze drifted back toward the Horns of Golgotterath.

Proyas stared at his fingertips, his soul roiling in horror and glee. His hands were shaking. His heart bobbled about his breast. His breath was nowhere to be found ...

He had not even begun his feast!

He joined in the man's westward vigil, peering at what had been their common destination ere this day had come, the fabled Horns, points of burnished gold, scorching the surrounding barrens for their brilliance. For so long they had seemed illusory, a trick on the horizon, golden and malicious. There was no denying their mountainous reality now.

And it seemed that together they understood, the King and the Leper, for what sparks of meaning that were struck from the stone of grief and the iron of ardour were the most profound of all. The Horns *were watching*. He punched the polluted Chieftain-Prince once again, forced his eyes east, so that he might see the Great Ordeal devour his fell parade of corpses. Together, they watched floods of limber shadows streaming about and between the ailing forms. Together, they heard the screaming grow into a tidal din.

As brothers, they watched brother revelling in the blood of brother.

"We ... walk ... together ..." the Scalded Lord of the Ordeal rasped. "*The ... Shortest ... Path.*"

Proyas stared at him, eyes weeping ... mouth watering.

"*We ... pace ... the beam ... of* Hell *... togeth—*"

The Exalt-General struck the Chieftain-Prince of Cepalor to ground once again, convulsed about the bliss that exploded from his loins.

He sucked drool ...

Pulled his knife.

⟨⟩

What Hell hath cooked, *he would eat.*

Honour ... Honour was ...?

And *grace* ... What was grace?

The mortification of what obstructed, what flinched, what bled and heaved and murdered, what quivered and throbbed, what dripped and cut and abraded.

What was grace if not the suffocation of what screamed?

And *honour* ... What was it, if not the sacrifice that best served the gluttony of your masters?

Perhaps it is you *I should fear then ...*

The Greater Proyas dwelt in the bloom of blind abandon ... and he saw that *he was free* ... that nothing in Creation could be more beautiful than ravaging the soul *with* the body.

"*So am I made whole,*" he whispered to the twitching form. He huffed and grunted for the gush of fluids about his delirious centre.

"*So I ... overcome ... my division.*"

⟨⟩

Even our weeping is broken.

Even our misery.

We lay siege to what is nearest.

Sap our own walls.

Eat our own hopes.

We chew our dignity to gristle.

And chew.

Until we become creatures that move, merely.

The counterfeit sons of rumoured fathers.

Souls needled into skin, across nakedness.

Murals where there should be Men.
Shades.
Holes filled with meat.
Gaps between faces, between stars.
Shadows in skulls.
Holes ...
In our hearts ...
Our bellies ...
Our knowledge — our speech!
Endless holes ...
Filled with meat.

CHAPTER SIX

The Field Appalling

Early Autumn, 20 New Imperial Year (4132, Year-of-the-Tusk), Agongorea.

Light like an eggshell shattering against novel ground, chips and flecks
bouncing incandescent. This time *she* fell to her hands and knees,
Anasûrimbor Serwa, the Saviour's daughter.

Sorweel stood above her, reeling for the significance as much as the sorcery of what had just happened. "You ..." he began, eyes wide with the recognition of truths that could blind. "You-you *knew* ..."

She pressed herself to her knees, gazing. "What did I know, Sorweel?"

"Tha-that he would see my-my ..."

He. Moënghus. Her eldest brother.

"Yes."

"That he would ... would leap!"

She closed her eyes as though to savour the eastward blaze of the sun. "Yes," she said, breathing deep, as if confessing something to herself.

"*Why?*" the Believer-King of Sakarpus cried.

"To save him."

He fairly sputtered for incredulity. "Spoken like a tru—!"

"Anasûrimbor, yes!"

Her effortless ouster of his voice chagrined, an unwelcome reminder of all the countless ways she transcended him.

"My father submits all things to the Thousandfold Thought," she said, "and *it* decides who's loved, who's healed, who's forgotten, who's murdered in the dead of night. And *it* cares only for the destruction of Golgotterath ... the Salvation of the World."

She pressed herself to her feet.

"You did not love him," he heard himself say.

"My brother was *broken*," she said, "unpredictable ..."

He gazed at her witless.

"You did not love him."

Was there injury in her eyes? And if there was, how could he trust it?

"Sacrifice has always been the toll, Son of Harweel. Is it so strange that Salvation would arrive decked as horror?"

The uncanny character of the land finally secured his attention. Dead flats, piling on and on. He found himself glancing about, searching for some evidence of *life*.

"Only we Anasûrimbor can see the Apocalypse," Serwa continued, "so only we Anasûrimbor can see how murder saves, how cruelty shelters, even though it can only appear as evil grasped within a human span. Sacrifices that boggle hearts are paltry to us, simply because we can see the dead stacked about us all, the *dead we will become*, should we fail to make the proper sacrifices."

The soil was lifeless ... exactly as he remembered it.

"And so Moënghus is your sacrifice?"

"Ishterebinth broke him," she said, her tone declaring an end to the matter. "Frailty is a luxury we children of the Aspect-Emperor are denied every-where, let alone here, on the dead plains. The Great Ordeal can probably *see* the Horns of Golgotterath ..." She raised her index finger to the horizon. "Much as we can."

Sorweel turned to follow her gesture ... folded upon his knees.

"And I," she said, now behind him, "am my Father's daughter."

Min-Uroikas.

Absurdly *small*—golden antlers set as a pin upon the horizon's seam—as well as perversely *immense*, something so mountainous as to peer over the World's very edge. Fragmentary memory swamped his thoughts, shadows charging void, horns signalling ranks of smoke, Wracu dissolving into wraiths. Dismay. Exultation. And it thrashed within him, the stumps of what had once wrestled that gilded apparition, that horrid, despicable, wicked place! Incû-Holoinas! Unholy Ark!

She brought her lips close to his ear. "You *feel* it ... you who have worn the Amiolas, who can remember the outrages suffered there. You feel it the same as I!"

He gazed, riven by a horror far more ancient than his own ... a hatred he could scarcely fathom.

Ciogli! Cu'jara Cinmoi!

"Yes," he murmured.

Her breath fell moist upon his neck. "Then you know."

He turned, swiveling up to seize her lips with his own.

The Horns of Golgotterath gleamed soundless for distance, airless. And it seemed an incomparable miracle, to discover himself stone inside her, the daughter of the Holy Aspect-Emperor, to feel her tremble, shudder for enclosing the root of him, for sucking the breath from his mouth, the in-credulity from his veins. They cried out in unison, voices drenched, deliri-ous for the thrust and grind of *youth* amid such ageless desolation.

"Why make love to me?" he asked afterward. They had fashioned a mat-tress of their clothing, and now they sat naked upon it together, he not so much wrapped as spangled about her. He dragged his boy-bearded chin along her neck to the outside of her shoulder. "Does the Thousandfold Thought decree it?"

She smiled. "No."

"Then why?"

She craned about within the gangly circuit of his knees, gazed into his eyes for what seemed like a long while. Her observation, her otherworldly intellect, was no longer divided by Moënghus, the youth realized. He was the sole object of her scrutiny now.

"Because I see only *love* when I stare into your face. Impossible love."

"And that doesn't weaken you?"

Her look darkened, but he plunged forward regardless, chasing the idiot impulse that was the undoing of so many young men in the hot tumble of passion—the will to know regardless.

"Why love anyone at all?"

She radiated a density so profound that he felt like a kerchief wrapped about a stone. "You want to know how you can trust an Anasûrimbor," she said, looking to the wasteland, abdominal stretches rising to ribbed heights. "You want to know how you could trust *me*, so long as I lay every soul at the foot of the Thousandfold Thought."

He did not so much kiss her shoulder as press his lips to her skin, and a sad part of him was amazed at the innumerable ways of connection, the fact the tethers could never be counted.

"Your father ..." he said, expending a breath that made him feel far older than his sixteen summers, ancient even. "He chose me because he knew I loved you. He told you to seduce your brother, reasoning that jealousy and shame would rekindle my hatred of him, so that I might satisfy the conditions of the Niom ..."

"Were my father *one of the Hundred*," she said, resting her cheek upon the forearm she had propped on her knee, "what you pose as manipulation becomes the God's work ... *meaning*, does it not?"

"What are you saying?"

She turned to regard him, and it seemed mad to be so intimate with any woman so beautiful, let alone an Anasûrimbor.

"That *faith*, not trust, is the attitude proper to the Anasûrimbor. That to be sacrificed in the name of my father *is the greatest glory that this life offers* ... What higher meaning could there be? You are a *Believer-King*, Sorweel. The degree of your degradation is the degree of your sacrifice is the degree of your glory!"

This chastened him, reminded him of the perilous stakes. If she were to learn that *he*, the inconsolable orphan-king of Sakarpus, had been chosen as *Narindar*—that he was the knife that the dread Mother of Birth herself had raised against her family—then her father would know as much, and he would be put to death before the sun had set upon this endless tomb floor. The fact of his conversion, the fact that Oinaral had convinced him that the end of the World was truly nigh, and that her father, the Holy Aspect-Emperor, had indeed come to save it, would mean nothing. To kill him would be to unwind the machinations of an outraged Heaven; few murders in myth, let alone history, had purchased as much!

Anasûrimbor Serwa, the woman he loved, the daughter of his father's murderer, *would kill him without the least hesitation*, just as she had killed her brother *no more than a watch before*. No matter how utter his adoration, how pure his devotion, she would end him were it not for the Dread Mother's glamour ... Her divine spit upon his recreant face.

How long would that unearned blessing last? Would he carry it to his grave? Or would it be rescinded, the way all things unearned seemed to be rescinded, the instant he needed it most?

He reeled, only now grasping the absurd consequences of his conversion ...

How he had fallen in love with his executioner.

"What," he asked, "do they call women who love fools in your country?"

She did not so much as blink.

"Wives."

<hr />

She fell asleep and he remained awake, wondering that things so pale, so barely skinned as they, could be so fierce, so immune to whatever had slapped life from this ground. She had told him how some Nonmen called this land "Unnûrull," the Trackless Plain, because it swallowed footprints "like the beach between waves." And indeed, not a track could be seen, though the whitish gravel nearby had the cast of mealed bones. And it seemed proper, the impunity of their love-making, the exposure. To be as children. To exult in *what has been given*, especially beneath the spectre of Golgotterath.

To wander trackless ground.

"*Ware her, my King*," Eskeles had warned him that first day in the Umbilicus. "*She walks with the Gods ...*"

Their next sorcerous leap, he embraced her the way a lover might, breast to breast, pelvis to thigh, and it seemed *miraculous*, her face tipped back below him, her lids glaring rose, her mouth welling with *meaning*, spouting truths that blind the eye, that rewrite the Book-of-the-World, her hair fanning out into a silken disc, her skin darkening for glaring brilliance, her voice burrowing through the flesh of Creation, rising out. Her eyes closed molten pools, smiling.

He dared seize her passion, lower his lips to her Metagnostic song.

They stepped clear spinning parabolic lights. He found it disorienting, the way the plain remained unchanged despite spanning the length of horizons. Even the Horns remained fixed—a fact that brought home their distance, and so their lunatic immensity.

She was already scanning the horizon, and Sorweel caught his breath in apprehension.

"There!" she cried, throwing his gaze eastward with a pointing finger. He spied winking light, as though pulverized glass had been sprinkled across the distance. The Believer-King of Sakarpus cursed under his breath, only now realizing the idyll that had thrown them together could not possibly survive the Holy Aspect-Emperor and his Great Ordeal.

They spent the next few watches trudging into their elongated shadows, Serwa silent, entirely absorbed by their destination, or apparently so, Sorweel endlessly peering, squinting, asking what it was the specks in the distance *could be doing*. The parade of perils about to confront him assured the questions were little more than cover. What was he going to say to Zsoronga? And the Dread Mother—was she simply *waiting* to punish his treachery? Would she rescind her glamour before the implacable regard of the Holy Aspect-Emperor? He only became genuinely curious about the figures in the distance when he realized Serwa wasn't so much ignoring him as she was *refusing to answer*.

The reason for her refusal became obvious when they came upon the first of the blood-drenched Ordealmen, Karyoti by the look of them, severed heads impaled upon their manhood ...

Human heads.

Serwa pulled him to his feet. He followed her in a stupor, wending between scenes of carnivorous languor and crimson squalor, his jaw slack. He understood that this was an *occasion* for horror, for raving shouts. But the most he could do was shrink into the shadow of wilful incomprehension.

How. How could such a thing be? Just yesterday, it seemed, they had left an Ordeal of grim and pious Men, a host that paraded as much as marched, bustling with symbol and insignia, stacked across the distance with ponderous discipline; only to return today to find ...

Abomination.

Every step had become a lever, a kind of effortless toil. He looked, even as his soul averted its gaze, saw them congregated like vultures about the blasted dead, feeding, caressing, rutting with wounds ... man after man, their hair matted, their beards wild and frayed, their armour scabbed with rust, mired with filth and gore, on and on, rocking about body after mutilated body, on and on, doing ... *things* ... things too ghastly to be ... possible, let alone witnessed. He thought he recognized several of the faces, but could not summon the will to defile *names*. The tickle in his gut unsheathed feline claws. Nausea scratched through him. He vomited. It was only in the burning, coughing aftermath that the horror finally managed to squeeze whole into him—and with it, a kind of crazed, moral outrage, a sense of disgust so raw as to be *excruciating* ...

Even Serwa, for all the reptilian serenity of her Dûnyain blood, had blanched. Even the Grandmistress of the Swayali walked, pallid and shaking, her eyes pinned on the blessed abstraction of forward.

A myriad of faces turned to their passage, their beards slicked in blood, their eyes hollow with a kind of incredulity, their mouths taut with swollen bliss. Sorweel's gaze fastened upon a man, an unkempt Ainoni, who had pulled the head and shoulders of a corpse across his lap. He watched him seal his lips about the breathless mouth, hover in a prolonged and grisly kiss ... before seizing the deadman's bottom lip in his teeth, jerking and tearing with the ferocity of a battling dog.

Madness. Anomie unlike any he had ever experienced.

This *place* ... Where there were no tracks to follow.

A shadow caught his eye, a patch of raggish black blown like something ethereal across the ground. He looked up, saw a stork wheel white and pristine where vultures should have been.

Yes ... something whispered. And it seemed he had known all along.

"Recall," Serwa said from his side, "our *destination* ..."

He turned to look in the direction she nodded, saw Golgotterath, the great golden idol that somehow made all this *holy* ...

"Father understood ..." she said, and he could almost believe that she spoke to fortify her own resolve. "Father *knew*. He realized that this must happen."

"This?" Sorweel cried. "*This?*"

An unknown part of him had intended his tone to be a rebuke, a slap, but she had retreated into her old, implacable manner. He would be the one to flinch ...

He was always the one who flinched.

"The Shortest Path," the Princess-Imperial said.

He followed her even though he suspected that she wandered aimlessly. They picked their way between the camps congregated about fire pits of maimed flesh. Men eating. Men languid in their obscenities, almost as if they seduced the corpses they desecrated. And Men frenzied, hooting and cheering the brutal fury of their kinsmen, falling upon their victims in gangs. The plain resounded, but the voices were scattered across so many registers—from grunts to shrieks (for some victims still lived) to sobs to laughs to murmurs to faraway calls—that the silence that rendered them distinct loomed over all, creating a crazed and contradictory din. The stench was unbearable, so much so that he breathed through pursed lips.

The thought came to him quite unbidden. *He is a demon ...*

Ciphrang.

And she said, "It is good that you believe."

Despite everything, her cool gaze added.

Despite. Even. This.

He did not believe. But then, neither had he *disbelieved*. He had vacillated, dangled from the words, the exhortations of other souls. Porsparian. Eskeles. Zsoronga. Oinaral ... and now this *woman*. He had staggered reeling from conviction to conviction—worse than a court buffoon!

And now ... now ...

What greater testimony could there be?

Evil.

At long last he understood the power of enigma, the reason why priests and gods were so jealous of their mysteries. *The unknown was immovable.* So long as doubt and confusion draped the Aspect-Emperor, he belonged to the doubt and confusion that shrouded the Whole. Short of genuine knowledge, he could not be sorted from the blackness that framed all things. He *had* to seem elemental, even *divine*, for the simple want of some mortal interval, some fact that bound him to the midden heaps of what was known.

But this ... This was *knowledge*. Had he possessed the most fanatic, contrarian will, Sorweel would have been unable to deny it. For here it was ... Before his very eyes ... Here. It. Was.

Evil.

Evil.

A wickedness so unthinkable that mere *witness* courted damnation.

The viscous glide of penetrations. The tremulous kiss of tongue tips. The masticating teeth. The savaged carcasses. The bowel grunt, the seizure of seed jetting across skin and crimson meat.

Yesss ... a voice cooed through a shuddering gasp. *Sooo lovely. Sooo-sooo-sooo lovely.*

These things stamped him with bodily force. They blew through the flimsy sheets of his soul and set upon the raw things, making snakes of his innards, knives of air ... He need only open his lips to gag. He need only blink to loose the tidal outrage swelling within, a fury indistinguishable from judgment, a violence that was justice distilled—the very essence of holy retribution! It seemed he need only raise his fists to the sky, cry out the wrath and disgust shaking him apart from within, and the skies would answer with cleansing lightning ...

It seemed ... so it seemed ....

But he had learned enough to know that the Gods could do little more than whisper in this World, that they were diminished by their interventions—that they required *instruments* to enact their eternal designs, tools ...

Like Prophets. Like *Narindar*.

The stork still lingered in the far sky, wings hooked about unseen rivers of air, slowly circling the degeneracy that dimpled the sepulchral plains.

The Believer-King of Sakarpus stumbled to his knees, senseless of Serwa's alarmed glare. He huddled over his retching.

Welling dismay.

I understand, Mother ...

Anguished repentance.

At last I see.

They made their way to a knoll that rose as if upon the back of an earthen wave. A single man occupied the hunched summit, sitting crouched above a lone corpse. Sorweel was several blinks in recognizing him, such was the transformation of his appearance: his once-impeccable beard a matted morass, his skin nearly as black as Zsoronga's for filth and dried blood, his brown eyes bright and wild—so very wild.

It was the legendary Exalt-General ... King Nersei Proyas.

Serwa stood above him, leaning across the sun so that he glanced up at her, blinking. The bestial cacophony hung upon the breeze, the sounds of the living plumbing the dead.

"Where are my sisters?" she finally asked.

Proyas flinched as if stung upon the neck. Sorweel glimpsed hair lashing a gob of scalp upon his Circumfix pendant as it swung over his shoulder.

"B-back—" the Exalt-General stammered, only to be choked by his own throat. He coughed, spit a shining web across the dirt. "Back in the encampment ..." The man's canny brown eyes, which had only ever emanated confidence before, clicked earthward for a heartbeat, before returning as an outraged glare. "Going *mad*."

She pitched high a skeptical brow.

"And what do you call *this*?"

A drunkard's smile. His look became heavy-lidded, even flirtatious.

"Necessity."

The once-regal man affected a laugh, but the truth sat unconcealed in his eyes, begging openly.

Tell me this is a dream.

"Where is Father?" the Grandmistress snapped.

His gaze sagged, his chin dipped.

"Gone ..." the man replied on a blink. "No one knows where."

Sorweel found himself upon one knee, gasping, tripping backwards for his nearness to the carcass mire. What was this? Relief?

"And my brother ..." Serwa snapped after a heartbeat. "Kayûtas ... Where is he?"

The Exalt-General cast a senile glance over his shoulder.

"Here ..." he said in the distracted way of someone engaged in a different conversation. "Somewhere."

The Swayali Grandmistress turned away, leapt skidding down the knoll's defilade.

"Please! Niece, I beg you!" Proyas cried, rolling his head while staring at the stripped corpse before him: some other savage Three Seas lord, only puckered and hairless, like something boiled for too long.

"What?" the Princess-Imperial cried, her cheeks silvered for tears.

The sight caught Sorweel's throat in a toddler grip.

"Should I—?" the Exalt-General began.

He paused to swallow, made a sound like a speared dog.

"Should I ... *eat* ... him?"

Both the Grandmistress and the Believer-King stared at the man dumbstruck.

"You have no choice," a familiar voice called from behind them.

They whirled to see Kayûtas—or a barbarous incarnation of him—on the opposite incline, grinning, leaning against a knee. Blood and gore, Sorweel could not but notice, soaked his Kidruhil underkilt about his groin.

"*Something* must be eaten."

———— ∞ ————

"*I am rarely ...*"

Sorweel fled, abandoned the brother and sister, revulsion scraping his thudding bones, his breath stabbing ...

"*I am rarely what my enemies expect ...*"

All along, the Son of Harweel realized. He had fled across this very plain all along.

This place. The Field Appalling.

He lurched more than walked across the degenerate landscape, so numb had he become.

To be a Man was to be a *Son*, and to be a Son was to shoulder the burden of kin and race and *history*—history most of all. To be a Man was to be *true to who you were* ... Sakarpi, Conriyan, Zeumi—it did not matter.

Who ... Not what.

For this was what the Aspect-Emperor had wrought with his mass murder and machinations. He had bent their myriad ways into *one* way. He had struck the shackles that made Men *men* ... and loosed the beast within.

The what.

Foul gluttony, to eat and to couple without restraint or remorse. To pin screaming.

This ... *This* was the Shortest Path.

The way of Ciphrang.

Hunger without scruple or constraint.

He had hoped to escape the ravenous throngs, but he found himself wandering galleries even more congested with cannibalistic furor. He slumped to his knees on the lifeless earth. Brutality lay as thick as milk on the wind ... as viscous.

The thought of battle crossed his soul, the fervent hope that the Consult would pick this occasion to unleash their long-hidden might. Thoughts of doom. And for a time, it seemed (as it always seemed with thoughts of calamity) that it *had* to come to pass, that he hunched his shoulders against some groundswell of retribution. For no matter how indifferent the Gods, surely *sins such as these* must arouse them ...

But nothing happened.

He looked back across the debauched fields to the Horns, sun-bright above the simmering heights of the Occlusion. He could obscure them with his thumb, yet he still trembled for understanding—remembering—their inhuman dimensions. They possessed a derelict sterility, a silence, and he flinched for the premonition that they were *dead*. Had they marched Eärwa's brutal length to besiege *nothing*? Had they, like woebegone Isholom, undertaken the most epic of trials in vain?

He stumbled onward. The passage of time, normally an empty frame, had become a rushing sewer, a channel clotted with filth. Pollution sloshed and soaked. He could scarce blink without glimpsing some unspeakable tableau. Corruption steamed. Mere breathing had become repugnance. He wept tears he could not understand, let alone claim as his own.

Shush, my Sweetling.

He found himself upon a floor. A stork stood before him, a vase lobed in dulcet white, still as beauty, silent as purity. It cast the shadow of a scythe across the hard earth.

"Mother?" he rasped.

It regarded him, the yellow knife of its bill pressed against its serpentine neck. Blood, he realized, fell in crimson beads from the orange tip.

Do you see, Sorwa?

"Wha-what I must do?"
No, my child … What you are.

The countless banners marking the difference of tongue and nation had been reduced to a spare fraction. What had been crisp ranks of tents and many-coloured pavilions, now sprawled like rubbish kicked from a heap, congested here, scattered there. The encampment was a foul shambles, scarcely a mockery of its former glory. It was also abandoned.

In a peculiar way, Sorweel found wandering the chaos almost as heartbreaking as the lunacy of the plain. The light was failing. The shadows were dark and drawn, throwing the discord of tent and belonging into sharp relief. Disregard littered his every glimpse. Discarded horse bones. Sagging canvas. Impromptu latrines. Soiled blankets. He could almost believe the camp had been overrun by a fleet and barbarous race, for things raised in haste and neglect speak of ruin as surely as things gutted and plundered.

Every tent a hollow, vacant, derelict. Every surface bearing some indecipherable stain.

He wandered aghast, quickly despaired finding anyone or anything. The Circumfix hung everywhere, as before, but bled of colour and frayed about the margins, the symbol of some vestigial God. It occurred to Sorweel that the lunacy on the plains might very well be *fatal*, that the diabolical compulsion commanding the Men of the Circumfix might refuse to relinquish them …

Perhaps this was the shameful end of the Great Ordeal. Perhaps the Host would die discovering it had been its own enemy all along.

The first verse he heard he deemed a senseless trick of the wind, the low howl of air drawn through wrack. But he needed only wander several footsteps toward the sound, it seemed, for the true source to rise clear. Men, their voices bowed in communal prayer.

> *Sweet God of Gods,*
> *Who walk among us,*
> *Many are thine names …*

The King of Sakarpus passed a series of three pavilions, canted and slack, sad with faded colour, and saw a knoll rise from the bristle of crammed shelters surrounding. Kneeling Men encrusted the slopes, all facing the summit, where a savage-looking Judge led them (one of the few yet living, he would later discover), dark face uplifted, hands held to the scalped heavens.

A congregation of those who had refused to *eat*.

The prayer concluded, and all souls lowered their heads in silence, Sorweel found himself fending shame for standing so indifferent, so conspicuous. Despite their harrowed and deranged appearance, he knew these once illustrious Men of the Three Seas. He knew the Ainoni from the Conriyan, the Shigeki from the Enathpanean. He could even distinguish the Agmundrmen from the Kurigalders, such was his familiarity. He knew their great cities, and the names of their kings, their heroes ...

"*Return him to us!*" the anonymous Judge suddenly howled to the heavens. Passion cracked his voice as violently as his face. "Please, God of Gods, *send us our King of Kings!*"

And suddenly all of them were crying out, wailing to the vacant sky, lamenting, cursing, and *appealing*, begging most of all ...

For Anasûrimbor Kellhus.

The Demon.

"*Horse-King!*" a voice bawled, so cracked for incredulity that the whole congregation fell silent. And it seemed to Sorweel that he saw him before his eyes managed to pick him from the helter of sun-blackened faces ... his friend ...

His only friend.

Zsoronga, standing gaunt and astounded.

They embraced and then, quite without shame, wept into each other's arms.

Night fell steep on the Field Appalling.

Zsoronga no longer cast his pavilion whole, but rather lived within the space afforded by a single pole. What had been spacious, even sumptuous, had been folded into oblivion by hewn canvas. He had lost all that remained of his retinue. "They never returned from Dagliash," the Successor-Prince of Zeum said without making eye contact. "The Scald took them. After you left, Kayûtas kept me as a runner, so ..."

Sorweel stared at him like someone realizing they had been *deafened*. The Scald?

"Zsoronga ... What happens here, brother?"

Hesitation. A look with a volatility wandering beneath.

"Such things ... Such things I have *seen*, Sorwa ..." The man dropped his head inexplicably. "Done."

"What things?"

Zsoronga meditated upon his thumbs for several heartbeats.

"You look *grown*," he said, affecting a mischievious glance. "Nukbaru. You have flint in your eye, now."

Sorweel set his jaw.

"How do you fare, brother?"

A look of hunted perplexity, one that would have been comical absent knowledge of its history.

"*Hungry* like everyone ..." he muttered. Something murderous flashed through his gaze. "*Strong*."

Sorweel watched him carefully. "You hunger because you starve."

"Tell that to your poor horse! I didn't promise to save him, did I?"

Sorweel was undeterred. "I'm speaking of the *Sranc*."

A queer grimace, followed by a croaking groan. "What do you think has fattened us so?"

"The skinnies nourish only the body ... the appetite ..."

The Sakarpi knew the perils of consuming Sranc. Life on the Pale was too hard. Scarce a winter passed without some debauched tale reaching Sogga Halls. But tales had been all that he had ever heard.

"The soul starves ..." Sorweel continued, "perishes. Those who subsist on them too long become raving beasts."

Zsoronga was watching him intently now. A hard moment passed between the two young men.

"They taste like fish," Zsoronga said, drawing his chin from his clavicle to his shoulder. "And lamb ... My mouth waters for merely mentioning it."

"There is a *cure*," Sorweel murmured.

"I am not sick," Zsoronga said. "The sick ones went out ... followed the Exalt-General to their damnation."

Then, with an exaggerated air of recalling something momentous he popped to his feet and began rooting through the tent, seized upon his matins satchel.

Sorweel sat reeling, the pinprick of Zsoronga's dismissal lost in the stab of a far more momentous realization. For the first time he understood the mad *straits* of the Great Ordeal, how these blasted lands meant they *had nothing to eat* ...

Aside from their horses ... their foes ...

Themselves.

For several heartbeats it seemed he could not breathe, the dread logic was so clear.

The Shortest Path ...

All of it, he realized, even these *sins*, as deranged and abyssal as they were, *had a place*. They were naught but sacrifices exacted by circumstance, lunatic in proportion to the dire ends they subserved ...

Could it be? Could what he had witnessed—acts so loathsome as too strike vomit from righteous bellies—simply be ... an unavoidable expenditure?

The greatest sacrifice ...

His heartbeat counted out the span of his breathlessness.

Had the Aspect-Emperor known that their *souls* would have to be abandoned on the trail?

"*Yes!*" Zsoronga cried in savage jubilation. "*Yes!*"

And what did that say *about his enemy*? The Consult ... and the boiling rumble of ancient half memories.

"Here it is!"

Could *they* be so wicked, so vile—could *anything* be? An evil so great as to warrant any crime, any *atrocity* contributing to its destruction ...

"*You can* feel *it* ... *you who have worn the Amiolas* ..."

Sorweel stared numbly at the pouch Zsoronga had pressed into his palm, stiff as a dead man's tongue, the pale pattern as intricate as he could remember it, crescents within crescents, like Circumfixes shattered and heaped into spilling piles. The Triple-Crescent, Serwa had called it. The ancient symbol of the Anasûrimbor.

His face scrunched about sudden tears, and he squeezed tight the Chorae within the ancient leather. He was High Keeper of the Hoard once again!

"Some say the Aspect-Emperor is dead," Zsoronga fiercely murmured, his eyes wild and wondrous with violent imagining. "But *I know he'll return*. I know it, because I know you are *Narindar*! That the *Mother of Birth* has chosen you! He will return because *you have returned*. And you have returned because *he is not yet dead!*"

Suddenly it seemed absurd, the weightlessness of the thing and the iron Chorae within it, like fluff ...

He knew nothing in that moment, save that he wanted to weep.

What do I do?

Thick black fingers closed about his pale hand, then tightened, forcing him to grip the pouch.

A sluggish heat leapt into the air between them.

"This is how I know ..." Zsoronga exhaled.

His body, long and sinuous, trembled, much as Sorweel's own.

"Know what?" the youth murmured.

A wooer's smile.

"That we dwell in a land without sin."

Sorweel did not shrink in his shadow—and that was as much cause for terror as anything he had seen or thought this day. His gaze wandered across his friend's scalding aspect, taking a numb inventory.

"What do you mean?"

A glimpse of something dead in his brown eyes.

Mu'miorn?

"I mean we have but one rule to constrain us, but one sacrifice to make! *Kill the Aspect-Emperor!*"

A long gaze, one urgent, the other pretending not to see.

I weep because I missed you.

"All else is holy ..." Zsoronga gasped with thrilling fury. And it truly seemed that all things had been decided. The Zeumi Prince pinched the lantern light into oblivion.

Strong hands in the dark.

Naked in the tented gloom, sweating despite the chill.

Even when they finished, it was not done.

It was all a sham, living a life. Forever stumbling, lurching, chasing resolutions that you name as your own, forever coming after *what you are*. Difference spews from the oblivion of the same, and events forever tumble, delivering twists, turns, surprises that are in no way surprising, and *there you are*, suffocating in the aching heart of it, ducking across the numb perimeter, coming to *be* only in the lee of your questions, that ghost fools call reflection.

You awaken with a start, gasp about a missing heartbeat, and find your-self ... doing ... things.

You wonder if you ever had a father.

Zsoronga's body seemed endless, vast and hot in the tangled dark, feverish with vigour, humming, pulsing. A greater hand enclosed his wrist, drew sense-less fingers to the stubborn, granite arch of his phallus. The mere act of clutch-ing made the World buzz and roar—even spin with languor and impossibility. Zsoronga tensed yet again, groaned and coughed through clenched teeth. He discharged his heat yet again, pulsing strings that looped through the black, pinning him, binding him, with nameless and unspeakable passions.

"*Mu'miorn* ..." he whispered, dragged through Ages as dense as water.

They lay. For a time all Sorweel could hear was his friend's breathing. His throat ached. Beyond the canvas planes, all creation slumped and top-pled in slow silence.

"It is a thing of shame for you sausages," Zsoronga finally said.

It was not a question, but Sorweel elected to treat it as such.

"Yes. A great shame."

"In Zeum it is thought holy for the strong to embrace the strong."

Sorweel attempted to snort in the old way—to make light of what could not be lifted.

Something diabolical hemmed the man's laughter.

"When our wives are quick with children, warriors turn to one another, so that we may fight as lovers upon the field ..."

These words left the Sakarpi King gasping.

"One need not think, dying for one's lover."

Sorweel relinquished his grip, but the greater hand clamped his wrist, forced his fingertips to trawl the length of the turgid horn, from root to summit. And he knew—understood with a philosopher's profundity—that his will was unwelcome here, that he lay in the jaws of an appetite that had devoured his own.

That he had been and would be ravished, as certainly as a daughter of a conquered race.

"You are strong ..." the ebony man said to the pale.

That he would rise to, even celebrate, his repeated violation, as certainly as any temple whore.

"And you are weak ..."

That shame would devour him whole.

"*I am here*, Sorweel," Zsoronga said, raising a thick-fingered hand to his breast. "*Here*, beneath the madness of what ... what we have eaten ..." He paused as if to secure evidence of his victim's belief. "And I will *die* to protect you ..."

He angrily wiped at tears the Son of Harweel could not see.

"To shield what is weak."

There is a clarity to ancient things that all Men seek to emulate. To read about one's forefathers is to read about Men who possessed fewer words, and so lived more concentrated lives, following codes that were ruthless for the brute fact of *simplicity*.

Clarity. Clarity was the gift of their innocence—their ignorance. Clarity was what made them the envy of their seed. What was, for them, *was*, something there to be seized, not something to be groped for behind curtains of disputation. Good and evil shouted from their worlds, their acts. Their judgment was as harsh as that belonging to the Gods. Punishment was without exception and cruel, even sadistic, for it could only be good to bring down evil upon evil, corruption upon corruption. No time was allotted for appeal, for no time was needed. Guilt was axiomatic, indistinguishable from accusation ...

So did they seem Godlike, as well as Godly.

And so did the Ordealmen *turn away from their ancestors* with the compounding of their crimes. To a soul they had either lost or stowed their ancestor lists following Swaranûl and the fateful decree to eat their foes. If asked why, they would cite "bother," but the truth was they could no longer at once bear the weight of their past and breathe. Where their forefathers had derived clarity from genuine ignorance, they relied on numbness and distraction.

One by one the Men of the Three Seas fled their abominable deeds, stealing as thieves across the night plain. They pawed at gore-caked faces with slicked hands, sought to cleanse filth with pollution. The meat they had bolted, the blood they had sucked, wrenched their guts as violently as their commissions wracked their hearts. Many found themselves on their hands and knees hooked about vomit that would not come, gagging on misery and horror, thinking, *Sweet Seju ... What have I done?*

And it crackled as lightning through them, this question which sorts all beasts from all Men, stopping hearts, clenching teeth and eyes.

What have I done?

Anxious horror passed for sleep, and the following day found their souls too far from their legs to march the last miles remaining. The day was given over to an awakening like no other, a *coming to see themselves*, lighting voices as timbre stacked for the pyre, a growing chorus of shrieks and lamentations. They gaped about the fact of their atrocities. And their shame divided them as they had never been divided, rendered them each the butcher of their own hearts, the one most hated, most loathed and feared. How? How could such memories be? Of those who could not bear to live *and* remember, most refused to remember, but more than six hundred Ordealmen would refuse to live, casting themselves into damnation's maw. The rest shrank into the shadows of their rangy shelters, where they warred with despair and incredulity and terror—all who had eaten of human flesh.

The Umbilicus remained abandoned, the avenues and alleyways deserted. Cries rose as if from beneath thousands of pillows, as things too sharp to be smothered. And beyond it all, the Horns reared as mountainous ghosts from the rotted teeth of the Occlusion, glinting in the pitiless sun, laughing it seemed, *gloating ...*

The second morning, they awoke from such sleep as anguish afforded to find the horror that had paralysed now pursued, hunting them with a lunatic terror of *place*. None could bear the ground that bore them. Fleeing the Field Appalling had become the only way to breathe. The Horns caught the morning before the sun had even risen, smoldering with diurnal gold above the ragged summits of the Occlusion. It was inevitable that all eyes turn toward it, that all souls gaze agog.

No hymns were raised, no prayers called ... Scarce a wonder was voiced.

They dismantled the camp, such as it was, and resumed marching, migrating toward the impossible spectre climbing the horizon before them. Not a soul had uttered an order. Not a tribe, cohort, or column marched together, let alone in formation. Not a man understood what he was doing, aside from *getting away*.

And so the Great Ordeal of Anasûrimbor Kellhus did not so much march toward Golgotterath as flee.

Sorweel would have whooped through the wood, had not his father taught him the ways of Husyelt the Hunter. So he crept across the dappled floors instead, mimicking the grim expression of his father's Boonsmen. This was the only reason he found the thing: a ball of grey fur, no larger than a walnut, laying at the base of a cleft oak. Though the incident itself would be lost to him, the fascination he would never forget, discovering, as he had, what seemed some magic residuum of life.

How he had cherished those solitary expeditions—especially after the death of his mother. There was a laziness in that wood—at least during those summers the Sranc shunned the Pale. He could sprawl across the leaves and be so reckless as to doze, daydream while rotating his gaze between high craning limbs, ponder the fork of the great and singular into the frail and many. He could listen to things creak and coo through the hollow chorus of the canopy. His body, as slight as it was, would seem strong enough, hale enough, and he would feel as hidden without as obvious within. And it would seem that nothing could be more common and more holy than a boy alone with his wonder in the sunny wood.

So he deemed the small ball of fur a *gift*, nothing less than a puzzle-box left by the Gods. He marvelled at its weightlessness, the way the breeze could tug it on his palm. He held it even to his eyes and stroked it with a fingertip. The fleece was marred by something poking from within.

The ball pulled apart with the ease of bread drawn from the oven, and bundled within he found *bones*, as white as a child's teeth, a motley the size of leaf stems and insect legs. He drew out a skull smaller than the nail of his pinky, held it between thumb and forefinger ...

For several slow and thick heartbeats, he felt like a God, an eye rendered pitiless for mad disproportion.

He cleared a patch of earth, arranged the contents across it. Children are forever inventing diverse tasks and the imaginary worlds that give them meaning. He was a priest in that moment, ruthless and old, scrying telltale traces of the future in the debris of the past. Fur and bones, as crucial to life as pole and canvas were to shelter. A whip-poor-will called out from the forest deep.

With a start he remembered his father telling him that *owls* did this, regurgitated the hair and bones of their prey. All along he had known it was a mouse, but he had believed otherwise. He looked up, peered between the oak's raised arms searching for some sign of the nocturnal predator.

Nothing.

Nothing, he had thought in a haze of inexplicable alarm, for it no longer seemed that he was playing. *Nothing* had devoured the mouse.

Digesting all that lived.

Spitting out all that mattered.

———— ⦾ ————

One could tell them apart by midmorning, the Upright Horn soaring on a curve pulled erect, and the Canted Horn leaning out over unseen tracts. Both arms climbed ever higher, balled into feminine fists, parting clouds as golden oars might part murky waters, rising above the hanging cliffs and gorges of the vast crater rim the Nonmen had called *Vilursis*.

The Occlusion.

Sorweel and Zsoronga laboured with their packs, wandered with the others in endless roping chains, Men in their tens of thousands, freighted with arms, rancid and grim, drawn as fish to flashing silver. All hearts sloshed in same cold dark water, it seemed. There was no prayer, no hymns, no cries of relief or exultation. Some looked as though they could not so much as blink, let alone speak. He and Zsoronga scaled the slopes of the Occlusion, peered in wonder at the ruins of the Akeokinoi upon the summits, beacon towers from Far Antiquity. They crowded through the canine slots, then joined the myriads stumping down the dusty gravel ramps on the far side, gazing mute and agog as they fanned across the interior waste.

Their bowels quailed. Their thoughts seized. Their hearts kicked as roped foals.

"Such a thing ..." the Zeumi murmured.

Sorweel had no reply.

They skidded down the gravel slopes, two upon a conveyor of descending thousands, mostly Conriyans above and below, and thousands of others, on and on, all transfixed by the image ... the insane image.

The Incû-Holoinas.

Rearing monstrous from the mathematical heart of the Ring, reaching up to dwarf the crimson setting sun ...

The Ark.

Aching for *leaning*. Blinding where it was burnished, great tracts of mirror-gold ablaze hoisted ever higher, casting leagues of crimson across the lifeless plain—across the appalled nations of Men.

Blood etched their toiling shadows.

How ... How could such a thing be? Ishterebinth was but a crude totem in comparison. How could mere *intellect* raise such arms, great and golden, to the very *clouds*? How could a contrivance, a mighty *city* encased in swan-curved hulls, crash from the limit of the sky, crack the very ground asunder, and still remain intact?

A chill shimmied through Sorweel's bones, mounted his heart, his soul. It was the Amiolas, he realized. He *knew* this place, not as anything he could recall or relate, but as the boot-print knows the heel. Though he had lost all that had belonged to Immiriccas, he had not lost his memory of plumbing those abyssal memories, nor the bent of having once been twisted about such a life. *He knew this place!* The way an orphan knows his father. The way the dead know life.

This place ... this *accursed* place! It had stolen *everything*.

A cancer. A blight. An evil that eclipsed imagination!

Fields of gawking Men descended about him, bearding the slopes with dust.

Immensity has a way of exposing silence, pulling it nude from the immeasurable background. For all the thousands tramping and murmuring about him, Sorweel could *hear* it, as surely as if he sat perched upon the cloud-wreathed summit, the *hush of transcendence*, of looming beyond the compass of human comprehension, and sharing bones with the very World.

The Unholy Ark. The great terror of legend, fallen from the Void, gleaming mountainous above a great network of fortifications, squat towers and black-curtain walls. Min-Uroikas.

Golgotterath.

"*Real* ..." Zsoronga gasped.

Sorweel understood, well enough to whiten his knuckles about the realization. The *name* had always been there—since before King Harweel's fiery murder, *the name of this place had crouched above all*. The pretext. The rationale of innumerable atrocities. For all the bluster of the Sakarpi Horselords, for all their vainglorious conceit, he knew they had all asked themselves the same question gazing across the stupendous host that had gathered to throw down their walls ...

How? How could wife-tales and nursery rhymes deliver us to destruction? How could the whole Three Seas go mad?

All of them upon the ramparts, King and Boonsmen alike, had resigned themselves to die defending their city. And all of them had marvelled and lamented that madness and fancy could seal their fate ...

A fantasy that had been real.

A hammer struck his heart, and he gasped, reeled upon liquified limbs. Zsoronga seized him before he pitched headlong, steadied him, drew him forward as though he were a little brother or a wife.

Nothing. Harweel had died for pride and folly ... for *nothing*.

Exactly as Proyas had said he would.

The ground levelled. The ghastly masses floated into the limits of his periphery about him, a silent, mortal tide. The desolation of the plain encompassed them, and Sorweel squinted out across its tracts, near and far, puzzled that it should be pale rather than black. But the horror that was Golgotterath did not brook distraction—the eye could no sooner deny it than it could an upraised fist. It compelled, even as its vast proportions boggled, rumbled with dire *possibilities* if not sound, premonitions of doom and infection, of pollution without compare. It seemed something catastrophic had to happen, that at any moment a new Horde would disgorge from the black iron gates, that Consult sorcerers would step singing from the gold-fanged barbicans, howling wicked lights, that Dragons would explode swooping down from the Horns, tossing them in fire and teeth ...

He was not alone. All Men stood as if strangled for expectation. But moment followed moment, heartbeat replaced heartbeat, and nothing happened—save that his gaze was drawn ever higher ...

The Horns. Two great golden arms raised to the clouds and *reaching them*, fists frosted for altitude.

The sun shimmered across the monstrous, vertical surfaces, drawing out light and pattern and colour like an overlay of foils, precious and complicated. *Script* haunted the soaring, the apparition of alien figure and symbol, somehow etched without grooves, somehow iridescent without wink or glitter, almost as if their shadow dwelt *within* the otherworldly metal.

Crows flocked about the Horns' lower regions, issuing from points across the black fortifications. Otherwise, no life could be spied apart from their own.

"*Real* ..." Zsoronga repeated in a harrowed voice, one close enough to a sob to kick Sorweel's own throat.

Everything. Hailing all the way back to the Scions. All the words they had shared during the long watches of the march, all the bitter recriminations, the declarations both pompous and shrewd, all the spasms of conviction and doubt, bone-rotting incredulity ...

All of it *ended here*. Caught upon the teeth of this place. Now they stood before the bald *righteousness* of their Enemy's cause ...

And the penury of their own.

The Men of the Ordeal drifted to a halt before the spectre. Rot hung pulverized in the air. Innards quavered for standing in the shadow of things too vast, too precarious.

How?

How could such a thing be?

Sorweel stood in the dust, transfixed for the apprehension of *what transcended* human apprehension. For awe, the inkling that flattened Men upon their bellies, that saw bulls twist as smoke into the heavens. What was spectacle if not unconscious worship?

His right hand clutched the Trysean pouch the way others clasped Circumfixes and other fetishes: as a soundless cry for rescue. Beside him, Zsoronga held hands to either temple, bawled out in Zeumi, his voice among the first to perforate the astounded rumble. Cacophony followed. The lowing of cattle. The howling of apes.

Sorweel didn't know when he had dropped to his knees, but he understood *why* as clearly as anything in his murky, misbegotten life. Evil. Where before he had thought, endlessly questioned and interrogated the fact of this place, at long last he could *feel*. Evil, burnished and monolithic. Evil stacked upon evil, until the very *ground* bowed against the beam of Hell. All the wickedness he had witnessed, let alone the abominations of the past days and nights, was but a narcotic lapse compared to this place, a doting drunkard's indiscretion ...

He could *feel* it.

In their surviving tens of thousands, the Men of the Ordeal cried out in wonder and horror and, yes, even jubilation, for they had marched to the very ends of the World. Their Holy Aspect-Emperor had spoken true.

They began falling to their knees in violent remonstration. And the

Believer-King of Sakarpus rocked and sobbed among them, wept for so very many things ... Shames. Regrets. Losses.

And the dread fact that was Golgotterath.

They gathered upon the inner rim of the Occlusion, the Sons of the Race of Men. *Humanity*, whose lives wilted so soon after budding, whose generations passed as storms and gentle rains. Ephemeral, yet fertile, and so forever *new*, casting nations like mantles, as ignorant of their origin as they were terrified of their demise. Humanity had arrived in all its turbulent, amnesiac might, come to obliterate Golgotterath. Thunyeri dwarfing Shigeki, their skin jaundiced for being so fair. Galeoth cowing Scarlet Schoolmen for the violence of their demonstration. Nansur Columnaries standing immobile, deaf to any officer's cry. Ainoni caste-nobles pawing white upon their cheeks. Thousands upon thousands gazing, witless for incredulity, paralytic for shame and horror, alien gold pricking their eyes ...

Men, the cracked vessel from which the Gods drank most deep.

Some had been petty unto murder in their past lives, knifing brothers for the merest slight, while others had been generous unto folly, abiding faithless wives, starving to carry witless parents. It did not matter. Gluttons and ascetics, cowards and champions, reavers and healers, adulterers and celibates—they had been all of these things ere they had taken up their Holy Aspect-Emperor's Great Ordeal. And for all their numberless differences, they need only look to fathom one another, to *know* whether they would be greeted or ignored or attacked. To be a Man is to understand *and be understood* as a Man, to blindly honour expectation so that others might gamble accordingly. For it was the way they *repeated* one another that made them Sons of Men. Despite their numberless feuds and grudges—for all their divisions—they stood as *one* before the heinous image.

The Great Ordeal ... nay ...

Humanity, horrid and beatific, frail and astounding, come to collect their future from wicked debtors.

One race, come to fathom the Ark with sword and fire, and to at long last exterminate the Unholy Consult.

CHAPTER SEVEN

The Leash

To speak truth to another is to set aside interest and ambition, to either possess faith in another's estimations or be indifferent to them. The honour of truth is indistinguishable from the horror.
— *The Third Analytic of Men*, AJENCIS

Early Autumn, 20 New Imperial Year (4132, Year-of-the-Tusk), The Leash.

The face rises from the depths of a pool, pale through the greenish cast of the water. Throughout the surrounding darkness, caverns intertwine, like the thin tunnels one finds beneath large stones pulled from the grass. Just beneath the surface, the turquoise-eyed youth pauses as though tugged by some deep restraint, smiles, and raises his mouth. With horror, the King-of-Tribes watches as an earthworm presses through the smiling lips and pierces the water. It feels the air like a blind finger. Watery and obscene, the bland pink of hidden places.

And always, his own inarticulate hand drifts over the pool and, in a quiet moment of insanity, touches it.

The pop of axes hewing wood, so many as to sound like corn thrown upon a fire. The deep shouts of men, voices upbraiding, teasing, declaring in some incomprehensible tongue.

Anasûrimbor Moënghus awoke to the bite of chains, the prickle of blood-starved extremities, and further pains too numerous to warrant complaint. He blinked against filtered light, saw greased hides rising on wooden ribs. He was naked ... bound. His feet had been shackled at the ankles, and his hands at the wrists. A chain girdled his torso, crude iron links looped his white-skinned torso, pinning his elbows to his gullet, and leashing him to a birch that had been shorn of all its branches, hacked into a prisoner's post.

The day was summer-hot with the bright and arid vacancy of autumn. The yaksh should have been stifling, but something, the dust in the leather and wooden crevices, perhaps, or the vent in the conical ceiling, lifted all breath and odour from the air. He felt ... *clean*, he decided, the cleanest he had been since Ishterebinth. The claustrophobic shriek and clamour persisted, but buried in the blackness beneath his feet. The *Scylvendi* had him—the People of War!—and despite all the atrocities history had shovelled about their feet, he had no fear. What pain could they inflict upon one who had survived the Ghouls, endured *Harapior*? And what could they take when life hung like lead ingots from him? The Scylvendi had him, the Sons of his father's race, and even if they refused to acknowledge his kinship, he had been born knowing theirs. No matter what fate they visited upon him, no matter what degradation, he would die knowing it had been clean and fair.

He was free! That was all that mattered ... The madness of the Ghouls and the Anasûrimbor *both* were behind him. If his remaining span be brief, then let it be lucid—clean!

He held himself rigid, lest he rouse something, he could not say. A male and female voice warbled through the staccato chopping, and he lowered his head, pricked his ears. They spoke Scylvendi, a lilting version of the barking one heard in the camps. Moënghus understood nothing of what they said, but he somehow knew they were discussing him. He saw wedges of the man squatting outside the entrance flap, drawing two fingers through the earth then raising them to his lips. He glimpsed a scar-grilled forearm.

Then his captor was ducking through, standing upright in the dulcet gloom, a beautiful blond woman in tow. The man was old yet panther-lean, and almost entirely armoured in *scars*, plaque after plaque wrapped about his arms and neck, climbing his high cheeks. An *animus* coiled within him, a lethality that prodded hackles and tightened chests, warned of imminent mayhem. His very body was his provocation—his astonishing war-cry. Shoulders stooped to the saddle, arms the density of graven oak, inked in sinew, crossed about hands harder than horn. And swazond without number ...

The ground momentarily tipped beneath the chained Prince-Imperial. His shackles chirped for saving his balance.

His captor regarded him, blinking turquoise eyes. He raised the blade of his hand and the woman scuttled to Moënghus's side, brandishing a crude key to undo his shackles. Her proximity simply confirmed her unearthly beauty.

"Do you know me?" his captor barked in Sheyic.

Moënghus licked lips still broken for Ishterebinth. The woman had become a rattling shadow to his right.

"You ..." he coughed, surprised by the pain of speaking. "You are Cnaiür urs Skiötha."

The most violent of all Men.

The glacial eyes regarded him. "And what did he tell you about me, the Anasûrimbor?"

Moënghus stammered for the enormity of the turn.

"Tha-that you ... you were dead."

"He knows you're his sire," the young woman called from Moënghus's side. "He trembles for it."

A murderous intensity crept into the man's glare.

"Do you know who she is?"

"No ..." Moënghus muttered, gazing into the girl's face. "Should I?"

Cnaiür urs Skiötha's laugh was born of butchery, a deranged, sneering thing.

The woman leaned across the dry light to stroke Moënghus's cheek, a divine handmaiden.

"You were just a baby," she said, smiling regret.

The King-of-Tribes kept him hooded during the day, his arms bound behind his back, so he continually lurched in his saddle forever surprised by the ground crossed by his foul-smelling pony. The hood was removed only at day's end, when he was returned to his yaksh. The shackles were removed only when the Norsirai concubine was present, the young woman, barely in her flower, who claimed to be his *mother* ...

Serwë ... A name had forever been a chill breath upon his heart.

Such a mad pantomime they played, night after night. The girl hanging upon the details of his day, showering him with chaste affections. The berserker King-of-Tribes not so much playing his father as watching while such games were played.

"I think you showed wisdom. Restraint. Your father is too quick to anger, to instill fear, so that Men who should confide *in* him whisper *about* him instead ..."

Moënghus understood what happened. He had seen the sane pandering to the witless or insane enough, arranging beliefs like feathers then strutting according to their false plumage. He just never believed he could ever be party to it, that he would exchange dignity to allay a terrifying eye. And the ease of it dismayed him, answering her maternal curiosities, never condescending to *confirm* the pretense, but then never daring to contradict them either. How does a soul walk such a line, forever communicate what lies between fact and deception?

His accursed sister, he had no doubt, would ask how a soul could do anything else. But madness was madness *because it carried a toll*, one catastrophic in proportion to the heights it ascended. Madness in the fields or the agora generally ended with the hurling of stones to bludgeon or the stacking of wood to burn. But madness in the palace usually ended in the ruin of all.

"Cease this lunacy!" he roared the third night after crossing the Leash. "You are *not* my mother!"

The alluring waif clucked and smiled as if at his naiveté. Perhaps this was when he realized she wasn't entirely human.

"Why?" he snarled at the shadowy spectre of his father standing arms crossed just inside the threshold. "Why do you play this mad game?"

Moënghus could almost believe that Cnaiür had loomed invisible above him in sooth, so suddenly was he struck. A yoke-hard forearm pressed his cheek to the lifeless dirt. And he could feel the *heat* of the legendary warrior, smell the bestial musk, the bull-snorting exhalations.

"You are *Anasûrimbor!*" the most-violent-of-men grated in his ear. "You have no right to complain of games!"

His spit made black glyphs of the dirt before the Prince-Imperial's face.

A grunt occasioned each blow across his ear and cheek. It was the place of fathers, beating sons.

He could hear her laughing, his mother.

Cnaiür was watching him when Moënghus regained consciousness, sitting naked in the light showering through the yaksh entrance. The King-of-Tribes slouched forward, his arms hooked about an upright knee. His swazond appeared to *scale* him—such was the contrast between shadow and the white morning bright—rendering him something crocodilian.

"Scylvendi children," the man said, eyes as bright as opals held to sky, "are taught to hate but a single thing." He nodded as if admitting fault in a wisdom that had to be obeyed regardless. "Aye ... *weakness* ... Weakness is what sparks the father's cane! Woe to the child that weeps!"

The most-violent-of-all-men cackled, a sound far too docile, given the grimace accompanying it.

"That's the cunning of it, boy, for nothing is impervious. All power shits. All power *sleeps*. Strength must be *aimed*, and so are all things exposed, all things weak. To despise weakness is to loathe *existence itself* ..."

And Anasûrimbor Moënghus understood what it seemed he had known all along. Cnaiür urs Skiötha rode for Golgotterath, *for the Unholy Consult*, bent on settling the mortal grudge he bore Anasûrimbor Kellhus. Finding Moënghus en route, the very son his enemy had stolen, *here*, upon the very threshold of his vengeance ... It would be too much for any man to credit, let alone one so rent by spite. How could he not presume some devious conspiracy to overthrow him?

"And so is the *World* made hateful, boy, transformed into yet another thing to be strangled and beaten."

"I know hate," Moënghus said warily.

The King-of-Tribes flinched, spat into the filtered morning glare.

"How could you?" he grated. "You had only *mothers*."

"Bah!" the Prince-Imperial scoffed. "All Men ha—!"

The Scylvendi leapt to stand chiselled and rank before his son. "*Thiiss!*" he roared, swatting palms against his scarred chest, thighs, and abdomen. "*This is hate!*"

He struck Moënghus full on the mouth, throwing his head back on the arc of the chain, down hard to harder earth.

"You are lettered!" Cnaiür urs Skiötha sneered. "Civilized! You abhor the harm that comes of cruel sport! You are sickened by those who whip horses, murder slaves or beat pretty wives! Something numb cramps within you, and you think it hate! But you *do* nothing! Nothing! You pule and you ponder, you worry loved ones, beat water and scream at skies! *You! Do! Nothing!*"

Moënghus could only gawk at the elemental figure before him, cower.

"*This!*" Cnaiür urs Skiötha boomed on climbing veins. "*Read it!*" He raked clawed fingers from his abdomen to his chest.

"This! This is the history of Hate!"

It took four bowlegged warriors to pry his stake from the earth. He could not understand the least word of their banter, but he was certain they called him a woman for his unscarred skin. They secured his arms about an ash bough against his back, then he was bound to a train of yaksh-dragging ponies, left to stumble with the chattel and the supplies. They flogged him for sport that evening, tormented him until darkness. And it seemed a *relief*, compared to what he had suffered at the hands of the ghouls. His hacking laughter unnerved them, as did his sobbing grin. What began with whooping derision soured into silence and grave faces.

He saw no sign of his father or his consort during this time.

Finally they hauled him staggering through firelight toward the apparition of the White Yaksh, which wavered as a reflection in water. They wrestled him in, leaned knees upon his head while chaining him to a new stake. Then the reeking brutes were gone, and he lay alone, broken lips against the soothing earth. He cackled for reasons he would never know, and wept for reasons he could not *unknow*. A lone taper—plunder from some Nansur temple—illuminated the interior. He rubbed his jaw, saw what seemed a helter of baggage across the welter of soiled rugs in the gloom. He noticed furs twined and tangled into a nest no more than two steps from his feet. The taper sputtered, sent light and shadow fluttering across the cone of the weather-stained walls, then everything went black.

Even though it recalled the horror of the Thresholds in Ishterebinth, the darkness seemed to mend him, as if wounds unseen instantly healed. A body is naught but a clouded eye, a vision born into cataracts, pleasure and pain for bright, numbness for dark, everything shapeless and obscure. His skin had seen too much of late, and darkness was his only salve.

He drifted, his body pulsing, alive with aches and flares and winces. His breath pressed a cold spoon against his heart, and he awoke from his doze, realizing he, Anasûrimbor Moënghus, was chained to the foot of an un-couth barbarian's *bed*. Like a dog.

This should have occasioned fury, but the limb required had been hacked from him, leaving the fact in the hands of melancholy wonder. He understood why he had fled Serwa. He understood why he had fled *here*, of all places. He even understood why his true father could do nothing but murder him, in the end. So why did his thoughts reel and stagger so? *Why was he perpetually baffled*, at a loss to answer some question he could not even ask? Was it simply because he was being beaten? Had his wits, like those of many old soldiers, been forever knocked from him?

The entrance flap snapped back, and Cnaiür urs Skiötha pressed through, bearing a lantern hooked upon a staff. He raised the light high, transferred it to a hook wired to one of the yaksh poles. Muddy illumination swung about the interior, more than enough to awaken Moënghus's weals.

The most violent of Men peered at the Prince-Imperial in the discon-certing way of those scrutinizing things near as if from afar. And for all his turbulent years, Cnaiür seemed far, far older still, like a barbarian scourge of old, the incarnation of Horiötha, the Scylvendi King-of-Tribes who had sacked Cenei and brought a whole civilization crashing at his feet.

Serwë ducked through the entrance behind him, slunk around stooping beneath the hide walls.

Moënghus pulled himself to his knees, the very limit of the chain's restraint.

"What do you want of me?" he cried hoarsely.

The barbarian placed his hands on his hips.

"What I always want. What I only want. Vengeance."

His instinct was to avert his gaze, but there was something *naked* in his father's blue-white glare, a famished intensity that demanded an answering stare—a matching exposure ...

"So you beat what shreds of *him* you find in me? Is tha—?"

A concussion snapped his head around, sent his torso swinging about its chain.

"Yes."

The Prince-Imperial pressed himself from the thatch, his eyes honey be-neath fluttering lids.

"Because murdering your own son in fact, murders him in effigy? Becau—?"

A backhand exploded high across his left cheek, and the yaksh interior swung up and about. Links bit into his throat.

"Yes."

Moënghus whirled back to the roaring figure.

"Fool! Mummer! Who spills their own blood to punish ano—?"

A strike high on his forehead sent him straight down.

The reply was grinding, demonic. "I do."

Moënghus snorted fresh blood, saw the beautiful waif kneeling nearby, watching him, her back too arched, her eyes dozing for arousal.

Serwë.

He spat blood, bits of teeth, wondered that it had taken so long for him to *realize*. What was the power of knowledge such that even the chained and battered could be freed?

"Momma?" he called on a grisly laugh.

He wricked his body stiffly about, so that he could apprehend his deranged father.

"So you make like dogs with *skin-spies*," he cackled at the shadow. "Is that it?"

Another concussion, this one chasing everything visible into the same tiny corner.

Yes.

Moënghus found himself hanging from the limit of his chain, breathing about an inner vastness, a void that pinned him to the empty air surrounding. It seemed the ground could plummet, and he would remain motionless, hooked to the void. Some time passed before he heard the King-of-Tribes screaming.

" ... so you had not the least inkling! *There* you dwelt—my blood! seed of my loins!—in *His very House*! and you had not the merest whiff of the abomination dandling you upon his knee. No. You *loved* him, adored him as your father even as your heart balked. You wondered that you could be so fortunate *to be his son*, a Prince-Imperial, struck from the bones of a living God! You gloated as all children gloat, *that you yourself were divine*, that Kings and Generals and Grandmasters had knelt and kissed your knee!"

A father's face should be a thoughtless thing, something too near to be seen, or at least studied, but for all the glory Kellhus had afforded him,

Moënghus was no more than a foundling in the end. The mien before him was a stranger's, even more alien for the ways it resembled his own, and not for the grills of swazond planking his forehead and cheeks.

"I have memories ..." he said to the visage, smiling heedless at the homicidal glare. "Memories that would crack your heart ... Never has the World seen such a family—such a court!"

A manic grin, savage for the carnivorous precision of his teeth.

"And this is supposed to surprise me? Overthrow my conceit? Nay, boy, it merely confirms me in my outrage, rekindles my conviction. Of course you loved him—worshipped, fawned and adored him. *He gave you meaning, and meaning, boy, is the gold that he tosses in the air.* And you are just another beggar, another mewling *cripple*, scratching dust at his feet!"

"And yet, *here you are!*" Moënghus shouted in incredulous retort. "Here you stand *wedded* to the selfsame goad! Soiling sheets with a Consult abomination! Bedding *Apocalypse!* The only gold that Kellhus throws!"

A growling cackle.

"Apocalypse? *That is my end.* Not his."

Moënghus tried to smirk through the thick of swelling.

"So what is his end?"

The powerful shoulders hitched in a shrug. "The Absolute."

The Prince-Imperial frowned.

"The Absolute? What's that supposed to mean?"

The plainsman spat to his right. "To know as the God knows."

"More madness!" Moënghus cried. "What foo—?"

"The Nonman seek the Absolute," the thing-called-Serwë said unbidden from across the yaksh. "They practice Elision, thinking they can hide themselves from Judgment, and so pass into Oblivion unseen, find absolution in the Absolute. The Dûnyain use the same word the Kûniüri inherited from the Nonmen, but enamoured of intellect and reason, they believe it to be a *goal* ..."

Moënghus snorted derision. "First you play my mother, and now you play my sister!"

Cnaiür's eyes whitened about cruel inspiration.

He strode to where his concubine loitered and clapped great, scarred hands about her throat. He hauled the slack-limbed beauty to a point immediately above the sagging Prince-Imperial. "I know your family, boy. My spies have never stopped watching! You speak of *Serwa* ... the witchqueen ..."

He brandished his consort's face as though she were a bulb ripped from a grandmother's garden, growling, "Yessss!" Sinew leapt from his banded arms, and thumbs burrowed into her pigeon-breast throat. Despite the crimped lines of anguish, her beauty arrested the Prince-Imperial, her face *became a world where he might live*, a place where strife yet suffered innocence—that is, until the visage unravelled into arachnid fingers, becoming a series of spastic clutches.

"She is every bit as *inhuman* as her namesake!"

Moënghus kicked back and around in involuntary terror. "*Madness!*" he cried. "You! You're the one who lies with monsters! With beasts!"

Cnaiür threw the thing-called-Serwë to bald ground, spat as it scuttled to the safety of leather walls.

"But what of you and your monsters, boy?" he replied with a malicious grin. "What of the lone piglet in a brood of Anasûrimbor wolves?"

"I-I don't understand ..."

"Pfah! I see the knowledge in you, the knowledge you would deny to preserve your golden life. How could you not feel the gulf between their souls and our own? So quick as to prick your hackles. So canny as to make you forever fear the treacheries dwelling in your face. Never forgetting, so greedy are they for munition! They cozened you with soft words and embraces, draped you in the bangles of their glory, so that you might caper as one of them, and still you knew their *defect*, what made them more abomination than human!"

The old Scylvendi Hero-King spat again, raised arms to the conical ceiling and its morning-glowing seams.

"Had they faces like fingers, you would cry out for swords and fire. But no, they possess *souls like fingers* instead. Their perversion can only be guessed, argued, and never seen!" He spoke with savage gesture, arms low and wide, snapping into fists and bladed palms. "My beast has been contrived to listen to secrets, while yours has been fashioned to *speak them*, bred—bred like fighting cocks!—to wind through the gut of our souls, to eat with our mouths, shit with our anuses! Bred to tangle the chambers of our heart, twine about our pulse, *to own us from within*, to nest in the pitch black of our follies, our conceits, our hopes, *our loves!*—all our womanish weaknesses!"

And he stood there, his true father, a mangled soul housed in twists of meat, slicked in sweat, grinning for blood, shining about his edges for the morning bright, scars like silver nails.

"You know of what I speak!"

This little black-haired boy.

This wolf-eyed foundling ...

Who was he?

"*Do not worry ...*" the Ghoul-most-hated had said. "*You shall be my son, after this.*"

So cold, that blackness. So clean.

"*Those who call you brother, you shall know not.*"

He lay across the dirt, as naked as his father but for his shackles. He lay, starving limbs a tingle, his temple pressed against the cool earth, a sand like the sodden sand on the strand's limit, only dry. He spoke without tone or intensity of what had happened, how he had come to Ishterebinth, what he had endured, and how that had delivered him to this place. He found it astounding how he could talk of Harapior without raging, how he could recount his grievances the Scylvendi way, with precision and hate. He told them of Serwa's seduction and their subsequent incest, how she had used him in an attempt to make the King of Sakarpus hate. He told them how *she had sang* while he had gagged and shrieked. With slow, measured words, he recounted the details of his sister's monstrosity, her resemblance to her arachnid father, and he found it absurd that he fought Cnaiür urs Skiötha's argument, mad even, given that it was his own.

"Everything," he conceded, "is as you say."

And it seemed nightmarish, the way the world within the yaksh simply snapped back to the mad pantomime he had just stripped away, his true father sitting cross-legged without comment, his attention utterly welded to his son's voice. His inhuman mother attending to his broken face.

They even kept him chained.

The black-haired boy. The wolf-eyed foundling.

Moënghus awoke in the predawn light, lying perfectly still in the way of animals upon predatory plains. The unseen camp was silent, as mute as the grey light filtering down from above. He knew his father was absent before he looked about simply for the chill in the air. He likewise knew the Consult skin-spy was present, but how, he would never understand. No alarm occasioned finding her face in the vapid light. The gloom consumed her body.

They stared at each other for what seemed an immeasurable time, mother and son.

"It surprises you that he knows what I am," the thing-called-Serwë finally said.

"And what are you?" Moënghus croaked.

"Malleable. What he needs me to be."

A pause filled with soundless breathing.

"You ... You're the perplexing one ..." She smiled angelically. "The *Anasûrimbor*."

The Prince-Imperial nodded. "And if he doesn't kill me, what then, beast?"

"But he *will* kill you."

Moënghus rolled onto his side, carried as much of his agony upon his right shoulder as he could.

She could have been a statue, so motionless had she remained. This too was a stratagem.

"I am a child of the House of your enemy," he said. "I am the very voice he must not hear. You *need* him to kill me. But you fear that he knows this as well as you ... that he'll keep me simply to *deny you*."

An intensity crawled into the disembodied visage.

"Perhaps ..." the thing conceded.

Anasûrimbor Moënghus grinned through lacerations.

"You really should kill me *now*."

The immaculate face withdrew as if on a stalk in water, vanished into adjacent shadows.

CHAPTER EIGHT

The Lament

*Verily, he stood beneath them, made bold demonstration of his will, and
yet still he kneeled, as did his kin, as did all assembled across the plain,
for It was too vast not to smite their hearts with knowledge that they were
gnats, merely, lice roaring.*
—"Third Fathom of Pir Minningial," Isûphiryas

Early Autumn, 20 New Imperial Year (4132, Year-of-the-Tusk), Golgotterath.

The madness was lifting, though the taste lingered.

You did it ... the Greater Fraction whispered.

Did what?

Carcasses jerked beneath libidinal fury.

What had to be done ...

Anasûrimbor Kellhus smiled as a toadstool of fire and pitch boiled to
the very arch of Heaven behind him.

What did I do? Tell me!

The lozenges of flesh so hot as to seem more tongue.

Something unbearable ...

Lips mashing lobes, teeth shaking blood from skin and meat.

What? What?

Licking the sewer reek.

You raped and consumed them ...

Convulsing upon his wounds.

What? Who?

Sibawûl, called Vaka by those who had come to fear him …

The Scalded … the Rotting Men.

Supping upon his flayed face.

Thinking it tasted more of pig than lamb.

———— ∞ ————

Camp was raised where Fate had mustered them along the eastern rim of the Occlusion. Despite the fears of the Imperial planners, water proved both unpolluted and plentiful. Springs pricked the heights, forming rivulets that wept orange and black down the slopes. The Ordealmen fasted, merely drank that evening. Together they transformed the inner ramps of the Occlusion into a mighty amphitheatre that took Golgotterath as its cancerous stage. Nary a soul among them spoke. The sunset possessed the autumnal clarity that transforms the loss of light into the loss of warmth and life. The Horns *burned* for embracing the sun, ere its descent became absolute. The intervening leagues seemed no less clear for the quick rising night. Beneath the gold-mirrored immensities they could easily discern the disposition of the bulwarks, no more than glue and paper compared the Horns, but as great as those ramparts belonging to Nenciphon, Carythusal, or any other great city of the Three Seas. They could count the thousands of golden teardrops that fanged the battlements. They could see Domathuz and Corrunc, the hated towers that flanked mighty Gwergiruh, the Gatehouse of Ûbil Maw, which loomed as a blight across so many tales of ancient woe. They could see the stepped fortifications of the Oblitus rising to a monstrous citadel crouched against the inner thigh of the Upright Horn, the High Cwol, barbican of the Intrinsic Gate.

The light receded over the raised edge of the World, faded to a dwindling crimson patina high upon the wrists of the Canted and Upright Horns. Every soul watching thought the stronghold would explode with horrors upon the sun's final gloaming, but since no soul dared speak, each man assumed he alone suffered this terror, and further despised himself as a coward. They sat and stared in their tens of thousands, bodies buzzing for shame, stomachs churning for fear and incredulity, jaws aching for slow, gnashing teeth.

Perhaps in some dim corner some few realized the perverse *thrift* of their straits, how *only an evil so great* could hope to redeem *souls so wretched as their own*. Even as Fate sharpened the World, their lives had been whittled to a point of private apocalypse. Perhaps a handful understood it well enough to speak it, the murmuring of possibility in their veins, the hope, the *prayer*, that they had committed those unspeakable crimes to better *know* the goad that drove them, to better *hate* the stupefying abomination that so commanded their gaze. And at some level, all of them understood, no matter how dimly, that they must somehow conquer, destroy this ancient and obscene vessel from the Void, *or be forever damned*. So they sat, they watched, and they took loathing stock of themselves. They prayed as strangers among strangers.

The sun eased against, then melted into the rugged shoulders of the Yimaleti. The burnished rims of the Horns flared brilliant even as their bulk blackened into violet obscurity. The broken circle of their shadow reached out across Shigogli and embraced the multitudes, bore them into the greater arms of the Void, the sky beyond the sky, the Endless Starving.

Night fell without incident, without so much as a faraway flicker of movement. Poised upon various heights about the Occlusion, Schoolmen cast their sorcerous lenses to better see, but nary a soul cried out for some glimpse of their foe. For all anyone knew, the fell stronghold lay abandoned.

The Ordealmen possessed little will to organize, such was their awe and turmoil. Many slept on the ground upon which they sat. The Horns loomed impossible in their fluttering vision as they drowsed and drifted, monuments to the boggling power of the Tekhne, the golden levers that had toppled whole civilizations.

They dreamt unkind dreams.

"Though you lose your soul ... you shall gain the World ..."

A simple phrase, but Proyas could tell speaking it had broken Drusas Achamian's breath in twain.

He had recited the words while walking, as they often did during Instruction, the idyllic wooded ways of the Ke in Aöknyssus. Years afterward, Proyas would come to realize the ancestral reserve was where he was typically the most dismissive of his arcane tutor, the most arrogant, cruel even. For whatever reason, he found license in the wash of wind through bobbing leaves, in the sunlight fracturing about branches, forever flashing in some corner of his eye, forcing the squint he would subsequently take to Akka's claims and assertions.

"But what does the *World* matter?" Proyas had snapped.

Achamian shot him a shrewd and disapproving look, the one he reserved for childish answers to mannish questions—the one that never failed to remind the young prince of his king father. Proyas would punish the Schoolman for this imposture as well.

"If the World were shut against the Outside," the rotund man said, "what would happen then?"

"Pfah! You and your Apocaly—"

"*If*, Prosha. I said *if* ..."

A scowl ... the very one that would be aged into his face.

"'If,' you say, 'then'! What does it matter, if such a thing can never come to pass?"

How he had hated the man's knowing smirk. The strength it betrayed. The pity.

"I see," Achamian replied. "So you are a miser, then."

"Miser? Because I observe the Tusk? Because I commit hand and breath to the God?"

"No. Because you see only gold, and nothing of what makes it precious."

Derision. "So gold is no longer gold, now? Spare me your riddles!"

"Would you throw gold to sailors wrecked at sea?"

There is such *heat* in the boyish soul, such *need* to declare for and against. To be a child is to be heard as a child, and so to be sealed in, to have no way of invading the World with your voice. So he, like so many other proud unto arrogant boys, defended his meagre circuit with zeal—at the cost of smaller truths if need be.

"Never! I'm a *miser*, remember!"

And *that* would be the first time ...

The first time he would glimpse genuine *worry* in Drusas Achamian's eyes. And with it the question ...

What kind of King will you be?

The World's shadow retreated across the rolling face of the World.

Night drained from the rising ground of day, receding across the horizon implacable and soundless, and where trapped, evaporating into oblivion. The pinnacle of the Horns caught the sun before anything and lorded it over the nations of slumbering Men, jaundiced the gloom in the shadowy lee of the Occlusion. No birds sang. No dogs barked.

Some had found reprieve in work. The previous evening, a company of Shrial Knights discovered the wain bearing the Interval abandoned on the Agongorean side of the Occlusion. They dismantled the cart and its contrivances and carried them through the passes—some twelve men and ropes were required to drag the great iron cylinder and its skin of etched benedictions. They worked through the entire night reassembling it. Unable to find the Prayer Hammer, they sounded the thing with a battleaxe, marring the Invitic inscription. And so the Interval tolled for the first time in three days, its far-ranging hum eerily resonant in the desolation, its ring, some would swear, sharpened for the Horns.

Men wept in the thousands.

The fire of dawn ignited the mighty golden hulks, slowly burned downward, even as the shadow of the Occlusion retreated across the Furnace Plain. The long-suffering Men of the Ordeal roused, climbed stupefied to their feet, not so much more themselves than less what they had been. Once subsumed in the bestial morass, the old facts of individual character seemed to stir and reassert.

So it was that the most irrepressible among them, Halas Siroyon, spurred Phiolos out across the crazed earth of Shigogli. He rode as if to outrun the broken glass in his breast, the shame that so lacerated his heart. He rode the Famiri way, his nut-brown chest bared to both wind and foe, his ravaged Circumfix standard raised high in his right hand. He passed beyond the shouts of his brothers, dwindled into a speck against the waste. He found peace in the interval, felt the ghost of his galloping youth. He rode until the gold-hanging immensity became *palpable*, and he had to arch his back and set his shoulders against the urge to cringe.

The fortifications stacked beneath the unholy Ark loomed large upon the cliffs of the Scab, the great black tumour that served as the Horns' pedestal. The General tacked to the south, calling, "Do you see it, old friend?" to his steed. "The stopper of the World!" The stoneworks were, for all that he could see, devoid of life. They were titanic by any measure, black bastions like Shigeki ziggurats, black walls whose height dwarfed those encircling Carythusal or Aöknyssus.

Clinging to Phiolos, he plunged feckless into their shadow, then veered to pace their circuit, then, as was the custom of heroes on the Famiri Plain, he leaned back against his cantle, raised high his arms, and offered his naked chest as a flying target for his foe. Not a shaft fell from the brutal heights. He laughed and he wept. He followed the circuit marvelling, peered into the recesses between the gold-fanged battlements. He felt like a runaway child. He felt daring, reckless with what was holy. He would be remembered for this! He would be inked in scripture! He came to the famed Field of Ûgorrior, the plate of dust where the scarps failed, and the fortifications stood knuckled directly upon the plain. He rode about the stumped immensity of Corrunc, then pulled Phiolos toward the legendary Iron Gate of Ûbil Maw.

He would be redeemed!

Man and horse slowed as they came to the storied ground immediately below the breastworks of Gwergiruh—the hated Grinning Gatehouse. Siroyon drew Phiolos to a halt not five paces from where, in days of Far Antiquity, General Sag-Marmau had issued his final ultimatum to Shauriatas, and where foul Sil, the Inchoroi King, had struck down Im'inaral Lightbringer, Hero of Siol, in days more ancient still ...

So young! Halas Siroyon was naught but a child—could be nothing but in the malevolent shadow of such a place. How bold must Men be! To raise pride and defiance against such a spectacle! Such a place!

Mortal. Skin so soft as to welt for the hurling of stones.

Gwergiruh towered only half so high as Corrunc to the north or Domathuz, her monstrous sister to the south. Even still it dwarfed both for its breadth and depth. The whole took the accursed shape of a pentagon, with Ûbil Maw lying at its mathematical heart, doors of ensorcelled iron opening into a murderous gorge some thirty paces deep. Siroyon's daring ended at the mouth of this gorge. Peering, the overawed man could see the wicked portal, doors as tall as a carrack's mast, stamped with oil-shining reliefs, figures bound to one another in poses of anguish and abjection, the misery of one becoming the frame for the lament of the other ...

Just as described in the *Holy Sagas*.

He warred with scarred Phiolos, managing only to pull him into stomping circles. He gazed across the soaring scarps of masonry, felt a sudden prick of nude vulnerability.

"*Show yourselves!*" he cried out to the black heights.

The great steed wagged its mane and settled.

Silence.

Faraway water trailed from the outer curve of the Canted Horn, which hung like a mountain's belly above. The rising sun had set the rims of the Horns afire: an eerie light jaundiced everything that could be seen.

The grasswives claimed that Halas Siroyon had been born the same day and watch as the great Niz-Hû, and that the ancient Famiri hero haunted his bones as a result. The General himself scoffed at such rumours, even as he affected an archaic manner to promote it—for he understood that *mystique*, as much as glory, raised a man in the jealous estimation of Men. His innards quailed for being dwarfed in so many ways, and yet he *laughed*, howled the way Niz-Hû had once laughed at the ancient King of Shir.

"Throw open your granaries!" he bellowed. "Send forth your Sranc—your skinnies!—so that we might *dine* on them!"

There is power in base savagery, in the *desire*, let alone will and capacity, to commit monstrous acts. All violence is equally ancient. To match a wicked foe abomination for abomination was to whisper in his ear while he slumbered—for the righteous were no more potent than when *they were ruthless also*.

"Anasûrimbor Kellhus!" Siroyon cried, craning his head as if to toss his defiance over the soaring parapets. "The Holy *Aspect-Emperor* has come!"

Monumental silence. Vacant heights. A murder of crows screeched from some unseen distance. The air stagnated for want of wind.

"To conquer!" he roared, at last feeling the weight of his own fury. "To *consume!*"

He thrust his makeshift banner into the earth, and at last gave Phiolos license to peel away in pursuit of their mutual terror. From the rim of the Occlusion, the Men of the Ordeal watched astounded. They made a choir of Shigogli with their cries, roaring with an exultation that unmanned them, so fevered was its wonder and fury.

And it was a thing of desolate glory, the Men thundering across the plain as Golgotterath hoarded darkness against the climbing sun. Swords hammered shields. Spears pricked the sky.

Siroyon's leaning banner—a Circumfix stitched black on white, tattered and gore-stained—leaned like a dead yeoman's scarecrow for the length of the day, ere night fell ...

And it was never seen again.

⸎

Prosha ... the pious and precocious little boy, the beautiful one, who had inherited the face and eye of his mother—just as the poets said. The pompous boy. The *ridiculous* boy, who had brought his father joy only when observing him unseen.

For Seju knew his tongue had brought the man only grief otherwise!

"Where, Father?" he had asked after hearing the last of House Nersei's ancestral rivals, the Nejati, had been executed. "Where lies the honour in murdering children?"

The long look of a father afflicted by the very thing that made him most proud. "In sparing my sons and my people war ten years hence."

"You think you will be *forgiven* this?"

"*Prosha* ..." The tone of a father long resigned to the condemnation of those he loved. "Prosha, please. You will understand soon enough."

"Understand what, Father? *Atrocity?*"

A fist hammering the table.

"*That power* is *damnation!*"

He flinched for the force of that memory no matter what occasioned it.

Why? Why was he the one to fear damnation so? It all seemed so clear, no matter how much confusion Achamian had poured into his ear. *This life was but a flicker*, a vista glimpsed in a flash of summer lightning, then gone. There were *a thousand Hells* for a hundred Heavens—so many more ways to drown in fire and anguish than to wander meadows in paradise. How? How could anyone be so low, so base, as to willingly sacrifice their *very souls* to monstrous Eternity?

How could anyone *embrace* wickedness?

But his father had been right. He *had* come to understand given the fullness of time. Piety was simple, and the World, woefully complex. What was virtuous, what was holy: these were verities that only the simple and the enslaved could know with certainty. For the Lords of Men, they were riddles beyond fathoming, perils that gnawed souls into the deepest watches of the night. If his father had spared the sons of Nejata, what then? Vengeance would have been their inheritance, discord and rebellion the consequence. The piety that would have spared them was the piety that would have put other, nameless innocents on the altar.

Piety was simple, too simple to not amputate life.

———— ✺ ————

The taste of salts—human salts—licked from carcass skin.

The Interval tolled, calling the Lords of the Ordeal to the Umbilicus—to reckon the unthinkable. Awaiting them, Nersei Proyas, Believer-King of Conriya, Exalt-General of the Great Ordeal, spat memory across the carpets below the Holy Aspect-Emperor's bench. He bent forward, elbows on his knees, warring against the urge to wretch. He raised his head to the gloom of the Umbilicus, wondered that for all their debility, enough men could summon enough routine, to drag let alone assemble the monstrous pavilion, mallet the tiers, hang the banners, unfurl and hoist the Ekkinû. He wondered even though he was one of those men, souls inclined to express adoration in simple labours. Somehow he had dragged the Great Ordeal across Agongorea and assembled it upon the porch of Golgotterath.

It still reeked, he decided, of the corrupt smoke of Dagliash.

The glint of his dead father's signet ring hooked his gaze.

The madness, a fraction observed, impassive. The madness of the Meat was lifting.

The memories were not.

He sat gnawing on his knuckles, which ached. He hunched gagging, his mouth shedding spit about rhythmic convulsions. He wept, for shame that his son should have such a father. He even cackled for a time, as it seemed an evil man should. He had succeeded! He had discharged the dread task of his Aspect-Emperor! And the glory of it was such that he could only laugh—claw his beard and hair sobbing, shrieking.

Eating Sranc. Lying with Men. Cannibalism. Rutting with corpses ...

No-no-no! The mere inkling of these things made chill knives of his lungs, maggots of his heart. *What?* some fraction shrieked and shrieked. *What have you done?* His lips parted, his teeth clamped, and his limbs waved like a corpse tumbling in surf. Something like a worm twisted from his gut to his skull, something hateful and weak, snivelling and blubbering ... *No! No!*

His lips, plush and cold, releasing threads of blood and spit bowing in the wind.

Wishing it all back ... Railing. Shrieking.

The hair of his cadaverous pubis trembling. Skin so pale beneath the haze. The *taste* ... so ...

What was this wretched instinct? This will to blot out *all existence* in the name of undoing the irrevocable?

Like something boneless and amphibian, cold against the hot curl of his tongue.

How? *How?* How had such a thing come to pass? How could ...

Coughing, vomiting for convulsive violence, so intense was the *insertion*, hot and bulbous, thrusting aside the chill paste of viscera. Grunting, blowing air, bull-huffing, bellowing—

How—

Sibawûl ... drowsy and almost dead, slack beneath his monstrous exertions, his head rocking to the pelvic violence, bobbing like a drunkard fending oblivion.

Sejenus says ...

What? What was happening? Just the day previous, it seemed, he had *gloated* over these selfsame acts, abused himself while wallowing in their miscreant memory, laughed at the horror of his blackened seed ... exulted.

And now? *Now?*

Now he sat upon the throne of a far *mightier* father ...

And the madness of the Meat was lifting.

He slumped from the seat to his knees. A great fist clenched within his breast, yanking his every tendon, every ligament, from the muck of his flesh. He rocked to and fro, keening, spit whistling from his teeth, air pinching his gums. A God seized the nape of his neck, thrust him forward. He convulsed about spittle, choked on threads of burning mucous. Obscenities wheeled, glimpses through smoke. Taking. Touching. *Tasting ...*

"No!" he croaked, his expression alive and jerking, as if hooked by strings to battling birds.

"*Noooo!*"

Yes.

———— ⌗ ————

Proyas? Proyas Vaka?

The premonition struck him with the force of a physical blow. He looked about wildly, blinking rheum from his eyes ... peering ... was it? Yes?

A form in the Umbilicus gloom, a golden, gliding apparition, hands outstretched, fingers spread between luminous rings ...

Yes.

And the velvet arms were about him, and he was clinging, clutching with the guileless ferocity of a child plucked from mortal terror. Again and again, the great fist hammered his innards, beating sob after sob from his breast. And with his face buried, *Nersei Proyas wept*, for all things it seemed, for there was no limit to the dragon roaring, no limit to the injustices endured. He wailed into dulcet cloth, gasped scented, reverend air, and no matter how violent his spasms, the form he clutched remained unperturbed, not so much immovable as *fastened* to what was necessary and pure. The chest rising beneath his mashed cheeks. The torso broad and buoyant within the desperate circuit of his arms. The beard like crushed silk against his scalp. The arms iron boughs, with palms hot as wonder ...

And the voice, humming more than speaking, reciting hymns in tones of warm water, viscid with love and comprehension.

Safe, a shuddering exhalation whispered. Encircled and safe.

"I—" he tried to say, but the crash of remorse was tidal. Wincing shames and biting terrors.

The humming trailed.

You have achieved the impossible ...

A breath like dropping through gossamer tunnels. Tears like acid.

Secured a glory that none will know.

"But th-the ... the things—!" he croaked. "S-such *wicked, wicked ... things!*"

Necessary things ...

"*Depravities!* Things that cannot be *undone!*"

No act can be undone.

"But can-can th-they be *forgiven?*"

What you have surrendered ... can never be reclaimed ...

He ground his forehead into the delusion's hallowed shoulder, clenched the fabric of the robe with a will that could not quite tear. An entire life come to this, a numb fraction realized ... All of it, the terror-lust-exultation,

turbulence concentrated into a fevered tingle, blasting through the bottle-
neck of this moment, this final ...

Revelation.

The tracks you have left ... are eternal ...

For an instant he was the little boy he had once been, only wrecked and
desolate, devoid of the least pious spark. A child, open for the utter absence
of wile, as he had to be, given that it was a question Proyas-the-man could
never speak.

"Am I damned?"

And he could feel it, the regret and the pity, passing through the glorious
form like a relaxation of a breath too long held.

The World is saved.

⟨∾⟩

An opiate air clung to each sounding of the Interval, a sense of not quite
awakening. The first Lords of the Ordeal began filing into the gloom of the
Umbilicus. Proyas watched them and did not watch them. He cared not
what they made of his stooped posture or the rictus of anguish that passed
for his expression. Nor did he need to, for they were likewise grim, likewise
maniacal, some more, some less.

The madness of the Meat was lifting.

So much must be done!

If the Consult were to attack *this very moment*, what then?

He heard Siroyon's name mentioned, but otherwise could not decipher
their growling banter. No matter what face his errant attention plucked from
the growing assembly, he could see it, the horror of souls reclaiming what was
irredeemably polluted. Wringing hands. Eyes darting or downcast or blank
for inward peering. Some, like the Earl of Cuarweth, wept openly. A handful
even screeched like spurned wives, and so compounded their degradation. Lord
Chorgah began sawing away his beard with a knife, plait by rancid plait, staring
out as if perpetually hung upon some untoward awakening, tidings of heartbreak
delivered in the dead of night. No one embraced—indeed they seemed to cringe
from one another, the sensitive shrinking from the proximity of the numb.

But they all looked to *him*.

So he stood the way an old king jealous of his fading dignity might, with
forced bravura. He looked out across the once-magnificent assembly, breath-

ing, it seemed, no deeper than the ache in his throat. He blinked. Tears like razors split his cheeks.

Those that could fell silent.

The madness of the Meat was lifting.

"If ..." he began, looking out to the assemblage of poles and wires that pinned the blackness above them. Even as he spoke, he spied the bereaved son of Harweel on the tiers, newly returned from Ishterebinth ... bearing tidings no one cared to hear. "If the Consult were to attack *this very moment,* what then?"

"*Then we shall be blotted,*" Lord Grimmel screamed, "*and justice—justice!—will be done!*" Out of all of them, he had always swung furthest from the rope of the Meat, but he was not without sympathizers. The Lords of the Ordeal erupted across the tiers. Wagging fists. Straining fingers. Cries, some outraged, others beseeching, bewailing, urging, resounded through the high-canvas hollows. It did not matter, the violence or the stupor, whether the man was a Grandmaster or a barbarian prince, *they all mouthed the same cry* ...

How?

All of them, that is, *save Sorweel.* He sat in the violent shadow of the Zeumi Successor-Prince (who stood howling with the others) cringing more for disgust than fear, a kind of hole in the furor, a pocket of incredulous cold.

"*Sin! Grievous sin!*"

"*My own hand did this! My hand!*"

"Heed me!" Proyas shouted, trying in vain to secure their attention, or at the very least their silence. "Heed!" He stood before the clamour, the theatre of gesticulating arms and anguished faces rising across the tiers ... mouths open ... hungry ...

Again he glimpsed Sorweel ... and he fairly threw out his arms out in warding, so sharp was the *accusation* in the youth's look. Yes-yes—the Sakarpi Believer-King *had been there,* had witnessed what he ... what he ... Proyas's eyes rolled of their own volition across the Circumfix banners, black fabric and emptiness. His voice caught upon a nail of agony in his throat.

The insertion. The welling blood. The wheeze of other incisions. The *heat* ... *Sweet Seju ...What have I done?*

For several heartbeats, he floated upon the anguished clamour, bobbed thoughtless on bubbling images of unthinkable deeds ... commissions ...

acts beyond the pale of redemption. He heard, but did not register, the sorcerous murmur ...

"ENOUGH!"

All eyes found Anasûrimbor Serwa standing with her brother, Kayûtas, just within the entrance of the Umbilicus. The Swayali Grandmistress had recovered her wardrobe and now stood decked in a jet-black billows twined into tentacles about her slight form. And it was nightmarish, the sight of *unsullied* dress—the gleam of Imperial magnificence—in this polluted and depraved place.

Proyas gawked, astonished as any. She too had *survived* something, he realized, something more than whatever had blackened her left eye. A trial of some kind had been stamped into her once-immaculate beauty, sucking what had been rounded with youth into stern lines. She looked hard—pitiless.

"*Recall* yourselves!" she cried in her mundane voice.

She too had *witnessed*, Proyas realized, recoiling at the memory. She had *been* there ... on the Field Appalling. Shame seized him by the glottis, and he nearly doubled over for gagging.

Cruel old Lord Soter rushed her, crashed to his knees at her feet, crying, "Sweet Doya! Please! What happens to us?" in his lilting Ainoni accent.

She looked sharply at Apperens Saccarees, whose eyes fairly bounced in horror.

"The Nonmen speak ..." the Mandate Grandmaster began, his voice fluted and frail. "The-the Nonmen speak of this ..." The Schoolman trailed. He had raised two fingers as he spoke, the way a man lost in memory is prone to comb his beard while lost in rumination, only left hanging in indecision before his face. He now gnawed on them, hunched and apprehensive.

"You have been beasts!" Serwa snapped in irritation. "You have floundered in the muck of animal desire, choked on your own most destructive appetites, unable to do anything save gloat and exult. And now, absent the Meat, your soul is rekindled, you finally recall *who* you were ... You awaken from your rutting nightmares ... and lament."

The assembled Lords of the Ordeal gazed aghast. Even the weepers fell silent.

"No ..."

All eyes turned to Proyas, who stood baffled, not knowing from whence his words or voice arose aside from some perverse will to truth.

"This ... this is no-no *awakening*," he stammered, scowling, perhaps even sobbing. "The ... the *beast* that committed ... those—those atrocities—*I am that monster!* What I-I recall ..."—a grimace—"I re-recall not as though from some dream, but as clearly as I remember any day I would call my own. I committed those deeds! I *chose!* And *that*"—a swallow to unscrew a rictus grin—"that is the horror, m-my Niece. That is the origin or our lament: the fact that *we hang upon* these foul-*foul*, heart-cracking deeds ... that *we*, and not the Meat, are the author of our lunatic sins!"

Cries and moans of recognition. "Yes!" King Hoga Hogrim bellowed above the chorus. "We did this! We did! Not the Meat!" The Swayali Grandmistress glanced toward her brother, who shook his head in warning. She strode to the foot of her father's throne, sparing the Exalt-General a hard look as she did so.

Don't be a fool, Uncle ...

She smelled of mountains, somehow ... places far more clean than this.

And then, spontaneously it seemed, the assembled Lords of the Ordeal began calling out for *Him*, Anasûrimbor Kellhus, their beloved Holy Aspect-Emperor, clutching for some connection between his absence and their malfeasance.

"Father cannot help you!" Serwa cried out to the Believer-Kings. And then, in tones closer to a shriek, "*Father cannot cleanse you!*"

A chastised hush eventually overpowered them.

"This! This is the *toll!*"

How many times? How many times had they hung upon their Holy Aspect-Emperor's words *thinking* they had understood his warning ... Had the circumstances been different, it would have sparked laughter rather than the wringing of hands or hair, the stupefaction of finding oneself oblivious to *what was known all along*. It was not for nothing their expedition had been named *Ordeal*. The assembled Believer-Kings, the battered glory of the Three Seas, gazed at the Princess-Imperial aghast.

"What? Did you think Golgotterath—*Golgotterath!*—could be purchased with cuts and sore feet?"

"*Uturu memkirrus, jawinna!*" Kayûtas cried out to her.

"We sit upon the stoop of the Consult," she said in cool retort to her brother. "The *Consult*, Podi! The Incû-Holoinas—the horror of horrors!—squats upon the very earth beneath our feet! I fear wallowing is a luxury we can ill-afford!"

"What?" Proyas heard a ghastly voice croak—his *own*. "What ... toll?"

She seemed impossible, the woman who turned to him ... the little girl he had once swung in his arms. These children, a fraction of him realized, these *Anasûrimbor* ... He had fathered them more than he had fathered his own.

And *they had seen* ... Witnessed his transgressions.

Who was this? Who was this shaking fool?

"Uncle ..." she said, her manner suddenly vacant, as if about the whinge of some remorse.

"*What toll?*" he heard his old voice ask.

Her gaze failed her. It seemed the greatest terror he had ever endured—watching her turn away.

"Saccarees?" she said, her face averted.

"I-I ..." the Mandate Grandmaster said, speaking as if otherwise absorbed in some tome. He turned scowling to the emaciated, yet well-groomed sorcerer standing at his side—*Eskeles*.

"You have paid ..." the once-portly sorcerer said with blank apprehension, "with your immortal souls."

Damnation.

They had known it. All along they had known it. For this very reason, they filled the black-canvas hollows with shrieks and bellows.

The madness of the Meat was lifting.

They stood upon bottomless earth, yet it seemed the Umbilicus rocked and heaved like the hold of a ship foundering in some tempest.

King Nersei Proyas wept alone in their raucous midst, for himself and no other. For where his brothers had yielded their souls for their shared God, he had done so for ... something unknown.

"*The World is granary, Proyas ...*

Images of his wife sleeping, negligent curls crushed against her cheek, arms about a child he would no longer recognize.

"*And we are the bread.*"

And again he found his gaze, like a thing plucked from a fire, lingering upon the boy-become-a-man, the Sakarpi Horse-King ... Sorweel. The Exalt-General sobbed, smiled through the ache and snot and snivel, for he seemed *so blessed*, so pure ... for the mere fact of his prolonged absence ...

For the fact of his *own* damnation.

King Sorweel remained motionless, save for when his gesticulating and shouting Zeumi companion yanked at him, demanding an attention that he would not, perhaps could not, yield. The youth did not notice the Exalt-General's scrutiny, staring instead at Serwa with something that could have been malice, were it not so obviously love ...

Love.

The thing King Nersei Proyas would miss most of all ...

After certainty.

Once again he looked to the skeleton of ash poles, iron joints, and hemp suspending the airy void above them, and once again he wondered that Men could ache as he ached, sob as he sobbed, *yet carry on*. And that wondering nudged him *away* somehow, as if his soul had been a skiff run aground. The skein of horror remained, as did the images of obscenity, like a frenzied chewing, at once sharp and glutinous, but somehow he was able to breathe about the latter and laugh through the first, a crazed kind of cackle, but so raw with sincerity as to draw the eyes of several. These would be the first to join him in his unconscious recitation ...

> *Sweet God of Gods, who walk among us,*
> *Numberless be thy many names.*

More looks found him, including that of the Swayali Grandmistress and her Prince-Imperial brother. Proyas raised his hands as if to seize their divided attention ...

> *May your bread silence our daily hunger.*
> *May your rains quicken our deathless land.*

Words they had known before they had known words.

> *May our submission be answered with dominion,*
> *So we may prosper in your glorious name.*

Those watching began mumbling and murmuring in unison, a sound scarcely audible for the surrounding cacophony at first, but a rut so deeply worn that the wheels of thought could not but fall into it. Soon even those most immured in terror and self-pity found themselves gasping about the absence of their lamentations. And, in the crazed manner of all unexpected reversals, the Lords of the Ordeal began reaching out, one to another, and clasping tight their neighbour's hand, drawing solace from the pull of manly strength against strength. And descending from aching throats to hoarse lungs, their voices began to climb ...

> Judge us not according to our trespasses,
> But according to our temptations.

Nersei Proyas, the Exalt-General of the Great Ordeal, stood upon the dais of a far, far greater father, and smiled about the booming crescendo that had gathered within the roof of his voice. He spoke to them, spoke the verses, the simple labours, that had miraculously made their souls one.

> For thine name is Truth ...

And the words seemed all the more profound for the fact that he did not believe them.

The Lords of the Ordeal stood breathing, gazing upon their Exalt-General with countless confusions. For the first time, it seemed, Proyas noticed their reek, his own reek, a smell so human his stomach hitched. He looked out across the expectant Believer-Kings and their vassals, scooped spittle from his lip on a knuckle.

"He-he *told* me this would happen ... But I didn't listen ... I didn't ... understand."

Foul breath and rotted teeth. Rancid fabric and soiled crotches. Proyas pinched the bridge of his nose, blinked. For a heartbeat the Lords of the Ordeal seemed little more than apes garbed in the plunder of some royal crypt. Diamonds iridescent against frayed embroidery. Pearls gleaming from brown-blooming stains.

"He said that it would come to this ..."

Proyas glanced at the Imperial siblings standing expressionless side-by-side. Kayûtas, at least, nodded.

"This ... is not simply our *toll.*"

He looked out to his brothers, Men who marched to the very brink of earth and history—to the very ends of the World. Lord Embas Eswarlû, the Angle-Thane of Scolow, whom he had saved from a Sranc javelin in Illawor.

Lord Sumajil, Grandee of Mitirabis, whose hand he had seen struck from his wrist at Dagliash. King Coithus Narnol, Saubon's elder brother, with whom he had knelt and prayed more times than he could remember.

Teus Eskeles, the Schoolman who had condemned him to hell.

He nodded, even smiled, though grief and horror yawed within him still. These Men, these Lords and Grandmasters, noble and ruthless, learned and base—these *Zaudunyani* were his family. They always had been, for twenty long years.

"We are *Men of war!*" he cried out by way of exhausting admission. "We cut down what we call wicked ... call ourselves Men of God."

He snorted in what seemed the old way. He would never know where the monumental *indignation* came from, or how it came to own him so absolutely, only that this would be the most fierce moment in what had been a relentlessly ferocious life. He could see it kindling the rapt eyes about him, expressions igniting, as if his words had become sparks.

He was not who he was. He was stronger.

"We are bred to destroy what we have become."

His eye happened upon King Sorweel, who remained seated high on the uppermost tier. Rigid. Eyes dull and sharp, like flint.

"What? Did you think the God would come to you, miserable, mortal wretch that you are, as another spoil—as *flattery?* Horror! Horror *is* your revelation! *Shame is your revelation!*"

He was not who he was.

"Dwell within it, and you dwell in the *very presence of the God!*"

He was something *greater,* the Proyas that perpetually outran his soul, that forever dwelt in the darkness that came before. Here, with these grim and battered Men, his *brothers,* beloved companions in the ways of wickedness and war. Here *in this place.*

"*You have been your Enemy*! You know Him as even the Gods cannot! Now you, alone of all Men living, know the value of salvation! The beauteous miracle that is honour! The breathtaking gift that is justice! As warriors understand peace, *so you understand evil!* You know it as you know yourselves, and *you hate it as you hate yourselves!*"

The Lords of the Ordeal erupted, not in acclaim or any bellicose affirmation, but in *recognition.* They hollered as orphaned brothers conjoined in the paternity of Death, as those who knew only each other, and so despised and feared all other things. Serwa and Kayûtas looked about, remote as always, but also gladdened.

They had feared him lost—that much was plain. And somehow Proyas knew their father had instructed them to seize power should he succumb— should he fail. Proyas, the one most pious ... and least aware.

The caste-noble assembly roiled. The very extremity of their passion, wailing as old women one moment, whooping as young boys the next, oppressed them, and for all their frantic gratitude the Lords of the Ordeal found themselves turning, as all manly souls turn, to anger and contempt. He had imbued their terror and despair with *holy meaning*, offered it up as a mathematician offers up equations, a ledger where wrath could suffice for redemption. Holiness is never so cheap as when bartered for lives, and they were, in the end, violent, hateful Men.

Sinners.

So they began baying for the blood of their foe. Proyas could feel it as much as they, the need to affix their sin to more disposable souls.

"Brothers!" he called, hoping to gather them once again within the harness of his voice. "Broth—!"

I feared what I might find ...

A voice spoken through the cracks between spaces, making a million mouths of the pores in their skin. It literally plucked air, strummed hearts. Eskeles was so startled he tripped and crashed backward, bearing Saccarees tumbling with him to the ground. Petals of luminance emanated from the back of the tented chamber. As one they whirled—save Proyas, who had been facing the proper direction all along, and had seen the light kindle from nothing. As one they saw *Him* step down from the highest of the nearly vacant tiers, near enough for Sorweel to lean out and touch. It seemed the sun itself descended upon its own ray, a beam bearing the twin ink stains of the Decapitants. Golden hair flowing, draped in one of the bejewelled vestments Proyas had seen in the baggage room weeks previous.

"*How my heart is gladdened,*" the shining figure said.

The Lords of the Ordeal slumped to astounded knees, dropped their faces to the ashen earth of Shigogli.

Only Proyas and the Imperial siblings remained standing.

"Sound the Interval. Let the faithful rejoice, and the unfaithful fear."

CHAPTER NINE

The Great Letting

So they cast down the innocent with the guilty, not out of folly, but for the stern wisdom of knowing what cannot be sorted.
—Journals and Dialogues, TRIAMIS THE GREAT

Early Autumn, 20 New Imperial Year (4132, Year-of-the-Tusk), Golgotterath.

Anasûrimbor Kellhus ...

The Holy Aspect-Emperor returned at last.

Brilliance, and the corresponding sweep of shadows. Dumbstruck, Proyas watched his Lord-and-Prophet step down the tiers leaving Sorweel and a handful of others astonished in his wake. He did not so much emit light as shed it in skins. Then he was down and among them, dimming to a glower, as if he were a coal drawn from the fire, before the gloom of the interior at last claimed him as one who belonged. Mundane light shone from the flaxen plaits of his beard, made snow and blue shadow of the folds and creases of his robe.

He paused to regard the men bunching like wasps at his feet, then, grinning, at last looked to his Exalt-General ... who had yet to fall to his knees.

"M-master ..." the Exalt-General stammered.

Fraud.

Kellhus had battered this truth into him the weeks preceding Dagliash. Proyas *knew* the mad beam of his deception—that even this entrance was mummery—and yet still his heart leapt, his thoughts dissolved into adoring foam. No matter how much his intellect balked, his heart and his bones, it seemed, obstinately continued to believe.

"Aye!" the Holy Aspect-Emperor called across the prone assembly. "Indeed my heart is *gladdened!*" Simply hearing the pitch and timbre of his beloved voice seemed to ease some long-cramped muscle. "Let no man claim that I bore the Great Ordeal upon *my* back!"

Proyas could do no more than gaze blinking, his body—no, his *being*—afire with ... with ...

"Rise, my brothers!" Kellhus boomed laughing. "Rise and speak! Such occasions suffer no ceremony! We stand upon dread Shigogli—the very threshold of the Place-Most-Wicked!"

The entire shape of what followed, it seemed, lay packed in the subsequent heartbeat of hesitation, set as a spring or a snare. One by one the Lords of the Ordeal climbed to their feet, raising their voices with their frames, calling out in relief and anxious exultation. Soon they were clamouring about their Prophet, boisterous as children about a father missed and not simply returned. Kellhus laughed a hero's laugh, reached over those near to clasp outstretched hands.

Proyas stood transfixed, scarcely able to breathe.

At last ... a voice whispered. *At long last.*

He felt a sloughing of weights so onerous as to seem celestial—the falling away of dread charges. A tremor passed through him, and for a moment he feared he might swoon for sudden weightlessness. He blinked hot tears, smiled against the imprint of more fraught expressions ...

At last ... Impostor or not, *at last he could follow.*

Then he glimpsed Sorweel sitting isolate upon the tiers, shoulders cupped against a chill only he seemed to feel. He glanced at the Imperial siblings standing side-by-side, conspicuous for their reserve.

"But what is this?" the melodious voice of the Holy Aspect-Emperor exclaimed. "Hogrim? Saccarees? Siroyon—*brave rider!* How can you, the strongest among us, weep so? What is this shadow that so darkens all your hearts?"

Some seventy souls crowded about their Holy Aspect-Emperor's miraculous return, but they might as well have possessed a single throat for the way these words collectively throttled them.

Silence, save the huff of involuntary sobs, the keen of those biting back shrieks.

The Holy Aspect-Emperor's scowl faded into a kind of leonine vacancy, as if in recognition, grand and patriarchal, of fears once entertained but long ago dismissed. His stature was his dais, allowing him to search faces across the entire congregation.

"Something happened in my absence. What?"

Proyas glimpsed Kayûtas touching Serwa's sleeve. Weightlessness became immateriality—*smoke*. Memories of Kellhus's carnal strength welled as fire through the Exalt-General. The violating thrust. The lip-gnawing wince. He thought of Cnaiür, the tormented Scylvendi, for what seemed the first time in years. He thought of Achamian upon the Juterum all those years past, wild and blooded, edges singed like a scroll fetched from the flames.

No one dared answer. Everything became as milk and shadow about the Holy Aspect-Emperor.

"What have you *done?*"

And Proyas glimpsed it, then, in the hole where his terror should have been. He saw the way power coupled with adoration *cleaved*, set each soul apart from the others. Despite everything they had suffered *together*, for all the bonds between them, *nothing mattered save the judgment of Anasûrimbor Kellhus*.

There he stood, the point of focus, the hook that snagged every thought, every eye. Tall. Imperial. Decked in the regalia of his ancient Kûniüric ancestors. Pale and golden ...

"Will no one answer me?"

There he stood, the *Dûnyain* who had usurped everything that had once existed between Men. He had raised them the way mathematicians raised temples, lines of force parsed and suspended, loads summed, conserved and redirected, until everything hung from the shoulders of a single post ... One inscrutable intellect.

"What?" Kellhus exclaimed. "Do you forget *where* you stand? The accursed *ground* beneath your feet?"

The nearest of the Lords shrank from Him, answering to some cue too subtle to perceive. Some even scrambled.

"*Must I remind you?*" Anasûrimbor Kellhus thundered. His eyes flared white. A voice, inverted and unintelligible, traversed alien planes of comprehension. He swept his right arm on a grand arc ... The *air itself snapped,* a concussion that blooded noses, and the westward wall of the Umbilicus *vanished*, a flake of ash blown from a bonfire. Fresh air laved them, bore some portion of their stench away. Men squinted against the sudden, grey-blue glare, gazed out.

Overcast skies ...

The slums of the encampment, descending on a vast curve.

And in the distance, soaring from fortifications like insect excretions, the *Horns of Golgotterath*.

Soundless. Stationary. Two golden fists raised to the height of cloud and mountain, a tantrum frozen, endlessly preparing to crack the chalk spine of the earth. The monstrous Incû-Holoinas.

"*Damnation!*" the Holy Aspect-Emperor railed. "Extinction!"

How, King Nersei Proyas wondered ... How could relief and terror be so conjoined?

"The line of your fathers hangs upon the very end of the World! *We stand upon Apocalypse!*"

The Holy Aspect-Emperor's attention, so effortlessly divided among those immediately about him, suddenly yawned wide then clapped shut about the Exalt-General.

"Proyas!"

He leapt within his own skin.

"Y-yes ... God-of-Men."

The Lords of the Ordeal heaved and parted about their beloved Prophet's advance. The fury of his aspect fairly beat them from his path. Proyas resisted the sudden urge to retreat ... run.

"What happened, Proyas? What could so soil so many hearts?"

For all the years he had served him, the Exalt-General had wondered at the intensity of his presence, the way he could *swell*, somehow baring your every nerve, or shrink until he was no more than a fellow traveller. Kellhus's eyes fixed him with hooks of ethereal iron. His voice trilled, strummed the unthought rhythms of his heart.

"I ... I did as you charged."

Something must be eaten ...

"And what was that?"

Do you understand me?

"You ... You said ..."

A frown, as if at a pain inflicted.

"Proyas? You have no call to fear me. Please ... speak."

His heart yanked his breath short. A sense of stampeding injustices. How? How could events conspire *against*?

"Th-the Meat. It ran out just as you feared ... S-so I c-commanded what you ... What you said I *must*."

The blue-eyed gaze did not so much pierce as plummet through him.

"What did you command?"

Proyas glanced at the encircling carnival of expressions, some of them wilfully blank, others already rehearsing passions to come.

"That ... that we-we ..." His bottom lip twitched, refused to relent. He swallowed. "That we march upon those sickened by Daglias—"

"*March* upon them?" the Holy Aspect-Emperor snapped. It was peculiar, even nightmarish, for Proyas to find himself *inside* the crushing circuit of his scrutiny and interrogation. How many? How many proud Men had he watched Kellhus reduce to stammering impotence with this very look, this very tone?

"You told-told me ..."

He stood utterly alone, blinking the overlong blinks of a cornered child.

Immaculate from several paces back, the Holy Aspect-Emperor's appearance now betrayed the toll of whatever it was he had suffered during his absence. Broken filaments jutting from the plaits of his beard. Bruised crescents beneath his eyes. Scorching about his sleeves.

"Told you *what*?"

"You told me to ... to ... *feed* them."

Incredulity, dawning betrayal ... so meticulous, so exact, that fractions within Proyas roiled and recoiled, all but convinced that *he himself* was the deceiver here!

"Feed them? Proyas ... What *else* would you do?"

"N-n-no. Feed them ... to ... to *themselves*."

Until this point, Kellhus had assumed the attitude and manner of a father reaching out to his youngest son, the one most bullied, and so most beloved. But the forgiving air of entreaty vanished, first in scowling confusion, then in outraged comprehension—and lastly, *resolution* ... Judgment.

Futility crashed through Proyas then, crown to root. A farce. A mummer's travesty ... all of it. He could almost cackle, let his eyes roll after floating hands ...

Madness ... All of it ... From the very beginning.

"I fed them! I did what you charged!"

He could traipse and cartwheel ...

"You think this"—an inhuman glint in his gaze—"*amusing*, Proyas?"

The Lords of the Ordeal crowed in outrage. A place had been prepared, and they fairly fell over themselves in their rush to occupy it. Proyas would have wept had not the capacity been scraped from him. So he smiled a false monkey smile instead, the one persecuted children use to incite yet more persecution, and consigned his grimace to the organs about his heart. Thus he gazed at them, his brothers, the illustrious Believer-Kings of the Middle-North and the Three Seas.

One need only ponder cowardice to unravel the complexities of Men—the reflex, like gagging, to forever be the one aggrieved. Who had suffered more than them (save the Scalded)? Who had endured more (save the murdered, the raped, the eaten)? In the absence of their beacon, they had wandered and then they had *erred*. They had turned to the one who dared claim the light of their Holy Prophet as his own ...

They had trusted.

So it was their Exalt-General had *led* them into depravity, *commanded* the commission of acts so foul, so wicked, they could scarce be imagined. He had *exploited* their confusion, *preyed* upon their hunger, anguish and disarray. He had *made* a feast of their honest and open hearts ...

And betrayed all that was sacred and holy.

"How long?" the Holy Aspect-Emperor cried in tones of heart-cracking defeat. Twin rivulets, silver for the shining blank of the sky, slipped across his cheeks, so profound was his staged grief.

Proyas could summon no more than a wild look in reply.

"Tell me!" the face that had been his temple cried. "Traitor! Miscreant! False"—a breath breaking about convulsive passion—"*friend!*" Anasûrimbor Kellhus raised the blade of a gold-rimmed hand, held it shaking in the simulacrum of scarce-restrained violence. "Tell me, Nersei Proyas! *How long have you served Golgotterath?*"

And there it was in his periphery, dominating the barren tracts of Shigogli—gold knifing skyward from leprous foundations—the threat that was to redeem all evil.

"*When did you first cast your number-sticks with the Unholy Consult?*"

And Proyas understood then, the truth of the altar that had owned his every aspiration, so greedily consumed his every sacrifice. He saw what it was Achamian had seen, so very many years ago ...

The False Prophet.

It was, a fraction of him realized, his first *true* revelation, the way light piled upon light, begetting ever more profound understandings. He saw that Kayûtus had known and that Serwa had not. He saw that all the World was oblivious otherwise—though oh-so many suspected. He realized, even though he lacked the words to voice it, that he stood upon *Conditioned Ground*.

That a place had been prepared.

All was riot and confusion, the queer, celebratory outrage that accompanies the undoing of truly catastrophic crimes. Hands struck him, seized him. He was borne off his feet, a doll rendered in human skin and human hair. The faces of his beloved brothers, his fellow Zaudunyani, floated about him, bobbed like inflated bladders jamming the surface of white rushing waters—some, like that of King Narnol, pale for pity and confusion, others, like Lord Soter, demented for outrage. He need not see his Lord-and-Prophet to know he waded through the commotion immediately behind, for it was the rare Lord of the Ordeal who did not continually, and quite unwittingly, glance at Him, so intent were they to express his will as their own. Proyas kicked back savagely, surprising the hands clamped about him, and he glimpsed the man, Anasûrimbor Kellhus standing upon an upside-down ground, in the thick of his Believer-Kings, yet somehow remote, untouchable. Their gazes locked for the merest of moments, Prophet and Disciple ...

You planned this.

The blue eyes saw as they always saw, a glance that was at once a peering, a terrifying scrutiny.

Then he was raised up. Golgotterath surged and a subsided. Gold sheered against white across wailing skies. And beneath the thundering invective of the Holy Aspect-Emperor, King Nersei Proyas was carried forth to the multitudes ...

So they might rejoice in his suffering.

———— ◈◈◈ ————

King Sorweel, heir to the Horn-and-Amber Seat, sat unmoved through all
of it, tingling for how *near* the Most Holy Aspect-Emperor had passed. He
looked down, saw the Triple-Crescent Pouch laying in his left palm, though
he had no memory of pulling the thing from his belt. Three Sickles. Some
time passed before he realized what was happening, how his father's murderer had scaped King Proyas for the Field Appalling. He could only wonder
at the spectacle of the man protesting his innocence with dwindling conviction, not in his claim, but in the truth. He could only marvel at the Lords
of the Three Seas, their canine eagerness to be cleansed in accusation, to
find reprieve in threats and jabbing fingers. Even Zsoronga dissolved into
the general uproar heaving across the Umbilicus floor, leaping with pious
demands for retribution, shouting to the rhythm of brandished fists, no
different than any Three Seas Believer-King.

On it went.

Sorweel looked to the gaping hole in the eastern wall, almost gasped for
the premonition of looking *down* the miles to Min-Uroikas. He clutched
the skin-polished wood. Absent direct sunlight, the hairline etching along the
waist and length of the vast cylinders seemed clearer, promising symbols to
the peering eye, but collapsing into scribbles rather than resolve. The World-
Curse, his Siolan brothers had called it, a prayer for our destruction
dropped from the stars ...

Immiriccas lowered his face, convulsed for disgust ... rallied for hatred.

When the youth finally looked up, the last of the backs were vanishing from
the Umbilicus—a few so bold as to leap through the hole, loping like boys about
the tumult's eager edge. Then the grand pavilion was empty, save for Anasûrimbor Serwa standing in the middle of the floor with her back toward him.

"Has it winded you at last?" Sorweel asked.

"No," she replied, turning to face him. Her cheeks shone white for tears.
"I merely mourn another sacrifice ... A deep one."

"And when He comes to you," Sorweel said, standing and stepping down
the tiers much as her father had several mad moments before. "When the
Holy Aspect-Emperor places *you* on the altar of the Thousandfold Thought
... What then?"

She closed her eyes, lowered her face.

"You know we cannot be together ..." she said, "that what happened on
the mountain, on the plain—"

"I know that it was *beautiful* ..." Sorweel interrupted, advancing nearer, "that it made me feel, not as a man, but as a *boy*, something tender, easily broken, something that could *leap*. I know that our fire burned within a single pit, that we could not be told apart, you and I ..."

She gazed stupefied, retreated from him one step.

He followed. "I know that *you*, an Anasûrimbor, *love me*."

The Triple-Crescent Pouch puzzled his left palm.

When?

"That look upon your face!" she suddenly cried. "Sorweel, you must make it go away! If Father sees it—if he sees *me* like this! I am too important to him. He *will end you*, Sorweel, the way he will end any and all liabilities before assaulting Golgotterath! Do you und—"

Thudding feet yanked their gazes to the entrance. Suddenly *Zsoronga* was seizing his shoulders, huffing for breath, his eyes wild with panic. "Sorweel! Sorweel! Something *has gone wrong*!" The Successor-Prince glanced wildly at Serwa, pulled his friend toward the great rent in the eastern wall.

Sorweel fought to disengage himself. "What is it?"

Zsoronga stood rapt before the image of Golgotterath, his great chest heaving, his eyes clicking between him and the Swayali Grandmistress. He licked his lips.

"Her-her father ..." he said, swallowing for want of wind. "Her father *claims*"—a grimace of incredulity—"claims that my-my *father* has violated the-the terms of their treaty ..." He closed his eyes as if waiting out some pain. "That-that he sent an emissary to help the Fanim attack Momemn!"

"So what does this mean?" Sorweel asked.

Zsoronga stared only at Serwa now, his expression crumpling for the remorselessness he found there.

"It means," the Princess-Imperial said without inflection, "that we all make sacrifices this day."

Zsoronga leapt for the image of Min-Uroikas, only to be caught on a gaseous shout, pulled spread-eagled by interlocking circlets of light about his wrists and ankles. Sorweel found himself rushing the girl, not to assail but to importune. The white eyes and sun-brilliant mouth turned to him, and something shattered across the length of his body, sent him whumping backward. He fell as a thing connected to limbs merely.

He did not so much kneel before the blackness as trip into it.

———— ⚬∞⚬ ————

Scripture, the Great Kyranean once observed, is history inked in madness.

The Lament had not been confined to the Lords of the Ordeal. Far from it. Not a soul among the Host of Hosts had escaped unscathed, for fairly all had consumed the Meat of necessity. Nevertheless, not all had joined in the obscenities visited upon the Scalded. Those righteous few who had somehow held fast crossing the wastes of Agongorea now found themselves perplexed by the shame of their fellows.

A Host uncannily divided received word of the Holy Aspect-Emperor's return. Those in the clutches of the Lament became wary, and many skulked aimlessly rather than make display, fearing the judgment of their Lord-and-Prophet. Those few still in the thrall of the Meat, however, made loutish demonstration, howling in exaltation, proclaiming a joy that was more mercenary than pious, for Golgotterath had become a granary in their eyes, and their Lord-and-Prophet's return an occasion to finally seize the Meat sheltering within. They formed wild, unruly mobs, made lewd celebratory displays. They scoffed at those in the throes of the Lament, took umbrage at their condemning gazes. More than sixty souls would perish in brawls.

A crazed night followed. Throughout the encampment, innumerable thousands huddled in vertiginous remorse, unable to sleep for horror and the sound of intemperate revels on the air.

The Interval sounded upon the desolate dawn. The Men of the Ordeal crawled from their blankets and tents, milled about the messes and latrines, wondering. Then, for the first time in weeks, the prayer-horns blared deep and elephantine, calling all souls to Temple. Men gazed about, wondering. On the southern outskirts of the encampment, a band of Nangaels spied the Holy Aspect-Emperor walking alone in the shadow of Occlusion. They turned to one another in astonishment, realizing their Lord-and-Prophet had *beckoned them* with a waving arm. Helical lights consumed the mirage utterly, and deposited the holy figure more than a mile to the south. "He bids us!" the longbeard warriors began bawling. "Our Lord-and-Prophet bids us follow Him!" The cry reproduced like mosquitos, leaping from throat to throat, and soon, clouds of Ordealmen were trekking southward.

Hours passed before they had fully assembled. The skies were woolen, the sun obscure. Golgotterath lay sullen in the distance, the golden Horns thrust into what seemed a high-hanging fog. The Holy Aspect-Emperor stood immobile upon a promontory jutting from the foundations of the Occlusion, a ramp of stone like a thumb, famed in legend. *Himonirsil*, the Nonmen had called it, the Accusatory, and evidence of their ancient works encrusted the terrain above and about its root, basalt wrack marbling the slopes, streaking and staining the whole formation from a distance. The Accusatory had once graced the Arobindant, the legendary Siolan fortress that had anchored (albeit in different incarnations) both the First and the Second Watch, in days older than old, when the exhausted Nonmen had whiled away centuries guarding the Ark. The ramparts had long been razed, and the Accusatory, which had once pointed from the fortress's heart, now jabbed out of its grave.

So did Anasûrimbor Kellhus, Aspect-Emperor of the Three Seas, stand upon the self-same precipice as Cû-jara Cinmoi, King of the House Primordial, only now, the *Sons of Men* packed the broken slopes below. They choked the ravines, then spread and spread, a vast and soiled blanket, across the dead plain. To a man they looked to their Holy Aspect-Emperor on the Accusatory, thronged with their backs to the dread spectacle behind them, knowing it was enough that He could see.

Though only those on the pitch of the Occlusion could see the number of those still trekking from the camp taper, the entire host fell silent of its own accord, somehow knowing the assembly was complete. Their Lord and Prophet was little more than a speck against the heaped wreckage of the Occlusion, yet even the farthest afield understood He was about to speak.

The Holy Aspect-Emperor stood monumental before them, garbed in robes of voluminous white, his flaxen hair drawn back into an antique war-braid, his beard squared and woven. Intermittent flashes revealed the halo crowning his head, as if an otherwise invisible plate of gold wobbled beneath some otherworldly sun. A retinue milled behind him, largely obscured by the Accusatory's rising bulk.

"*Who?*" his voice cracked across the barren scarps and plains. "Who among you has not returned to find your hearth *untended*, your home *disordered?*"

Nearly every soul drew breath.

"And who has not been wroth?" he boomed. "Who has not reached for the *rod?* Who among you has not *laid hands* upon those most beloved?"

Individual cries dissolved into a gaseous roar.

"So I have found *my hearth*! My *home*!"

Palms waved. Voices wailed in involuntary expostulations of sorrow and shame. What was cacophonous swelled into a singular, thunderous howl ...

The Holy Aspect-Emperor's words dropped through it like iron through sodden tissue.

"I took my leave following the Scald ... And I returned *home* ... to the *Three Seas* ..."

The Great Ordeal crashed into miraculous silence. It seized their hearts, that word, *home*.

"I returned to Momemn and the glory of the Andiamine Heights. I returned to what we would save, and I *found that turmoil had claimed my house*!"

It clutched their throats, gouged their bellies. How long? How long since they had squeezed their children? How long since their wives had last seen them weep?

"So I took up the rod ... I set *right* what had been overthrown!"

Cheers rose in tepid squalls from various quarters, only to collapse into anxious silence ... The night had been fat with rumour.

"And now I have returned to the Host of Hosts to find the same!"

A party of four stone-faced Pillarians resolved from the small crowd behind Him, dragging forward a powerful Zeumi youth, naked with his elbows bound behind his back: Zsoronga ut Nganka'kull, the Successor-Prince of High Holy Zeum, and hostage of the New Empire.

"*To do the same!*"

The Pillarians brought the Satakhan's eldest son forth to their Holy Aspect-Emperor, beat him to his knees.

"Accursed be Zeum!" the holy figure thundered above the lacerated boy. "Accursed be Nganka'kull, Great Satakhan of Zeum, for he has cast his sticks with Fanayal and his heretical marauders—and so cast his honour and our treaty into the flames!"

The far-flung assembly roared in outrage, and exultation, a veritable sea of howling mouths and wild gesticulations. Pillarians had been toiling behind the back of the Zeumi youth even as Kellhus spoke. Now the Holy Aspect-Emperor raised a sandalled foot to Zsoronga's forehead, and the booming trilled with illicit anticipation, as much for those in the throes of the Lament as for those yet in the thrall of the Meat. Men caught their breath for the suddenness of the fall. The Successor-Prince bounced from the limit of the rope, dangled insensate from his elbows, his head down, turning on a slow rotation, first one way, then the other. A stone struck his thigh, and he kicked as if from a dream. Almost immediately a shower of missiles rose from the crowds roiling below. A moment of confusion and consternation followed, as the Pillarians struggled to raise and tie him off higher.

But the Holy Aspect-Emperor gestured, and another nude figure—this one pale and olive—was brought forward. He was carried then violently thrust upon the gravel and stone where the Zeumi prince had grovelled but moments before. The hail of stones trailed, and a hush clipped the Great Ordeal's indignant roar. Men bid one another to be silent, to the point of cuffing fools if need be, and they gazed in wonder at their Lord and Prophet, who stood erect and glorious before the cringing figure.

"Accursed—!" he began only to stumble upon the crack in his sacred voice ...

"*Accursed be Nersei Proyas!*" he boomed with a savagery none had ever heard, a bark that seemed to pluck hairs from arms, the injury and incredulity belonging to fathers betrayed by beloved sons. An avalanche of cries rose from the Great Ordeal, roars that were at once snarls, building into a crescendo that nearly matched the hellish clamour of the Horde. But the din in no way diminished or hindered the Aspect-Emperor's thunderous voice.

"Accursed be my *brother*! My *companion* in faith and arms! For his treachery has thrown the *pall of damnation upon you all!*"

The countless thousands seethed, stamped feet and brandished fists, scratched at skin, scalp, and beards.

"Accursed be he ..." the Holy Aspect-Emperor cried upon a failing breath, "who has *broken my heart!*"

And what had been tumult and uproar surged into riot, the violence of Men so maddened they must punish what was near to exact vengeance upon what lay far.

The Pillarians once again laid hands upon the disgraced Exalt-General. He slumped against their brutal ministrations, his head lolling like a murdered maiden's. They trussed him the way they had Zsoronga, then cast him from the Accusatory ledge. The hemp jerked him short, swung him hard into the chapped stone faces. He hung swaying by his elbows above the howling masses.

Occupying the point between the two criminals, the Holy Aspect-Emperor stood upon the thumbnail precipice, his gold-shining hands outstretched. The Great Ordeal answered in what seemed a vast, collective paroxysm, the rabid fury of those who had fallen upon the Scalded, and the wild lust of those who yet starved in the clutches of the Meat. Men wept and raged, screamed flecks of spittle at either of the two hanging figures, or howled adoration at the God who had condemned them.

The very World screamed, a sound so loud that the sky itself smelled of teeth. And the miraculous voice—*His voice*—somehow passed through all clamour and struck their ears to the quick ...

"Accursed be the Great Ordeal!"

A voice so mighty as to transcend sound, to make a cavern ceiling of void, a *croak* that made a throat of Creation, and a tongue of each and every listener. The Host's roar faltered, trailed into the whisk of dust-devils. The Men of the Ordeal stood dumbstruck, stupefied, as if the sheer loudness of their Lord and Prophet's declaration had cracked the words and made mud of their meaning.

"For the commission of acts obscene and unspeakable—transgressions that beggar the heart, the intellect!"

And in their tens of thousands, they stood naked and hanging. Wails began poking the astonished silence ...

Not a soul spared any thought of Golgotterath behind them.

"For the iniquity of brother raping brother! Of kin slaying kin!"

Others cried out in shame and grief, rocking, tearing hair and scratching skin, gnashing teeth.

"Aye, *accursed*! **Damned**! *Damned to the eternal furnaces of Hell!*"

And what was a broken chorus of lamentation swelled into a thunderous furor, whole nations, peoples, races, *beseeching* ...

"*Cannibal treachery! Unholy congress!*"

"What *outrage!*"

"What **abomination**!"

To a man they convulsed or wept or shrieked or cast out warding hands. Admission, denial, it did not matter. Like inconsolable children they threw themselves against their neighbours, thrashed as if against the grip of the very World.

How? How had such a thing happened? How had *these* hands ...

How *could* ...

High upon the rock, the Holy Aspect-Emperor gazed down upon them, white and golden, a shining aperture. The chalk scarps of the Occlusion soared about him, flecked with black. And though he was little more than a mote to endless outer thousands, it seemed they could see the scowl of incredulity and indignation, feel the cudgel of divine judgment, the knife of fraternal disappointment ...

How? How had his children wandered so far?

High upon the Rock of Accusation, their Lord-and-Prophet watched, waited, becoming as inscrutable as the overcast heavens. And one by one the Men of the Ordeal exhausted not so much their grief or loathing as the absolute license they had yielded to it. Soon they stood silent save for the mewling of those too far broken to be retrieved. They stood dead of heart, thought and limb, begrudging even the bare need to breathe. They stood awaiting the judgment of the beacon shining before them.

Yes. Let it end.

Even damnation, it seemed, could be blessed, if the past were blotted.

Though none could say from whence they came, cups appeared among them, small cones cut from papyrus and vellum sheets of scripture. And with the mass compliance peculiar to crowds, each repeated the actions of their fellows, taking one cup and passing the stack along. And it calmed them, this simple, communal act, as much as expectation made them wonder. Many craned their heads to peer across the masses, while others peered at the fragments of text scrawled upon their ad hoc cups. Still others gazed to the promontory, awaiting some sign from their Holy Aspect-Emperor ...

Not a soul looked to Golgotterath rising in malignant glory behind them.

Thousands continued to weep, inconsolable. A few called out, while others simply wondered aloud. A conversational rumble swelled across the near tracts. Those who had been injured in the heaving madness were raised up and passed outward upon thickets of upraised hands.

"Many still weep among you ..."

His voice fell upon them as rain, windless and warm.

"The souls most *guilty*."

And something in his voice—a resonance or an inflection—pricked the ears of each and every one of them. Many of the weepers caught their hitching sobs, arranged their shoulders and stood erect, squeezed away tears with the balls of their thumbs, peered blinking in feigned weariness. But the vigilance of their neighbours was such that it did not matter. They had been branded by their lamentation.

"They lay as shadows across failing light ..."

Screeching was rekindled within the rumble. Many of those marked by their wanton displays cast about, either bewildered or seeking lines of flight.

"They pollute ... They *foul* ..."

But some even *welcomed* their degradation, called out sobbing and smiling, *beckoned* the mortal judgment about to crash upon them.

"Seize them!"

The masses, which were too raucous with detail to be anything other than homogeneous, instantly bloomed into thousands of flowers large and small as myriad regions set upon the weepers in their midst.

"*Seize them!* Raise them so that *I might see!*"

Flowers of concentrated violence, bending ingrown, then leaning out and back, offering countless figures to the scrutiny of the sky, some writhing, some battling, some limp ...

"*Make a spigot of their throats!*"

And the flowers contracted, shrank from whitening extremities, scored by the radial striations of thousands reaching ...

"*Drink!* Drink deep their iniquity! Bathe your heart in the heat of their damnation!"

Men battling forward, holding forth cups cut from scripture. Men shrinking away, hunched over their crimson wages. Men throwing their heads back ...

"And prepare! Set aside all that is weak!"

And he flared radiant from the very point of the Accusatory, pure before the noxious gold immensity of the Unholy Ark.

"For behind you lies your only hope of redemption! The Holy Task that the God of Gods has set before you! And you! Shall! Spend! *All!* Every pain! Every fury! Maimed you shall crawl, stab the stomping maul, gore the groin, pierce the thigh! Blind you shall grope and grapple, knife the squealing black! Dying you shall spit, bellow curses!"

The bodies of the weepers were tossed as rags upon them, grisly flotsam in the tempest.

"You have battled across the World! Witnessed what no Man has seen in an age!"

The flowers dissolved like figures of sand beneath waves.

"And now you stand upon the very cusp of Redemption! Glory everlasting!"

The Host of Hosts clenched and surged in all its miles, for at last it had turned, away from the tossed ramps and precipices of the Occlusion—away from the cruel judgment of its Holy Aspect-Emperor.

"*Golgotterath!*"

Away from itself.

"**Golgotterath**!"

And toward.

"All fathers beat their sons!" the Holy Aspect-Emperor cried, his voice scoring the vault of creation.

"**All fathers beat their sons!**"

CHAPTER TEN

The Great Letting

To be false is sane when the truth will get you killed. To be false is insane when only the truth can save you. Thus is Reason is the father of Glory, and Truth little more than a pompous sibling.

—*Antitheses*, PORSA OF TRYSË

Early Autumn, 20 New Imperial Year (4132, Year-of-the-Tusk), Golgotterath.

Days of bodiless terror, fury, and lamentation. Days of moaning without voice, shrieking without breath, gnashing without teeth.

Days of *floating* ... drifting as smoke in the black.

The great and terrible Anasûrimbor Kellhus had pursed Malowebi's soul. Nothing was left for him save to watch the pageant of dangling glimpses. The wastes crossed. The wrecked Empress, her gaze forever chasing the outlines of things. The son always skulking the camp's margins. And now the commotion and fury of returning to the Ordeal ... All glanced rolling from the thigh of the Aspect-Emperor.

The Thought-dancer ...

He could scarce contemplate it: though bodiless, the passionate tumult poets so often blamed on the flesh remained, burned as fierce as he could remember, the terror, the fury, remorse lashed to the eye-gouging limit.

Likaro, wherever he cringed, should have been reduced to cinders for the curses heaped upon him!

Like all wreck survivors, Malowebi had taken account of his supplies, what might sustain him. He could feel. He could see. He could think and reason. And he could remember what *he had once been* ... before ... before ...

He could still curse Likaro.

He still possessed all his faculties—he *remained* Malowebi, only shorn of his every physical connection, and locked into one of the Decapitants bound to the Aspect-Emperor's waist—or so he told himself in the beginning. The more he rehearsed the cataclysmic occasion of his imprisonment the more he realized *no such transfer had taken place.* He clearly remembered the Aspect-Emperor affixing one of the Decapitants to the spouting stump of his neck. If the man had imprisoned his soul in the remaining demon, *then he should be bouncing alone across his thigh*—he should be *in the thing*, not staring at its blasted mien.

Which meant the Anasûrimbor hadn't so much stolen his soul *as his head.*

The greater horror of this lay in the finality it betokened. If a demon possessed his body, then *repossession* remained a possibility ... He had been stolen, yes, but he had not been destroyed. No matter how pathetic, he could still plot escape, he could still take aim. But realizing his *very own head* swung from the Anasûrimbor's hip transformed what had been a prison into a trophy, a probing soul into a mummified gaze.

What was he going to do? He couldn't entertain this question without lapsing into tirades of disembodied fury, cursing Fanayal for his crazed conceit, Meppa for his heresy, and Likaro for his pulse, his criminal ability to breathe.

The prophetic irony wasn't lost on him. It seemed he could see the Yatwerian witch as clear as sunlight in his soul's eye, Psatma Nannaferi, watching him from her mirror, daubing lamp-black across almost closed eyes, young lips communicating an old and wicked grin.

"And now you wish to know your part in this?"

If anything, he had obsessed over this encounter even more than the one with the Anasûrimbor, realizing—with greater assurance as the days passed— that he suffered the very doom the accursed witch had prophesied: to *watch*, to witness as a reader might, unable to touch, unable to save.

And only now, swinging from the Aspect-Emperor's hip as he exhorted the debased multitudes from the pulpit heights, did Malowebi fathom the mad *object* of his curse.

Only now ... gazing upon Golgotterath.

He had no heart but the heart he *felt* was cinder and ash.

Not even the sudden appearance of *Zsoronga* upon the Accusatory could knock him from his horror. Of course the boy had survived this far. Of course his life was forfeit, given that his father had commanded Malowebi to conspire with his captor's enemies. Whatever he might have felt for the Successor-Prince was blotted, suffocated by the golden abominations rearing lucent into the clouds beyond his ailing form ...

Golgotterath! *Golgotterath was real.* Woe to those who are fool enough to deny it! And woe to those who throw their sons as number-sticks against it.

"All things abhor you!" the battered youth cried, cringing for the hovering menace of the Pillarians, all but blind to the violations goring the shroud of Heaven beyond. The insult to dimension, artifice become blasphemy for unthinkable scale. The sense of cataclysm hanging in perpetual arrest, like golden knives endlessly falling into the breast of the World.

And Men sheeted the earth before it—Men!—stamped and shouted from across Shigogli.

Zsoronga was bound into a ceremonial posture of submission then summarily kicked from the side of the Accusatory. Malowebi saw it all quite clearly, given the angle the Whore afforded him, every wince and grimace, all the folds and creases that token anguish and outrage. But the Horns pillared the very Heavens behind the sobbing boy, the Incû-Holoinas ...

And Malowebi could only think, *All along ... He spoke true.*

Implication blew as void through him, opened cavities once shut by ignorance, hollows once choked with hope and conceit and ancient fancy.

Anasûrimbor Kellhus had spoken true.

Now the whole World had be rewritten—beginning with the Satakhan's eldest son.

How long had it been since Achamian had last seen them? How many *centuries* past?

Crossing the Leash had been more a matter of poling than paddling, forcing the crude raft he had wrought through the soaked dead. They had turned away from what was deep ... what was *beneath*. It was enough to feel the sponge-sodden carcasses roll like apples beneath their strokes, break like bread. So they had studied different points on the opposite shore as they continued toiling, their gazes fixed, lustreless, the look of souls wandering outside resignation.

Upon reaching the far shore, they had done much the same, cleaving directly north into the lap of the Yimaleti, rather than northeast to the wasted abdomen of Agongorea. At every juncture they encountered, Achamian elected what he deemed the most *secretive* route, the path that revealed them to no horizons, and so revealed no horizons to them. They had turned away from what was *far*, what lay in the *future*, and had looked to their feet, following ravine after ravine, never climbing, never daring any height that might lay their wicked destination plain on the horizon, the dread golden vision ... Anochirwa. The Horns of Golgotterath.

And now, at long last, he, Drusas Achamian, stood upon the foot of the Ring Mountains, the Occlusion. Climbing was all that remained, all that lay between him and the dreaded sight.

"Come, Akka," Mimara said, her gaze worried, searching.

"Yes—yes," he said, not moving from where he stood.

For all the torment Mandate Schoolmen inherited for reliving Seswatha's tumultuous and tragic life, there was respite to be found in reliving his frailties and failures. Men are ever stranded with their own cowardice, the implacable facts of their petty schemes and deceptions. They were quick to play the game of silent accusation, of course, to charge others for crimes wholly their own. But for every sentence meted, the implicit measure of their own guilt grew—and with it the terror that *only* they were so weak. Mandate Schoolmen knew otherwise, thanks to their Dreams, knew that even the greatest heroes among Men harboured terrors all their own ...

That courage was the work of flawed tools.

"More rest, little ones," Mimara murmured to her gold-scaled belly. "Your father's heart is winded ..."

The old Wizard fumed, but remained just as rooted.

"He hauls too much history to climb ways so steep."

Rather than find passage between the Occlusion's shattered teeth,

Achamian insisted they climb an ancient switchback stair leading to one of the ruined Akeokinoi. Mimara asked for no explanations, even though the climb was far more onerous for her given her condition than for him. Had she asked, he would have muttered something about prudence, of needing to *observe* the Great Ordeal before daring it, all the while knowing she wouldn't believe a single mumbled word.

The wind harboured the promise of wider and wilder spaces as they gained the heights. The sky extended its vacant span. The Nonman watch-tower was little more than a wrack-strewn podium. The ancient craftsmen had used basalt quarried from elsewhere, a dense black stone that still, after thousands of years, stood in stark contrast to the high-heaped sandstone and granite comprising the Ring Mountains. Evidence of its destruction lay scattered about a shallow peak, as dark as coal in dirty snow.

Pressing hands against knees, Achamian surmounted the final steps, strode gasping into the ancient shell. He saw the Horns immediately, though his soul pretended otherwise for several heartbeats. He stood sway-ing, blinking away what seemed an immovable stupor.

He could hear Mimara at his side, sobbing, and aye ... *laughing.*

For *there they were* ...

Canted and golden. Opposing swan necks, heads thrust high into the blank.

The old Wizard slumped to the cracked floor. And she was there, Mi-mara, the image of Esmenet, the Judging Eye of the God, kneeling at his side, clasping him, weeping, laughing ...

Gazing at her, he could feel them give way, all the small terrors, and he coughed for violence of passion, blinked hot tears. He could swear he bled, so violent was his smile. He croaked in laughter, a crooning cough that be-came a lunatic cackle ...

For *there it was* ... The dread image. The wicked emblem that had summed Evil for what seemed the entirety of his life. The horror that had supped upon his tender heart, feasted upon his compassion. The malig-nancy that had corrupted every breath he had ever drawn.

Incû-Holoinas, the Ark-of-the-Skies ...

Min-Uroikas, the Pit of Obscenities ...

Golgotterath.

Golgotterath! The Fell Stronghold of the Unholy Consult ...

Cradle of the No-God.

TELL ME ...

Breathlessness seized his heart, tore it from his laughter.

WHAT DO YOU SEE?

Mimara slipped his grasp, her look anguished and alarmed. He could see her murmur, *Akka?*

WHAT AM I?

He had clutched his temples. He had never laughed, it seemed. Only shrieked ...

Tsurumah! Mog-Pharau!

But she was clinging to him, shushing, and smoothing, *weeping* new tears, *his tears*, knowing, *believing*, with and for ...

Understanding.

And it stilled him like nothing he had ever known, understanding that she *understood*—and with a profundity that eclipsed his own, for what he had lived as Seswatha, *she had apprehended through the Eye.* A slackness breathed through him, uncoupling every ligament, every organ, and he slipped into what seemed her cradling even though she huddled within his arms. She drew his right hand to her gold-armoured belly ... said nothing.

Hearts beating.

They lay like this among the rounded blocks, he upon his rump, she on her knees, curled into him, like a child's hand cupped within a father's callused palm. Breathing. Their unborn gestating between them, their world spinning off into desolate irrelevance far about ... and their beauty *something essential*, another ore.

What was it, this union they had been unearthed between them? Too desperate to be love ...

Too near ... too *profound.*

They swooned for a time, dozed beneath the rising spectre of Anochirwa.

Hearts beating.

She was the first to hear it, the faraway voice. He heard it the instant her alarm cracked the bliss between them. The warble of a human crying out, baffled by stone scarps and disembowelled by breezy distance. Leaning each against the other, they stood, gazed once again at Golgotterath. Never had Achamian felt so ancient and so young. Together they hobbled the remaining paces to the lip of the black-stone ruin.

The volume of the voice bloated out of disproportion to their advance. It had resounded all along, the old Wizard realized, ringing through the empty air above them. The bruise of sorcery was plain.

"A glamour of some kind," Achamian muttered, replying to her questioning look.

They crested the heights, stood numb and dizzy, gawking out over the grim reaches. It seemed impossible (as much for the Dreams as in spite of them), the way the mountainous curve of the Occlusion followed a perfect compass line, extending out below brumous skies, the rim of a concavity so vast as to defeat vision. Rising from ulcerated foundations, the Ark lay at its centre, dull-gleaming, miraculously intact given its cataclysmic arrival. The fortifications about its base, even the hulking towers of Domathuz and Corrunc, seemed burnt pastry in comparison, wicked only for the ten thousand little teeth of gold fanging the ten thousand battlements. The plain of Shigogli radiated out from the Horns' bower, as flat as marble floors, and betraying the meaning of its ancient name, "Inniür," for it was now more the colour of bone than the charcoal it had been in previous ages ...

High to their left, they saw the greater mountains of the Yimaleti pile into cerulean obscurity to the northwest.

And to their right, in the east, they saw the *Great Ordeal* strewn along the Occlusion, steaming with dust, sizzling with indistinct activity, its southern flank so near that even Achamian could discern individual figures. The thunder of it lay viscous on the autumn air. The voice they heard somehow floated upon the rumble, a harangue that suffered no deaf ears. They stood numb ... gazing more to accustom their souls to the spectacle than to scrutinize or see. And as they watched, pockets of turmoil erupted within the undifferentiated mass, crude rings, as if it were a pool beneath a hail of gravel.

Screams complicated the striate roar.

"What happens?" Mimara asked.

Achamian fought for wind. He spared her a passing squint, nothing more.

"Your stepfather," he said upon a shuddering exhalation.

To come so close.

Proyas thought of girls with stooped shoulders and bold eyes, peppercorns crushed upon honeyed quail, the dust hanging about the blue-dancing feet of the priests of Jukan. He thought of children discoursing with grand authority in another room, unaware of any parent listening. He thought of clouds bloating above him, crisp white upon hazy blue, soundless and soundless and soundless ...

He thought of love.

The pain did not so much subside as swell into something too great to be apprehended. Even the stings had been blunted into spheres.

Only the flies truly plagued him.

The ground below rotated first to the left, then to the right, but for no reason he could fathom, for the air had been gutted of all motion. Some torsion in the rope maybe? Some imperfection ...

He could feel the slack weight of it, hanging from his bones ... the meat. So cold to *be* ...

And so hot to touch.

The more he pondered the broken ground below, the more it became a conclusion.

At one point he thought he saw Achamian—or some ancient, crazed version of him, shoulders heaped in rancid furs—standing upon the arc of his rotation, squinting up. Proyas even smiled at the image, croaked ...

"*Akka.*"

Though it knifed his chest doing so.

Then the apparition was gone, and only his conclusion remained.

He found bliss in dozing.

Then he was being hauled upward. He had no awareness of it until he saw his companion *below*, the Zeumi youth, the friend of Harweel's son. Remorse skewered him to the pommel. Then he was spinning in the orange glare of evening, drawn relentlessly upward, grip by grip. It dawned on him as he was heaved across the promontory's lip that the man's *strength* had shouted his treachery all along ...

The fact that he was inhuman.

The white clad image spiralled about him, luminous for the haloes about his head and hands, stained for the cadaverous contradiction of the Decapitants. Then serrated ground ... warm water rinsing his face with cool, slaking his thirst.

"Gaze ..." the beloved voice said—for even after everything, it was still beloved.

"Gaze upon Golgotterath."

And Proyas saw them out across the Shigogli, the Horns rising colossal on a tangent to the furnace orb of the sun, black burnished in smoldering gold.

"Why?" he croaked. "Why do you show me this?"

He did not need to turn to see the Aspect-Emperor hesitate. Golgotterath had become his face.

"I'm not sure ... The closer I come, the greater the darkness grows."

Swallowing had become laceration, but Proyas grimaced more for confusion. His entire life, it seemed, had been apportioned equally between this very day, and all that had gone before.

"You bid me ... bid me commit those abominations."

"Yes. To accomplish the impossible you had to commit the unthinkable.

To bring such a host this far through lands so perilous ... You have wrought a *miracle*, Proyas."

The Exalt-General wept for a time.

"I needed you *weak* ..." his Master explained. "If you had been strong, you would have sought alternatives, you would have gambled on some way, *any* way, to avoid taking the monstrous actions you took."

"No! No! If I-I were strong ... you need only *command* me! I would have committed any atrocity in your name!"

A rueful breath. "That is the universal vanity of Men, is it not? To presume they can know *all their decisions*, past and future ...

"No, old friend. I see more of you than you can fathom. You would have balked, assumed that I had to be testing you somehow. If you did not question me, if you *assumed me good*, then you would have questioned my command. This is why I tore down your conviction. To be uncertain is to embrace the expedient. By trammelling your faith I assured you always reached for the nearer club, that you always found for *hunger* when you cast your sticks."

Golgotterath ... Even so distant, it nevertheless managed to *loom*, to stir some kernel of primeval alarm.

"Then ... *why denounce me?*"

The beloved face did not flinch. "Because your life is worth the lives of millions ... the lives of Miramis, Thaila, and Xinemus."

Proyas closed his eyes about hot tears, sputtered for relief and outrage both.

"How then? How does ... denouncing me ... change ... anything?"

"By healing the hearts of those who continue the battle. By giving me Men who fight as Men *reborn*."

A line of southward-bound geese crossed the intervening sky, drawn into a cryptic rune.

"So am I *saved*? Or have I ... have-have I ... *damned* myself?"

Anasûrimbor Kellhus shrugged.

"I am no prophet."

The other Proyas hissed between clenched teeth. Affront blotted all distinctions.

"False!"

"The seeds are cast and I say which grains will grow, no different than any Prophet."

"Lies! Deceit and deception—all of it!"

"Truth," the shadow of the Holy Aspect-Emperor said in a voice that was also a shrug. "Lies ... For the Dûnyain, these things are naught but tools, two keys to two different arenas of the World. Tell me which is greater: The truth that sees Men extinct, or the lie that sees them saved?"

The deposed Exalt-General spat blood. "Then why not lie *now*? Why not say, Proyas, yours is the lot most blessed? You shall sup with Heroes, lay with virgins in Holy Chalahall!"

"Because if I were to lie to you, I would not know what I was *lying for* ... The darkness all but owns me here ... The darkness that comes before. Any lie I might utter would serve ends I cannot know ... I speak the truth to you, Proyas, because truth is all I have left to speak."

Heat cupped the fallen Believer-King's eyes, a sting he could not swat away.

"So these are my wages?" he cried on the welling edge of anguish. "*These are my wages?* Betrayal? *Damnation?*"

The white-robed figure stood without reply, or perhaps replied *by standing*.

Proyas looked back to Golgotterath, the tyrant that had commanded this final betrayal in sooth. And it seemed the most mad thing, both in and of itself, and relative to him and his yearning. At long last he could *scry the distance*, pace the cubits, between *here* and the dread end that had given meaning to every instant of his life.

To come so close.

All that Malowebi knew of Nersei Proyas was the residue of what passed through the Satakhanic Court, rumours of politic melancholy, godlike appearance, and ferocious conviction, the very image of the great man bound to a legendary vocation—not much, but more than enough to know it was no small murder the Holy Aspect-Emperor committed here at the very ends of the earth.

"Let me die," the man begged. "Please, Kellhus."

The Anasûrimbor's voice fell as edict from the overarching oblivion, as it always did given Malowebi's skewed vantage.

"No, Proyas ... The World holds no torment that can compare to what awaits you. I have *seen*. I know."

"Then ... be *done* with it!" Proyas sobbed. "If I am ... to be your witness ... tell me ... tell me your truth *so that I might condemn!* Curse you in turn!"

Blood and swelling had made a horrid smear of what looked to be handsome features, but the nobility of the ruin was indisputable.

"But you know my truth as well as you know my lie," the occluded presence said. "I have come to save the World."

Broken lips grimaced about missing and broken teeth. A grisly smile. "And that is why ... the *Gods themselves* hunt you!"

Malowebi cringed. Images of Psatma Nannaferi drowned his soul's eye, an old crone flooding nubile fields.

The Holy Aspect-Emperor replied as if this were the very clay to be cracked and sifted. "As they have to! The thing—the most horrific thing to understand, Proyas, is that at some point *the Inchoroi must win*. At some point, perhaps this year or ages hence, the whole of humanity will be butchered. Think on it! Why did Momas strike Momemn, his namesake city, and not this infernal place? Why is Eternity *blind to Golgotterath?* Because it stands outside Eternity, outside *what the Gods can see*. And that blindness is nothing short of *breathtaking*, Proyas! Our actions, our Great Ordeal, follows a *doom outside of doom!* We undertake a pilgrimage that *rewrites the Hundred* with every step!"

And Malowebi reeled hearing this, both for the turmoil of unwelcome understanding, and for the realization that the Yatwerian witch, despite her absolute contempt for the future, *did not know it* ...

"When they attack me," the Anasûrimbor continued, "their assassins are doomed since Creation to succeed, and then they fail as they were *always doomed to fail*. Eternity is transformed and the Hundred with it, oblivious to the transformation. The Unholy Ark is the disfiguring absence, the pit that consumes all trace of its consumption! To the degree it moves us, we pursue a Fate the Gods can never see ...

"Do you see, Proyas? *We act outside Eternity*, here ... in this place."

Lacking any body immune to convulsions of understanding and passion, Malowebi floundered. A doom outside of dooms?

"Aye, if the Absolute is anywhere to be found, it is *here*."

Dizzied, the Mbimayu Schoolman clung to the macabre image of the man lying broken upon the Accusatory, the peril of the Horns conjoining the sky and plain beyond him. The Believer-King of Conriya seemed curiously unconstrained, despite the cruel way his elbows were trussed behind his back. His eyes followed random tracks across the distance.

"And the *God of Gods*?" the battered face gasped.

The view pitched and rolled to the left as the Holy Aspect-Emperor set a sandalled foot upon his beloved disciple's shoulder. Malowebi's view rolled with his severed head; the barren arc of the Occlusion replaced the captive, towering heaps of wrack veering across the distance with compass precision.

"As blind to His Creation," the Anasûrimbor said, "as we are blind to ourselves."

Malowebi heard hot skin scuffing across stone. The scene dangled back to the Accusatory and distant terror of the Horns—absent Nersei Proyas. The hemp rope snapped tight across the rock.

Anasûrimbor Kellhus stood motionless upon the promontory for a time, as always entirely occluded from view. Still reeling, Malowebi averted his attention from the narcotic emblem, the *Ark*, followed its wicked shadow, the blackness reaching for the scabrous outskirts of the encampment, the Great Ordeal. He saw the Host of Hosts, and it seemed nothing more than the teeming of insects ... beetles scrabbling in circles beneath the gaze of Anasûrimbor Kellhus.

How could such an enterprise be a madman's errand? Who would enslave a civilization to wage war against mere *fables*?

Anasûrimbor Kellhus had upended the World *for a reason*, one wholly as dire as he claimed.

A night. An age.

The second drop has broken things. Cuts murmur and abrasions moan. It will not be long now.

The slow twist reveals his brother, Zsoronga, who hangs dying with him, then takes him away.

The sun breaches the summits rearing behind them, and looking out and up from his meat where it dangles, the Skeptic-King *sees* it.

Truly sees.

A golden crown for a head greater than any mountain, a *laurel*, set upon negligent earth ...

An infinite abdication.

Breathing hurts. Breathing is difficult.

He swings, the hemp creaking like wood. He swings seeing ...

He knows impossible things, dying. He understands that his father had understood all along. On his deathbed, proud Onoyas had called for his son *knowing* he would not come ... And yes, even *hoping* ... Because it mattered not at all, what a life makes of a soul.

Not at all.

Proyas can see it now, though he must raise mountains to lift his brow.

The World is more real, parsed into light and shadow. The distances are more distant ...

And we are less embroiled.

Impunity leaps from the cracks between us ...

And we punish whom we will.

CHAPTER ELEVEN

The Occlusion

Inked the heart's verses,
on the peak, in the light;
stole a lover's breath,
in the deep, in the night;
caught a child's tumble,
on the peak, in the light;
dried a mother's cheek,
in the deep, in the night;

blinded an ally's children,
on the peak, in the light;
murdered a brother's wife,
in the deep, in the night;
choked a mansion's hope,
on the peak, in the light;
grasping to seize, merely,
in the deep, in the night;

So are my hands more accursed,
than blessed,
more violet than white.

—Song of the Violet Ishroi

Early Autumn, 20 New Imperial Year (4132, Year-of-the-Tusk), Golgotterath.

There was a feeling to the sand, a sterility that made meat of other earth.

The Son of Harweel sat without ceremony, his boots and legs askew, his shoulders slumped, his hands insensate. The Occlusion ramped before him, piling into the cracked joists that raised the bulk of the Promontory like the tip of an accusing finger.

His friend hung dying above. Mu'miorn ...

His solitary Boonsman.

He understood that he wasn't thinking clearly. He understood, in a sideways manner, that he had endured *too much*: too many uncertainties, too many indignities, too many maddening, ingrown anxieties—and now, at last, too many *losses*.

All of this was clear to him.

What he couldn't fathom was *what he was doing*. Did he mourn? Did he plot or ponder? Disintegrate?

Did he *wait*?

The cramped shrieks, the blood beneath his fingernails ... these were clues. And Mu'miorn, the adorable fool, *refused to shut-up*. Natter, natter, natter. Yatwer, Yatwer, Yatwer ...

"Why did you love me!" he heard his lungs bellow in reply. "*Why?*"

Couldn't he see? To love him was to *die*. That was his curse ...

But no, his friend insisted. Stupid sausage! To love him was to be *murdered* ...

True, that.

The sun at last outran the woolen shield of clouds. It fell as a hot breath across his back. The blood trickling from his friend gleamed crimson across the stones.

An old Ketyai draped in rotted pelts stood near him for a time, staring up at the deposed Exalt-General—a man whose name Sorweel could no longer remember.

"What happened?" he asked in a voice like bark.

"Innocents ..." the Son of Harweel replied on a gurgle. "Innocents were sacrificed."

The old man studied him, his gaze bald enough to beg hostility.

"Yes," he finally rasped in reply, flinching from a glance toward Golgotterath over his shoulder. "So the guilty might prosper."

He hobbled several steps toward Sorweel, bearing an intensity sharpened ever more into the point of a knife. A nimil hauberk swung between and beneath his pelts, the shimmer of countless herons. The man stopped, *braced*. Eyes more silver than white glittered from a battered, bearded face—one that could have belonged to an ancient Eskeles.

"Worry not, son ... *Judgment* has come to the Aspect-Emperor."

With that, the wild stranger turned as a heap and began trudging toward the encampment sprawled below the Occlusion.

"*Whose judgment?*" the King of the Lonely City had screamed at the retreating figure. "*Whoooose?*"

But he knew. He had been here *before*, and the old man and Mother had told him precisely the same thing.

The day waned. The raining blood slowed to a spit, then stopped altogether. Where violet became black, red became brown, and this troubled him not at all. Sunlight trickled down to its dregs, drawing the stork's shadow ever more gracile upon the stone tumble.

He had noticed the white bird immediately, but for whatever reason a watch passed before it fell within the ambit of his soul's gyre. When he finally turned to gaze at the thing he had to fend the wild urge to seize its feathered heat, to bury his head beneath one great wing ...

To hitch and sob.

Mummy ...

Be brave, Little One ...

Mimara walks. The Ordealmen gape at her, as much for her unborn child as for her parentage.

Some ... a few, remember to fall to their faces. The others follow out of ignorance or exhaustion, and this relieves her more than anyone can know ...

Relieves the Eye.

Her memories of fleeing the Andiamine Heights scarce seem real anymore, but they possess more than enough substance for her to worry over the irony: that she had fled the Andiamine Heights, run the compass of the World, to the very shadow of *Golgotterath*, only to find the Imperial Court *awaiting* her.

Or its monstrous remnants, anyway.

A kind of stupor fell across her and Achamian trudging across the chalk expanse of the Shigogli. She recalls quarrelling over Qirri. Otherwise, she has no recollection how, only *that* they parted ways. Traversing Shigogli became its own trial, with the Horns boggling her periphery, continually prying at the feeble latch that kept all the screams inside, and with the encampment a growing labyrinth of wreckage before her. Images of her past life confounded any focus she mustered, a thousand little razors, each glimpse another bleeding nick. Slaves buttoning girdles. Dignitaries watching her on the sly. The *whole of her life* awaited her in those canvas slums— everyone she had fled the previous winter ... Serwa ... Kayûtas ... What would she say? How could she explain? And her stepfather—*what would Anasûrimbor Kellhus do with what he saw in her face?*

And the Eye. What would *it* see?

When one is numb enough, terror ceases to exhaust and begins to sustain; if anything her fears quickened her already unnatural gait. Two shadows had accompanied her passage the entire time, hers distinguished for the black orb that was her waist, rippling ever longer across the trampled dust—and then ... *there was only one.* They simply parted, drawn apart on oblivious angles, and she found herself alone, clasping her golden-armoured belly ... returning to a place she has never been.

Walking among the Damned.

Her horror of them, and her weeping especially, simply makes it worse, makes *them* more desperate to inquire, to relieve whatever could be ailing her—not understanding that *they* are what ails her, they and the dizzying obscenity of what they have done. Not all suffering raises in the Eye of God. Not all sacrifice is holy. She can scarce discern their nations, so potent is the blot of their crimes, and so alike. Conriyan, Galeoth, Nilnameshi—it does not matter. No history, no ageless compact of bone and blood, could mitigate their infernal doom. Their sins had pitched them beyond peoples.

She sees it as if refracted across colourless glass, a shadowy pageant of atrocities, abominations, of *Men making as Sranc*, not simply with Sranc, *but with Men.* Orgiastic apparitions, warriors supping upon the living and rutting with the dead, linger like smoke about a hellish glare, light become terror, impossible visions, torture combed into feathers, a thousand thousand strands ...

Ciphrang masticating, chewing souls as meat. Sin like naptha. Endless, blistering fire.

At last the latch is thrown and she flees sobbing, clutching her belly as she runs.

She waddles and scrambles through the slum alleys, between camps that were little more than strewn belongings, beggars' nests. She keeps her face down so none might see her resemblance to her mother, her pelts thrust forward to conceal her bulbous abdomen, but word of her presence has spread, and no matter what precinct she flees to, she is recognized; the infernal masses fall to their knees and cry out in wonder, utterly insensitive to the crushing yoke of Eternity.

She walks among them, the damned Men of the Ordeal, turning the Eye away as best as she can manage. And impossibly, *she grows accustomed* to the company of demons, the servile fawning of burning souls. For this, she realizes, is what it means to possess the Judging Eye, to walk among, and not flee, the damned, and to find some way to help them see. Why should *she* flee? And it astounds her, the disproportion of her return, how someone who was little more than a spark kicked from a worldly flame, could return *as the very sun*. It flabbergasts, even terrifies her, knowing that soon—so very soon!—she will stand before the Holy Aspect-Emperor, and that *she* will be the immovable one, the *one most holy*, the one to pass sentence ...

Give voice to the Judging Eye. The Judgment of God.

And she stumbles for the realization ... even though it seems to her that she has always known. All this ... all the damned kings and warriors and sorcerers ... the *Great Ordeal* ... and its dread task ...

All of it *belongs to her*.

No matter what she sees when the Eye falls upon Anasûrimbor Kellhus, upon the Dûnyain who has usurped the whole of the Three Seas ...

She, the child-whore, the waif, the mad, melancholy runaway—*Mimara* ...

She is the only true Prophet here.

Achamian would never know what had compelled him, only that he had been a fool.

They had picked their way down the Occlusion then set out across the chill reaches of the Furnace Plain. He recalled feeling years accumulate with each and every footfall, and how announcing as much led to an inevitable feud over the Qirri. They paused, isolate in the vast expanse. Apertures opened in the woolen skies above, allowing shafts of lucid sunlight to trawl the distances. Silent pockets of summer, the kind that spark yearning, skimming into oblivion. The Horns of Golgotterath glowered more than gleamed ... as they had in horror of his dreams.

Titanic gold.

The two of them partook of the Last Nonman King in the old way, with their mouths. The ash was sweet. Then they resumed their trek, skirting the wastes where they had watched the Great Ordeal roil and howl watches previous. Step after step they laboured, Golgotterath a nauseous looming to their left, the encampment a midden heap kicked and raked across the landscape before them, the Occlusion fencing all visible creation.

They walked.

The Qirri had restored their wind, but left their confusion intact. Perhaps it was the obscurity, the uncertainty of what was about to happen. Perhaps it was the finality. Perhaps their transit had damaged them too profoundly to countenance any destination, let alone the one pinioned between Golgotterath and the Aspect-Emperor.

His thoughts were too watery to congeal into memory, let alone anything resembling reason. Anxieties and images sluiced through senseless channels. Walking had become the one abiding thing, the myriad of aches and stings and discomforts. As was so often the case on the long trail, the toll of incessant movement became the one truly motionless thing, the blind anchor of blind being.

As they crossed the scuffed tracts he turned to peer at the thumb of stone where Kellhus had harangued the Great Ordeal. The Accusatory, he had realized on a dull flare of wonder, suddenly seeing the shadow of the Arobindant in the black whorls and encrustations across the surrounding slopes. Peering, he glimpsed the two figures hanging from its blunt terminus, as well as the loose collection of souls keeping vigil below. For some reason, he could not look away from the image, and as so often happens when vision strays, his path strayed as well. Something about the sight *itched*, for some reason. The great, chapped finger pointed not so much *at* him as over, toward Golgotterath beyond, two nameless victims strung from the point of its cryptic accusation. It was only as he neared that he had realized it was the figure trussed and hanging to the *left*, the paler one, that he sought ...

He fairly panicked when he realized that Mimara had not followed his straying.

She had the Qirri.

Even still, his eye was drawn back to the wretch strung to the left—to the direction his strides already took him. The kernel of all madness resides in the *clarity* of its unreason. Doubt is ever the ballast of sanity, what opens the course of Men to the correction of other Men. This was why Achamian now feared more for his *intellect* than his sanity, because it seemed he had stepped *out of void*, that his origins had been stripped from him. *Why?* Why had he come *here?*

He walked, gums tingling, clamouring for more cannibal ash.

To find Ishuäl? To discover the truth of Anasûrimbor Kellhus?

He knew he was sane because *confusion* had always ruled him—he chased hazy inklings, not divine edicts.

He drifted to a stop below the promontory, peered up without blinking. He knew he was sane.

No matter how disjoint it felt now, he had not stumbled across Eärwa in a stupor ... but then neither had he sought out the origins of Anasûrimbor Kellhus.

He had come to recover what was stolen. A cherished wife.

A beloved student.

Head hanging down from shoulders wrenched back, elbows bound into the apex of an agonizing triangle. Creaking to and fro. Dripping blood.

Prosha ...

He stood staring at the strangeness and the familiarity. Locks of black hair hanging, satin with filth. Eyes sealed in rheum and misery. The old Wizard was not alone. In his periphery, he sensed the gaze of the blond youth who knelt nearby, beneath the Zeumi wretch who hung opposite his once-beloved pupil. Achamian did not so much ignore as forget the youth, such was his grief.

There was shouting.

He could not look away. His neck clamoured. He wanted to weep, and somehow, the fact that he could not seemed the worst misery of all. He wanted to scream. He even wanted—for a heartbeat at least—to put out his own eyes ...

Madness had its consolations.

But he was a Wizard far more than he was a Man, a soul bent to unceasing, unnatural toil. He understood that there was *meaning* here, meaning bound upon the tickle of the Incû-Holoinas in the small of his back. The tutor and the student of days bygone were anything but alone on this accursed plain. Other reasons dwelt here, some written into the very ink of what happened.

He had come to deliver Mimara, the Judging Eye.

Drusas Achamian suffered a *second* certainty then, one unlike any he had ever known. And somehow it made his remorse *holy*. He squinted at the one child he had loved most aside from Inrau. The second son he had taught and failed to keep alive.

"*My boy* ..." was the most he managed to croak.

Not so high above, the bound form of Proyas, blessed son of Queen Thaila and King Onoyas, swayed on slow revolutions ...

Dying in the shadow of Golgotterath.

———◆———

It wasn't a dream, the little Prince-Imperial realized upon awakening.

What he remembered ... It had happened!

The light become nausea and ground. The vast slum of shelters, the encamped Ordeal knitted like mould along the inner arc of a low range of mountains. The Horns rearing beyond—the *Horns of Golgotterath* soaring vast and unbelievable from the blasted lands. The Ordealmen streaming from all quarters, ghastly mockeries of the Men they had been. How they had blubbered and whooped upon their arrival. Sobbed and grovelled! Like foul beggars tugging at Father's robe. Some had even torn their beards for joy and grief!

Father abandoned him and Mother to them almost immediately, stepping back into the selfsame light they had just stumbled from. A company of crazed and filthy Pillarians took them in hand. Mother had to be carried, so violent was her illness—even Kelmomas had reeled and vomited. Father had pressed them *hard* across the final horizons. The Men bore them to a massive black pavilion with a kind of deranged reverence. Some had openly wept! Mother had been too sick to protest when they had installed him *with* her in a gloomy chamber—the Umbilicus, they had called it. And so he had lain exhausted and joyous—joyous!—his soul and stomach spinning, pondering the fact that after everything, he had somehow found himself *here* ...

Mother's chamber. Bellied black canvas walls, barricading the gloom. A single lantern light, plucking the geometry of empty and eclectic spaces from the black, illuminating palms of painted and brocaded pattern.

A lion. A heron. Seven horses.

A straw mattress laid out like corpses across the ground. Silk sheets, dull for the soil of unwashed bodies, but still gleaming, lines of white hooked across the restless tangle, sharp against the bruise of rose.

And Mother, the beloved one, sleeping.

Eyes closed in the grey ghost of lampblack. Lips sealed about an open jaw, slumped chin. Oblivious.

The little one watching. The fallen one.

The beauty of her was carved into his very bones. He had been drawn from her womb—hewn from her hips!—but he nevertheless remained *of* her in every way. The girlish tangle of her hair knotted him. The bare length of her left arm made tack and gum of his breath. The slow cycle of her breathing was a pang rising and falling within his own breast.

To gaze upon her was as near a soul such as his could ever come to worship. The Blessed Empress.

Mommy.

There was much he had refused to know—as of yet. The entire World now twisted from a solitary hair. And for all his Dûnyain guile, he possessed a child's feral understanding of powerlessness, the concessions that *helplessness* exacted from those, such as him, who were condemned to love. To be Kelmomas the Feared, the Hated was at once to be Kelmomas the Alone, the Unwanted ... the Doomed.

For what was love, if not weakness become blessing?

She. She was the one thing that mattered. The only mystery to be solved. All the rest, Father's return, the Narindar, the Earthquake—even Father's interrogation—mattered not at all. Not even the mad fact that he was about to witness the Great Ordeal assail Golgotterath! Only *she* ...

Only Mommy.

Slumbering as he had never seen her slumber before, her heart thrumming fleet, then ponderous, following deep and inexplicable patterns. Their miraculous journey across Eärwa had almost proven beyond her endurance. Father had carried her convulsing, retching spittle for a greater part of their mad and magnificent passage. She was weak ...

Worldborn.

She needs us ...

To protect her, yes.

The Prince-Imperial made no effort to feign sleep or otherwise conceal his scrutiny. He had always resided here, invulnerable and unknown, in the very bosom of her slumber. This was *his* place. And it always had been. The difference was that he had never before feared she might stir from her slumber. She would awaken, yet slumber still.

She hates us!

Hates you. She always loved me better.

The anguish was quite unlike anything he had known. There was the pain he had suffered following Uncle's palace coup, but there had been exhilaration and play as well. As desperate, as forlorn as he had been, he had had such fun-fun! There was the pain of being abandoned, he supposed, and then there was the pain of *being found*, and the latter was so much worse-worse—horrible! A loss without the hope of recovery.

No! Noooo!

Yes. She could always smell Him on you!

Him. Father. They had hidden from him so long Kelmomas had thought himself invisible. But Father had simply cast his eye across the curve of the World. He need only *look*, the way Inrilatas had looked, to see *all of it* ...

You mean the Strength. She could always sense the Strength in me.

Yes. The Strength.

Sharacinth. Inrilatas. Uncle. The hunting and the feasting ...

All the fun.

Father knows all—Everything!

Yes. He is the strongest.

And he had *told* Mommy. They had seen it in her eyes, the way it died, the one part he had sought to raise above all others ...

A mother's love for her poor little son.

What are we going to do, Sammi?

That isn't the question—you know this.

Yes-yes.

He knelt upon the corner of the mattress watching her, and he fairly swooned, so intense was the desire, so *cosmic the need*, to simply lay a cheek upon the maternal hill that was her hip, to hold tight what he had been, cling to the one soul that could save him.

What? What was Father going to do with his wayward sons?

Maybe the Consult will kill him.

To see is to follow. Mimara understands that now, understands why the blind are so prone to linger, to roam apart from the mob. She sees the tented slums of the encampment, follows impromptu ways that fork like old veins. The recognition belonging to that first soul on the encampment's perimeter pursues her like a famished dog, so that Men drop all about her wherever she wanders, some grovelling, croaking and moaning like demented beggars, others beseeching, importuning, crying across outstretched fingers. She goes so far as to cast arms against the leering visages.

To see is to follow. She speaks to no one, makes no queries, and yet finds herself standing before the Umbilicus all the same. It rears as a many-poled mountain range before her, the mottled grey of things once-black, more bruised than adorned with circumfixes, so mudded and tattered was the embroidery. It seems to flap and billow, though the air is absolutely still.

She comes upon it from the east, such is the Whore's perversity. *Golgotterath* rises beyond, monstrous and implacable.

As damned as the Ordealmen are, the Ark leans across the Eye in a manner almost too violent to comprehend, a vision that strums the scale of the spirit too profoundly to hear. All this time, she has thrown aside her face, shielded her gaze, lest she vomit, void her bowel.

But there is no avoiding it now, short of groping her way forward.

Evil. An alien malice as cold as the Void.

Mutilated babes. Cities heaped like so many beehives upon a bonfire. The Horns gleam static through imagistic clamour, rise against clouds of tangled violet, crisp and gleaming, massive and inanimate, scarcely reflecting the eruption of demonic atrocities below, the thousandfold glimpses of dying peoples, races, civilizations—crimes that break the back of imagination, multiplied unto lunacy across the span of lands and ages, so heinous as to draw Hell, like fat in famine, up through the pores of the World.

She stands shaking, a child drawn from the tub in winter. Urine sops her inner thighs. She smells burnt belongings, roasting horseflesh.

Please!

"Princess-Imperial?" a masculine voice exclaims. "Sweet Sejenus!"

And she sees *it*, blackness bound in whirling dust, towering across the Heavens ...

"Is it truly you?"

"Our Holy Aspect-Emperor," Apperens Saccarees said, affecting a brittle distraction. "Does he know you are here?"

The old Wizard shrugged. "Who can say what he does and does not fathom?"

That earned him a sharp look.

"Aye," the Mandate Grandmaster replied. The man set aside the tome he had been perusing, scrutinized the greatest traitor his School had ever known.

The Men of the Ordeal had been roasting horses when Achamian finally hobbled into the encampment, great shanks of meat slicked over fires fuelled by what belongings they had managed to salvage thus far. Few paid him any attention. They were grim, exhausted. Many were blackened for unwashed skin. Mangy black and brown stained every tunic. A kind of expectancy animated them, but tempered by the air of *survival*, of too many cuts endured, the fever, perhaps, of a lingering sepsis. Achamian recognized the look, or the nub of it anyway, from the siege of Caraskand. These Men of the Ordeal had suffered grievously getting here. They had burned and hacked the breadth of Eärwa, crossed an ocean of Sranc, and now they had reached the point of greatest dread for any host campaigning in hostile lands, the turn where they must begin consuming the very things that sheltered and conveyed them.

The old Wizard was neither troubled nor surprised.

Night had gathered almost all ere he had found the Mandate encampment. He had not known what to expect of his former brothers. Both more and less, he supposed, than the ring of ramshackle pavilions he found. The skies had cleared, baring all to the Nail of Heaven and the pallor of the infinite Void. He found breathing difficult, so convincing was the illusion of airlessness. Thanks to some perversity of his vantage, the Ark appeared to loom inscrutable over the encampment's immediate perimeter, its monstrous contours gilded by hooks of silver sterility. Resolve as he might, Achamian could not stop casting glances over his shoulder. *You're here!* a breath would cry within him. *Here!* And alarums would skitter across his skin, terrors would burr his thoughts, and yes, even *glee* would evanesce through his soul.

It was happening. The horror and anguish that he and every Mandate Schoolman alive or dead had dreamed night after miserable night—all of if could be redeemed! Vengeance—*vengeance!*—was finally at hand!

And yet the aura in the compound had been one of doddering ... numbness.

"However ..." the Grandmaster continued, "you *are* the legendary Drusas Achamian ..." He smiled. "The *Wizard*."

He had never known Saccarees personally, but he had heard of him. As irritating as teachers find prodigies in the room, they crow in their absence, quick to find evidence of their efficacy. Saccarees fairly had his masters falling over themselves in self-congratulation. Whatever the man's gifts, Kellhus had certainly recognized them quickly. Achamian idly wondered whether the Mandate had ever possessed a Grandmaster so young. The only thing more outrageous than his hairline was the fact his hair possessed so little grey.

Achamian smiled in turn. "And you are?"

Twenty years in self-imposed exile, months warring across the wastes, and there it was, as oiled and effortless and accursed as it had ever been: *jnan*.

"Please," the Mandate Grandmaster said, his smile revealing teeth that were far too even. He spoke, Achamian could not help but think, like a man struggling to awaken. "Things will go better if we speak plainly."

It boggled to think, but *decades* had passed since he had last suffered the company of the wise. There's a difference that learning makes, a manner the vulgar are apt to distrust, even despise. Apperens Saccarees, the old Wizard very quickly realized, was *enduring him*.

The old Wizard pursed his lips, exhaled. Everything, it seemed, reeked of tragedy—and hope.

"A shadow lies across this place."

The Grandmaster shrugged as if at errant absurdity. "We make preparations to assault *Golgotterath*, recall."

"No. Something *ails* you. Something ails all of you."

Saccarees looked down to his thumbs.

"Think of the *ground* you stand upon, Wizard."

Achamian frowned scoffing. "You've slept upon this ground every night of your life."

"Yes, but we quite literally *marched across the World* to get here this time, didn't we?"

Achamian blinked away images of himself swatting the fool.

"Why has Proyas been *condemned to die?*"

Had he learned something? Had he seen *through* Kellhus somehow?

Again the Grandmaster hesitated. Despite his urgency, Achamian found himself conceding that Saccarees was, when all was said and done, *a good man* ...

For it was plain that *shame* had conquered something in him.

The Grandmaster flattened his expression. "How is it, do you think," he asked, speaking to an abstract point to the right, "that so many Men have managed to journey so far?"

The old Wizard scowled, understanding the riddle, but resenting the misdirection.

"They *walked* ... same as me."

The sneer of someone who has hung from his limits for too long. "And what, pray-tell did you use to *nourish* your steps?"

Achamian had frequented enough opium dens during his years in Carythusal to know well the expression that lay cold as a claw upon his face. He had seen it many times on many addicts, the *look*, the one that raises fury and outrage to a perilous height, then dares others to risk the truth.

"What," the Mandate Grandmaster pressed, "*did you eat?*"

Cu'jara Cinmoi ...

"Forage."

Then Nil'giccas.

"And what *forage*, do you think, the Great Ordeal had available?"

So it came to the old Wizard at last, the doom he and Mimara had tripped into.

Two eunuchs minister to her. Both are damned.

She had been pampered as a slave, cosseted and beaten. She had been pampered as an Anasûrimbor, coddled and spurned. Perfume and silk and fussing hands had hung upon her every whim, maddening her from time to time, but comforting her far more. Even now, seeing the Judgment dwelling within all things, glimpsing demons clawing the false smiles and anxious looks, she takes refuge in the absurdity of other hands doing what her hands could plainly do.

She is *waiting*, she realizes.

Waiting for the Judging Eye to close.

It refuses.

Apparently water was in short supply, so they cleanse her with wetted cloth. Save for the odd murmured instruction, the eunuchs do not speak, leaving the air to the supple sounds of water and fabric. They have a stunned, astonished air about them, a desperation that has wrung all routine from their task. They do what they do with a religious intensity.

As they should, given the outrages they have committed.

With clean hands and soiled hearts, they daub and wipe the filth from her skin. She marvels at her nudity in the lantern-light, at the great sphere of her belly. After a muttered exchange in some Buskritic dialect, they elect to garb her in a silk tunic—belonging, no doubt, to her stepfather— embroidered white upon white with innumerable thorn-sized tusks. It fairly drapes to her ankles. An overrun fraction of her soul mourns the tent pitched by the mound of her belly, but only for a heartbeat. It is proper that she wear white.

One of them produces a silvered shield in lieu of a mirror, but she turns her face aside, not for the bulbous and elongated character of her reflection, but for the blinding glare of *holiness*. She bids them fetch her ensorcelled hauberk, her belt and Emilidic blade, her Chorae, and of course, the pouch containing Nil'giccas. She can smell her journey on these things, the tang of Lord Kosoter and the Skin-Eaters, the dank of Cil-Aujas and the Mop, the sweet reek of Ishuäl and the Library of Sauglish.

She avoids looking into their faces. She feels neither remorse nor pity.

A Pillarian wearing tatters of green, filth, and gold is waiting for her beyond the chamber flap: Meerskatu, Exalt-Captain of the Pillarians. He bites his lip like a disordered child, leads her without explanation down the leather-panelled corridor. He presses open a flap branded with elaborate scenes drawn from the Tusk and the First Holy War. She glimpses her stepfather hanging from the Circumfix in Caraskand.

She thinks of Achamian, suffers a pang of worry.

Meerskatu gestures for her to enter. "Truth shines," he says, working his mouth peculiarly. The Eye glimpses the groins his teeth have savaged.

She gazes at him in horror, unable to speak for revulsion. He fairly flees from her presence, somehow sensing, knowing.

She presses past the images of things dead and holy, finds herself in an antechamber of some kind. A second flap stamped with similar motifs lies opposite. A single lantern peers through the gloom, illuminating a haphazard tangle of Imperial baggage. Her skin tingles. To be cleansed, she thinks, is to be less real.

Light gleams across a thatch of golden thread, drawing her eye to what appears to be a heavy blanket crumpled across a cot—a kind of field settee to her right. She walks toward it, savouring the feeling of fabric beneath her toes. A terror leaps upon the summit of her breath. Her throat aches.

She clutches the blanket, draws it out like a matron inspecting wares in the market. For a time she draws no breath whatsoever.

The blanket is actually a small ornamental tapestry, supple for the extraordinary quality of the weave. The tapestry itself she has seen before, she realizes. It once hung in the Sartorials, the imperial feast hall near the summit of the Andiamine Heights. But the *image* ... that she has seen much more recently.

It seems she can even smell it, the moss and rotting bark, the air choked of all motion—the Mop.

A dank socket between trees. A rare shaft of moonlight. Her *own reflection* across a black pool ... only transformed by the Eye into the very image *she now holds in her hands* ...

A pregnant woman, her cropped hair all the more black for the plate of brilliant silver about her head.

Blessed.

She hears the whisk and ruffle of the far flap—freezes.

"Who are you?"

A feminine voice, husky for disuse, too exhausted to be alarmed.

Her extremities tingle. She cannot bring herself to turn. She cannot bear to look ...

A *curse*, Achamian said so very long ago. The Eye is a curse.

At last she understands.

"Mim?"

Her hands wring the fabric. The air buzzes about her ears, daring her to breathe.

Breath drawn, as if at a sudden cut. "*Mimara?*"

She turns, though all her will clamours against it. She *turns*, the very hinge of absolute judgment, a little girl pitched to sorrow's sobbing edge.

"*Momma ...*"

More gasp than voice.

There she stands before her, Anasûrimbor Esmenet, the Blessed Empress of the Three Seas. Haggard. Palace-pale. A rose-silk sheet clutched to her breast ...

Dark with the writhing, straining shadows of countless carnal transgressions. Glowing with the promise of paradise.

Tears ... An inarticulate cry.

Tears.

Sorweel wasn't sure when she had slipped into the squalid interior of his tent, but then he himself had no recollection of entering. Anasûrimbor Serwa stooped to the bellied slope of the canvas, bound in her Swayali billows, carved in the ink and gold of his solitary lantern.

"Zsoronga was your friend," she said, peering with the same impervious mien as her elder brother. But he no longer feared her scrutiny. At long last he *trusted* that she would see what was required of her.

"My father *murdered* him."

The otherworldly density of her presence disoriented, especially in such base surroundings.

"*Executed*," the youth emended, "in accordance with the terms of the treaty struck between Zeum and the Empire." He glanced at the wild old hermit over his shoulder, sobbing and raving as he did.

She crouched, her knees pinned tight by her gown, clutched his shoulders, and he jolted (as he had always jolted) at the shock of her touch, the miracle of her proximity. The scent of cinnamon.

She clutched his shoulders, and he leapt in his skin.

"How can you say this?" she demanded.

"I will *die* to protect you ..." Mu'miorn whispered, wiping away tears.

She clutched his shoulders, and he clawed at the brutal hand about his throat, swatted and convulsed for the pummelling hips, the jetting seed, looping cursive upon his skin ...

He stared at the white point, light conjured from the fat of skinnies, awaiting her arrival. He looked up, and saw her kneeling before him, beseeching—as far as the daughter of any demon could beseech.

"Sorweel? *How is it you still believe?*"

He knew not her motive. He knew not whether she entertained suspicions or genuinely cared for his well-being. He knew only that she saw the face the Dread Mother had prepared for her ...

The expression of a Believer-King.

The details of her beauty arrested him, the saddle of freckles about the bridge of her nose, the whitening of her brows from dark roots, the profile of the Empress on the Kellic ...

The sunburnt pallor of the Accursed Aspect-Emperor.

"Does it *matter*, Serwa?"

The Son of Harweel gazed into her imploring face, watched the openness of it tumble as from a parapet, falling into Imperial obscurity. He started at her clutch, the heat of her palms. He watched her bolt from the squalid confines.

"To shield what is weak," Mu'miorn cooed.

The assurance of a kiss, her face so close, then pitching back and away, dwindling, vanishing into the nocturnal nations. The scent of cinnamon. He sat, so very far from alone. He squinted for sunlight. He peered across the assembled Believer-Kings and their vassals, the battered glory of the Three Seas. He turned and saw her singing, luminance flaring from eyes rounded by horror. He smiled, stepped into the glittering violence of her lights ...

While all around the darkling World heaved and danced, the Southron Kings howling at the pillar of salt that had been her father.

Do you see, my sweet?

Skinnies. The Great Ordeal had consumed their foe. Sranc.

He should have run screaming to find Mimara, but the Grandmaster's story, when he began it, compelled him, held him riven with dismay. Dagliash. The Scalding. The Scalded.

"But *you* were there!" Achamian finally cried. "You could have counselled them! Told them what was happening!"

Laughter, sneering not so much out of condescension as self-loathing. "We all thought ourselves Seswatha! Mandati. Swayali ... Any who had clasped the Heart!"

And so he learned of the Meat and the nightmare that was Agongorea—how the Sranc had very nearly conquered the Men of the Ordeal from within. He listened blank with incredulity as the Mandate Grandmaster, his voice harrowed, described the crimes he and his brothers had committed.

Saccarees' second mention of the Scalded occasioned a long silence.

"What are you saying?"

A long exhalation. A grimace for a smile.

"We fell upon them, Wizard ... *Proyas* commanded it, claimed that it was the will of our Holy Aspect-Emperor! 'What *Hell* hath cooked for us!' he cried. I remember it ... like another mad Dream, I remember. 'We must *eat* what Hell hath cooked for us!'"

A shudder wracked the Grandmaster. He glared at nothing for one heart-beat ... two.

"We fell upon them, the leprous wretches, the Scalded. We fell upon them the way ... the way ... *Sranc* would fall—and worse! We-we ... *feasted* ... Gloried in ... obscenities ... degradations ..."

The man snorted in sudden, convulsive disgust, thumbed the tears from his eyes.

"*That* is why Proyas dies."

The little Prince-Imperial asphyxiated for dismay. How? *Here* of all places ...

You should have killed her!

And *now* of all times!

Kelmomas had lain next to his mother in the pretense of sleep, probing the leather-chambered complexity of the Umbilicus with his hearing. As far back as he could remember, his impulse was to *own* the detail of his circumstances, to *know* the ways, the souls, and the objects that populated his surroundings. He had known that someone had arrived, someone significant enough to send ripples of activity throughout the Umbilicus—and to command the reverence belonging to him and his family. He had heard the incredulity the arrival had evoked. He had even caught wayward tones of disapproval ...

But for all that the newcomer had *refused to speak.*

He had lain listening and waiting, and *waiting*, but *nothing*, not a word, nothing that would betray identity. He decided it couldn't be Kayûtas—his elder brother was far too fond of testing his voice. It could very well be Moënghus, who was given to long, sullen silences, but his fearsome aspect would have cast a wary shadow across the voices of those tending to him. That left his sister, *Serwa*, who had always unnerved him, not so much for her native penetration as her scrying *attitude*. Where others forever glossed their surroundings, she had a habit of peering at things *near* ...

She was like him, that way.

Then the guardsmen showed the newcomer to *their* chambers, and upon hearing the quaver in the Exalt-Captain's voice—the horror that was guilt and awe—Kelmomas knew instantly and irrevocably that someone other than Serwa had been delivered to them—someone *impossible*. He had lain reeling, so preoccupied with outrage that he failed to sense Mother stir. He almost cried out when she climbed upright, pulled herself to groggy feet. Instead, he lay slack in the pretense of slumber, knowing that she regarded him, blinking at the bleary turmoil that so disordered her heart. A pang of adoration throttled by grief and monstrous disbelief ... he could almost *smell* it.

See! She still loves!

He would have exulted, twitched and cooed as if suffering some onerous nightmare, affected the semblance of a child not so much bent by birth as afflicted by happenstance. For everything he had done, he had done out of *love for her*. Even Father had seen it, *attested* to it!

She would see! She *had* to!

She turned on an audible shiver, and trotted from the chamber as if across cold floors. She needed to make water, the young Prince-Imperial realized.

He heard her press the flap aside, knew that she ducked her head out of some old instinct. Then she vanished into soundlessness ...

And somehow Anasûrimbor Kelmomas *knew*.

"Who are you?"

His mother's voice, raw for loss and survival.

"Mim?"

A long moment.

"*Mimara?*"

Kelmomas lay transfixed, impaled by spears of catastrophic consequence. Never ... Never had he heard such wonder, such crazed *surrender*, in her voice. It was ridiculous—obscene even! She was *whole*! She ended at her skin—like everyone else! Why? Why play *half a soul*?

"*Momma* ..."

More breath than voice, remote in the manner of forgotten gods, and yet more near than near ...

It was stamped into him, that voice, down to the merest nuance. He need only hear it once to make it his own. But it was too late—far too late! They embraced, mother and daughter, slumped to their knees, keened and sobbed. And he lay raging, fuming, weeping. Here? Now? How could it be? He clawed the sheets. How much? What must he do? How much must he endure?

You should have killed her!

Shut-up! Shut-up!

Filthy slit! Crazed whore!

He pressed through the stamped leather, saw them, snivelling, mewling. He had no recollection of leaping from the mattress. He simply found himself standing, staring, breathing.

The two women clutched one another, balling fabric in fists. Mimara faced him, her cheek mashed into her mother's neck and shoulder, her face pinched about a thousand passions. "*I was so afraid*," Mother hissed, her voice cracked and muffled.

Mimara's eyes fluttered open, glittered for tears in white lantern-light. She somehow failed to see him, stared at what seemed to be Eternity instead. It sickened him, how much she looked like Mother.

"*I'm sorry, Momma*," she whispered through a shudder. "*I'm so-so sorry!*"

She blinked tears, peered as if through a sudden gloom, then with a perplexed air gazed directly at him.

"*Mim!*" Mother cried. "*Oh, sweet-sweet Mim!*"

Kelmomas saw the old, familiar tenderness crest his sister's expression, the insipid compassion that made her such a rank fool—as well as his most galling foe. Mimara smiled through her grimace ... *smiled at him.*

Something kicked bile into the back of his throat.

Mother's hand had roamed her daughter's shoulder and arm, as if confirming reality. Now it paused upon the bulge of her belly. "*How, sweetness?*" she asked, pressing her head back the merest degree. "*What ... What—?*"

Mimara beamed at him. Kelmomas felt his face reciprocate, *grin*, even as murderous urges romped wild through his veins.

"*Just hold me, Momma ...*"

"*Pregnant whore!*" Kelmomas heard himself cry.

The joy simply dropped from Mimara's face, like a burden bound to be jettisoned with ease.

He could spit for the outrage of her impersonation.

Mother went rigid, slowly pressed herself from her daughter's embrace—then *whirled*, flew at him. He could have blinded her, or crushed her throat, watched her choke on the meat of her own neck. Instead, he stood numb, motionless. She seized his arm, struck him full across his mouth and cheek with a clawed hand. He allowed the force to draw his head back and to the side, nothing more.

"*Mother!*" Mimara cried, bolting forward to catch a second eye-scratching blow.

"You have *no inkling!*" The Blessed Empress shrieked at her wayward daughter. "No idea what he has done!"

He savoured the sting where her nails had notched him, the welling.

"*Viper!*"

A thread of blood spilled hot from his nose. He grinned at the taste.

"*Abomination!*"

Mimara pulled Mother away, wrestled her wrists to her breast. A moment passed between them, or a look—a recognition of something. Sanctuary? Permission?

Mother went slack, slumped weeping into her daughter's arms.

"*D-deeeead ...*" she keened. "*All deeeead ...*"

Inconsolable sobbing. She clutched Mimara's shoulders, violently, suddenly, then screamed into her breast, breaking, at long last, about the savagery of all she had suffered.

Anasûrimbor Kelmomas retreated from the grotesque spectacle, slipped from chamber to chamber, gloom to gloom.

"*He killed them, Mim ... murdered ...*"

The little boy gazed at the portal that now lay between them, leather for iron. He saw his father upon the Circumfix, etched across what had once been living, bleeding skin.

Nobody ... it whispered on an airless, inner breath.

Nobody loves us.

———— ✺ ————

"Enough," the Grandmaster of the Mandate resolved on an exhalation. "He would *not approve.*"

"There are things I must tell you," Achamian said.

"You have told me quite enough."

A croak of laughter. "Your Dreams ... Have they been changing?"

This arrested the Schoolman's attention, if only momentarily.

"My Dreams have ..." Achamian continued. "Utterly."

Saccarees held his gaze a long instant, sighed audibly. "You are no longer Mandati, Wizard."

"And neither are my Dreams."

Apperens Saccarees pressed himself to his feet with a scowl, affecting the manner of someone disgusted for misspent generosity. Achamian reeled. The old desperation fumbled for his heart, the one he had all but forgotten, so long had it been: the wild need to be believed.

"Saccarees! *Saccarees!* All the World's wheels grind about this place—this *moment!* And you choose ignorance ove—?"

"Over *what?*" the Grandmaster snapped. "Blasphemy? Deceit?"

"I no longer suffer the past through Seswa—!"

"*Enough*, Wizard."

"I know the *truth of Him!* Saccarees, I know what He is! I know what He—!"

"I said, *enough!*" the Mandate Grandmaster cried, slapping both hands hard across the camp table.

The old Wizard glared up, matched the ferocity of his gaze. The fool!

"Why?" the Grandmaster exclaimed. "Why do you think He's suffered you all these long years?"

The question obliterated the horde of scathing retorts rising within, for it was one that had plagued him throughout the entirety of his Exile: Why he had been spared?

"Why do you think *I* have suffered you?" Saccarees continued. "A Gnostic *Wizard?*"

Achamian had always counted his life a bargain—but a sufferance?

"Because," he replied, his voice far more frail than he wished, "I always lose at benjuka?"

An old joke belonging to Xinemus.

Apperens Saccarees did not so much as blink. "The *Empress* ..." he said. "The Blessed Empress is the only reason you live, Drusas Achamian. Count yourself lucky she is *here*."

The Grandmaster drew out a crimson-clad arm, gestured to the sagging exit. But Achamian had already lurched to his feet, only to discover he needed to pause to recall the brute facts of breathing, walking ...

Yes-yes! a fraction reassured.

Mimara had the Qirri.

Such a lonely little flute he had been, an isolate soul twisting in the black, wicks of wane smoke on the Void.

Such a *chorus* he had *become*.

Standing with a stork upon his shoulder, and sitting alone in his tent, looking up, seeing Harweel, his expression rent between outrage and fear for his son, saying, "*My priests call him a demon ...*"

A cataract that transcended all glory ...

The White-Luck Warrior.

Wandering, following his own back through weltered alleys, across fields of slumbering human garbage, scavenge for the Ciphrang, turning to an insistent prod, seeing–*as it happened*–Porsparian standing upon mounds of dead Sranc, smiling as he dropped, the spearhead slipping into his glottis like a hand into a pocket. Only to crouch in the grass with Eskeles, squinting–*as it happened*–at the pottery shattered into shark teeth, the obese Schoolman saying, "*Our God... the God, is broken into innumerable pieces...*" rolling across the pinch of filth, hearing–*as it happened*–Serwa's hooked cries, seeing her buck and heave upon Moënghus, as Zsoronga squeezes tight his throat, feeling–as it happened–his iron thrust making delirium of his own, the Princess-Imperial saying, "*we can see the dead stacked about us all,*" as Nin'ciljiras ladled chill oil upon his scalp, gleaming like something furnace-glazed, heavy-lidded, pretending to be anything other than wrecked, saying, "*Do you think this is why the Anasûrimbor sent him to us?*" and he was there... as it *happened...*

Walking. Sleeping. Murdering. Making love.

Rushing in fathomless cataracts. Now and now and now and now ...

The White-Luck Warrior.

Alone on the edge of the encampment, looking out across the darkling plain at the carcass of a long dead evil, the pretext that would make a glutton of Hell.

Do you see? the stork whispered.

Harweel clasped his son's shoulder, grinned in paternal affirmation.

Ever has it been.

Shut the World? How, when all the future was drawn upon the same skin as the past ... Stamped. Written. When beauty and horror were bottomless.

And the ground so thin.

———∽∾∾———

Esmenet!

The sensation of falling plagued the old Wizard's nocturnal trek to the Umbilicus. Neither he nor Mimara had known what they would do upon reaching the Great Ordeal. Achamian had gone to Saccarees primarily out of what seemed an absence of alternatives but could have been a simple matter of self-preservation. It was only while imploring Saccarees that he understood the deranged extent of his fear, how the years of obsessive pondering had rendered Anasûrimbor Kellhus the sum of all horror.

He had imagined their arrival often enough, but in the vague way of hopes not quite believed. In his soul's fancy, he always stood beside Mimara as she delivered the Judgment of the Eye, the Holy Aspect-Emperor and his Imperial Court looking on ... and ...

What a fool he had been!

The fact of Proyas howled as much, but heartbreak had stoppered his ears, allowed him to prolong his daft sense of impunity. *They had the Eye.* The *Whore herself* was bound to what was about to happen here! Or so they had assumed in their exhausted fancies. Despite everything, Achamian had assumed the simplicity of *conclusions*, the clarity of scripture and myth, would occasion their arrival. *Fate* awaited them!

But Fate, as Protathis so famously declared, relieved only the augur's toil. It was a slaver's chain, not a king's litter—at least for the likes of him and Mimara. Fortune only sneered at souls such their own.

And what was more, Anasûrimbor Kellhus *was Dûnyain.* Complication was his accursed birthright. *Of course* the Great Ordeal was naught but a crossroad, a turn to a far more lethal and onerous toil. They tarried upon the very threshold of *Golgotterath* ...

Of course they lay in the jaws of mortal peril!

Of course *no one would believe them*, no matter what Judgment the Eye rendered ...

So Drusas Achamian walked, fulminating and cursing in the old way, as honestly perplexed by his oversights and failures now as he had been as a young man. He knew not what to do, only that he loved, and he was wise enough to take this as cause for terror instead of hope.

———— ❦ ————

Question crowded upon question ...

"We have come to judge *him*, Mother. Kellhus."

Esmenet gazed incredulous.

"*We?*"

"Akka and I."

They sat upon the matted floor, knee to knee, each slicked in contrasts of light and dark. Mimara had supped on water and roasted horse while Esmenet related all that had happened in Momemn since her flight, a tale that quickly turned into a hollow recounting of Kelmomas's horrific crimes and machinations. She had taken care with the words and the details, fearing they might trigger more paroxysms of grief and outrage. But like footsteps, they had borne her away instead, wandering from the walls and gutters and temples of the Capital to the wondrous fact of her eldest daughter. Alive!

It had wracked her, her sorcerous flight with her husband and her monstrous son across the Wild. The misery of it blotted any suffering she had known, and she had *welcomed* it. Losses were no different than luxuries. Heap them upon any one soul long enough, and that soul will come to see them as wages *earned*—aye, even *as justice*.

And then ... *Mimara*. This unaccountable gift, taken then returned ...

Herself a mother! Or almost one ... Bearing word not of losses, but *gifts* ...

That were also losses.

"You carry ..." Esmenet said over the buzzing in her ears. "You carry *Akka's* child?"

Downcast eyes, but no remorse or repentance whatsoever.

"I was the one," her daughter said to her thumbs. "I-I ... seduced him ... I wanted him to tea—!"

"*Seduced?*" the Blessed Empress heard herself snap. "So he is that simple? Or did you hold a knife to his throat? Coerce his seed?"

An angry glare, one that seemed to collapse the interval of unfamiliarity between them. All the old feuds had been renewed.

No-no-no-no ...

"Perhaps I did," Mimara said coldly.

"Perhaps you did *what?*"

"Bully his seed!"

"So you did use a knife then?"

No-no-no-no ...

"Yes!" her daughter cried on a hot gasp. "*You!* You were my knife! I used my *resemblance to you* to seduce him!" She even leaned forward, smiled as if warming to her old facility for cruel and cutting claims.

"He even cried your name!"

Too much. Too many insults. Too many hopes broken. The Blessed Empress was on her feet, barging past flaps, reeling through the leather-panelled gloom, glaring murder at any who dared accost her.

Too much. Too much. Enclosed spaces. Seams like stitched veins. The cloying regalia of an Empire crashing into ruin a world away. She fairly shrieked at the Pillarians who made to block her passage. Then she was out, free of the Umbilicus, stumbling to her knees beneath the vacant bowl of the night. At last!

Free—

The sight did not arrest her all at once. She became stationary in sliding, jarring pieces, it seemed. First her hands, drawn up, then her spine, arched back. It cut the strings of her expression, hooked her eyes, then pinioned everything else—thought, breath, heartbeat—against the granitic immobility of her form.

The black shadow of Golgotterath, rising serene and cancerous from the great grey bowl of the Occlusion.

She hung for what seemed a desolate season, thinking, *Is this what it feels like?*

She convulsed about a scraping inhalation.

Is this how it happens?

The end of the World.

The Ordeal barnacled the intervening terrain, canvas shanties clustered about the Occlusion's roots, fanning like spackle out across the flat tracts of the Shigogli. She could see Schoolmen stalk the heights about the perimeter. Across the desolation beyond, she could see the plumes of war-parties encircling the monstrous fortifications ...

And the Horns ... She could see the *Horns* ... the eldritch gleam.

Just as she had read.

"*We have come to judge him, Mother.*"

Initially, she overlooked the figure stumping up through the dark below the malevolent vista. She instantly recognized him when she did spy him, though heartbeats would pass before she could countenance her recognition.

He had grown old and skinny after all. So very different from the plump fool she had loved.

He recognized her as well, slowing. He stumbled as if besotted.

The smile came unbidden, like something older and wiser. She came to her feet, brushed her gown out of some numb need for dignity. She wiped her eyes out of fury.

He advanced, but slowly, as if dreading the detail the Nail of Heaven would add to his wild outline. With every step, he more resembled the madman her spies had described to her.

Drusas Achamian ...

The Wizard.

He hobbled close, his face inscrutable. The reek of him tainted the air.

She struck him, bloodied the lips hidden beneath the wire excesses of his mustache and beard. She raised her arm to strike him again, but he caught her wrist in a hermit fist, wrestled her into his embrace. They slumped together into the dust. He smelled of earth. He smelled of smoke and shit and decay. He reeked of things both whole and frail, of everything the Andiamine Heights had stolen. She wailed into the stink of him, somehow knowing that after this night, she would never weep again.

She heard Mimara shouting—at the Pillarians, she realized.

Her daughter's arms slipped about her shoulders. Jasmine. Myrrh. Her belly pressed warm and taut across her back ...

Esmenet, Accursed Empress of the Three Seas, wondered at the prod of a fetal kick. And she *understood* ... With a clarity and finality she never would have thought possible, she understood.

She belonged to *them*. She belonged to them now.

The ones that could love.

CHAPTER TWELVE

The Last Whelming

*Not all arrows miss an enemy unseen, but no arrow hits an enemy
unknown.*

—Scylvendi Proverb

*Before birth there is conception, and before conception there is maturation,
and before maturation there is birth. Thus the light passes from brand to
brand. For souls are naught but torches that burn as time and place.*

—Five Apprehensions, HILIAPOS

Early Autumn, 20 New Imperial Year (4132, Year-of-the-Tusk), Golgotterath.

All nations differ in their prosperity. The zenith of every people is a thing
distinct, the product of custom, belief, and expression imperious to the degree it contradicts those of its neighbours. It is *ruin* that divests them of luxury, *ruin* that strips away the florid dividends of power and ingenuity.
Suffering, be it war or famine or pestilence, grinds nations into a common
meal. The lamentations of the one are the wails of the other.

Thus they had come, the nations and peoples of the Three Seas, bound
by common prayer and insignia, yes, but taking haughty pride in their distinction all the same, what set them apart from their fellows. So the Ainoni
lords painted their faces white and scoffed at the silver masks donned by
their Conriyan counterparts. So the Galeoth laughed at the beards of the

Tydonni, who ridiculed the Nansur for their smooth cheeks, who derided the Thunyeri for their unruliness, and so on. Thus they had come, the Southron Kings of the Three Seas and the Middle-North, each the Son of an ancient and elaborate heritage, each hailing from cities fat with artifice and decadent age. Thus they had come, proud and debauched, their origins flashing brilliant in their carriage, their garb, and their armaments, each the distinct flower of a different soil.

Thus they had marched beyond the Pale of Men, across the trackless leagues, wandering so very far from home—in all ways.

A nightmarish transit ... as much *descent* as crossing.

And so they had reached the Furnace Plain having passed through the furnace of Eärwa, a kind of human plunder, an assemblage of ancient relics, heirlooms, broken up and melted down, re-forged into something unlike anything the World had ever seen—*recast*. Accursed, where they had been blessed. Damned where they had been saved. And *one* where they had been many.

A *new* people, grim for witness, fierce for desperation, pious for hunger, their ornament cast away, their garments stained by the soils of a thousand lands, their armaments scavenged from dead kinsmen. A monochrome nation, born of demented months instead of placid ages.

The night following the Great Letting, the Holy Aspect-Emperor went to each of his most illustrious commanders, sounding their hearts in seclusion. He offered no pardon for the atrocities they had committed, nothing that might dull the horror in their hearts. He spurned their protestations, begrudged them their beseeching. He had come to them in fury, harsh in edict and impatient in audience. According to rumour, he even struck Earl Shilka Grimmel, who could not cease his lamentations. Of all the sins, *unmanliness* had become the most egregious.

Tomorrow, he told them, the Schools would be loosed, and the Ark would be stoked as an oven!

"And when it is naught but a gutted hulk," he grated, luminous beneath sagging canvas, "we shall take what remains of our blasted hearts ... and *return home.*"

And in the breathless aftermath of his visitations, the Southron caste-nobles wondered at the strangeness of that word ... wept for it.

All Men yearn for home.

Mother and daughter led Achamian to the Empress's chamber in the Umbilicus. Their reunion was fraught, as charged with disbelief and gratitude as apprehension and injury. Reuniting souls once bound together amounts to the coupling of interlocking wounds, the pressing of scar to scar, scab to scab. So when Esmenet first refused to intercede on behalf of Proyas, Achamian presumed she nursed some grudge that only understanding and patient explanation could overcome. His every glimpse of Mimara heavy with child stabbed him, after all. He reasoned the same glimpses afflicted Esmenet with the outrage corresponding to his shame.

But the more he implored her, the more the fact of Proyas's straits clawed bubbles from the mud of his belly. Esmenet affected an attitude of forbearance reminiscent of their arguments in Sumna: the wilder his worry for Proyas, the more profound her pity for Akka. She had seen *thousands* "slung," she said, especially in Nilnamesh after Akirapita's first successes fomented rebellion. Men so bound and suspended never lasted more than several hours, strangled from within by the weight of their own bodies. "He's beyond everyone, now," she said, her cruelty as sharp as her glare. "You can't save him, Akka. No more than you could save *Inrau*."

Mimara had argued with him up to this point; now she looked at him with the wide eyes of a lapsed confederate.

"I'll simply take him then!"

"So what?" Esmenet cried. "Save him so you might die together?"

He felt so very old in that moment.

Both women watched him with sorrow and apprehension now, even more alike for gloom and the convergence of passion. Despite their damaged angles, they saw *one and the same man*, he realized. They *knew*. The urge to tear out his own beard bubbled from the edge of his fingertips.

The burden was too heavy.

"Akka! The *World* is our object now ... We recline in the shadow of Golgotterath!"

The toll too high.

Too much.

"*The very shadow my boy dies in!*" he cried, his heart overburdened, his senses swollen with imaginings of Proyas's anguish. And he was on his feet, barrelling through leather flaps, canvas halls, heedless of the women shout-

ing behind him. And then he was outside, in air too rank to impart liberation, beneath sky too grey to belong to day or night, *and the image of it
knocked him to his knees.*

Golgotterath.

The sun already smoldered from the heights of the Upright Horn, and
as he watched, the first sliver of diurnal brilliance lanced from the tip of
the Canted. The static flotsam of shelters and the bare miles of the Shigogli
lay jaundiced in a false dawn before him.

He doubled over, retched for the cancerous intensity of the gold, lay
braced on all fours and still falling, blinking at strings of spittle ...

Small hands set about each of his arms and pulled him with embarrass-
ing ease to his feet.

"Only *I* can save him," the Blessed Empress of the Three Seas said, plac-
ing her forehead to his temple. "I'm the only traitor my husband has ever
suffered to live ..." She looked to them with wonder and apprehension
both. "So far."

The little Prince-Imperial jerked upright on the tolling Interval, clutched his
cheeks for disorientation. The chamber was commodious but crowded. The
area about his cot was small, enclosed by leather panels on his left, and hedged
by heaps of stores and belongings on his right. Then he remembered: the
bitch Mimara had come back, and they had stowed him with the baggage.

Awakening has a curious way of bequeathing what has come before, of
granting ownership to events too tumultuous to be grasped in immersion. They
had *fled* the ruins of the Andiamine Heights, raced across the very abdomen
of the World, and he had reeled for dismay and terror and regret throughout. He had simply lacked the wind to fully reckon what had happened.

Now it seemed as though breathing were his only capacity.

We have lost this game, bro—

No!

At first he sat dejected, a rigid shell about silent, shrieking disputations.
Someone would come, he told himself. Someone *had to come*, even if only
a guardsman or a slave! He was *a little boy* ...

Nothing. No one.

His lantern had guttered through the night. Light pricked bright through a single seam across the ceiling and dull along the top of the outside wall. It was more than enough for *his* eyes, far brighter, in fact, than the bowel of the Andiamine Heights. He undressed, laid out his Amoti tunic—the crimson one chased with fine ropes of gold—across the cot. Then he took it up and dressed as if it were new. He wept for hunger.

He was *little*!

But nothing happened. No one came.

He sat on the corner of the mattress for a time, his heels kicked out, listening, sorting through voices, *searching*. Purchase—he needed some *purchase* on the catastrophe that had engulfed his World. On the Andiamine Heights he had always known beforehand when something was happening. He would lie warm and drowsy, savouring the way space and activity could bloom from the merest trickle of sound. Haste would clip the lazy sounds of routine, purpose would cinch the murmur of gossiping slaves, and he would make a game of guessing the nature and object of all the preparations. The Umbilicus differed only in the freedom the membrane walls afforded his prying ears. In the palace, marble and concrete had forced every clink and whisper to crowd the gilded corridors. Here, he need only close his eyes and the leather walls became as lace, transparent to the scratching, piping sounds of the souls who occupied it.

Silence became ranging space, emptiness animated by scattered pockets of solitary and collective industry. Two souls bickering over the lack of water. Meerskatu, Exalt-Captain of the Pillarians, giving perfunctory instructions. Someone hammering in the great cavity of the audience chamber.

He caught a voice murmuring, "*Which one?*" from a nearby chamber, somewhere to the rear of the great, rambling pavilion.

It was the *reverence* more than the servility that seized his attention.

"*The wolf's head ...*" a second replied.

Where the first voice had been youthful, its Sheyic marred by the barbaric twang of the Eumarnan coasts, this second was more seasoned and assured, possessing a lilting Ainoni accent that had been filed down by long years in the Nansurium. Both were hushed, overawed even, by the presence of a silent third ...

The little Prince-Imperial bolted upright, clasped his shoulders tight.

Father was here.

In a panic, he probed the murk for any sign of Mother—the bouquet of sounds he knew best of all, cherished above all the World's clamours.

Did she sleep?

Had she fled?

You did it! You chased her away!

No ...

She *had* to be somewhere near—*had to be*! He was her darling boy! Still just *little ...*

"Good," the second voice said. "*Now pass me the brush.*"

The sound of vigorous whisking. In his soul's eye Kelmomas could see *Him* standing motionless, his arms held out, while a murky body-servant stooped to brush the hems of his felt vestments.

"Father ..." he dared coo in the gloom. "N-no one comes for me."

Nothing.

Something like a little monkey claw clenched the back of his throat. He scratched his face.

"Father ... *please!*"

We're just little!

The rhythmic susurrus of brushing fabric continued uninterrupted, so like the slaves brooming the expanse of the Scuari Campus.

The traitors within the little boy made riot of his heart. Tears scorched his eyes. He coughed about an irresistible sob, blew spittle across the dark. A kind of feline keening prised open his mouth—

Forsaken! Abandoned and betrayed!

An then his father, the Holy Aspect-Emperor, said, "*The Believer-Kings assemble.*"

The brushing stopped.

"*You will attend your brother and sister.*"

Then resumed, now quick with wonder and terror ...

"*Heed them, Kel.*"

The sound of a slave attempting to vanish into the task assigned to him.

"*They know the nature of your crimes.*"

They set out across the predawn expanse of the Shigogli together, the mirror brilliance of the Incû-Holoinas lighting their way. Once they reached the Accusatory, the Blessed Empress would simply command Proyas be cut down. Once again, Mimara refused to relinquish her accursed trinkets, and so prevented him from walking them across the sky.

"Aye!" the old Wizard cried in mystified outrage, clawing the empty face of the sky. "Lest we *sa*—!"

"Look!" Esmenet cried. The finger of the Accusatory lay visible in the distance, still in the shadow of the Occlusion—a fact that made the faraway blue-white flare of Gnostic sorcery more visible ...

"Swayali," Mimara, the keenest eyed among them, said.

The old Wizard cursed the inevitability as much as the fact of it. The presence of Swayali meant that he indeed could do nothing without the Blessed Empress of the Three Seas. His thoughts raced, bubbled like the white upon ferocious waters. He began pacing a small circle, explaining, in what seemed a reasonable way, how he and Esmi could go ahead—

"And what?" Esmenet cried. "Leave your pregnant wife to waddle across Shigogli *alone*?" She whirled to Golgotterath in diminutive fury, crying, "Have you forgotten *where we are!*"

Drusas Achamian did scream at that point, his voice as ragged as papyrus fetched from the inferno. He roared at the empty tracts, at his predicament, and at his confusion, the utter absence of clarity, above all.

The two women watched scowling, then Esmenet turned to her daughter, her expression blank, and both erupted into laughter. The old Wizard stood gasping, staring in horror, determined to glare away their outrageous behaviour. But they closed upon him, foul heap that he was, hands squeezing, arms hugging tight, and suddenly he was laughing as well, cackling like an old loon, sobbing for relief, for gratitude, to find himself so beset by those he truly loved ...

A memory of the old vitality rose through him as a perfumed vapour. He extricated himself with the nodding air of men recovering their wits, if not their courage. "Let's see if he still lives," he said, at last admitting the possibility Esmenet had been arguing all along.

His sorcerous voice rose as mist about them. He saw the light of his mouth spark white in their beautiful eyes. With outstretched palms he oriented the sorcerous Lens toward the famed Himonirsil, the Accusatory, taking heart, the way he always did, in the demonstration of his power. A circular distortion fastened upon the distance and miraculously brought it near—showing the very thing his eye had sought, the very *terror* ...

Proyas hanging nude ... a thing like wet garbage, rubbish pulped and glistening ...

And *breathing*.

A deeper shadow fluting his flank, slow and steady ... indisputable.

Achamian gasped, cried, "*Sweet Seju!*"

"Kellhus hasn't ... *hasn't slung him*," Esmenet said, transfixed by the image. "See ... How the rope about the waist runs to his elbows? See the weight it bears? He wants Proyas to *live* ... not to die."

This occasioned a shared look, a recollection that there were no accidents here.

"To *witness* tomorrow's battle?" Achamian asked. "To show him the righteousness of his cause?"

Esmenet slowly nodded. "That's better than the other option."

"What other option?" he asked.

Mimara stood with her hands upon the white bulb of her abdomen, somehow more aware and less invested than either of them. "To *suffer*."

But the Blessed Empress of the Three Seas frowned. Like himself, Esmenet was not so quick to assume her husband *wicked* in addition to ruthless.

"No. To *lure* us ... remove us from the Great Ordeal."

This scraped a dagger point across Achamian's sternum.

"Why? What happens today?"

Esmenet shrugged. "The Great Ordeal makes ready ..."

Void brushed his stomach.

"How?" Mimara asked from his side.

"The Lords of the Ordeal are to gather in the Umbilicus to accept his benediction this afternoon," she said, looking from face to face. "He's calling it the Last Whelming."

The Son of Harweel watches himself turn to see himself watching as he navigates the crowds about the Umbilicus, at the very moment the Mandate Schoolman paws his arm.

"How-how—" Eskeles stammers, "how have you kept, your Glory?" The man isn't simply skinny, he's emaciated, but his smile is every bit as mealy as before. "I would have sought you out upon your return, but ... but ..."

Such a lonely little flute ...

He has been.

Eskeles, frowning as he and Mu'miorn laugh at his poor, belaboured pony. He reaches out through the milling crowds, clutches his elbow and says, "How have you kept, your Glory?"

Such a lonely little song ... a bewildered wail upon the abyss.

"I would have sought you out upon your return, but ..."

Sunlight flares and flared. The White-Luck Warrior frowns, then grins in recognition, saying, "This land eats manners." They embrace—something in the Schoolman's manner demands it. He looks past the *leuneraal*, sees himself kneeling before the Holy Aspect-Emperor, leaning forward to kiss the mountainous knee, the ancient pouch palmed in his right hand. The black sails of the Umbilicus encase the infinite blue.

"That motif ..." Serwa says, "the triple crescent ..."

"What about it?" he asks, tingling for the proximity of her gaze to his groin.

At last her eyes climb to meet his own. Her look is cool, remote in the way of old and prideful widows.

"That is the Far Antique mark of *my* family ... the Anasûrimbor of Trysë."

He turns to find himself encircled by damned Ordealmen, walking with the shrunken corpse of Eskeles, who says, "I would have sought you out upon your return, but ... but ..."

The Lords of the Ordeal howl in terror and incredulity.

The White-Luck Warrior grins, awaiting what has already happened. He glimpses the Son of Harweel watching him, mere heartbeats away.

What was a lonely wail has become a mighty chorus. His breathing lover ignites his flesh, makes a votive of him for the Dread Mother.

"This land eats manners."

Anasûrimbor Serwa had come unannounced, dressed in flashing ceremonial billows, trailing a Pillarian who bore a lantern and a joint of horse roasted the previous evening. Kelmomas immediately fell upon the meat, made like a dog sitting cross-legged on the mats, while she strolled about Father's baggage, scrutinizing him with shameless intensity.

"Did you murder all of them?"

Kelmomas spared his sister a melancholy glare, then fell back to his meagre repast.

"Only Sammi," he said with his mouth full.

The spare edge to her appearance was new, but not much else, save perhaps the bruising about her eye and a vague air of ... desperation, perhaps. Serwa had always been remote. Even as a young child, she'd always managed to express a certain grandiosity of image and character, effortlessly expressing a feminine noblesse that other girls her age could only ape. The battlefield, the little boy realized with no little annoyance, had honed that into something almost mythic.

"But then, not really," she said.

"No ... Not *really*. All I killed was his meat."

"Because you believe *you* are Sammi."

"Father knows. Father knows I speak the truth. And Inrilatas did too!"

"But Mother ..." she said, letting her words hang rather than asking an honest question.

Chewing. Swallowing.

"Blames me for everything. Inri. Uncle Holy. Even Thelli."

His sister visibly bristled.

"What do you care?" he cried.

"We are as crazed as cracked *plates*, brother. Our hearts are not bowls. They cup no compassion." She approached, becoming more the Grandmistress of the Swayali with every step, and less the girl who had so studiously ignored him ever since he could remember. "But our *understanding*, little brother. Our intellect! What we lack in compassion we recover in *sanity* ..."

He gazed at her for several placid heartbeats then fell back to his greasy repast. "You think me mad, then ..." his said, stuffing his mouth. "Like Inrilatas."

She resumed her arbitrary inspection of Father's stores. "Inrilatas was different ... He confused transgression with Godhead."

"And what of me, Grandmistress? What is my madness, then?"

Her reply terrified for being instantaneous. "Love."

The boy concentrated on the shanks glistening across his plate. Even meat had its own Unerring Grace. He exhaled slowly ... as slowly as he had exhaled while spying on the Narindar in the Andiamine Heights.

His sister continued. "Mother is forever beyond you now, Kel. Do you understand?"

He continued staring at his horseflesh, lest the will to murder breach his pouting facade—lest his grand and ruthless sister see.

"She plotted Father's murder," he said, more to vandalize her insufferable self-assurance than anything. "Did you know that?"

Serwa looked at him carefully. "No."

"She lies beyond Father now."

You giving too much away! Samarmas cried.

Serwa's eyes lost focus for but a single heartbeat, then returned as iron nails.

"And you think you can regain his affections because of this? I know you're not such a child as you look."

The Prince-Imperial continued gazing at his horsemeat, fairly trembling for the savagery of his fury—all of it, so plain for his sister to see!

The Grandmistress of the Swayali crouched before him. "You are precisely as Father says," she said, her face slumber blank. "You love our mother as a human boy would, but your scruples and attachments are Dûnyain in every other respect. Mother's love is your *sole study*, the only mission you could possibly pursue. All the World is but an instrument, a means to dominate her passion for you ..."

The boy glared down, chewing as loud as he could manage. He could feel her watching, a presence malevolent for being so angelic, so ruthless.

"You are a creature of darkness, Kel, a *machine*, even more than they are."

Now that was funny.

What does she mean? Samarmas asked.

The World had yielded too decisively too many times for him to be cowed by a cow's assessment of him ...

He looked up to her, trusting the purity of his hate to wipe the slate of his expression clean. "Can you *smell* them?" he asked. "Our sister and the Wizard?"

Serwa graced him with a small grin of sibling triumph, then popped to her feet with an ease that reminded him of her greater speed and strength. Humouring her little brother, she closed her eyes and breathed deep, striking a profile that was at once beautiful and weak.

"Yes ..." she said, her eyes still closed. "So she simply wandered in from the Wild?"

Kelmomas nodded about a gargantuan swallow. How ravenous he had been!

"As quick with child as that tapestry from the Feast Hall."

Serwa fixed him in her cold gaze.

"Is Father at all *concerned?*" the boy pressed. "She says she's come to *judge* him."

"Mimara was always mad," Serwa said, as if pointing out a mountain with no passes on a map.

She terrified him for a premonition of *altitude* at that moment. Was this what rendered souls inhuman, the hitching of too many cares to things too vast to resemble the particulars of life? Too much resembling God ... As Inrilatas had said.

"What do you think Father will do with me? Lock me up like Inri?"

She pursed her lips in thought, or the simulacrum of it.

"I don't know. Were it not for Mother, he would have had Inrilatas put to death—or so I think. Kayûtas disagrees."

"So he would kill his *own son?*"

His sister shrugged. "Why not? Your gifts are too fearsome to be trusted to the whim of passion."

"So *you* would have me killed?"

She paused, awaiting his gaze. "Without hesitation."

Something seized and twisted his innards; something like *reality*, as if everything had been just another nasty game up to now ...

What would death be like, I wonder.

Shut up!

"And Kayûtas? He would have me killed as well?"

"I have no idea. We are rather busy."

He affected the pose of a glum child. "You resent this, having to attend me?"

"No," she said in a distracted voice. She set aside the blanket once again, allowing her eyes to linger. "I trust Father."

"You would trust a father who would murder his own son?"

Her gown whisking, she occupied the position directly before him, glared down in her mild and damning way. Light winked across the golden Kyranean wings—the root of each blooming from the tip of another—embroidered across her billows.

"You imply I shouldn't trust Father because Father doesn't love," she said. "But you forget we are Dûnyain. Common *purpose* is all that we require. So long as I serve Father's ends, I need never fear or doubt him."

Kelmomas tore a mouthful of meat from the cold joint, chewed while staring up at her. "And *Proyas?*"

The name caught her like a hook. He knew very little of what had transpired upon their arrival—but he had guessed enough, apparently.

"What of Proyas?" she asked.

"Some ends wreck the tools that accomplish them."

An air of renewed appraisal tainted her look.

You show too much.

Let her see. Let her see how sharp a knife her little brother can be.

"So be it," the famed Grandmistress of the Swayali said.

"You would *die* for Father?"

"No. For Father's *end.*"

"And what is his end?"

She paused again. Of all his siblings, the little Prince-Imperial had always found Serwa the most inscrutable, even more so than Inri, but not because of the Strength. She saw neither so deep nor so far as he—but she remained fairly impossible to read nonetheless.

"The Thousandfold Thought," she replied. "The Thousandfold Thought is his end."

Kelmomas frowned.

"And what is that?"

"The great and terrible design that will deliver the World from this very place."

"And how can you *know* this?"

Yes. Be relentless ...

"I cannot. I can only *know Father*, know the peerless glory of his intellect."

"This is why you would render up your life?" he cried with naked incredulity. "Because Father is *smarter?*"

She shrugged. "Why not? *Who else* should guide us, if not he who sees the deepest ... farthest?"

"Perhaps," he said upon a swell of pride, "we should chase our *own* ends."

A pained smile. "There is no better way to remain *small*, little brother."

Unless, the once-secret voice said, *one compelled the very World ...*

Curiosity darkened her expression.

"Samarmas ... He really *is* there inside you."

Kelmomas dropped his gaze to his plate.

She was genuinely wary, now, he could tell, though no single sign betrayed it.

"You are mistaken, Kel, if you think you *own* the ends that impulse brings yo—"

"But I *do* own my ends! How ca—?"

"Do you now? Why then this *interrogation*, little brother? *What is your end*, pray-tell?"

Anasûrimbor Kelmomas stared down at his greasy thumbs, the flecks grey tissue, white fat.

What *was* he attempting to accomplish?

His sister nodded. "Desires arise from the darkness, the darkness that comes before. They *own you*, Brother. To indulge in them is to exult in *slavery*, to make blind appetite your mas—"

"Better a slave to the Thousandfold Thought?"

"Yes!" she cried, invested at last. "*Better a slave to the Logos*. Better a slave to that which delivers *mastery* over life!"

He glared at her, quite dumbfounded.

Clever bitch!

Shut up. Shut up.

"And *that* is why you would kill me," he cried heedless, "becau—"

"Because you know no end that is not our Mother."

He stared at the meat in his hands, the scorched extremities, the pink nearer the bone, layered like torn pudenda. It seemed sorcerous, the way the bone and cartilage gleamed.

"And if I *make* Father's end my own?"

He resumed gnawing.

"You have no command of your ends. You are like Inri in that respect."

He swallowed, sucked at his teeth.

"So I should resign myself to death then?"

The illustrious witch scowled. "I know not what Father intends. Perhaps even *he* doesn't know, given Golgotterath and the Great Ordeal. I fear you are the least of his cares, little brother. A mote, merely."

Apparently the World was about to end.

Yes! Don't you see? We have time!

Shut up!

Time to make amends!"

"And if you were in my straits, Sister, what would *you* do?"

Her look harrowed for its indifference. "Fathom our Father."

And it was a testament to their blood, the fact that she need say no more, for their blood had been the answer all along.

The little Prince-Imperial resumed chewing.

Two triunes of Nuns guarded the Accusatory, one occupying the heights, the other the broken terrain below. Achamian need not conjure another Lens to know the witches observed their approach with great interest.

Rather than approach from below, they climbed into the Occlusion, picking their way through the black basalt ruin of the Arobindant. Her husband's followers, Esmenet explained, had difficulty enough respecting her when she towered over them, let alone when she called up from gullies. But the climb, which appeared straightforward from below, proved taxing, especially for Mimara. The old Wizard's heart almost leapt from his mouth glimpsing her totter upon the slopes, her arms dancing out for balance, her belly a great pear.

"*Why?*" he could hear the Scylvendi snort. "*Why have you dragged your bitch across a thousand screaming, rutting leagues?*"

The Nuns most certainly knew he was a sorcerer, for his Mark was deep. But they made no sign of preparation as they scaled the final approach. They had cast their own Lens, after all, and so knew full well the Blessed Empress accompanied him.

Achamian hauled Mimara, who still looked miraculous for being clean, onto the gravel shelf with him and her mother. The promontory's root lay immediately above them.

"Let *me* do the talking," Esmenet said, though the old Wizard had no idea why she shot *him* the warning glare. "If I could have *surprised* them," she added, "I'm sure they would have ob—"

A feminine call in the near distance cut her short, followed by a disjoint chorus of sorcerous mutters. The three of them scrambled onto the levelled foundations of the Arobindant's ancient citadel, saw the Swayali triune arrayed some thirty cubits *above* the back of the Accusatory, their eyes and mouths flashing white, their billows *unfurled*, so that curlicues of golden fabric snaked through the open spaces about them ...

Esmenet cursed, gawking the same way Achamian and Mimara did.

"So much," the old Wizard muttered, "for occupying the high ground ..."

The image stupefied. The Accusatory pointed exactly as the legend said, not so much to the Canted Horn as to the Upright, vast and gleaming, a great golden axle for the desolation wheeling out about it. The Swayali witches hung as though pinned upon the monstrous tableau, their silk still shining despite months of insult, blooming like stalkless flowers, meaning glowing hot from their mouths and eyes.

Achamian turned to Esmenet, who seemed to be mumbling what she was going to say. He clutched her forearm, saying, "*Wait* ... Esmi ..."

She turned to him frowning.

"If Kellhus wished to ... to kill you ... to kill *us* ..."

"Then what?"

"I ... I could think of no better way than this!" Away from the encampment, where he could concoct any exonerating tale.

She smiled as if at his naiveté, drew two fingers from the height of his cheek down through his wiry beard.

"I've lived with him for twenty years, Akka. I *know* my husband."

"Then you know this could be a trap!"

She shook her head in gentle negation, seeming to see too much, the way she always had, of the desperate contradictions within him.

"No, old fool. I know that he needs no traps to murder the likes of you and me."

And then she was off, matronly in the white silk occasion that had been hemmed to fit her frame. He began shaking, understanding ... at last, that Esmenet, far from taking the easy road, had suffered more losses, that out of all their souls, hers was the most numb—the most capable. And he continued shaking, even after Mimara clutched his shoulders and waist, for it seemed nothing less than a miracle watching Esmenet stride thus, beneath the flowering threat of the Swayali, into the deeper lunacy of Min-Uroikas, walking as though *she* were the World's only terror ...

"They will not harm her," Mimara said, her voice hollow, her eyes as rapt upon the Blessed Empress as his own. "But neither will they heed ... We have come all this way for nothing."

"How can you know?"

Lightning sparked between the cerulean clouds snared upon the Horns' heights, and they stiffened, the old man and the woman.

"Because that's what she believes."

To live is to starve for want of the eternal.

The black sails of the Umbilicus swallow them, but the crowd does not abate within the Eleven-Pole Chamber. And the Son of Harweel can see it in every harrowed face about them, the *famine*.

"I'm sorry," Eskeles begins, "about ... about Zsoronga ..."

"We have all thrown love upon the funeral pyre ..." the young King of Sakarpus replies. "We have all made sacrifices."

The Schoolman looks uncertain. "You *understand* then ..."

"He was his father's wager."

Eskeles bows his face, acknowledging the wisdom. "As are we all, my young King."

"Indeed."

To live is to witness the rotting of instants and nothing else. To *be* the decay of presence, the forever failing light. Life is the damnation that anticipates damnation.

And now that he has outrun life?

"Such times!" Eskeles exclaims. "I can scarce believe ..."

He has become he who follows his following.

"How do you mean?"

The coming after that comes before ...

"To dream of the Apocalypse as we in the Mandate do, then to wake up and ... and witness the selfsame horror ..."

His every breath the most miraculous throw ...

"Golgotterath."

The White-Luck.

Terror. Servitude. Worship.

These were the wages of the Strength.

Anasûrimor Kelmomas stood some five paces to his Father's left, Serwa behind him, her hands resting on his shoulders in the simulacrum of comfort. The Lords of the Ordeal filed through the entrance to their right, fanned across the earthen floors to take their place on the tiers. They had the look of bandits, soiled to the pore and long-hunted by vengeful authority, cutthroats dressed in the plunder of more subtle castes and nations. Almost all of them gawked at the sight of him upon entering, and many continued glancing in his direction long after sitting. Some nodded and smiled in recognition. Others scowled in worry. And still more gazed at him in lingering horror, or worse yet, *yearning*. He found the attention oppressive, even terrifying—enough to weld his gaze to the cancerous image of Golgotterath through the broad rent in the western wall.

He understood why they stared. He was the first child any of them had seen in a year of arduous travel. What was more, he tokened their own children and grandchildren, the *home* they had thrown so far over the horizon. This was why Father had commanded his presence: to example what these Men had come to save—to make meat of what they had forgotten.

Kelmomas marvelled at the machination. He had almost forgotten how absolutely his father commanded these Men—the fathomless depths of his dominion. The Believer-Kings had come to make display of their fidelity and devotion, to secure their oh-so-mighty Lord-and-Prophet's blessing before the assault upon Golgotterath. They had come to be fortified and fortified they would be. But not a soul among them could hope to fathom the primary end of this gathering. If the Holy Aspect-Emperor harangued them, he *scrutinized* them more, assessed their reliability, so that he might know where best to use, to exploit ... the way Kelmomas himself was being used, exploited.

The hard work was about to begin. The tools must be inspected.

Kelmomas clutched opposite folds of his white-silk tunic, stricken for insight. All this time he had thought his father merely a stronger version of himself, someone who could do more of what he could do. Not once had he considered that Father could do things he could never hope to, things he couldn't even *think*.

Perhaps anything ...

The Holy Aspect-Emperor of the Three Seas strode from blackness to light, stepped before his bench. A golden nimbus hung miraculous about his head—and about each of his hands as well, which he raised in benediction and prayer. Despite the gloom of the Umbilicus and the overcast sky, he was somehow bathed in the light, his white-and-gold vestments bright unto squinting, the folds scored by shadows angled to an unseen, mid-morning sun.

"*Fathom our Father ...*" Serwa had told them.

The collected Believer-Kings and their vassals fell to their knees across the tiers. After a pinch from his sister, Kelmomas lowered his eyes to his feet. The Umbilicus rumbled to the chorus of warlike voices, a sound as deep and ancient as the sea. And they all seemed apes in the shadows, carnival wags, compared to their Holy Aspect-Emperor—even Serwa. *All of them* groped and thrashed in the black—save Him.

Save Father.

We were overweening ... Sammi whispered.

Yes. Greedy.

They had always been overmatched. He could see it so clearly now.

"Praise," his father boomed into the high-sagging hollows.

"Praise be the Meta-God."

Toying with the worldborn was no measure of his Strength. Any fool could command a kennel. The episode with Inrilatas had shouted as much, especially the ease with which his brother had seen through him—seen through *them.*

No. He would do what he should have done from the very beginning, what his elder siblings had done: transform himself into a *tool*. He would make himself useful ...

To survive, at first. Then to thrive ... perhaps even conquer.

And Mother? She had squandered her utility (as her absence now argued), fumbled whatever confidence Father might have had in her. Even her womb was barren! Let her fawn over her whore-daughter. Let her mewl and cling! She had become *cheap*. An aging bauble, something to be forgotten—traded for drink and song! Or even *given away*, should her wits grow addled ...

We will accomplish something mighty! Prove our Strength!

Yes ... Yes!

Then she would learn—the stupid bitch! Errant *cunt!* When even the slaves balked for cupping her drool, bathing her delicious secrets, for washing the rank shit out of her sheets! *Then* she would see, and she would love—love *as she should*—and caress and hold and say, "Oh, Sweetling, please-please-please forgive me!"

Yes. It seemed so clear watching the caste-noble cattle low about Father's long knife.

She will be our prize.

⟨ ❦ ⟩

"Ishma tha serara ..."

The menacing congregation rose at their Lord-and-Prophet's bidding, forming a bowl of expectant faces across the back of the Eleven-Pole Chamber. The contradiction of it tugged the child, the pathos of once strong souls frantic to recover decorum, dignity, and the grim aura of invincibility belonging to those who have survived unspeakable trials. They seemed at once ghosts, creatures of smoke and rumour, and an assembly of iron ingots, indestructible. The Eleven-Pole Chamber had suffered parallel indignities, what given the rent western wall, the scavenged lanterns, scabbed leather and rotted canvas. He recognized the two carpets banding the interval between them and the Lords of the Ordeal, for he had cartwheeled their length many times when they had lined the galleries of the Imperial Audience Hall. He knew they had been ornamental once, a lavish pictorial retelling of the First Holy War—the story of how Father became holy—but now they seemed of a piece with the blasted ground, the dirt of Golgotterath, their vivid imagery trammelled into stains.

"*You ...*" Father began. "Embattled. Weary."

The Sons of the Three Seas watched rapt as children.

"I ask you ... What miracle has brought us to this place?"

Absorbing even the questions.

"What miracle has brought us to the very end of Men?"

Proyas! Kelmomas silently japed.

"Ages past a knife was cast," Father said upon inaudible, yet palpable, thunder. "A knife was cast across the Void, tossed glittering in the black, sailing gulfs we cannot imagine before finally striking here. *Here.* It cracked the underworld spine of Viri, great among the ancient Nonmen Mansions. It threw up the mountains of the Occlusion, and cast out a fire that ignited the very sky above us, and all the skies surrounding ..."

Kelmomas craned his head about to spy his father, and found himself ensnared, by the mad profundity of his Mark, by the crisp glory of his felt vestments and white-silk robes, by the *haloes* about his hands and his head ...

"But the knife itself was not destroyed," Father said. "Intact, it began leaching its poison. A venomous thorn, thrust deep into the breast of Being, an infected tusk goring ours ... the Holiest of Worlds ..."

The long tails of the Ekkinû, the ensorcelled arras suspended behind his father's chair, waxed bright for no explicable reason. The boy glimpsed the mouths of the Decapitants masticating, as if the one murmured into the ear of the other ...

Serwa's palm upon his cheek pressed his face forward.

"For Ages we have bled, pierced, impaled. For millennia we have been *sickened*, and we have marked the passing of our Ages according to the wheel of our fevers. Whole civilizations have convulsed about its intrusion, first the Nonmen of yore, Cu'jara Cinmoi and his Ishroi, and then the Men of the Ancient North, the fury and might of my forefather, Anasûrimbor Celmomas and his Chieftain-Knights."

Kelmomas exulted hearing his ancient namesake—of course Father wanted him here! He embodied both home and *history*. Serwa had spoken true: there was *meaning* to be found in Father's dominion. Why had he always hated and feared him so?

Because he could see the game we were playing with Mummy.

"Both those great Kings stood, as we stand now, on these awful plains. Both raised arms and perished in the shadow of this *place*."

Because he scared us ...

"For want of God," his father said.

The warlike assembly erupted into a tempest of raw voices. Shouts. Cries. Murderous declarations. Men leapt to their feet across the tiers. And Kelmomas could *feel* it, the way they each vibrated as strings on his father's loom. For the first time, it seemed, he understood the beauty, the symmetry between his malformed soul and faith.

Yes! Samarmas exclaimed. *Father! Father!*

I will give myself to him! I will give myself to him and he will see! See that we're true!

It was so clear, the fool he'd been. Nothing save Father's distraction had afforded him his games. Such *Strength!* This was what these gulls celebrated, though they knew it not. The *mastery* of their master! Their own enslavement!

"We suffer no such want!" the Most Holy Aspect-Emperor boomed and the Lords of the Ordeal roared their affirmations, stamped their feet and brandished their fists in furious martial display.

"Mog-Pharau awakens—even now *the No-God stirs*! Even now, the Enemy congregates about His carcass, shriek tongues fallen from the Void, performs rites ancient, lewd, and more evil than any sinner can imagine. Even now the Consult beseeches Him!"

And the little Prince-Imperial fairly cackled for glee. There was *fun* in this! How could he have been blind to this, the *game of games*? And what was the difference between saving and *pocketing* the World?

"Aye, my brothers, *we are the bulwark*. I stand where Cu'jara Cinmoi stood. I stand where Anasûrimbor Celmomas stood! Ancient, obstinate souls. Proud. Domineering. I gaze upon *you*, my noble stalwarts, souls grim for slaughter, bright for vicious ardour, the way they gazed upon their most violent champions."

Father's voice resonated, thrummed and growled across registers that none save Kelmomas and his sister could hear, tones that plucked each according to how he had been tuned.

"And I say to you ... *We shall succeed where they faltered!* We shall smite the ramparts! Kick down the wicked gates! We shall raze the fell bastions! Crack open the citadels! We shall descend upon the Unholy Consult in *righteous* fury! For! We! Have! God!"

Men who had been battered blunt now roared on the keen edge of outrage and hatred, their eyes flashing as bright as razors.

"For between us we have gathered a Host *unlike any the World has seen!* A Host of Hosts for the God of Gods, the *Great Ordeal!* We shall seize our foe by his throat, cast his corpse from the golden heights!"

The Southron Men swayed and shouted and gesticulated, and the boy's eyes once again ranged out across the plate of Shigogli, to the *Horns* soaring into the woolen gullet of the sky. *Such a game!* he thought, blinking tears.

For once his brother was not cruel.

———— ∞∞∞ ————

Father stood immobile, not so much basking in the fanatical adulation as somehow *measuring* it, somehow urging the Lords of the Ordeal to redouble their howling demonstrations *without the least perceptible sign.* And then, somehow, he was *waiting*, and the chorus dwindled and sputtered, before trailing into silence altogether.

"You ..." he said, his voice at once cryptic and conversational. "It all lies with you."

He clasped his hands before him—a curiously disarming gesture.

"Last night I wandered among you. Many of you greeted me, enjoined me to partake of the comforts of your abode ... such as they were ..."

The rumble of laughter from the tiers. Father had trained them thus, the young Prince-Imperial realized.

"But I did not seek out the company of the great alone. I also walked among the camps of our vassals, those with mighty *will*, if not blood. I came upon an Ainoni, a youth named Mirshoa"—he turned the Believer-King of High Ainon—"one of your brave boys, Soter."

"That depends on what he said!" the Holy Veteran cried in reply.

Another swell of deep-chested laughter.

The Holy Aspect-Emperor wagged a finger and smiled. "He told me the story of his cousin, Hatturidas ..." He looked from face to face.

"You see, Mirshoa joined the Ordeal out faith as Zaudunyani, to save the World, where his cousin had joined *to keep Mirshoa safe* ..." The Aspect-Emperor trailed, seemed to hold his breath for every soul in the Umbilicus. "And as far as he was able, Hatturidas fulfilled his charge, battling at Mirshoa's side every encounter, risking his pulse time and again to save his beloved cousin's softer skin. And Mirshoa would wonder at his ferocity, for he thought *himself* righteous, the way all souls think themselves righteous, believed that he warred for the God, *that he fought for me* ..."

"And yet, here was his cousin fighting *harder ... for him* ..."

He allowed the concrete of this to set in the hearts of his audience.

"So I asked him why he thought that was." A rueful grin. "Verily, it's not often that an Ainoni is at a loss for speech ..." Another prolonged rumble of laughter. "But finally, Mirshoa told me how his cousin, Hatturidas, had died at Dagliash, felled by a javelin in the Battle of the Shore. Losing his cousin, he said, had *halved his heart*, showed him how he had been *fighting for Hatturidas* all this time, and not me ..."

His father turned as if envisioning young Mirshoa standing next to him. "*Bold*," he said, beaming admiration. "The way he stood. The way he spoke! Daring me—aye, *challenging me*, to deny him ..."

An interval of suspense, exquisitely timed to the syncopations of a hundred hearts.

"I did not," the Holy Aspect-Emperor conceded. "I could not. For he had spoken the truest words I heard last night ... Indeed ..."

His father looked down to his palms, and the haloes burnished the Kyranean intricacies of his beard. The boy could swear he heard the collective heartbeat of the congregation *slow*.

"The truest words I have heard in a long time."

The Lords of the Ordeal growled solemn affirmation, sobbed for their own fallen kin.

Serwa inexplicably squeezed his shoulder, and he craned his face back and upward, following her gaze to the shadowy spaces about the entrance ... where he saw *Mother*, her hair pinned severely back, wearing a priest's white occasion hemmed to her diminutive form. Kayûtas held her by the arms, but the new Exalt-General proved no match for the Blessed Empress of the Three Seas, who simply barged past her eldest son, whispering furiously as she did so. Kelmomas fairly chortled. Mimara followed in Mother's wake, looking preposterous for her girth, scanning the booming interior with anxious eyes. An ancient beggar hobbled immediately behind her, one blasted by the Mark. Kelmomas wriggled against his sister's grip in an attempt to follow his mother's passage after the intervening throngs engulfed her, but his sister conceded him nothing.

What happens?

More madness ...

As if to confirm his appraisal, Father abruptly folded his legs upon the bench, and *floated* ... a mere hand above the cushion at first, and then a cubit forward, so that he hung as something iron in the open air ... and using no sorcery that Kelmomas could see! All shadow steamed from him, so that he was *perfectly illuminated*, an image impossibly crisp, save for the two black smears hanging from his waist. Suddenly the reality surrounding seemed a bruised fruit.

"**What miracle?**" the Holy Aspect-Emperor of the Three Seas asked, his voice tickling the cavities of the ear. "**What miracle *has delivered us to this place*?**"

Not a soul among them could say what word their prophet was about to utter, and yet each, the boy realized, had prepared to receive it.

Father shook his head and smiled, blinked tears for these fools he so loved. He held forth his gold shining hands.

"*Each other*."

Shouts exploded across them, mouths howling from beards, eyes spilling for tears, faces reddened, fists closed and raised as hammers. Praising. Blessing. Cursing.

"**Because of you—*you*!**" his father's voice cracked godlike through the uproar, "**I know *Golgotterath shall fall in flames in ruin*! Because of you, I know the Unholy Consult shall at long last be broken! That Mog-Pharau, Tsurumah, shall be preempted—*stillborn*! By your individual will, individual might, *the End of Days shall be forestalled*!**"

This place.

And they shook and they heaved, the lost Southron Men, wild with renewal, with fury and hope ... until their apish stink became all but intolerable.

Kelmomas fought in vain for some further glimpse of Mother through the mobbed Lords of the Ordeal. Like dogs overanxious for the touch of their master, they had been slinking forward one by one, abandoning the tiers for hard ground, or the step above for the step below—almost as though they understood without knowing what their beloved Warrior-Prophet would demand of them next. When Father finally called, "Come to me, my brothers, and be *Whelmed*! Let *my hands* be the basin that cleanses you!" they fell over one another for naked urgency, imploding into a jostling ball that the little Prince-Imperial found both comic and revolting. Again he peered at the entrance, leaned forward and back in another futile attempt to find Mother, but Serwa flicked his ear—*hard*—saying, "Decorum!" on a harsh whisper.

But she too was gazing toward the entrance by this point. He studied her meditative profile against the bickering throng of Kings and Grandmasters. Before he could query, she was already kneeling beside him, somehow recalling the doom hanging over his head with a single sharp look. "Stay ... *put*," she murmured, then left him, withdrawing behind the Ekkinû arras and hastening around to the entrance ... So she might assist Kayûtas with Mother?

He could barely suppress his chortling. He quite *liked* the thrill of occasions such as this, he decided. The untoward always intervened—did it not?—no matter how great the Strength ...

No mastery was complete. Every act was a wager, even those belonging to Father.

We were such a wager ... the voice whispered.

Yes.

The caste-nobles who yet loitered on the bottommost tiers had taken to singing, some hymn the Prince-Imperial had never before heard. The words caught like sparks on tinder, and soon the whole chamber thundered.

The purple tempest, drowning brown and birthing green,
The darling rumour, revealing love that cannot be ...

The eight-year-old turned to regard the hanging emanation that was his mighty father, His Arcane Holiness, Anasûrimbor Kellhus I, Aspect-Emperor of the Three Seas, his shoulders arched back, his knees wide, his wrists balanced on his knees, the whole of him bright with otherworldly light. The boy's stomach bubbled for the way he simply floated—how he could so effortlessly contravene the shackles that bound the monkeys cavorting about him. That he could so *dwarf* the Sons of Men!

Even now, he throws the number-sticks.

Yes.

He watched a savage version of Lord Soter kneel then lean forward to kiss Father's right knee. Kelmomas strained once again for some glimpse of Mother or Mimara, but he could see nothing through the screen of bobbing torsos. He turned back to the pack of noble dogs vying before him, feeling, for the first time, the glum of boredom. And then he saw *him* ...

A balm to my heart, a lamp to my feet,
Guide me, O' Saviour, to the place I might sleep ...

There, naked in their midst, bold unto absurdity.

An Unbeliever.

———— ∞⟩⟨∞ ————

Any moment is but a snag upon a thread in a boggling weave. This is why the White-Luck Warrior is *dead*, even though this present moment continued to breathe. This is why the moment-once-called-Sorweel walks to himself the way one might walk toward a door. Life is but a mote compared to what comes after. To be Eternal is to be dead.

Eskeles is quick to smell the possibility of benediction, so the moment-once-called-Sorweel is already on the floor when the others surge to queue. They stand, singing the same booming hymns as the others. Patience absent all effort. Eskeles is joyous with bloodlust—the soft fronds of his character have been pulled away from his religious barbarism. "I have *never forgotten*, your Glory. I have never forgotten that it was *you* who saved me ..."

"Neither have I," the moment-once-called-Sorweel replies.

Time eats the queue's numbers; they draw closer. The moment insists that his companion precede him in the queue. Eskeles makes fatuous protestations, but is too careless to conceal a kind of miserly glee.

They approach the floating Demon, soul following soul, like beads about to be unstrung. The moment-once-called-Sorweel sings with the others. Eskeles is like a trembling curtain, his hair is so wild. The moment-once-called-Sorweel only stands revealed when the Schoolman kneels.

The Demon regards him.

The air cracks and hisses, such is the intensity of its hunger.

The Demon smiles.

It consumes the offering Eskeles has made, but it is displeased, the way it is always displeased, by the extremities of the man's passion. It thanks him for the long starvation that has made him thin, counsels as well as blesses, recalls the virtues of intellect, the false power of the Logos.

Then Eskeles is stumbling into nonexistence, and the moment-once-called-Sorweel is kneeling *directly before the Ciphrang*, breathing deep the sweet scent of myrrh. The infernal Decapitants hang askew, each angled against the other, the Zeumi so low that its stump twirls upon the carpets. The long tails of the Ekkinû frame the Invader, gold braided about black bearing the endless descent of writhing *text* that no one save he and the Demon can read. The shadow of the Sickle draws over all.

"Blessed be Sakarpus," the Unclean Spirit intones, its voice pitched so that the others might hear.

"Eternal Bastion of the Wild. Blessed be her Most Heroic King."

The moment-once-called-Sorweel smiles in gratitude, but not for any word the Abomination has spoken. The pouch slips from the sleeve, falls to the fingertips. His head bows forward as his hands raise to grasp the infernal knee, gently, the way a warlike uncle might touch the cheeks of a weeping niece. The Lords of the Ordeal sing and make bellicose demonstration. The pouch is tipped. The lips rise to the kiss. The Chorae slips into the right palm.

The Demon is aware—an irrevocable heartbeat.

The right hand closes about the knee.

The World is light.

The moment-once-called-Sorweel is blown back into his astounded peers.

The Demon is salt.

The Mother shrieks, "*Yatwer ku'angshir ciphrangi!*"

The Lords of the Ordeal are screaming, and the daughter sees him, sees what the Blessed Mother hath wrought. Her *gift* to Men.

At last the sorcerous fire combs him free.

Anasûrimbor Kelmomas scowled for peering. The man stood at the milling root of the impromptu line that had formed to receive their Holy Aspect-Emperor's blessing. Tall. Fine-featured. Blond hair once cropped for battle, but now grown into a greasy tangle. Beard and mustache thickening from juvenile haze. Eyes every bit as blue as Father's, and more so than his own.

The boy turned to Father, searching for some reassurance, some sign that he too had seen, but he was preoccupied, muttering low words of encouragement to King Narnol, who had just kissed his knee. Kelmomas could see nothing of Serwa or Kayûtas, but through the singing he heard some old man cry "*Proyas dies!*" from the quarter where he had glimpsed Mother.

Even though Father did not so much as glance in the direction, the boy imagined He tracked it with a precision that eclipsed his own.

Kelmomas stood rigid, followed the Unbeliever's progress with naked incredulity. The man was of an age with Inrilatas, even though he looked older for the onerous toll exacted by the trail. He wore the raggish remnants of a Kidruhil uniform emblazoned with the insignia of a Field-Captain, but he bore himself with the posture and bearing of a caste-noble. He sang with the others, acknowledged all their looks and pious asides, but in shabby token only, like a mummer who had come to despise his craft.

> *The little hand that does not doubt the great,*
> *The sweaty brow that does not flinch for hate.*

The Prince-Imperial began jumping, so desperate was he for some sign of his sister or brother.

> *A balm to my heart, a lamp to my feet,*
> *Teach me, O' Saviour, so that I might weep.*

Father remained absorbed by the souls kneeling before him. Even still, the boy saw him glance across the train of petitioners on occasion ... Surely he had set eyes upon the man numerous times. Surely, he had seen!

He knows, his brother whispered. *He humours him to some end.*

Perhaps ...

It was the sheer audacity that most confounded the little Prince-Imperial, the way the traitor—for he could be nothing else—cared so little for the observation of his fellows. It was a contempt that would have made him seem daft, even imbecilic, were it not for the way everyone remained utterly oblivious—including those with the Strength!

But does everyone humour him?

His brother had no answer.

Something is wrong.

Mother gives.

Mother *yields* ... strangles and suffocates.

The White-Luck Warrior need look ahead to see her.

"Sometimes, Sorwa," she coos, "a hunger from the deep breaks free."

He sits on her lap, his one leg folded, his other dangling. He is a little boy. The sun glares across the verandah, across tiles fired in ancient Shir. The air is so clear an eye can roam to the very Pale. His father still lives.

"A Ciphrang, Mama?"

A stork watches from the balustrade, white as pearl.

"Yes. And like a bubble in water, it rises ..."

"Seeking us?"

She smiles at his fright, blinks in the slow, lazy way of dying invalids and drowsy lovers.

"Yes. They take us ... take us to *take*, to feed their hunger."

"And that's why you struck me? Because it wasn't ... it wasn't *you*?"

Welling tears.

"Yes. I was-wasn't myself ..."

She clutches him tight, and they sob as a single soul.

Weeping makes one.

He bawls, "*Get-it-out-get-it-out-get-it-out!*"

She presses him back, smiles against her grimace. "Oh, Sweetling! I wish I could!"

"Then *I* will do it!" he savagely declares.

Eskeles, the sorcerer who was once fat, kneels before him, revealing the moment.

"I will do it, Mama!"

The Demon smiles.

"Oh, Sorwa," she cries smiling. "Oh my, darling little Prince!"

You already have.

"What ails you, Little Prince?"

Lord Sristai Croimas had lurched before Kelmomas as if from nowhere, so intent he had been on the dilemma of the Traitor. Croimas was Conriyan, one of those sycophantic souls who instinctively exploited all the possibilities of ingratiation, to the point of wooing slaves and children—the very inversion of his famed father, Sristai Ingiaban, by all accounts. Kelmomas found it amazing the man had survived the Great Ordeal's transit, given the stories, yet here he was, skinnier beneath his hulking mail and plate hauberk, bearish for the lack of grooming and the surfeit of black hair, and no more the wiser for his tribulations.

His breath reeked of rancid meat.

"You have lost much, I know," the man said, apparently referring to what had happened in Momemn. "But what you are about to witn—"

"Who is *he*?" Kelmomas interrupted. "That one. The young Norsirai behind the starved Schoolman ... There ... the Kidruhil Captain."

No small part of him *wanted* the traitor to notice his pointing and thus his scrutiny, and so abandon whatever game he thought he was playing. But no.

"That is King Sorweel Harweelson," Lord Croimas replied, turning back with a friendly scowl. "One of the most celebrated souls amo—"

"Celebrated?" the boy snapped.

The friendliness dropped from the caste-noble's scowl. Eastern oaf that he was, Croimas was not one to suffer youthful impudence. "He saved your sister's life," he said in a tone poised between flattery and reprimand. "And a whole fraction of the Ordeal aside!"

The Prince-Imperial persisted in peering around the fool.

"He alarms you?" the Palatine of Kethantei asked.

"Yes!" Kelmomas cried in exasperation. "Can *none* of you fools see?"

"What is there to see?"

Malice.

What's happening?

I don't know! I don't know!

Lord Croimas stood upright with the paternal air of rescinding a gift given. "After your father blesses him, I will call him over."

Kelmomas further insulted the fool by pressing him to the side, out of his line of sight. The Son of Harweel was now but two souls back from Father ... Kelmomas swept the Conriyan Lord and everything else from the plate of his attention, aimed his every sense, his every fraction, at the Traitor ... until he was all that could be heard, all that could be seen or pondered ...

The Son of Harweel possessed nothing of the anxious excitement that so animated the Men about him. He did not sweat. His heart did not palpate. He did not breathe, as so many others did, from below his clavicles ...

There was an air of ... *routine* about him. In a queer way, it almost seemed as if the novelty of what happened, let alone the enormity, left him entirely untouched.

His eyes did not dart, but remained fixated on the image of his Holy Aspect-Emperor, gazing with ludicrous confidence—and with a naked hatred.

Young Anasûrimbor Kelmomas understood Sorweel Harweelson was no mere traitor ...

He was an assassin.

I'm afraid, Kel ...

Me too, Brother.

Me too.

The Sickle has fallen. The Demon is salt.

The Demon smiles in false greeting, saying, "Blessed be Sakarpus, Eternal Bastion of the Wild. Blessed be her Most Heroic King."

The White-Luck Warrior looks up, sees himself kneel, lean forward to place his lips against the abomination's floating knee.

The Demon is salt. The Lords of the Ordeal are screaming.

He glances over his shoulder, sees himself—*as it happens*—joyous and exultant, crying out, "*Yatwer ku'angshir ciphrangi!*"

He stands in queue, patiently awaiting what has always already transpired, knowing and knowing and knowing ... Soon the Sickle will fall.

A thronging wall of Believer-Kings, Chieftains, Generals, Palatines and Earls, Grandmasters and their advisors all but surrounded them, leering and cadaverous. For several taut heartbeats, Kelmomas peered at Father in his periphery, his leonine profile imperious, at once proximal and remote. Judgment incarnate. The air thrummed for deep-throated song ...

> *The light that does not shine but reveals,*
> *The sun that leans gentle upon laden fields.*

Would that Kelmomas could scream it away, strike all sound and motion from the brawling carnival before him. From his position, the great rent in the westward wall and ceiling of the Umbilicus framed the head and shoulders of the petitioners. He could see only the canted Horn, shining morose in the sunless distance. The assassin's profile lingered beneath it for several heartbeats, obscuring sepulchral fortifications. It happened quickly, so quickly that none could have seen it save Kelmomas ...

A stork, angular and pristine white, flitted across the opening ... great wings wide.

What?

It was a glimpse so unexpected, so incongruous, that it could only refocus his attention on the immediate.

> *A balm to my heart, a lamp to my feet ...*

Kelmomas saw the starved Schoolman in front of the traitor stand and depart, drawing a crucial fragment of Father's care with him.

> *Teach me, O' Saviour, so I might finally weep.*

The Son of Harweel stepped forward and fell to his knees in the man's place, gazed up at his miraculous Lord-and-Prophet, his lip hooked in contempt, his eyes shining for lunatic *hate*.

Father hailed him—*welcomed* him as another Believer-King!

Anasûrimbor Kelmomas, the youngest son of the Holy Aspect-Emperor, glimpsed a hand clutch in concealment, saw a pouch branded with three sickles fall from a sleeve ...

Mimara is done with talk. They have been stranded at the congregation's shadowy perimeter all along, arguing first with Kayûtas and now with Serwa, peering at the glowing heart of the assembly from where the light failed.

"Enough!" she cries over the chorus of singing Lords. She has never liked Serwa, not even when the girl was a wobbling toddler. Mother would ceaselessly chide her for treating a mere child as a rival, but Mimara always knew that some part of Mother understood (or at least feared) her daughter's animus.

They were never quite *human*, her siblings. Always somehow *more*, somehow *less*.

And now here she is, Anasûrimbor Serwa, resplendent in her billows, a grown woman—a *Grandmistress*! The most powerful witch the World has ever known. And it *irks*—all the more for being petty. Irks that she's taller, by a hand at least. Irks that she's *clean*. Even the way her beauty cuts against the ferocity of her Mark irritates.

"We go *where* we will *as* we will!"

"No," Serwa responds terse and remote. "You go where *Father* wills."

"And Mother?" Mimara snaps. Mother was implacable when it was simply Kayûtas confronting them, but her resolve has wilted since the arrival of Serwa. "What of *her* will?"

"What of i—?"

"Father *will* receive you," Kayûtas hastily intercedes. "You need only *wait*, Sister."

How absurd he looks decked in their uncle's insignia and mantle—how tragic and corrupt!

"Have you *both* taken leave of your senses?" she cries—with enough violence, apparently, to earn Mother's wary hand on her forearm. "Proyas *dies*!"

she shouts for a second time, her voice brimming with disgust for it. "*Even as we speak!*"

This silences them, but they remain stubbornly planted in their path nevertheless. When Mimara makes to barge around, Serwa seizes the crotch of her arm.

"*No, Mim,*" the witch says firmly.

"What?" Mimara cries, yanking her arm free. "Are we not *Anasûrimbor*, the same as you?"

"*You* never believed so."

Mimara glares into her sister's eyes, all her prior resentments twisting like sparks in the smoke of her fury. How could she not be jealous? The daughter raised in pampered splendour and the daughter sold to slavers. The daughter tended, enabled, and the daughter neglected ... the daughter perpetually denied! She had been the prize of the brothel, the Empress! Allowed to pick and choose her abusers like suitors. That was the one thing Mother could never understand, the way she had been *condemned* by her rescue, a trampled weed replanted in the World's most glorious garden, her blood thick with caste-menial mud, always outwitted, always outshone by her golden brothers and sisters. How could she not be *ugly*, incarcerated on the Andiamine Heights?

How could she not be so obviously ... *broken* ...

She glares up into Serwa's face, struck yet again by the heinous profundity of the witch's Mark—as deep as any sorcerer of rank despite her tender years. A peevish instinct clamours for the Eye to open so she might *see* her younger sister's damnation ... and she recoils in horror from the thought.

Was any family ever so deranged, so insanely convoluted, as the Anasûrimbor?

She glimpses the bones of the Whalemothers, vertebrae in the dust, ribs heaped like broken bows.

Mimara suddenly laughs, not in any shrill, defensive way, but in the manner of those stumbling across glaring absurdities hiding in plain site. Why bandy words with Dûnyain? She surprises her witch-sister, brushes past and throws herself into the warlike mob beyond. Perhaps it isn't such a curse being the sole weed in the garden, the one soul broken. There is nothing they can do, no harm they could inflict, that she hasn't already endured—short of killing her.

And *that*, she knows, the God will not allow.

She answers to a higher power.

Heedless, Mimara barges through a gallery of masculine shock, of towering, warlike Men, unwashed and armoured, making way agog. They yield, it seems, as much to her pregnancy as to her paternity or sex, astounded by the sight of something so bound to hearth and home, to the hidden world of bullied or cherished wives, arising *here*, in the fearsome shadow of Golgotterath.

Serwa cries out and curses close behind. She seizes Mimara's shoulder just as she pushes clear the intervening caste-nobles, into the circuit of her step-father's light. The Swayali Grandmistress tries to spin her about, but Mimara resists ...

Together, they bear witness to a scene chiselled from Scripture. Lords and Schoolmen watch, some solemn and rapt, others cracking for passion, and still others singing, their heads back, their mouths merry pits in unruly beards. Her *step-father* floats cross-legged within their circle, illuminated from all angles, draping folds of the purest white, a plate of luminous gold shining behind his mane. A young Kidruhil officer, Norsirai, kneels before him, about to clutch and kiss the Imperial knee. And Kelmomas *moves* from his place beside his sire ... so fast as to scarce be seen ...

Gazes turn in singing faces. A knife is plucked from nowhere, agleam with reflected light. A leap ... unnatural for any human child.

Kelmomas lands with his back to his handiwork, immediately before Mimara and Serwa, his stance impeccable, the blade now missing from his hand.

Mimara catches the boy's gaze, even as the kneeling Norsirai jerks and sways behind him.

Murder ... is Mimara's singular thought. Serwa cries out *with real horror*, bolting past their littlest brother to the slumping Kidruhil officer. Shouts of alarm and dismay swallow the booming hymn. She glimpses the pommel jutting from the youth's temple the instant before her sister obscures the mortal image. Kelmomas turns to follow the astonished line of her gaze.

She knows Serwa loves the man ...

Then, impossibly, *he* is standing before her, the Holy Aspect-Emperor of the Three Seas. Her Mother's all-powerful husband, close enough to touch, and as always, taller than she remembered. He holds Kelmomas kicking and squirming beneath one arm. "*He was an assassin!*" the little boy is shrieking. "*Father! Father!*"

And in her soul she screams, *Open! Open! You must open!*

But the Eye refuses to listen. It is as stubborn as she.

And her step-father's mortal blue eyes *see* ... before waxing sudden, shining white.

Sorcerous muttering sets claws upon every surface, visible and invisible.

Lightning brilliance. And the Holy Aspect-Emperor is gone, leaving her blinking at the chaotic convergence of Men surging forward, the Lords of the Ordeal.

"*Breathe!*"

Her sister's shout?

Mother clasps her shoulders, crying out, staring at her feet.

"*Mimara? Mimara?*"

She looks down, craning to see past her belly, sees her shins and calves glistening, the dust soaked black. Only then does she feel the flush of heat and wet across her thighs and feet.

The first of the pangs strike, the clench and cramp of things too deep to be her own. It was too early!

She grunts in shock, cries out.

Proyas is dead.

Her mother has her.

Her mother has her.

Sorweel topples. The earth bruises his cheek. Blood spills as if from his ear.

Life is famine. To draw breath is to starve for want of past and future ... to suffocate.

He twitches prostrate across the rugs. The Lords of the Ordeal cry out astonished. He glimpses the Triple-Crescent Pouch through the trample of booted feet, sees it kicked into stamping obscurity, back into the nowhere from whence it came. He struggles to raise his cheek, but his head is an iron anvil.

To witness the rotting of instants and nothing else. To *be* the decay of presence, the forever failing light.

He has always burned as he burns now. The onlookers rush forward, a congregation of concerned shadows. Through fire, the beautiful witch watches him appalled. Serwa. She cradles his head upon her lap, coos reassurance, commands ...

"Breathe."

The Mother is bounty ... birth ...

"He is dead, Pri—"

"*Breathe!*"

The Mother is the bearer of all ...

"*Breathe, Horse-King!*"

Warm arms. A cradle of sunlight. Fields whisk endless and nubile green. The earth *aches* for monstrous fertility.

"*Sorweel!*"

A feminine humming ...

"*You must breathe!*"

Rising horrific from his bones.

Shush.

Shush, Sorwa, my Sweet.

Set aside the hammer of your heart ... the kite of your breath ...

Cease your work ... your play ...

I have you, Sweetling.

Doze in my holy arms.

CHAPTER THIRTEEN

The Occlusion

To spy your enemy from afar is to spy the very thing he is blind to: his place in the greater scheme. To spy yourself from afar is to live in perpetual fear.
— DOMILLI, *Rudiments*

Early Autumn, 20 New Imperial Year (4123, Year-of-the-Tusk), Golgotterath.

Surfaces vast and gold soared and plunged about the Inchoroi, who appeared sepia for reflected light, like something carved from an apple. He hung out from one arm, clawed feet braced against the Horn's impenetrable skin, so high his lungs ached for the emptiness of the air. Though he had been Grafted for this world, the frame of his body remembered its distant womb, or at least held fast some portion of it. His soul, however, recalled nothing of his origin, unless solace could be called recollection. He *dreamed* it on occasion, especially when novelty had commanded his day, as if all those ancient experiences, hidden as they were, remained essential to his understanding. But he could never remember these dreams. He knew only that *contentment* hummed deep within, hanging thus, stirring him to wonder at worlds with thinner air.

He was old, aye, so ancient as to be broken into multitudes by the Ages. Glorious Iskiak, Spear-Bearer to mighty Sil, the great King After-the-Fall. The legendary Sarpanur, celebrated King-Healer, the great Killer-of-Hells. The infamous Sin-Pharion, reviled Plague-Bearer, the Soul-Most-Hated ...

Aurang, the accursed Horde-General.

He remembered their hallowed vessel faltering upon the shoals of the Promised World, and the Fall, the Inertial Inversion Field piercing the crust to the pith, gouging the landscape, heaving it out upon a cataclysmic hoop, raising mountains to retard their descent ... just not enough.

He remembered the Weal that followed, how Sil had rallied the Holy Swarm from the brink, taught them how to prosecute war with the remnants of their once-dread Arsenal. Sil had been the one to show them how they might still save their eternal souls!

He remembered enough.

So many incarnations, so many *ages* labouring upon the brink! And *now it happened* ... at last, after uncounted millennia, the piling of years so numerous, the past could only be crushed into Law. So very soon!

Even from such heights, he could smell the shit of Men on the wind. He could see them plainly enough, smeared across the rim of the Occlusion, another Ordeal, come to break tooth and claw upon their Sacred Ark.

And he knew the sweet, sweet fruit they would pluck. He had wandered far over the plains and mountains of this World prosecuting Resumption. His soul had flitted through all the greatest cities of Men; aye, he knew well the pig fatted for the feast. The humid brothels, where the oils were both scented and bewitched. The temples, gilded and immense. The vast babble of the markets. The slums and alleyways, where gold was daubed in blood. The teeming streets. The cultivated plains. The soft-skinned millions awaiting their delicious ministry. The squirming. The screaming ...

The whirlwind walking, vast and black.

And his phallus hooked high across his strapped abdomen, a bow strung for war ...

And glory.

Each clasping an arm, Achamian and her mother hustle her from the uproar of the assassination into the partitioned rear of the Umbilicus. Appalled and appalling faces slide by, some gawking, others turning aside. Thighs she cannot see are slicked. Her feet skid and squish in their sandals.

No-no-no-please-please-please-no!

"What happens?" Achamian cries under his breath.

"The baby comes," Mother says, intent on steering them clear the looming Lords of the Ordeal.

This is the answer Mimara can tell he expects, yet he sputters in disbelief. "No. No! It must be something—food, maybe. Rancid horseflesh, per—"

"*Your baby comes!*" her mother snaps.

They trot through flaps, down a gloomy corridor. Mimara can feel them like straps so very deep within, muscles cinching, cramping, screaming ...

"Mimara ..." Achamian cries, genuine panic in his voice. "Perhaps if you vomit?"

"Fool!" her mother curses.

But if anything, Mimara shares the old Wizard's incredulity. It cannot be. Not *now*. It was too early! This *couldn't* be happening now! Not on the stoop of the Incû-Holoinas—Golgotterath! Not with Proyas hanging from the Accusatory, leaking like a waterskin. Not when they stand within a toss of completing what they had set out to do!

Judging *him*, Anasûrimbor Kellhus, the Dûnyain who had conquered half the World ...

She does want to vomit, but for the idea of delivering a newborn soul—her *first child!*—to such straits, to such an evil time and place! Had any cradle been more ill-omened, more terrifically malformed? But it happens nonetheless, and as appalled as she is—cannot but be—an invincible *calm* dwells within her, a corporeal conviction that *this one thing is true* ...

A life lies within her ... and it must out.

They cross the antechamber where she had first found Mother, press into the bedchamber beyond.

Must and gloom.

"Per-perhaps ..." the old Wizard stammers as they ease her onto the mattress. "Perhaps we-we could try ... try ..."

"No ..." Mimara gasps, grimacing in an attempt to smile. "Mother is right, Akka."

He leans stooped over her, his face slack and ashen. Despite everything they have endured, never has she seen him more terrified, more broken.

She clasps his hand instinctively. "This too is part of what happens ..."

It has to be.

"Think of it as a *Cant*," Esmenet snaps, fussing over pillows. Mother fends her own dismay and horror, Mimara realizes ... over the murder they had just witnessed.

And the fate of her mad little son.

"Only blood instead of light," the Blessed Empress huffs, raising a cool, dry palm to her forehead. "Life instead of ruin."

—⟨⟨⟨⟩⟩⟩—

There was violence to his Translocations—Malowebi could tell as much by the flurry of light and shadow—and yet experience insisted that *he had not moved at all*, that the very World had been torn down and reassembled around him, plank by plank, in the twinkling of an eye.

So it was the shouting turmoil of the Umbilicus fell away as a page turned, revealing the nocturnal barrens of the Shigogli, which also fell away as leaf bound to a common spine, returning to the encampment, only higher on the slopes, before the entrance of a sagging pavilion, one with panels like leopard skins for mouldering discolouration.

The little Prince-Imperial wailed as they plunged into the black interior. The Anasûrimbor conjured light with an indecipherable murmur, inking the evacuated interior in blue and white.

"His *face*, Father! I could see it on his face! He w-was going to-to assassinate, *assassinate* you."

Malowebi spied a great screw hook anchoring a set of rust-pitted shackles to the barren centre of the floor.

"No, Kel," the ever-hanging shadow said, pinning the child to the ground next to the plate. "He loved me the same as the others—more than many, in fact."

The cherubic face was swollen for injustice and incredulity. "No-no ... the *hate* ... You *had* to see it, Father! Why do you pretend?"

The Holy Aspect-Emperor had crouched such that Malowebi could see little more than his hands deftly manacling his son's ankles and wrists. It almost seemed he caressed fluttering shadows, so intense and artificial was the contrast between light and dark. Great veins inked across tendons. Tiny hairs aglow.

"So much raw ability," the occluded presence said. "All of it yoked to darkness."

"It was there! The hate was *there!*"

Anasûrimbor Kellhus stood erect, and Malowebi watched the boy bolt back in his shackles, his innocence too pale, too raw for a demonstration so bestial.

"You are a fascinating child."

"You're going to kill me ..." A wild, flaxen maul about a face of anguished rose and sniffling pink. Wet blue eyes sparking for the dismay of the unloved and betrayed. "You're talking the way you would if you were going to kill me!"

"You believe the one speaking is Kelmomas," the Holy Aspect-Emperor said, "and that the one whispering is Samarmas, not realizing the two of you continually trade places."

The boy watched as blank as a thing of sugar—and as fragile.

"You *are!*" he gurgled as much as screamed or wheezed. "You are! You're *go-going* to kill me!"

The occluded presence stood inscrutable. A clenching in the passage of time.

"I'm not convinced there's anyone to kill."

The Anasûrimbor stepped into a wider stance, rolling Malowebi along his thigh.

"Look-into-my-my-face!" the little Prince-Imperial cried, reaching out as if to catch a slamming portal.

Metagnostic singing—still pinching the Iswazi sorcerer despite the absence of living ears. Reality vibrated like sand on a drum-skin, a sound that blew through the drooped ceilings, echoed as rain through shuttered windows.

"My-my *face!* Pleasssee. Daddy. Look into my face, *please-Daddy-please!* You can-can seeee! Serwa *convinced* me! I serve yo—!"

The Cant of Translocation cut the darkness along a different set of angles, made a shadowless plate of the little boy's face, glutinous for remorse, bright for sneering—

Then the page turned and everything was different, and Malowebi alone remained unmoved.

———— ❦ ————

Drusas Achamian mooned about the entrance to the leather-walled chamber, fear clenched like an anxious fist in his breast. He found breathing difficult. His heart had become rot and slurry—something beaten for merely beating.

Simple *being*, it seemed, had become a question.

How had it all come to this?

Agony seized the beloved voice, held it high upon a screech, then smashed it into hacking shards.

"It hurts ..." Mimara gasped from the mattress. "It *huuurts*!"

She shrieked again.

She lay naked and gleaming, a soiled sheet across her mountainous abdomen. Her shadow writhed as she writhed, drawn long across the chamber ... like a *spider*, Achamian could not help but think, black, elongated limbs flexing about a black, bulbous thorax.

"Too much!" she cried in the spasm's wake. "Some-some-something is wrong, Momma! It hurts too-*too much*!"

Esmenet sat cross-legged at her side, daubed her forehead with a wetted rag.

"Nothing's wrong, my Sweet," she said, smiling as best as she could manage. "The first is always the most painful."

She drew the cloth down either cheek, and the image caught the old Wizard's breath, for on certain angles in certain casts of shadow and light, only their ages distinguished them, as if one and the same woman had been divided between times.

"Shhh ..." the Blessed Empress continued. "Pray this one isn't so stubborn as you were, Dewdrop ... I screamed for two days!"

Mimara grimaced—a smile, he realized. "Don't ..." she said about a huff. "Don't call me that!"

"Dewdrop-Dewdrop-Dewdrop ..." the Blessed Empress chimed. "I called you that when yo—"

"*Don't call me that!*" Mimara shrieked in abrupt fury.

It was her third such mercurial outburst, but Achamian started as violently as he had at the first.

Esmenet, however, scarcely blinked, continued smiling after catching her lips in a firm line, continued her soothing ministrations.

"Shush ... shush ... Let it pass. Let it fade."

"I'm s-sorry, Momma."

Something within him clawed and clamoured for escape. Esmi had demanded that he stay, that he *assist*, even though he had yet to do anything but wring his hands. "This is *your* doing!" she had accused. And he knew from her look and tone that she had only nominally forgiven him for loving her daughter. So he had stayed, and he had stood, watching mute, feeling for all the world like an earthen jug filled with ever more insects, his insides crawling as palpably as his skin. This was no place for any man, let alone one so old and as put upon as himself. These were *womanish* mysteries, too fraught, too pungent with truth, too raw and wet for the odourless, arid heart of a man.

Besides, *this wasn't even supposed to be happening.*

Mimara's breathing eased, then became inaudible altogether. Another long lull in the spasms had begun.

"See?" Esmenet murmured. "*See?*"

With the relaxation of suffering came the easing of obligation. Perhaps that was why it overcame him at that moment, the eye-rolling aversion, the irresistible urge to *shirk* ...

He fled, though he would never admit as much, batted aside the stamped leather flaps that passed for doors. The air was too close, he told himself. The sights were too delicate ... for a stomach so ... so *wet* as his.

He found himself outside, dizzy with guilt and confusion. The Horns climbed impossible in the nocturnal distance, the northernmost trailing a skein of clouds the way a stick might trail foam in a river.

Curse Esmenet and her sentence! Who was *she* to judge?

He leaned against his knees, breathing as if he *really* required the open air he had used to justify his cowardice. He need not see the two Pillarians to know they stood behind him—given the Chorae bound to their navels. They were omnipresent around the Umbilicus otherwise, garrisoned as they were adjacent to the grand pavilion and stationed throughout. It was the *premonition of the Mark* that drew his eyes upward, one deeper and more limned in errant peculiarities than any he had ever apprehended—including that of the Nonman King.

He saw a figure striding directly toward him from the shadowy mouth of an avenue. The old Wizard loosed a long, shuddering exhalation, warred with a far different urge to flee ... knowing. He stood upright, his breast a beehive for terror and incredulity, and watched *Anasûrimbor Kellhus* resolve from obscurity ...

The Holy Aspect-Emperor of the Middle-North and the Three Seas.

How long had it been?

He had seen the man thrice during the benediction and the subsequent uproar—three glimpses, merely, each a cold knife, so sharp were the pangs they sparked. For most souls, there's no arrangement, no clarification of charges, no enumerating of the accused or apportioning of the guilt. For most, gall is a kind of dwelling, a place where pangs and images resolve from the inarticulate gyre of outrage that has outlived its season. Most souls are illiterate, and so cannot hope to use words to pin the shadows racing across their hearts. And even when they can, they loathe framing their resentments with any clarity that might make them disputable.

Not so Drusas Achamian. For *twenty long years* he had practiced and prepared for this very moment: the words he would say, the pose he would strike, the stratagems that would reclaim his trammelled honour ... his ... his ...

Instead he found himself batting at his ringing ears.

No. No. Not like this.

Haloes, every bit as miraculous as Shimeh, like gold-glowing plates serving a sewage head and sewage hands. Achamian could scarce see the mundane fact of the man, so hideous was his Mark, so corrupt. He was taller than he remembered, dressed in the same white vestments as earlier, his golden beard squared and braided in the manner of the Far Antique Kyranean High-Kings. The peculiar pommel of his blade, Enshoiya, jutted above his left shoulder. The legendary Decapitants swayed gangrenous from his hip, bound to his nimil-scaled girdle by their hair. Eyelids twitched in deep sockets, revealing glimpses of glass, oiled and black. Ingrown lips masticated about teeth like black nails, as if murmuring.

Achamian shuddered, realizing that Kellhus *truly had fathomed the Hells* as rumour said. The floor of the World groaned, the joists of existence creaked, such was the *density* of his presence. Each advancing step fell upon his breast as much as upon the accursed ground, crushing the breath from his lungs ...

So much *power* so concentrated! Never had the World seen the like ...

And he, Drusas Achamian, had been the one responsible, the fool who had betrayed the Gnosis *to a Dûnyain!*

Twenty long years ago.

Anasûrimbor Kellhus came to a halt a mere four paces before him, a vision throbbing for memory as much as for arcane intensities. The Pillarians stationed at the Umbilicus entrance had fallen to their faces, and when Achamian failed to do the same, the nearer guardsman barked some threat he couldn't hear for the thunder in his breast and ears ...

The old Wizard stood gaping.

"You spoke with Saccarees," Kellhus said in ancient Kûniüric. No solic-itation. No jnan. "You troubled him."

"Not nearly enough," Achamian replied in numb kind.

The figure did not so much emanate light as refashion it into something worn at angles orthogonal to the World.

"You told him of your Dreams."

Achamian nodded warily. "As much as he would listen."

The pale eyes fixed him the way he remembered, as if he were a bauble hanging upon an abyss, not simply the last thing existing, but the only thing.

"Will you tell me?"

"No."

Anasûrimbor Kellhus had requested it, thus it must be denied.

"Your hatred has not waned."

"Cnaiur's lesson."

A heartbeat of bottomless regard.

"So he lives."

Dismay. The old Wizard's hackles pricked and needled, for he under-stood the folly of this encounter. There was no way to deceive the man be-fore him, no way to influence or outmanoeuvre. And the longer he stood inside the circuit of his inquiry, the more he would inevitably betray—even secrets he himself did not know!

It was axiomatic.

"I've seen Ishual," he said out of instinct, whether idiotic or canny he did not know.

The epic being before him paused, and for the space of a breath all the night seemed a glass for his preternatural scrutiny.

"So you know of its destruction."

Achamian nodded, swallowed, thought of the Qirri stashed with Mi-mara's belongings.

"I watched your *son* leap to his death."

A nearly imperceptible nod.

"Did anyone else survive?"

"I know what it means to be Dûnyain!"

The transformation was nothing short of miraculous: what was remote became warm and familiar, the smirk of a friend long accustomed to the irksome wiles of a damaged friend.

"To be ruthless?"

"No!" Achamian spat in sudden fury. "*Wicked!* An abomination in the Eye of God!"

A perplexed frown ... one that recalled Xinemus.

"The same as *you?*"

Achamian stared witless.

Kellhus abruptly turned toward the great pavilion's entrance, as if keen to something only he could hear. A fraction of the old Wizard balked at following his gaze, convinced this was but another accursed Dûnyain ploy, another way to rattle and misdirect, bewilder and dominate. But he looked regardless, his chin answering to an instinct more decisive than his nattering soul. The Pillarians remained prostrate, hunched like green and gold scarabs to either side of the once-ornate flaps. The flanking braziers lapped and sparked, indifferent. The leather planes of the Umbilicus climbed beyond their meagre light ...

And, like some miracle from the Tusk, *Esmenet* pressed through the shadowy cleft.

Her irked look immediately fastened upon Achamian, the truant soul she sought, only to be waylaid by the sight of her monstrous husband ...

Her right hand reflexively clasped her left, covering the bruise that was all that remained of her conjoined-snake tattoo. Achamian could almost weep for how she stiffened, for the way her expression melted into a blank imitation of her Imperial Husband's own. In that slender moment, it seemed, he saw the very sum of all she had lost and endured in the interval between this moment and Shimeh. Anasûrimbor Kellhus had been the greatest blight, the most onerous yoke she had ever suffered, and she *hated* him as she hated no other ...

Achamian saw this as surely as if he were Dûnyain.

"Where is Kelmomas?" she asked in the crisp, caste-noble Sheyic of the Andiamine Heights, with only the merest burr betraying her caste-menial blood. She referred to the boy, the old Wizard realized, *her* boy, the one behind the furor that had occasioned Mimara's labour.

"Chained," Kellhus said, "to a stake in Lord Shorathises' pavilion."

She searched the implacable face. An air of defeat had already crept into her manner. For all her matronly sturdiness, she suddenly seemed willowy, frail, standing in the shadow of her godlike Emperor.

"What happened?"

"You saw. He murdered Sorweel, Son of Harweel, the Believer-King of Sakarpus."

He could feel it then, the *enervation* of dwelling overlong in the shadow of such inhuman vacancy. And he understood how profoundly it had *mangled* her, being the human portal for the emergence of inhuman souls, loving what could only manipulate her in turn. Another Whale-mother. A clamour to *save* her inflamed him, to rescue not so much their present as their *past*, to pluck her from the catastrophic consequences of decisions entirely his own. He would do anything, in that moment, to *go back*, to yield to her beseeching, to stay and make love to her on the sweaty banks of the River Sempis all those years ago ...

Anything but abandon her for the Library of the Sareots.

"But *why*? Did he even know him?"

"He thought him an assassin. He says that he could see murder in his face, and he believes what he says."

There was tenderness in Kellhus's voice, even affection, but it was muted, dulled by the years, and careful as well, like all lies crafted in awareness of ineluctable disbelief.

"And was there?" she asked, her voice tight. "Was there ... murder in his face?"

"No. He was a Believer ... Among the most devout."

The Blessed Empress simply stared at him, inscrutable save for the anguish bruising her eyes.

"So Kel just ... he just ..."

"There is no reclaiming him, Esmi."

She looked down in thought. Then she turned on her heel and strode back toward the Umbilicus.

"Leave him be," Kellhus called after her.

She paused, did not so much look at him as turn her chin to her shoulder.

"I cannot," she said in hollow reply.

"Then *ware* him, Esmi, *attend to the limit of his chain*. He is more hunger than human." His voice welled for a wisdom indistinguishable from compassion. "The son you loved never existed."

Her eyes scraped the image of her Lord-and-Prophet. "Then I shall ware him," she said, "as I ware my husband." The Blessed Empress turned and vanished into the great tent of her husband.

Kellhus and Achamian stared after her, and for a heartbeat, it seemed not a day had passed, and they stood as they stood in the First Holy War, boon companions on a murky trail, and the old Wizard found that no courage was required to speak.

"In Ishuäl we saw where you kept your women ... *how* the Dûnyain kept their women."

The haloed face nodded—more to the recollection than the words, it seemed. "And you assume this is how I have used Esmi. As another Dûnyain woman, a means to multiply my power through my issue."

The old Wizard shrugged. "She assumes as much."

"And what of you, old teacher? As Mandate Schoolman, you saw souls as tools as well, instruments of your ends. How many innocents have you placed on the balance opposite this wicked place?"

The old Wizard swallowed.

"Not those I loved."

A smile that was both sad and exhausted.

"Tell me, Akka ... What was the *penalty* for harbouring a sorcerer in Sumna during the Ikurei Dynasty?"

"What do you mean?"

Now the Aspect-Emperor shrugged. "If the Shrial Knights or the Collegians had discovered you all those years ago, what would they have done to Esmi?"

The old Wizard fought to purge the injury from his glare. This was what Kellhus always did, a mad part of him recalled. Always exhuming shallow graves. Always murdering what piety you hoped to raise against him.

"Dif-different times!" he stammered. "Different days!"

Anasûrimbor Kellhus, Holy Aspect-Emperor of the Three Seas, loomed as the incarnation of tempest, as drought and plague. "*I am a tyrant*, Akka, the most terrible soul to walk this World in an Age. I have butchered whole nations merely to terrorize their neighbours. I have authored the death of a *thousand* thousand souls, glutted the Outside with the fat of the living. Never has a mortal been so feared, so hated, *so adored* as I ..."

"The *Hundred themselves* raise arms against me!"

He actually seemed to swell as he spoke, bloat across dimensions of dark import.

"I am the very thing *I must be*, **if this World is to survive.**"

What had happened? How had his cause—his righteous cause!—become smoke and conceit?

"For *I know*, Akka. I know as a father knows. And so knowing, I *compel sacrifice*, I punish those children who stray, forbid those games that corrupt, and aye ... I *take* what *survival* requires."

Be it lives or wives.

Futility crashed upon Drusas Achamian then, all the more agonizing for its inevitability. He was nothing but an old madman, a crank who had nursed too many grudges for too many years to hope to see beyond them. Where? Where was Mimara? It wasn't supposed to happen this way. Not like this! How? *Why?* Why deliver her to the Ordeal, only to chain her to her body? Why shackle her to her womb at the moment of their greatest need?

Why? Why would the God pluck his own Eye *now*, on the very eve of the Second Apocalypse?

All the years Dreaming, fretting, reliving the greatest Terror the World had known, toiling without sanction or purpose, drinking, raging, whoring, laying in mortal dread of slumber. And now ... *now* ...

"Yes," the Aspect-Emperor of the Three Seas said.

It wasn't supposed to happen this way.

"But *it happens* nonetheless, Akka. A reckoning like no other."

Trembling. Shaking about an old man's entrails, about the shame of being *seen* shaking.

The blasted figure nodded. "You gave me the Gnosis because you believed I was the *answer* ..."

"I believed you were a Prophet!"

"And you saw through that guise, saw that I was Dûnyain ..."

"Yes! Yes!"

"So you recanted, repudiated, thinking me false ..."

"You *are* false! Even here! Even now!"

"No. Merely *ruthless*. Only what I *need* to be ..."

"More lies!"

A look of exquisite pity.

"Did you think *justice* would save the World?"

"If not ju—"

"Did justice deliver the Nonmen? Did justice deliver the Ancient North? Look! Look about you. We stand before the very gates of *Min-Uroikas. Look.* Regard the Host I have assembled, the Factions and the Schools I have recruited, the might and glory that I have led across the desolate breadth of Eärwa, across innumerable leagues of screaming, rutting Sranc. Do you think *goodness* could have accomplished this? Do you think *honesty* could have compelled so many fractious souls? That *fear of myth and legend alone* could have served as my goad?"

And he had looked—how could he not, *knowing where he stood*. His whole life he could only cry "Golgotterath!" and stamp his feet, knowing what was for him ages of history and horror was but an absurd word for others, a chit belonging to a lost game. And now *here Achamian stood*, hearing his very own cry on another's lips, and turning ...

And *seeing* ...

"The Gods are witless," Kellhus pressed, "blind for seeing all. The God of Gods is naught but their bewildered sum."

The nocturnal immensity, menace soaring to the stars, gleaming sterile beneath the Nail of Heaven.

"No," Achamian gasped.

"Only a *mortal* can conceive what lies outside the sum of all, Akka. *Only a Man* can raise eyes to, let alone arms against, the No-God ..."

"*But you are no Man!*"

So uncanny, his haloes, so *impossible*.

"I am the Harbinger," the glowing vision said, "a direct descendant of Anasûrimbor Celmomas. Perhaps, old friend, I am just human *enough* ..."

Achamian raised hands to either side of his head, staring so that the Holy Aspect-Emperor and the Incû-Holoinas complicated either edge of his vision, opposing augurs of woe, each shining as if oiled, each noxious as much for their Mark as for their hated memory.

"Then *show* it!" he cried, throwing his hands out in sudden inspiration. "*Cut Proyas down!* Show mercy, Kellhus! Demonstrate the very *salvation* you have promised!"

Each inhuman.

"Proyas is already dead."

"Liar! He *lives*! and you *know* he lives! for you intended it! So *show it*! Suffer one snarl, one loose thread, in your accursed weave! Act as a human would! *Out of love!*"

A bereaved smile, twisted into something leering by the Nail of Heaven.

"And what are *you*, Holy Tutor, but a snarl, a loose thread that I suffer?"

The Harbinger turned away, began striding toward the warren of beaten pavilions fencing the slope immediately below. Achamian opened his mouth in idiot protest, once, twice, like a fish left gasping in the dust. His voice, when it came, cut for desperation.

"Please!"

Drusas Achamian *fell to his knees* upon wicked Shigogli, old and wrecked and more confounded than he had ever been. He opened his arms, tears spilling hot, *beseeching* ...

"*Kellhus!*"

The Holy Aspect-Emperor paused to regard him; an inked apparition, wrenching for the carrion profundity of his Mark. For the first time Achamian noticed all the faces peering from the shadowy slots about them, men squinting at the dark, wondering at the truth beneath the ancient tongue Kellhus had used to conceal their exchange.

"This *one thing* ..." Achamian cried. "Please ... Kellhus ... I *beg*." Sobs shook him. Tears spilled. "This one thing ..."

A single heartbeat. Piteous. Impotent.

"Tend to your women, Akka."

The old Wizard flinched, coughed for the pang in his breast, flew to his feet upon bursting rage. "*Murderer!*"

Never had a word seemed so small.

Anasûrimbor Kellhus looked to the Horns rearing into the firmament, the vast and malevolent gleam.

"Something," the monstrous entity said, glancing back, "must be eaten."

"Mummy?" the little blot of blackness called.

Esmenet lifted the hood from her lantern, held the light out and away more to spare her eyes than to probe pavilion's interior. She glimpsed bare corners, bellied seams, hanging swales of canvas bleached and mottled for long months on the trail. She smelled must and dank, the melancholy residue of some dead owner.

There was something nightmarish about the way his image simply materialized from her blinking, bright against the bare dust floors, avid of expression, keen in the way of children newly awakened. He fairly radiated need and contrition. But the look repelled far more than beckoned, attached, as it was, to the hip of so many atrocities—so many outrageous crimes and deceptions.

What was she doing? Why had she come?

She had always found joy in the *smallness* of her children, their compact, wagging, wriggling bodies. The reckless, careless dancing. The heedless running. With Serwa, in particular, she had marvelled over the calm she found simply watching the girl traipse through the Sacral Enclosure. A kind of profound contentment, the comfort that *bodies* take in the apprehension of bodies *they* have made. But as much as Kelmomas's appearance summoned the memory of that joy, it was also freighted by the insanity of everything she had since discovered—*bloated*, as if his image were a bulge of some kind, an evil cyst on the neck of the World. The little boy before her, the form she had so cherished and adored, had become a living receptacle, a philter brimming with chaos and poison.

She exhaled, fixed him with a resolute gaze.

"*Mummee-mummee please-please-please liste—*"

"You will never know ..." she interrupted, calling as if she were at market. "Ne-never understand what it is to have a child."

He was bawling now.

"He-he was *going to kill Father!* I-I wa—"

"*Cease your blubbering!*" she shrieked, bending, elbows to her waist, fists clenched. "*Enough!* I have had *enough* of your deceit!"

"But it's true! It's true! I saved Father's li—!"

"*No!*" she cried. "No! Cease *pretending to be my child!*"

This struck him as surely as a man's fist.

"I *am* your mother. But you-*you*, Kel, *are no one's child.*"

There it was ... the same blank look that she had learned to see as wariness in her other children. How was it she had never seen it before?

He was as mangled as the others. More, for his ability to appear otherwise ... to mimic the living, the human. And it returned to her, then, the enormity of all that had happened. The deaths. The destruction. The bestial truth of the child before her.

She fell to all fours on the dust, retched what little horseflesh she had been able to eat. She blinked tears, but she did not cry. She half expected him to seize upon this weakness, to cajole or to berate or to wheedle and insinuate—or even, as Kellhus had warned, to murder her.

"*Attend to the limit of his chain ...*"

But he merely observed, as indifferent as any truth.

She spat into the dust, noticed what seemed to be a finger bone breaching the powder. She looked up to him, raised a sleeve to wipe spittle from her chin and lower lip. Her white sleeve was stained yellow.

"Why would he pretend?" he asked in a small voice. "Why would Father pretend that I lie?"

The Blessed Empress regained her feet, brushed dust from her knees and sleeves, kicked sand across her vomit. Numb. She wondered if she had ever felt this numb.

"I think—" she started roughly, only to be stymied by a thickness in her throat or tongue. She blinked, cleared her throat. "I-I think he believes that you believe."

A single heartbeat of calculation.

"He thinks me mad, then. Like Inrilatas."

She pulled back her hair, spared him an evasive glance.

"Yes."

Another heartbeat.

"No one found anything in his hand."

"He was a *believer*, Kel ... Just like the others."

The wide eyes narrowed. The cherubic face lowered.

Shining from the ground, the lantern transformed the dust floors into a manuscript, every scuff and track a fragment of ink, shreds of some long-lost meaning. Kelmomas stood isolate in this mad sigil, like the last significant thing ... Small. Frail.

Her sweet, murderous little boy.

He looked up, his expression far too composed for his heart to be anything other than wrecked.

"Then why have you come?"

Why had she come? It seemed an act of necessity, as natural as water pooling. She simply had no other choice. To be a mother was to migrate between perspectives, to become a vagrant nation, forever pursuing desires, defending interests, and suffering hurts proper to what were, ultimately, *other* souls. Sometimes those souls reciprocated, but so much was given in the end, so much surrendered and forgotten, that rank injustice was all but assured.

Perhaps this was why she had come. *To be wronged* was the lot of mothers, to dwell with imposters, to give against any hope of recompense, to be deceived and ridiculed and exploited ... and to be *needed*—with a desperation that dwarfed any one skin.

Perhaps she had come to *mother*.

Perhaps—

"I see ..." he said.

The turmoil fell away, and she gazed at him with unflinching wonder, this child that perfumed slaves had pulled from her loins. She paused before fleeing, reached beneath her robe, withdrew the small file she had pilfered from the Umbilicus. The sight of her tattoo arrested her hand, but for a heartbeat, merely. She tossed the implement to the ground at his little feet, where it seemed to smoke for tendrils of dust.

Her final gift ...

Borne of the love most radical.

Migagurit urs Shanyorta sat perched high on the Occlusion, occasionally glancing out across the plain to Shaita'anairull, the Grave-that-is-Golden, but for the most part studying the camps scabbed below. The fires were few. To an untutored eye, they could only deceive, give the impression of scant numbers spread thin. But Migagurit was an old hand at the ways of war. The Southron host, he knew, had taken to burning its own shelter and accoutrements, much as it had taken to consuming its own horses. All good omens.

The King-of-Tribes would be pleased.

As a memorialist, he knew well the lore surrounding this place. He had always believed in Lokung, had always assumed that Shaita'anairull was real. What shocked him was how much his belief depended on the *unreality* of the thing. For when he set living eye upon the Grave-that-is-Golden, he quailed rather than rejoiced, felt his innards spoil for apprehension. And how could he not gaze upon it, when it proved the horror was real, that he had truly worshipped murder all along? At last he dozed, his dreams troubled by the terrors that steamed up from the rocks ...

Lokung had not died easily.

He jerked awake sputtering, wincing, rubbing his brow above his left eye. Something, a stone, had struck him while—

He sat blinking in supernatural dread ...

A *little boy* crouched at his feet, flaxen hair shining white beneath the Nail of Heaven.

"Are you *Scylvendi?*"

Migagurit smiled harmlessly, then made to seize the apparition. The child vanished. The memorialist rolled to his feet and whirled, his senses afire. He clutched at his knife only to find it missing—

He fell grunting, his calves flexed into unanchored balls in the crotch of either knee. A warmth in his heels bloomed into agony. He knew he was dead, but his body thought him a fool: everything became grunting panic. He dragged himself back on his elbows. His legs didn't seem real. The child bounced as a shadow upon a string. Cuts fell as visceral pricks through a fog of bestial misery. Migagurit thrashed and convulsed, wagging hands and crossing forearms that only served to spark more musical laughter. His will finally stranded him upon the scarp's edge, his back bent across the hump of a downward leaning rock, gasping in immobility.

The blond child paused to regard him, smeared blood across his cheek for wiping his nose.

"An-Anas—!" Migagurit sputtered through blood. "*Anasûrimbor!*"

He could feel the fall pulling at him. He knew that blood drained about his head and shoulders, glazing the nub of the boulder ... greasing his way ...

The boy leapt upon his chest, where he crouched like a monkey, peering into his eyes. The plummet pulled upon the tonguewalker's bulk, threatened to peel him from his every point of earthly contact.

"Where do Scylvendi go?" the boy asked with insouciant curiosity. The Nail of Heaven conjured a silver nimbus about his head.

Migagurit croaked and blubbered. With belief, came terror.

The boy nodded. "Somewhere *scary* ..." he said musing.

"Like everyone else, then."

The man tried to cry out, but the boy had crushed all breath remaining. The fall continued clawing at him.

"*Leave him,*" a feminine voice called from somewhere above.

A rib popped in the meat of him, so violently did the boy leap in reaction.

Outrageous agony, but mealy with the promise of respite. Migagurit somehow drew his head up from his paralytic misery. He saw the boy, knife brandished, his stance wide and wary, standing before a figure garbed all in black. A once-beautiful woman growing long in her years ...

The Empress?

The drop clutched at him, fumbled for some purchase ...

"You're not my mother," the boy declared.

A cross smile.

"I can be whatever you need me to be."

The woman reached out her hand ... a *man's* hand.

The plummet firmed its grip, then yanked the Son of hard-hearted Shanyorta over the edge.

The Men of the Ordeal traded tales and rumours, as all soldiers are prone. Fire was forbidden everyone save the Great, so they congregated in the pallid illumination of the Nail, each absorbed in some point of maintenance as they spoke—be it sharpening an edge, binding a seam, or rubbing some tarnished sheen. They sat in intimate proximity, their voices hushed out of some nameless reverence for the moment. And as was so often the case, the fact of *telling* proved far more significant than the facts told. The wits sought only to contribute, never to disrupt. Those who stammered found their voices unstopped, bold and clear. Those who loathed communal scrutiny found themselves speaking feckless, their hearts bare. And even when a man faltered, he received only encouragement, the wry hectoring of elder brothers, a hand upon the shoulder, or the scalp, mussing hair. For in the many trials of their affliction, they discovered *abundance*, and so destitute, denied everything but the least hope of redemption, they found occasion to give.

Ordealmen of all nations spoke of their wives and their children at some point. Reminiscence stole across the camp in stages, the reverence of Men recalling sunlit mornings, their eyes lost in recollection, hearing the trill of feminine voices, glimpsing faces floating bright and joyous about all that was needed. They laughed at the excesses of the wee ones, the temper and tenderness of their wives. Gales of lustrous laughter blew through the sagging dark, sparking here and there across the encampment. Men held out their hands to empty space, recalling the heft and wriggle of young sons, or the trembling compliance of lovers. They confessed a longing that made many listeners weep. They made heart-cracking resolutions, swore public oaths of damnation.

And so, one by one, did they commit *their eternal souls* to the morrow—to the destruction of foul Golgotterath.

They pondered the nocturnal burnish on the rim of the Horns, the void recapitulated in mountainous reflection. They groused about their night terrors, for Shigogli troubled the sleep of all.

Not one soul dared mention their hunger.

And so it was they regained their *fellowship* that night, the memory that was camaraderie, a forgiving look, a teasing grin. They had become far more than mere companions in strife and carnage. *Sin* had conjoined them in a manner more profound than faith: they need only commute the judgment they had passed upon themselves to recover one another.

To become *brothers* once again.

They were sinners ... responsible for horrid, degenerate acts, obscenities they could scarce credit, let alone fathom. Guilt had become their yoke, shame their lash. *Crime* had become their communion, sin and damnation. And like all Men wrecked by criminal burdens, they had seized upon the way offered, the track that would redeem, not their souls, but *all they had taken*. They would make a gift of their courage, their lives, their fury—they would render their final heartbeat, yield their ultimate breath. They would *give*, not for the sake of some arcane exchange, but for the sake of giving ...

For the love of their brothers.

And if this impulse was mad, they did not see it. Nor did they ponder the deranged condition that had brought it to fruition. To dwell in brotherhood was to set aside all questions, all yearnings trivial and profane. To dwell in brotherhood was to stand for a time *outside* the cares of time—to discover the Eternal, not in the heroism of faith, but in the sleep of trust.

They passed flasks of precious water. Mere breathing had become the breaking of bread. They sang hymns together, botched jokes and recited prayers. The encampment sprawled on and on beneath the stars, the debris of Men spilling from the pubis of the Occlusion out across the sunken abdomen of Shigogli. Golgotterath's bastions hunched in the crisp shadow of the Horns, bereft of light or any sign whatsoever. They turned their backs on this monochrome World, spurning it as a task for the morrow, and they remained intent upon one another, upon the light of the *generosity* they had kindled in lieu of any campfire. And each had occasion to reflect on the souls about them, to gaze upon their comrades and see a beauty that eclipsed their own, souls at once precarious and invincible. Each had the opportunity to say, *This man ... I throw my sticks for him.* And it moved them to wonder. For brotherhood was not the discovery of oneself in the breast of another, but *of someone better.*

Night waxed. They embraced, and those who were canny murmured gentle assurances, realizing the mad ferocity to come. Some were bellicose, others grandiose, but all were forgiven their excesses—their gorgeous *humanity.* The Men of the Ordeal discovered a different kind of awe, communing in the shadow of Golgotterath, one that did not so much humble as make whole. They filed to their shelters through murk, warmed against the chill. They slipped into troubled slumber, knowing that for one night in their fearsome journey, at least, they had been blessed.

Galeoth thanes, Shigeki surgeons, Ainoni warrior slaves, Nansur columnaries, Khirgwi marauders ... it did not matter. For a span of watches, they knew *Grace* ...

And in the shadow of Apocalypse, that was gift enough.

CHAPTER FOURTEEN

Golgotterath

We, the sons of past sorrow,
We, the heirs of ancient trow,
We shall raise glory to the morrow,
And deliver fury to the now ...
                    —"Hymn of the Pyre-King," *Shimeh Songs*

Early Autumn, 20 New Imperial Year (4132, Year-of-the-Tusk), Golgotterath.

A chevron of geese drawn long and ragged fled across the bluing skies.

Daybreak. The sun blackened the scarped bulwarks of the Occlusion, burnished the gleaming enormity of the Horns. Gold lanced down the cracked heights, graced the encampment with the memory of its many-coloured splendour ...

The highest of the high-hoisted Circumfixes flashed white.

The Interval tolled for the final time, a bright-humming resonance that hovered in the stationary air. The mazed thoroughfares of the encampment remained vacant for its duration. Spears and lances leaned in the sand. Lords and officers could be heard bawling out lonely commands from unseen quarters, but nothing more. Then the Men of the Ordeal issued forth, sluiced in their myriads into the tangled ways and byways. Silence became booming intercourse. Absence became teeming industry.

The Witches and Schoolmen formed up within the grounds of their respective enclaves, organized themselves into triunes. Given the colours of

their billows, they seemed flowers to the pickets stationed across the heights
of the Occlusion. Even the most aged and decrepit shimmered with vital
glory. The mundane soldiery secured what sustenance they could, then
joined the mass exodus to the encampment's perimeter, where their kin
and countrymen assembled beneath the stern regard of their commanders.
The near distances bristled for the transport of arms, dazzled for the play
of sunlight across polished miscellany. Everywhere, pockets of Men knelt
in communal prayer. Hymns floated and filtered throughout the bustling
tracts, songs of memory and distraction, praise and outrage. What Judges
survived assisted the priests with Whelmings.

Despite all the grievous insults and injuries the Whore had meted, the
Great Ordeal remained a martial wonder. Scarcely one-third of those who
had embarked from Sakarpus had survived. A full quarter of their number
had been lost at Irsûlor. Another quarter had perished at Dagliash, if not
in the Scalding, then in its nightmarish consequence. The vagaries of disease, murder, and attrition had consumed the rest. And yet, fairly one hundred thousand souls assembled across the blasted tracts of Shigogli, half
again as many Men as Anasûrimbor Celmomas had mustered in Far Antiquity, and at least three times the number of Cu'jara Cinmoi's Ishroi.

The Host of Hosts formed up across the smoking leagues. For the sentinels across the Akeokinoi, it seemed time itself had been inverted, watching miraculous *order* congeal from the streams and clouds of Southron Men.
Phalanx upon shining phalanx assembled across the waste, the flanks bowed
about the sepulchral presence of Golgotterath in the distance. Signs and
devices drawn from across the Three Seas adorned the formations. A thousand variants of the Circumfix hung slack in the morning chill.

The Host's ponies had either been eaten, or lingered beyond the Occlusion starving, too weak to bear a child let alone an armoured knight. Only
the Lords of the Ordeal remained mounted. Decked in those warlike accoutrements they had been able to salvage, they paced their formations, inspected and harangued their charges. Answering shouts boomed out over
the desolation.

The Holy Aspect-Emperor had divided the Ordeal into three Trials, as
he called them, each charged with its own violent objective. The Men of
the Middle-North under King Coithus Narnol formed the centre, charged
with assaulting Gwergiruh, the cyclopean gatehouse guarding the famed

Ûbil Maw—the Black Mouth of Golgotterath. The Sons of Shir under the cruel King Nurbanû Soter formed the right flank, charged with taking the Tower of Corrunc north of Ûbil. And the Sons of Kyraneas under Prince Inrilil ab Cinganjehoi formed the left flank, charged with taking Domathuz, Corrunc's monstrous sister to the south of the Gate.

The great shadow of the Occlusion shrunk from the gold-fanged parapets, and began its slow retreat to the lee of the scarps, not so much dark as ochre and saffron for the foul brilliance of the Horns. The clamour of assembly gradually faded into the hiss of the morning sun. Soon only the shouts of a few unruly souls could be heard. The Holy Aspect-Emperor himself could not be seen, but his banner stood high and visible to all at their fore, a black Circumfix once intact, but now an empty circle, having lost the image of their divine Prophet to the rigours of the sky. The gazes of all returned to it, and the hearts of all were comforted, for it was scourged as they were scourged, all their differences worn into a singular principle, one aptly signified by the perfection of the threadbare circle.

A lull settled across the Holy Host of Hosts. In one booming, gaseous voice, the Men of the Ordeal recited the Temple Prayer.

> *Sweet God of Gods, who dwell among us,*
> *Hallowed by thy Many Names ...*

The chorus rumbled out across Shigogli, and the Men heard what their ancient forebears had once heard—as the Nonmen had heard before them: the way the Horns reflected shredded echoes, and so mocked all collective declaration. The voices of some faltered for puzzlement, but those who were strong continued, and by example incited their brothers to declaim even louder.

> *May your bread,*
> *Silence our daily hunger.*
> *Judge us not according to our trespasses,*
> *But according to our temptations ...*

It was a prayer they had learned before they were born, words so well worn as to become invisible, and therefore immovable, stamped into them before they were themselves. So they were rooted as to the infinite as they recited it, and for all its vertiginous immensity the Ark seemed naught but a mummer's conceit, a trick of perspective and foil.

Trumpets peeled across the desolation, fading into the onerous, oceanic groan of the *ghus*. As one, the armed and armoured fields began advancing, dark and brilliant against the powder of the Shigogli. The very floor of the World seemed to move, such was its extent. For those still breathing on the ruined circuit of the Akeokinoi, the Men seemed to dissolve into the obscurity of their own dust. The Great Ordeal became a host of shadowy apparitions, an assembly of wraiths, with only the rare wink of reflected sunlight to attest to their frail reality ...

Thus did the Believer-Kings of the Three Seas advance westward, toward the pale, water-colour curtain of the Yimaleti Mountains beyond the Occlusion—and the grim and golden spectre of Golgotterath beneath.

So did the End of the World begin.

Im'vilaral, the Nonmen of Viri had called them so very many indignities ago, the "Horizon-that-has-teeth." The High Norsirai purloined this name the way they had so many others, beat it until it became a thing of comfort on their tongues—if not their hearts. So Im'vilaral became "Yimaleti," the name for the range of mountains that barricaded, for sheer immensity, the north against mortal reckoning.

To own a thing was to know it. All the World's unplumbed pockets made the hearts of Men anxious, but few could claim to command the terror belonging to the Yimaleti Mountains, for they became, far more than Golgotterath, the true womb of the Sranc. The Nonmen had sought to cleanse them in the gouged aftermath of the Cûno-Inchoroi Wars. For years it was the lot of the most heroic Quya and Ishroi to climb into the scarps and hunt the miscreant progeny of their foe. But as years past and names vanished what had once been deemed a courageous undertaking came to seem reckless. And as so often happens, bravery found itself broken upon the boney knee of futility, and the strategy was abandoned.

The High Norsirai would seek to clear the monstrosities from the shoulders of the Yimaleti in their turn. For a time, no mercenaries in the World were so feared or so prized as the famed Emiorali, or the "Bronzemen," so-called for their great gowns of bronze armour. Their Aorsi cousins from the plains, however, had another epithet, Kauwûttarim, or "Broken Strong"—a name originally given to those driven mad by battle. As quick as they were to invoke them as brothers in outland company, they eschewed the Emiorali otherwise, remained aloof in the brittle manner of weaker, yet far more numerous Men. Though the Bronzemen were notorious for stingy dealings, taciturn manner, and melancholic fury, the truth was that their kin begrudged their fame and feared their strength. "What is to stop them?" the suspicious asked about the failing way-hearths, when the faces of all grow crimson and the soul turns to things bloody and dark. "Men such as these ... Why live the hard life? Why feed their sons to the scarps and gorges, when they need only pluck what is ours?" Thus did they render inevitable what they feigned to prevent, such is the madness of Men.

In the Codicil Councils of Shiarau, the wisest among the Aorsi had assumed that the Sranc population would eventually collapse, so great was the toll the Emiorali had exacted defending their Hooded Redoubts. Perhaps the creatures did dwindle for a time, but the fealty of the Emiorali to Shiarau dwindled quicker. The Bronzemen eventually grew impatient, even disgusted, with the fat ways and absurd condescension of their southern cousins. They became the stock of sedition, a people known for rampaging bandits and usurping generals. In 1808 Year-of-the-Tusk, High-King Anasûrimbor Nanor-Ukkerja VI finally decided the Sranc and Bashrag were the lesser evil: all ninety-nine of the Hooded Redoubts were abandoned, and the Yimaleti were ceded entirely to the Foe.

None knew why these mountains proved such fertile breeding grounds. They stood twice the height of the subdued Demua, as monstrous, as wricked and ragged as the Great Kayarsus itself, and pitted with numerous, largely barren vales. The most ancient Nonmen records spoke of an infinite wasteland of ice and snow beyond the Yimaleti; a continuation of what Men called the Vastwhite to the east. The Bashrag hunted game, but the Sranc sucked their meat from the very earth, and could not sustain themselves on land too long frozen. The Vastwhite was proof enough of this. Some Far Antique scholars claimed the secret lay with the western Ocean, citing mariners who had explored the seaward sockets of the western Yimaleti, daring souls who described innumerable, deep-barrelled fjords warmed by the Ocean and so overrun with Sranc that the very landscape itself shivered as with maggots. *Pitarwum*, they called them, Beast-cradles.

One of these scholars, a King-Temple Historian known to posterity only as Wraelinu, proposed that these Pitarwum anchored cycles of exploding population, which in turn drove endless migratory invasions across the northern back of the Yimaleti. This was why, he claimed, the Sranc in the eastern extremes of the range were invariably so much more emaciated than those spied in the west. And this was why the Yimaleti Sranc differed from their southern kin, shorter of stature, slower across open ground, but more powerful of limb, more ferocious than vicious; the Pitarwum, he argued, bred them the way herdsmen bred cattle. There they remained until exhaustion drove them forth into the mountains, which belonged, in sooth, to the Bashrag. It was this cycle that had proven so ruinous ...

Only the greatest of mobbings, he claimed, could incite their pestilential descent upon Men.

The Great Ordeal traversed the intervening desolation.

There was foreboding among the Men, but there was exultation as well. *Golgotterath* hung in the distance before them, the trudging object, not just of their present exertions, but of anguished months of campaigning and toilsome years of preparation. Few pondered the fact explicitly, for doing so robbed the air of its sustenance, the will of its direction. Golgotterath—the end for which whole peoples had been put to the sword. Golgotterath—the warrant of so much peril, so many privations of the heart, spirit, and flesh. Golgotterath—the subject of so many outraged prayers, sinister tales, and anxious, nocturnal musings.

Golgotterath. Min-Uroikas.

The Wicked Ark.

The greatest evil the World had ever known, bloating by imperceptible degrees, step by dusty step.

There could be no denying the holiness of their undertaking. There could be no questioning the righteousness of raising arms against such a place—a cancer so foul, so *obvious*, that it compelled excision.

There could be *no doubt*.

The God of Gods walked with them—*through* them. The Holy Aspect-Emperor was His sceptre, and *they were His rod*, the very incarnation of His curse, His violent rebuke.

The song, when it arose, seemed to spark in all throats at once ...

> *By the waters of Siol,*
> *we hung our lyres upon the willows,*
> *and abandoned song with our mountain.*

And it seemed a miracle within a miracle, a glorious compounding of Providence, that this, of all the lays they had committed to memory, would be the song to seize their hearts now: the *Warrior's Hymn*.

> *Ere the doom of Trysë,*
> *we hoisted our sons upon our knees,*
> *and counted scabs upon our hands and heart*

None knew its origins. It possessed as many verses as the World possessed bone-fields, which made its subtleties all the more remarkable: the melancholic honesty, the obstinate manner in which it sang *around* battles instead of about them, bundling the violence in depictions of *respite*. It never failed to move, even when raised during the most interminable of marches, for it sang to the commons between them, the vigil that all warriors kept in the shadow of atrocity. They sang as brothers, a vast assemblage of coincident souls, and they sang as *sinners*, the authors of abominable deeds, isolate and astray ...

> *In the fields of Cenei,*
> *we broke bread that we had stolen,*
> *and tasted the love of those who were dead.*

And it was the *same* for all of them. The Knights of Hinnant, their faces white for paint, their eyes bred to the hazy expanses of the Secharib Plains and so strangely comforted by the flat plate of Shigogli. The iron-mailed Agmundrmen, carrying their longbows likes stocks across their shoulders, their wrists hooked high. The Massentian Columnaries, their shields like halved barrels emblazoned with the Circumfix and the Sheaf, yellow upon yellow. The two-hearted Holca tribesmen, conspicuous for their stature and the fiery crimson of their beards and manes, marching, as always, at the fore, where their battle-madness was both most useful and most safe.

Golgotterath! *There* before them! Inexorable and impossible. No matter what the nation, no matter what the names scrawled on the ancestor lists, it was the same for all. *Golgotterath* had become the World's only portal, the one defile that could deliver them from Hell. They had pitched themselves from the precipice, leapt into the void ...

And so the Wicked Stronghold loomed, sinister in aspect, as alien in *scale* as in appearance. The Horns reared impossible, commanding all, the two great Oars of the Ark goring the belly of the sky. Their golden skin roiled with morning brilliance, so bright as to cast palls of jaundiced light across the stoneworks below. Their hearts, which had been rooted in immobility, continuous with the very God, became progressively unmoored. Not a soul among them did not quail in some fashion, such was the premonition of enormity, of weights too vast hung upon heights too perilous. They became as *gnats*. And to a man they thought what every mortal had thought stumping across Shigogli's bitter plate ...

No Man belonged in such a place.

The proof of its manufacture was plain in the great abrasions marring the Canted Horn. All could see the radial beams through the stripped-away planking, glimpses of bulkheads and frames similar to those in wooden ships. The Incû-Holoinas, the dread Inchoroi Ark, was a contrivance, a Void-faring *vessel*, the product of innumerable, *inhuman* wrights and artisans ... Aliens that revelled in filth and atrocity.

From *where?*

To a man they asked this, because to a man they instinctively understood the *power of origins*, that the truth of a thing lay in its genesis. But like the Nonmen, this thing, this mountainous Ark, had outrun its beginnings. It was *enigmatic*, incomprehensible, not merely in the way of miracles and cataclysms, but in the way of madness and mayhem. *A thing from nowhere* was a thing that should not be. And so the Ark, in their eyes, became an outrage against existence, an object so fundamentally accursed that hands became papyrus for simply gazing upon it ...

An intrusion like no other ... A violation.

The *rapist* that had despoiled the maidenhead of the World.

And so it was that *disgust* hooked their lips, *revulsion* propelled their voices, that *abhorrence* and *loathing* steeped their hearts as they cried out their battlesong. They gnashed their teeth, stamped their feet, beat sword and spear against their shields. Hatred and fury filled them, the lust to strangle, to cut and to burn and to blind. And they knew, with a conviction that made some weep, that *to do evil to this place* was to be holy. They became as cutthroats in the alley, murderers in the night, souls too dangerous, too deadly, to fear the machinations of *any victim* ...

Even one so monstrous as this.

The Horns loomed ever more immense, the fortifications ever more near—close enough to reflect their shouting fury and so impart a demented, echoic resonance to their song. Soon the World rang as if across metal.

> Beneath the Ark of horrors,
> we saw the sun rise upon gold as night fell,
> and mourned the captivity of tomorrow.

Trumpets crowed upon this, the ultimate verse, and the chorus cracked into the rumble of innumerable disjoint voices. The outer echelons of each Trial paused, then filed behind the centremost formations, creating three great, articulated squares. Thus the Host of Hosts arrayed itself across the plain the ancient Kûniüri had called Ûgorrior; and the Nonmen, Mirsurqûl, immediately below the jaws of the Ûbil Gate.

Golgotterath loomed wicked directly before them—*at long last!*—so close its stench hung as a corrupt emanation on the air. The Horns soared in hazy stages above, the alien traceries of the World-Curse clear for all to see. Abstract figures, unintelligible and vast, etched into the casing. Bands of evil symbol. From a distance, the fortifications below seemed a crude afterthought, the Horns so overshadowed them. But now the Men could see that they rivalled, even surpassed, those of the greatest Southron cities. The cataclysmic Fall of the Ark had occasioned some kind of igneous upheaval, creating a series of cliffs and scapular heights, black and blasted, about the submerged base of the Horns—what the ancient Kûniüri had called the Scab. A great curtain wall wandered its outer compass, towering more than fifty cubits in places, folded and knotted into a cunning series of bastions and bulwarks. The whole consisted of mighty black rocks hewn from the Scab's interior heights, with the sole exception of the battlements, which had been adorned with tear-drop shanks of gold. The Lords of the Ordeal had reckoned they were some kind of salvage drawn from the Ark and affixed as a form of hoarding. Since no ancient texts made mention of them, the Men of the Ordeal dubbed them *incisori*—for the way they resembled golden fangs perched upon black-rotted gums.

The greatest gate in the evil circuit was also the only gate, the legendary Ûbil Maw, so named for the myriad Ishroi it had consumed during the Cûno-Inchoroi Wars. The Nonman had razed the hated original long, long ago, but the lay of the Scab was such that Golgotterath could possess but one orifice, one point of egress and ingress. Rugged cliffs skirted the black formation everywhere save the southwest, where it had been scalloped into a ramp very nearly as broad as the Sempis, one that eased from the very summit to the desolate plate of Shigogli. So while the walls upon the stronghold's high perimeter had a plummet for their foundation—and were all but impregnable for it—those guarding the southwest stood upon Ûgorrior, the same dusty earth as the Men of the Ordeal, or very nearly so. Thus their cyclopean immensity. Thus the monstrous proportions of Gwergiruh, the infamous Gatehouse of Ûbil, which squatted every bit as immense as Atyersus. Thus the flanking towers, Corrunc and Domathuz, whose gold-fanged crowns reached as high as the summit of the Andiamine Heights. And thus the famed Oblitus, the network of ascending walls that terraced the slopes from Ûbil's black iron to the horrific immensity of the High Cwol, the fortress raised about the fabled Intrinsic Gate the terrestrial entrance to the Upright Horn.

The stronghold hung in its evil sum upon this axis between inner and outer gateways. Thus the menacing immensity. Thus the iron-strapped stone. Thus the mad piling of Wards upon Wards—an arcane laminate so deep, so intricate, it stung the eyes of the Few.

For all their passion and conviction, the Men of the Ordeal were daunted. An attempt to rekindle the Hymn faltered, dissolved into a chorus of disparate shouts: individuals attempting to rekindle the ardour of their brothers.

They knew the tales. Short of stealth or captivity or collusion, no *Man* had *ever* gained Golgotterath. With the Sohonc, the Knights of Trysë had contested Ûbil, the Extrinsic Gate, for the space of a single, ancient afternoon, but at a cost so grievous that Anasûrimbor Celmomas bid them withdraw before nightfall. Only the *Nonmen*, Nil'giccas and his allies, had managed to overrun this, the most wicked of all places.

An eerie, almost numb, silence fell across the entirety of the Great Ordeal. The morning sun climbed behind their backs. Their conjoined shadows, thrown long before them when they first assembled, shrunk to the height of grave-markers. The titanic gold of the Horns cast a yellow pall across skin, fabric, and sand.

Not a soul could be spied on the black ramparts. But the Ordealmen could *feel* them, it seemed, wet eyes watching, dog-chests panting, inhuman lips sucking drool ...

The sentinels scattered across the heights of the Akeokinoi were all dead by this time. Near naked Scylvendi now watched in their stead, their skin painted the grey and white of the Occlusion.

Luminous, the Holy Aspect-Emperor rode to the fore of the host, paused upon the foot of the incline so that he and his retinue of Believer-Kings might be seen. Cheering erupted among the nearest ranks, then passed like a wave outward to the extremities. His head was bare, his leonine mane braided tight to the back of his neck. Unlike his warlike companions, he had no armour; he wore some kind of grand, scholastic billows instead, white silk so lambent it seemed mercurial, bound to his form with a serpentine black sash. Unlike his sorcerous advisors, he was armed; the pommel of his famed sword, Enshoiya, jutted above his left shoulder.

The Decapitants swayed from his hip, as always, smudges of black and thistle.

The roaring faded.

His back to Golgotterath, he assessed the mighty fruit of his labour, the *Great Ordeal*, and it seemed to those who were near *that he wept*, not for fear or regret or loss, but for *wonder*.

"Who?" he cried in a voice that somehow closed the distance between him and the most remote of his followers. "Who among my Kings will offer our Enemy terms?"

Hringa Vûkyelt, Believer-King of Thunyerus, stepped forth from the Aspect-Emperor's immediate entourage, keen to repeat and so secure his dead father's glory. Passing his Lord-and-Prophet, he strode alone across the dusty interval, stopping beneath the monstrous shins of Gwergiruh. He wore his famed father's coat of mail, which was black, and weighed two thousand kellics of copper. He hoisted his grandfather's legendary shield, the ensorcelled Wark, an ancient heirloom of his family. He peered up at the parapets, and seeing nothing, allowed his eyes to roam the Horns, the breathtaking bulk, climbing into haze and heaven, higher and higher ...

He feigned losing his balance, tripped into a mock pirouette.

The Men of the Ordeal roared, first for laughter, then for exaltation. The skies rang.

The Believer-King whirled from his pantomime, cried, "*Yeeesss!*" to the vacant parapets. "We *laugh at you*! We *mock!*" He turned back to grin at his hundred thousand brothers.

"The choice is simple!" he bellowed to the black heights. "Open this gate, live as slaves! Or huddle behind it"—he threw a glance over his shoulder—"and *burn! In! Hell!*"

Ûgorrior boomed with pounding shields and vibrant cheer.

The black parapets remained empty, the ramparts unmanned.

The Foe made no answer.

King Hringa Vûkyelt stood waiting, scanning the battlements, his grin fading into a frown. After several heartbeats, he shrugged, and slinging Wark over his shoulder, began strolling back to his brother Believer-Kings. Even as he turned a great, paint-and-fetish-adorned Sranc leapt from the blackness and cast a spear as thick as a weaver's beam, shrieking, "*Mirukaka hor'uruz!*" in the corrupt tongue of his race.

This, the first glimpse of their enemy, astounded the Host. The shaft struck the Believer-King in the small, drove him to his face. Thousands among the Men gasped, certain he was dead. But Wark had preserved him, just as it had preserved his grandfather and his grandfather's grandfather before him. Grimacing, the Believer-King of Thunyerus hoisted himself back to his feet.

Once again, the Great Ordeal roared.

"Is that '*Yes*'?" Hringa Vûkyelt called to the lonely Ursranc, "or '*No*'?"

Stung by tears of hilarity, Men clutched their sides, even swatted their cheeks.

"*Well?*" the Thunyeri shouted to the creature.

Rather than speak, his foul interlocutor stiffened about a spasmodic start, spouted violet blood across the stone. He was heaved upward, his limbs flopping in unison. The Great Ordeal drew collective breath, for a *Nonman* held him high overhead, his face indistinguishable from his victim's, but his nude form the very image of inflamed, porcelain perfection. He heaved the Sranc out over the parapets, laughing as he did so. The carcass crashed in a shamble to the ground, popped like rotted fruit.

Silence claimed the reaches of Ûgorrior. The Nonman's ridicule trailed into a crazed murmuring. He raised his face to the sun, turned it from side to side as if to warm either cheek.

"Who," King Hringa Vûkyelt cried, "speaks for the Unho—?"

"*Yoouu!*" the nude Nonman raged in deformed Sheyic. He raised a foot upon the battlement, scanned the whole of Ûgorrior, glared for what seemed an eternal moment of incredulity. "You have *wrecked* me!"

The hard-bitten Thunyeri peered at the figure, scowling. "Don't look at me! I have no idea what happened to your clothes!"

The gales of warlike laughter seemed to focus the Nonman's attention. He stood bold, raked the distant formations with bald contempt. Then he made Hringa Vûkyelt the prize of a sneering gaze, one that bespoke ten thousand years of racial contempt.

"The World holds no terror for me," the Nonman said. "I stand naked as the falling sword!"

He closed his eyes, shook his head in pity. His body seemed oiled for beauty. "I am the terror ... ***Yimral'emilias simpiraccas ...***"

Twin suns glared from his waxen skull. Great arcs of Gnostic energy encompassed him ...

Hringa Vûkyelt reached for his Chorae. But somehow, his Holy Aspect-Emperor *was there*, at his side, staying his han—

A dazzling tempest seized them, erupted across blind angles, Quyan assaults twisting and cracking across Gnostic defenses. The Men of the Ordeal blinked in the wake of the onslaught, their eyes adjusting ...

The Holy Aspect-Emperor stood unharmed, his Believer-King kneeling at his side. A wild mane of scorching formed a perfect circle about them, blackened earth still smoking.

The Host of Hosts erupted in jubilant fury.

The Nonman looked to the cheering masses, imperious, but more for incapacity than presumption. Neither smiling nor sneering, he had the air of a drunk parsing suspicions of affront, one who imagined himself too cunning to yield any reaction. Let the World wait, *he* would be the one to decide ...

Whatever it was that happened ...

Anasûrimbor Kellhus commanded Hringa Vûkyelt to clutch tight his Chorae and withdraw. Robbed of his swagger, the Thunyeri hastened back to his Household, leaving his Lord-and-Prophet alone beneath the dwarfing turrets of Gwergiruh.

"**Cet'ingira!**" the Holy Aspect-Emperor called up to the nude figure. His voice fell upon the air like a cudgel upon pottery. "**Mekeritrig!**"

An old and wicked name, attached to innumerable legends, a curse upon innumerable lips.

The Evil Siqu inclined his face downward, but his dark eyes lingered on the masses beyond.

"They *laugh* ..." he finally called down, as though uncertain whether to be wounded or offended.

"Do you recall me, Man-traitor?"

The eyes clicked down. A lucid interval passed between them.

"*You?*"

Peering, as if vision were naught but memory. Then the dawning of delight.

"Yesssss," the ancient Erratic said. "*I remember* ..."

"Do you repent your obscene iniquity?" the Holy Aspect-Emperor boomed across the wastes of Ûgorrior. "Will you embrace your damnation?"

Cet'ingira smiled. His eyelids fluttered. He rolled his chin upon his breastbone. "Can you *mean* such things?" he marvelled. "Or do you speak this for *them?*"

"Do! You! Repent!"

The Evil Siqu thrust out a cramped hand, a curious gesture toward the assembled masses. "So the nettle condemns the oak!"

"I am the voi—!"

"Pfah! You are scarcely a child! I am *older* than your languages, your histories, your duping Tusk! I am *older than the names* you give your tapeworm Gods! The soul that now regards you has witnessed *Ages*, mortal!" Deep laughter echoed down the ramparts, offensive for its sincerity. "And you would presume to be *its* Judge?"

Serene of mien and pose, the Holy Aspect-Emperor paused in the manner of those awaiting an interruption to end. All across Ûgorrior, Men of the Ordeal caught their breath, for he seemed to *glow* in the instant, in a manner too profound for eyes. There he stood, the Warrior-Prophet, overshadowed by monstrous stoneworks, scorned as a child ... and yet it was *he* who was the mightier by far.

He shrugged, raised his palms from his thighs. A nimbus of gold flashed about his outstretched fingers.

"I am," he said, "but the vessel of the Lord."

Cet'ingira cackled for what seemed a long time. "Oh, you are far, far more *Anasûrimbor* ..."

There was a great thrum of bow-strings. Myriad negations of Creation pocked the open air, rising from points across the black ramparts and falling on a menagerie of arcs, climbing, falling, converging on the circle the Non-man had scorched upon the earth ... striking as a furious hail.

But the Holy Aspect-Emperor was no longer there.

Cet'ingira snapped his gaze skyward, to a point just above the white stab of the sun ...

For it was upon this angle that the Ciphrang fell roaring.

———— ⌘ ————

Shrieking, they plummeted, falling from the sun's blinding white well, Ciphrang summoned from across the Hells, bound with cruel and subtle sorceries to the agony of the Created. Puskarat, Mother of Perversions; foul Hish, the Great-Jawed Glutton, who shambled as a living heap of fire and putrescence; and monstrous Hagazioz, the Feathered Worm of the Pit, a Godling the size of two galleys set end upon end; mighty Kakaliol, Reaper-of-Heroes, armoured in the glory of the damned; and appalling Urskrux, the vulturous Father-of-Carrion, whose vomit was pestilence—and two dozen other malformed demons from the abyss, slaves of the Daimos, arcane puppets of Iyokus and his Daimotic confreres. The Ciphrang hooked wide their folded wings, scooped wind to slow their descent. They swooped over Gwergiruh, screeching in a chorus that clutched the throat and clawed the ears, plucking every tone on the scale of human terror. A heartbeat saw them over the Oblitus, sailing to the root of the High Horn, where they fell shrieking upon the High Cwol, dropped as balls of iron through floors, igniting interlocking Wards ...

The Men of the Ordeal stood dumbstruck, blinking, peering after glimpsed monstrosities, watching the blossoms of fire erupt across the High Cwol above the shoulder of Corrunc. One soul whooped ... and the whole of Ûgorrior boomed in reply, a roar that was almost a collective scream, such was the passion vented.

It was happening. It was finally happening!

Somewhere deep in Golgotterath, bestial arms hammered gongs, and a cacophonous racket made hash of the skies. Their deception spent, the Ursranc surged onto the heights of Golgotterath's walls, armoured in hauberks of black scale, their cheeks branded with Twin Horns, hooting in their corrupt tongue. But the holy ghus sounded also, so deep as to roll under all other sounds. Archers and crossbowmen burst from the forward ranks of each of the three great Trials: Agmundrmen for the Sons of the Middle-North; Eumarnans for the Sons of Kyraneas; and Antanamerans for the Sons of Shir. In what appeared an act of reckless lunacy they dashed out exposed onto the dust, and before their unruly Foe could organize, they nocked their shafts and bolts, raised their weapons—*released* ...

The gold-fanged parapets seethed with activity, bristled with black iron. Howling white faces crowded the embrasures—but nary a shaft fell upon them. Without exception, the shafts and bolts fell short, clattering across the sheer faces and squat foundations of Corrunc, Domathuz, and Gwergiruh. White lights flared across the fortifications, implosions. And a sound climbed into the collective bewilderment, one unlike any heard by Mannish ears, like a thousand mastodons charging across the drum-skins of Soul and World ...

Wards cracking, unravelling, dissolving.

Golgotterath had been raised with ensorcelled stone. Fell Quyan sorceries strapped and permeated the fortifications, some binding structure, others set like springs primed to burn and concuss, and many more applied like coats of arcane lacquer, shielding exposed faces from the violence of Cants. The Chorae Hoard rained upon and across them, each sparking a violent dissolution, explosions of salt. Blocks cracked. Joists groaned. The Ursranc on the parapets were thrown from their feet.

The Schoolmen had already begun their muttering song at the command of their Exalt-Magus, Anasûrimbor Serwa, the Witch Most Holy. Even as the bowmen fled back into the great phalanxes, *hundreds* of Triunes stepped from them, climbing into the vacant heights—the greatest concentration of sorcerous might the World had ever seen. One thousand Schoolmen, their faces—and thus the telltale light of their singing—obscured by deep cowls. One thousand Kites, as the Ordealmen had come to call them, fairly every sorcerer of rank the Major Schools of the Three Seas could muster.

The Mandati under Apperens Saccarees, their red billows monkish for their simplicity; the Imperial Saik under Temus Enhorû, their gold-trimmed gowns as black as ink, glossed with deep shades of violet, scored with the white of reflected sunlight; the Mysunsai under Obwë Gûswuran, their garb eclectic save for their cowls, which resembled those of Amoti shepherds, white striped with sky-blue; the decimated Vokalati, their white-and-violet numbers dwindled to a mere handful for the travesty of Irsûlor; the Scarlet Spires under Girûmmû Tansiri, their garb an iridescent play of crimson upon crimson, like blood upon autumnal leaves; and of course the Nuns, the Swayali Sisterhood, the most numerous and certainly the most bewitching in their gleaming saffron gowns, their voices complicating the ponderous, masculine chorus with a high-drawn, feminine keen.

One thousand Schoolmen, the greatest concentration of sorcerous might the World had ever seen. As one, they unfurled their silk billows, became as flowers in the gleaming sun.

The Men below roared in jubilation.

Brilliant explosions pimpled the distant ramparts of the High Cwol.

The Scylvendi assassins watched from afar upon the Occlusion, breathless for awe and dread.

The Triunes formed three lines at the fore of each phalanx, tentacular blooms hanging the height of mighty oaks. Their skulls cauldrons of light, the witches and sorcerers began singing in *unison* ...

"*Imrima kukaril ai'yirarsa* ..."

A sudden breeze whipped their hair about their faces, tugged at the extremities of their billows. Chaos and terror ruled the black walls and towers before them.

"*Kilateri pir mirim hir* ..."

And as one the Schoolmen paused, inhaled, and *blew*, puffed as a child might blowing fluff from a dandelion ...

A great gust of air exploded before them, blasting the hard floor of Ûgorrior, scooping vast quantities of sand and dust, tossing it into a vast pluming curtain that boiled upward and outward. Within heartbeats, Golgotterath's savage defenders could see naught but grey. Even their fellows had been reduced to ragged silhouettes in the murk. The Ursranc howled in frustration and terror, for they knew the Schoolmen had merely begun their catastrophic song.

Vile angel.

It knows not this place. The animals scurry from its smoking onslaught, squealing and grunting. Kakaliol shrieks for agony and fury, stamps them like rats beneath its horned feet, lays its lash upon them, lays them out as burning bundles, blistered pulps, flesh like paper thrashing in the flame.

Surcease! it screams.

The galling *implacability*, the needling obstinance, the knifing *reality*, cutting and cutting and cutting, sawing them, it, as a carpenter might, joint from joint, limb from limb, over and over and over again. What *torment* was the World—what shrieking agony! Pricking it point by point, every thimble of diabolical substance, pinning it to these monstrous solidities, these pealing, stabbing, *details* ...

Surcease! the Carrion Prince bellows to the Blind Slaver within. **Surceeeease**!

After your task is complete ...

Blind worm! How I shall care for thee! Love and invert thee!

I fear more horrific souls have claimed me.

I shall kindle a furnace in thine heart! Sup on thi—!

Discharge your obligation!

Vile angel.

It screams, for the Slaver has spoken a word and the sharp-sharp needles of this World have answered. Kakaliol, the great and dreadful Reaper-of-Heroes, Seducer-of-Thieves, screams sulphur, weeps pitch for fury, and punishes the pageant of soulless meat, visits destruction on the mewling animals that scurry and squeal from its path. It stalks the great corridor, a crimson light in the smoking dark, trailing sizzling ruin in its wake. The flesh now flees before it, gibbering and yammering as if it were real. A different flesh replaces it, far greater in height and girth, draped in clanking gowns of iron. Bellowing they fall upon Kakaliol, spear and cudgel its scaled limbs, but they too fall away, puling hoarse and glutinous, burning and broken.

And it strides forward, stone cracking beneath its feet ...

Vile angel.

The meat lies smashed and smoking about it. Nothing opposes it—save a lone hooded figure occupying the centre of the grand hall ...

Beware ... the Blind Slaver whispers.

A roar shivers up through rotted stone.

At last ... Kakaliol croaks on a poisonous fume.

A soul.

———❧———

Helplessness was fury for Men.

"*She is your wife!*" Esmenet cried.

Words meant to scratch the heart.

The old Wizard gazed at her incredulous. Despite everything he had en-dured, despite all the deprivations and indignities of the trail, it seemed nothing compared to the night he had suffered: the slurry of the watches, slipping into slumber only to be yanked clear, riven by alarm, gazing helpless as Mimara, stumbling to and fro to discharge Esmenet's commands, some-times barked, sometimes gentle, fetching water, boiling water, cleansing rags, wringing and applying, always confused, always anxious, always *out of place*, an interloper, always averting his eyes *for no good reason*, save the contradic-tion of the girl's posture, whorish and natal, the lustful and lascivious *turned inside out*, transformed into something too round, too deep, not to pain the flat hearts of men, force unwanted wisdom upon them, knowledge of the primal, feminine toil that stood at the very *origin* of life, the mealy divinity, swollen and bleeding and anguished beyond masculine comprehension ...

A World ending. A life beginning.

"I'll be right back," he explained. "I just-just *need to see*."

Something was wrong. With Mimara, Esmenet was nothing but reassur-ing, cooing encouragement as the seizures waxed in cruelty, then telling sto-ries of her own travails in the lulls between, especially regarding the birth of her beloved first, Mimara herself. She cajoled her terrified daughter, made her laugh and smile with whimsical appraisals of her fetal obstinance. "*Two* days!" she would cry, her look one of laughing adoration. "*Two days* you denied me! 'Mimara!' I would cry, 'Please, my Sweet! Please be born!' but, *noooo* ..."

But for every indulgence she afforded her daughter, she exacted some penance from *him*, the man who had quickened her womb, the man she still loved. Several times now, at the grinding pinnacle of some particularly torturous seizure, she had all but stabbed him with her eyes, so hateful was her look. And each time, it seemed Achamian could read the movements of her soul as plainly as he could his own ...

If she dies ...

The stakes were mortal—he knew as much. The stakes were always mortal where childbirth was concerned. And for all the times Esmenet contradicted her daughter's tearful protestations *that something was wrong*, it was plain that she too believed as much. Her daughter's travail was too taxing, her seizures too ferocious ...

Something *was* wrong. Horribly wrong.

And this made Drusas Achamian a murderer in waiting.

"I need you here!" Esmenet spat in reply, her indignation imperial. "*Mimara* needs you!"

As was often the case in familial feuds, exhaustion had become indistinguishable from selfish will.

"Which is why I'll return!"

Esmenet blinked, obviously shocked. An answering wildness animated her look, but only for a heartbeat. At the draw of a single oar, she became remote, cool—looking *down* far more than up, as if he were but another petitioner begging favour at the foot of the Blessed Empress.

"You need to change out of that filth," she said. "I need you to be *clean* ..."

"I'm *informing*," the furious old Wizard replied, "not begging your permission, *Emp*—!"

And with that, they found themselves standing in a different future, one where Esmenet had struck him. Hard enough to bloody his mouth ...

So much lay between them. A lifetime bound by common desperations, the half-mad ferocity of souls *that have nothing but each other*. And then a second lifetime, constant in the manner of ascetics and potentates, bound by nothing save that continuity, be it the wilds of Hûnoreal, or the splendours of the Andiamine Heights. A new lifetime condemned to dwell in the ruins of the old.

And now here they stood ... reunited in turmoil at long last.

Achamian wiped his mouth across a filthy sleeve.

"You owe me this," Esmenet said softly.

"I fear you are the debtor," he replied on a momentary glare.

"You owe me *your life*!" she exclaimed. "Why do you think Kellhus suff—?"

"*Mother!*"

It was Mimara, her voice frayed to the hemp for grunting and screaming. Both of them flinched for the realization that she lay watching.

"Leave him, Mother ... Let him be ..."

She had sensed it as well, Achamian realized. The smell of sorcery borne on a different wind.

"Mim ..."

"*Someone*, Mother ..." the girl gasped, at once irked and beseeching. "*Someone must see.*"

It fell upon their skin, seized them hair by hair. It rose from the nethers of their gullet, steamed from the margins of their sight. It fell as mist from the heavens, shivered up as tremors from the sands. It twisted hearing, bewildered heartbeats. It cracked thought wide open, allowed the ink of madness to seep in ...

And it wrung light and destruction from vacant air.

Sorcery.

The Triunes advanced into the roiling veils they had swept into the air, vanished one by one. Not a soul among them hesitated. The long months fencing with the Horde had taught them how to estimate shrouded locations and distances, how to count off paces in the air. Their enemies screeched and clamoured across immovable walls, their positions fixed, *known*, while they ranged high and low, all but invisible.

They could scarcely see one another in the murk; their billows transformed them into octopus shadows, their cowls concealed their light. Their singing seemed stolen from their lips, their lungs, and braided into the greater, choral impossibility. Each sang Ward after Ward, sheathing themselves and their Triune brothers in ethereal defenses, either abstract or metaphoric. Each silently counted the counterfeit steps taken ...

Missiles fell as an indiscriminate hail, but more about them than upon. Each could sense the arc of Chorae through the air, small holes of nothingness whipping from obscurity into nowhere. One struck a Mysunsai sorcerer-of-rank, the bent-backed Keles Musyerius, upon his cowled head, and he simply dropped, salted to the pith, shattered across the ground. Three others were superficially salted by Chorae striking their billows, and had to be born back to the Ordeal by their comrades. The yammering parapets drew near, the sounds preposterously *close*, and more disconcerting still, falling from *above*, so colossal were Golgotterath's defenses. Spears and javelins joined the violent downpour. Great, iron-tipped bolts cracked against the Wards of many. But the Triunes continued their blind advance, converging upon the one thing they could clearly sense in the swirling grey monotony: the fallen Trinkets of the Chorae Hoard, strewn about the base of the very stoneworks they had exposed and weakened ...

The great cloud they had cast into the eyes of their enemy dissipated, enough for the defenders to discern their congregating shadows. The barrage of missiles concentrated, became a hellish racket. Seventeen Schoolmen toppled, flopped to earth, salted. Fifty-three others had to be carried back, some shrieking, thrashing, others immobile ...

The massed remainder struck.

For the Men of the Ordeal, the gold-fanged crowns of Corrunc and Domathuz where the first structures to resolve from the screens of grey, little more than battlemented silhouettes against the far more enormous bulk of the Horns. They glimpsed the Ursranc clustered like white-skinned termites along the crest, frantically casting spears and loosing slings and bows at the unseen Schoolmen below. The sorcerous unison abruptly dissolved into a many-voiced clamour, one that swatted ears for booming urgency. Substance itself croaked in hellish tongues, including their own flesh. Lights flashed in rapid succession from the murk, white upon white ... blue, crimson-violet, each revealing the mangled shadows of the Schoolmen and their billows. Clacking thunder tingled across bare and bearded cheeks, resounded over the whole of Shigogli.

And though many cheered, many more caught their breath, *for they saw the summit of Corrunc slouch.* The parapets dipped to the right, as though in mocking obeisance to the north, then simply toppled, first outward, then straight downward, as the evil bastion slumped into its own obliteration. The shock wave bulged, then blew out the last of the obscuring haze, revealing the Scarlet Schoolmen and the Mandati hanging about the crashing surf of Corrunc's destruction, their Anagogic and Gnostic Wards pelted luminous for showering debris.

The Ursranc of Golgotterath shrieked and wailed across the adjoining turrets. The Sons of Shir cheered and bellowed like beasts, brandished spear and sword. Horns screeched through the residual rumble, and the swart Men of Ainon, Sansor, Conriya and Cengemis surged out across Ûgorrior ...

The Canted Horn reared on an ethereal scale behind the collapse—no less than a dozen souls were trampled for gawking at its heights. Gwegiruh hunched stubborn to their left, hulking works beneath a tempest of scything lights—the ministry of the Nuns. Mighty Domathuz beyond cracked even as they ran, sloughed its eastward walls—revealing stacked floors that crawled as a broken beehive, a glimpse of a thousand inhuman throes, before all dropped howling into the smoke and ruin below.

The Sons of Kyraneas loosed their own booming cheer, and the Men of Nansur and Shigek, Enathpaneah, Amoteu and Eumarna raced out across foul Ûgorrior ...

The Gatehouse of Ûbil Maw alone remained standing. Half the height and twice the girth as Corrunc or Domathuz, evil Gwergiruh was simply too sturdy to collapse of its weight. Their billows twining into golden ligature, the Swayali were forced to pummel and to rend, to obliterate the ancient structure by degrees. They hung like fey swans about the monumental edifices, clawing at the bastion's innards with geometries of light—the Third and Seventh Quyan Theorems, the Noviratic Warspike, and the High Titirgic Axiom. They scourged the scratching heights, blasted the smoking bowels, slicked the debris with violet ruin. Behind them, the battlehorns sounded, and the Middlenorthmen let out a mighty shout, the warcries of violent and gloomy nations, then charged in a single mass of 30,000 souls, the Sons of Galeoth and Cepalor, Thunyerus and Ce Tydonn, come to avenge their ancient kin ...

The Ursranc upon the islands of intact wall screeched in terror, howled in lament. Lights erupted between the gold-fanged battlements.

And so the Great Ordeal accomplished what no other Mannish host could. The Extrinsic Gate was cast down in smoking ruin. For the first time in history, the belly of Golgotterath lay exposed to the licentious fury of Men.

———— ◦⊗◦ ————

The Umbilicus was entirely abandoned, but the old Wizard had already guessed as much. It was the emptiness of the *encampment* that terrified him, the sight of the slovenly precincts reaching out and out, a worn mosaic devoid of any sign of activity or life ...

They were *alone*—stranded on the rim of *Shigogli*, no less!

But the Whore afforded him no more than heartbeats to ponder the consequences, for beyond the encampment, beyond the desolate tracts of the Furnace Plain, lay *Golgotterath*.

And it seemed he had heard it all along, the chorus of hundreds of Schoolmen singing.

Breathless, he gazed. He could see the Great Ordeal *entire*, massed in three great squares before a vast smear of smoke or dust. He could see the flicker of arcane lights, like discharges of lightning buried within a distant thunderhead only many-coloured: white, blue, and vermillion. Then he saw *Corrunc stumble*, tip and slump into smoke and oblivion ...

Corrunc! Foul, murderous, and so tragically stubborn! The Eater-of-Sons *destroyed*!

The fraction of his soul that was Seswatha cried out for joy and terror, for it seemed impossible that he should witness something so hated, so *unconquerable*, overthrown. For it was *he*, Seswatha, who had convinced Celmomas to raise arms against the Consult, to dash the lives of noble thousands against its remorseless walls. It was *he* who had commanded the Sohonc to dare the Chorae Hail, who had sent so many of his beloved brothers to their doom. It was *he*, Seswatha, Lord Librarian, *who bore the greatest portion of blame*. And to see such a thing now ... to *witness* ...

It had to be some kind of cruel dream!

The old Wizard gasped, staggered. Up-welling passion cracked the strength of his legs, dropped him to his knees.

It was *happening* ...

And Kellhus! He ... He ...

Blinking, peering, he saw Domathuz sheer in half, then topple into far-away ruin. Deferred thunder rumbled across the plain.

Kellhus had spoken true.

Drusas Achamian wept and cackled, whooped with a wild, even lunatic joy. He leapt to his feet, danced a howling jig. He averted his gaze, then peered and peered again, like a besotted drunk testing the reality of his visions. And each time he dared gaze *he saw Golgotterath falling* ... There! There! The twinkling ranks surging across Ûgorrior; Men—tens of thousands of Men!—streaming through the breaches. Schoolmen *in their hundreds* raining incandescent destruction upon the stronghold's interior—striding the very gullet of Min-Uroikas! He slapped his forehead in disbelief, hooked hesitant fingers in his hair, his beard—and he *exulted*, croaking and dancing like a mad old beggar with a diamond.

Sobriety came with the sound of Mimara's wail rising hoarse from the Umbilicus behind him. His soul scrambled to recover its habitual decorum, its martyred air. Without quite realizing he had wetted a finger and poked it deep into the pouch, which he had somehow pilfered from Mimara's belongings. Qirri ... his cannibal vice. His old, old friend.

He sucked at the ash greedily—swallowing more than he had ever dared in Mimara's critical presence.

He closed his eyes to calm his racing heart, steady his arrhythmic breathing. He savoured the earthen bitter, glimpsed Cleric—Nil'giccas—in his soul's eye, melancholy and ruthless for the profundity of his confusion.

So much had happened. So much *had yet* to happen ...

Steady old fool ... Think.

Mimara shrieked once again, her voice frayed into anguished threads. The clack and roar of arcane ruin shivered out to the bowl of the Occlusion. Smoke swam about the monstrous foundation of the Horns. Sorcery sparked and glittered. Achamian did not move, captivated by the vision, arrested by what seemed innumerable claims upon his hope and attention.

And suddenly he understood Esmenet's mulish resistance, why she had pressed with such vehemence to prevent him *from standing in this very spot*. She had always been the wiser, the soul more shrewd. She had always known him in ways he could only recognize afterward. He had dwelt his entire life in the punishing shadow of this moment, this *time* ...

Now.

She knew he would stand where he stood.

And that the World would claim him.

CHAPTER FIFTEEN

Golgotterath

What trespass could be equal,
the woe you have brought upon us?
What sin could be so foul as to balance
our grief upon your ruthless Beam?
For we have praised thee, O Lord,
We have struck all that offends thee.
Why quicken our fields, our wombs,
only to set alight our granaries,
and crack our strong places asunder?
What sin could be so grievous,
that our children should be rendered,
to the raving of Sranc?

—Unknown, "The Kyranean Lament"

Early Autumn, 20 New Imperial Year (4132, Year-of-the-Tusk), Golgotterath.

The Sons of Shir raced forward. The mass deformed, stretching more and more into a spearhead as it neared the heaped foundations of Corrunc. The Mandate Triunes had struck ahead, and already assailed the lower terraces of the Oblitus, while the Scarlet Schoolmen had divided to attend to the intact walls on either flank. What few missiles that rained upon the rushing Men were sporadic and ineffectual. Those Ursranc that did not flee shrieking, burned such. The Scarlet Schoolmen clustered above the breach, laved the gold-fanged heights with golden fire, the brilliant issue of dozens of Dragonheads. The Sons of Shir gained the mounds below, led by the Knights of Conriya, whom the Holy Aspect-Emperor had tasked with redressing the shame of their King. They clambered up the ruin, roaring. The Marshal of Attrempus, Palatine Krijates Empharas, would be the first to crest the ruins of Corrunc, and the first to leap down, and thus, the first Man to set foot within Golgotterath. Shouting behind their silver warmasks, he and his household slaughtered what Ursranc they encountered. Glints of Gnostic destruction rolled like oil across their helms, shields, and hauberks.

The Sons of Shir streamed unmolested into Golgotterath. The Ark hung as a second, impervious ground above them, tracking the least detail in reflection. Beyond the curtain wall lay what the Ordealmen would come to call the Canal, a broad avenue finned with ruin and humped with refuse, and webbed with filthy hovels—warrens that the Schoolmen promptly set aflame. Smoke boiled toxic and black, its stench unmanning. Massed upon an isthmus of ruin surrounded by inferno, the Conriyans had no choice but to assail the far wall of the Canal, the First Riser, the lowest, fortified step of the Oblitus. Chains and hooks were called up, and the Southron warriors stormed onto the terrace unopposed, found the ground clotted with bodies burning as candles might. Their billows lacing the heights, the Mandate and Scarlet Schoolmen wracked the terraces above with catastrophic lights.

The ruins of Domathuz witnessed a different series of events. For reasons unknown, Temus Enhorû refused to lead his Imperial Saik against the Oblitus, electing instead to tarry above the breach and cleanse the flanking walls—the task assigned Obwë Gûswuran and his Mysunsai. The first Sons of Kyraneas to broach Golgotterath were Prince Cinganjehoi and his heavy-mailed Eumarnans. Unlike the Conriyans to the north, they found themselves pinned beneath a hail of missiles from the First Riser of the Oblitus and suffered grievously. Chaos ensued, with those at the rear forcing more and more of their kinsmen to brave the killing grounds below the Oblitus. Temus Enhorû only realized his error after Cinganjehoi ordered his Men to fire on the aging Saik Grandmaster from below. An inadvertent consequence of this was that the Sons of Kyraneas, bent on seeking cover, would be the first to seize the orphaned wall between Domathuz and the Evil Gate, where the javelin-bearing Nansur Columnaries, in particular, were able to inflict horrible losses on the Ursranc defending the First Riser.

They would also be the first to reach the imposing rump of Gwergiruh, where the Middlenorthmen found themselves stalled, locked in pitched melee with their bestial foe. Anasûrimbor Serwa and the Swayali had passed over the monstrous Gatehouse, thinking they pursued the defenders into the Oblitus. But the Unholy Consult, knowing the unreliability of their slaves, had gone so far as to *chain* some thousand Ursranc throughout Gwergiruh's honeycombed interior. King Vûkyelt and his bellicose Thunyeri had clambered into what they had assumed was a vacant hulk, only to find themselves in the hacking thick of battle. As with the breach at Domathuz, the eagerness of those in the rear proved lethal. The roaring Thunyeri were pressed into the black cleavers of their foe—many died for simple want of room to swing axe or sword. The adventitious arrival of General Biaxi Tarpellas and his Columnaries from the south put a quick end to this tragic waste. The Ursranc, crazed for terror, all but threw themselves upon the Nansur spears. Vûkyelt, Believer-King of Thunyerus, and Tarpellas, Patridomos of House Biaxi, would embrace in the fell shadow of Ûbil itself, which, seized and strapped by evil sorceries, remained shut despite being overthrown.

The Men of the Circumfix thronged in their thousands across the First Riser and into the Canal, kicking over leprous shelters, stamping out flames. Tens of thousands more massed and clamoured about the breaches at Domathuz, Corrunc, and the overthrown Gatehouse of Ûbil Maw. Only the Chorae archers who had initiated the stupendous assault lingered upon Ûgorrior. The ramparts cleared, they scoured the skirts of the ruin, as well as the ground where the Holy Aspect-Emperor had parlayed with Mekeritrig, searching for exposed Chorae. Luthymae, the Collegians charged with managing and recovering the Chorae Hoard, paced the desolate plain across the entire range of Ursranc archery, pointing out those they sensed or sighted. Any bowman recovering a Holy Tear of God would immediately set to affixing it, using prepared shafts and kits. Soon a great number could be seen, one knee down in the dust, their hands working furiously.

They would be the only ones to escape unscathed.

The Exalt-Magus, Anasûrimbor Serwa, hung above the fray, her billows like an intricate lily suspended in sun and water. She did not hesitate.

"Ware the First Riser!" she cried on a sorcerous boom.

Fairly every soul in the Great Ordeal ceased what they had been doing.

Three Triunes of her Gnostic Sisters hung about her, billows agleam and undulating. Dozens of like formations extended like wings to either side. The Oblitus reared imposing before her, step by monumental step, a god-stair climbing to the base of something greater than gods. But for all the threat of its stacked ramparts, it was the First Riser some thirty cubits beneath her feet that commanded her attention. Something ... No ...

Nothing. She sensed nothingness ... *Moving* nothingness.

And yet only ash and entrails remained of the skinnies who had stood upon the parapets ...

"Assemble!" she cried. *"Assemble against it!"*

Her voice dropped like cudgels upon every soul visible. Those along the remaining sections of curtain wall had already set their shields against the rising Oblitus. Confusion ruled all others, however. Eager to join what had seemed easy slaughter, the Men of the Ordeal had fallen into disorder, pressing heedless into the Canal, the slum-choked interval between the cyclopean outer walls and the bottommost terrace of the Oblitus. They formed a vast, elongated bolus, a motley of nations, steaming for the smoke of stamped out fires, bristling with arms and bereft of purpose. She watched with cool wonder as they spontaneously formed into impromptu ranks, shield locked to shield, all facing the blank wall of the First Riser.

She scanned the air above the Host, searching for some sign of her father. He would know.

At a thought, she dropped, alighted upon the first terrace, her billows drawn out behind her, across the burned and twisted carcasses. She closed her eyes, focussed on the tickles of oblivion floating like bubbles beneath her. Chorae, without any doubt, moving as if bound to things lumbering and alive ...

She caught her breath.

"Bashrag!" she cried, her voice fractured into something inhuman by a conspiracy of masonry. *"Concealed in the Ris—!"*

Monstrous impacts. A series of them, erupting along the entire length of the Canal, here thudding, there cracking, shattering. Dust and grit exploded from mortices. Men cried out, raised arms to protect their eyes. Skirts of masonry exploded outward. Whole sections of wall sloughed away, disgorging horrors ...

Dozens of orifices had been smashed across the sheer walls. Bashrag fell from them as vomit, leapt into the pallid ranks of Men, bull-bellowing, swinging pole-axes as thick as war-galley oars. They towered above their scrambling victims, obscene amalgams, motions hooked to their deformities, but no less deadly for it. Shields and arms exploded. Helms were stoved, rib-cages crushed. Armoured knights were thrown, sent like cartwheels above the massacre. The din was as instant as it was deafening. Serwa leapt back into the air, rejoined her witch sisters. The cunning of the attack was not lost upon her. Fairly all the Swayali gazed dumbstruck at the screaming turmoil below, the vision of Bashrag wading like monstrous adults into roiling mobs of children, reaping them as wheat, murdering them. And there was nothing to be done, no way to strike without killing their own. She saw the standard of Tarpellas fall. She saw the bearer and honour guard hammered to pulp against stone. Despite her Dûnyain blood, Anasûrimbor Serwa hesitated ...

Where was Father?

The mere thought of him spurred the recovery of her senses. She whirled about to face the Oblitus, which had entirely fallen from the Host's attention. She need not see to know the activity that brewed upon them. The Consult had not so much lost their legendary walls, she realized, as they had *given* them ...

"**Retreat!**" she cried on a crack of thunder. "*To Ûgorrior, Sisters!*"

Like variations in the sound of a waterfall ...

This was the most the Blessed Empress of the Three Seas could hear of the assault from within the chambered interior of the Umbilicus: a near featureless roar, a yawl woven across different registers of mass violence. A faraway cataract, booming with death instead of water.

Death and more death. Always *death*, these past twenty years. Even the lives she had delivered had simply added to the heap of murderers.

Only Mimara ... the dazzling little girl who had so adored the smell of apples. *Only she* had been Esmenet's one true gift to life.

So now it was her turn to die.

"*He'll return ...*"

Esmenet started. She had been sitting cross-legged to the side of the mattress, drifting in that upright way that made one feel like a sail pulled by unseen winds. She had thought her daughter unconscious, for the severity of her last travail as much the sleepless watches since her womb's draining. She looked down upon the girl's drawn face, noted, as she always noted, the saddle of freckles across the bridge of her nose—but one of so many things she had inherited from her whorish mother.

Too many.

"Mimara ..."

She hesitated, found herself fixed in her firstborn's brown-eyed gaze.

"I ..."

Her wind failed her. She flinched, looked down and away, though it seemed her every fraction clamoured that she endure. Several heartbeats passed. Her daughter's gaze became palpable, a tingle across her temple and cheek. She braved it once again, only to be overwhelmed by its implacable intensity—and to look down as she once had in the presence of caste-nobles.

Mimara reached out, caught her hand between her own.

"I never understood until now," she said.

Esmenet looked up, meek in the way of failed mothers and lovers, her breath so shallow it hurt. Her daughter's smile was dazzling—for its incongruity, its authenticity, yes, but for its *certainty* most of all.

"All that time, ever since you plucked me from Carythusal, I punished you. Everything I had suffered, I had heaped upon your name ... upon the dim image of a mother exchanging her little daughter for coins ..."

These words seized her heart within their fist.

"They said you would be a weaver ..." she found herself saying, "but I suppose I didn't believe them." Her eyes had become burning spikes. "The gold was just an accursed ornament. We-we were *ropes*, you and I ... starved to the bloody gum, and I *thought I was saving your life*. They had food. You could see it in the fat on their faces. The grease staining their insufferable tunics ... Their grin. I nearly swooned for thinking I could smell the food *in them* ... isn't that mad?"

How could it burn so, matching a child's gaze?

"You speak as though to absolve," Mimara said smiling, blinking tears, "to explain ... even though you think you deserve neither absolution nor understanding ..."

Ringing silence. Numbness.

"Yes ..." she said, her heart beating cloth. "Kellhus said the same."

"But Mother! I *see you*, Mother—I see you as the almighty *God of Gods* sees you!"

The Blessed Empress of the Three Seas flinched.

"That's funny," she said, reaching out to flatten bedding, "you sound just like Him ..."

A smile, crazed and beatific. "Because he pretends to be *what I am*."

"I liked you better when you were in pain," Esmenet said.

Her daughter's gaze did not so much catch as *arrest* her, absolutely, as if she only *existed* so far as Mimara could see her.

"You know ..." the beloved face said, "You *know* what it is I'm going to say ... and yet you cannot bear to hear it ..."

Esmenet found herself standing, her back turned to her daughter, her whole skin bewildered and afire.

"Perhaps it is best, then," she said stiffly, her voice nearly cracking on a sob that her breast refused to deliver.

"What is best?"

She turned, but could not bring herself to look directly at her prostrate daughter. She forced a smile.

"That we only have each other."

Esmenet could do no more than stare at a point to the left of the pregnant woman, the prophetess—the *stranger* ... She could only guess at the pity and adoration upon her face.

"Mother ..."

Esmenet knelt, raised a bowl of water to Mimara's lips, wondered when she had become so numb to the perversities of her lot. So many afflictions—too many, one would think, for any one soul to bear.

And yet here she was.

"Mother ..." The woman's look had a gentle urgency, a maternal conviction in certain things. She was the strong one now. The knowing one. From this moment, the mother would follow the daughter. "You can *let it go*, now, Mother."

A narrow smile. "Hmm?"

"Mother ..." Gelid brown eyes, seeing what no mortal should. "*You are forgiven ...*"

Life slowed about its most inflamed gear.

"No ..." Anasûrimbor Esmenet said on a smile far too honest for her liking. She wiped at her cheeks, expecting tears, found nothing save the grease of exhaustion and worry. Where? she wondered madly. Where had all the weeping gone?

"Not until I say so."

The Soldiers of the Circumfix were *hard* Men, as inveterate as any in history. For a great many, the mad trek across Eärwa was but the most recent episode of an entire life spent embroiled in violence and war. They had celebrated triumphs. They had suffered reversals—even wholesale routs. They had ravished, plundered, and butchered innocents. They had made cruel sport of their captive foes. They had trudged through tempests of archery. They had thrown back the glittering charge of Orthodox knights, and they had been scattered, ridden to earth. They had been scorched. Many even bore the puckered and inflamed scars of sorcery.

So it was they suffered no true terror as they watched the wall of the First Riser bow and buckle. Swells of laughter could even be heard as wits called out ribald encouragement. A good number of Men grinned for *anticipation* as the sheets of masonry fell away. No experience they possessed could prepare them for what followed.

Of all the Inchoroi abominations, none were so *unnatural* as the Bashrag. They spilled from the cavities, poured like sewage into the gleaming stew of Mannish nations crammed into the Canal, shambling monstrosities, shagged with great black heads of hair, possessed of malformed, tripled limbs, armoured in gowns of iron weighing ten thousand kellics or more. The Men were scarce more than armed and armoured children before them. Even the tallest of the Tydonni stood no higher than their elbows. Only the Nansur Columnaries under General Tarpellas managed to impede their bellowing egress, releasing volleys of javelins in numbers that could bring down mastodons. But the breaches continued discharging the beasts, who leapt and stomped into their midst, squealing and grunting, heaving their shield-sized cleavers. Not a single grin survived that initial onslaught, but there was no shortage of bravery—at least at first. Men stabbed and hacked and speared. But the quarters were too close, the Bashrag too ferocious, too powerful, for them to slow, let alone contain, the rampage. Armour crumpled like foil. Skulls shattered like pottery. Shields were little more than vellum, things swatted and ripped away. The swinging axes halved Men where they stood, tossed whole torsos over the screaming tumult.

The Schoolmen watched from on high, dismayed for the mayhem, paralysed for want of any course of action. The cunning of their Foe was obvious, as was the objective. Attack the beasts from above, and they killed their own. Attack them from the ground, and they risked their own lives, for hundreds of the creatures bore Chorae. The ambush's immediate objective was nothing more than to inflict losses, to murder as much of the Great Ordeal as possible on the doorstep of Golgotterath. Then Anasûrimbor Serwa, either succumbing to womanish fear or savvy to some other threat, commanded the Schools *retreat* ...

Those who could looked up, saw the Grandmistress, her billows soiled with soot and violet, lead her Swayali back out over Ûgorrior. For all their hardness, *panic* seized the Men of the Ordeal.

Within heartbeats, it seemed, the Nasueret, Selial, and Circumfix Columns all but ceased to exist. The hallowed Nansur standard—the legendary breastplate of Kuxophus II, the last of the ancient Kyranean High Kings—was overthrown. Tarpellas, who stood upon the debris heaped against the rear of Gwergiruh bawling futile commands, was struck from the shoulder to the pelvis. Death came swirling down.

Maranjehoi, Grandee of Piralm and companion to Prince Inrilil, lost his right arm nearly at the shoulder, on a blow so swift that the dismemberment left him standing. He simply stumbled backward, fell onto his rump and back across the corpses of his kinsmen, gazed unblinking at the sky-hooking enormity of the Horns until he could do nothing else.

Bansipitas of Sepa-Gielgath fell. As did Orsuwick of Kalt and Wustamitas of Nangaelsa, both undone by anvil-sized hammers.

Death and more death, sweeping down and away ...

Men began fleeing, or attempting to do so, for thousands found themselves trapped in the scrum about the breaches. Exultant, the Bashrag loosed a sinusoidal roar and stampeded into them, worked a great and grisly slaughter.

The surviving Believer-Kings in the Canal lamented, began crying out to heavens, calling for their Holy Aspect-Emperor ...

⌘

A cry of masculine agony, muffled, yet near enough to hear the raw of it, the crack and gurgle of phlegm.

It yanked the Blessed Empress from her nodding reverie, sent her leaping to her feet. She stood blinking, listening, knowing in her bones that it had come from *within* the Umbilicus. She cursed Achamian, suddenly understanding that *this* was what had made his presence mandatory. No soul was more vulnerable than the birthing mother's—save the infant she delivered.

She clasped the knife she had set aside for the birth-cord, crept to the threshold, pulled aside the image-panelled flaps.

"Mumma?" Mimara sobbed after her. Another seizure was nearing.

She shot an annoyed look at her daughter, raised a finger to her lips ...

Then pressed through.

She crossed the antechamber. Her ears pricked, she strained to discern any sound over and above the background cataract, the distant chorus of killing and dying.

She slunk into the corridor, crept down its length, holding the knife point directly out before her.

She heard muttering voices ... then a cough, apparently grievous for the pain it inflicted.

She slipped into the Eleven-Pole Chamber, crouched low behind her husband's bench and dais, waited for her eyes to adjust. She crinkled her nose at the smell, noticed the Ekkinû Arras was missing ...

"*Here?* Are you sure?"

She nearly cried out for recognition, but stifled her voice out of fugitive habit.

"I need ... to keep ... watching ..."

She peered into the airy interior.

"But there are beds!"

"It is ... better ... to *see* ..."

Indirect light streamed through the missing fourth wall, the one Kellhus had torn away to reveal the wicked glory of Golgotterath. It fell across the raised wooden tiers, too diffuse to cast shadows, yet concentrated enough to darken the gloom surrounding. With his back to her, Achamian sat high on the arm of tiers opposite the great rip ... ministering to someone laying naked and prostrate across the planks, his head across the old Wizard's folded knee.

"You ... you were right ... all along ... Right about him."

Proyas?

"No-no ... my boy. I was *wrong!*"

Esmenet fairly convulsed for the intensity of her shame—and relief. Of course he had left—as she had feared. And of course, *he had returned ...*

He was Drusas Achamian.

Even still, she found herself voiceless and immobile, spying upon yet another luminous clearing from yet another murky bower—*hiding*, as she always hid, loathe to afflict others with her fraudulent presence ...

The lesser reality of her soul.

"But *he is false ...*" the ailing King of Conriya gasped, "He is ... *Dûnyain* ... Just as you said!"

Achamian raised an arm to the brightness, revealed his wiry profile for the merest of instants. "Look for yourself ... Golgotterath *falls!*"

She could see nothing of the spectacle, given her angle ...

"Does it?" Proyas asked on a heaving shudder.

And it astonished, even appalled, to realize that she *had turned her back on the Apocalypse ...*

"Well it certainly *burns ...*"

Anasûrimbor Kellhus, her accursed husband, played number-sticks for the very World—and *she did not care ...* so long as Mimara remained safe.

"Ah ..." Proyas said, his voice regaining, even if only for a heartbeat, something of its old warmth and confidence. "Yes ... It must be *nectar ...* for you ... Narcotic even ... A spectacle ... such as this."

Achamian said nothing, continued daubing his old student's face. Pallid light showered down upon them, inking their undersides, bleaching them of colour, etching them in the monochrome facts of their mortality. A king dying upon a sorcerer's lap ... as in days of old.

Esmenet swallowed at the ache of her cowardice, her abject inability to either reveal herself or steal away. She remembered spying him unawares in Amoteu so very long ago, after reading *The Holy Sagas* for the first time ... after spurning him for the delirium of Kellhus's bed. She remembered the heartbreak of finally *understanding* him, the beauty that was his all-too-human frailty ...

And it seemed nothing compared to this.

"Can you—?" Proyas began, only to have his voice stolen by some whistling pain.

"Can I what, dear boy?"

"Can you ... you ... *forgive me* ... Akka?"

An insincere laugh.

"A wife's curse is as worthless as a sorcerer's blessing. Isn't that what you Conriyans sa—?"

"No!" the King cried, obviously preferring the anguish of violent exclamation to any demurral or making-trite. "My *name* ..." he continued on a grimacing voice, "will be *the* name ... the name ... that my children ... my children's children ... will *curse* in their prayers! Don't you see? He did not simply betray my body! I'm *damned*, Ak—!"

"*As am I!*" the old Wizard cried in smiling contradiction. Esmenet saw his shoulders hitch in a helpless shrug. "But ... one learns to muddle."

She understood then what a gift this was, the ability to negotiate terms with death.

"Yes ..." Proyas replied, his voice once again wavering about the memory of an easy nature. "But this ... Akka ... This ... is *me* ..."

The old Wizard shook his head in slow incredulity. The two Men laughed, though only Proyas was punished for it. He gasped and wheezed about some pain, arched his back, revealing, for a heartbeat, the black maul of his pubis. The old Wizard clutched his beloved student's scalp in his right hand, slowly drew his wetted cloth along the man's chest, neck, and shoulders with his left. He continued doing this until the convulsions subsided—the same as she had done, and would continue to do, with Mimara.

Long moments passed in silence. Esmenet dropped from her crouch to her knees for discomfort.

"Such arrogance ..." Proyas eventually said, his tone glassy, and alarming for it.

Achamian's attention had drifted to what vistas his view afforded. "What?"

"Such ... such *arrogance* ... you would tell me ... Such reckless, simple arrogance ... to make *guesses* the measure ... of *worth* ..."

Achamian sighed, at last resigning himself to Proyas's need to confess.

"Children often take me for wise. Children and idiots."

"But I *didn't* ... I took you ... for a fool ..."

Achamian said nothing—evidence of some old and unaccounted bruise, Esmenet assumed. Such are the burdens we impose upon one another. Such are the plots we leaved unweeded, untilled.

"Can you ..." Proyas asked on a tremulous voice forcefully breathed. "Can you *forgive* me ... Akka?"

The old Wizard cleared his throat ...

"Only if you hang on, my boy. Only if you *li—*"

But Proyas had pushed aside Achamian's ministrations with the purple grotesquerie of a hand. He arched forward, gazing out to riot on the plain, only to be stalled by agony.

Esmenet caught her breath, loud enough to earn a momentary, backwards glance from Achamian.

Their eyes locked for but a heartbeat—two blank faces.

"*Look!*" Proyas groaned and gasped, waving an arm at Golgotterath, "Some-something ... *happens* ..."

She saw the old Wizard turn to the missing wall—and blanche.

Apart from the Scylvendi occupying the Akeokinoi, the Mysunsai and Saik Schoolmen reforming above Ûgorrior were the first to see ... though initially many refused to credit it.

To the west, the Occlusion extended on a perfect arc, reaching out into hazy colourlessness, fencing all that was visible, until dwarfed by the wreckage-of-earth that was the Yimaleti piling white upon cerulean. None other than Obwë Gûswuran, Grandmaster of the Mysunsai, spied them, his eye drawn by a wick of dust or smoke ...

Sranc, streaming down a gully in the western face of the Occlusion. More appeared at a different interval fairly a league to the south. More again at a point nearly between.

Then another greater mass to the north. An outpouring of thousands.

The Schoolmen traded shouts of alarm and consternation. Temus Enhorû dispatched triunes of Saik to inform Serwa, Kayûtas, and Saccarees. But it seemed they could already hear it, despite the hellish racket of battle below ...

A titanic yammering, howling madness multiplied into a heaven-cracking sum.

The all-encompassing roar of the *Horde*.

Then, abruptly, like water breaking its bead, Sranc *flooded* the clefts and slopes of the far Occlusion, a writhing deluge of what seemed maggots in pitch. Teeming figures engulfed all save the most precipitous heights, in many places falling in sheets down cliffs and breakneck slopes, hundreds becoming thousands, thrown to their deaths by the vast surge. The dead and maimed tumbled down the mangled inclines, accumulated and accumulated, choking gullies, matting slopes, forming great ramps of carcasses, until those that toppled *began leaping up*, rejoining the rush—until the Occlusion became naught more than a collection of isolated summits in a cataract that heaved and rushed across *leagues*, pooling below and washing outward, a foul seepage of innumerable thousands ...

The Schoolmen watched dismayed and incredulous. Some, those with more youthful eyes, sighted *a lone figure standing upon Shigogli* as if awaiting the torrents. They watched with wonder as the roiling masses advanced on him, raising plumes and curtains of dust ...

Only when the ground beneath the floating figure began belching geysers of ashen sand, flinging Sranc in blooms of white and violet wreckage, did they recognize their Holy Aspect-Emperor ...

Standing solitary against the Sranc Horde.

Vile angel.

Its triumphant screech brings down a haze of dust and flaked mortar.

Kakaliol, Reaper-of-Heroes, dandles the thing in its fiery talons. Lolling limbs, head hanging as if from a stocking. Soft skin blistered or abraded or shorn away, a bladder for gelatinous innards and absurd quantities of blood, like an unwrung rag.

But where? Where is the *soul?*

Cast it aside, the Blind Slaver commands.

I would keep it for my token.

It runs a claw across the porcelain scalp, skinning it like rotted fruit, seeking ...

Discharge your task!

The Arch-Ciphrang roars, clacks and stamps in impotent defiance. How? How can it pain him so? A world like bread. Like soap or cake. A world filled with dolls of meat!

And yet impregnated with pins, edged with teeth.

The pleasures I could have rendered thee, mortal ... The delights.

I render here.

The Seducer-of-Thieves stalks into vacant blackness, bearing the carcass across a horned shoulder. Its hide sheds a baleful circle of illumination, one that pulses larger upon each bull-huffing exhalation. But nothing more than crude-cobbled floors are revealed, so immense is the chamber. Only as the burning trail of its blood lengthens are the limits—and the purpose—of the great cavity revealed: the cyclopean blocks, the massive square pillars ... and the vast *wall of gold* ...

Vile angel.

Kakaliol pauses between two pillars, rakes the gloom with its infernal eyes. It allows its prize to slop sizzling to the floors.

Yes ... the Blind Slaver murmurs.

They stand deep in the bowel of the High Cwol, the point where the ponderous stone of Golgotterath marries the impenetrable skin of the Inchoroi Ark. The curve of the High Horn climbs vast before the demon, liquid with reflected crimson and seething, scintillating gold. A great chasm, some thirty paces wide and too deep to be fathomed, separates it from the floors, so that it plummets as deep as it soars high. The surface, however, is far from intact. A bridge spans the abyss, black stone raised across girders of gold, linking the floors to a gigantic rent in the Ark's shell, one sealed and barricaded by stone bulwarks as mighty as any in Golgotterath, as if masons had bricked shut a rupture in a ship's hull.

Behold, the insidious whisper declares, *Ûbil Noscisor* ...

The Intrinsic Gate.

The stench of human entrails permeated the air. The Canal convulsed the whole of its glutted length. Ordealmen in their thousands formed dark clouds about each of the three breaches, blots that twinkled for countless sharp edges. The Exalt-Magus led her sisters out over the mobbed ruin of Gwergiruh beyond the shattered circuit of Golgotterath's outer defenses.

The Scarlet Spires had surmounted the Scab and secured their right flank, while the Imperial Saik was in the course of doing so on their left. Even as her sisters stepped back onto Ûgorrior, the Mandate sheltered behind the northern island of intact wall, and the Mysunsai—those who heeded her call—did the same behind the monolithic southern. The Ordealmen cried out in dismay below, cursed them as craven, but Anasûrimbor Serwa had eyes only for the sinister stages of the Oblitus. The Bashrag attack was no mere contingency. The Unholy Consult had *yielded* evil Ûbil and her monstrous towers ...

The ambush was part of a larger deception. A greater catastrophe loomed.

But where?

Dozens had ignored her call for a general retreat, most of them Mysunsai, but two of her own as well: Hûtta-mimot and Sapharal, older, headstrong souls, women who had pursued witchcraft under the threat of torture and death long before the Shrial Repeal and the founding of the Swayali. They lingered with their triunes as their sisters retreated, either loathe to abandon the Men dying below, or wedded to some course of action they thought decisive and heroic.

Serwa forbid any effort to contact them or their subordinates. For the nonce, knowledge was the paramount objective—her mission.

Plumes of smoke continued to rise from the gold-fanged parapets of the High Cwol, forming fans across the base of the Upright Horn, sheets of liquid black balding across mountainous gold. She conjured a Lens, scolded a handful of her sisters for wandering into her line of sight. Then Mirûnwe announced that the Mysunsai had spied *another Horde* spilling down the northwest slopes of the Occlusion. As catastrophic as these tidings were, Serwa had eyes only for her Lens and the image of Nonmen Erratics stepping from the parapets of the Ninth Riser—*Quya*, their skulls shadows for semantic incandescence.

Ghouls.

The tickle of oblivion drew her attention below: constellations of unseen Chorae borne by unseen hands. She waved the Lens down to the Third Riser, scrolled across loping companies of Ursranc archers.

"Stand fast!" she cracked across the cloudless heavens.

She barked orders to her triune, whom in turn signalled the other

Grandmasters, as well as her brother Kayûtas, the Exalt-General, and the contingents of Chorae bowmen below.

Mannish shrieks and huffing Bashrag wrawls pealed through the air. The Ursranc archers formed batteries along the parapets rimming the third terrace.

Nothingness rained down on the malingering Witches and Schoolmen.

Serwa batted away the Lens. Hûtta-mimot and her triune vanished in flickering succession. Sapharal and her sisters fared far better, with only one, Herea, struck ... in the mid-billows, it appeared.

But the Quyan Ghouls were instantly upon them. More than a hundred of them descended the Oblitus, some naked save for the beading of cere-monial scars or myriad lines of ink script, others garbed in Ishroi glory, agleam in silk and nimil, and still others bound in rot and rags—all howling their madness in geometries of light and fire.

The timing troubled the Exalt-Magus.

"**Hold!**" she boomed.

Of the stranded Swayali, only Sapharal hung with her billows fully ex-tended. Mipharal, her sister in fact of blood as well as witchcraft, clutched the injured Herea. The woman looked up and found herself at the blinding intersection of two dozen Quyan Cants. The two Witches lasted scarcely ten heartbeats. Though spared the brunt, Sapharal fell back to the surviving section of wall between Domathuz and Gwergiruh. The Ghouls pursued her with howling light, a brilliant welter of Cants, Illarillic Primitives and Thimioni Aggressives, chosen less out of sense than fury. Sapharal fled the cataclysmic advance, her tattered Wards sailing ethereal about her. But the Ghouls closed, scraping and spearing and hammering at her with lights bright enough to throw shadows in the full sun, killing all the hapless Men she passed—the Men who did not matter.

Just then, the first of the rearmed Chorae archers began surmounting the stranded islands of wall, scuttling for what cover the wrack afforded, crouching and firing. Old beyond reckoning, lusting for ruin and heart-break, the Quya Erratics had not sensed their Chorae through the wall's intervening bulk. Many paused to regard the new threat, but many more continued hounding Sapharal, who dove beneath a golden fang laying wedged in debris.

What followed bruised the hearts of all those who Dreamed the First Apocalypse, and so knew the Ghouls as they once were—as Ishroi and Siqû,

Cûnuroi of ancient old. Only the Anagogic Schoolmen were so callous as to cry out in exultation. The Chorae bowmen began finding their raving targets, and one by one the Quya began falling as salt and statuary, crashing across the First Riser or into the churning length of the Canal. The ghoulish sorcerers began shrieking their inhuman songs, raked the archers with torrents of fractal light, killing many for the violence of secondary, mundane forces. But for every one they killed, two more slipped between the battlements. And lo, the Men of the Three Seas loosed a second Chorae Hail, one avenging the tragedy of the first more than two thousand years ago.

"**On them!**" the Exalt-Magus thundered.

And with that she led her arcane sisters over the teeming ruins of Ûbil Maw, back into the cauldron of Golgotterath, even as the Mysunsai and the Mandate floated out across either flank, their skulls furnaces of meaning, their singing an existential cacophony, the song of five hundred stone-cracking Cants.

It was a sight unlike any seen. Slaughter become beauty and light.

Dazzling Primitives, ghostly Reality Lines and blinding Inessences ... all of them snuffed for the fury of Abstractions and Analogies, winking into burning, blasting existence, then fading on the smoke of dropping, burning forms. So died Sos-Praniura, Lord-of-Poisons, accursed Founder of the Mangaecca; and Mimotil Cravenhearted, Bearer of the Copper Tree at Pir Minginnial; and the mercurial Cu'cûlol, the impossibly ancient kinsman of Cu'jara Cinmoi. So fell Risaphial, nephew of Gin'yursis, and so many others, in reckless immolation, battling for the very evil that had so scarred their hearts, murdering for memory's sake.

So fell the remnants of an entire Age.

Fairly two dozen Ghouls survived that initial onslaught. They could have fled the advancing triunes of Men, but nearly all of them persisted, some laughing, booming taunts in their melodious tongues, others simply shrieking out Cants, battling wraiths from their past, perhaps, shadows of ancient heartbreak. Hanging resplendent in their billows, the Magi of the Three Seas laved them in killing lights, tore away Quyan Wards like tissue, knocked the Erratic Quya from the skies, sent their blazing corpses crashing to earth.

Even as Bashrag hacked and Men howled below their slippered feet.

It opens and closes now, the Eye ...

Dilating with the arrival of her birthing pains then squinting at their passage, and sometimes, more rarely, blinking and peering in the calm between, like a napping dog noting unexpected arrivals.

Mimara seizes the hand of the luminous angel that is her mother, screams, though her voice is little more than rope, rigging on a beached wreck. She hears herself whimper, sob. She gazes into the angel's diamond eyes, begging, not for anything tangible or intangible, not even to make the agony stop, just begging, beseeching without hope or object.

She does not need the Eye to know the Blessed Empress thinks her daughter is dying.

It seems she must be dying, so excruciating the pain has become, so fruitless the ordeal. Mimara had not thought such anguish possible, the piling on of ache and twisting cramp and laceration and bulbous rupture. Her womb has become a great claw, alien and relentless, clenching and unclenching about the palm of her belly, kneading and crushing her very centre, again and again and again, until her screams are the screams of a stranger.

The latest series relents, and she actually cackles, so out of proportion is the pain, so lunatic. Her mother shushes and soothes. She falls to panting. Her eyes flutter, and the leather-walled chamber—gritty gloom slicked in pale lantern light—reels and revolves in aching delirium. Her mother is talking, she realizes ... to someone hidden behind the shadows battling like starlings across her periphery ...

"No. *Impossible. Her canal ... It must unshut ...*"

Achamian, she realizes ...

Akka!

She raises her head against the cramping, sees him at the foot of the mattress, bickering with Mother yet again. The ugliness of his Mark is enough to kick bile to the back of her throat, but the beauty of his presence is ... is ...

Enough.

You can come out now, little one. Father has returned.

The Blessed Empress does not share her relief. "I *forbid* it!" she is crying high and shrill. "You will no—!"

"*Trust me!*" the old Wizard booms in irascible fury.

Her mother flinches, notices her scrutiny. Achamian follows her gaze.

They are *ashamed*, she realizes, even though quarrelling over the dying has ever been the lot of those who love. She tries to smile, but can only feed the grimace that tyrannizes her face. "I ... I t-told *you* ..." she gasps to her Empress mother. "*I told you ... he would come ...*"

The old Wizard kneels at her side, his smell pungent and unforgiving. He is trying to smile. Without explanation he wets his finger, prods it into the *pouch* ...

How could she forget it?

He pulls an ash-furred fingertip from the maw of the thing, proffers it ...

"Akka!" her mother protests. "Mimara ... *don't* ..."

Mimara looks to him, the one Man she has ever trusted with her weakness, her father, her lover ...

Her first disciple.

He cannot bring himself to smile; they have travelled far, beyond the need for compassionate deceptions. He does not know whether the Qirri will harm her or her child. He knows only that she has no choice.

Are you sure?

His nod is almost imperceptible.

She takes his hand, swallows his finger to the second knuckle, sucks at what is bitter and strong.

Nil'giccas ...

Priest of Waste and Wild.

The Canal had become an abattoir.

The Men had exhausted the initial, inhuman fury of the Bashrag—by dint of numbers if nothing else. The giants had sheered through the ranks effortlessly at first, hacking broad swathes clear of all save the dead. When the Men had taken to panic, they had trampled and hewn, chased the survivors into disparate clots of resistance, or to the great bladders of Men about the destroyed towers and gate. But as their ferocity lapsed into labour, the massacres evolved into battles, which became more and more pitched.

The violence of the assault had been far from even. The bulk of the attack had come in the centre, where the Bashrag appeared intent on retaking ruined Gwergiruh. But here they confronted the legendary Sosering

Rauchurl, High-Thane of Holca, along with two hundred and seventy-three of his tribal kinsmen. The Holca were the fiercest of the Sons of Thunyerus, though their cousins scarcely thought them human. They were famed for many things: their fiery hair, their prodigious strength, their battle-madness—and the fact that each possessed *two hearts*. The lands of Holca lay on the very frontier of Mannish hegemony, high on the waters of the mighty Wernma, in the violent shadow of the Wilderness the scalpers called the Mop. They were suckled in the shadow of the Sranc, veterans of countless mobbings, and like very few Men, they counted Bashrag among their ancestral foes.

Their heads great, wiry swags, their limbs pocked with cancerous moles, the Bashrag cudgelled and cleaved their way through the crush about Gwergiruh, where Rauchurl had assembled his kinsmen along ruined heights. As the grotesqueries lurched neared the base, the Holca leapt upon them, a shouting rain of battleaxes and red-flushed limbs. Obscene skulls cracked. Violet gushed from great scale gowns of iron. The Bashrag wavered. Seized by a berserker fury, Rauchurl closed with foul Krû Gai, a chieftain renowned among his misbegotten kind. They roared at each other, Inchoroi obscenity and unnatural Man, the one lurching and dark, mucose and pallid, the other flushed with wild vitality, trembling with red-rimmed *life*, both screaming a fury more primal than thought or soul. Rauchurl leapt, swung his battle-axe wide on its leather strap ... and caught the monstrosity's jaw, portioning the vestigial faces on either cheek, sending the elephantine head backward. The High-Thane of the Holca did not so much holler in triumph as he *screamed*, adding his spittle to the descending haze of violet.

So the Holca closed with the Bashrag, leaping into them with hacking fury, hewing their tripled ankles, picking their chariot breasts, axing their cauldron skulls. They moved with the lethal alacrity of cats despite their hulking frames, possessed of a ferociousness that was as insane as it was unconquerable. Even disembowelled, they stood and raged and battled. The Sons of Holca fought crazed, and the Bashrag, in their dim way, were astonished. They croaked and mewled to their brothers. They assailed the Crimson Men in ever greater numbers and fell, grunting, pawing gouts of violet with three-handed hands.

The lumbering obscenities numbered at most some few thousand, and for all the punishment they had meted, their numbers had been whittled down. As more and more of the beasts answered the alarums raised by the Holca, the bloody contests began to turn across the entirety of the Canal.

So the battle hung poised when the Nuns and Schoolmen assailed the Quya. Be they black and rheumy or white and clear, all eyes turned upward to the vaulting of wicked lights, incandescent and ephemeral. And for a miraculous moment they simply stood wondering, Man and Bashrag, shedding shadows that spun about their feet. And as the Quyan Ghouls began dropping, blasted and burning, the soulless hulks were seized by terror. The Soldiers of the Circumfix let out a mighty shout, charged en masse, and began avenging the thousands that had been killed.

Not a soul among them at this point knew of the Horde descending from the west.

The foremost triunes stayed low, striding scarcely above the heads of the Men massed and advancing below. They sang continuously and in unison, their heads inclined to the threat of the Oblitus, great plumes of sorcerous smoke materializing from their outstretched hands, drawn high into obscuring shrouds on the wind. Perched on the islanded walls, meanwhile, the Chorae Bowmen began methodically pelting the terraces of the Oblitus with their Trinkets, bringing down vast systems of interlocking Wards. The Believer-Kings and their vassals surged onward and upward using hooks and chains, climbing from the carnage and shadow of the Canal, seizing first the Second and then the Third Riser, where their arms and armour flashed newborn in the nooning sun.

And they understood the wicked might of the Consult had been broken. *Golgotterath lay open*, helpless before their righteous fury. An eagerness seized them, a predatory knowledge that whetted their lust for blood and destruction. Men whooped, cried out triumphant, rushing over the abandoned tiers of the Oblitus. Anasûrimbor Serwa remained suspicious, even though she understood their conviction. Their Holy Aspect-Emperor had overthrown every place he had coveted. Why should Golgotterath prove any different?

Unless the ancient and monstrous intellects of the Consult played a far different game.

One that turned on *timing*.

She had already signalled her concerns to her elder brother, Kayûtas, who concurred. The newborn *Horde* was the cornerstone of the Consult's design, not the gold-fanged bulwarks of Golgotterath, which need only occupy the Great Ordeal long enough for the Horde to descend upon it ...

This was why Father stood alone upon Shigogli, luring, cowing, wreaking untold destruction.

To purchase her and her brother more time.

"**Seize the heights!**" the Exalt-Magus thundered, her voice resonating across the Horns. "**Storm the High Cwol!**"

A sovereign brilliance, one glaring more *against* the noon sun than for it ...

The Holy Aspect-Emperor hung low and solitary above the desolate plate of Shigogli, facing the intersection of the Occlusion and the blue towering Yimaleti.

The very vista before him *crawled*, teemed with masses so great as to baffle the eyes, dupe the immovable frame of sky and earth into decamping. Sranc and more Sranc, nude save for crusts of muck, gibbering and yammering, brandishing crude axes and cruder spears, their canine members taut across their abdomens, stained violet for blood. They had swamped the northwest Occlusion. Pallid cataracts now draped the shoulders of every summit, cascading down and flushing out across the wasted plain, a thousand strands of turbulence convolving into one vast and loping onslaught ...

Into the Blessed Saviour's furious light.

In their rutting thousands, He smote them. And still they continued raging, continued running, tidal surges of innumerable, screeching faces, white beauty crushed into vicious, bestial inhumanity. They scratched and scrambled across the carcasses of the slain, leapt screaming into his armatures of scything light. Limbs and torsos erupted as autumn leaves about lines of brilliant white.

The Horde surged below and the Holy Aspect-Emperor hung above, flashing as a beacon, singing the only hymns the septic masses could reckon, genocidal Abstractions that carved tracts of ruin from the festering rush, Metagnostic disputations that consumed legions across the span of a league. Hearts exploded from myriad breasts. Skulls spontaneously imploded, wrung like rags. Wherever He walked, the Blessed Saviour trailed skirts of luminous destruction, plastering whole swathes of the plain with smoking, twitching dead. But they were pockets, merely, for the Sranc deluge swelled across the horizon, encompassed more and more of Shigogli.

Soon He stood stranded, hanging above an earth whose every ground had been overrun by white screams and raving appetites.

The Shroud engulfed first the Holy Aspect-Emperor, then his miraculous light in billowing obscurity. And for all his divine might, the Horde descended upon Golgotterath as if unhindered.

There are regions, *places*, gloaming tracts between the cruel edges and the mists—between the living and the dead. Hooks allowing the soul to linger beyond the moist endurance of the body.

Proyas lies breathing, naked and limbs askew upon the tiers, showered in the light of the very images that compel him.

The Horns soaring high as lightning. The black crab of Golgotterath, smoking.

The Shroud of another Horde, vast rags of ash roiling sunlit about gloom and darkness ... nearing.

A silhouette appears below the spectacle, at the base of the breach in the leather wall—a physically powerful man, a *warrior*, sporting a Kianene helm. Even though he stands outside the Umbilicus, Proyas somehow knows the man belongs to the shadow play *within*, understands that he has *always* belonged, despite the madness and mayhem shouting the contrary.

The figure strides into the airy gloom, accumulating menace with warlike visibility. An entourage of armed wraiths follow, but they are obscured by his approach. Wild black mane. Stooped carriage. Scars upon scars upon scars—swazond without number. High cheekbones ... and the eyes. His eyes. His unravelling look.

Cnaiür urs Skiotha strides up the tiers, rises to blot the smoke-roped vista of Min-Uroikas. His corded chest and torso lay bare in ritual display. Swazond are stacked in puckered sheaves across his entire skin, the record of his murderous life, *shelling* him. They encase his neck, a corded filigree that climbs the gunwale of his jaw, and reaches no higher than his lower lip ... as if he were about to drown in his homicidal trophies.

The most violent of all Men.

Proyas gazes, blinking, but not for want of faith in his eyes. He lies beyond incredulity. Were it not for his anguish, he would have laughed.

He feels the thud of the man through the timber stringers. Cnaiür halts his climb upon him, as though he plans to prod him with his boot. Proyas could have been either blank earth or a murdered loved one, so titanic is the man's gaze, so numb.

"I *asked* ..." Proyas pants upon a grimace. "I-I asked ... *Him* ..."

The same eyes, irises blue unto white, pupils as bottomless as Carythusali greed. The same wild, ransacking gaze.

"Asked what?"

Even his voice has aged savage.

Proyas blinks, tries to swallow.

"How you died."

The eyes narrow.

"And what did he say?"

"With *glory*."

Another man would have balked at such a cryptic answer. Another man would have pressed, asked for details, laying out the entrails of the encounter, seeking to isolate some clear meaning. Not the most violent of all Men.

"He did this to you?"

A meeting of cracked lips. "Yes."

There was something stronger than iron in their mutual regard, something heavier than ground.

The Scylvendi King-of-Tribes turned his head and spat.

"I was never such a fool as you."

Again Proyas smiles, somehow anguished and serene.

"So ... the *argument* ... unfolds."

The savage mien winced. "Aye. My feud is ongoing. But yours, Outland King, *leaks* from your insides."

Proyas does laugh then, and weep. "Give it ... time."

The World is grey now, spaced in blurs of looming light ... His mother giggles, teases him for having such lustrous curls ... and *there*, clear as linen warming in sunlight, stands the Scylvendi barbarian who had delivered Anasûrimbor Kellhus to the Three Seas. Somehow stronger, the violence of his intensity more keen, for the leathery ruts about his eyes, the hide of beaded swazond, and the intervening decades of atrocity.

"From the beginning," Cnaiür growls, "I hated."

"And so ... you were *known* ..."

"He is the *coal* that kindles my wrath," the Scylvendi retorts, "the *knife* that compels my will. Do you think I do not see this? Do you think I am numb to his depraved yoke? *From the beginning!* From the beginning he has ruled my obsession ... And *knowing* this, I have thrown my own number-sticks. Knowing this, I have raised myself—*by my own hair* I have wrenched myself!—from his innumerable snares."

And Proyas sees it, not so much the truth of the Scylvendi as the truth of *tragedy*, the doom of all doomed souls. To believe themselves set apart. To think all floods subside at their feet.

"He told me ... He told me ... you were coming ..."

A look of sullen thoughtfulness.

"He is no God," Cnaiür urs Skiotha said.

"And what is ... he?"

A scowl.

"The same as me."

Proyas understands the imperative to be wary, to measure the potential offense of each and every word in his savage presence. Malice flexes beneath his every movement, his every expression, a serpent awaiting the merest provocation to strike. His hulking stature and iron-strapped arms merely assure the outcome.

The Believer-King understands these threats, but feels nothing of their urgent clamour. It is a measure, he realizes, of where he stands on the circuit of death.

Proyas swallows, gasps against the plucking of something deep within his chest. "Do you truly ... think ... all *this* ... is a *ruse?*"

Cnaiür drops as if to grapple or throttle, his teeth clenched, the pouched skin of his neck taut about flaring tendons.

"*He!*"

A granitic fist cracks the wood next to Proyas's right ear.

"*Is!*"

A second thuds across the fabric spilled next to his left.

"*Dûnyain!*"

The most-violent-of-all-men arches like a lover over him.

"And I shall *dog* him! Snap at his heels! Bay through the watches of his sleep! I shall wait upon his outrageous arrogance, cast upon the obscene gluttony of his Mission! And when his diseased tools are spent, when he is battered and bereft, then—*then!*—I shall reveal the dread beam of my vengeance!"

"You ... would risk ... al—"

"What? Your great cities? *Midden heaps!* The fat of Three Seas? The People? Creation? Fool! You appeal to reason where there is none! You would put my hatred upon the balance with my desire—show me the mad wages of my design! *But my hatred is my desire!* My ribs are teeth, my heart a gut without bottom! *I am fury incarnate*, outrage become stalking sinew and flesh! My shadow cracks the earth, falls upon Hell itself! I smoke for the murder of innocents! And I shall *sup* upon his humiliation! I shall put out is eyes! Make adornments of his fingers! his manhood and his teeth! I shall hack him *into the worm!* the worm that is the truth!—*truth!* of his nature! For he is naught but a maggot feasting upon carrion and corruption!

"The meat of you!" he howls, yanking high *his knife* ...

Cnaiür urs Skiotha freezes, hangs as if upon the rawness of his own voice. And Proyas wonders at his own detachment, that he could see his life wobble upon a point, and not care, let alone fear.

The King-of-Tribes stands from his murderous crouch. "And *you!"* he spits, sheathing his knife. *"Who are you* to bandy reasons? You who have been trampled, you who have been thrown underfoot! When do the *slain* argue the righteousness of the slayer?"

The light greys. Proyas feels the empty air in his mouth, the absence of words or spittle. He sees ... *Serwë* ... standing two steps down. Unaged. Slight, waifish even, despite the barbarism of her costume. As beautiful as she was the day Sarcellus murdered her in Caraskand.

The mad King-of-Tribes bends his head from side to side in pursuit of a kink. The Sack of Golgotterath plays out in bright miniature against his profile, and Proyas finds his eyes drawn to what now seems a submarine drama. The Shroud of the Horde rears across the background, obscuring the far reaches of the Occlusion, challenging the Horns for the Heavens.

The light is dimming.

He glimpses intermittent threads of crimson, then the grilled face blots the spectacle once again, grimacing for perpetual disgust.

"He has used you up."

And Proyas sees it across the encroaching gloom, images struck in the light of a less jaundiced sun. A different Age. A different Holy War. A Norsirai garbed like a beggar, mannered like a king—and a *Scylvendi* ... "Yesss ..."

And it seems impossible, the *carelessness* of that moment, that he had once held the *Holy Aspect-Emperor* and the *Scylvendi King-of-Tribes* within the compass of his mortal judgment. Had he felt it then, youthful fool that he was? Had he sensed the tickle of *this* mortal instant ...

Way back then?

Turquoise scrutiny. Shit escapes the broken body below him, hangs animal. The light is dimming. The madman looks up into the gloom, his eyes counting the Circumfix-entangled insignia hanging from the void of the Eleven-Pole Chamber. He throws out his neck-breaking arms. "*Burn it!*" he roars, as if darkness and empty air were also his thralls. "*Burn this place!*"

Cnaiür urs Skiotha turns away, strides down to the grave shadows milling below—becomes a hulking silhouette once again. He barges through them, passes through the breach into swazond sunlight.

And Proyas lies breathing, as before, crafting each inhalation into shapes that might slip unnoticed between the swelling agonies.

He gazes through what seems a darkling glass.

Evil Golgotterath, like a wicked idol, squatting, watching beetles scurry about its horned feet.

Scylvendi throng in the foreground just outside, yelling, running, casting brands at the rotund walls of the Umbilicus ... The light dims.

Moments pass before Proyas realizes one of Cnaiür's spectral entourage has tarried ...

Another silhouette. Another neck-breaking physique.

It approaches, parting smoke like ethereal waters. Once again, identity comes in stages. Once again, a familiar mien obscures the epic gleam of the Incû-Holoinas and the whorls of battle beneath. But this face is different, the ware of a more refined potter. The brutality bequeathed by the father has been tamed by the beauty of the mother, drawn into a more aquiline manliness.

"Mo-Moënghus?"

The dark Prince-Imperial nods. Obscurity plumes and bloats about his edges. The Shroud-of-the-Horde has become his halo.

"Uncle."

And it seems proper, that this too, should be real. Geared in the accoutrements of the People, it is undeniable, the fact of what Moënghus is. *So ... something whispers within him. All truth shall be out this day ...*

"How?" he coughs. "What are ... you doin—?"

"Shush, Uncle."

Fire leaps through the Eleven-Pole Chamber. Anasûrimbor Moënghus hesitates, then raises a hand as great as his father's, clamps it about Proyas's mouth and nose.

"*Shush* ..." he says with what seems an ancient melancholy. He has pondered this. He has resolved.

Convulsions wrack bloated flesh.

"You have lingered overlong."

His strength scarcely seems human.

"And I will not let you burn."

The Skeptic-King of Conriya suffocates. Light and image dissolve. His lungs cramp. A burning flashes from his bones. His flailing astonishes him, for he had counted his body dead.

But then the animal within never ceases battling, never quite abandons hope ... Faith.

No soul is so fanatic as the darkness that comes before.

This is the lesson we each take to our grave—and to hell.

None knew who had stacked the great basalt megaliths upon the summit of the Upright Horn. For watches, the Horde-General had crouched beneath the greatest of them, sheltered from the sun under the veined canopy of his wings, gazing down over the burnished rim of the plummet, watching the play of pieces great and small across the immense, circular benjuka plate below. The Canted Horn reared vast to the south, his only companion in the yawning vacancy of the sky, a stooped and stunted sister, hazed more than obscured by the scant clouds breaking upon it.

How *long* had he waited? Even for a being so deformed, the passage of time seemed no less miraculous. Millennia had become centuries, and centuries had become years ... and, now, *mere watches remained.* The sun would set upon their Salvation ... at long last. *Resumption.*

The ancient Inchoroi terror stood erect upon the summit, heedless of the plummet, little more than a wick against the oceanic onset of the Shroud. His Horde had engulfed the western plains, drawing the dark promise of the Shroud across the western skies. Soon, so very soon, it would put out the cruel eye of the sun. Soon, so very soon, the Derived would fall raving upon the Trespassers, mount their labile corpses, and cleanse their filth from the stoop of the hallowed Ark.

Their chorus inflamed him. Chill wind scoured the golden pitch, knifed at his great lungs. On a whim, he raised his wings, allowed it to buffet him as a kite, raise him to the pinnacle of the massive stone. Looking out, he could see the very curve of the World, and he moaned for a sudden yearning to be raised higher, ever higher—to be pitched into the bosom of the infinite Void ...

To walk above and between worlds.

A thread of scintillant crimson yanked his regard back to the beetles beneath him.

⸎

Fire consumed the Umbilicus, flames binding like momentary muscle, wrapping and unwrapping liquid bones. Anasûrimbor Moënghus wandered the perimeter of the conflagration, clenching and relaxing hands that would not cease shaking—especially his right, which still tingled for the mash of his Uncle's beard. And he wondered at the smoking skin of the pavilion, how it heaved upon sheets of clean fire and plumes of noxious black, how it trembled and *writhed* as a living thing.

It was, he decided, a fitting pyre for King Nersei Proyas.

The Holy King-of-Tribes had led his barbaric entourage higher on the slope, where they now stood fairly encircled by more burning wrack, the rubbish that remained of the Great Ordeal's belongings. Either custom or madness had granted his father three paces, for he stood encircled as much as accompanied, stripped to the waist save his nimil vest. Only grizzled Harlikarut, eldest living son of Oknai One-Eye, dared stand at his side. His Consult mother, the thing-called-Serwë, stood apart for a change, gesturing toward the very thing tyrannizing their communal barbaric regard: Golgotterath.

The constellation of puzzled squints sparked no curiosity in the Prince-Imperial. He had just suffocated a beloved uncle—a fact that did not so much occupy his thoughts as obviate any need for them. Some fury is simply too great to be perceived, too deep of keel, too broad of beam not to vanish into life. And so Anasûrimbor Moënghus had not the least inkling that he was about to murder his father.

"You would *burn him alive?*" he heard himself scream as he approached. "The man who *saved you* twenty-years ago?"

Several faces turned to him, but only those nearest. His father, a beacon of brutality even in such brutal company, made no demonstration of hearing ...

His wasn't the only outrage, Moënghus realized, glimpsing his counterfeit mother gesticulating between the taller Men. The load of gazes blunted, then finally heaved his glare in their direction. He peered over the burning tracts of encampment out to Golgotterath, Horns gleaming beneath the sky-climbing Shroud.

A line of luminous red flickered from the thigh of the Upright Horn to the termite confusion below.

"*That is the sign!*" his false mother cried and in *Sheyic*, no less. The assembled Chieftains scowled for incomprehension.

"*The Holy Spear of Sil!*"

Even swamped by roaring flame and whooping warbands, her words rang as clarions.

"*You are sworn, Son of Skiotha! We must strike!*"

The Prince-Imperial climbed among the outermost Chieftains, peering at the preposterous beauty of his mother, wiping his palms against his foul Scylvendi breeches.

The Holy King-of-Tribes loomed before her, banded limbs taut, hands clenching emptiness.

"You think I believe your nonsense?"

She seemed so slight in his overpowering shadow, so tragically beautiful, an emblem of a world desired, but never possessed ... Never enough.

"Everything ..." she cried, poised to flinch, to ward. "Everything you promised me! *You swore an oath!*"

The Holy King-of-Tribes reached out into her trembling aura, pinched an errant lock of her hair between thumb and forefinger.

"You think," he grated, "your lies reek *less?* That you might succeed where a *Dûnyain* has failed?"

He clamped his right hand—scarred, burnt dark for cruel seasons of sun—about her swanish throat.

She gasped, raises ineffectual hands to the great wrist. "I am *everything ...*" she coughed, "everything you need me to be!"

"You think I am so bent, *so disordered?*"

Both hands were about her neck now, thumbs digging not so much for her windpipe as her carotid.

"Lover!" she cried. "Assa–!"

"You think I beat you out of shame! *Out of depravity?*"

"*Gnngh*–!"

"*Disgust!*" the King-of-Tribes screamed, wrenching her neck. Shadow inked the crevices of his forearms, the striping of scars, the twining of veins. And he *squeezed,* driving thumbs like iron hooks, palms like grinding stone. "I battered you for obscenity's sake!" he barked, his face a lunatic mask. "I tormented you to make you believe! Punished you to gull! *To deceive!*"

Her manhood arched turgid in her leggings. Noises cracked from her throat. Convulsions wracked her whipcord body. The alabaster perfection of her face *perforated,* flexed like some horrific gill ...

Cnaiür urs Skiotha hunched over her now, corded as hemp, trembling with exertion, huffing air and spittle. His concubine's body flailed cartilaginous for a heartbeat, an eruption of blind reflexes.

Moënghus barged between the last chieftains intervening, saw his father hoist her ear to his lips, murmur as much as rave: "I trained you as a *beast!*– trained you *for this very moment!*"

Moënghus blinked for the glimpse of *smoke* wafting from the ligature of swazond that encased his trembling arms.

"To wait out advantage ..." the most violent of men gasped on a furious exhalation. "And wait ..." he murmured, sucking air, titanic exertion creaking on his voice. "And *waaait* ..."

He thrust her down as an axe or hammer ...

"*Until only death remained!*"

The body folded like a marionette. A noise too meaty to be a crack— its neck ...

Serwë's angelic face fell open on glistening, knuckled articulations.

Cnaiür urs Skiötha stood so as to sweep arms to the uninvaded fractions of the sky. The Chieftains of the People roared in frenzied approval about him, even clasping one another in celebration.

Still lathered for his exertions, the breaker-of-horses-and-men turned to seize his girl-skinned son's shoulders. The grasp firmed when Moënghus cringed.

"Leave my side again," the Scylvendi King-of-Tribes grunted, "and your limbs shall be struck from you."

It happened the instant Serwa had ordered the assault on the High Cwol. It lasted for a heartbeat, soundless for the din of battle.

A line of light, dazzling, as perfect as any Gnostic Cant, but *crimson* ...

And in no way stained by the Mark.

A Scarlet Schoolman dropped, dragged his flaming billows into the ramparts of the Oblitus. Thirümmü Sek was no more.

The whole of the Great Ordeal stopped for horror and wonder, including Anasûrimbor Serwa.

Another line, soundless and blinding, conjoined Myrathimi—another Scarlet Schoolman scourging the parapets—and a point hanging on the High Horn's inner thigh, above the reach of any sorcery. A simple pulse, bright enough to induce warding arms, then she was watching Myrathimi plummeted between blinks.

Tekne.

"Sweet Seju!" Mirûnwe exclaimed in horror from her side. "The Heron Spear!"

A third pulse followed, and another Scarlet Schoolman, Ekompiras, spiralled to earth, his fiery billows breaking up like straw.

"*Interpolate!*" the Exalt-Magus cracked through the furore.

The triunes of her Command instantly began shrinking toward her. She was already singing with her flanking sisters ...

A fourth pulse, like a sun become milk—light that gutted the haphazard Gnostic spheres, concussions that pinked cheeks for mere proximity. Air whooshing.

"*Father!*" she boomed.

A fifth pulse. Light striking with the force of Wûlri, the Gall-Spear of Hûsyelt, clapping Wards into smoke and splinters, punching breath from guts, igniting the extremities of their billows.

The Swayali continued singing, the blood weeping from their noses black for the light of their mouths.

A catastrophic sixth pulse, glaring across the back of hapless sorceries.

"*Scatter!*"

She cried this even as Kima toppled from the sky, a white moth afire. All their billows burned. The sunlight glared, and she glimpsed the Men of the Ordeal packed across the Oblitus, gazing up awe and horror. She pulled the sash binding her billows to her waist, slipped from her flaming gown ...

Even as a seventh pulse passed through it as tissue.

She landed among a company of astounded Nangaels, already singing, simultaneously batting at the embers on her hair and shift. She expected the Men to flee, but they *piled* before her instead, shields raised in pitiful gallantry against the vast scarp of the High Horn.

But no eighth pulse came—not for her. An incandescent line conjoined the golden heights with a cluster of Mandati and Scarlet Schoolmen hanging before the black parapets of Cwol. Four burning figures plummeted from the arcane assembly, followed by a flailing fifth. She heard Saccarees command they scatter as well. She bid the bearded warrior behind her, a grim and strapping man wearing an iron hauberk, to raise his kite shield.

She did not see the ninth pulse, only her momentary shadow across flagstones.

She nodded to the Tydonni Knight, then leapt, using his shield to vault the summit of the Riser. Like an acrobat, she swung herself into a handstand, threw herself into a crouch on the precarious summit of the battlements. The Men on this terrace, Galeoth Gesindalmen, cried out for shock. She dashed out along the lip of the parapets, racing southward. So she ran the length of the Sixth Riser, sprinting like a gazelle with slender grace, her slippered feet making a blur of the crude battlements. To her right, the Soldiers of the Circumfix flew beneath and fell away, a gallery of gawking fools ...

Those nearest died in the eleventh pulse.

Serwa rode the shock wave, pirouetting, alighting like a swan, running with even more speed. The Galeoth on the terrace began casting their shields into the air behind her, seeking to obscure her passage.

She sang out on a luminous voice, still racing. Black roiled through empty air behind her, blooming like lobes of ink through water. The rope of the battlements shrank to nothing. She leapt, legs scissoring into emptiness ...

The terminus of the Sixth Riser erupted behind and beneath her, slapped her spinning. The twelfth pulse.

But she caught the ground's sorcerous echo, began walking over empty space, ascended the scarps of the Scab. The encampment floated across her periphery, distant slums and rubbish splayed across the feet of the southwest Occlusion. The pluming dust and flashing arms were what caught her attention—faraway tendrils and streams spilling down along multiple points, overrunning tents and pavilions.

Human ... she realized.

Scylvendi?

But the Exalt-Magus turned away. She had no time. The arcane smoke had baffled the invisible Spearman merely—or so she had to assume. She soared over the black and broken heights of the Scab. The Canted Horn reared titanic before her, daylight glimmering through its chapped hull. The Horde had bloated far beyond its obscuring bulk, drawing a great curtain of darkness, ash, and ochre across the West. Hundreds of streamers radiated out from the tumult, the nearest fairly reaching Golgotterath's ramparts: Sranc bands, she realized, the most famished and fleet. Behind them, the masses churned across what seemed the whole of the west, mob piling upon mob, a teeming that became ever more colourless and indistinct as the Shroud reared to consume everything, including the sky ...

Even still, she glimpsed it: glimmering light, flashing from a socket in the twining screens and plumes.

"Father!" she boomed again, calling, beseeching, her voice cracking the distances asunder ...

Just as the thirteenth pulse found her.

———— ✑✒☙ ————

All Creation wailed. Dust vaulted into a high-hanging pall, swaddled them in shadow. The light of destruction became the only light, revealing Sranc, pale as fish in murky waters, packed unto trampling, howling, surging across the very bourne of visibility ...

And it beggared Malowebi's dispossessed soul.

The terror was a constant, as was the corporeal disorientation. Even though Malowebi *knew* he gazed from the sockets of a severed head, he *felt his body nonetheless*, dangling and paralytic, alternately dragged over earth and whipped about air like cords of weightless silk, a scribble across the face of the thronging plains ...

The Horde.

Decanted across the great grey distance, flying in loose gales at the fore, surging into a tempest that encompassed heaven and earth, not so much covering the land as *becoming* it, mass upon frenzied mass, churning up plumes and veils that closed the distances, blotted the sun ...

The *Horde* ...

Smote by sorceries Malowebi could scarce conceive, *Abstractions*, like those belonging to the Gnosis, but unlike any Cant described in any text. Silvery hoops broad as bastion-towers, shaking everything within like images in kicked reflecting pools. Fractal blooms, lights replicating outwards, one become six, six become dozens, severing, *detonating*, laying out whole regions of dismembered ruin.

The Horde.

Countless raving faces becoming smooth with white wonder as death and light falls. Nightmarish. Vertiginous in ways the Iswazi mage could never articulate, a *captive* soul, swinging as a purse from the dread Aspect-Emperor's girdle, watching him cast the very sum of his might into the wretched, earth-eating multitudes.

———— ❦ ————

In their thousands, the Ṣons of Men set about gaining the Scab and securing the black curtain walls. Others were tasked with barricading and manning the breaches. Though some Lords-of-the-Ordeal balked at the notion of *defending Golgotterath*, they need only glimpse the western reaches of Shigogli to grasp its mortal necessity ...

Lord Sampë Ussiliar and his Shrial Knights had taken the vanguard in the south, racing across the parapets in the wake of the Imperial Saik, who burned and blasted any Ursranc too foolish or maddened to flee. Seizing the gold-fanged heights proved remarkably bloodless. The mayhem and grim butchery were confined to the towers, where nary a footfall went uncontested. Though nowhere near the size of their famed cousins overlooking Ûgorrior below, the structures were brutal affairs, at once squat and cyclopean, raised from blocks of crudely-hewn rock. Given the need for haste, the Saik Schoolmen were called on to scourge the halls and to blast the iron portals, clearing a path to the adjoining parapets so that the rush might continue while a force remained behind to finish clearing the structures.

But the convoluted, almost hive-like, layout of the towers, combined with the raving ferocity of the Ursranc, transformed each into a pitched melee requiring hundreds of souls. The heavily armoured Shrial Knights howled and hacked their way down treacherous stairs and along narrow, lightless corridors. Those too reckless ran afoul traps and ambuscades, for the Ursranc were far more cunning than their wild kin. Men bled out in the corners, limbs tangled in the corpses of their foe. Grandmaster Ussiliar had scarce travelled five towers before the simple lack of manpower forced him to concede the advance to General Rash Soptet and his more lightly armoured Shigeki.

Progress in the south quickly ground to a halt. But once the first tower on the heights above the ruins of Domathuz had been cleared, Nansur Columnaries and Eumarnan Grandees began spilling onto the lobed back of the Scab. The initial plan had been to form up below the walls, then secure the heights in full array lest the Consult ambush and overwhelm them. But the Horde—which the assembling Men could see consuming more and more of Shigogli—denied them this tactical luxury. With General Biaxi Tarpellas dead, command of the Nansur Columns had fallen to General Ligesseras Arnius—though he would be some time learning as much. By all accounts an impulsive yet gifted field commander, he grasped the peril instantly. Who knew what secret gates the Consult might possess? He understood well the tragic lesson of Irsûlor: Should this new Horde gain the interior of Golgotterath, all would be lost. Trusting his example would count as communication enough, he led his Columnaries in a disorganized mob across the Scab, bearing beneath the crotch of the Canted Horn toward those towers directly overlooking the approaching Sranc menace. Quick to grasp his intent, General Inrilil ab Cinganjehoi commanded his mail-draped Eumarnans to do the same. To a man, his Grandees and their households gazed at the spark of white and turquoise light hanging above the nethers of the Shroud: their Holy Aspect-Emperor standing alone before the catastrophic onslaught. "To the western walls!" Lord Inrilil bellowed to his wondering kinsmen. "They have by far the better view!"

Despite its rampaging disorder, the Horde moved as if possessing a will and intent all its own. For those battling on the walls, the way it consumed ever more of the *World* between glances seemed a kind of nightmare. But rather than simply swallow Shigogli whole, it *penetrated* the desolate expanses, funnelled toward the southern extreme of the dread stronghold, winding into a tendril as vast as Carythusal, fields of commotion so immense that the Shigeki watching from the southern parapets felt the ramparts drift westward beneath their feet.

With such terror streaming below them, how could they know their doom hung above?

⎯⎯⎯⎯⎯ ❧ ⎯⎯⎯⎯⎯

Kakaliol, Reaper-of-Heroes, stands gazing upon Ûbil Noscisor.

Vile angel.

Scales smoking. Wounds weeping pitch and fire for blood.

Beware, the Blind Slaver whispers. *Great and terrible sorceries lie coiled within the bri—*

What, it croaks on wheezing fire, **is this place?**

The Blind Slaver is taken aback. The Carrion Prince can feel his soul twist in momentary, febrile confusion, like a minnow thrashing on a string.

Kakaliol screams for the outrageous perversity. A world ruled by bladders of muck! A world where *souls* hang upon the sufferance of slop and meat! A world where lice drive lions!

Discharge your Ta—!

What is this place?

The Blind Slaver hesitates. And Kakaliol, the demon-godling of the diseased slums and gutters of Carythusal, *can feel it:* the indecision, the bewilderment, the dawning fear ...

All the delicacies of mortal *weakness.*

You stand upon the threshold of the dread Ark ... the Blind Slaver replies. *The Incû-Holoinas.*

Hard doth it lean upon the threshold ... the Seducer-of-Thieves says, for it can feel the smouldering torsions, the remorseless yaw in directions orthogonal to the accursed lines of harsh reality, as though it were a coal upon a blanket, burning through, filament by despicable filament.

Yes ...

Vile angel.

And it realizes. Kakaliol apprehends. It *can feel it sinking,* all about, like a hulk upon the waters. The Reaper-of-Heroes raises its scimitar talons, roars with laughter, expelling the shrieks of a thousand thousand souls.

All it need do is *scratch*, tear away the cutting paper of this accursed World ...

Now discharge your Task.

Nay.

Discharge your Task!

The Blind Slaver dares speak it, the *word*. And it can *feel* the torments the Manling would inflict upon it were it *elsewhere* in this accursed World. But *here*, in this place, *Hell itself steeps the air*, making *whole* what the frail sorcerer's magicks had halved. Here, *in this place*, it cannot be sundered.

The Reaper-of-Heroes cackles, shrieks in diabolical triumph.

What does it matter, the punishing of a Desire identical with its Object?

Your Oath! the Blind Slaver cries upon blind panic. *Your Oath is your Task!*

Nay ... the Carrion Prince rumbles across the edges of existence. **Thou art my Task, mortal.**

And upon this, Kalakiol, the Reaper-of-Heroes, *involutes*, reaches through itself, and seizes the Voice of the Blind Slaver, plucks the nubile wisp that is his soul. How the insect flails! Roaring exultant, it collapses into a writhing heap of centipedes, chitinous multitudes that spill out twitching and scratching across the floors, and begin boring through the flaking paint that is this World ...

The vile angel is no more.

❮❯❯❮

None other than Lord Soter had been the first to assemble his kinsmen beneath the turrets of the High Cwol. The Ainoni had taken up positions, preparing to follow the Schoolmen once the gold-fanged bulwarks had been entirely cracked asunder. The sky immediately above was fairly clotted with sorcerers and their silk-twining billows when the first pulse struck. Suddenly the air tasted of acrid things burning—smelled of pork. All was confusion, Men jerking their gaze to and fro in a panicked search for answers. Then Myrathimi fell burning, and shouting choruses erupted among the ranks. Those still baffled followed the arms and fingers pointing almost directly upward, to the hanging enormity of the High Horn ...

Only to be nearly blinded by the third pulse.

Sorcerous singing clawed at the bowels. The Thousand Schoolmen were in disarray, some clustering to concentrate their defenses, others scattering—and all shrinking from the battered ramparts of the High Cwol. A young Ainoni caste-noble, Nemukus Mirshoa, was the first to realize the burden of Apocalypse had fallen upon *them*, the Soldiers of the Circumfix. While all others peered skyward, he cried out to his Kishyati kinsmen, shamed them for their sloth. Then shrieking their ancestral warcry, he charged forward, quite alone, into the black and blasted maw of the High Cwol.

Moved to wonder, the Men of Kishyat followed, first in scattered flurries, then en masse. Black arrows rained upon them, studding their shields and shoulders, but killing few, given their flaring helms and hauberks of heavy splint. They assailed a great breach due to the death throes of Hagazioz, labouring up pitched slopes of debris. There they found Mirshoa and his cousins battling scores of foul Ursranc in the gloom.

Lord Soter, a bellicose man by nature, immediately grasped Mirshoa's impetuous wisdom. "As they reap, so are they reaped!" he cried to his vassals. "We cower behind sorcerers no more!"

So did the Palatines of High Ainon leave the Schoolmen to fend the unseen Spearman. On a disordered tide of shouts, they stormed the cracked bastions and scorched corridors of the High Cwol.

Since their presence had counted for naught, they were not missed. Seeing Serwa's flight across the Oblitus, Apperens Saccarees commanded triunes of Mandate Schoolmen to surmount the High Cwol and rush the mountainous trunk of the High Horn. "Save her!" he cried. "Save the Daughter of the Lord!"

Upon the Cwol, the sorcerers saw the Horde, an endless deluge of Sranc descending upon the whole of the Furnace Plain, the Shroud churning skyward from the masses surging at the fore, steaming up to choke the very Vault. Fending horror and dismay, they threw themselves forward, crying out their ancient and holy inheritance, the Gnosis. They harangued their foe with Seswatha's own Argument, the dark corpus of the School of Sohonc, the dread Cants of War. Great combs of brilliance swept up and scissored across the sheer, golden expanses—Third Looms, Thosolankan Intensities. Jaundiced reflections leapt and danced across the sheen in counterpoint, as if the Upright Horn had become a greased mirror. Radiance clawed ever higher up the cyclopean pitch, reaching for the Spearman's perch ...

But they could not so much as scorch the platform he stood upon, let alone test his Wards.

Nearly vertical pulses counted out the howling Schoolmen with combusting billows. Like flowers, they twirled to ground aflame.

The Men across the Oblitus watched spellbound, crying out curses and heavenly pleas. Frantic shouts across the Ninth Riser drew all eyes to a flickering above the Sixth—to the radiant glare that delivered the Holy Aspect-Emperor ...

The Soldiers of the Circumfix roared in exultation.

He hung the height of a Netia pine, immaculate in his white gowns, gyres of smoke swirling out and about his miraculous coming-to-be. He held his hands palms up, flattened into blades, and his face bent skyward, so that it seemed he prayed as much as peered, searching for the dread Spearman ...

A thread of crimson brilliance leapt between him and the High Horn.

For a span of two heartbeats, the brilliance and subsequent glare obscured him. Thousands cried out for premonition ...

But their Saviour hung intact and unmoved, gazing precisely as before.

Another pulse, consuming vision and air. Men glimpsed the multiform apparition of his Wards, wicking energies, glowing across fathomless dimensions.

Again the Spearman struck. The air crackled for errant discharges. The interplay of convexities waxed brighter, reducing the Holy Aspect-Emperor to a penitent silhouette.

And another pulse, this one obscuring him altogether. The Wards now hung glaring, an ethereal object that jarred the intellect as much as the eyes.

Only those gazing up at the dizzying immensity of the Horn saw the luminous point appear on the tubular heights ...

Another crimson pulse.

The Wards crumbled into smoke about the point of impact, entropy cascading outward, through all the incandescent reticulations, spinning into spaces more profound than empty air. And the Great Ordeal cried out for terror, save for those few peering upward, who first gasped for wonder, then cried out in delirious triumph.

For they saw their Holy Aspect-Emperor step from the ether *above* the Spearman, standing upon the platform's slim echo, bellowing his Metagnostic song. They saw the rain of catastrophic Abstractions, the cracking flare and shimmering implosion of the Erratic's Wards. And they saw their Saviour fall as vengeance upon him, cast him shrieking from the impossible heights ...

They watched their Holy Aspect-Emperor *take up the Spear*.

The Soldiers of the Circumfix boomed in triumph. Across the Oblitus and the captive walls, Men fell to their knees and gave praise. They cried out the hallowed name of Anasûrimbor Kellhus, their all-conquering Lord-and-Prophet.

The triumphant shout shrugged aside the caterwaul of the Horde, resounded deep into the shattered halls of the High Cwol, where it further inflamed the heart of Mirshoa and his Kishyati kinsmen. They hacked and hammered at the raving, Ursranc throngs, until their white-painted faces were all but violet for their foe's blood. They battled down corridors narrow and wide, pressing ever closer to the Intrinsic Gate. Like all warriors alive in the moment, they could feel it, the leakage of their enemy's resolve. And this incited them even more, until Mirshoa and his kin laughed and roared like gods having lethal sport.

Tumult had engulfed all that was visible. The Horde crashed upon the westward ramparts of Golgotterath, bearing south. Vast legions of Yimaleti Sranc encompassed all the western tracts of Shigogli, churning up vast curtains of dust, screens woven into the impenetrable obscurity of the Shroud. To the east, the encampment *burned*, and divisions of *Scylvendi horsemen* had formed across the outskirts—what looked to be *thousands* of them. Within Golgotterath, Men ran from all quarters, scrambling to seize and secure the outer walls.

The Holy Aspect-Emperor raised the Spear ... cast it.

Greater and greater it loomed, a vista of ruined ramparts and smoking sockets beneath the surreal enormity of the Horns.

"Fleeing!" the old Wizard cried out in dismayed indignation. "Fleeing *to Golgotterath!*"

For madness it was. They hobbled across the waste with Mimara braced between them, in the Throes or between Throes—he did not know, for the Qirri had afforded her a vitality all her own. Golgotterath loomed nightmarishly before them, the Horns reaching, burnished unto blinding in the direct sunlight, the Shroud engulfing ever more of the skies beyond. Incredulity numbed him to the pit—to simply witness the image let alone *scramble into it*. For they desperately needed to reach the gold-fanged bulwarks and the security of the Great Ordeal. Achamian suffered a clutch of panic each time he made note of the Shroud's progress. Even with the blessed ash, even with the cannibal vitality quickening his limbs, they had no hope of beating the Horde to the breach where ancient Corrunc had once stood.

They were too late. He could feel it in his bones.

They could have walked the sky, had Mimara been willing to relinquish her accursed Chorae. But she insisted that she needed them. He had relented without protest: the Scylvendi were already burning pavilions by that point, and his greatest concern was to slip from the encampment unnoticed.

But very soon now, she would have no choice.

Very soon.

"Someone pursues us!" Esmenet cried over the growing howl.

The old Wizard followed her terrified gaze. At first all he could see was contradiction, the contrast of the lean vista they fled from with the black and brooding turmoil they fled to. Then he saw the far precincts of the encampment burning, the Scylvendi myriads fanning through the whorls and clots of canvas hovels as though flushing game from a meadow ...

And closer still, a war-party numbering in the hundreds, galloping hard on their trail.

"Move! *Move!*" he exclaimed.

Mimara cried out for anguish, and somehow they managed to quicken their pace. But a shambling, stumbling trot was not going to save them. Within heartbeats, the People of War had gained enough ground to begin testing their bows. A shaft sunk into the ash to the right of them—then another just behind. The third glanced his Wards, skidded burning. Then a continuous hail of archery began flashing across the back of his Gnostic defenses ...

It was time.

"Cast aside your Chorae, Mim!"

"*No!*" she barked savagely.

"Stubborn wench!" the old Wizard cried, fairly tripping for disbelief. "Yield them or die! It is *that* sim—!"

"Wait!" Esmenet hollered, looking over her shoulder as she hustled. "They're turning about! They're ... The—!"

"*Look!*" Mimara croaked on a hook of agony.

Achamian had already turned, his gaze compelled by a crimson dazzle across his periphery.

Even though leagues distant, the Horns of Golgotterath nonetheless *loomed*, impossibly monstrous. The Great Ordeal had overrun the fell stair of the Oblitus—a sight that was itself breathtaking—and was even now assailing the High Cwol—the great citadel of the Intrinsic Gate! And there it was: a glittering bloodred line, conjoining a point low on the profile of the High Horn with what had been a Schoolman. A light miraculously unpolluted by sorcery's Mark ... a *killing* light.

Tekne.

"What is it?" Mimara cried. "The Heron Spear?"

Could it be? No. The Heron Spear had frequented too many Dreams for him to mistake it.

"The colour is wrong ..."

A different Inchoroi weapon of light? A different Spear?

Speechless, they limped and raced across Shigogli's desolate beam. The Spear flashed and flashed again, counting out their progress with burning Schoolmen ...

Until Kellhus at last appeared.

———— ❧ ————

Suspended high, a thread of ruby brilliance pulled perfectly taut ... striking not the lurid convolutions of the Horde, nor the turrets of the High Cwol, but the inner thigh of the *Canted Horn*—where the golden shell was most decrepit.

A crack slit the sky's throat. The echo rumbled like Fanim drums-of-war.

The Holy Aspect-Emperor cast the Spear again.

And again.

The sight was one the Soldiers of the Circumfix simply could not credit. For many, standing beneath the Horns stirred memories of dozing at the root of some ancient tree, the trunk a great and heavy bulk upon their brow, the curvature climbing to obscure whole empires of the sky. The forces, the torsions did not matter. *Permanence* was utterly assured, such were the proportions. Mountains did not leap, and the Horns *did not fall*.

And yet, the Canted Horn shuddered, wagged like something suspended from a line, then *dipped*, no more than the slightest declination—what would be counted an insult in jnan—but catastrophic nonetheless.

The sky teetered.

A sound like a dog's yawn groaned across all Creation. The pinnacle swayed out, sheering through the cloud hooked about its gleaming neck. *The Horn toppled.* The eyes of many simply refused to believe, such was the scale. The ground seemed to heave beneath their feet, yanked as cloth torn between dog and master. The structure revolved in a ponderous pirouette, then sailed on an imploding hinge out across the plain. The sun burnished its golden descent, a bead of brilliance drawn over leagues of unearthly gold. On the plain below, Sranc wailed in the sudden shadow, legions scattering for terror into countless other such scatterings. A sound like coins zipping across fine mail—an enormous, airy *whisk.* Then a series of yawing cracks, concussions that swatted exposed skin—deafened. And there, before infidel eyes, *the very sky plummeted*, a vast, deformed cylinder, ribbed like the hull of a ship, obliterating Golgotterath's ramparts, *thumping* the plains with geologic violence ...

Casting Sranc like dust into the erupting air.

The impact threw Men from their feet. Blood popped from their noses, flecked the whites of their eyes. The ground shook as though quaked for more than *thirty heartbeats*—the time required for the structure's monstrous crown to join its monstrous nethers. The Canted Horn hammered the very drum-skin of the World, and all Creation resounded. As far away as Carythusal, napping babes started awake, began bawling.

The Horde fell silent. A great gust of lucid air galloped into the belly of the Shroud—revealing the endless, virulent masses ... white-faced and agog.

The Men of the Ordeal did not have time to wonder—they scarce had time to regain their feet. Showers of ejecta followed hard upon the shock-wave's clarity, a tempest of gravel and grit that pinched throats and pricked eyes. They milled in a stupor, coughed and called out, daubed noses or swatted ears. One by one, the Sons of Men squinted through the lifting screens, saw the Great Ordeal intact and the Horde grievously wounded. Prince Inrilil ab Cinganjehoi raised his eyes to his Holy Aspect-Emperor standing high upon the Spearman's perch, shrieked in crazed and unmanly exultation.

And all the surviving Soldiers of Circumfix joined him.

CHAPTER SIXTEEN

The Incû-Holoinas

To understand beatings is to hate brave brothers.
       —Celestial Aphorisms, MEMGOWA

Early Autumn, 20 New Imperial Year (4132, Year-of-the-Tusk), Golgotterath.

Cataclysm, crashing and golden.

The tink and clatter of debris trailed into the hiss of raining sand.

Astonished silence ...

Across the terraces of the Oblitus, along the gold-fanged walls and the bulbous heights, the Soldiers of the Circumfix climbed to their feet coughing, squinting, peering across the devastation. The Canted Horn lay like a boned limb across the Shigogli, a train of shattered cylinders, some buckled, others impossibly intact, larded with vast, freestanding hoops, sections of skinless girding that reached higher than the Occlusion despite the calamity they had endured. Dead Sranc encircled the ruin, an enormous halo of carcasses tangled like string, bleached into a vast frieze for the dust settling across them.

Dawning comprehension.

Cries of triumph cascaded across the heights of Golgotterath, swelled into a single, booming roar. As one, the Men of the Ordeal turned to their Most Holy Aspect-Emperor standing high upon the Spearman's pulpit, their voices broken for incredulity and adoration. Windswept, Anasûrimbor Kellhus raised the gleaming convolutions of the Spear above his head in reply.

The Men of the Ordeal howled in adulation, wept for jubilation.

Many glimpsed the rock plummeting down the length of the High Horn, gasped for incomprehension. The Holy Aspect-Emperor glanced up—

Hurtling granite exploded against unseen convexities—Wards—shattered into a wilting bloom of debris. The Soldiers of the Circumfix cried out.

Some saw the winged horror of the Horde-General flitting down and about, then darting like a sparrow into obscurity. Some saw the Aspect-Emperor slip like a coin from a slashed purse, only to vanish into the oblivion of sorcerous light. Some saw the Spear topple out into the void, trailing a rope attached to some kind of metallic coffer ...

A yammering susurrus arose across the great plate of Shigogli, a raw and virulent murmuring. The Soldiers of the Circumfix looked to the packed leagues about Golgotterath across the pale and rapacious *millions*. A sound like chattering teeth climbed into the very pith of the sky, the rattle of snakes without number. Then the crazed yowl resumed, lust bound to hatred bound famished frenzy, thread twisted into caterwauling thread ...

The Lords of the Ordeal bellowed what commands they could.

The broken silhouette of Golgotterath loomed before the three ailing refugees.

"*Get up* ..." the old Wizard wheezed—as much to himself as the others, for he hacked spittle on his hands and knees. He could scarce hear his own voice for the whine clawing at his ears. "Get up! *Hurry!*"

A shadow fell across him. He glanced up, saw Mimara towering across the hazed disc of the sun, her hand held out. Esmenet was already pressing herself to her feet, blank-faced and blasted white with chalk. The old Wizard clasped the pregnant girl's wrist.

The three refugees stood gawking as the aftermath resolved from the dust.

"We should keep moving ..." Achamian murmured.

No one so much as twitched.

"Is it possible?" Esmenet said in a flat voice.

Achamian had no wind to reply. He scarce had wind to conceive ...

Ajencis famously spoke of the way the soul could make anything a marker of anything else—how all human signs were *arbitrary*. Even when it came to sorcery, he argued, what mattered were the *meanings*. But some symbols, Achamian knew, were indistinguishable from their meaning. Some symbols tyrannized, others galvanized, not by virtue of what they *meant*, but because of what they *accomplished*.

A sword was such a symbol. As was a shield, or a Circumfix ...

The dust settled like sand kicked in a tidal pool, baring details that seemed nude for the brilliance of the sun and the dark contrast of the Shroud rearing beyond. Golgotterath lay exposed before them, like the skull of some mountain-headed beast, half-buried in desolation, only one great antler remaining ...

One Horn.

The School of Mandate had made fetishes of many things, for theirs had always been a desperate cause, and the desperate were forever bent on anchoring their preposterous hopes with more tangible items. But the Horns of Golgotterath had been their one and only *idol*, the image they had perpetually prayed *against*. For it was *always there*, a shadow thrown across the curve of the entire World, lingering on the extremis of every glance, every gaze, no matter how trivial or epic the occasion, a memory of horror that had become horror, a leering token of itself.

A symbol of terror that was terror, distilled and embodied.

And it had been *broken* ...

The sight stole his breath. The Canted Horn lay strewn into a mountain chain of barrelled ruin, shining golden in the sunlight, like a brace of ceremonial armbands spilled and trampled across the dirt. A stinging seized his eyes—sand. A peculiar vertigo reeled through him, an impulse to repair what he saw via some adjustment of vantage, as if a tilt of his head or gain in elevation might somehow bring the two Horns back together.

Esmenet was clutching his hand, shushing reassurance. Mimara smoothed his shoulder and back.

He couldn't breathe. Why couldn't he breathe? He thought of how the God-Kings of Ûmerau would execute criminals by ratcheting hoops of bronze about their breasts tighter and tighter. He heard the dry sobbing of someone old.

"*We—*" he began, only to feel an infant's hand clench the cords of his voice.

No matter how violently he blinked the grit remained.

Mimara cried out, folded about her great abdomen. He heard the roaring of thousands upon thousands of *human* throats—the Great Ordeal howling in triumph.

"Come!" Esmenet was calling into his ear, compassion belied by urgency. "We need to *keep moving*."

But she was already too late.

More than Sranc had been killed by the cyclopean collapse. None of the Shigeki or Saik Schoolmen on Golgotterath's southern ramparts had known of the Spear or the turmoil it had caused across the Oblitus. The bulk of the Canted Horn, hanging like a mountain above them, had occluded all. Only when the Holy Aspect-Emperor began using the ancient Inchoroi artifact did they turn from the dire spectacle of the streaming Horde and gaze up toward the crack and thrum of the vast forces suspended above. General Rash Soptet had stood with Grandmaster Temus Enhorû atop the ninth tower, straining to shout over the swelling howl of their foe. Together, they turned squinting, for the high sun blazed across the rim of the Horn's immense belly. They felt the ground fly up toward it, so massive was the structure. The old Grandmaster screamed some kind of Ward, but it availed him no more than the General's outflung arms. The golden ground clapped down, folding all life and light in infinite gloom.

Grandmaster Ussiliar had been locked in a vicious melee deep in the bowel of the fifth tower when the Canted Horn smote the floor of the World. Walls buckled. Dust and debris rained from the ceilings. Even jammed shoulder to shield, the Shrial Knights were knocked from their feet. The Ursranc were quicker to recover, as the Whore would have it, and they worked a terrible slaughter before the Men regained their wits and ferocity. A slavering chieftain, nearly as tall as a Man and draped in a coat of iron chains, fetters that had been soldered into a crude hauberk, assailed the disoriented Ussiliar, goring him in the thigh before the Shrial Grandmaster finally stoved the obscenity's skull.

"To the parapets," he commanded the Knights who propped him in the battle's aftermath.

With no little dread, he ascended the stair, climbed into dust-filtered sunlight. The vast cylinder of the Horn lay bellied across the Scab, looming mountainous over the shattered walls, and strewn into a vast, golden cordillera across the plate of Shigogli. One of his retinue cried out at the sight of the naked woman curled in the southeast corner of the tower, still breathing despite the horrific burns that ulcerated her skin. The Men gathered incredulous about her. Lord Ussiliar was the first to fall to his knees.

"Princess Imperial," he called, daring to reach for an alabaster shoulder. "Exalt-Magus ..."

Anasûrimbor Serwa seized the Shrial Grandmaster's wrist, then floated to her feet as if thrown by hands. She peered at the contortions of gold towering above, then swept her gaze out across the tortured distance, the numberless white-skinned wretches. Incredulity passed into assurance without residue. The Shrial Knights fell to their knees, pressed their faces to the stone as much out of horror as respect, for she was clothed only in anguish. Her once-luxurious hair had been burnt to shags. Her right arm was greased in weeping ulcers from shoulder to fingertip. The intact portions of her face, once the image of aquiline perfection, formed the outline of a hand about her eyes and nose. Everything else, her brow, her cheek, had been cracked and welted, including her mouth. Only her shanks and the downy curse of her sex had been entirely spared.

"Lord Ussiliar," she said, her voice somehow untouched by the rising clamour. "Recruit every soul still breathing. Leave the walls to the wounded. Defend the *ruin* with the hale ... Make sure nothing passes through the wreckage of the Horn!" She leapt upon the battlements with feline ease. "*Quickly!*" she barked in sudden anger. "While your voice can still be heard!"

And with that her eyes and ruined mouth flared brilliance, and the Exalt-Magus of the Great Ordeal strode out across empty air.

Nemukus Mirshoa and his Kishyati had battled their way deep into the High Cwol ere the Felling of the Canted Horn. They pressed down shattered hallways, cleared reeking storage chambers, long barracks crowded with refuse and offal. All was grunting strain and threshing fury in the murk, notched swords beating down black iron cleavers. The Men knew nothing of what transpired under the sun, for Ursranc packed the gloomy halls, their ferocity waxing more violent with every cubit they surrendered. The contest possessed no clear front. The devastation wrought by the original Ciphrang assault had complicated the labyrinthine interior, linking levels with shattered ceilings and floors, mazing corridors with blasted walls. What was more, they encountered Ursranc of a *different breed*, more mannish in stature, far less given to frenzied demonstrations, more want to rely on skill and grim determination. These were the dreaded Inversi, palatials armed with swords looted from the crypts and reliquaries of Ishterebinth, decked in iron-scaled hauberks and bearing shields emblazoned with a golden tracery of upside-down flames. More and more the Sons of High Ainon found themselves battling foes as lethal as themselves—even moreso, given the Ursranc's greater stamina. What had been a steady advance ground into vicious stalemate. Urdrûsû Marsalees, the once-obese Palatine of Kûtapileth, renowned for his mighty cudgel, fell to an Ursranc bearing an ensorcelled Cûnuroi blade, the famed Pitiril, which sliced through his shield as if it were paper. Grinar Halikimmû, Sacred Hewer, the famed castemenial champion of the Sranc Pits, was likewise felled by an arcane relic of the ancient Cûno-Inchoroi Wars, immolated by Isiramûlis, the eldest of the Six Cinderswords known to be forged by Emilidis.

Death came swirling down.

The High Cwol was given over to screams and slaughter. The Men were driven relentlessly forward by the masses surging behind them, until they found themselves on the masticating front, straining cheek to jowl with the Ursranc, stabbing, grappling, killing and being killed. Ever at the fore, Mirshoa and his Kishyati kinsmen found themselves battling across the bottom of a well that had been smashed through five different floors. Melees of varying intensities knotted each of the floors exposed above, and the Kishyati, ghoulish for the white paint smeared across their faces, endured a continuous rain of projectiles. Mirshoa lost his right ear to an Inversi Captain after a block cast from above robbed him of both his balance and helm. The young man would have perished, had not a second block struck the creature as it lunged for the kill.

Then the floors slapped the bottoms of their boots.

The Incû-Holoinas had *tipped*, such was the mass of the Canted Horn. The dead bounced. The living fell. Sheets of masonry sloughed from the ceiling, crashed down the walls. Mirshoa and his brothers scrambled to find their footing, only to be overthrown once again as the Canted Horn crashed across Shigogli. The roof of the well collapsed, a cataract of morticed debris that killed indiscriminately. Wan sunlight filtered down. The Soldiers of the Circumfix cried out for dread and horror, for the presentiment of disaster. The black-armoured Inversi saw only Men in disarray, sweet vulnerability, and with lust larded by hate, they threw themselves upon the dismayed Sons of High Ainon ...

Screams and clanking reverberated through the cracked halls.

Suddenly Mirshoa and his kinsmen were battling for their very lives. Even as their brothers on the Oblitus roared in exultation, the Sons of High Ainon found themselves beaten backward throughout the High Cwol.

But they had not been forgotten. Apperens Saccarees, Grandmaster of the Imperial Mandate understood the importance of seizing the Intrinsic Gate. Even as the Ainoni faltered before the fury and weaponry of the Inversi, the first of Seswatha's Heirs stepped singing through the sunlit aperture, and began floating down the well wreaking sorcerous ruin. Five were lost to Chorae—Mirshoa was himself nearly killed by the plummet of a Schoolman salted to the pith. But at every stage of their descent, the sorcerers blasted and scourged the exposed halls with intricacies of Gnostic light, until they at last they turned their dread regard upon the Ursranc palatials contesting the bottommost floor. "*Vengeance!*" Mirshoa howled to his kinsmen, who now numbered only in the dozens. The Inversi shrank from his leaping blade, then broke altogether, mewling and shrieking as they bolted. The slaughter was fierce. And among the Ursranc slain by Mirshoa was the fell creature who had struck down Halikimmû and so many more of his countrymen ...

Thus did the young caste-noble come to possess the sword Isiramûlis—Hearth-slayer.

Some five Schoolmen pursued the fleeing Ursranc, and Mirshoa and his kinsmen pursued them in turn, plunging into the gloom of a broad, processional corridor, one already strewn with burnt and dismembered dead. The company of young knights whooped in triumph as they ran, crying, "The High Cwol! The High Cwol has fallen!" But their jubilation was almost instantly knocked from them. Without warning, the discharge of sorceries dazzled the throat of the processional before them, slicked the crude masonry with light. Then, abruptly, the five points of eerie illumination they pursued became *four*. The surviving Sons of Kishyat skidded to a halt, peered apprehensively. Mirshoa glimpsed what seemed a nimil hauberk about an elephantine chest, the portion of a pale leg longer than a man was tall ...

Four lights became three.

Now it was the Mandate Schoolmen who raced *toward them*, fleeing whatever had extinguished the light of their two comrades. "*Runnn!*" one of them urged the mundane company. To a man they obliged, for what a sorcerer fled, only a fool would dare.

Mirshoa, however, remained.

He could scarce see in the wake of the sorcerers, but he need only desire light ... Isiramûlis flared into sudden brilliance, striking his inhuman adversary from the darkness as much as illuminating him, revealing him in all his nightmarish particulars ...

A Nonman Erratic, at least two cubits taller than a Bashrag, draped in great skirts of scintillant nimil, wearing a helm like a fuller's basin, and possessing hands that could dandle a man like toddler. The Cindersword's sudden glare dazzled the giant, allowing Mirshoa to easily sidestep the swooping anvil that was his cudgel. He whirled around as the iron carried the Ishroi's swing, then leapt about the great frame, plunging his blade into the monstrous Erratic's face. The point chipped across cheekbone, slipped into the eye-socket. The giant's momentum carried him crashing forward, yanking Firebrand from Mirshoa's hand.

Mirshoa raised himself winded from the floor, peered for utter blackness. He stumbled into the Cindersword across the uneven flagstones. At his touch the reflection of flames leapt brilliant across its length. Holding it as a torch before him, he continued alone down the carcass-strewn corridor, stalking the Intrinsic Gate.

Malowebi was no stranger to battle, unlike that craven Likaro. He understood its spasmodic rhythms, the tumble of complacency into panic, the passage of hacking violence into bleeding lull and then back again. The "Drunken Father," Memgowa had famously called it, given the petty caprice of its punishments and rewards.

But this ...

He would have babbled in idiot horror, were it not for the absurdity. He would have loosed his bowel had he possessed one.

One instant, he was watching one of Golgotterath's Horns drop as though in water, unravel in cataclysmic ruin across leagues of thronging Sranc. The next he was dancing on an arc from the Anasûrimbor's hip, toppling from a plummet, the stone-regimented earth swinging about his disorder, death flying upward—

Only to find himself plummeting from the absolute vault of the sky, so high that the whole the Occlusion could be glimpsed ...

Falling, utterly helpless as the head that was his vessel floated and lolled. He glimpsed the other Decapitant, saw scaled cheeks and a line of iron horns jutting from black hair, orange eyes that could have been as dead or alive as his own. And he glimpsed the Aspect-Emperor, plaited beard climbing his cheeks, his mouth a furnace, his expression impossibly serene.

Falling and falling, until he felt a bubble, a soul tethered by a single infernal hair—

Only to be yanked to a violent standstill, his gaze wagging as he and the other Decapitant bounced like bangles from the Anasûrimbor's waist, seeing only the obscurities of the Shroud—

Swinging about on his captor's sudden whirl, his soaring field of vision dazzled by Gnostic geometries, lines sketched with the precision of compass and rule, inked with the brilliance of naked sunlight.

A winged shadow sparked through the weir—

Then they were plummeting from on high once again, the Shroud splayed like a cancerous smut across the breast of the World—

Only to slip through yet another impossible threshold and emerge in the chalk and ochre pall once again, this time mere lengths above a winged monstrosity, a creature with skin like spit hanging in water ...

Inchoroi ... Malowebi realized in horror.

And the Anasûrimbor hunted it.

The Mbimayu sorcerer had witnessed a pageant of legends since finding his soul captive, and as numb as he had become, this one *pricked* like no other ...

There was no more doubting the intent of Anasûrimbor Kellhus.

The alien hung above the roiling multitudes, rising and falling with every beat of its ragged wings, its gaze twitching from point to point with anxious alacrity. Only the Aspect-Emperor's Cant alerted the hideous creature to their presence. The uproar was such that only sorcery could be heard, intonations that travelled angles sideways to the Real. The thing whirled as if upon a wire. At first, Malowebi thought the creature blind, for the sockets upon the great, oblong skull were packed with bloodless flesh. Then he saw the misbegotten face cramped into the skull's maw, the glitter of black eyes—suddenly glaring bright with semantic intent ...

Perhaps the thing sought to strike, or perhaps to simply reinforce its Wards—Malowebi would never know. He had recognized little of the sorcery he had witnessed this day. The creature was too late either way. Threads of blue-white brilliance leapt from the aether, lines that extended across arcs, winding about unseen axes, forming spirals that etched, with greater and greater complexity, a sphere about the Inchoroi *and* its Gnostic Wards. Astonished, the Mbimayu sorcerer saw the Inchoroi begin to *revolve* ...

It was as if space itself had been decapitated, snipped into a polyp of emptiness, something the Aspect-Emperor could spin like a top—and so overcome his foe without tearing a single Ward asunder.

The revolutions accelerated, turning became whipping, until the Inchoroi became little more than a shadowy blur within a sphere of pulsing, reticulate light, until its limbs and wings were pulled outwards in a grim parody of the Circumfix, their sockets yanked along infinite lines of flight.

The Anasûrimbor strode toward the uncanny spectacle, then, miraculously, *into it*, breaching the sphere, somehow seizing the blur, plucking it into grotesque immobility—

Tossing the Inchoroi senseless to a golden platform beneath their feet.

All was burnished brilliance, soaring planes of gold mirroring the sun. Heartbeats passed before Malowebi realized precisely *where* they stood.

No ...

The Shroud engulfed the High Horn.

Sikswarû Maragûl, the Far Antique Sohonc scribes of Ûmerau had called it, distorting the name given to them by their Siqu teachers. The Obmaw.

The dread Intrinsic Gate, the terrestrial threshold of the Incû-Holoinas.

Mirshoa strode into a great chamber, drawn forward by the reflection of his own light across what turned out to be *the Ark's golden hull*. A great chasm, some fifty cubits wide, lay between it and the crude-cobbled floors. He halted before setting foot on the bridge—black stone girdered with gold—that spanned it, and so preserved his life from the Wards coiled as springs within it.

The unearthly metal of the High Horn's shell soared high and low, outrunning the ceiling above and the light below. But where the golden surface followed curves smooth as juvenile skin elsewhere, here it had been buckled and breached. A rent as long as any of the Scarlet Spires were tall scored the hull on an angle. Black masonry, blocks as cyclopean as any in Golgotterath, sealed the gash in its entirety, crude compared to the immortal polish of the hull.

The Intrinsic Gate lay in the centre of this stonework ...

Open.

The reek was palpable for being so raw, so *alien*, a putrescence that only his stomach, it seemed, could smell. The Kishyati noble caught his mouth and coughed, stood peering into the pitch-black maw, his jubilation bleeding into horror. The resolutions of young men are mercurial things, abstract for want of hard experience, and thus as weightless as any whim or fancy. He had charged the High Cwol ...for what? To inspire his brothers. To discharge his sacred duty. To save his miscreant soul ...

And yes, *to be first*.

The first to lay eyes upon the Intrinsic Gate.

The first to violate the Ark.

The prospect of consequences had not occurred to him—for like many young men he instinctively understood the way *acting made irrevocable*, how simple doing could throw a man beyond the pale of cowardice, strand him with courage and glory as his only companions.

And now he stood stranded ... shieldless, bearing a magical sword, and wracked with fear and indecision.

What lay *within* the Incû-Holoinas? What perversities of sense and reason?

He thought of the degenerate sins he had committed under the spell of the Meat, the atrocities against human decency and divine writ. He thought of his damnation, shuddered for the force of his revulsion, blinked tears ...

A yawing creak issued through the black portal.

The young caste-noble fairly jumped. But in the receding flush of alarm, the old fury was returned to him, the one that barred all fear.

"'And they *quake* in their wretched holes!'" he cried, quoting scripture for the want of any words of his own. "'For they hear Judgment groan upon the planks of Creation!'"

He stood with Isiramûlis held high, watching the blackness between the iron doors ... breathing.

He wondered at the Ûmeri runes engraved into the stone frame.

A monstrous snout materialized from the void, followed by jaws like skiffs and eyes like emeralds afire, beady beneath the horned flanges that passed for brows.

Wracû.

Mirshoa stood transfixed.

The head rose with the soundless grace of a python, glittering black, revealing a mane of white spines as long as spears, and a serpentine neck as thick as a mastodon's waist. It towered the height of a masthead, then lunged with the swiftness of a twitch, yanking its head back on a feline hiss. Incinerating fire engulfed the head of the bridge—consumed the witless young caste-noble.

And yet swept about and over Mirshoa as no more than a warm breeze. Stone cracked, popped like the joints of a living thing. The young Kishyati stood as before, crying out for wonder and terror.

The Great Wracu reared anew, the crimson of fury rimming the obsidian shields scaling its neck. The spines rose about its majestic crown, and began clattering as iron rods. It grinned, revealing teeth that wept smoking spittle. Mirshoa had assumed it would roar in outrage, but it *spoke* instead ...

"**Aungaöl pauth mûwaryesi ...**"

The Kishyati caste-noble, who could scarce believe he still lived, laughed as an adolescent might after rising unharmed from a mortal tumble. Anagke did favour him!

He could hear the shouts of his kinsmen echoing down the processional behind him.

"Behold righteousness!" he bellowed at the Beast. "*Only the wicked* burn on this day!"

The malevolent Wracu regarded him by the incandescence of Isiramûlis, rising higher and higher against the vast golden plane, so immense that the young man's body quailed beneath the skin of his shrill bravado, for where the soul hoped, the body *knew* ...

"For they hear Judgment!" Mirshoa cried in tearful defiance. "Judgment groans upon th—!"

It struck with the eye-blink speed of a cobra, swinging down as a hammer strike, clapping its maw about the hapless boy—for that was all he was in the end. It paused for but a heartbeat, long enough for Mirshoa's calves and right forearm to flop to the cobble. Then, just as quickly as it had struck, it shrunk back into the void of the Intrinsic Gate—vanished ...

Skuthula the Black.

Worm-Tyrant. Wingéd Conflagration. Glutton of Obmaw.

Keeper of the Intrinsic Gate.

Anguish has its ways. It can foreclose on the World, roll a harbouring soul into a little ball about itself. Or it can prick the bubble, peel back the membrane and cast the soul as paint across the spiny back of the Real.

"*Run!*" the old Wizard cries.

He is frantic for terror; Mimara is not.

"*Do something!*" her mother screeches over the ascending wail.

The things that should belong deny her, and the things that should deny her now belong. The empire of her body has dissolved, stranding her with limbs like so many provinces tipping into rebellion. And yet everything—the gold-thorned battlements, the climbing stages of the Oblitus, even the alien enormity of the Upright Horn—*tingles* like extensions of skin ... until it seems she is as wide as Creation ...

Mimara fleeing from Mimara into Mimara.

"*Cast away those blasted Trinkets!*" the old man snarls. "*Let me save us!*"

She sees the Sranc on the plain, twisting like maggots across ground-that-is-meat. But her gaze lolls away, across the intact Horn soaring upward, silken with sunlight. Slowly, gracefully, she draws the Shroud across its gracile immensity, for she is—and always has been—a modest whore.

The beautiful ones always are, you see.

She looks down upon the three desperate souls, as tiny as beetles clicking across the temple floor.

The little Mimara is screaming, hands about her burning, cramping, shrieking womb. *There is life within her*, and her body chokes and convulses about it.

The greater Mimara communes with God as God.

Malowebi watched the Shroud swallow the void that was light and deliver foetid darkness, gloom. The bottomless vista disappeared, leaving only their small platform stranded upon a vertical plane extending indefinitely in all directions. What relief Malowebi found in the reduction of riot to simple lines was overthrown by his terror. They stood upon the Vigil, he knew, a platform set high upon the eastern face of the Upright Horn—the very stoop, the ancient poets claimed, of the *Golden Room* ...

The innermost sanctum of the Unholy Consult.

At least the gate appeared barred against him. A crude monolith of iron had been set into mirror gold, stamped in rows of script, tall enough to admit an Inchoroi's high-hooking wings, broad enough to accommodate two men abreast. In terms of brute scale it seemed modest enough; *metaphysically*, however, Malowebi had scarcely seen anything more monumental. Its Mark boiled with the intimation of potent Wards, sorceries anchored to the iron's very essence and thrown in fractal webs across the Horn's curve.

The Inchoroi abomination lay curled unconscious at the Aspect-Emperor's feet, carrion wings folded like hands in prayer, black veins pulsing beneath the intestinal skin, membranes fluting. The Anasûrimbor stepped over the powerful frame, pinning the wings beneath his right boot. Malowebi dangled above, so close to the body that both wings had been *amputated* before he even realized the Anasûrimbor had drawn his blade.

The creature awoke on an appalling shriek, snapped from a foetal hunch into a convulsive arch.

The Aspect-Emperor stepped out of reach. Malowebi bounced with his macabre perspective, alternately glimpsing void and the soaring casements of the Horn. Shadow and pallor animated the mirror polish, a murky, watercolour procession. The Inchoroi writhed on the platform, kicked, wailed into the ambient baying of the Horde. The thing seemed to recuperate in stages, finally climbing with puling breaths to kneel before its conqueror. The face embedded in the jaws of the greater skull turned up, slicked in mucous, twitching between boredom and a rictus of anguish ...

He was watching *Aurang*, the Mbimayu Schoolman realized, the Horde-General so reviled by the Ancient Norsirai authors of *The Sagas*.

"I will *love* thee ..." it exhaled.

And Malowebi glimpsed a dawning *allure* in the wretched and piteous face, a promising tenderness. Its strapped frame, which had repelled for the intimation of pallid rot mere moments before, suddenly emanated carnal glory. What had been foul mucosity became slick with the promise of oily congress. Malowebi glimpsed its pendulous member rising turgid across its thigh ... and was not repelled.

If anything, the sight *seized him*, infused him with a curiosity that was at once a yearning, an innocent need to know, and charged with the giddy promise of *release* ...

"Throw open the Portal," the Anasûrimbor replied.

"I will *adore* thee!" it gasped. Images of ravishing and being ravished twined beneath his soul's eye.

"Throw open the Portal, *now*, or join your Horde below."

It stood as erect as its phallus, towered over the Aspect-Emperor, grinned as if conceding its inhuman ardour—as if *yielding* to corporeal desire. Even without hands, Malowebi instinctively made to *clutch* its member, to attend to its swollen needs.

Then it turned to the Portal, revealing the grievous amputations upon either shoulder ...

And the back of Malowebi's lewd madness was broken.

He felt the heave of phantom viscera, gagged for revulsion. The thing had *ensorcelled* him, he realized, picked his soul as a lock with some kind of wanton and loathsome glamour.

Malowebi wished a plague of boils upon Likaro and all his kin.

The alien abomination chipped talons across the iron barricade, lowered its elongated skull to mutter something inaudible. Tar oozed from the stumps upon its back, sheeting its backside. Energy pulsed through the great system of magicks—an ethereal heartbeat.

The dark World howled. The iron monolith glided to the left without sound.

The Portal was open.

The Vigil's height was such that the sun could not be denied entirely. Light filtered into the rectangular maw, revealing the depth of the stone frame, the glimpse of shadowy, skewed golden surfaces beyond, but little else.

The Incû-Holoinas ...

The Ark of Apocalypse!

The Inchoroi slumped to one knee, its obscene life draining from the roots of its dismembered wings. The face in the great-grinning jaws turned from the ink of the entrance's throat.

"Save me, Anasûrimbor," it rasped through mucous and reeds. "I can *show* you ... Death ... damnation can be conquered!"

"Conquered?" the Holy Aspect-Emperor replied. "You are the terror of Hell made flesh, become terror in this World. Hell has conquered you in every way possible."

A clicking that was carnal laughter. Milk-grey membranes shuttered eyes of oil and obsidian. "You will bleed," the monstrosity wheezed, "such will be the intensity ... the *vigour* ..."

He could not see his captor, so Malowebi would never know precisely what happened, only that the shrouded World flew as if upon a string, the Vigil and the Horn bobbing on the margins of oblivion, and when all had settled, the Holy Aspect-Emperor stood alone on windswept heights.

He heard a diminishing shriek, an alien wail pursed in a far mightier roar.

Aurang, the ancient and malevolent Horde-General of Mog-Pharau, was no more.

Not like this ...

But even as the thought occurred to him, Achamian understood this was precisely the fate Anagkë *would* apportion him. For his life had been nothing but a long march of perversities ...

A death march, as the Whore would have it.

Mimara, he decided, had been deceived by the sheer immensity of Golgotterath—what other explanation could there be? The Horn leaning across the whole of Heaven, an impossible immensity. The gold-fanged ramparts half-again greater than those ringing Momemn. She had looked and, addled by her travail, decided they were closer to the refuge of the Great Ordeal than they in fact were, close enough to reach the nearest of the breaches before the masses of Sranc rising from the south.

Now the Shroud had engulfed the High Horn, and the first Sranc had gained the shattered remains of Corrunc. More followed—more than more! A veritable deluge of skinnies sluiced across the desolation, Sranc more brutish than any he had ever seen, bent on trampling all the Furnace Plain.

The three of them ran despite the manifest futility, cramps knifing their flanks, breathlessness scorching their throats, their limbs numb as loamed clay. They could no longer hear one another save for bellowing directly into hands cupped about ears. And it seemed a horror to the old Wizard, the sight of Mimara, teetering great with child, her cheeks shining for tears, her brow pinched for anguish, her mouth working about *soundless* cries.

Yet onward they hobbled. The old Wizard marvelled at the stubbornness—the delusional extremity! Anasûrimbor Mimara would joyfully lob the three of them—or *four* of them?—into the maw of certain death! She would sooner cast him to the Hells than *heed* him!

Skinnies in their tens of thousands flooded the intervening ground. The Shroud consumed the white spike of the sun, towered before them as a progression of phantom cliffs, ethereal faces as tall as the sky, compounding until the Upright Horn was naught but a shadowy silhouette, the only point of reference remaining. Spared the sun's afflicting glare, the first of the Sranc spied them. Within heartbeats, the whole of the Horde—or what they could see of it, at least—bore directly toward them.

"Obstinate wench!" Achamian cried to the girl. "You've killed us all!"

But he couldn't even hear himself.

Esmenet was weeping, her face averted from the mad spectacle. Achamian could not look away, staring as if transfixed by the brute fact of their foe, the canine heave, the violent jerk and gesticulation of pallid limbs, the endless progression of white faces, graven beauty imploding into expressions of lunatic lust and fury. The Horde crashed upon them, each raving figure a fragment of hurtling debris, lethal both individually and in monumental sum ...

And still they limped onward ...

Directly into the maelstrom.

Achamian fairly cast Mimara into Esmenet's arms, raising his voice in arcane song before the two had even crashed to the dust. Flailing white bodies plastered the limits of his incipient Wards, skinnies crushed against his defenses by the irresistible surge of their wretched kin. Gnashing teeth. Grinding hips. Hacking limbs and weapons. The Blessed Empress of the Three Seas lay on her rump, clutching her riven daughter between her legs, sobbing as she threw her gaze about.

The Shroud encompassed them.

Within heartbeats the skinnies had inundated the arcane hemisphere, and they were plunged into a gloom more terrifying than any they had known—far more so than the mobbings they had survived in Kûniüri. The old Wizard sang with weeping abandon, knowing that it was only a matter of time before either his strength gave out or some Chorae-bearing skinny simply leapt into their midst. The semantic incandescence of his conjuring limned every surface—everything from mashing phalluses to the round of Mimara's belly—in an eerie and indiscriminate blue light. He blasted the lunatic welter, threw them from his Wards as so many sodden leaves. He ignited the meat of them, transformed them into thrashing candles. He inscribed the spaces they occupied with geometries of Gnostic light, and left them twitching and dismembered. And yet more and more surged over the greased and smoking carcasses, threw themselves at his Wards with the same thrashing intensity.

Esmenet had lowered her chin to Mimara's shoulder, and now rocked to and fro with her daughter, cheek to cheek. Dust clotted the tracks of their tears, painting black trees about eyes clamped against all that was visible.

Drusas Achamian watched them as he sang, saw their terror blunt for realizing, as he did, that it was not such a bad thing ...

Dying in the arms of those one loved.

He set aside his song, fell to his knees beside them, gathered them in his embrace. Mimara clutched his hand. Esmenet cupped his grizzled cheek. The Sranc vaulted their smoking kin, flew at his Wards, each misbegotten form stealing an increment of murky light. Blackness engulfed them. Achamian pressed his face against their scalps, closed his eyes, and with the ease of an exhalation, surrendered whatever reserve of regret and resentment he yet possessed ... He breathed deep the union of love and resignation.

Wept for gratitude ...

For Esmenet. For Mimara.

These two, at least, had *believed* ... had forgiven.

I have toiled long enough.

The Horde howled.

The light, when it came, was brilliant enough to shine through sealed lids. He opened his eyes blinking, threw an arm against the dazzling glare. Squinting, he saw *her* hanging against the shifting obscurities of the Shroud, a girlish slip clothed only in raiments of blistered, ulcerated skin, singing Gnostic Cants unlike anything he knew.

His beleaguered Wards had been cleared, as had been a great swathe of the raving tumult beyond, almost a ghastly road of sorts, paved in bulbous torsos, jutting limbs ...

"Run!" her voice cracked across Creation.

To shout at what you see is to club what you *do*, to *act otherwise*. For days he had swung from the Anasûrimbor's girdle, and even though his impotence was vertiginous for being so complete, he nevertheless found it impossible *not to shout*. Several times, now, he had thrown himself against the implacable course of the Anasûrimbor's actions—but never so violently as he did now upon the Vigil.

They lure you! he cried into the silence of his captivity. *The Consult* beckons *you!*

Aurang was dead. The Portal had been thrown open.

Likaro was going to pay for this.

The Aspect-Emperor tarried upon the platform's rim, singing sorceries the Mbimayu sorcerer could not fathom, but supposed were Metagnostic Wards of some kind. The man prepared.

You have won your Argument, Anasûrimbor!

Even though Malowebi knew he possessed no body, some fraction of his soul once again refused to countenance this knowledge. Even now it kicked and clawed at the encapsulating oblivion.

I know you can hear me! Why else bear me upon your hip?

Void yawed all about them, heights and pitches lost to the obscurity of the Shroud. The Horn's burnished hull gleamed through the gauze, seemed endless for outrunning visibility, something that spanned the sum of Creation.

The Aspect-Emperor stepped before the threshold. It seemed they stared down a pit and not a corridor—into a more profound and horrific ground.

Nooo! Malowebi howled. *This is folly! You have to know as much!*

An obsidian floor extended mirror-black into the murk. The walls that flanked it for the first several cubits were both stone and square, rising to brace stone lintels, likewise square. But beyond this the interior world was at once golden and *turned three quarters*, with bulkheads rising at acute and obtuse angles, likening the floors to pitch pooled across the basin of a capsized vessel.

You play number-sticks with Apocalypse! The end of all things!

Then the impossible happened: the Anasûrimbor laid palm and fingers across the Decapitant's cheek ... The captive Schoolman could scarce feel the touch, but it triggered paroxysms of terror and grief still.

"Fear not, Iswazi," the Holy Aspect-Emperor said—*to him*. "I am the greater mystery."

Something flashed between the play of pale gleams down the hall, like a cuttlefish in the deep.

"I walk Conditioned Ground."

And so was Second Negotiant Malowebi carried reeling into the horror of the Ark.

CHAPTER SEVENTEEN

The Upright Horn

The more cunning the Lie, the more it exhibits the form of Truth, the more it lays bare the Truth of Truth. So do not fear the Scriptures of other Men! To drink deep from the Cup of Lies as the Cup of Lies is to grow drunk on Truth.

—*44 Epistles*, EKYANNUS I

Early Autumn, 20 New Imperial Year (4132, Year-of-the-Tusk), Golgotterath.

Far more souls would perish in the tribal wars subsequent to the Battle of Kiyuth than in the legendary contest itself. Infighting, hunger and squalor would all but consume the People of War. Across the Hallowed Steppe, the old mothers began openly cursing those bearing recent swazond, calling them the Fa'bakilut: those who grow fat on Misfortune.

Then Cnaiür urs Skiötha had ridden out of the smoke of the Carathay, a lone Utemot encased in scars from cheek to toenail, bearing more swazond than *any among the People*, past or present. His "Norsirai concubine," far from blotting his honour, simply added to his mystique. She was a daughter of Lokung, he claimed, and none dared contradict him. The old mothers even began calling her *Salma'loku*, a name of legendary dread among the People. Rumours rode the winds, of course, tales of scandal and shame, but they impeached the tellers far more than the souls told. The

Utemot had been scattered unto the corners of the Holy Steppe. And what was more, this man was so obviously the very *incarnation* of the Old Honour. A warrior who had reaved at Zirkirta, survived Kiyuth, and had struck out seeking to redeem the People, battling in Outland wars for Outland Kings, bathing in rivers of outland blood ...

More importantly, *he was the one* the memorialists *extolled* in their tales of the Hated Battle, the solitary chieftain to dare raise his voice against Xunnurit the Accursed. And now *he had returned* bearing the death rattle of hundreds in his veins, on his skin, and declaring *the People were one*. Cnaiür urs Skiötha ...

The Most Violent of all Men.

Some said he seized the Steppe in a single day, and though this was not at all the case, it was very nearly true, for none who resisted him possessed a fraction of his will, let alone his cunning or prestige. In the span of a single furious summer he crushed all who found advantage in fratricide, murdering only those who needed to be murdered. The blood of the People was too sacred, he said, to be squandered. He apportioned the widows to the mightiest, enslaved all who were barren. A tempest was upon them, he claimed, and the People would need all her Sons.

How the old mothers had crowed. They would weep for the privilege living so long to see his Coming. They would stoop to earth before him, clawing the grasses, baring the soil to his feet, so they might be *one*, the Steppe and the man they had called Wrencûx ...

Redeemer.

A savage reflection of his sworn foe.

The soul, like the body, knows how to cringe and huddle, how to shelter itself *within itself* according to what is most tender or precious. And as with the body, it is the *face* that is always buried deepest. So Anasûrimbor Esmenet held her free arm over her face as she skidded and tripped, hauling her daughter. Her inability to witness had become the inability to expose, so ghastly had her world become.

Carcasses ... burnt and eviscerated, mangled and amputated, a wan and beautiful vacancy in their faces, eyes limpid and dark, pools the size of pennies, gazing into mudded ground or scissored flesh or out across the blank face of Creation.

Carcasses ... twitching like fish spilled across the docks.

And there, just beyond the riddled Wards, the surge of endless thousands from all directions, howling without sound, wagging weapons, then perishing in incandescent upheavals, becoming silhouettes within blooms of molten brilliance, slumping or flying apart.

And she picked her footing and hauled, picked her footing and hauled. She was a mother, and her daughter was all that mattered.

The daughter, that is, she dragged over carcasses. The daughter above, she failed to recognize.

She picked her footing, her sandalled feet sometimes sinking to the knee, and heaved her anguished daughter forward, always forward.

Until a treacherous fraction whispered, *I know these beasts ...*

For she had been fending them the entirety of her life, their hunger as bestial as their judgment ... Things naked and twitching.

She let slip Mimara's arm to cast both arms across her face, only to lose her footing upon the macabre tangle. If she cried out no one heard it. She fell into the pockets of slick nudity, flailed at the wet skin, and at long last began kicking her dread and confusion.

You remember this ...

The shriek was deafening.

Golgotterath became an island in a threshing inland sea.

The Horde crashed upon the western approaches, the greater part hying south, where it careened into the ruin of the Canted Horn, and was slowed to a trickle by the need to funnel through the gold-ribbed devastation or to circumnavigate it altogether. More and more of the clans hied to the north as a result, until the wicked stronghold—and the Great Ordeal within it—was engulfed in its entirety.

The long-suffering Soldiers of the Circumfix besieged and were themselves besieged. Everyone save the Sons of High Ainon were either called to the roiling perimeters, or assembled in reserve, lest any of their brothers falter. The last of the towers were cleared of Ursranc and manned. Shield walls were raised about the breaches, phalanxes arrayed dozens of Men deep in many cases.

The Knights-of-the-Tusk defended the southernmost breach, the gullet of the Canted Horn's ruin. A vast, impossibly intact section of cylinder lay cracked upon the cliffs, overlooking the mountainous spine of shattered gold—or what could be seen of it through the Shroud. Draped in iron-mail, their Tusk-and-Circumfix shields interlocked, the Knights stood but a pace back from the edge, spearing and stabbing the endless upswell of inhuman faces rising from the lip. The interior of the section lay stacked in utter ruin behind them. Unbeknownst to them, however, the impact had crevassed the scarps below, producing defiles beneath the ruined segment, which otherwise lay braced against bowed and cracked curtain walls. Were it not for the prudence of their Grandmaster, who had stationed pickets through the cavernous ruin to guard against just such a contingency, the Shrial Knights would have been doomed. As it was, these pickets were quickly overrun, but a dozen survivors managed to gather across the lip of a shelf more than a hundred and fifty cubits above and behind where Lord Ussiliar had deployed, screaming, waving their arms, throwing debris, yet unable to gain the attention of any of their brothers in the titanic din. It was only when they began *throwing themselves*, leaping to their deaths, that Lord Ûssiliar at last saw them and fathomed the threat. Using tap-signals to communicate, the rear ranks were turned about so that the whole could form a tortoise thousands strong. An avalanche of missiles and debris crashed down across the carapace. Sranc surged from the gutted hollows, gushed in gesticulating streams. The Knights-of-the-Tusk knelt beneath their impromptu bulwark, propping their shields with their shoulders and their broadswords, and stabbed at the hacking clamour upon them with their Cepaloran long-knives. But shields and arms were broken, and more and more of the raving creatures cracked through, creating inlets and puddles of pitched melee. Men screamed unheard in the hunched and closeted gloom. Many muttered what they believed were their final curses and prayers, until they glimpsed the play of many-coloured lights between the joists of their shields. The Imperial Saik, once their most hated rivals, had saved them. Forsaking the edge, the Knights-of-the-Tusk fought their way into the ruin, deeper into the mountainous segment, gawking as the Schoolmen transformed the floor of the great hoop into a fiery cauldron behind them.

The Judging Eye comes to her knees amid the char and wet skin—looks up ...

Sees a slender Ciphrang hanging as high as the future, showering the earth with death—a *witch*, wet with the fires of damnation, burns heaped upon her burns.

It turns ... sees an old woman who beams angelic grace and an old man who wheezes fire, a thrice-damned cinder.

It glances out ... sees the Sranc, though they are scarce more than apparitions sketched in coal, falling as black hair in the polluted radiance of the witch's craft.

Then, at so very long last, it looks to her belly ...

And is struck blind.

The breaches to the southeast were the easiest to secure and defend, at least in the early going. King Hoga Hogrim and his Tydonni Longbeards held the ruined foundations of Domathuz with battleaxe and kite-shield. Red-faced and roaring, the Thanes of Nangaelsa, Numaineiri, Plaideol and more, defended positions some thirty paces beyond the black ramparts, arrayed across heaps and swales of rubble. To the north, King Coithus Narnol and his Galeoth defended the ruins of Corrunc. Unlike her sister Domathuz, Corrunc had collapsed as a whole, producing a radial flange of debris that extended almost as an oblong bastion beyond the gold-fanged circuit, providing the bellicose Northmen the footing they needed to form a traditional phalanx, and thus a proper shield wall. And so they weathered the rabid, yammering assault with disciplined equanimity.

King Hringa Vûkyelt and his barbarous Thunyeri were charged with defending the most complicated, and therefore most treacherous, of the three breaches: the shell of Gwergiruh, the monstrous gatehouse of the Extrinsic Gate. Here the ruins afforded no obvious line of defense. The hindquarters of the gatehouse remained intact, with only the forward bastions battered down in differing degrees. Interior floors hung exposed. Blocks the size of hovels lay cracked. Intact sections of wall reared solitary and indefensible. Rather than deploy across the perimeter of the wreckage, the Thunyeri Believer-King elected to defend the ruined hulk instead, stationing his black-armoured Men through the very halls and chambers they had wrested from the Ursranc mere watches previous. This ad hoc deployment should have meant casualties, but the Thunyeri were weened on the blood of skinnies.

By dint of upbringing and bloodthirsty temperament, they far preferred depending on their kinsmen's axe over his shield. They knew how to shatter the Sranc stampede, how to *hew into the rush* in a manner that sent the creatures reeling, allowing them to reset. And so the gutted galleries of the Extrinsic Gate became a grisly abattoir.

But even their toll paled before that of the Mysunsai Schoolmen. Hanging in triunes above and about the breaches, they assailed the tormented plate of Ûgorrior with the dread Nibelene Lightning of yore. They were the first to spy the Exalt-Magus approaching through the leaves of the Shroud, gesticulating wildly, singing at the very pitch of her ability, drawing combs of exploding brilliance across the Sranc masses. Despite her straits, she moved with anxious sloth, as if pacing someone who crawled. Soon the glow of Gnostic Wards appeared *on the ground below her*, a luminous bowl that stumbled after the wreckage of her pulping, charring song.

Those upon any height of Gwergiruh could see it ...

And then it inexplicably stalled.

Anasûrimbor Serwa hung as a living light above a *living gyre*, a landscape that scribbled and heaved, that relentlessly surged inward no matter how violently she gouged it. She wracked the earth, unleashed whipping parabolas of razor sharp light. Whole war-bands simply slumped upon their amputations, writhed across their thrashing kin, flailing.

The Men roared in voices that could not be heard, some in triumph, but more in warning, for any fool could see she merely dug sand underwater.

And as if hearing, the girl suddenly whirled to face them across the thronging plain.

"Your Empress needs you!"

Once again it was Lord Rauchurl who seized what favour the Whore had to offer. Without the least consultation, he led his Men in precarious file along the peak of the blasted inner wall of the Gatehouse, thence down to where they could leap directly into the thronging Sranc masses. One by one, the great-shouldered Holca landed, two hundred and thirteen in all, their skin as crimson as their hair for berserker rage, their blades blurring for whirlwind savagery, breakneck violence. With grim deliberation, the High-Thane of Holca led them into the shrieking bedlam of the plain. Nine triunes of Mysunsai shadowed their advanced, scoring the tumult with brilliant white swatches of Nibelene Lightning.

Thus did they slash and burn their way through the threshing tracts, a terrestrial circle of hacking barbarians beneath a floating ring of conjured shadows, all illuminated in flickering sheaves of lightning. The mighty Holca heaving to and fro, great arms snapping, battle-axes throwing blood that glowed violet when glimpsed against discharges. For those with the luxury to watch, standing upon Gwergiruh or the adjoining parapets, it seemed as much a horror as a miracle, a scrap of divine grace that made stark the scale of their plight. For some, all the World seemed to hinge upon the lunatic transit, for despite the unnatural strength and savagery of the Holca, nothing was assured. Not a breath passed, it seemed, without some glimpse of a warrior falling, bludgeoned and cloven, blooded faces dragged howling into the ghoulish frenzy. At any instant, it seemed, the battle-circle could implode beneath the rutting fury.

But then *they arrived*, gained the bright beacon of the Exalt-Magus. They tarried for more than a dozen fraught heartbeats, and then began relentlessly *cutting their way back* to the shell of Gwergiruh, now moving even more quickly for Anasûrimbor Serwa and her astounding Metagnostic might.

Tears clotted the eyes of those Men who could see: The Blessed Empress was saved!

Sosering Rauchurl himself carried her cradled in his great arms, bore her over the blasted remnants of Evil Ûbil to the safety of the Canal.

Only one hundred and eleven of his Holca had survived to follow him.

The Incû-Holoinas.

The deeper the Anasûrimbor penetrated, the more Malowebi had the impression of *sinking*, as if they dove into a golden wreck at the bottom of some black sea, so viscous was his terror.

Everything was capsized, twisted so as to contradict down. But he could not, given the combination of gloom and his abject vantage, discern the limits of the space, let alone make sense of it. He knew only that they had entered a vast, golden room, one illuminated by what seemed a monstrous, upside-down brazier the size of the Healing Pools of Phembari, strung from great chains to form a ceiling of sorts above the polished obsidian floors. Pale wicks of flame roiled and twisted across its surface, blue waxing baleful orange and sparking white—only *lapping downward* ...

Wonder had him straining at the margins of his vision to decode the flames at first, for in no way could he sense the stain of sorcery in the unnatural burning.

Avert your eyes ... a presence instructed.

Whether the voice was his own or belonged to the Aspect-Emperor, he did not know, but it bent the arrow of his attention as if it were his own ...

Away from the uncanny flames and across the mirror blackness of the floors to the spectre of a *throne* arising out of a massive array of horned cylinders and convoluted nodes and grills. The Chair-of-Hooks, he realized, the wicked Throne of Sil. It fluted out upon a myriad of angles, flaring into preposterous dimensions as it bulged into cavernous murk. The floors, he suddenly realized, ended just beyond the great seat, dropping into spaces too vast to be hidden from heaven. Gleams inhabited the abyss, etching the back of shadow with the intimation of staggering structure. Old Zabwiri had shown him the inner workings of a water-clock once, and Malowebi suffered that selfsame sense of peering into an unfathomable *mechanism* now, of seeing what had to be the joints and conduits of mundane force without the least inkling of what those forces might be ...

Aside from unimaginably vast.

And the captive Zeumi Emmisary found himself wondering about the ancient Ishroi of Viri, mulling whether something similar had passed through Nin-janjin's ghoulish veins upon first witnessing the wonders of the dread Ark. Had he experienced the selfsame awe? The same speechless incredulity? *For this was the Tekne*, the mundane mechanics that Malowebi and his ilk regarded with such contempt, only refined to pitches that beggared the intellect, made crude barbarity of their sorcerous barks. The dread Ark, he realized, was a water-clock of unimaginable subtlety, a titanic contrivance driven by its own principle of animation, causes tyrannizing effects, energies hounded through labyrinths, all arranged ... just ... *so* ...

What fools they were! Malowebi could even see them cavorting in the Palace of Plumes, the Satakhan sorting nuts in his palm, Likaro decanting the poison he called wisdom at his side, and the rest of his cousin's festooned inner circle, drinking themselves into oblivion, trading slanders in the pursuit of petty grudges—growing even more fat and stupid, all the while utterly convinced that *they* decided the fate of the World. Such idiot arrogance! Such *conceit*! Layabout, ingratiating souls, anchored to thighs and pillows, addled with wine and hashish, courting favour by calling out ribald condemnations of the Aspect-Emperor—*by cursing their Saviour!*

What shame! What disgrace they had called down upon High Holy Zeum! This was why he hung from the hip of the Anasûrimbor—why he was doomed! *This was why Zsoronga was dead ...*

He gazed upon the dread ligaments from within. And his revelation upon witnessing the Incû-Holoinas from the promontory stood revealed as half-hearted, the skin of something far deeper. The "world" was murdered and the *World* rose up in its place, *a new, deeper ground* of believing. Unknown. Terrifying. Sharp where there had been murk, and impenetrable where there had been flattering phantasm. At last he understood what it was the preachers his cousin executed had experienced: the becoming myth of what had been scripture, and the becoming *question* of what had been myth.

What *were* the Inchoroi? The Nonmen said they descended from the Void, that they sculpted their flesh the way potters fashion clay. But what did that mean? What *could* it mean? Were they truly *older* than humanity?

And what was the Ark? A ship for sailing ... between stars?

It was too much ... Too much too fast.

This was why the last thing the Second Negotiant discerned in the gloom was what should have been the first: *a ghost-white face* peering from the hooded confines of the wicked Chair ...

A hand floated up with a poet's fey sloth, obscured the brow.

Mekeritrig, saying, "It was Sil who fashioned this place."

The Grandmaster of the Imperial Mandate had no choice but to call on the Exalt-General—for he was at a loss as to how he and his Schoolmen might overcome the Intrinsic Gate. They began by attempting to clear the Wards on the bridge, only to watch it slump into the void of the chasm. Then they set upon foul Obmaw itself, wracking it and the adjacent stonework with a catastrophic array of sorceries. They battered the masonry into avalanches of debris, casting the ruin so as to choke upon a narrows in the chasm. The edges were cudgelled down. Wrack was blown as leaves, as the most powerful continued blasting the ensorcelled iron of the portal itself, Abstraction after battering Abstraction, until it too finally sloughed into the choked crevice, leaving only a gaping void where Sikswarû Maragûl had once barred their way ...

The Ark had been pried open.

And so, deep in the husk of the High Cwol, the Men of the Three Seas boomed celebration, save that the stench surpassed description; it bloomed through the chamber like a fog of rotten grease, silenced the cheer. Violent retching could be heard over the eerie resonance of the Horde.

The one hundred and fourteen surviving Schoolmen of the Imperial Mandate arrayed themselves, billows bound, in an intricate formation, facing the soaring golden wall above the chasm's edge. The rent in the Ark emanated darkness as much as inhuman reek.

A causeway dropped from the footings of the hole, then climbed on a steep saddleback to the High Cwol. Five triunes advanced upon the black hole of the Obmaw, walking the arcane echo of the ridge of debris. They sang as they approached, layering their Gnostic Wards, for they knew that a mighty Wracu kept the gate. The breadth of the rupture was such that only one triune at a time could pass. The glory of the van was accorded to the triune of Iërus Ilimenni, a childhood prodigy who had recently become the youngest member of the Quorum. The remaining Mandati watched as the triunes passed as threaded pearls into the mouth and throat of the Intrinsic Gate. Sorcerous chanting hung upon the empty air, resonating, in its peculiar way, *inward* rather than out ...

Brilliance flared from the Obmaw, followed by a breath-stealing whoosh. Shrieks pealed through the opening, cut short on some thunderous impact. "Hold!" Saccarees cried to keep the more impetuous in check. All present stood transfixed, anxiously peering ...

A solitary Schoolman materialized from the blackness, running across mundane ground, arms flailing, billows ablaze. He staggered ten paces out upon the causeway then collapsed in an inert heap. Heedless of his own safety Saccarees raced out to attend to the man: Teüs Eskeles, who had been one of Ilimenni's triunaries ...

"*Skuthula!*" the man gasped, raising a hand that had been salted to the pith.

Death came swirling down.

Death lay heaped as midden throughout the Canal.

Bashrag rose like speared bales; Men webbed all the spaces between. Blood had drowned all the depressions, forming pools with cracked ceramic rinds.

The Exalt-Magus simply stood watching her wards. There was no talk, no reproaches or expostulations of gratitude, simply because there was no sound that could be heard through the monumental wail. The three refugees lay huddled, the two women upon some wall-hanging they had managed to rescue from the encampment, Drusas Achamian on blood-slicked stone. The old Wizard grimaced as he tore fabric from the corpse of an Imperial Columnary—to bind about his ankle, Serwa realized. Her mother lay slack and almost entirely witless against the wall. Mimara knelt at her side, attended to her despite the paroxysms of agony that wracked her. Serwa watched her pregnant sister thrust a finger into a leather pouch that she held cradled in a shuddering hand, withdraw it covered in dust, then press it between their mother's lips ...

This small task completed, Mimara slumped onto her rump, surrendered to her anguish ...

Or was about to, for her look immediately fastened upon her younger sister standing above, clicked from point to point about her nude form, lingering on the blisters and ulcerations that were her only garb. Pity and horror. After a covert glance at the old Wizard, she proffered the pouch, wincing about some pang as she did so.

Serwa hesitated.

What is it? she asked with a look.

She need only see her elder sister's lips to hear his name.

Malowebi struggled to recover his inner composure.

"Before Sil," Mekeritrig said, "it was Ark who commanded, Ark who apportioned, Ark who judged ..." A wan and predatory smile. "And the Holy Swarm hung upon It as a babe from the teat."

The Evil Siqu leaned into the wavering fullness of the downward-burning light. He drew his hips forward, lowered a bare foot to the mirror-polish of the floor. There was a glory to his nude body, a perfection of

manly form and proportion that was disconcerting. He reached to the left
of the wicked Chair, stroked the long curve of what Malowebi saw was a
scalp ... the greater skull of *another Inchoroi*, resembling Aurang in every
respect, save for its meek bearing. Where the Horde-General had imperi-
ously consumed the space surrounding, this creature—*Aurax*, the Mbimayu
sorcerer realized—shrank from it, as if simple emptiness were indistinguishable from mortal peril. It huddled against the Chair-of-Hooks as if stranded
over a lethal fall.

"A machine," Anasûrimbor Kellhus said. "The Inchoroi were ruled by a
machine."

Mekeritrig smiled. "Aye. But then the Inchoroi held that *all* are machines
... not unlike the Dûnyain. Ark ruled simply because Ark was by far the
mightier machine."

"Until the Fall."

The Nonman retrieved his hand, gazed without blinking at the
Anasûrimbor. Aurax made as if to follow the caress, then shrank back to
its grovelling station.

"They were wrecked for losses," the Evil Siqu replied. "Yes. But they were
wrecked for the ruin of Ark most of all. They had become—How would you
say?—*parasites* ... Yes. Worms in the vast gut of Ark."

He stood to reveal the alabaster magnificence of his form—a beauty that
rendered all mortality decrepit.

"It was Sil who first climbed free of their stupor, who rallied the Divine
Inchoroi Swarm. It was Sil who fashioned this place ..."

"Before Sil," the Holy Aspect-Emperor said, "it was Ark who commanded."

Malowebi found himself confused by the repetition, until he realized
that the Anasûrimbor *tested* the ancient Erratic, probed the limits of what
must have been an ailing memory.

A bleary, scowling look. An ancient indecision.

"It was Sil who raised the Inverse Fire from the Bowel," Mekeritrig continued, "installed it here, so that all who petitioned him might fathom
the Onus."

"Yes ..." the Anasûrimbor said with peculiar distraction. "The reason all
mention of this room was struck from the *Isûphiryas*."

It seemed clear the Inverse Fire was the brazier hanging inverted and
elephantine above them—as was the fact that the Anasûrimbor (whose face

remained hidden) gazed into it. What perplexed and worried the Mbimayu sorcerer was the Evil Siqu's triumphant sneer ...

"I cannot but envy you," Mekeritrig said, stalking about the gossamer phantasms reflected across the floors. "And mourn. Yesss ... Seeing the Inverse Fire for the very first time."

Aurax shuddered at his departure, lowered its chin to its feet, seemed to whimper.

"We entered from over there," the Evil Siqu declared. He cast some Quyan version of a Surillic Point on an arcane whisper, threw it out upon a flung arm. The white light made liquid of the obsidian floors and fractured confusion of all else, thousands of shining white points slipping like oil across myriad intricacies of gold. It paused above the first in a series of six stairs that simply plummeted into the black sheen. The original golden room had been a juncture of some kind, Malowebi realized, opening onto a dozen or so corridors that, capsized, had become stairs, six descending from the level of the new floor to their left, and six ascending to their right.

"There were three of us," Mekeritrig continued, raising his eyes to the Inverse Fire. "Wise Misariccas, cold and cruel Rûnidil, and myself. We were wary. Sil had managed to turn not just Nin-janjin, but *all* of the *Viri*— a people famed for their mulish will! We knew it had something to do with *this* place ..."

The Nonman glanced back toward the Anasûrimbor in a covert manner— dark humour flashed in his eyes ... and satisfaction.

"But nothing more."

As far as the Mbimayu sorcerer could tell, the Aspect-Emperor continued peering into the flames ...

What was happening here?

"How *well* I remember!" the Evil Siqu gasped, raising his face as if to some morning sun. "Such ... glorious ... *horror* ..."

What *was* the Inverse Fire?

"Misariccas stood where you are standing ... transfixed ... unable to tear aside his gaze ..."

Some kind of sinister weapon?

"Rûnidil—always so harsh, so contemptuous of display!—he fell *there* ... began weeping, bawling ... grovelling on his belly and crying out gibberish!"

Were they already doomed?

"And *you?*" the Anasûrimbor asked.

It was not manly, the gratitude that washed through him for hearing the man speak.

Look away! he cried in his thoughts. *Turn down your eyes!*

The smile that hooked the Nonman's lips was as unseemly as any the Mbimayu sorcerer had ever seen. "Why ... I *laughed* ..." A sudden frown seized the porcelain features. "What else does one do, learning they had lived and murdered for the sake of *lies?*"

Mekeritrig gazed back up into the Inverse Fire with an attitude of sharing something sacred—miraculous.

"I am *whole* in its presence," he said on a profound sigh. "Present."

The Anasûrimbor remained conspicuously silent—and motionless.

He deceives you! Lulls you!

"You should have heard my stalwart Ishroi brothers rant upon our return! We're deceived! We are deceived! We're damned all of us! Condemned to eternal torment! *The Inchoroi spake true!*"

Laughter, peculiar for its fragility.

"Such fools! Speaking truth—unthinkable, unlivable *Truth!*—to power, *any power*, let alone that of a Nonman King! Oh, Nil'giccas was wroth, demanded that I, the silent one, the cryptic one, explain their blasphemy. And I looked to them, Misariccas and Rûnidil, their eyes so certain that I would confirm their manic claims, certain because we had become *brothers* the instant we had gazed up into these flames, brothers possessing a bond that no coincidence of blood and bone could rival. They looked to me ... eager ... dismayed and disordered ... and I turned to my wise and noble King and said, 'Kill them, for they have succumbed as Nin-janjin had succumbed ...'"

Another laugh ... this one intentionally false.

"And so was Truth saved ..."

The Evil Siqu looked down once again, blinking as if at some arcane disorientation.

"For Nil'giccas would have murdered me as well, had I not."

And it seemed to Malowebi that he floated, his every experience nothing more than a bubble drifting through cold horror. For he at last understood *what it was*, the Inverse Fire ...

And the object of the Anasûrimbor's enraptured gaze.

Damn you, look away!

"What was I to tell him? That the hallow Between-Way was a fraud? That everyone he had lost, his comrades-in-arms, his son and daughters, *his wife!* Was I to tell him *they all shrieked in Hell?*

"Look!" the Evil Siqu cried, gazing upward, hands drawn up in horror and incredulity. "*Look,* Dûnyain! Look at the heinous *madness* of their crimes, the way they *unravel* you! Suck the grease of anguish from your very thread! Unthinkable trespasses! Raped to the being! Decanted into screams!"

"Nay ..." he suddenly laughed, a mania shining through his gaze. "There was no explaining *this.* Not to Nil'giccas—or any Nonman King. That was what Misariccas and Rûnidil failed to reckon: the Inverse Fire cannot be *told* ..."

Cet'ingira fixed his darkling gaze on the Anasûrimbor.

"It must be *seen.*"

⸺ ⟳ ⸺

"Skuthula!" the Exalt-General bellowed into the cracked throat of the Obmaw. "I would parlay with you!"

The sooty blackness remained every bit as inscrutable.

Apperens Saccarees stood at his side, but no one else, some twenty paces out on the saddled causeway. Over one hundred Ainoni Knights had just died attempting to swarm the Intrinsic Gate: their charred and smoking corpses matted the floors both about and within the blasted hole.

"*Skuthula!* Speak to me, Black Worm!"

A lesser man would have yelped at the sight of great, serpentine *eyes* opening in the darkness, black slashes for pupils, embedded in irises that flexed like a weave of golden blades. Even Saccarees shrank back a step before recalling himself. Anasûrimbor Kayûtas merely stood as inscrutable as before.

"**Whooo?**" the Wracu intoned on a gaseous croak. A malefic orange glow revealed the breadth of its jaws, made one hundred silhouettes of its scimitar teeth. "**Who believes reason might prevail where sword and sorcery fail?**" An incandescent grin, like a blazing furnace seen about a corner ...

Laughter like tumbling heaps of coal.

"Anasûrimbor Kayûtas! Prince-Imperial of the New Empire! Exalt-General of the Great Ordeal!"

"**Ahhhhh ... Namesake of the Accursed Slayer.**"

"What binds you, Wracû? How have you been enslaved?"

"You would bait me with your insolence ..."

"You are chattel, a dog chained to the stoop of your master!"

"I am no more a slave than you are the Slayer."

"Indeed, Wracu, I am not my namesake—any more than you are Skuthula the Black, the Great Obsidian Worm!"

The golden eyes snapped shut, then reopened narrow with malice, hatred, and suspicion.

"I shall savour thee, manling. Cunning makes the flesh swee—"

"What happened to the great and terrible Wracu of legend?" Kayûtas interrupted with shouting violence. *"The Skuthula I know* roosted upon the summit of mountains, tyrannized the very Heavens! Who is this *imposter* who skulks and snaps from a badger's hole?"

The Exalt-General's voice peeled across the soaring gold faces, hung for a heartbeat before vanishing into the Horde's ambient wail.

The Wracu's eyes narrowed ever further, became slits bent into shining bows. Orange light waxed behind the cage of teeth, limned the crocodilian scowl ...

Then the leering visage disappeared.

The two Men stood waiting, peering.

"Just as the legends say," the Mandate Grandmaster finally murmured. "Bodies scaled in iron, souls skinned in gauze ..."

The Obmaw hung slack and ruined before them, utterly empty.

"Too much so," Kayûtas said. "I fear he will die before relinquishing Obmaw now."

"Perhaps not," Saccarees replied. "Perhaps he has already abando—"

The twinkle of light in the portal's black gullet stole the Grandmaster's words ...

Spewing, exploding brilliance engulfed all else.

"Have you found yourself?" the Evil Siqu asked, his voice silken and oceanic. "Everyone who looks finds themselves, everyone who has dared any kind of greatness in this accursed World."

The Mbimayu sorcerer howled in voiceless fury, as much for impotence as for what transpired.

Avert your eyes!

"Do you *see*, Dûnyain?" Mekeritrig screeched with sudden intensity. "Do you see the necessity of Resumption! Why Mog-Pharau must walk! *Why the World must be shut!*"

The Anasûrimbor had not moved in the slightest.

"Tell me that you see!"

Malowebi might as well have been bound to a post.

"I see ... *myself* ... Yes."

A scowl hooked the Evil Siqu's zeal into something less certain.

Malowebi found himself caught on wonder.

"But you feel it ... like a memory that resides in your veins ..."

Deny him! Please!

"Yes."

What was happening? The Mbimayu sorcerer wanted to believe that the Anasûrimbor had somehow prepared for this threat. But Mekeritrig so utterly *assumed* the Inverse Fire would reveal ... What? The truth? Could a deeper, far more horrific layer of revelation lay beneath what he had already grasped ...

Could the Aspect-Emperor be deceived?

Schoolmen were loathe to ponder Hell. They built innumerable habits of avoidance into their lives.

The infamous Nonman Outlaw gazed back up to the Inverse Fire—what for Malowebi remained a play of spectral incandescences across the mirror-black floors. Convections cast shadows like liquid or smoke across the length of his chiselled white frame. After several heartbeats, an opiate glassiness emptied his look.

"After a time," he said vacantly, "the sheer *profundity* of it, the monstrous scale of the anguish ... it becomes soothing ... sublime ..."

The sluicing of firelight across white skin.

"And never ... never *repeating*, always different ... like some kind of broken arithmetic ..."

Horror cracked the white enamel of his expression.

"We call it the *Goad*," he continued, a ferocity cracking through his voice. "It is what has *bound* our Holy Consult these thousands of years ..." A seizure of anguished fury. "*To see the crimes committed against us*! That is what drives us to blot the foul abomination that is this World! The torments revealed by the Inverse Fire!"

He had fairly screamed this, and now he stood riven, sinews finning his neck and arms, his hands clutching emptiness.

"But I suffer no torment," the Anasûrimbor said.

Malowebi hung in numb oblivion. Mekeritrig was several heartbeats blinking before he could properly peer at him.

"So you think the Fire *deceives?*"

"No," he replied. "This artifact senses the continuity of the Now with our souls as they exist outside of time. It siphons it like sap, boils it into an image the Now can comprehend. The Fire burns true."

Pained scowl. "Then you see *that you are my brother?*"

The Golden Room swayed across the belly of Malowebi's visual field: the Holy Aspect-Emperor had finally turned to face the founding soul of the Unholy Consult.

"No ..." the Anasûrimbor replied once again. "Where you fall as fodder, I descend as *hunger*."

Death.

So cool in the harem tangle. A Bashrag lay with its black-shag head in the crotch of its triune arm, like a child counting in a game of hide-and-seek. A Nansur Columnary sweated beneath, sprawled like something dropped from the sky. Another reclined almost as if snoozing, save for the unnatural crook of his neck where his head pressed against the trousered thigh of the former. A severed arm reached out, intent on tickling his ear ...

And it all ... *tingled.*

There was a simplicity to things dead, a stillness that was singular for perching within the husk of motion. And it struck her as the most beautiful thing, the *immunity*. To live was to grind possibility into an endless thread of actualities, to slough moments like a serpent shedding an infinite, anguished skin. But to *die* ... to die *was to be*, to dwell with the ground *as ground*, an obdurate and impervious extension.

Imagine never having to breathe!

She gazed at the decapitated head of a handsome man, young, with fulsome lips and straight teeth set in a lantern jaw. How she had once prized young, handsome Men, wondered how even their filth could feel so *clean*. She imagined catching his eye in some gilded corridor on the Andiamine

Heights, upbraiding him for some contrived oversight, a naughty old queen, flirting ...

But then her gaze caught upon an Ursranc pinioned between human legs, and she found her fancy overthrown ... for the creature was more hand-some—and all the more repellent for it.

Tingling ... within her and without.

She drew a finger across her lips, and blinking, turned to the commotion to her right, saw her daughter, Mimara, screaming soundlessly at her side, and her lover, Achamian, holding the pregnant girl's hand, shouting words no one would know. She reached out, laid a tentative palm across her dis-tended abdomen, wondered that it was so *warm* ...

Birth.

And on a sharp intake of breath, her macabre tranquillity was expelled, and all the riotous urgency of living crashed through her once again.

All the dead eyes about her, even those cooked to snot in blasted sockets, turned away.

The Evil Siqu regarded him narrowly.

"Subterfuge!"

"So I am the first?" the Aspect-Emperor asked. "Have no others resisted the Goad?"

Mekeritrig said nothing, retreated to the Chair and its frame of wicked hooks. He leaned upon one buttock, pulled his legs onto the cushion the way an adolescent girl might. Aside from a hand upon his knee, shadow obscured all save his forehead and brow.

"Not even the famed Nau-Cayûti," the Nonman eventually replied from shadow. "The Great are always flawed. Always damned ... I had assumed the same of you."

Aurax bobbed its great crown at the Evil Siqu's knees, like an abused dog seeking favour, only whispering scarcely audible syllables ...

"*Gassirraaaajaalrimri ...*"

Malowebi *wanted* to rejoice, but too many worries harried his thoughts—the fact that a *window into Hell* hung immediately above the *least* of them! What would *he* do, were he to *witness* the facts of his damnation? Embrace it?

Or embrace *them*?

The Anasûrimbor had said the Fire burned true, and *he would know*. He had been to Hell—or so his Three Seas enemies had claimed ...

The Evil Siqu seemed to have no inkling of what he should do, as if his faith in the efficacy of the Inverse Fire had been complete. With silence, came the spectre of unrequited violence.

"Where is Shauriatis?" the Anasûrimbor demanded. "Where is your Halaroi master?"

Mekeritrig leaned from the Chair's shadowy hood. "That will avail you nothing," he said. "*Baiting.*"

"Why?"

"Because I am eight thousand years too old."

"And still chained to the post," the Aspect-Emperor snapped. "I tire of this shallow posturing. Tell me, witless Cûnuroi dog, *where is Shauriatis?*"

The alabaster figure remained motionless, save for the pulse of a single vein high on his illuminated forehead ...

Then, as if draped across cobwebs, a new voice fell upon the room.

"*Calm ... old friend ...*"

Followed by another voice ...

"*He knows all the ancient legends ...*"

Also frail, as if spoken on breathing's final allotment.

"*And you all but told him ...*"

"*How the Inverse Fire rekindles your zeal ...*"

Five *different* voices had spoken, each cast of its own alloy and yet scratched into the unanimity of rust by hoary age. The Anasûrimbor had remained motionless, as if absorbed in some arcane scrutiny of their content or timbre. Now a subtle shift in position told Malowebi that he returned his gaze to the Chair-of-Hooks, and to the *golden platform* that floated down from the void above it ... resolved as if *growing* as much as nearing.

Shauriatis?

The platform was the length and breadth of a skiff, shaped and curved like a great shield, but far too large to be wielded as such by human arms. At first it appeared to bear ten great *candles* set in a circle, wax gutted and knobbed and pale as bacon fat, each set within a stone pedestal ... Except these candles clearly *moved*, and possessed (as quickly became obvious) *living faces*, rutted and as hairless as prunes, mouths like masticating sphincters, eyes like sparks set in mucoid shadow. The pedestals, he realized, were in fact perverse *cradles*, stone sconces for *bodies bereft of limbs* ...

Ten senescent, larval forms had been welded upon the back of some great soggomantic shield ...

The revulsion intensified as the thing neared, then settled next to the Chair-of-Hooks—just beyond the ghostly reflection of the Inverse Fire across the floors. Aurax grovelled beneath Mekeritrig's feet.

"At *lasht* ..." one of the ancient worms crooned.

"*Our disparate Empires meet* ..." another gasped in completion.

This? This was *Shauriatis*? The legendary Grandmaster of the Mangaecca?

Cet'ingira exploded from the Chair, his face as seamed for fury as any Sranc. Semantic brilliance waxed from the apertures of his face. An apricot glow charted the fork of veins through his cheeks and sockets.

Anasûrimbor Kellhus was utterly unsurprised, already turning, already seizing the Evil Siqu with a Metagnostic whisper that was a hairline of blinding white that leapt to the Nonman like lint to wool in winter, sheering through his Incipient Wards, then cinching his throat, an arcane noose hanging him nude and kicking beneath the wavering, infernal landscapes.

"I am Master here," the Holy Aspect-Emperor said.

Malowebi whooped into the nowhere imprisoning his soul.

"*Yesh* ..." one of the senile larva cooed from beyond the Mantraitor's thrashing form.

"*Our master* ..." another Larval croaked, his torso a swallowing throat.

The Anasûrimbor strode past the wheedling heels of Mekeritrig directly to the abomination that was Shauriatis. He fairly leaned over the near edge, so close that Malowebi could see everything: the trails of offal greasing the metal from the base of the chipped cradles to the bevel; the magisterial Inchoroi figures stamped across the gleaming curve; and varieties of skin, this one velvet and lobed like petals, that one harassed into fibrous wisps, this one dimpled with ruby lesions, that one drawn amphibian thin across veins like black string. He understood the nature of the contrivance at once, for the totem-lore of the Iswazi told of many Mbimayu who had sought to save their souls from damnation.

The legendary Shauriatis, the sorcerous architect of the Unholy Consult, *did* stand before them, his soul tumbling and forever deflected, roosting like a sparrow for but a breath in each wretch before capsizing into another. Such cunning! *Dying* vessels, denuded souls, gouged of some vital passion, allowing him to alight *whole*, rather than be drawn and divided across the Outside like other Proxies ...

Shauriatis!—not so much the wretches themselves, as the *intervals between*.

"Tell me, Archidemu," the Anasûrimbor said. "How long has it been since you were usurped?"

Usurped?

There the image was, the horrid obscenity that were the Larvals, as pitted with grisly detail as anything the Iswazi mage had ever seen, and he watched the Aspect-Emperor *pass his haloed hand through them*, saw miniatures of the scene sweep without the least substance across the man's palm and fingers ...

Less than smoke. Phantasm.

Malowebi cursed the Great Sage.

Tekne.

"Brother!" the Exalt-Magus cried upon seeing Kayûtas standing with Saccarees and Lord Soter.

"*She lives!*" one of the numerous Mandate Schoolmen cried. Hundreds of worried faces turned to follow her floating descent. Her passage over the crowded ranks of Ainoni had sparked commotion through the ruined halls of the High Cwol, for her prolonged absence had been noted by all. At some point the Soldiers of the Circumfix had begun falling to their knees and crying out, "Serwa! Serwa Memirrû!"—the antique Ainoni moniker for heroes reborn. She watched, with a kind of harried wonder, as the sorcerers took up the call in turn.

She came to ground immediately before her brother. His look fastened upon the grievous burns that she had taken as her garb. He too had survived some kind of fiery assault, but only his beard and crimson Kidruhil surcoat appeared to have suffered.

"Serwa—" he began.

"We have no time," she interrupted. "I saw Father *upon the Vigil*."

A heartbeat of passionless scrutiny.

"So soon?"

"We need to storm the Ark *now!*"

"Easily said," Kayûtas said scowling. "A Wracu guards the threshold."

"Then *kill* it!" she cried.

"Skuthula," Saccarees croaked on a ragged breath. He too sported glistening burns, though nowhere near so severe as her own. "*Skuthula the Black* defends the Intrinsic Gate ..."

She looked to the Mandate Grandmaster for a moment, then back to her brother. The legendary Black Worm had very nearly killed them, she realized. She turned to the battered maw of the Intrinsic Gate, and peering with her prodigious arcane sight, sensed Chorae ... a faint constellation of voids hanging in spaces unseen.

"Father ..." she said, thoughts racing.

A grave nod from her elder brother. "For the nonce, he confronts the Unholy Consult alone."

The Aspect-Emperor strode *into* the visible reality of the Larvals, waded *through* the gold-gleaming intricacy of the floating shield, paused in the very centre of the wretches. The image hung impossibly static, with each of the grotesqueries caught upon some infirm expression.

"Reveal yourselves!" the Anasûrimbor cried out to the blackness.

Despite his turmoil, Malowebi could only marvel at the *substance* of the mirage, which was *nothing at all,* and yet somehow duped the eye into seeing onerous matter. Drool hung like ice, from the chin of the nearest, reflecting a past stage of the Inverse Fire on a molten thread.

"Set aside your vain ornaments!" the Anasûrimbor boomed into the metallic gloom.

As if in cryptic reply, the Larvals winked out of existence.

What was happening? Who did he think he was calling?

Aurang had been cast to its death. Aurax cowered against the Chair-of-Hooks, clinging to its knees, keening in terror, riven in the manner of dogs beaten unto madness. And the sounds of strangulation meant that Meker-itrig still hung kicking behind them ...

Shauriatis?

"*Cease this pantomime!*" the Anasûrimbor cried.

Had the Consult indeed succumbed to the toll of ages? Grown so decrepit as this?

The man whirled to his right without warning, tossing Malowebi's field of view on a precipitous arc. The Aspect-Emperor strode from the oily immediacy of the light, slowed to a pause beside a rising fin of golden metal: some kind of partition the ancient renovators had raised the obsidian floor around, rather than remove.

The gloom defeated Malowebi at first. One would think hanging *Hell* from the ceiling would afford better lighting! But the glints and contrasts slowly morphed into structure and detail the longer he peered. The mirror polish of the floors extended into the jaundiced murk, ending at a curved golden wall. Six equidistantly spaced shafts punctuated the intersection of the tipped floor and the suspended wall—corridors become stairways. Six sets of obsidian steps rose from the black polish to meet them, devoid of handrails or any other ornamentation.

Five forms descended them, moulting shadows step by relentless step ... horrifying the Mbimayu Schoolman by stages.

Led by the King-of-Tribes and his girl-skinned son, a file of Scylvendi warriors on horseback finned the gravel heights of the Occlusion. The Umbilicus burned as a gutted ulcer amid the fields of smoking char below. The Horde enveloped Golgotterath in vast tentacular masses beyond, concealing all in chalk obscurity in its wake, lest anyone witness the inevitable atrocities committed.

"The skin-spy ..." Moënghus called to his father. "She wanted you to throw the Tribes across the plain?"

"Aye," Cnaiür urs Skiotha replied, gnawing on his ration of amicut.

"To seize the breaches before the Ordeal could defend them?"

The Scylvendi King-of-Tribes leaned to spit a wayward fragment of bone. He wiped his mouth with a swazond-ribbed forearm, glared at his son with a murderous intensity.

"Aye."

The young man did not flinch from his scrutiny—and why should he, dwelling as he had beneath the Dûnyain's bloodless gaze?

"Then the People would have been fed to the Horde?"

Cnaiür urs Skiotha spat again, this time for the sake of spitting, then peered at the High Horn's shadow through ponderous skirts of chalk and ochre.

"Everything," he said, "will be eaten here."

CHAPTER EIGHTEEN

The Golden Room

Nay, the world is not equal in the eyes of the God.

—Scholars 7:16 Tractate

Fall together, land alone.

—Ainoni saying

Early Autumn, 20 New Imperial Year (4132, Year-of-the-Tusk), Golgotterath.

Earth and sky wailed, a chorus so featureless as to sound angelic, so titanic as to *become* the voice of every Man who dared open his mouth to breathe, let alone howl against it.

Dusk lay watches away. But for some reason the chalk dust of Shigogli, which had been pale as bone upon the ground, *blackened* as it hung in the Shroud, spinning a pall that had blotted the day and unleashed the night. Dragonheads vomited brilliance both within and beneath the Canted Horn's immense, metallic husk, fire that seethed gold across wracked heights and feathered the Shrial Knights in endless parade of fading shadows. Nibelene Lightning glared and flickered from points across Ûgorrior, illuminating the Sons of the Middle-North in fluttering white. While along the western ramparts, myriad Gnostic Abstractions waxed and smouldered, throwing incandescent blue like paint, bending shadows about the Eumarnan's booted feet.

Golgotterath had become an island of slaughtering lights.

Inhuman thousands scaled the ramparts at any given time, but the surfaces were too treacherous for the creatures to overwhelm the parapets. Individual Schoolmen roamed the heights, and were quick to visit destruction upon any Sranc threatening to test the defenders. The battle turned on the *breaches*, on the Men assembled across pitches of gore and debris, and on the sorcerers singing in cracked voices above, wracking the murky throngs with meanings damned by God. It was a battle of violent surges, great waves crashing across breakers of sorcery and iron, the survivors slinking back in thin sheets as the Horde recoiled to surge forward anew. Again and again, the Men of the Ordeal stymied the foul onslaught, crying out the names of Gods and loved ones in voices they could not hear. Again and again, they slumped to knees or staggered against their fellows in the gasping wake.

The logic was simple: those who grew too weary, fell. The ferocity of the Sranc combined with the thrashing density of their bodies, required *enduring* strength, a tenacity that not all Men, no matter how inveterate, possessed. None other than King Hoga Hogrim died this way, electing to remain at the tumultuous fore with his Men despite his sapped limbs. A hulking creature barrelled into the Believer-King, knocked his greatshield to the side, then clove his thigh to the bone. The nephew of the famous Gothyelk fell gouting blood, shaking uncontrollably as the immediacy of his circumstances drained away. Dismayed faces floated above him for a time, then death came spiralling down ...

Bore him wailing to the fire.

Only a minority of the Yimaleti clans carried javelins—and archery was all but unknown to them. But periodically, concatenations of these Sranc came against the breaches, and the Men of the Ordeal found themselves enduring absurd showers of the weapons. As crude as they were, the black, fire-sharpened shafts always managed to murder a select handful through a variety of cruel flukes. This was how King Coithus Narnol was maimed and forced to retire back to the Canal, and how Thane Sosering Rauchurl was felled from the heights of Gwergiruh. He was grinning to his compatriots when the missile dropped from the void of his left, piercing his cheek, breaking his teeth, and pitching him headlong into the frenzied threshing below. Death came spiralling down ...

Bore him wondering to the brace of Gilgaöl.

The Sorcerers of the Circumfix hung immune for the most part, but they did not escape unscathed. Seven among the most elderly Schoolmen, all hailing from different Schools, simply slumped from the air, undone by their exertions. Along the breaches facing Ûgorrior, where the bulk of the Chorae Hoard plundered from Sakarpus had been expended to neuter the ensorcelled walls, more than two dozen Mysunsai were struck from the sky over time. The sheer number of carcasses had raised a second ground upon the ground, one far more grisly, and far more treacherous to stand upon. At some point, the Sranc trapped in the press began hacking their dead cousins into pieces, hurling them remarkable distances, either ineffectually at the Schoolmen punishing them from above, or across the armoured ranks arrayed against them. Soon, torrents of limbs and spinning heads— even organs and roping entrails—rained down upon the Men of the Ordeal. Roiling among themselves, the Sranc had begun *hurling themselves*. Sheets of slicked meat fell upon the Mysunsai triunes especially, a charnel deluge, and periodically, either by happenstance or for some witless cunning, a Chorae would find itself within the soaring mire ...

The brilliant and irascible Hagnar the Elder was felled this way, his leg salted to the bone. As was Parsalates, one of the Mikka Surconsuls, and some twenty others. Points of nothingness pricked the macabre hail, Wards became as fumes, and Schoolmen were tossed into the infernal pit ...

Darker and darker the Shroud grew, even though the sun was mere watches past its zenith. The chalk dust blackened, biting eyes and throats, obscuring more and more of the sepulchral tracts, until each Man found himself stranded within a dwindling island of turbulent visibility. And with the encroaching black came a horror and a dismay, a premonition of doom that no heroism or fervour could dispel, that for more and more souls resolved into the breathless tingle of *futility* that was the certainty of defeat.

To smother sight is to strangle hope, for direction is the bounty of vision. At points across the ramparts and the breaches lone Swayali witches began to appear, Nuns with their billows bound and meaning flashing from their mouths. But rather than delving into the lunatic fray, they hung behind the bristling ranks of Men. One by one, *blinding white pillars* appeared between their outstretched arms, lancing up through the smothering locks of the Shroud ...

Bars of Heaven anchored the circuit of Golgotterath's mighty curtain walls, puncturing as much as glaring through the Shroud, throwing shadows of it across its own seething veils, and cutting wedges of visibility into the engulfing blackness, disrobing the heaving multitudes, the endless raving that was the Horde. Bright unto blinding, the incandescence made silhouettes of the Schoolmen, dazzled the eyes and blunted the viciousness of the endless inhuman surge.

And the Men clutched shoulders for wonder.

Dared to *believe* once again.

"How long have you known?" the nearest and perhaps most hideous figure asked.

They were *Men*, Malowebi realized. *Mutilated* Men.

They stood upon their individual stair some three steps from the floor, each garbed in quilted robes of grey silk. Each had recently shaved their scalps, and each was pallid for want of sun. But the similarities ended there—catastrophically so.

The speaker looked as if someone had skinned him in tempestuous seas, so webbed was he with the residue of near-fatal burns. His eyes glared from sockets lidless for whatever fiery maelstrom he had endured. Unable to blink, he pinched them between brow and cheek every few heartbeats, a convulsive flexion, unsettling for its speed.

"Since Dagliash," the Anasûrimbor said. "But I have suspected this eventuality all along. I assumed Ishuäl would be found once my existence became known. I knew the Consult would assault it with due fury, and that our Garden would succumb, eventually ..."

Question after frantic question lurched from a fog of Malowebi's misapprehension. Who were these Men? How had they come to rule—*rule!*—the Ark?

And more horrifying still, why did the Anasûrimbor *know them*?

"How long did it take to purge the Thousand Thousand Halls?" the Aspect-Emperor asked.

"One thousand six-hundred and eleven days," the second figure replied. He alone appeared unscarred and intact, though his attitude was so remote as to be cruel.

"We could not cope with the Erratics," the third added. This one bore two great scars on his head: the first a vaginal pit in lieu of his right eye;

and the second more subtle, a slash the length of a hand-scythe, rimming the perimeter of his head from crown to throat, as if someone had abandoned an attempt to remove his face.

"That is," the Aspect-Emperor said, "until they took you captive."

And it came to Malowebi on a bolt of numbing terror: Dûnyain.

These Men were *Dûnyain* ...

The Thought-dancers described by Drusas Achamian in his heretical treatise.

"I always knew that *some* of you would be captured," the Anasûrimbor explained, "that you would begin, as I began, by pandering to the conceits of your decrepit masters ..."

Did that not mean they stood before five powers *equal to Anasûrimbor Kellhus*?

"I always knew that you would master your captivity, the way Dûnyain master all circumstances ..."

Curse Likaro! Curse him and his conniving deceit!

"And very soon, conquer the Unholy Consult from within."

"What do you eat?" Kayûtas asked. "Medicine?"

"Nil'giccas," Serwa said without sparing him a glance. The powder was as chalk on her tongue, tasted of char and ash, no more. Even still, a tingling suffused her almost immediately ...

It occurred to her that she would have her audience with the legendary Nonman King after all.

"What do you intend?" her brother pressed.

She tossed the pouch to the wary Exalt-General.

"To save our Father," she said, finally matching his gaze. "Our *World*, Podi."

In many respects, Serwa was much the same as her sister Theliopa, differing more in proportion than kind. If her intellect had never burned as bright, then neither had her passions entirely guttered. She had always been more their mother's daughter. Where Thelli could only grasp the intricacies of human concourse in abstract outline, Serwa could *feel* the visceral tug of things like apprehension and regret ...

Love and duty.

"Sister, no. I forbid it."

As could Kayûtas.

They had always regarded each other as twins, even when their difference in age had yawned between them. Each had always known that the other dwelt in the same wan twilight ... the point where caring, *hurting*, almost mattered.

"Who are you to gauge the compass of my power?" she asked.

His eyes clicked to her weeping skin, the lament and anguish of her nakedness.

"Serwa ..."

"I know how to set aside bodily pain."

Kayûtas ... Kayû. He looked so much like Father, and yet he was so much less. It was the curse of the Anasûrimbor, to dwell perpetually overshadowed in one another's eyes.

"Nevertheless, I forbid it."

She graced him with a sad smile.

"You know better."

Saccarees was yelling, berating those who gawked at the vision of the Exalt-Magus rather than keeping a vigilant eye on the Obmaw.

"Any fool can see that you're dying, Sister."

"Then what does it matter?"

She could feel him now, Nil'giccas, his ancient vitality kindling her marrow, palpating her tissues.

"Saccarees," Kayûtas said to the scorched Grandmaster. "You will apprehend the Exalt-Magus should she attempt to enter the Intrinsic Ga—"

"What are you doing?" she cried. "Why do you think they have hidden a Wracu so great as Skuthula *here*?"

"To guard the Intrinsic Gate," he replied scowling.

"But against whom?" she asked. "Certainly not Father."

It seemed their souls merged on the hard look that followed. The Prince-Imperial looked down, the resignation in his eyes as profound as any grief she had witnessed this accursed day. It was always only a matter of time with the two of them, the sharing of unwanted insight.

Apperens Saccarees, however, was a different matter.

"What are you saying?"

For all his gifts, he was no Anasûrimbor.

"The Consult ..." she explained. "They know the Great Ordeal stands or falls with its Holy Aspect-Emperor."

"So this is a *ploy?*" he asked, wincing for the way his burns punished his frown. "They *mean* to hold us at bay, while ... while ..."

The man blanched.

Saccarees, she realized, had never honestly countenanced the possibility his cherished Lord-and-Prophet could *fail*. In his eyes, they did not so much stand stark upon the abyss as swaddled in the bleeding ink of scripture. Despite all his metaphysical erudition, despite all the lunatic tribulations he had endured, he was but another Believer in the end, committed unto death, assured unto idiocy ...

Unlike her brother.

"Here ..." Kayûtas said, drawing a broadsword—an *ensorcelled* broadsword —from his girdle and extending the pommel. It was Cûnuroi, pre-Tutelage— older than Ûmerau given the archaic triangularity of the blade and the absence of any hilt. She took it from him, testing the balance and heft while studying the intricacies of its Mark. She glanced back at her brother in wonder: there was no mistaking the craft of the Artisan, Emilidis, the Siqu Father of the Mihtrûlic, the School of Contrivers.

"*Isiramûlis ...*" she murmured, reading the spidery Gilcûnya runes etched across the mirrored surface.

"A Cindersword," Saccarees said, nodding.

She swept it high overhead, took satisfaction in the razor whisk.

"Truth shines," Kayûtas said, commending her to whatever future remained with a lingering look.

She blinked at him in the old way, the way she would when making sport of some all-too-human combination of irony and folly. He merely nodded. Clasping the haft of Isiramûlis tight, she turned to the blasted orifice of the Obmaw, stalked the causeway. What cloth of skin she yet possessed tingled for the cool. Tears beaded across the deeper nakedness of her burns. The dead Nonman King flowered through her veins.

Deep in the ravaged shell of the High Cwol, the Sons of Men roared.

Bars of Heaven fixed the wicked stronghold with pillars of scalding white, snatching details from the swamping black. The High Horn towered mountainous, clearly visible for being skinned in a dozen brilliant reflections, the Bars bent to its vast and unnatural frame, skewed gibbous across its impossible bulk. The light glared outward, over the loathsome tracts, salvaging nightmare glimpses from the edges of steaming obscurity, Sranc shoaling, their alabaster skin shocking the gloom, their beauty horrid for the bestial throng, clans stamping upon invisible earth, alternately straining toad-forward or brought about by some pallid tide, howling lust and malice. Here and there seizures marred the ponderous gyre, gibbering multitudes that cohered *against* the grain of the greater Horde, shattering the spiral tow into clouds, regions that sizzled with furious, white-skinned gesticulation ...

Golgotterath became as a raft upon a vicious, churning sea.

And they were not alone: different lights wandered the darkling plain.

The Saik Schoolmen were the first to glimpse them through the inky murk. They were obscure at first, wavering and delicate, ponderous and smeared, bruising more than illuminating the Shroud's bowel, like the glower of candles through oiled linen. Those Saik within the vast throat of the Canted Horn saw nothing, such was the kaleidoscopic brilliance of their Dragonheads reflected across the reefs of gold that soared about them. Those stationed in the shadow of the hulk's exterior, however, saw them clearly, exhalations of luminance moving in slow and random concert, like lightning buried in a faraway storm front ...

But only for a time.

Velvet silence—though all the World spit and screamed about the Horn.

"We didn't conquer the Consult ..." the one-eyed figure said.

"We *subsumed*," the fourth of the figures continued on a voice like bundled reeds. He also possessed a myriad of scars, scars *upon* scars actually, but was most distinctive for the iron brackets scaffolding his head and shoulders.

"Shauriatis alone raised arms against us," the fifth figure explained. Like his neighbour, countless scars puckered his visible skin, only smaller and more numerous, as if he had taken many more far less dramatic risks. But something grievous had happened, for nearly two thirds of his lower lip had been sheered away, revealing shining gum and teeth beneath the canopy of his upper lip.

"So Shauriatis alone was undone."

"The others," the unscathed one said, "merely found our Cause irresistible ..."

"As will you," the burnt one declared.

Dûnyain ruled Golgotterath—Dûnyain!

"But this is precisely the issue to be decided," the Anasûrimbor replied. *"One* of us possesses the Greater Cause. Consult or Ordeal, *one* of us stands upon ground *belonging to the other.* And yet we both proceed on the presumption that we are that ground's sole possessors."

Though Malowebi scarcely understood the significance of what was being said, he understood enough to know that a *genuine* battle was being waged, not a metaphoric one.

"But the simple fact remains," the unscathed Dûnyain said, "that *we* have scrutinized the Ark."

"And you have not," the burnt one concluded.

Where words were almost always dross among Men—the "convoluted costumes of avarice," as Memgowa called them—*here,* among Dûnyain, they possessed the heft and hardness of iron tools. Bastions could be raised upon one breath and demolished on another *for all parties.*

There was something miraculous in that ... and alarming.

"I concede as much," the Anasûrimbor said—without the least reluctance.

The unscathed Dûnyain raised an arm—a gesture that startled for the strict immobility that preceded it—beckoned to the spaces beyond and behind the Aspect-Emperor. "Aurax!" he called. "Come!"

The Anasûrimbor turned from the waist—to assure nothing untoward had been signalled, Malowebi supposed. The Mbimayu sorcerer's field of view hitched then rolled to an angle *orthogonal* to his bearer, so that when the man turned back to the Mutilated, Malowebi found himself facing the golden fin rising from the black floor—looking at his own *image* among the gold-tinted reflections.

"The Inchoroi have outlived their origins," the one-eyed monk said.

There he was ... Staring out from burlap skin, strung from hair like ink from Anasûrimbor Kellhus's girdle ...

Curse him! Curse Likaro! May all his wives become lepers!

"Where we raised walls against our history," the wire-headed Dûnyain continued. "They rendered theirs irrelevant."

It throttled the Iswazi mage, staring at what he had become, strangled with vertigo, the intimation of void where his throat and viscera should be. Curse him! Curse his conniving hide! He tore his gaze from the Decapitant, looked into the black and golden world as reflected across gold—the very glint of avarice multiplied into something cloying and vile. The Aspect-Emperor stood erect, his stance wide, his leonine head watery for imperfections in the metal, the long pommel of Enshoiya a slash of ink above his left shoulder, the immaculate white of his vestments refracted into shades of voluminous yellow. The Mutilated receded into the depths of the room before the Anasûrimbor, each more diminutive than the previous.

"Tell him, Aurax."

The Inchoroi stood upon a dimple in the reflection and so looked both wretched and absurd, its torso hooked into a blade of grass, its claws drawn like melted wax.

"*Wheeere?*" it rasped upon a seditious moan. "*Where is my brotheeeer?*"

The melted image advanced a step, and a semblance of Aurang emerged from crazed distortion.

"Tossed upon the Horde," the Anasûrimbor said.

The thing wheeled to the burnt figure. "*Yoooou!*" it shrieked. "*You gave me your oath!*"

But the thing's defiance had crumbled into mewling servility even before the Dûnyain turned to regard it. It scuttled back into its dimple, its image bifurcating and balling into something crustacean.

Thought-dancers! *Forming a new Consult!*

One that had *Inchoroi* grovelling for terror ...

"What you see," the teeth-baring Dûnyain slurred, "is the fruit of the Tekne. The very structure of its flesh bears the imprint of intellect."

"They were a warrior-caste," the burnt one continued, "bred to lust and to hunger for all forms of trespass, to heap such damnation upon themselves that the merest glimpse of the Inverse Fire would reignite their ardour."

What good did cursing Likaro do?

"So they are *themselves* a kind of Sranc?" the Anasûrimbor asked.

But what else was there?

"Their mission," the caged Dûnyain replied, "has likewise been branded into them."

Better hatred than despair!

"Irrevocable *belief* has been branded into them," his one-eyed brother added. "An Inverted Faith, one meant to hoard damnation as a goad to salvation."

Even though it dwarfed the images of the Mutilated, the Aspect-Emperor's reflection was somehow the least clear. It was as if globules of pitch lay suspended within the fin of Inchoroi gold, compressing elements of the man's image.

"And how," the Anasûrimbor asked, "had their ancient progenitors earned *their* collective damnation?"

"The Fathers of the Inchoroi?" the teeth-baring Dûnyain asked. "Surely you've already grasped the answer ..."

"I fear I have not."

The Mutilated paused to count one another's eyes.

"For straying so near the Absolute," the burnt one answered.

Absolute?

"I see," the golden reflection of the Aspect-Emperor said.

Serwa began sprinting up the ragged ramp of the causeway, felt her burnt skin crack into island archipelagos, and though she could count out each blistered atoll, she begrudged them not, for she was as the wind, too fleet to be grappled to earth by pain. Her agony shambled after, incentive to run ever faster into the cobwebs her apprehension had spun before her. She saw her myriad shadows shrinking into a fluttering thicket before her, until absorbed into her alone: a slender girl conjugating blackness. She saw the savaged Obmaw gaping, then engulfing, battered black stone hanging and jutting from the flying golden veneer. She breathed a reek so noxious as to kick one cough from her—then two.

She was in the Ark.

She slowed in wonder, hesitated. She could barely hear the Horde.

Had she managed to slip through undetected?

A monstrous crocodilian face grinned in the light of its own vomit ...

She threw her arms up, crouched to one knee.

Fire burst, flung through with saliva like naptha or exploding phosphor. It slipped as water from oilcloth about her ravaged skin and away, heat like a childhood memory, a terror from long ago. She leapt backward and to her right, kicking in a somersault that carried her above the exhalation, and in that heartbeat she absorbed *everything illuminated*, plotted her lines of flight, for she could *feel* the ninety-nine Chorae hanging about her—she knew the strings would twang before the inhuman archers who had drawn them. She was already racing by time the points of oblivion began flying, running across a ground of cracked and pulverized bone ...

An inner earth of corpses.

Residual wicks of flame danced for small circles of admiring offal. A single grey lane emanated from the breached Intrinsic Gate. Otherwise, complete blackness inhaled all space, leaving only time and memory ...

The only two things a child of Anasûrimbor Kellhus required.

A vast atrium lay beyond the Obmaw, a shaft some hundred paces across, enclosed by a tremendous scaffold of columns bearing floors stacked upon floors, all of them pitched like the deck of a foundering pleasure barge. Perhaps the place had been glorious once, some kind of iridescent testament; it was little more than rubbish and hovels strung about a missing mountain now. Midden and debris had levelled the floor she shared with Skuthula, but all else was draped, including endless batteries of rotted cloth and hide—hammocks—hanging from the pitched ceilings.

The Wracû coiled near the atrium's vacant heart. At least a dozen companies of Ursranc palatials, Inversi, had assembled across the skewed heights and about the outskirts of the corrupt ground ... Far more than she had hoped.

Eighty-eight Trinkets remained.

Absolute ...

Ajencis had used the term to refer to the collapse of desire and object, Thought and Being.

Memgowa held that it was nothing other than Death, the reduction of being to the plurality of beings—the becoming thing of existence. But Malowebi had no clue what a *Dûnyain* meant by the term, aside that it was some kind of prize, the end shared by the Mutilated and the Anasûrimbor alike ...

"The progenitors called it the Illumination," the unscathed Dûnyain said, reflected in gilded miniature. "The age that saw the Tekne become their faith, the idol they raised above all others. They turned their back on their old Gods, their old temples, and raised new ones, great houses dedicated to unravelling the wellsprings of existence. Cause became their one and only God."

Of all the shadowy images, the burnt Dûnyain loomed the largest apart from the Anasûrimbor. "*Cause*, Kellhus."

"For through it," the wire-headed one declared, "they believed they could overcome the darkness preceding all things, and so become Gods."

"Attain the Absolute," the teeth-baring figure concluded, his reflection as tiny as a thumb across the polish.

But what is sunlight to a mole? In their curious, collective manner, the Mutilated told how the Tekne so transformed the problems faced by the progenitors that all the old ways became impossible. It raised them from their traditions, struck the shackles of custom from their intellects, until only their common animality constrained them. They worshipped themselves as the measure of all significance, gave themselves over to wanton gluttony. Nothing was forbidden them, short the obstruction of others and their desires. Justice became the calculation of competing appetites. Logos became the principle of their entire civilization.

"By imperceptible increments," the one-eyed Dûnyain said, his face strange and glaring, "the Tekne unfettered their desires, allowed them to plumb ever deeper perversions."

The Tekne. Yes. The Tekne lay at the root of their argument.

"They began moulding *themselves* the way potter's mould clay," the unscathed one said.

The Tekne and the transformations wrought by its bottomless potency ...

"They stood upon the very brink of the Absolute," the teeth-baring Dûnyain called. "It pricked their fingers, it was so near!"

How, in relieving the Inchoroi of want and deprivation, it had stripped them of everything sacred ...

"There was only one riddle they could not solve," the lone unscarred Dûnyain said, "one ancient enigma the Tekne could not fathom ..."

"The *soul*," his teeth-baring brother gasped.

Three heartbeats of silence followed—silence and tumbling revelation.

"It became their Mystery of Mysteries, the focus of their most cunning intellects."

It no longer mattered who spoke—for the *Mutilated did not lie*, and the Truth spoke with but one soul.

"And when the soul at last yielded its secrets to their scrutiny ..."

And *there he was*, a beehive head slung from the Aspect-Emperor's imperial reflection. How? How had he found himself in such wretched straits?

"They discovered their entire race damned."

Curse Likaro!

About the ruins of Domathuz, the Bars' brilliance threw the shadows of Men across the soulless thrash, toiling shadows, hacking and spearing, hunched shoulder to shield. Again and again they heaved the Sranc back, gore effigies more than Men, locks pasted about their cheeks, beards sodden about gasping mouths, eyes darting, caged by urgency, even panic. Again and again, the Sranc rushed heedless into the rakes of Nihelene sorcery, surged over the heaps and swales of charred dead, threw themselves upon the beleaguered Norsirai, slobbering, crazed and innumerable, narrow-shouldered frames hewn from pale wax, eyes shining like black olives in oil, their assault as much a rapine obscenity as a wailing fury. Soundless clatter. Soundless grunts and howls. Again and again, the creatures slumped or spun to the tangle beneath their horned feet, their pelvises counting out their final breaths.

It was here the wandering lights glimpsed by the Imperial Saik to the west reappeared. The Mysunsai Grandmaster himself, fierce Obwë Gûswuran, would be among the first to spy the arrhythmic glow, flashes of dimension cutting hollows into the belly of the Shroud. He stood at the fore of ruined Domathuz, both where the Sons of Ce Tydonn were most sorely pressed and where the greatest number of his fellow Schoolmen had been felled by Chorae. He doubted his eyes at first, but a glance at his triunaries assured him the phantasms were very real.

Any fool could see the Mark. The lights multiplied in number and intensity, pocking the murk with swatches of detail, cavern glimpses of the Horde, regions shivering like countless maggots in ink ...

Sorcerers ... *Dozens* of them by the pyrotechnic density and intricacy of the approaching lights.

Obscure smouldering became a hazy glow, which soon waxed into Gnostic brilliance—or so the Grandmaster initially thought. And then, one by one, they emerged from the roiling plumes, walking some twenty cubits above the tortured plain, some naked for madness, others gowned in archaic and voluminous robes, the mouths and sockets of all shining with arcane brilliance as they blasted and wracked the raucous tracts below.

"Ishterebinth!" Gûswuran's voice cracked on arcane thunder. *"Ishterebinth joins the Great Ordeal!"*

The Quya advanced in a haphazard arc, drawing curtains of scintillant destruction across the far-flung heave. Mightiest among them were Vippol the Elder, Far Antique Siqu to Atrithau and the Sons of Eämnor. And Cilcûliccas, another true son of Ishterebinth—and among the Lastborn, so in possession of his faculties. It was he who struck down the fell Dragon of Knives, Murathaur the Silver, during the Investiture. And there was the notorious Sûjara-nin, an Ishroi of High Siol, who the ancient chroniclers had called Bloodless for the extremity of his pallor, and who had once wandered the nations of Men as the Red Ghoul, the Vizier to mortal Kings ere he became Erratic, and sought the pardon of Nil'giccas, King of the Last Mansion. He alone had some connection to the Mysunsai, for his Near Antique predations had motivated the founding of the Mikka Council, and his methods, though the Mysunsai knew it not, had inspired their mercenary mission. It was he who had first demanded a philter of blood from his patrons, holding it as hostage until remuneration was received—the selfsame practice of the Mysunsai. And it was his moniker that had inspired Men to refer to all Nonmen as ghouls, eaters of the dead.

None of the souls watching recognized any among the Quya, whose deeds were older than old. They saw only Cûnûroi, the False Men of the Tusk, beings whose might and beauty shamed, and whose faces could not be distinguished from Sranc. Ghouls. Even still, the sheer glory of the display moved to wonder all those not embroiled in the squalor of pitched battle. These were no depraved Erratics such as those they first encountered, bent upon extracting shreds of torment they might remember. These were the last of the Intact, decked in ancient glory! The legendary wrath of the Quya had been roused!

The Nonmen of Ishterebinth had hearkened to the call of their Holy Aspect-Emperor!

Their songs flashing from their skulls, they sailed over the apoplectic fields assuming the antique posture, chest forward and arms back, as if pulled by their hearts through water. At the penultimate moment they would snap their arms forward, invert their pose as if catapulting their Abstractions. And Sranc died the way they once had died, when they were young and the obscenity of their Derivation lay fresh as atrocity. Parabolas of light whipped them into slop. Radiant combs ignited them as candles. And they shrieked as they had once shrieked, yowled at the floating spectres *who were there fathers*, their upward-turned faces imploding like silk clenched in fists, seeing and hating—as Men themselves hated—the existence of a more perfect rule.

But where abjection imposes uniformity, mastery affords diversity. Some thirty-three Quya advanced upon the breach, and for all the uncanny similarity of their features no two shared the same expression. Each was riven, be it by murderous cold, wailing grief, or convulsive laughter. Even the Intact displayed some besotted rictus, for the many Quya held that battle was *Ri*, beyond all law and restraint. Hunched above the brilliance of their Theorems, they wept and cackled, screamed and calculated, punished the white-roiling tracts beneath them.

Obwë Gûswuran possessed the bravery of the thoughtless, famous sort, even more than was common among Men of his dour and domineering ilk. Where others wandered the labyrinth, he unerringly strode the golden path, turning, choosing, and stepping out of what he necessarily saw as necessity.

He was far quicker to perceive slight than to recognize peril.

The howl and clank of the Ursranc Palatials reverberated through the metallic void.

"**Many times,**" the great and terrible Skuthula croaked, "**have we supped upon the virgin daughters of Man ...**"

Anasûrimbor Serwa whipped through the black, vaulting over the rubbish and debris revealed in the last guttering wicks of light, hearing the scrape and clap of some hundred or more Inversi spread across the very impenetrable gloom she hurtled into. The lowermost gallery was scarce more than a cave given the skew of the floors relative to the ground, which was gullied where it verged upon the canted original floors. The ceiling declined in parallel, leaving little more than a slot exposed to the great atrium where the ancient Wracu stomped and reared.

"**But we do not smell your maidenhead ...**"

Not one of the creatures had the least inkling of her presence, at least at first. She ran among them with the ease of a child popping bubbles. Isiramûlis leapt in acrobatic counterpoint. The Ursranc merely grunted or screamed, toppled to ground pawing mortal wounds. She had killed five before coming upon the lone Chorae bearer. He died every bit as witless, but his death throes summoned the others, who came rushing at once ridiculous and dangerous for the way they hacked blindly. With nothing left to hunt, she simply ran back the way she had come, chased by a riotous, caterwauling band ...

"**Are you a wife**," the mighty Wracu wheezed, "**or are you a *whore*?**"

Back out to the luminance shining through the ruined Obmaw—where she crouched for but a heartbeat, long enough to burn her slender image in the eyes of all those who would hunt her. She could feel the raising of Chorae across the galleries opposite, the aiming. She could hear the whisk of the Dragon's horned crown, sense the shiver of his bulk. She could see the Inversi erupting from the gallery she had just fled, Nonman faces pinching in outrage ...

She set herself, poised for the leap that would see her thread the Chorae and their intersecting trajectories.

"*I am!*" she cried with shrill calculation. "*A witch!*"

Fire. Fire boiled across everything about her, making glass of dirt, igniting fragments of bone, and immolating the company of leaping Palatials.

Hitherto she would have to contend with the light of burning bodies.

The count was now Eighty-seven.

He could remember her well, the Sawdilli whore he and Likaro had shared as youths. *Ware that jackal!* she once warned him. *For he will be your doom!*

Ferocious words, spoken with a weariness indistinguishable from wisdom. Even still, Malowebi doubted she had quite envisaged *this*.

Headless. Hostage to the Unholy Consult—or rather, the Dûnyain terror that had consumed them.

Nothing less than *humanity* lay in the palm of their disputation, the sum of all love and toil. Arguments like gears and wheels, observations piling upon observations, assessed, not according to the jealousies and anxieties of the speaker, but in compliance with *what was*—no matter how it contradicted *what was holy* ...

"Do you see, Brother? *Logos is Tekne.*"

The danger of comprehension was one that *Second* Negotiant Malowebi knew all too well having witnessed Likaro steer their addled royal cousin through decision after decision. To grasp was to be *moved*. To understand was to linger upon the threshold of *belief* ...

"Do you see our Cause?"

He could feel it even now, mulling the possibility that the True and the Sacred *were not the same*. How Ajencis would have gloated and crowed!

"*Damnation* is the impediment ..."

But as much as his Intellect balked, Malowebi's Heart foundered upon what seemed an even more profound realization: *These were not Men.*

"The obstacle."

As the Inchoroi were versions of the Sranc, bred to believe *as they were wrought*, so too were these Thought-dancers—these *Dûnyain*—bred to the union of conquest and comprehension.

"The World must be Shut, Brother."

To attain their enigmatic Absolute ...

"The Will of the Ark must be realized."

To become *self-moving souls*.

That poor wretch Drusas Achamian had said as much! All this time the Court had puzzled over the Aspect-Emperor, trying, again and again, to extract some kind of *reason* from his perplexing actions, attributing, again and again, crude motives belonging to their own souls. Had a demon possessed him? Was he the "Kucifra" that Fanayal and that Yatwerian monster had claimed? Not once had they considered the possibility that he embodied a *principle*, that he, *like the Sranc*, simply executed an imperative stamped into his soul's foundation.

The eradication of everything *other* ...

"The circuit of souls must be breached," the teeth-baring Dûnyain said, his miniature visage absurd for his solitary lip. "Mankind must be hunted to the edge of extinction."

Mad, mad sausages! The Mbimayu Schoolman reeled, not so much because anything so insane could be conceived, but because anything so insane *could be true*. By far the greater terror was knowing the Anasûrimbor could be *convinced—not by cunning, but by reason!*

Could it be so desperate as this? Had *delusion* always been the bastion of Mankind—ignorance?

How heartbroken poor Zabwiri would have been ...

"And this is why you woo me," the Anasûrimbor's reflection said.

Heartbroken and amused.

"Yes," the burnt Dûnyain acknowledged, his webbed skin alarming even reflected in small. "To resurrect the No-God."

The choral wail *dimmed* into something less than deafening.

Those Longbeards upon the ramparts dared the slots between the gold-fanged battlements, gazing out, while those arrayed about the breach, cried out for an unexpected respite. The tens of thousands of Sranc massed about ruined Domathuz had fallen silent. The Quya floated out from the steaming occlusions, a ragged line punctuated by semantic construct and corresponding explosions of terrestrial brilliance. The Mysunsai Triunes, meanwhile, hung upon their stations, their billows coiling like ink in water, their Nibe-lene Lightning whisking life from the ground with stark light. And the Sranc roiled like a vast school of fish between their arcane lines, darting both to and from the monolithic black walls, packed so thick that even the most anaemic Cants worked vivid slaughter. Despite the sorcerous sheen of the cleavers, it was butcher's work all the same.

The Sons of Ce Tydonn howled in unison—a cry that they could *hear*. They began clapping axes and broadswords upon their raised shields.

Obwë Gûswuran stepped forward, led his Triune *toward* the Ishtere-binthi, believing it his prerogative and obligation. The Triunes stationed adjacent moved to accompany him. A vestment of lead-grey felt anchored the complexity of the Grandmaster's billows, bearing the tripartite symbol of his School in iridescent gold embroidery: the Bent Scroll of the Oaranat above the Bow-and-Quill of the Nilitar between the Compass of the Mikka. Some fifteen of his Schoolmen strode the empty heights on either flank, many of them likewise adorned.

Among the Quya, Cilcûliccas had guessed the intent of the Grandmaster's approach and attempted to alert Vippol the Elder, but to no avail. The Madborn wracked the heaving press, screaming, crying the name of his long dead brother. And so it was with many others: Lost to whatever loss that trammelled their memory, they relived battles they had endured *thousands of years past*: Imogirion, Pir Minningial, Pir Pihal, and others. They hollered the names of the beloved dead, mourned and avenged calamities older than the languages of Men.

As the Whore would have it, the Red Ghoul would be the first to receive the Mysunsai Grandmaster. Given his legendary lust for destruction, Sûjara-nin had wandered far ahead of his fellows, alternately cackling and sobbing, hanging resplendent in his gown of ensorcelled crimson nimil, Orimuril, the famed "Immaculate Rim," which the Men of the Three Seas had named the Scarp in fear and envy centuries past. He battered the earth with Viritic Inflationaries, flung Sranc on the back of exploding spheres, gouts of them, flying on arcs that fell mere cubits short of his sandalled feet. He seemed to notice the Schoolmen only when they were upon him, so deep had he fallen into the pit of himself. Frowning like a man just awoken, the Red Ghoul hung peering as the Mysunsai formed about him ... then saw the gold-embroidered Compass adorning the chest of Obwë Gûswuran ...

The Grandmaster's defensive Analogies, which he had cast only to shelter against mundane missiles, proved no match for the Abstractions of Sûjara-nin. Spectral stone crumbled into smoke, and Obwë Gûswuran fell burning, his body kicking itself into portions about the scything white brilliance of Mimtis Rings.

Death came swirling down ... bore his essence to the loins of Hell.

Sûjara-nin slew another Mysunsai in the astonished heartbeats that followed, felled two more as the remaining ten frantically sang to duel. The surviving eight turned as one upon the raving, crimson-armoured Nonman, wracked him with the Nibelene Lightning that had become their reflex, caged him in a thicket of blinding white threads, then sent him crashing into the raucous throngs below—for he too had cast only the Wards he had needed to turn aside spears.

The Red Ghoul was no more.

Like a mouse in the shadow of a fire-spitting cat, she darted across the carrion earth. Great stones clacked through Skuthula's outraged roar. Molten sputum sloshed about her and the surrounding ground, mushroomed into whooshing brilliance.

She leapt beyond it.

"Maidenhead is *all* I smell!" she cried on a gasp. "Could it be *yours?*"

She clasped ropes, swung into the circus gloom of the second gallery.

Fire flooded after, roiling like a living, *seeking* thing. Isiramûlis firm in hand, she slipped as a ghost from the incendiary tentacles. The glare yanked a heartbeat of structure and detail from what had been no more than shreds of polish winking in the murk. She found herself on a battered catwalk, racing constellations of lucent orange beads, peering into a world as labyrinthine as it was crude. The skew was such that terraces and walkways had been strewn throughout, some heaped from stone and carcass dirt, others rendered out of wood so rotted in regions as to hang like cobwebs—the extent of all circumscribed by the pitch of the golden ceilings. In some cases, four or even five terraces occupied the length of any given slope, with two or three shrunken floors tucked beneath each. It was as if some savage world had parasitized the gut of a more fundamental and yet contradictory frame—an irretrievable hulk.

"**The very ground reeks of cunny!**" the magnificent serpent boomed on a croaking laugh.

She ran, skimming the plummet, as close to the atrium as she could manage. The bodies of the Palatials she had lured below burned with bonfire brilliance, etching her nude form in red and pastel orange. She added six to the Count this way ... Seventy-four.

"**They say ten million died in the Falling,**" Skuthula roared, "**laying earth such as this throughout our Mother's womb!**"

But even now, more Palatials swarmed across the decrepit network, racing to catch or intercept her.

"**Our Most Holy Ark!**"

Here—emerging clear enough for her to spy the upside-down flame adorning their shields. There—a flitting stream of shadows in the niggard light below. She ran as if seeking their embrace, ducking or leaping five more whistling Chorae that lanced from points across the void of the Atrium.

She leapt from the planked walk on the edge to one of dirt and stone lower down the Skew, and *halted*, stood motionless in a false pocket of calm, concealed from the Wracû, but entirely visible to the upward-welling Ursranc. The vigour that was Nil'giccas lay like pins in her deepest veins, and it seemed she could *sense it all*, the swords and cleavers wagging on the run, the claws kicking the mire, the rattle of the crest, the ramming bulk shouldering aside putrid air. A bottomless host of telltale signs all closing upon this ... one ... *place* ...

Conditioned ground.

She saw the Palatials scuttling up from the murk, their Nonmen faces disfigured by grinding malice and lascivious contempt. And somehow, she saw the ponderous crown of the Wracû rise behind her *in their counterfeit faces*—the details of his aspect scattered across the myriad manifestations of shock and terror. She watched them skid and tumble to a halt. She clutched Isiramûlis to the cleft between her breasts, for she had seen the Wracû's fire in the gold glittering in their eyes.

Was this what it was like for Father?

Seeing *behind the head.*

The roaring vomit burst about her. She felt it tousle the remnants of her hair, buffet the remnants of her skin. She watched it consume the Ursranc as surely as any other instrument of her will ...

The wretches screamed like drowning swine.

Then she was leaping out over the Skew, slipping the iron-clap of Skuthula's jaws, brushing the ceiling, sailing over the wood and stone welter into the crotch of the gallery. Two of the Inversi she left behind had possessed Chorae ...

"And pray tell what," she cried, laughter lilting across vague armatures of gold, "would a *Dragon* know of cunny?"

Sixty-seven remained.

"Mog-Pharau," the Anasûrimbor said.

The name fell hard.

A sorcerous mutter, curious for its cadence, gasped from all points. Light dazzled the image of the teeth-baring Dûnyain, transformed his remaining lip into something drawn from a glassmaker's furnace. The reflections of the Mutilated turned in unison to the darkness ...

Malowebi saw *it* almost at once, emerging black from the black, soundless, a great *sarcophagus* some nine cubits by four, rendered of ceramic or some strange metal, floating in upon its obsidian reflection ...

This was happening *now*, he realized. Happening!

The gleaming bulk whispered past each of the farthest three Mutilated.

The distorted twist that was Aurax whinged at its passage, barked some kind of cough. It loomed monolithic before the Aspect-Emperor for a heartbeat, its inky surface veined and contoured with what seemed the shrunken effigy of some face or great city—and Malowebi squinted for the way the obscuring blackness in the Anasûrimbor's reflection melded with the thing. But it tipped backward with the same soundless precision, until it was wholly horizontal, as deep as the Aspect-Emperor's waist for hovering a hand above the floor.

The *Carapace* ... Could it be? Most sources claimed that Chorae had been set into it ...

"Behold the Object," the burnt Dûnyain announced on a grim call.

The surface revealed itself to be a lid like those found on sarcophagi, a graven plate that spontaneously lifted then tipped to draw down one side, where its ink-black polish fractured and reorganized the light of the Inverse Fire.

Malowebi could see nothing of its interior ... nor could he assemble any coherent thought.

"But why anything so elaborate?" the Anasûrimbor asked. "If the extermination of Men is your goal, then why not use the weapon you employed in Dagliash?"

And Malowebi could only think, *No-God* ...

The No-God lay before him.

"We could restore only one," the unscathed Dûnyain said, mirrored in gold. "Even if more existed, they're too indiscriminate, especially when used in numbers."

"Our Salvation lies in the *art* of human extinction, not the fact," his burnt brother explained

"Only the Object can Shut the World against the Outside," the one-eyed Dûnyain explained.

"Yes ..." the Aspect-Emperor said, "the one hundred and forty-four thousand ..."

"The Object is a prosthesis of Ark," the teeth-baring Dûnyain continued, his reflection no larger than a pinky for his position at the end. "A code lies buried in the ebb and flow of life on this World. The more deaths, the brighter this code burns, the more Ark can read ..."

"So the Ark is the No-God?" Anasûrimbor Kellhus asked.

"No," the burnt Dûnyain replied. "But then you know as much."

"And what is it I know?"

"That the No-God collapses Subject and Object," the one-eyed monk replied. "That it *is* the Absolute."

The Holy Aspect-Emperor of the Three Seas lowered his head in thoughtful affirmation. The reflections of the Mutilated paused in collective anticipation of his next words. For all the image's curious distensions, Malowebi could plainly see the Anasûrimbor gazing down into the Carapace ...

Mulling?

Yearning?

"And you think *I'm* the missing piece?" Kellhus asked. "The Subject that will revive this ... system?"

Was that why the Chorae had been removed from the Carapace? *For him?* It seemed to Malowebi that he strangled ...

The nearest of the disfigured Dûnyain, the burnt one, nodded. "The Celmomian Prophecy foretells *your* coming, Brother."

The wail owned all but the most booming voices. Moënghus had yet to test his own, for he stood as dumbstruck as most of the others, his fingers numb upon the black parapets of the Akeokinoi. The Scylvendi tongue defeated him, but what happened was clear. As the boggling size of the Sranc host became apparent, his father had ordered the People to shelter on the far side of the Occlusion (using their Excursi to bar the passes), while taking up position with his chieftains and commanders here ... watching sights that unmoored as much as unmanned.

Rising like gaseous gums from the Horde's forward teeth, the Shroud had gradually drawn the whole of the Shigogli within its fetid embrace, a pale gauze that had *turned black* in the afternoon glare, becoming ever more impenetrable, until they could no longer discern the surviving Horn's gleam rising through the veils. Save for sorcery glimmering like silver kellics deep in nocturnal waters, the Shroud was all that could be seen, sheets braided with more septic plumes, fat as the Occlusion and as high as the blackening Vault of Heaven.

And it dismayed the Prince-Imperial, bruised with a profundity that evil Harapior could only pretend to ... for he had been *raised* on tales of this, the ultimate moment, the day when the Fate of Men was at last sorted. The meaning of all their souls would be stamped this day! It reeked of conspiracy, how the Shroud fit into the radial arms of the Occlusion, like a receptacle embracing a dark and epic offering ...

The land itself had become an altar to horror!

Kayûtas was in there ... *Serwa!*

"Surely your plan wasn't to chew rations and watch!" Anasûrimbor Moënghus boomed over the Horde's wail.

The Holy King-of-Tribes turned on him with an intensity both grinding and homicidal. "The *plan*, whelp, was to *surprise* the Ordeal while *still encamped*, to seize the Chorae Hoard and butcher your entire family!"

The words were meant to provoke him.

"And you expecte—?"

"I expected what I always expected when vying with *Him!*"

The other Chieftains looked on stone-faced above crossed arms.

"And what might that be?" Moënghus asked, chastened. For all his life, he had always been the most intemperate, the most *driven* by inner fury, hardened and impelled.

The barbarian grinned a charnel house grin. The scars about his mouth smiled in vertical counterpoint, and Moënghus had the disconcerting sense that *all* the man's countless swazond grinned with him.

"That I will *fail*."

"That is madness!" Moënghus blurted before thinking.

"Madness? But that is the *very kernel* of it, is it not? The very insult his existence inflicts upon us! The very excrement he smears across our cheeks— our nostrils! That we be as gripe-moths on the plain, *forever jumping from the tracks*, stepping sideways, leaping blind to all inclination, laughing as blackbirds spear daisies. *That we must be mad to be free!*"

"You *are!*" Moënghus cried horror. "You are *insane!*"

"Yessss!" the Holy King-of-Tribes roared, clapping him about the nape, glaring with bloodthirsty hilarity. "Because it alone is *sane!*" he boomed on a cackle, turning back to the grim spectacle of the Shroud towering black above them all. Cnaiür urs Skiötha spat down the sheer ramps of the Nonman ruin. He raised both hands, thumbs and finger cupped ...

"Until I see His shadow," the most violent of men cried to the ponderous maelstrom, "I do not leap!"

All was uproar. At last Vippol the Elder was roused from his stupor—only to fall into another possessing far more horrific consequences. He turned to the isolated clutch of Mysunsai, his eyes coin-wide for rabid fury. "*Sioli tiri himil!*" his voice cracked from the shrouded heavens, "*mi ishorioli tiri himil!*" Only Valsarta, the sole Swayali witch upon the breach, understood the dread import of his words ...

"The blood of Siol is the blood of Ishoriol!"

The Madborn stalked the Mysunsai, who yielded space as he advanced. They recalled well the tragedy of Irsûlor, where the Vokalati and the Mandate had gored each other for the act of one madman, Carindûsû. Like some primeval wraith out of myth, the deranged Quyan Archmage bore upon them, queer for the array of wire screens that he wore affixed to a harness about his cadaverous gowns—his archaic Chorae armour.

"*Ishra Vippol!*" Cilcûliccas boomed. "*Insiqu! Siralipir jin'sharat!*"

The Madborn hesitated, hung blinking, his image fogged for his seething Wards. He looked to the cyclopean ramparts, the High Horn soaring into occlusion, its mountainous mirror faces scored with chiaroscuros of dancing white and gold. He glared as though bewildered across the gaping spaces once blotted by the Canted Horn ...

"*Ishra Vippol!*" Cilcûliccas bellowed across registers beyond sound and hearing.

The Madborn finally turned to his Intact kinsmen.

And so was one disaster averted even as another, greater catastrophe took root. Facing the prospect of sorcerous combat, all the Mysunsai about Domathuz had ceased scourging the roiling plain. Pitched melee churned the ranks across the spangled entirety of the breach. For the first time, the Sons of Ce Tydonn bore the hacking, thrashing brunt of the Horde *entire*. They had been trained for this, endlessly drilled, and they had endured such assaults previously, but the Sranc they faced were of a fiercer, more sturdy breed. They fell upon the Longbeards as rabid apes, stabbing, flailing as if afire. The shield wall dissolved into stabbing, grappling desperation. And so did the price of evil old Domathuz climb. Men fell, so quickly that the commanding Thanes began spanking the helms of whole companies, commanding them to advance.

But the Sons of Ce Tydonn did not break. And how could they, with the stacked glory of their nation packing the breach behind them? The Nangaels suffered the worst, for they held the foremost swale of debris beneath the sky Obwë Gûswuran had occupied and then abandoned. Even when the Mysunsai resumed ransacking the plain with their arthritic skeins of light, the Nangaels remained exposed to the undiluted violence of the Horde. Death scraped at them as iron against coal, and even though they did not break—could not break—protracted loss sucked the marrow from their bones, afflicted them with the grim assurance of death no matter what outcome claimed the field.

Their Longbeard cousins, Canutishmen, were the first to begin pointing, perplexed as to what they were seeing. Buried in the agitated heave some hundred paces beyond the Nangael's roiling position, out where endless white faces bayed and innumerable cleavers and clubs shivered like insect shadows, Sranc had begun ... flying?

Or was it *dropping*?

From all points of the compass they rushed *inward*, as if assailing *something in their midst*, something that flung them airwards even as they hacked down, pitching them on a line that ran perfectly *parallel* to the plain, *accelerating* for more than a hundred paces. The scene baffled the eyes: a terrestrial nucleus of Sranc in their hundreds continually imploding about a point that hurled each of them above and *out*, as if down the face of a cliff. Scrabbling white figures plummeted in all directions as if over some kind of *sorcerous edge*, at last whipping with neck-breaking effect into the radial masses ...

And it *moved* ...

———⦿———

"Emilidis, the Accursed Smith, was cunny, and we knew him!"

The Dragon's retch had sparked an inferno, for the wood was little more than tinder. Sealed in the bowel of the Ark, the ramshackle network of posts and platforms and catwalks had never seen moisture, aside from mould and urine, perhaps. But as quickly as the flame sprinted from point to point, the Exalt-Magus out-distanced it with ease, her feet slapping through the septic mire in the trough of the gallery.

"The tender wheeze of his meat!" the magnificent beast roared. *"The brittle temper of his bones! We devoured the maker of your little sword!"*

Her drumming feet kicked offal into a spray, cracked open fumes that would have overcome any other man. But she slipped through it all as though untouched—indeed, as something *untouchable*.

"**Yesss ...**"

Never had her task been so clear.

"**We ...**"

"**Like ...**"

"**Cunny ...**"

Despite her gifts, she had always fended clutter, always battled to keep pace with the World's frenetic surge. Always and everywhere, she had been hemmed by things obstinate and mercurial, trapped within the urgent cage of what was here and what was now—forever thrown back upon herself *by what was other*.

"And so Skuthula woos *Skuthula!*" she cried, pitching her laughter to chime through the crackling roar.

Nothing could touch her simply because *she was everything*.

The white-glowing gash of the Obmaw. The mounded carcass earth. The Great Atrium, ascending on the Skew to fathomless heights, louvered by countless floors. The Ursranc Palatials clustering about the rim of the lowermost galleries, yammering and gesticulating, a thousand squints hungry for her merest sign ...

And of course the Dragon.

"**Insolent whore! We shall see what songs you sing when I pluck your legs from your hips!**"

"You would not like *my* songs, dirtsnake!"

She backtracked the instant of her call, began leaping up the Skew, toward the whooshing bowers of the fire. She glimpsed a score of Ursranc shrieking and puling as they ran ablaze. Holding Isiramûlis tight, she plunged into the hairy brilliance, climbed timbers skinned in coals.

"**A witch?**" Skuthula croaked in saurian incredulity. "**Of all the might the realms of Men have assembled, they send a scrag witch to test our might?**"

The flame fell like wetted rose petals from her skin. The soot stained her, but the smoke was toothless, unable to bite her eyes or breath no matter how viscous the acrid swirl. In heartbeats, she emerged where she had vanished, standing upon the Great Atrium's rim hundreds of paces from her adversaries' expectation, her skin and burns wreathed in sluicing smoke.

The fire had made a vast, burning grin of the gallery, slicking every golden surface with replicas of its image, etching the void in reams of fractured light. Coiled before the aperture of the Obmaw, Skuthula the Black stood revealed, the enormity of his form glossed in the light of his own violent manufacture.

"*Send us your* **Heroes**!" the black monstrosity roared. "*Send us your Men, so that we might martyr their courage, light them as votives to the True Holy!*"

No soul living knew how the Inchoroi had spawned Dragons, the devious alchemy of their concoction, for like apples, their seed gave rise to different fruits, variations upon the same gargantuan theme. It was none other than Skuthula who had inspired the Nonmen of old to name their race "Worms," for he was the most serpentine of the Wracu. His monstrous bulk hung barrelled about a frame that consisted almost entirely of spine and ribs, save for the spindly legs arrayed beneath, dozens of them, rising and falling in centipedal waves as the creature moved. He was skinned in countless black scales, the length and breadth of Norsirai shields across his length, shrinking to the size of broaches about the skittering articulations of its legs. His wings lay clasped as lateen sails about his elongated back, rising from two massive swales of muscle that alone lent shoulders to his dread form. Spear-long quills maned the back of his neck, a crest of stark white spines forming a thicket about his massive, gored crown.

"*Feed us those who can* **bear** *the burden of our glory! Who can hoist our legend upon their shoulders—raise it by their measure!*"

But his lethal magnificence lay more in his hue and grace than in the bald facts of physiognomy. His scales were at once nacreous—shattering light into an iridescent dance—and absolute, consuming illumination without residue, so that he seemed mirror shards strung about an absence, a phantasm lacquered across void. And he stole through space as an eel through water, here hanging slow like a frond, there little more than a blur upon a flexion. He did not so much move as *pulse*. Combined with the uncanny black, this made him seem more wraith than monstrous lizard, a thing of ink slipping across a greased world.

"Alas, that World is dead!" she hollered, "I fear Dragons are the stuff of *little girls* now!"

Screeches greeted her reappearance. The Sranc teeming about the downward-hanging rims of the galleries opposite began hooting and gesturing. Skuthula's snout snapped toward her, the baleful green eyes narrowed.

"**So says the delicacy**," the Scourge of Ages boomed, "**to the teeth!**"

And it was all ... so ... clear ...

"*So says the hero!*" she cried with lilting derision.

Dangling jibes like lures of silver, baiting the reptilian intellect, slowing it with the need to calculate irrelevant points of honour ...

Dangling her body like a dockside whore, baiting the Ursranc archers, a pale and brutalized temptation ...

It was all so clear because she *was* that reptilian intellect, coiled vast about immemorial grudges, just as she *was* each and every one of the masticating archers, loins taut against her floating image, hunched about the raving promise of congress. The Qirri had flung her veins, nay, her *bones*, across all the intervening hollows, all the false holes in being that had rendered her isolate and vulnerable ...

The Qirri had revealed what she *was*, what she had always been ...

A waifish dance about Chorae, whistling from strings released by fingers aimed by eyes tracking a waifish dance ...

A slender leap through an incinerating exhalation ...

A wolfish lunge and a fleet sprint ...

A clapping maw and a ducking roll ...

Wheels spinning wheels. Anasûrimbor Serwa, Exalt-Magus of the Great Ordeal, divine daughter of the Holy Aspect-Emperor—*she* was what happened here.

She was this place.

And so was the Count whittled to twenty-one.

To live is to be sodden. There is nothing arid about existence, nothing laundered or distinct. To live *is to reek*, to forever seep into circumstances. All gateways to the human stink. The ears. The mouth as much as the anus, for some.

And the *eyes*, the eyes most of all.

To live is to consume and to exude, to excrete and to chew, to turn upon a thousand hidden alchemies, rheumy transformations of what we lust into what we abhor ... or love.

And so life convulsed and life was expelled from the socket, drawn sheeted in blood from the suffocating real, the very muck of amniotic origin, and held exposed to the scrutiny of cold Void, the hospice of prayer ...

So that some *essence* might alight ...

Some breath be drawn and screamed.

The Mutilated told a different tale, how the Unholy Consult had never truly understood their faith, let alone the implements propping them. They knew only that the Carapace *required a soul* for the No-God to awaken. So they began feeding Subjects to the Object, chaining their captives in great lines, and dragging them across this very floor so they might be entombed in the Carapace—and killed by it—one after another. They did this for more than a millennia before the First Apocalypse, murdering tens of thousands, casting the corpses down the great shaft of the Abskinis, the Groundless Grave ...

"And then," the reflection of the burnt Dûnyain said, "they inserted *Nau-Cayûti* ... the famed son of their mortal adversary."

"My ancestor," the Holy Aspect-Emperor said.

"That is the *meaning* of the Celmomian Prophecy," the caged Dûnyain explained.

His neighbour finished the thought without the least hesitation. "Your return augurs the No-God, brother, because *you are the No-God.*"

Absent limbs, Malowebi heaved and flailed.

"You are Mog-Pharau."

Run! the Mbimayu Schoolman cried without voice. *Flee this obscene place!*

But the reflection of the Anasûrimbor across the golden fin stood motionless before the regard of the Mutilated.

"You are your own salvation," the unscathed Dûnyain said. "The salvation of us all!"

Horror pimpled the nape of a neck Malowebi no longer possessed. *Mog-Pharau ...*

"But I am already saved," the Holy Aspect-Emperor said. "And I fear your souls are blasted beyond reclamation."

Whatever relief these words occasioned for Malowebi was scuttled by the vision of figures slinking as silent as clawless cats over the obsidian floors behind the Anasûrimbor, each dressed in ashen black, each bearing a pin-prick of oblivion bound to their palms.

"I have walked the infernal deep ..." the Anasûrimbor said, either unaware or unconcerned. "I have struck treaties with the Pit."

Each possessing pale aquatic fronds instead of a face—or rather, *digits*, Malowebi realized, long crone fingers extending, then clenching into crude human approximation, again and again.

"The Hells are *blind* to this place," the burnt Dûnyain declared. "Even if they watch you, they cannot see where you stand."

Consult *skin-spies* ... one after another, emerging from the black, more than a dozen that Malowebi could see—and that the Anasûrimbor could not.

The Lord-and-Prophet of the Three Seas actually *smiled*. "You seek to starve the very Gods," his reflection said. "Brothers, things so great need no light to cast shadows."

"How do you mean?" the teeth-baring Dûnyain demanded.

"Some have always smelled your *absence*."

"At most," the unscathed figure retorted. "They Intuit rather than Reason. They lack the Intellect to *question*."

Malowebi saw more black-garbed assassins surfacing from the darkness reflected in the fin. There had to be a *hundred* of the creatures now—spiderfaces!—all of them bearing Chorae in their palms. It scissored his senses, looking forward to see reflections of the vacancies he sensed floating behind him.

"Which is why," the Holy Aspect-Emperor said, "they needed *me*."

The Mutilated regarded him. The scores of faceless assassins paused where they crouched.

It seemed to Malowebi that nothing breathed.

"An Inverse Prophet," Anasûrimbor Kellhus said. "A revelation ... sent by the Living to the Dead, by the now to the Eternal."

The Tydonni guarding the ruins of Domathuz warned one another with claps on the shoulder and pointing arms. A *precipice* of some kind *walked* through the Horde—*toward the breach*. Somehow, gravity was tipped and skinnies began falling *horizontal*, over their slavering kin, and in all directions. Streams of them began crashing into the Nangaels elevated upon the debris, pocking the ranks like catapult stones.

Among the Mysunsai, confusion reigned. Every bit as bewildered as the Tydonni, each assumed that *someone* knew better when no one did.

That is, save a Swayali witch, Valsarta.

What escaped her was the profundity of the Mysunsai's turmoil. The sideways rain of Sranc was already pelting Golgotterath's walls by time she realized *they weren't going to act at all.* By time she sailed, her billows boiling about her, to the heights above the beleaguered Nangaels, it was already too late. The peril of being cast *at* had become the peril of *being cast.*

For Lord Woyengar, the Earl of Nangaelsa, the approach of the precipice was nothing short of surreal, Sranc pitched out on whatever direction their momentum carried them, as if they fell over some scarp's edge, *only from every point of the compass at once,* each twisting and kicking down an impossible horizontal abyss. The Sranc assailing Woyengar's forward rank slackened and thinned, then vanished altogether, and between iron helms of his vassals, the Earl of Nangaelsa watched the precipice step clear of the Horde ...

The *Red Ghoul* emerged, Sûjara-nin miraculously intact, his crimson nimil gown agleam, his eyes and mouth windows into the furnace cauldron that was his Erratic soul. The Sranc shrieked and thronged behind him, a lunatic rush that saw each descending club and cleaver pitched with its possessor over some non-existent plummet. Sûjara-nin did not so much as pause at the sight of the grim Northmen, but continued stepping from carcass to carcass, directly into the first rank ...

Lord Woyengar saw his Men raise shield and sword, then simply trip into the air and cartwheel into the occluded depths of the Horde. And then *he himself* was upon the mad Quya, *standing* where all others had been thrown—for the Chorae bound against his navel a fraction of him realized.

Cackling, the Erratic parried his swooping broadsword, chased the deflected impact into the Earl of Nangaelsa's exposed face. He yanked his ancient blade clear. Howling Nangaels fell upon him from all angles, only to fall over the Immaculate Rim ... topple headlong into their doom.

And so the Red Ghoul advanced across the heaped ruin, throwing all who rushed him deep into the nightmare heave of Ûgorrior. By the simple act of walking, the mad Nonman cut a broad furrow in the Tydonni ranks ...

The Yimaleti Sranc surged upon his catastrophic wake. They came as a yammering, threshing flood, instinctively gaining the flank then leaping deep into the shattered ranks, where they hacked with the nimble savagery of cats. In a matter of heartbeats, roiling violence had engulfed the Tydonni root and bough beyond the breach. Hanging above the chaos, Valsarta and the Mysunsai had no choice but to abandon the breach to Sûjara-nin. Saving the far greater numbers imperilled by his passage was more than toil enough.

And so the Red Ghoul climbed all but uncontested into the ragged socket that had once housed Domathuz. He stood upon the slung summit of the debris, sobbing and cackling for reasons thousands of years dead. He looked out across the appalled Longbeards, Plaideölmen, forming in the Canal below.

"**Why?**" he thundered in Sheyic, shrugging aside the all consuming din. A grimace fluttered about, then consumed, his flawless white face.

"*Why did you wait so long?*"

Blinding white. A shaft with a Trinket affixed had struck him full upon the cheek—a "Spank" as Chorae Bowmen called it, an impact square enough to salt a sorcerer through to his marrow. Perfectly balanced at contact, Sûjara-nin remained standing in perfect salt effigy, his expression a rictus of chalked fury, his famed armour yet hanging in links of intricate crimson ...

The infamous Red Ghoul was dead, this time forsooth.

The Sons of Plaideöl stood dumbstruck for wonder, somehow understanding the World had become less. They had yet to realize what was about to follow.

The statue bowled forward and toppled, trampled beneath the stampeding of horned feet.

The Breach of Domathuz had fallen. Like a chitinous flood of termites, the depravities gushed into the evil precincts of Golgotterath.

Once a vast crypt, the Atrium had become a scintillant furnace.

Wild with rage, the legendary Wracu whipped and struck and vomited fiery blindness. Skuthula hounded the young Grandmistress to the exclusion of all else, bent on punishing, on *showing*. Roaring with deranged saurian indignation, he pursued her into each gallery she vanished into, thrashing through Sranc, crushing them, consuming them—and *burning* them, burning them most of all, setting gallery after gallery alight. Lines and arcs and planes of Inchoroi gold bristled for reflected fire, while smoke boiled across the ceilings, streamed up into a cataract great enough to choke the vast skew of the shaft.

And she ran and danced not so much from as *with* those who would murder and desecrate, no more than a moment in a far greater automata, a system of systems ...

She understood the truth of heroism, how it collapsed action into reaction, *how it simply moved* careless of fear or bravery.

She understood her father's power.

The Ursranc Palatials hooped and screamed, many diving from the heights to crash like bundled leaves afire. Save for a scant handful, those wretches bearing Chorae now fled the fire and the dragon. She could feel each of the points of oblivion scattered across the Horn's bowel, the ones that threatened jerking through spaces high and low, before falling still, joining those already laying fallow.

And a fraction of her counted.

Fourteen ...

Thirteen ...

The joists groaned for the bulk of the Wracu, wending like a monstrous serpent from level to level. Skuthula began using his immense length to herd her down to the trough of the Skew, where he tried to crush her with blind thrashing. The unearthly metal thrummed for titanic impacts ...

She floated in flawless counterpoise, naked save for her burns and her Cindersword, passing as an apparition through perfumed sheets of flame. Time and again, Skuthula materialized from the fiery shrouds, reared with iron-hooked grace, lamellar scales rimmed in crimson wrath, lacquered in oily ghosts of the conflagration.

Time and again she held her ensorcelled sword tight ...

Seven ...

Six ...

Isiramûlis ... Hearth-slayer.

And she *laughed*, danced beyond the clacking violence of his jaws, like a moth dangling on a wire affixed to the mighty Wracu's snout. She laughed with an implacable mirth, and in a voice honed to echo and resonate and filter throughout the great slanted gullet of the Atrium ... the laughter of a little girl making sport of the most fearsome dragon to have ever lived.

Skuthula the Black howled and raged and flailed its immense, serpentine frame.

And Anasûrimbor Serwa slipped and eluded, counted the Ursranc dying and misfiring.

One ...

Zero ...

"**Now!**" she cried upon a sorcerous thunderclap, a voice that made a harp of the ancient Wracu's roar.

Light.

Cold.

Terror ...

Breath.

A convulsive wail of arrival ...

Lost in the deluge of those departing.

Malowebi looked to the diminishing line of the Mutilated reflected across the fore of the soggomantic fin, then to the assembly of gulping, gripping faces reflected across the rear.

"I bore word of the temporal to the divine," the Aspect-Emperor said. "You aren't so hidden as you think."

The burnt Dûnyain swept his hand high on a graceful arc. Sudden light flared from what seemed a thousand points scattered across the cavernous deeps, revealing *leagues* of arcane mechanism, shapes so intricate as to be an alien language to the Mbimayu Schoolman. "You would compare your burnt brick temples to a cathedral such as this?"

"The *Ark* is our argument, Brother," the lone unscathed monk said. "Would you deny the material incarnation of Logos?"

The Holy Aspect-Emperor did not so much as glance at the gulfs of golden reticulation. "And if the Logos no longer moves me ..." he said, his greasy resemblance at last turning to survey the skin-spies assembled across the margins of the Golden Room. "What is your contingency then?"

The great frame of lights fell dark, and the gold was muted to gleam, threads in abyssal blackness. For the first time, Malowebi found his gaze hooked on the *other* diabolical head hanging with him against the Aspect-Emperor's thigh—the other Decapitant. For the first time, he noticed the *same* obscuring distortion that marred the Anasûrimbor—like globules of ink hanging in quicksilver—marring it.

What he saw stopped his ethereal heart ...

"Coercion, of course," the teeth-baring Dûnyain replied.

Gibbering, hitching terror.

"You are utterly overmatched, Anasûrimbor," his one-eyed brother said.

Antlers, savage and knuckled, rising mangled as if scribbled by a drunk or a child. *Four* of them ...

No ...

"And yet you forget," Anasûrimbor Kellhus replied, grinning.

His reflection raised a knee, stamped a sandalled heel down ...

A cataclysmic *thump*, mazing the obsidian polish with concentric fractures, resounding through the mountainous bones of the structure, where it reverberated and returned to rock them all ...

Without uttering a word of sorcery.

"I am Master here."

Terror kicking like a frenzied mule.

Second Negotiant Malowebi wailed, his repentance unheard ...

Forgave Likaro all his countless flaws and sins.

⌘

The very World had become as a mill about her, every city, every soul wheels spinning within wheels, murmuring in places, groaning throughout. And in all creation Golgotterath was the most violent grinding gear.

The place most *unpredictable*.

"Now, Kayûtas!"

She sensed it even as she shouted, *the prick of oblivion*, no more than two paces to her right, just *appearing* as if drawn from a pocket ...

She did not need to hear the click.

The quarrel barely stubbed her knuckle, and yet it was enough—more than enough.

The ancient Cindersword did not so much fall from her hand as *with* ...

The Princess-Imperial slumped to her knees, cradling her stumped right forearm. Blood welled, melting salt as snow.

One hundred, she thought, looking up to the rising menace of Skuthula, the fire-spitting grin ...

One hundred stones.

She knelt on the ashen edge, crouched over her arm. The great serpent hung above her, its elephantine skull declined, the spines on its crest clattering for jubilation. Slather fell in blazing strings from its maw. The globed emerald of its eyes burnt for admiration.

"Long has it been," the legendary Wracu croaked, ***"since we supped upon a hero such as you ..."***

The Princess-Imperial drew upright on her knees, matched its baleful gaze. "I'm a witch."

The strands of her thought parted. *Meaning* made black shadow of her skull.

In a single motion, she retrieved Isiramûlis with her left hand.

Skuthula the Black vomited Hell.

Singing into the furnace, she raked lines of mercurial brilliance across the region before her.

She felt a sound with her heart, an impact that transcended the scale of hearing.

Then she was falling, tumbling with cracked ruin toward the trough.

Everything was falling, everything slung or mortared across the skewed frame of the Ark, the dross of *ages* of inhuman squalor, the encrustations of millennia raining down the massive shaft of the Atrium. She glimpsed it as she toppled, the plummet of tremendous curtains beyond the gallery, heaps bearing the roaring Dragon-Prince down, more carrion for the false earth, before crashing *into* the slot above, a galloping surge of debris, coming down as an avalanche upon her—

Father!

The Sranc exploded from the breach as hard-pent waters, leapt hacking and stabbing into the astonished Tydonni thanes. Cleavers made clay of faces. Stone cudgels made bread of bones.

The Sons of Plaideöl were as stalwart as any soul in the Host of Hosts, but the alchemy of events had plotted their undoing. The suddenness of the collapse. The disorder of the Mysunsai. The baffling terror of the Red

Ghoul. These would have sapped the resolve of any soul whatever their mettle. The forward ranks dissolved in the threshing torrent of skinnies. Thane after thane fell in the frenzied heave: Lord Emburalk, famed for his monstrous stature, and for wielding a cudgel other Men could scarce heft, let alone handle; the fanatic Lord Byrikki, called the "Candlemaker" for all the Orthodox he had burned for heresy during the Unification; and many others lesser known. Plaideölmen, however, were a *vengeful* folk, more incited to outrage than terror by the fact of grievous losses. They would have rallied about their fallen kinsmen ...

Had not their legendary Earl stood at their fore. For all his storied feats in the First Holy War, Werijen Greatheart was no match for the rigours of the Horde. The tribulations of the Great Ordeal had whittled his age into doddering frailty, and like many warlike souls who had outlived their strength and glory, he yearned only for death in battle—verily, this was the reason Anasûrimbor Kayûtas had stationed him in reserve. He found gratification in the first moments of the onslaught, toppling beneath a Sranc who had vaulted upon his shoulders. The bestial creature made a soup bowl of his skull ere his bereaved householders killed it.

Death came swirling down ... bore him as another wailing prize to the gluttony of the Pit.

So the ancient House of Rilding vanished forever, and the Red Sword standard of Plaideöl dropped to the carcass mats. Like cream spilled, hope is almost impossible to retrieve in the turmoil of battle. Loss begets loss begets loss. Terror is compounded. The resolve of the whole sags, slumps, then unravels into countless mortal coincidences. So did the long-bearded thanes waver upon the vestiges of their hatred before dissolving into horror and dismay.

The vile surge *consumed* their floundering ranks, overran the Sons of Plaideöl entirely.

The raving multitudes sluiced crashing into the Canal, fell upon the Sons of Ingraul, frantically forming ranks behind the shattered hulk of Gwergiruh ...

It could not be ... the horror Malowebi saw boiling across the soggomantic sheen.

Zeum was an ancient and imperial nation, pure of race and language, bound by strict law and subtle manner, steeped in millennial erudition. How could her Sons *not* hold the Three Seas in contempt? With its mangled maps and polyglot confusions, its perennial internecine wars over garden-plot provinces, its perverse need to forever dispute the sacrileges of their fathers. It was the nature of sausages to eat sausages, to undo what they could not outdo. So *of course* Malowebi had looked upon Fanayal and his motley court as *barbarians*, superstitious fools believing whatever their vainglorious agendas required—even more so when the man took Psatma Nannaferi as his concubine. A bandit Padirajah and an outlaw Mother Supreme! The dregs of yet another overthrown order ...

How could he entertain anything such outcasts might say? Especially when it confirmed Likaro ...

And now ... there He stood.

"Our differences are contingent," the dread image of the Anasûrimbor said, "artifacts of where we fell once cast out of Ishuäl ..."

The Demon.

"You were delivered to the machinations of the Tekne. And now you see it as the consummation of Dûnyain principles, the truth from which your very sinew and intellect are hewn. You think our error was to confuse the Logos with the movements of our souls, when in sooth it belongs to the machinery of the World. Your revelation was to understand that Logos *was nothing but Cause* as concealed by the darkness that comes before. You saw that *reason itself* was but another machine glimpsed in the blackness, a machine of machines."

There He stood! Malowebi could actually see ...

See *Him*.

"You realized the Mission was not to master Cause via Logos, but to master *Cause via Cause*, to endlessly refashion the Near to consume and incorporate the Far."

His reflection twining and coalescing *inward*, sparking more and more with boiling discharges, bloating about glowering exchanges of submerged ... *power*.

"But where you were delivered to the Tekne, I was brought to the *Gnosis*."

Incorporeal, yet somehow *more real* than the pallid echelon of the Mutilated on their stairs, the bulbous distortion that was Aurax, or the masticating faces of the skin-spies thronging ...

"I seized temporal power, usurped the Three Seas as you have usurped Golgotterath. But where you saw antithesis in your damnation, a goad to resume the ancient Inchoroi design, *I saw fathomless power.*"

The Four-Horned Brother had come ...

"Where you immersed yourself in the Tekne, took up the generational toil of recovering what the Inchoroi have lost, I mastered the *Daimos*, plundered the Houses of the Dead."

The Thief-of-Souls had found a way.

"Where you would shut the World against the Outside, and so secure your souls against damnation, *I would conquer Hell.*"

He had broken into the granary of the Living.

"Where you would strike the Outside from the hip of the Real, *I would enslave it.*"

And was about to plunder all.

The Mutilated regarded the boiling image.

"And if we choose to contest you?" the teeth-baring Dûnyain asked.

Cinder black about the raging furnace within, the Four-Horned image of the Anasûrimbor raised its hand.

Mekeritrig abruptly appeared from the nethers of the golden fin, clawing at the incandescent noose about his throat as some invisible force or entity dragged him across the obsidian polish, then hoisted him naked and gagging for the benefit of the expressionless Dûnyain. One of the mightiest Wills to walk the world, pinned to empty air, held upon the threshold of asphyxiation, utterly helpless.

When the Infernal figure spoke, his voice rumbled as distant thunder.

"You lured me here assuming the Inverse Fire would seduce me as it had seduced you. Failing this stratagem, you assumed numbers would serve you, that five would have no difficulty overcoming one. You need only cast my blasted carcass from the heights, and the Great Ordeal, dispossessed of its Prophet, would scatter to the winds."

Ajokli ... the Appalling Father ... Prince of Hate ...

"You lured me here because you assumed that *this* place, the Golden Room, *was your place ...*"

A God of the Tusk!

"Even now you still believe that it is I who stand upon your Conditioned Ground."

Woe! Woe! An Age of untold woe was about to descend upon Men!

"And how," the burnt Dûnyain said, gesturing to the silent throng of skin-spies, "could it be otherwise?"

Low growling laughter, terrifying for its immediacy, as if someone probed his ears with a knife-point.

"*Because in all the World*, no place has witnessed more terror, more obscenity, brutality, or sublime trauma. Your Golden Room is scarcely more than a bubble floating upon the Transcendent Pit. *Hell*, my brothers. Hell pollutes its every shadow, smokes from its every surface, creeps through its every brace ..."

Again the creak of mighty torsions. Again the groan of warring angles. Like a troubled pool, the congregated reflections blurred for the passage of impossible forces.

"Because, brothers, *this* place, more than *any other on the face of this fat World* ..."

The infernal image's hand fluttered. Cet'ingira's headless body flopped twitching to the black-mirror floors. The right hands of the skin-spies were yanked *down* in perfect unison, falling with the Evil Siqu's decapitated head. The Chorae bound to their palms now nailed them to their obsidian reflections.

The Anasûrimbor's head dissolved into a jetting torch.

"*Is my place.*"

Malowebi screamed.

The old Wizard could not breath.

Not grey. Not purple.

Becoming pink, flush with soundless shrieking.

A son.

Head craning, gazing through phlegm at the horror surrounding.

He had a *son* ...

Stupefied perfection.

Esmenet was laughing soundless, weeping soundless, cradling the infant for him to see.

He had become numb unto vacancy, a hole blinking at a nascent soul.

Miniature fingers, clutching bosom air, already reaching, grasping.

And all he could think was, *Another candle that would be lit.*

Another pyre that would be burned.

Shame sent his eyes fleeing to Mimara, who lay gasping knees askew, her head vertically braced against the fell stone of Golgotterath. Her eyes had been seeking his, despite everything she had suffered. There was none of the exhausted relief he might have expected had he lived a life that could bear such expectations. Inhuman blood matted her scalp and cheek. Her face was drawn, funeral-swollen. Gone was the crutch and club of her anger, the obstinance of her mad ordaining. Gone was the indifference, the calluses of resignation worn into her by tedious months on the trail. No, *acquiescence* and acquiescence alone radiated from her look, a blameless will to yield her own life, even in the delicate glare of another's dawning.

He understood instantly what she said, even though he could hear nothing beneath the Horde's savage choir.

There's another.

He glanced back to Esmenet to communicate his alarm, saw the Canal beyond her—

Glimpsed the first of the skinnies leaping like apes above the shifting forests of Men.

Terror ... stoked to such extremity as to be identical to agony. Had Malowebi possessed a body, he would have hung as if from a spike hammered into the back of his throat, kicked and clutched.

"**You shall be my angels,**" the Ciphrang-God grated in a voice that was the exhalation of countless damned.

The skin-spies heaved about them, the articulations of their obscene faces clenching for exertion, but their hands lay as welded to the obsidian floor. The reflected Inchoroi, Aurax, had scuttled from his dimple to cringe, behind the teeth-baring Dûnyain upon the farthest stair, his wings raised in a pathetic canopy. The Mutilated stood absolutely immobile, transfixed by the infernal apparition churning ink and fire before them.

"**You shall be my goad, the scourge of nations. Children shall keen for the simple rumour of your coming. Men shall rage and weep. And whatever horror and anguish you should sow, I shall reap.**"

"He *hides* here," the one-eyed Dûnyain said, his face blank. "His siblings hunt him and he thinks he can hide fro—"

The God's reflection raised a clawed hand, and the reflection of the Dûnyain *imploded* as if upon a point, skull crumpling like foil, limbs cracking and bursting as if wrenched through a twig-thin embrasure. In a heartbeat, scarce more than mucous ruin remained.

"Four brothers," the Prince of Hate mused. **"*Four Horns*. Together we shall gore this World, drink of it as a pierced fruit raised high."**

The very frame of the Golden Room yawed about the diabolical intonations. The lament of ages filtered in from the encircling darkness.

The four remaining Dûnyain exchanged looks.

"The Inverse Fire is naught but a window into my House," the Dark God-Emperor said. **"You have seen what awaits you. *Adore me*, or suffer eternal damnation ..."**

The Mutilated stared, their disfigurations their only expression. The skin-spies brayed, wagged and thrashed for terror. And Malowebi saw, impossibly, a *little boy* threading the spaces between their wild exertions, following a path that vanished behind the Grinning God's infernal reflection. The Prince-Imperial? Several of the creatures began hacking at their pinned wrists.

Malowebi sobbed, thrashed and flailed against his captivity.

"I *alone* ... Brothers ..."

But nothingness and nothingness alone was his prison.

"I am the Absolute."

What could not be grasped could not be broken.

CHAPTER NINETEEN

Resumption

And she shall wail, cry out to Us in the Heavens.
For We would know what soul that mother hath delivered, and when.
—Canticles 38:2, The Chronicle of the Tusk

The King declared all revelation unlawful, citing the unrest of the masses
and the lives wasted for fanatical distraction. Thus did water divination fall
to the witches.
—The Annals of Cenei, CASIDAS

Early Autumn, 20 New Imperial Year (4132, Year-of-the-Tusk), Golgotterath.

There are places that Men are brought from which they may never be retrieved, irrevocable places that, no matter how distant in years or leagues, will forever shackle them to terror and desperation.

The old Wizard grasped a spear, hauled himself to his feet.

A son.

He managed to surmount the chest of a felled Bashrag. He teetered over the carnage, steadied, then stood peering down the Canal.

He had a son.

Sorcerous lights bloomed wondrous across the stepped walls of the Oblitus to his right. Fluttering white. Pulsing turquoise. Glowing vermillion. To his left, Gwergiruh stacked into the soot-black sky. Ingraulish axemen teemed across the wrack some forty paces or so before him, hastening to reinforce the great phalanx of their kinsmen bracing the throat of the Canal beyond. The Longbeards thrust and chopped across the fore of the black formation, toiling to stem the white-skinned deluge, Sranc masses leaping, popping like surf upon breakers, becoming a sizzle of maggots beyond the violet haze ...

So many. Too many.

He had a son! Achamian realized.

Suddenly lights flashed *within* Golgotterath's ramparts. The old Wizard watched awestruck as *Quya* strode from the breach of Domathuz into the regions above the thronging slot, their skulls ablaze with blasphemous meaning, the canyon below erupting for their lethal ministry.

The slaughter was absolute. The Canal was transformed into a great, rolling furnace, first engulfing, then incinerating the white masses. Panic overcame the remaining Sranc. Chaos dissolved into something more chaotic still. The Canal became a trough that boiled with ingrown lines of flight, a heaving in all directions. The iron-draped Ingrauls surged forward, hewing and thrusting.

The old Wizard stood agape, his own Cant forgotten. None other than Lord Vippol himself floated at the fore of the Quya, decked in his antique wire armour, singing with the fury of those insane for growing old ... And there!—there was Cilcûliccas, the Lord of Swans, the far-famed slayer of the Knifedragon ...

Kellhus *had* called on Ishterebinth, a numb fraction of him realized.

The creatures fell as millet before the scything Sons of Ingraul; they burned as pitch-sodden torches beneath the singing Sons of Eliriqû. Sword and fire consumed the remaining skinnies. The Ingrauls raised their gored weapons in triumph, began streaming over the long oven floor to retake the breach.

He had a son!

By some caprice, Achamian caught the eye of Lord Vippol hanging above. The darkling gaze held his for a heartbeat, then turned away in disorder ...

And then it happened ... the all-conquering roar of the Horde crashed into impossible *silence*.

Ringing ears.

A babe wailed ... and it dizzied, so impossible was the sound.

The very ground seemed to yaw for unreality, so ambient and overwhelming had the sound been. Though it had stopped his ears for mere watches, it had become a thing primordial in that short time, a peer of Creation.

The old Wizard cast about bewildered, saw every other soul doing the same ...

"*It flees!*" some Longbeard cried from the parapets above. "*The Horde! Fleeeeees!*"

A babe wailed into the wake of the man's ravaged voice, a cry like a bleeding reed.

Achamian turned to the two women, Esmenet, crouched between the knees of her daughter, who grunted and keened. "D-do you he—?"

A thunderous explosion of masculine voices seized all that was visible. Cheers, Achamian realized. *Cheering.* The Men of the Three Seas threw out their arms, seized one another in disbelief, or simply dropped to their knees and wept. Golgotterath boomed and resounded. Exultation cracked into unhinged exhibitions of incredulity and joy. Men curled into keening, snuffling balls. Men huffed and bellowed like beasts, beat their chests, kicked and stomped carcasses. Men seized elbows and danced their grandmother's jigs.

The blackness of the Shroud thinned about the back of the northern wind, became as smoked glass. A second daylight broke upon them, one not seen by mortal eyes in an age.

The babe wailed. The mother sobbed. The second birth would be mercifully quick.

Furtive in the celebratory uproar, Esmenet hurriedly cut the cord with Chipmunk, then bundled the blue slip in a swathe of cloth torn from a corpse. The old Wizard would never know what became of it, the dead twin.

Holding the first bundle to her chest, Mimara wept uncontrollably.

The old Wizard hobbled down from the Bashrag's great chest, made a seat of its cauldron head. He propped his elbows on his knees, lay his eyes in his palms. Tremors wracked him.

When was a thing over? When was tribulation complete?

Drusas Achamian had a son.

Sunlight fell as a healer's hand, fingers breaking through the tatters of the Shroud, blessing pockets of ruin with dulcet illumination. Those touched looked out and wondered, their faces blackened for soot and gore. They saw rays as enormous as the Horn only spectral and pure, threading slow mountains of smoke and dust that tumbled orange, black, and dun to the rib of the sky, glowing through septic fumes.

Those defending the western walls—exhausted Nansur Columnaries, Eumarnan Grandees, and others—watched the Sranc recoil from the stronghold of their Makers, race as shoals of fish beneath the retreating haze of the Shroud. "So the Soulless bolt," General Inrilil ab Cinganjehoi bellowed in rapture, "from the wrath of the Souled!"

More than a million carcasses webbed the ashen plain, very nearly all Sranc, heaped into slopes and gutters about the gold-fanged ramparts, strewn in vast, radiating skeins. Bodies burned as bonfires at dozens of points, trailing smoke like black hair in water. Golgotterath rose as a burnt canker from the mayhem, the chambered socket of the High Horn, which soared into impossible clarity once again, dazzling for the fingers of the sun. The Canted Horn lay sectioned and shattered across the Shigogli below, a range of burnished wrack and ruin.

Dispersed across the blasted circus of the interior, the Men of the Great Ordeal cawed and wept for relief, for triumph—for *salvation*. Exhortations rang raw at different stations throughout the fell enclosure, cheers rising from one quarter of the fortress to blot the cheers rising from others ... all the different tribes of Golgotterath.

Then the keen-eyed spied *Him*, and jousting cheers became a tempest of ecstasy and adulation.

The Holy Aspect-Emperor stood upon the Vigil, high on the eastward face of the surviving Horn. In their thousands, Men peered, the maimed as much as the hale, each crying out as their eyes fastened upon his heavenly figure, casting their voices as lots into the singular roar. And He stood sheltered in the Horn's shadow, gazing down upon them as though from a mountain summit—and they could see that He was glad.

What had been ecstatic became crazed, frenzied even.

Passion maddened the air. The thunder of thousands rang across the soaring curvatures of Inchoroi gold. It warbled only when they saw the Holy Aspect-Emperor step from the Vigil into void ... only to be redoubled when

He *floated* rather then plummeted, descended as dandelion fluff in motionless air.

A war-trumpet peeled across the heights about the Horn's base, ringing crisp and bright. The martial call for Temple. In the wondering lull, a solitary Conriyan Knight stranded on the gold-fanged parapets to the north began singing the famed *Warrior Hymn*,

> *By the waters of Siol,*
> *we hung our lyres upon the willows,*
> *and abandoned song with our mountain.*

Perhaps it was the quaver in his voice, or simply the haunting intonations of the hymn itself, which seemed to thread the very bourne of melancholy and joy ...

> *Ere the doom of Trysë,*
> *we hoisted our sons upon our knees,*
> *and counted scabs upon our hands and heart.*

For it leapt from soul to soul with unnatural alacrity, radiated out and across the blasted tracts of Golgotterath, absorbing voice after cracked voice, transforming thousands of mudded droplets into a single lucid pool. They were Men who had seen the God's will *through*. They were and would forever be *Ordealmen*. They understood the way, knew the harshest toll, and this song was *for such as them* ...

> *In the fields of Cenei,*
> *we broke bread that we had stolen,*
> *and tasted the love of those who were dead.*

So the New Inrithi sang as Anasûrimbor Kellhus, the Most Holy Aspect-Emperor of the Three Seas, floated down from the heights, for it was the want of Men to surrender their borders in song, *to cease to be* and so to cease to be *alone*. They sang to their Prophet to be indistinguishable from one another.

In the absence of edges lies the sum of divine grace. Fields of open palms were raised to brush his distal form. And they screeched as much as they cried the ultimate verse, for it bound the horrific sum of the toll they had paid ...

Beneath the Ark of horrors,
we saw the sun rise upon gold as night fell,
and mourned the captivity of tomorrow.

How many times had they sung this? How many dreary watches had they spent cycling through the Warrior Hymn's countless verses, always irresistibly drawn back to this very one, the words bearing the weight of *their water*, their experience, boiled down to a single fraught verse. How many times had they squinted through the shifting thickets toward the horizon and *wondered at this very moment?*

For here they stood, *hands raised ...*

Witnessing their salvation.

Salvation ... such a peculiar word.

One that made babes of Men.

For some, it was simply too much to bear, so much suffering and speculation come to such a finely honed point. They staggered, or even swooned outright.

But others found their passions even further inflamed. *"Our salvation!"* they began crying out to their Prophet, shouting, roaring, disjoint choruses resolving into thunderous clarity.

"Our salvation!"

"Our salvation!"

Men packed the terraces of the Oblitus, blood blackening their skin. Men gathered across the bulb of the Scab, crowded any section of the outer wall that afforded them a view. Some sixty thousand voices cried out in unison, engulfing their own porcelain echo, transforming the chant into something that *struck*, that punched and kicked the skies.

"Our salvation!"

"Our salvation!"

The Most Holy Aspect-Emperor fell as a mote through immobile air, seemed to flicker or waver for some otherworldly light.

"Our salvation!"

"Our salvation!"

He passed from the shadow of the Horn, flared with luminance in the gloaming sun ...

"Our salvation!"

"*Our salvation!*"

And sank into the reverberations, his hands outstretched within discs of shining gold.

"*Our salvation!*"

"*Our salvation!*"

"*Our salvation!*"

————— ✺ —————

Hands ...

Hands bear her.

Mimara's gaze lolls about the surface of the mad surge.

The very ground has become deranged with jubilation, faces pale and swart, all of them drugged with weariness and gloating exultation.

"*Our salvation!*"

They have seized her, the brutish Men, lifted her upon lacerated arms, and now they are bearing her in the wake of her Imperial mother. The anguish of her loins is beyond describing, and she is paralytic with exhaustion, but she *feels* it, nevertheless, the residue of the Nonman King, like a wire strung through her from pith to extremity. She hangs from Nil'giccas as a beggar's laundry.

"*Our salvation!*"

She turns, sees the old Wizard floating upon hands beside her, cursing his bearers, nearly lost in his rancid bundle of animal skin for struggling. She feels the nausea that is his Mark. She realizes he has been shouting her name.

"*Our salvation!*"

Her mother marches on foot with singular purpose before them, her grandson held tight to her breast. She is diminutive in the shadow of the Ingrauls wedging apart the masses before her.

"The Blessed Empress!" they bellow as they lurch to and fro. "Make way! Make way!"

"*Our salvation!*"

She sees *them*, the Men of the Ordeal, the pageant of damaged faces ... falling to earth as their bodies drop them to their knees.

"*Our salvation!*"

Following the eyes of those more distant, she sees *Him*, glorious for the paint thrown by the setting sun, descending from on high.

"*Our salvation!*"

She sees the High Horn, its mirror immensity throwing sundogs across her periphery.

"*Our salvation!*"

She worries that she has just given birth, and yet feels no yearning for the bundle in her Empress mother's arms. She wonders what has happened, and why, surrounded by such joyous extravagance, she feels only desolation.

"*Our salvation!*"

She sees the whorl of warriors across the battered terraces below, the gutter of coal and cinder that is the Canal. She sees the curtains walls, like a saw with golden teeth. She sees the smashed maw of Ûbil, the Extrinsic Gate, the barrows of debris where Domathuz and Corrunc had once loomed impenetrable.

"*Our salvation!*"

She glimpses the great, deformed curve of the Fallen Horn hunched on a mountainous, gleaming arc over the back of the Scab. She sees a scatter of garnets taking flight ... crows and vultures riding thermals.

"*Our salvation!*"

She stares out across what would be holy scripture.

She sees *Him* ...

"*Our salvation!*"

Anasûrimbor Kellhus, the Most Holy Aspect-Emperor. She sees Him descend into fields of reaching ...

The old Wizard is shouting her name.

The stupor of calamity is the stupor of an undertaking too enormous, the idiocy of not knowing where to begin. Achamian relinquished all thought, allowing his feet to step over bodies, his gaze to chase glimpses in the absence of intent or design. He stumbled after. He looked about witless. Puddled blood shivered for the violence of the Ordealmen and their demonstration ...

"*Our salvation!*" like a hammer strike across Inchoroi gold.

"*Our salvation!*" mapping their Lord-and-Prophet's descent, becoming a booming stair ...

Until He alighted upon the ground belonging to all, and *tranquillity* stole across Golgotterath. His very image twitched for unearthly power, the lines of him scribbling for a heartbeat, then no more. Silence flew out across the Ordeal as a ripple in a pool.

"Our salvation!" resounded once more, absent any centre ... then dissolved into an oceanic murmur.

Suddenly Men who had been too desperate to recognize let alone attend to the three refugees threw themselves to their knees amid the carcasses, begging to serve their Most Blessed Empress. Hobbled, Achamian could only stand and gape, watch blinking as Esmenet—holding his infant son bundled in her arms—commanded the Ingraul who had been their bulwark to convey them to her divine husband. He did not protest when the towering warriors hoisted him from his feet and began passing him across their heads. He *should* be thrown bodily as upon a flood, it seemed. Buoyant upon warlike hands, he remembered how he had floated thus some twenty years previous in Sumna ... as the Holy Shriah railed against the iniquities of the Fanim.

He did not swoon as he had that day—or at least not in the same manner. Incredulity was but the margin of what he suffered. His life—and since seizing Seswatha's Heart, his *being*—had been a creature of this place. For all our sovereign pretension, we are welded to what we fathom. The degree to which events knock us from ourselves is the degree to which we are indistinguishable from our knowledge.

Absent some horizon, a compass needle is no compass at all.

So he was bourne to the uttermost tier of the Oblitus, at once insensate and alert, alive to every excruciating detail of his transit. Wounds. The spirit-crushing bulk of the Horn above. Drying gore. He remembered crying out to Mimara, either at the behest of some agency other than his own, or out of stupid reflex for catching glimpses of her miraculous face.

The Ordealmen crowded across the steps of the Oblitus, eyes lunatic with exaltation, or dull with disbelief. The Schoolmen had alighted like crows along the protuberant heights of the Scab, many-coloured sorcerers-of-rank crowding the ledges with their sword-wielding brothers. Men knelt in prayer or exhaustion. Men sat transfixed, rigid about their own breathing. Men stood and craned their heads, straining for some glimpse of what transpired. Men milled and conversed, animate for joy and expectation. Here and there individuals pricked the old Wizard's rolling gaze: a bloody-headed Galeoth whetting his blade, a Shigeki heaving the dead about to check faces, an Ainoni sitting and rocking as he repeatedly stabbed his own thigh.

So the old Wizard was passed as a coin from hand to hand. Hemp ropes draped the Risers, hoists either bound to wicker baskets or knotted into simple nooses. Thus he was hauled up scorched-stone faces. His handlers, no matter how savage their appearance, accorded him the same reverence they accorded their Blessed Empress. The vista of the Oblitus and the ruined hulk of Gwergiruh became more vertiginous with each tier he surmounted. As the Ordealmen heaved him up the penultimate wall, he saw Mimara below, a view so unobstructed, so lucid, that he could not but recall some portion of what was happening ...

And who he was.

She looked up, hearing the one shout he had not voiced. He could weep for the dark oval of her face.

Then callused hands seized him once again, drew him about. He was lifted between battlements, wheeled around to stand on his good leg ...

So that he might gaze dumbstruck across the summit of the Oblitus.

The sound of weeping larded the hush.

A Carythusali proffered him a spear he might use as a crutch. He took it.

Everything lay in the chill shadow of the Scab. Circumfix devices hung slack in the evening lull. Only the Men working the hoists stood and toiled—for their sakes, no less. Otherwise, a field of prostrate Men extended from his feet, radiated out to encompass the whole of the terrace. Shields and backs and bowed heads clotted his every glance. Believer-Kings beside Schoolmen. Caste-nobles wedged between menials.

A recess scalloped the black scarp that loomed over the uppermost tier, the Ninth, creating the likeness of hands cupped about something that might cut or burn. A great shard leaned out from the hollow ...

His rostrum.

There He stood.

There He stood, his smile canny, staring directly at him.

Anasûrimbor Kellhus.

The Holy Aspect-Emperor of the Three Seas.

Lord of Golgotterath ...

His image fairly dazzled, cast tangles of gold across innumerable obsidian fractures, glimmered over myriad surfaces of metal and enamel.

It bore no Mark.

The old Wizard coughed to breathe ... to sob. Hot tears flooded his cheeks.

He had been ... cleansed ...

Saved.

Achamian started at the small, warm hand that clasped his own. He tore his gaze from Kellhus, expecting to see Mimara, but found *Esmenet* instead, his son in her arms, her eyes wondrous ... avid with the revelation they all shared. Tears coursed her cheeks, leaving lines that refracted the Holy Aspect-Emperor's otherworldly light.

Something stepped through him—something greater than thought.

Could it be?

Could it be that all he had lost, all he had lamented ... *begrudged* ...

His School ... His cause ... His student ...

His *wife!*

Had his throttling sacrifice ... his *heartbreak* ...

Had it saved the World?

He spoke true ...

Drusas Achamian trembled as he had never trembled before.

It's over ...

The Holy Aspect-Emperor inclined his head to the two of them—a look that was an impossible blessing—then swept his cerulean gaze out over the assembled ...

His will has been done.

The voice of Anasûrimbor Kellhus fell as warm rain, bracing even as it soothed ...

"Man ..."

It hummed across the mountainous nethers of the Horn, made warm what was vast and empty ...

" ... *would sooner weep before God than his brother.*"

Achamian made to join the impossible congregation, only to teeter. Esmenet caught him, helped him ease to his knees, then joined him. That was when Mimara staggered past, her look plundered. He reached out to clasp her sleeve, but his fingers fell short. Swaying for the rigours of her travail, she picked her way forward between the prone Men of the Ordeal.

"*He cowers beneath the rod that never falls ...*"

Her babe gurgled in her mother's arms.

"To better convict his brother of pride ..."
Blood flushed the backside of her borrowed gown.
"To better beat him into submission."

———⸎———

Her feet are bare ...
    It does not matter.
    She lurches past Akka and her mother ...
    It does not matter.
    She sees her brother approach from the High Cwol bearing her sister's blasted body in his arms ...
    It does not matter.
    The Judging Eye is open.

———⸎———

The Holy Aspect-Emperor speaks from a black dais ...
    Anasûrimbor Mimara advances through the kneelers, stumbling onto the backs of some, hauling herself onward without acknowledgement, let alone apology.
    They do not matter.
    At last the soles of her feet scuff across the inexplicable line where no soul dares approach further ... no soul save her own. She cannot breathe. Heat drops through her, slipping like sheeted water from her crown to her toes. A hand clutches her elbow, tries to pull her about, *but the gaze is unbreakable*, as implacable as the sun ...
    So the old Wizard hobbles to her side instead, looks to the Most Holy Aspect-Emperor frowning down at them from above ...
    All the World has fallen silent.
    "Mim ..."
    "Akka ..." she replies, still staring into the golden regard of Anasûrimbor Kellhus.
    A sob kicks through her, makes ropes of her bones. The old Wizard steadies her, turns her body about, though her eyes remain soldered to the image of her stepfather.
    The assembled nations of Eärwa watch in wonder, the mightiest Sons of the Tusk.

"He spoke true, Mim ..." Achamian murmurs. He slaps astounded hands to his wild hermit hair. He cackles for incredulous joy, cries, "The Consult *has been destroyed!*"

A ragged cheer erupts from the Soldiers and Schoolmen of the Circumfix. The Zaudunyani upon the debris heaped about the High Cwol, along the lip of the Scab some thirty cubits above, cry out.

"No ..." she says.

But a crazed elation seizes the Host of Hosts, one that sends brutalized thousands to their knees, sobbing, reaching for the shining image of their Lord-and-Prophet, their all-conquering Holy Aspect-Emperor.

"*Nooooooo!*"

Achamian clutches her hand, his flush draining into pallor. "Mimara?"

"Can't you see?" she screeches. "*Looook!*"

Her tone is so wild, so stricken, that it claws the fabric of every soul in earshot. The cheer cracks and dissolves into bewildered peering. Achamian might have been toothless for the way he gaped.

The Most Holy Aspect-Emperor stands luminous in the sunshine of a different day, a different World. He nods in forbearance.

"Daughter?" he calls on a smile.

And she blinks and she blinks and yet *still* it hangs there ... scarab shining ...

"What is it?" Anasûrimbor Kellhus says, though he is nowhere to be seen. "What ails thee, Mimara?"

A *sarcophagus*, iridescent black, hovering where her stepfather stands robed in shining white ...

His leonine image smiling ...

Forgiving ...

Saying ...

"Tell me ..."

The Upright Horn groans with cataclysmic power. The first gust falls upon a vast and chilling gyre.

"*What do you see?*"

Skirts of dust leap and skid across the Shigogli.

The old Wizard lets slip her hand for trembling.

WHAT AM I?

CHAPTER TWENTY

The Furnace Plain

Twas words that packed the earth.
Twas words that flung the sky.
Twas words that made us beautiful,
ere our Faith became our lie.

Twill be words that crack the earth.
Twill be words that low the sky.
Twill be words you hear us wailing,
ere the day we die.

—The Heaver's Song

Early Autumn, 20 New Imperial Year (4132, Year-of-the-Tusk), Golgotterath.

Ever does oblivion whisper deceit to time, flattening afternoons into heart-beats, stretching blinks into mornings. Malowebi awoke as from death. It felt like watches had passed, or even more, the rolling of the days, the tumble of years. But mere instants had passed in sooth.

He hung as before, his hair bound to a warrior's girdle. He could see his crazed prison mirrored in the soggomant as before, the ovoid smears of the Decapitants strung from the hip of a ...

A statue?

Tall before the black depths. Bearded in the antique manner. Helmless, with hair braided across his nape, wearing what seemed an elaborate robe ...

The pillar of salt that was the Aspect-Emperor.
Anasûrimbor Kellhus.

———⊗⊗⊗———

A *feeling* ... thus began the new Years of the Crib. A feeling not known since Far Antiquity, since the weal and woe of the Apocalypse.

It was identical in all souls in all places, be it the rice-paddies of southern Zeum, the humid canal-ways of Invishi, or the looming turrets of Attrempus. Whether alone or in their thousands, Men *leapt* ... then turned to the northern horizon, peering. Wives caught up crying children. Priests trailed mumbling into silence, clutched fetishes in palsied hands. *Every soul living* caught their breath, their tongue, and hung upon the *feeling* ...

Like falling.

Like a great inhalation of *essence* from the World.

Not a soul could reckon the feeling in ancient days, at least not initially. Some even dared laugh in wonder, marvel at the absurdity of a horror without object, a knowing with direction only, a passion that *moved all souls as one.* Only when the first mothers began shrieking could they fathom the significance of what would be called the Boding. All souls recognized it now, at least in those nations celebrating *The Holy Sagas* as scripture. For the faithful of the Three Seas, the Boding dread was itself dreaded, the thing wives and mothers prayed most ardently *against.*

And so wailing filled the great fleshpots of the South, the lament of believers confirmed in disaster and unbelievers dismayed, doubly overthrown. Families gathered on the rooftops, made demonstration of their grief. Riot embroiled temples both humble and great, so desperate were souls to entreat and repent. The Hagerna in Sumna, already battered for the quaking wrath of Momus, was set alight, burning above the city it had forever starved. Only the mad took to the streets and alleyways, otherwise, crying out what every heart already shouted. The Boding! Sweet Sejenus, the Boding was upon them!

The Great Ordeal had *failed!*

Very few heard the mothers shrieking this time, so universally did souls call out their own grief. And those who could hear them, their midwives, found themselves too astounded, too mortified, to minister as a Yatwerian priestess should. No womb-prayers were offered, no name-tiles were cracked and pestled. The condolences, such as those that were given, were distracted, for they, and they alone, could recognize the feeling as *one they had suffered before*, as a feeling uniquely their own, the anguish of a stillbirth guessed and not yet known. The Bode of legend was *their boding*, the premonition both of tragedy and the necessity of running tragedy's course ...

The feeling of birthing the dead.

And they wept, knowing that every womb was now a grave, and they had become diggers.

The Death of Birth.

It towered so high over them one had to kneel to apprehend—kneel to see!

The Carapace.

Hanging coal-black above the mobbed terraces of the Oblitus, drawing curtains of dust on vast and invisible rings across the Shigogli. Hanging as it had in so many of the Dreams, only absent the eleven Chorae once affixed to its seams. There! In *waking* life!

Mog-Pharau.

Obsidian against mountainous gold. The sky groaned and clotted above the Upright Horn, clouds piling outwards and up, obscurity belching obscurity. Bluff winds sent detritus scratching across faces of stone. The first tendrils of black began circling Shigogli.

Mimara had folded about her screaming, her gaze fixed at a deranged tangent, her face quivering for exertion, howling out spit and outrage and incredulity, as if she aired each and every indignity—from flints in her sandal to mad Nonmen kings—she had suffered the seasons previous. Achamian and Esmenet hauled at her, pulled her down the direction of general flight. The babe squalled in the Blessed Empress's arms. His living, breathing son.

Hundreds, nay, *thousands* ran with them, Ordealmen bowling between other Ordealmen standing like posts in cement, faces raised in witless confusion, fixed in the aimless rush. It was the same throughout the smoking hulk of Golgotterath. Upon the stranded walls, over the matted dead, the Men of Three Seas cracked as if upon some inner joist, dividing into those too dismayed to yield their ground and those too dismayed to hold it. A filter fell across the sun, made ochre of gold, wax of nimil. The Upright Horn throbbed so deep that only marrow could hear it. Gusts laved them, throwing hair across mouths, flicking grit into eyes. Faces took to grimacing when turned into the gyre. Those upon the heights raised the crotch of their arms in warding.

And it towered over them, a black so deep as to mirror the terror beneath.

The old Wizard sobbed as he hobbled about and over the corpses, spat at the bile. A crazed diversity of shouts scraped the air, cries that washed into ocean surf for sheer numbers. Towering warriors barged about and between them. His leg shrieked. He passed a Cuarweshman wrenching his beard from his bloody jaw. He passed an Ansercan Columnary squatting upon his helm, cackling into his palms and calling out numbers. He passed faces beaten to swollen clefts, and faces without a fleck of blood. He passed faces squinting up as though to gauge the morrow's weather, and faces breaking ... about losses, realizations, limits, all those things peace cannot bring.

He slowed not so much for understanding as *recollection*.

Mother and daughter swivelled inward in alarm, but his reassurance exploded about an impact from behind, and he found himself gulping air on all fours, staring into the upturned face of a Nonman, cold and flawless as porcelain, propped so as to bestow a drowsy, open-mouthed kiss. And *he could feel it*, the plummet hanging in the sky above all of them, the fatal fall made incarnate, and he did not despair.

This time it was Mimara exhorting him, begging, tugging on his rancid furs. He did not so much see her as see her stained hands, shaking, fumbling the pouch, spilling the cannibal ash—the Qirri. He fairly gagged for the amount she jammed into his mouth, hacked muck between clenched teeth, reflexively swallowed ...

A babe squalled.

He snorted the ash of Nil'giccas from his mustaches. Lightning fell through him in shivers. He reared back on his knees. A Swayali strode out across the emptiness above the panicked terraces, wreathed in golden incandescence. He saw her gaze into the sky. He saw numberless, windblown grains explode into smoke across her Gnostic Wards. He saw that *she was Seswatha*, beaten and weary, hounded across the back of the World, and so very, very old.

Drusas Achamian did not so much understand as *belong*.

"**Irjulila ...**" he began chanting, "**hispi ki'liris ...**"

His voice glared across the wrack, and he glimpsed his hermit-wild face reflected in the Quya's dead gaze, his eyes sparking blue under birdnest brows, his mouth a hole of brilliance in a whitewater beard. He shrugged aside the ministry of small hands, turned his back to the Bode, hobbled out beyond the wrecked battlements of the Ninth Riser. Wind flailed his eyes, his skin. He looked out over the surging channels of Men, out beyond the revolving shrouds of grey and black, and saw the Horde's grotesque rim closing upon Golgotterath once again ...

And he thought, *Yes ... I have been here before.*

His voice cracked the ribs of the horizon.

"Flee! Flee, Sons of Men!"

And for a heartbeat all the beleaguered and begrimed faces turned to him, gazed upon the pelt-heaped aspect of the Wizard. His arcane shout fell upon them as Heaven's own Rod. Those already fleeing surged, while those yet loathe to run crumbled into the tide of their brothers. What had been erosion suddenly became a landslide, currents of men loosed within packed masses, spilling out and down, splashing into pitched battle across a descending array of blockages. Within heartbeats, castaway shields scaled the visible ground.

"The Second Apocalypse!"

He looked back to the astonished faces of the women he loved, saw their beauty flinch for the thunderclap that was his shining voice, the calamity that was his black declaration.

"The Second Apocalypse is upon us!"

And from the heights of the Oblitus, it seemed the ground moved backwards, so vast was the exodus to escape it.

Still floating, Drusas Achamian reached for Esmenet, who deftly joined him upon the phantom plate, slipping one hand about his waist, while holding her wailing grandson tight to her breast with the other. He turned to Mimara, grinned as Seswatha had always grinned in the twilight of ruin, a smile that only intimates of doom know, souls stripped to the bald fact of love.

She gawked at him, shrugged about a sob. *How?* her look did not so much ask as ache. *How could this happen?*

The Upright Horn towered, seized frost from the empty heart of the sky, a bulk that forever plucked the instinct to cringe. The Great Ordeal drained from the cracked black bowl that was Golgotterath, spilled toward the east. The winds crossed some threshold of violence, and Esmenet buried her face in the old Wizard's pelted shoulder.

Mimara, for mad reasons all her own, endured the pinprick lashing, glared at the father of her child, weeping freely, asking *how* ... Sweet Seju ... Why?

Achamian extended his hand. "*Please*," he called across the bloating roar.

There is knowledge in our manner, *ways to prove* that utterly elude the apparent sunlight of speech. Sorcery does not exhaust the miracles of the voice: with one word, it seemed, he had demonstrated to her what tomes of disputation could never do.

Apocalypse was his birthright.

Horror yawed above them, a light that struck only souls. She pawed at her tears in fury, withdrew the pouch bearing her two Chorae, the one that had saved them in the bowel of Cil-Aujas, and the one she had looted from Kosoter's corpse at Sauglish. In a single motion, she pulled the thread about her head and cast the pouch out over the void of the Oblitus. No eye followed their descent into the wrack and panic. Her last proof against him.

Anasûrimbor Mimara stepped teetering to the brink, then took his sorcerous hand.

The Aspect-Emperor was dead.

Never had Malowebi been so immobile, so windless within. To be bodiless and still is to cease to exist.

Memory retrieved him, hoisted him on the back of images across indeterminate cavities. Ajokli—the *Four-Horned Brother!*—not simply *here*, but inhabiting *Anasûrimbor Kellhus*. The clawing implications, the retching *terror*, the soundless shrieks, the intimation of slaughtered futures ...

And then the *little boy* had appeared, Anasûrimbor Kelmomas ... *there he was*, scampering between the skin-spies nailed to the floor by their Chorae ...

Malowebi assumed, according to his terror, that the boy belonged to Ajokli ... One of the *Hundred* stood manifest before him! Of course the boy was his!

Except that he *wasn't*.

"He can't see me *either*!" the little boy chortled.

The geyser of incandescence that housed the Grinning God's visage sputtered ...

The four remaining Mutilated watched with disfigured fascination. Aurax grovelled.

The glare vanished from the shoulders, leaving only *Anasûrimbor Kellhus*, blinking as any mortal man, swaying, peering at his youngest son ...

"K-Kel? How di—"

The nearest skin-spy clapped the Chorae in its palm about his ankle.

And the Aspect-Emperor was no more.

"See!" the child gurgled, squealing for preposterous joy. "I told you! I *told* you! They can't see me! The Gods! *The Gods can't see me!*"

Unable to think, Malowebi witnessed, watched it all in golden reflection, how the Mutilated seized a begging Kelmomas, first with sorcery, then with hands lacking five fingers, how the child had wailed and kicked and shrieked, realizing he had traded one tyrant for four. Malowebi glimpsed the flutter of small limbs as the Dûnyain thrust him into the great black sarcophagus, heard the porcine shrieks of bodily violations, the heartbreak of his blubbering, his whimpering cries, as the great face of the Carapace closed upon its ancient seal ...

"Mu-mu-mum-meee ..."

He could *remember*! The Carapace climbing soundlessly upright ... The very root of the Horn roaring.

The Aspect-Emperor dead.

Never had Malowebi been so immobile, so windless within.

<hr />

A vision like straps about your chest.

You see a chip shining black, hanging within the watery distortions pulsing about the remaining Horn. You see the dust devils have ceased their random scrawl, and now orbit the great black plate of the Shigogli. You see *Men* spilling like iron filings and grains of quartz, pouring through the very breaches they had wrought mere watches previous. You see Magi like seeds detaching in a different wind, this one blowing not around, but toward *you*. You see the Horde amassed upon the far line of the Occlusion, following the miracle of its retreat with the cataclysm of its *return*. You see the pallid stampede chasing the same, second wind.

And you know because you can *feel* it, the dimple in what Men cannot perceive, an absence beyond the sensible, beyond horror. You know the *Whirlwind walks*.

The No-God has returned.

"You must *do* something!"

You scream this, but your father stands stationary, like a statue, you would think, were it not for the way his immobility *raved*. Indifference, bottomless indifference, combined with an umbrage that could humble Gods. Your father's grudge could not be more personal, more clotted with the blood and hair of human outrage, and yet, somehow, it remains apiece with the spectacle before them.

Tsurumah ... Mursiris .... Mog-Pharau!

"What?" you cry scathing. "The great King-of-Tribes stands witless? Undone by the undoing of all things!"

And when your father—your true father—finally turns, *you are taken aback*, so keen is the edge in his gelid gaze, so murderous. His lips vanish, so wolfish is his sneer. His teeth are too small, too even, too white. And you understand, at last, that you are to this man what your brothers and sisters were to their true father, a lesser light wrapped in a coarser cloth.

He turns to his chieftains, and *too much seems to move*, as if the countless cat-rib scars were in fact *stitches*, something binding him to his place. And on a bolt of horror you realize he is no longer a Son of Man, your father. Sin and hatred have cut his soul from his mortal frame, and now Hell suffuses the whole.

"It matters not," he tells his proud chieftains, "what you see when you look upon this boy. *He!* He is your King-of-Tribes, now."

He swivels his gaze, grinning at each many-scarred warrior in turn. You don't see madness so much as the limits of reason shining in his turquoise eyes.

"Dare not doubt me ... *Look!* Gaze upon me, my cousins, admit what you have always known, what your drunken kinsmen murmur when the fires burn low. Look upon me and know the fell potency of my curse. Dare betray *him*, blood of my blood, and *I shall visit thee!*"

The words pinch your heart between thumb and forefinger. He turns his back on *all things*, it seems, and you stand every bit as astonished as the others and even more confused. Together you watch him, your legendary sire, *Cnaiür urs Skiötha*, the breaker-of-horses-and-men, descend the inner rim of the Occlusion and walk out alone into vast and distant machinations of doom. You even weep.

Only their terror of your father keeps you alive.

No knowledge runs so deep as knowledge of calamity; no name is more primal—or final. It is what infants wail and homicides rave. It is what old men groan as sight dwindles, and what mothers weep. It is what poets lavish with spit and pearl. *Tribulation is our maker*, the foe that so hounds us as to craft us like clay. Think on it! Tales of murder would not so enthrall us, were we not the children of survivors.

The Men of the Ordeal could feel it in the crescendo of the winds, the confluence. They could feel it in the groan that tingled through all substance. And they could feel it in the nauseous void pressed against their spine, always *there* no matter how far they managed to run, the premonition that something ... something ...

The vast flock of the Aspect-Emperor hobbled and sprinted across the Black Furnace Plain, casting aside weapons, sawing at armour. For many, shock precluded the possibility of emotion, left them little more than automata shambling across the flats. Others wept, bawled and raged as little ones bereft of some childish prize. Still others clenched their jaw against the gibbering extremes, refusing to unlock the passions rocking them.

Sheets of blasting grit soon swept the whole of Shigogli. Blood became black as oil. Grimaces were inked into faces, down to the blackened teeth, so that each was at once wretched and a mummer mocking the wretched. More and more fell to their knees convulsing for the *taste*.

Thus the Ordealmen fled, ever more obscure, ever more harrowed, a great mob drawn as a comet across the Black Furnace Plain, the infirm and the unlucky trailing the hale and the lucky, all of them running to the encampment they had seen burning. The Horde closed upon Golgotterath behind them, a chitinous rush *across all that could be seen*. The Whirlwind seized upon the sky-high billowing of the Shroud, began to feed upon it, and rags of blackness began scribbling about Golgotterath and the Upright Horn. An obese funnel climbed from great sweeping skirts of noxious black, obscuring the glint of the Carapace. The roar battered aside all hearing, save ...

TELL ME ...

Howled through the throats of thousands upon thousands of Sranc, a flood inexorably encompassing the interval separating them from the injured and the encumbered. These wretches were doomed—clouds and clots of them stumbling, even crawling through the trampled dust. The Witches and the Schoolmen, the only souls that could hope to save them, had leapt so far ahead they could no longer be seen.

Those Ordealmen at the fore of the rout called out in dismay, and stopped in the smoking ruins of their encampment. Climbing echelons of them were transfixed for the image of the Whirlwind about the Horn, gouging the Shroud from the Horde to the Vault of Heaven. They could not move. The encampment was not so much a vestige of home, the illusion of security that comes with familiarity, as a point requiring *decision*, and no one knew where they should go or what they should do. And so was each refugee undone by the indecision he found awaiting him. The bands of congestion grew deeper across the encampment's scrag perimeter.

"**Run!**" a sorcerous voice cracked—the same voice that had chased them from Golgotterath. "**For the Occlusion!**"

And rolling eyes found a figure, fur-bedecked and hermit-wild, hanging above the fugitive fields. The Holy Tutor ...

The Wizard.

"*Run for your lives!*"

⚭⚭⚭

Once, when Cnaiür was a child, a whirlwind had roared through the Utemot encampment, its shoulders in the clouds, yaksh, cattle, and lives swirling like skirts about its feet. He had watched it from a distance, wailing, clutching his father's rigid waist. Then it had vanished, like sand settling in water. He could remember his father running through the hail to assist his kinsmen. He could remember beginning to follow, then stumbling to a halt, transfixed by the vista before him as though the scale of the transformation had dwarfed his eyes' ability to believe. The great rambling web of tracks, pens, and yaksh had been utterly rewritten, as though some mountain-tall child had drawn sweeping circles with a stick. Horror had replaced familiarity, but order had replaced order.

This was a different whirlwind.

And he was no longer that child.

He was of the People, one who had so eaten of the Land as to become the Land. He was a Chieftain of the People, one who had put so many souls to dirt as to confound numbers! He was a King of the Chieftains, a descendant of Ûthgai who smashed ancient-old Kyraneas as pottery; and of Horiötha, who burned Imperial Cenei as a pyre. Their blood was his blood! Their bones were his bones! *Utemot*, the most wild and holy of the many tribes of the People.

Cnaiür urs Skiötha strode down the slopes and out across the flats heedless of the refugee masses parting about him. He stared only at *it* as he walked, his long knife in hand, cutting away his own armour and clothing piece by piece, revealing the horrendous sum of what he had taken from the World, the thousand sons and daughters violated, the thousand hearts stopped, the thousand eyes blinded. Finally he pressed his blade down his hairless pubis, and sliced away his loincloth, baring his manhood to the sting. And so he walked, a solitary man, naked save for the swazond grilling his limbs and torso, numberless totems of those *murdered* and not merely killed.

The wind scoured his striate skin, wricked his black mane. Existence was caterwaul and thunder, darkness and obscurity, vast discharges of brilliance high above, and whipping, knifing obscurities below. Existence turned upon and against the cyclopean gyre, corruption whipping blurred about glimpses of the Upright Horn.

Squinting against the maelstrom, he plunged forward. Smoke coiled from his swazond like blood from gills in rushing waters.

"KELLHUS!" he roared in no human voice, a shout that cracked the Horde's howl, that struck dust from open air.

The Whirlwind continued to feed upon the Shroud, rending and inhaling, ripping it from its roots in the Horde, spinning it into the great bulbous pillar. The creatures were almost upon him.

"I COME TO YOU AS HATE!"

Ordealmen continued to materialize in their hundreds from the shrouded tracts before him, all of them wounded or bearing wounded, all of them monkey-grimacing, faces toppling out of the maelstrom, each as bright as any *now*, any *here*, each a silvery angle on Creation.

"AS OUTRAGE AND HEART-CRACKING HUNGER!" he roared in no human voice.

A Shrial Knight emerged from the whipping murk, his white surcoat reduced to violet rags, standing at the side of a body already duned for immobility and wind. The sky had become a tortured wheel, inner rending outer, and the man hung upon the image as though straining to read, his lips moving. Beyond him, where all was shadows, the scabrous masses engulfed all, imploding about each and every flailing Ordealman. Whether heedless or oblivious, the Knight-of-the-Tusk stood motionless as the inhuman avalanche surged toward him.

Cnaiür urs Skiötha laughed as the first white-skinned figures fell hacking upon him, laughed as the screaming fish-white masses loped toward *his laughing.* thousands upon raving thousands. He laughed and spat.

"MY BREAST HAS BECOME AN OVEN, MY HEART A BLINDING COAL!"

All the World thronged with shrieking forms, white where not soiled black, a vast wave that swallowed all the survivors hobbling before it, transforming each into flowers of shaking savagery as the masses swept onward. The Whirlwind soared beyond, a monstrous fat-bellied funnel, rising distinct from great smoking sheets.

"MY THOUGHTS BURN AS OIL AND FLAX! TOO FAST! TOO FAR!"

Naked and unarmed, Cnaiür urs Skiötha, the most-violent-of-all-men, strode laughing into the Horde of Mog-Pharau ...

And it *parted* ... not for the smoke steaming from his numberless swazond, nor for the crimson glow poisoning his turquoise eyes, nor even for the shadowy presentiment of *four horns* rising about his head. The creatures did not so much veer from his infernal path *as did the Horde itself*. The abominations screeched and streamed and gesticulated as before, only in the spaces about him.

Cnaiür urs Skiötha laughed and sneered and spat fire.

"ANASÛRIMBOR!" he roared in no human voice. "HEAR ME, DECEIVER!"

Upon his every step a screaming transit opened before him, and so he walked *between* the Horde, an entity unseen, striding ground trammelled trackless.

The winds began chewing his naked skin.

"I SHALL HAVE MY OWN PORTION! MY OWN PRIZE!"

And it was mad to see so many iterations of one thing, let alone a thing so obscene as Sranc, fields of them, *plains*, unnatural teeth gnashing, beauteous faces sphinctering—fields upon fields of them!

The barbarian laughed, stood untouched amid great, wheeling shoals of the beasts. He spat fire upon them, laughed more as the creatures kicked and were ruthlessly trampled.

"YOU SHALL SUFFER AS NO SON OF MAN BEFORE YOU!" he boomed to the black tunnelling heavens, his eyes now spikes of crimson brilliance.

And in the heart of the Whirlwind he glimpsed rumours of it, the black shining jewel. He leaned back to face the heights, scarred arms askew, corded and smoking.

"A THING FOREVER PASSED AS MORSELS IN THE PIT!"

The winds had become abrasion; blood began weeping from his swazond. Smoke fluted from a thousand slits across his body.

The No-God walked ... walked to *him*.

"ANASÛRIMBOR!" he roared, his voice bestial with fury. "REVEAL THYSELF TO ME!"

A million throats answered.

TELL ME ...

The Whirlwind blotted all Creation before him, blowing bodies outward and sucking bodies up as it advanced. A million blasting needles sheared the scars from his skin, leaving his windward surfaces striped in living fire. And they roiled like burning grease within him, the indignities he had suffered, the grudges and grievances he bore! Such a toll as only murder could redeem!

"SHOW THYSELF SO THAT I MIGHT STRIKE THEE!"

Skin pealed back from tissue, sloughed as parchment. Bleeding was struck into mist.

WHAT DO YOU SEE?

Even as it blinded the wind *laid bare*, exposing structures, devouring them, displaying the lurid layers beneath. With *Hell's own eyes*, Cnaiür urs Skiötha peered up into the void and saw ... nothing.

"REVEAL! *REVEAL THYSELF!*"

Flesh disintegrated. A vicious black climbed over all things, grew numb.

WHAT AM I?

———— ❦ ————

Awe is the heart aimed at all horizons.

Awe is how we belong to what beggars our conception.

Awe redeems the vacancy of our imperium, lets us hope and hate as our fathers had hoped and hated, to strive for what the honest heart can comprehend. Awe dares souls to swell beyond the horizon, to shrug away the demented iterations, *to believe in what cannot be seen*. It calls on us to be what we were and what we remain: Men who can kill for the tale's sake.

So we might dwell in the husk of ancient certainty unto the end of our bloodless days.

So we might tremble at beauty, numb to truth.

———— ❦ ————

Noxious fumes roped the last remaining light, blackening the face of Heaven, and the roar waxed louder, though pain alone betrayed as much, and the Horde came before the Whirlwind, an oceanic flood of iron, flint, and claw. Ordealmen vanished in scrambling thousands beneath the surge, spurring those toiling ahead, the clouds hobbling through the gutted encampment, condensing into pitched chaos at the Seven Passes. The obscene multitudes rushed the slopes below, loped shrieking, howling, phalluses bent and pinked across their sunken bellies, and the Sons of Men threw back their heads, their mouths pits in their beards, their looks shining and hopeless, eyes that mirrored the flailing that is the final recourse of all blooded things. The threshing edge heaved up. Over. As hornets on honey, Sranc caged them in convulsive thrusting. Punctures welled and spouted. Skulls fractured, and faces bulged like pillows ...

Ere Hell opened and Death came swirling down.

The Horde came before the Whirlwind, aye, a deluge swamping the inner foundations of the Occlusion, and the Ordealmen began trampling their brothers, so frantically did they force the backs before them. All the guises of anguish and lunacy lunged motionless about them, faces, all of them slicked, pinched into the shapes of overthrown souls; here an Ingraul with finger bones knotted through his longbeard, his upper teeth missing; and there a splint-armoured Karyoti swaying like a sunflower with the crush and careen, lampblack running his cheeks into his plaited beard, brown eyes peering out across the continent, so that he might smile upon his children in their uncle's garden, giggling when they should be napping.

The Horde rose up, flurries become packed masses, waves swallowing wrack of tents and baggage, waves that abruptly *burned* in geometric cages of light ...

A motley band of Witches and Schoolmen hung pinned above the passes, voices gravel for abuse, singing sorcery brilliant in proportion to the murk, dispensations small as silver needles beneath the black immensity of the Whirlwind, yet sparking as beacons across the Shigogli all the same, illuminating countless raving white faces, numbers like the sands about the sea.

The Ordealmen trapped in the gullies of the Occlusion rejoiced, loosed a cry that could be seen if not heard, and some dared turn to exult in the spectacle of masses convulsing afire.

But the Sranc came before the *Whirlwind*, and the Horde, which would have shovelled itself howling into such Gnostic furnaces before, fell still ... utterly still ... leaving only the cyclone booming about vacancy.

The Shroud was inhaled from the depravities, league after league, revealing a million godlike faces impassive beneath overarching cataclysm.

The Sons of Men traded their cheers for stupefied wonder.

Mog-Pharau, the Whirlwind, *walked*, robed in tempest, crowned in lightning, and the Horde shrieked forward, terrifying for the singularity of its animating will. The Schoolmen resumed coughing and crying out their songs, disgorging fires, spinning lattices, and watched appalled as the abominations *leapt into* their phosphorescent ministries en masse, running heedless of torment, faltering only for gruesome incapacity. They advanced as a continuous, pestilential surge, flinging themselves into thrashing heaps of char and tallow, fires that grew ever fatter, ever more liquid. The Schoolmen traded warnings, retreated to what seemed more secure positions, unaware that *thousands of Chorae* had been scooped from the wrack of Golgotterath and cast with all violence forward, again and again, passing as a cloud through the body of the Horde, until taken up in slings at the foot of the Occlusion.

The surprise was all but complete. The sorcerous lights—and the scenes of riot they struck from the hip of blindness—disappeared across the Black Furnace Plain. The flesh of kings and their captains lay spilled as treasure and splendour at the feet of the Derived, meat for their rapacious hungers.

So did the Great Ordeal of Anasûrimbor Kellhus perish in salt and butchery.

APPENDIX ONE

The Encyclopaedic Glossary

Author's note:

Steeped in the classics, Inrithi scholars commonly rendered names in their Sheyic form, opting for native forms only in the absence of antique Sheyic analogues. So, for instance, the surname Coithus (which is mentioned twice by Casidas in *The Annals of Cenei*) is in fact a Sheyic version of the Gallish "Koütha," and so is rendered as such here. The surname Hoga, on the other hand, has no extant Sheyic form, and so is rendered in the original Tydonni. Kyranean place names (such as Asgilioch, Girgilioth, or Kyudea) are a notable exception.

The vast majority of the following proper names, then, are simply transliterated from their Sheyic (and in some instances Kûniüric) form. They have been translated only where their Sheyic (or Kûniüric) version does likewise. So, for instance, the Ainoni "Ratharutar," which has the Sheyic form "Retorum Ratas," is given as "the Scarlet Spires," the literal meaning of *ratas* ("red") and *retorum* ("towers"). The etymological provenance and translated meaning of place names can be found bracketed at the end of certain entries.

These would be the names as Drusas Achamian knew them.

A

Abbarsallas (4068–4106)—Mimara's owner during her first five years in Carythusal.

Abenjukala—The classic treatise on benjuka, written anonymously in Near Antiquity. Because of its emphasis on the relation between benjuka and wisdom, many consider it a classic philosophical text as well.

Abskinis—"Groundless-Grave" (Ihrimsû). Vast well plumbing the Upright Horn, where the Consult casts the bodies of those killed in the Golden Room, by the Carapace or otherwise.

Absolute, the—Among the Dûnyain, the state of becoming "unconditioned," a perfect self-moving soul independent of "what comes before." See *Dûnyain* and *Conditioning, the*.

Abstractions—An epithet for Gnostic sorceries. See *Gnosis, the*, and *Metagnosis, the*.

aculmirsi—Literally, "milestone man," the epithet used by Near-Antique dramaturges to describe those who travelled for the sake of travelling.

Adûnyani—"Little Dûnyain" (Kûniüric from Ûmeritic *ar'tûnya*, or "little truth"). The name taken by the followers assembled by Kellhus in Atrithau.

Aenaratiol—"Smokehorn" (Aujic). The mountain housing the derelict Nonman Mansion of Cil-Aujas.

Aëngelas (4087–4112)—A Werigdan warrior.

Aenkû Aumor—Ancient Meöri fortress that once guarded Kelmeol, capital of the Meöri Empire.

Aenkû Maimor—Ancient Meöri fortress that once guarded Telmeol, now a scalper entrepot called Fatwall.

Aethelarius VI (4062–4132)—(Sheyic form of Athullara) The King of Atrithau, last of the line of Morghund, killed leading his Men against Cnaiür urs Skiotha and his Scylvendi at the Battle of Eels.

Aeviternal Seal—A great, ornamental plaque unique to every Nonman Mansion, typically set behind the king's throne, widely thought to be the most sacred of their relics. According to the *Holy Juurl*, the primary scripture of the Nonmen, Imimorûl, who had hacked off his shield arm to create the Nonmen, took Siol, the House Primordial, as his shield against the Starving (sky). As a symbolic "Shield of Imimorûl," each Seal was thought to be invested, if not imbued, with the essence of its respective Mansion. "Crack the Shield," an old proverb went, "sunder the Mountain."

Agabon, Coithus (4124–4132)—Ordealman and youngest son of King Coithus Narnol, among the first to perish on the Great Ordeal's trek across the Istyuli Plains.

Agansanor—A province of south central Ce Tydonn, noted for the lengthy beards and martial zeal of its sons.

Age of Bronze—Another name for Far Antiquity, during which bronze was the dominant metal technology of Men.

Age of Cenei—The era of Ceneian dominance of the Three Seas, from the conquest of Nilnamesh in 2478 until the Sack of Cenei in 3351. See *Ceneian Empire*.

Age of Kyraneas—The era of Kyranean dominance of the northwestern Three Seas, beginning with the Kyranean victory at Narakit in 1591, and ending with the Breaking of Mehtsonc in 2154.

Age of Warring Cities—The era following the dissolution of Kyraneas (c. 2158) until the rise of Cenei as a dominant power in 2349, characterized by perpetual warfare between the cities of the Kyranae Plain.

Aghurzoi—"Cut Tongue" (Ihrimsû). The language of the Sranc. It was long disputed among the Cûnuroi whether the Sranc could be said to possess any language at all given their *lack of souls*. Among those who had long, hard experience of the Sranc, their possession of language was a murderous fact. But Quya sages such as the venerated Yi'yariccas asked how Sranc words could *mean* given their lack of experience altogether. What could a language without meaning possibly be? The answer that eventually became dogma was that the Sranc tongue was a form of "Dark Speech," speaking without consciousness of speaking, exchanging "Dark Meaning," which, although nowhere allowing reflection, or *choice of words*, served the bestial requirements of the Sranc quite fine. Damial'isharin—a Siolan Ishroi who found himself trapped for five days (hidden in a dead fall) in the heart of an itinerant clan camp—famously claimed the Sranc possessed social customs and regimes very nearly as complicated as their own. Based on his account, several scholars (such as the famously heretical Lurijara) went so far as to argue that *all language was dark*, and that meaning was the province of the sorcerer and the Gods alone. Few lent credence to such extreme views, however.

Agmundr—A province of northeastern Galeoth, located beneath the Osthwai Mountains, south of Bayal.

Agnotum Market—The main bazaar of Iothiah, dating back to the days of Cenei.

agoglian bulls—Ancient Kyranean symbols of virility and fortune. The most famous examples are found in the Hagerna opposite the Vault-of-the-Tusk.

Agongorea—"Fields of Woe" (Kûniüric). The famed "Field Appalling" in the days of the Ancient North. The blasted lands to the west of the River Sursa and north of the Neleost Sea. Given extant Nonman accounts of Arkfall, most Three Seas scholars believe (as, indeed, their Far Antique counterparts believed) that Agongorea was an unnatural consequence of the debris thrown up by the impact of the Incû-Holoinas.

Agonic Collar—A sorcerous artifact of the Ancient North, reputedly crafted by the Mihtrûlic Gnostic School. According to Mandate scholars, the purpose of the Agonic Collar was analogous to that of the Uroborian Circle utilized by the Anagogic Schools of the Three Seas, namely, to inflict excruciating pain on the wearer should he attempt to utter any sorcerous incantation.

Agonies—The name for the Gnostic Cants of Torment, a reputed specialty of the Mangaecca.

Ainoni—The language of High Ainon, derived from Ham-Kheremic.

Ajencis (c. 1896–2000)—The father of syllogistic logic and algebra, held by many to be the greatest of all philosophers. Born in the Kyranean capital of Mehtsonc, he is reputed to have never once left his city, even during the horrific plagues of 1991, when his advanced age made his death a near certainty. (According to various sources, Ajencis bathed on a daily basis and refused to drink water drawn from city wells, claiming that these practices, combined with a distaste for drunkenness and a moderate diet, were the keys to his health.) Many commentators, both antique and contemporary, complain that there are as many Ajencises as there are readers of Ajencis. Though this is certainly true of his more speculative works (such as *Theophysics* or *The First Analytic of Men*), his work does possess a discernible and consistent skeptical core, primarily exemplified in *The Third Analytic of Men*, which also happens to be his most cynical work. For Ajencis, Men by and large "make their weaknesses, not reason or the world, the primary measure of what they hold true." In fact, he observed that most individuals possess no criteria whatsoever for their beliefs. As a so-called critical philosopher, one might have supposed he would eventually share the fate of other critical philosophers, such as Porsa (the famed "Philosopher-Whore" of Trysë) or Kumhurat. Only his reputation and the structure of Kyranean society saved him from the vicissitudes of the mob. As a child, he was allegedly such a prodigy that the High King himself took notice of him, granting him what was called "Protection" at the unprecedented age of eight. Protection was an ancient and hallowed Kyranean institution; the Protected were those who could say anything without fear of reprisal, even to the High King. Ajencis continued speaking until he suffered a stroke and died at the venerable age of 103.

Ajokli—The God of thievery and deception. Also known as the Four-Horned Brother. Though listed among the primary Gods in *The Chronicle of the Tusk*, there is no true Cult of Ajokli, but rather an informal network of devotees scattered across the great cities of the Three Seas. The lack of any organizing institutions has transformed the Cult into the skulking, criminal embodiment of its skulking, criminal Master. The high priests of the Cult, insofar as it possesses any, are its Narindar, the most deadly of the most deadly assassins.

Ajokli is oft mentioned in the secondary scriptures of the different Cults, sometimes as a mischievous companion of the Gods, other times as a cruel or malicious competitor. In the *Mar'eddat*, he is the faithless husband of Gierra. In the *Book of Gods* he is nothing less than the dread enemy of mankind, the one God too hungry to remain in the Outside. In the *Book of Hintarates* he is the same, but depleted for his endless grasping, and so reduced to craft and insinuation. The fractured image presented in the scriptures is expressed in the sheer number of names used to reference him or his work: the Trickster, the Thief, the Four-Horned Brother, the Bald-faced, the Grinning God, Immortal Malice, the Prince of Hate, the Rake, among others.

Ajowai—A mountain fastness in the north Hinayati Mountains that serves as the administrative capital of Girgash.

akal—The defunct base monetary unit of Kian.

Akeokinoi—The fortress watchtowers the Nonmen raised upon certain peaks of the Occlusion during the Second Watch.

Akirapita, Shoddû (4099–4123)–Eldest son of Shoddû Rapita III, King of Nilnamesh, and perhaps the most brilliant and resourceful Orthodox general of the Unification Wars.

Akkeägni—he God of disease. Also known as the God of a Thousand Hands. Scholars have oft noted the irony that the Priesthood of Disease provides the primary repository of physicians for the Three Seas. How can one at once worship disease and war against it? According to the scriptures of the Cult, the *Piranavas*, Akkeägni is a so-called Bellicose God, one who favours those who strive against him over sycophants and worshippers.

Akksersia—A lost nation of the Ancient North. Though the White Norsirai of the north shore of the Cerish Sea lacked any sustained contact with the Nonmen, they gradually became the second great seat of Norsirai civilization. Akksersia was founded in 811 by Salaweärn I, following the dissolution of the Cond Yoke. Though originally confined to the city of Myclai, her commercial and administrative capital, the nation gradually extended its hegemony, first along the length of the River Tywanrae, then across the plains of Gâl and the entire north shore of the Cerish Sea. By the time of the First Great Sranc War in 1251, it was the largest of the ancient Norsirai nations, incorporating almost all the White Norsirai tribes save those of the Istyuli Plains. It fell to the No-God after three disastrous defeats in 2149. Akksersian colonists on the Cerish Sea's heavily forested south shore would form the nucleus of what would become the Meörn Empire.

Akksersian—The lost language of ancient Akksersia, and "purest" of the Nirsodic tongues.

Akkunihor—A Scylvendi tribe of the central Steppe. As the tribe closest to the Imperial frontier, the Akkunihor are the traditional brokers of Three Seas rumour and knowledge among the Scylvendi.

Algari (4041–4111)—A body-slave to Prince Nersei Proyas.

Alimir–"Divider" (Ihrimsû). The legendary ensorcelled sword of the Kûniüric High-Kings, famed for possessing the Edge Peerless, and when wielded with skill, capable of halving mammoths. Lost at the Battle Eleneöt with Anasûrimbor Kelmomas in 2146.

Alkussi—A Scylvendi tribe of the central Steppe.

"All heaven cannot shine through a single crack ..."—The famous line attributed to the poet Protathis suggesting that no man can be trusted with divine revelation.

Allosian Forum—The great judicial galleries located at the foot of the Andiamine Heights.

Allosium Mandala—Famed Nilnameshi prayer-tapestry prominently displayed in the Allosium Forum, famed for being the first to incorporate concentric design motifs.

Am-Amidai—A large Kianene fortress located in the heart of the Atsushan Highlands, raised in 4054.

amicut—A ration used by Scylvendi warriors on the trail, consisting of wild herbs and berries beaten into dried sections of beef.

Amiolas—Sorcerous, face-encasing helm allowing the wearer to understand Ihrimsû, widely regarded as one of the most powerful Emilidic artifacts. Despite the miracles of sorcery, *translation* had (and has) remained stubbornly impervious to arcane facilitation. The genius of Emilidis was primarily metaphysical: he grasped the *continuity of meaning and souls*, how a sorcerous understanding of Ihrimsû entailed a *sorcerous unification of disparate souls*. Inventing new forms of sorcery as he proceeded, Emilidis imbued his helm with the soul of Immiriccas Cinialrig, the infamous Malcontent, an Injori Ishroi condemned to die by Cu'jara Cinmoi, and given the choice by Nil'giccas between risking the Hells or dwelling forever as an amputated, interpreting soul.

The Amiolas surfaces in human histories at several junctures, including protracted periods where Kings and Grandmasters refused to wear what the Umeri called the Embalming-Skull, and the Kûniüri, the Cauldron, fearing it to be a weapon (which it almost certainly became on occasion). According to Sohonc scholars, the Amiolas melted the contents of Immiriccas into the warmer waters of the wearer's soul, creating a composite, a morass that would dry out for some, deepen for others. Ihrimsû would come effortlessly, only twisted in every respect about the hard fibre of the Malcontent, the architecture of his ancient old soul. Though no records exist of wearers admitting to what had to be a profound transformation of identity, Mandate scholars report that Seswatha forever regretted demanding it from Nil'giccas, even though the information it provided allowed him and Nau-Kayûti to steal the Heron Spear, and so save the World.

Ammegnotis—A city on the south bank of the River Sempis, raised during the Kyranean New Dynasty.

Amortanea—The merchant carrack that bore Achamian and Xinemus to Joktha.

Amoteu—A governorate of Kian, located on the southern edge of the Meneanor Sea. Like all the nations in the shadow of the Betmulla Mountains, Amoteu, or Holy Amoteu as it is sometimes called, grew in the influential shadow of Old Dynasty Shigek. According to extant inscriptions, the Shigeki referred to both Xerash and Amoteu as Hut-Jartha, the "Land of the Jarti," or as Huti-Parota, the "Middle-Lands." The Jarti were the dominant Ketyai tribe of the region, to which the Amoti and several others were tributaries before the Shigeki conquest. But with the extensive cultivation of the Shairizor Plains, and the slow rise of Shimeh and Kyudea along the River Jeshimal, the balance of power slowly shifted. For centuries the Middle-Lands found themselves the battleground between Shigek and her southern competitors, Eumarna across the Betmulla Mountains and ancient or Vapartic Nilnamesh. In 1322, Anzumarapata II, the Nilnameshi King of Invishi, crushed the Shigeki and, in an effort to secure his conquests, transplanted hundreds of thousands of indigent Nilnameshi on the Plains of Heshor, an act that would long outlive his brief empire (the Shigeki reconquered the Middle-Lands in 1349). With the collapse of Shigeki regional dominance in 1591, the Jarti attempted to reassert their ancestral control—with disastrous consequences. The resulting war gave rise to a brief Amoti Empire, which reached the length of the Betmulla to the frontier of the Carathay Desert. All the Middle-Lands would fall under the power of Kyraneas in 1703.

With the dissolution of Kyraneas, c. 2158, Amoteu enjoyed its second—and last—period of independence, though now the Xerashi, the descendants of Anzumarapata's settlers, had become its primary competitors. This second "golden age" would witness Inri Sejenus, and the slow growth of the faith that would eventually come to dominate the Three Seas. After a brief period of Xerashi occupation, Amoteu would suffer a long succession of foreign overlords, each leaving its own stamp: first the Ceneians, who conquered the Middle-Lands in 2414, then the Nansur in 3574, and finally the Kianene in 3845. Despite the peace and prosperity enjoyed by other conquered provinces, the early years of Ceneian rule would prove particularly bloody for Amoteu. In 2458, while Triamis the Great was still in his infancy, Inrithi fanatics led the province in a vicious rebellion against Cenei. As punishment, Emperor Siaxas II butchered the inhabitants of Kyudea and razed the city to the ground.

Amoti—The language of Amoteu, a derivative of Mamati.

Amrezzer the Black (1753–1897)—Legendary Surartu Grandmaster responsible for securing the river fortress of Kiz in Far Antique Carythusal, c. 1800, called the "Black" for his propensity to burn down the homes of those opposed to him.

Anagkë—The Goddess of fortune. Also known as "the Whore of Fate." Anagkë is one of the primary "Compensatory Gods," which is to say, one who rewards devotion in life with paradise in the afterlife. Her Cult is extremely popular in the Three Seas, especially among the higher, political castes.

Anagogis—A branch of sorcery that turns on the resonances between meanings and concrete things.

In Kellian metaphysics, there is the *meaning that is being*, the meaning that is your angle upon the world, and then there is the *meaning that inflects being*, merely. This latter we know as everyday writing and speech, whereas the former is the province of sorcery and religion. To be a soul is to be at once an angle *on* the world and to *be the world*, but one small angle that existence possesses on existence—on itself. The so-called Many, given their blindness to being, cannot close the circuit of thought and being. The Few can see the onta, however, and so can, given the proper rigour and training, close the circuit of thought and being, work what appear to be miracles. As it turns out, there are two quite different ways of deriving being from thought, one analogical (as with the Anagogis and the Iswazi) and the other inferential (as with the

Gnosis and Metagnosis). So where the Gnosis deals directly with abstract forces, the Anagogis deals with substances embodying those forces. The Anagogis is, once again deferring to Kellian metaphysical parlance, a *phenomenological* sorcerous art, relying on the densities of experiential meaning as described to drive the manifestations. The Gnosis, by contrast, is a *formal* sorcerous art. Both rely on the same intellectual gymnastics (essentially, speaking and thinking different yet intricately interrelated things simultaneously), but they draw their semantic force very different sources, much as poetry and mathematics do.

Throughout history, the Scarlet Spires has consistently been the most innovative of the Anagogic Schools, which is why a good fraction of the Anagogic Canon is derived from their research, Cants such as the infamous Dragonhead or Houlari Twin-Tempests.

Analogies—An alternate name for Anagogic sorceries.

Anasûrimbor Dynasty—The ruling dynasty of Kûniüri from 1408 to 2147. See *Apocalypse*.

Anaxophus V (2109–2156)—The Kyranean High King who wielded the Heron Spear against the No-God at Mengedda in 2155.

ancestor scroll—A scroll kept by most pious Inrithi, bearing the names of all the dead ancestors who might intercede on their behalf. Since the Inrithi believe that honour and glory in life brings power in the afterlife, they are particularly proud of renowned ancestors and ashamed of known sinners.

Ancient North—The name given to the Norsirai civilization destroyed in the Apocalypse.

Ancilline Gate—One of the so-called Lesser Gates of Momemn, located to the immediate south of the Girgallic Gate.

Andiamine Heights—The primary residence and principal administrative seat of Nansur Emperors, located on the seaward walls of Momemn.

Anfirig, Thagawain (4057–4114)—Man-of-the-Tusk, and the Galeoth Earl of Gesindal.

Angeshraël (?–?)—The most famed Old Prophet of the Tusk, responsible for leading the Five Tribes of Men into Eärwa. Also known as the Burnt Prophet for bowing his face into his fire after confronting Husyelt at the foot of Mount Eshki. His wife was Esmenet.

Angka—The ancient Norsirai name for Zeüm.

animas—The "moving force" of all existence, typically analogized as the "breath of God." Much ink has been spilt over the question of the relation between animas, which is primarily a theological concept, and the sorcerous concept of "onta." Most scholars are of the opinion that the latter is simply a secular version of the former.

Anissi (c. 4089–4113)—The favourite wife of Cnaiür urs Skiötha.

Ankaryotis—A demon of the Outside, one of the more manageable Potents controlled by the Scarlet Spires.

Ankharlus—A famed Kûniüric commentator and high priest of Gilgaöl.

Ankirioth—A province of south central Conriya.

Ankmuri—The lost language of ancient Angka.

Ankulakai—The mountain on the southern limit of the Demua that cradles the city of Atrithau.

Anmergal, Skinede (4078–4112)—Man-of-the-Tusk. A Tydonni thane, slain at the Battle of Tertae Fields.

Annals of Cenei, The—The classic treatise of Casidas, covering the history of Cenei and the Ceneian Empire from the Imperial City's legendary foundation in 809 to the time of Casidas's death in 3142.

Annand—A province of north central Conriya, known primarily for its silver and iron mines. "All the silver in Annand" is a common Three Seas expression, meaning "pricelessness."

Anochirwa—"Horns Reaching" (Kûniüric) An early mannish name for Golgotterath.

Anphairas, Ikurei—See *Ikurei Anphairas I*.

Anplei—The second-largest city in Conriya after Aöknyssus.

anpoi—A traditional drink throughout the Three Seas, made of fermented peach nectar.

Ansacer ab Salajka (4072–4116)—The Sapatishah-Governor of Gedea. The Black Gazelle is his totem.

Ansansius, Teres (c. 2300–2351)—The most famed theologian of the early Thousand Temples, whose *The City of Men*, *The Limping Pilgrim*, and *Five Letters to All* are revered by Shrial scholars.

Anserca—The southernmost province of the Nansur Empire.

Antanamera—A province of High Ainon, located on the highland frontier of Jekk.

Antareg—The westernmost mountain of the Urokkas, at once the roof of ancient Viri and the foundation of Dagliash.

Anûnuarcû—Ancient Kûniüric province located west of Ûmer and south of Far Wuor, famed as a Sranc frontier and the birthplace of heroes.

Anwurat—A large Kianene fortress to the south of the Sempis Delta, constructed in 3905.

Anyasiri—"Tongueless Howlers" (Ihrimsû). An early Cûnuroi name for the Sranc.

Aöknyssus—The administrative and commercial capital of Conriya. Once the capital of the long-lost Shiradi Empire, Aöknyssus is perhaps the most ancient of the Three Seas' great cities, with the possible exception of Sumna or Iothiah.

Aörsi—A lost nation of the Ancient North. Aörsi was founded in the 1556 partitioning of Greater Kûniüri between the sons of Anasûrimbor Nanor-Ukkerja I at his death. Even contemporaries recognized Aörsi as the most warlike of the ancient Norsirai nations, though her ambitions remained uniquely defensive rather than expansionist. Sparsely populated save for the regions surrounding her capital, Shiarau, Aörsi faced considerable and unrelenting pressure from the Sranc and Bashrag tribes of the Yimaleti Mountains to the north, not to mention the Consult legions of Golgotterath across the River Sursa to the west—a challenge that would spur the construction of Dagliash, the greatest fortress of the age. It is no accident that the word *sursa* came to mean "front line" across the Ancient North.

Aörsi's history is one of ingenuity and determination in the face of never-ending crises. Perhaps it is fitting that her destruction in 2136 (see *Apocalypse*) was due more to the betrayal of her southern Kûniüric cousins than to any real failure on the part of Anasûrimbor Nimeric, her final King.

Aparvishi—Fortress protecting the Invittal, the great belt of cultivation feeding Invishi.

Apiary—The highest halls of Ishterebinth, the only enjoying sunlight, though at the price of wasted air and deep chill.

Apocalypse—System Initiation. The protracted wars and atrocities that obliterated the Ancient North. The roots of the Apocalypse are many and deep. Mandate scholars (who, popular opinion to the contrary, are not the recognized authorities on the subject) argue that they are older than recorded history. More sober accounts reach back no further than the so-called Nonman Tutelage, which eventually led the Gnostic School of Mangaecca to the site of the Incû-Holoinas, the Ark-of-the-Skies, where it lay protected, hidden by Nonmen glamours in the shadow of the western Yimaleti Mountains. Accounts are incomplete, but it seems clear that what were called the Great Sranc Wars were a consequence of the Mangaecca occupation of what would come to be called Golgotterath.

Traditionally, scholars date the beginning of the Apocalypse with Anasûrimbor Celmomas's call for a holy war against Golgotterath, his Great Ordeal, which is to say, with the beginning of the accounts found in *The Sagas*, the primary historical source text for this cataclysmic event. Legend has it that Nonmen Siqu informed the Grandmaster of the Sohonc (the pre-eminent Sauglish School) that the Mangaecca, or Consult as they had come to be called, had uncovered lost Inchoroi secrets that would lead to the world's destruction. Seswatha in turn convinced Celmomas to declare war on Golgotterath in 2123.

There has been much debate regarding the next twenty years, and much criticism of the pride and bickering that would eventually destroy the Ordeal. What most fail to realize is that the threat facing the High Norsirai of Kûniüri and Aörsi at this time was entirely hypothetical. In fact, it is surprising that Celmomas was able to hold his coalition, which included Nonmen as well as token contingents of Kyraneans, together for as long as he did.

The first great battle, fought in 2124 on the Plains of Agongorea, was indecisive. Celmomas and his allies wintered in Dagliash and forded the River Sursa the following spring, catching their foe unawares. The Consult withdrew to Golgotterath, and so began what would be called the Great Investiture. For six years the Ordeal attempted to starve the Consult into submission, to no avail. Every assault proved disastrous. Then, in 2131, after a dispute with King Nimeric of Aörsi, Celmomas himself abandoned his own Holy War. The following year disaster struck. Consult legions, apparently utilizing a vast subterranean network of tunnels, appeared in the Ring Mountains to the rear of the Ordeal. The coalition host was all but destroyed. Embittered by the loss of his sons, Nil'giccas, the Nonman King of Ishterebinth, withdrew altogether, leaving the Aörsi to war alone.

The following years witnessed a string of further disasters. In 2133 the Aörsi were defeated at the Passes of Amnerlot, and Dagliash was lost soon after. King Nimeric withdrew to his capital of Shiarau. A year passed before Celmomas acknowledged his folly and mobilized to relieve him. By then it was too late. In 2135, Nimeric was mortally wounded in the Battle of Hamuir, and Shiarau fell to the Consult legions the following spring. The Aörsic House of Anasûrimbor had perished forever.

Now it was Kûniüri that stood alone. His credibility destroyed, Celmomas was unable to rally any allies, and for a time the situation seemed bleak. But in 2137 his youngest son, Nau-Cayûti, managed to rout the Consult at the Battle of Ossirish, where he earned the name Murswagga, or "Dragonslayer," for killing Tanhafut the Red. His next victory, within sight of Shiarau's ruins, was more complete still. The Consult's remaining Sranc and Bashrag fled across the River Sursa. In 2139 the young Prince besieged and recaptured Dagliash, then launched several spectacular raids across the Plains of Agongorea.

Then, in 2140, Nau-Cayûti's beloved concubine, Aulisi, was abducted by Sranc marauders and taken to Golgotterath. According to *The Sagas*, Seswatha was able to convince the Prince (who was once his student) that she could be rescued from the Incû-Holoinas, and the two of them embarked on an expedition that is almost certainly apocryphal. Mandate commentators dispute the account found in *The Sagas*, where they successfully return with both Aulisi and the Heron Spear, claiming that Aulisi in fact was never found. Whatever happened, at least two things are certain: the Heron Spear was recovered, and Nau-Cayûti died shortly after (apparently poisoned by his first wife, Iëva).

In 2141, the Consult returned to the offensive, wrongly thinking the Kûniüri crippled by the loss of their greatest and most beloved son. But Nau-Cayûti's mead-brothers proved themselves able, even brilliant, commanders. At the Battle of Skothera, the Sranc hordes were crushed by General En-Kaujalau, though he died of mysterious causes within weeks of this victory (according to *The Sagas*, he was another victim of Iëva and her poisons, but again this is disputed by Mandate scholars). In 2142, General Sag-Marmau inflicted yet another crushing defeat on Aurang and his Consult legions, and by the fall of that year he had hounded the remnant of their horde to the Gates of Golgotterath itself.

But the Second Great Investiture proved far shorter than the first. As Seswatha had feared, the Consult had been merely playing for time, nothing more. In the spring of 2143 the No-God, summoned by means unknown, first drew breath. Across the world, Sranc, Bashrag, and Wracu—all the obscene progeny of the Inchoroi—hearkened to his call. Sag-Marmau and the greater glory of Kûniüri were annihilated.

The effect of His coming cannot be overestimated. As numerous independent accounts attest, all Men could sense his dread presence on the horizon, and all infants were born dead. Anasûrimbor Celmomas II had little difficulty gathering support for his Second Ordeal. Nil'giccas and Celmomas were reconciled. Across Eärwa, hosts of Men began marching toward Kûniüri.

But it was too late.

Celmomas and his Second Ordeal were destroyed on the Fields of Eleneöt in 2146. The Heron Spear, which could not be used because the No-God refused to give battle, was lost. Kûniüri and all the great and ancient cities of the River Aumris were destroyed the following year. The Nonmen of Injor-Niyas retreated to Ishterebinth. Eämnor was laid waste the following year, though its capital, Atrithau, raised on anarcane ground, managed to survive. The list continues. Akkseisia and Harmant in 2149. The Meöri Empire in 2150. Inweära in 2151, though the city of Sakarpus was spared. The Shiradi Empire in 2153.

The Battle of Kathol Pass, fought primarily by the remnants of the Meöri and the Nonmen of Cil-Aujas in the autumn of 2151, would be mankind's only victory during these dark years, one which was entirely undone when the Meöri turned on their benefactors and sacked the ancient Nonman Mansion the following spring (which gave birth to the myth that the Galeoth, the descendants of those Meöri refugees, were forever cursed with treachery and fractiousness).

Though defeated at the Battle of Mehsarunath in 2154, Anaxophus V, the High King of Kyraneas, managed to save the core of his host and flee southward, abandoning Mehtsonc and Sumna to the Scylvendi. The Tusk was evacuated and brought to ancient Invishi in Nilnamesh. Though the historical record is scant, Mandate scholars insist that it was at this time that the High King admitted to Seswatha that his knights had rescued the Heron Spear from the Fields of Eleneöt eight years previously.

Perhaps no single event from these dark times has inspired more acrimony and debate among Three Seas scholars of the Apocalypse. Some historians, the great Casidas among them, have called this the most monstrous deception in history. How could Anaxophus conceal the only weapon that could defeat the No-God while the greater part of the world died? But others, including many belonging to the Mandate, argue precisely the opposite. They admit that Anaxophus's motive—to save Kyraneas and Kyraneas alone—was more than a little suspect. But they point to the fact that had he not hidden the Heron Spear, it would surely have been lost in the catastrophes following the Fields of Eleneöt and the destruction of the Second Ordeal. According to extant accounts, not once did the No-God expose himself to battle during this time. It was the years of attrition that forced him to intercede in the Battle of Mengedda.

Whatever the case, the No-God, or Tsuramah as the Kyraneans called him, was destroyed by Anaxophus V in 2155. Freed of his terrible will, his Sranc, Bashrag, and Wracu slaves dispersed. The Apocalypse had ended, and Men set out to recover what they could of a ruined world.

Apple Garden—A courtyard grove of the Fama Palace famed for the ancient dolmens found within it.

apples—Galeoth slang for severed heads gathered as trophies.

Apportioning—Once the ritual division of spoils between conquering Ishroi, now debased into a slave auction.

Araxes Mountains—A range forming the eastern frontiers of both Ce Tydonn and Conriya.

Arcastor, Linnû (4095–4132)—Ordealman, Earl of Gesindal, killed and the Battle of Imweor.

Archipontus of Wûl—Bridge on the River Nary once famed across the Ancient North, now a ruin in the Meori Wilderness.

Architect—An epithet used by skin-spies to describe their Consult makers.

Arithmeas—The Prime Augur to Ikurei Xerius III.

Ark-of-the-Skies—See *Incû-Holoinas.*

Arobindant, the—Traditional name given to the now-obliterated Siolan fortress overlooking Golgotterath during the First and Second Watch.

Arsoghul, Nepimit (4097–4132)—Ordealman, Satrap of Hawis'amparesh, killed in the days preceding the disaster at Irsûlor.

Arweal (4077–4111)—Man-of-the-Tusk. One of the Nascenti, formerly a client thane of Earl Werijen, claimed by disease at Caraskand.

Ascension—The direct passage of Inri Sejenus to the Outside as described in "The Book of Days" in *The Tractate.* According to Inrithi tradition, Sejenus ascended from the Juterum, or the Sacred Heights, in Shimeh, though *The Tractate* seems to suggest that Kyudea and not Shimeh was the location. The First Temple was purportedly raised on the very location.

Asgilioch—"The Gate of Asga" (Kyranean from Kemkaric *geloch*) The great Nansur fortress, dating back to Far Antiquity, guarding the so-called Southron Gates in the Unaras Spur. Perhaps no Three Seas fortress can claim such a storied past (which includes, most recently, stopping no fewer than three Fanim invasions). Over the years the Nansur have coined many epithets for the famed stronghold, among them Hubara, or "the Breakers."

Aspect-Emperor—The title taken by Triamis the Great in the twenty-third year of his rule (when the Shriah, Ekyannus III, formally institutionalized the so-called

Emperor Cult) and adopted by all his successors. The title also taken by Anasûrimbor Kellhus I following the capitulation of Shimeh to the First Holy War.

Athjeäri, Coithus (4089–4112) — Man-of-the-Tusk. The Earl of the Galeoth region of Gaenri, and nephew to Coithus Saubon. Legendary hero of the "Pommel Psalms," a series of lays recounting his many deeds of valour during the First Holy War.

Atikkoros — "Tower of Horses" (Kyranean). Oldest structure in the Petotic, the traditional residence of the Conriyan Kings, originally the citadel of the ancient Shiradi fortress of Impuxû, and famed to this day for its megalithic "tower wall" construction. The Kyranean name dates to the time of the Ceneian Empire, when the citadel was renamed to commemorate the 2543 defeat of the Famiri on the Plain of Shorimurra.

Atkondo-Atyoki — The language group of the Satyothi pastoralists of the Atkondras Mountains and surrounding regions.

Atkondras Mountains — Perhaps the greatest range west of the Kayarsus, running from the Sea of Jorua to the Great Ocean, and effectively sealing Zeüm from the rest of Eärwa.

Atrithau — The ancient administrative and commercial capital of what was once Fämnor, and one of two Norsirai cities to have survived the Apocalypse. Atrithau is peculiar in that it is built upon what is called "anarcane ground," which is to say, ground that renders sorcery impotent, found at the foot of Mount Ankulakai. It was originally founded *c.* 570 as the fortress Ara-Etrith ("New Etrith") by the famed Umeri God-King Carû-Ongonean.

Atrithi — The language of Atrithau, derived from Eämnoric.

Atsushan Highlands — The arid hill country of the Gedean interior.

Attong Plateau — "Missing Tower" (from Kyranean *att anoch*). Also known as the Attong Gap. The famous opening in the Hethanta Mountains, and the traditional invasion route of the Scylvendi.

Attrempus — "Tower of Respite" (Kyranean). The sister fortress of Atyersus, founded in 2158 by Seswatha and the nascent School of Mandate, and held in trust by House Nersei of Conriya since 3921.

Atyersus — "Tower of Warning" (Kyranean). The sister fortress of Attrempus, founded in 2157 by Seswatha and other Gnostic survivors of the Apocalypse. Atyersus is the primary stronghold of the Mandate.

Auja-Gilcûnni — The lost "ground tongue" of the Nonmen. See *Languages of the Nonmen.*

Aujic — The lost tongue of the Nonmen Aujan Mansions.

Aulyanau Cawa-Imvullar (*c.* 1091–1124)—Emperor of the Pseudo-Ûmeri Empire, known primarily for his defeat at the hands of the Scintya, and the crippling tribute he and his successors were forced to pay.

Aulyanau the Conqueror (895–950)—Legendary ruler of the Cond who defeated Cel-Ongonean at the Battle of River Axau, leading to the Breaking of Ûmerau and the beginning of the Cond Yoke. His subsequent campaigns would unite the Norsirai for the first time since Uskelt Wolfheart. Since references to Aulyanau typically signalled pan-Norsirai sympathies among Middlenorth caste-nobles (particularly the Tydonni), Anasûrimbor Kellhus declared an Excision in 4128, striking all record of his name and famously executing several notables who continued to pretend that such a personage had ever existed.

Aumri-Saugla—The language group of the ancient Norsirai peoples of the Aumris Valley.

Aumris River—The primary river system of northwest Eärwa, draining the greater Istyuli basin and emptying into the Neleöst Sea. The River Aumris is also the cradle of Norsirai civilization. Over a relatively brief period of time, the High Norsirai tribes that settled the rich alluvial plains along the lower Aumris founded the first cities of Men, including Trysë, Sauglish, Etrith, and Ûmerau. As the result of trade with the Nonmen of Injor-Niyas, the power and sophistication of the Aumris River civilization grew quickly, culminating in the Trysean Empire under the God-King Cûnwerishau in the fourth century.

Aurang (?– — "The Warlord" (Kûniüric). A surviving Prince of the Inchoroi and Horde-General to the No-God during the Apocalypse. Very little is known of Aurang, save that he is a ranking member of the Consult and the twin brother of Aurax. Horde-General, Sin-Pharion ("Deceiving Angel"), and Sarpanur represent some of the more significant names he has earned over the ages.

Aurax (?– —A surviving Prince of the Inchoroi. Very little is known of Aurax, save that he is a ranking member of the Consult and the twin brother of Aurang. Mandate scholars speculate that it was he who first taught the Tekne to the Mangaecca.

Auvangshei—Famed Ceneian fortress on the extreme western frontier of Nilnamesh, often symbolically invoked as the limit of the known world, which is to say, the Three Seas. Successively occupied and abandoned over the years, it would be rebuilt by Anasûrimbor Kellhus in 4123, following the Zaudunyani conquest of Nilnamesh.

Avalunsil (c. 820–c. 860)—The legendary, Far Antique Ûmeri princess who murdered Symaul—the Skettic Chieftain who had executed her father, Wulta-Ongorean—with a fish knife, so giving birth to the family of Bardic lays called the *Harsunci*, or "fish knives." She would go on to be the first (and only) Empress of the All, or Ûmeri Empire. According to various tales in the cycle, she was called the "Twice-Flowered" for her refusal to marry, and was ultimately assassinated by one of her suitors.

Avowels—The classic text by Olekaros, which poses as a "spiritual exploration" but is in actual fact little more than a collection of wise sayings from various thinkers in various nations. Its Sheyic translation enjoys widespread popularity among caste-noble lay readers in the Three Seas.

B

bagaratta—The "sweeping way" of Scylvendi sword fighting.

Bajeda, Straits of—The straits separating the southwestern tip of Nron from the southeastern extremities of Cironj.

Balait urs Kututha (4072–4110)—A Scylvendi warrior of the Utemot tribe, and Cnaiür urs Skiötha's brother-in-law.

Bandit Padirajah—See *Fanayal ab Kascamandri*.

Bannut urs Hannut (4059–4110)—A Scylvendi warrior of the Utemot tribe, and Cnaiür urs Skiötha's uncle.

Bardic Priest—In the traditional folk religions of the Ancient North, a type of wandering priest who earned his living reciting scriptural lays and performing priestly functions for various gods.

Barisullas, Nrezza (4053–4119)—The King of Cironj, at once admired and maligned throughout the Three Seas for his mercantile ingenuity. He is notorious for surviving and managing to reverse Shrial Censure not once but three times.

Barricades—One of the Sublime Contrivances of the Artisan, Emilidis, the sorcerous portal barring the only entrance to the Incû-Holoinas that Nil'giccas and his Quya could not seal from within. Though easily the most significant of the Artisan's Aporos defying works, the Barricades remain largely a mystery. The few extant descriptions that remain are apocryphal and inconsistent.

Batathent—A ruined fortress-temple dating back to pre-classical Kyraneas, and destroyed by the Scylvendi shortly after the fall of Cenei in 3351.

Batrial Campus—Imperial parade and drill ground to the north of the Andiamine Heights, bounding the Guest Compound.

Battle-Celebrant—An honour bestowed by the Gilgallic Priesthood on those most responsible for victory in battle.

Battlemaster—Among the Inrithi, the traditional rank assigned to those commanding coalitions.

Battle of Anwurat—A pivotal battle of the First Holy War, fought in the summer of 4111 about the fortress of Anwurat south of the Sempis Delta. Despite early setbacks, the Inrithi under Cnaiür urs Skiötha managed to rout the Kianene host of Skauras ab Nalajan, allowing the subsequent conquest of southern Shigek and opening the road to Caraskand.

Battle of Caraskand—Sometimes called the Battle of Tertae Fields. The desperate and pivotal battle in 4112 between the host of Kascamandri ab Tepherokar, the Padirajah of Kian, and the First Holy War under Anasûrimbor Kellhus, where the Fanim, despite outnumbering the diseased and starved Inrithi, found themselves incapable of slowing or stopping the First Holy War's general advance. Many attribute the Inrithi victory to the intercession of the God, though a more likely explanation is to be found in the revelatory events immediately preceding the battle. Nersei Proyas is particularly effective in his descriptions of the maniacal morale enjoyed by the Inrithi as a result of the Warrior-Prophet's Circumfixion and subsequent vindication. That the Kianene were overconfident is amply demonstrated by the Padirajah's decision to allow the First Holy War to assemble its ranks unmolested.

Battle of Eleneöt Fields—The great battle between the Horde of the No-God and the Second Ordeal on Kûniüri's northeastern frontier in 2146. Despite having assembled the greatest host of their age, Anasûrimbor Celmomas and his allies were unprepared for the vast numbers of Sranc, Bashrag, and Wracu gathered by the No-God and his Consult slaves. The battle was an unmitigated catastrophe, and signalled the eventual destruction of Norsirai civilization.

Battle of Imogirion—The disaster that ended Illisserû's attempt to surprise the Vile with a sea invasion. Scarcely one hundred Ishroi survived to sail back to their mansion. Of these, all but one—the famed Moryror—would die in the tempests that wracked their return.

Battle of Imweor—Also known as the First Battle of the Horde. The inaugural battle between the Great Ordeal and the Horde in the summer of 4132, so named for the ancient province that witnessed it. After spending several weeks retreating before the advancing Great Ordeal, sheer numbers and starvation triggered the Horde to attack. Unbeknownst to the Ordealmen, the Consult had shadowed their progress with several Yokes, divisions of chained Sranc that they unleashed in the Ordeal's rear as the Horde descended upon them. The battle would have proved the expedition's first great disaster, were it not for the Scions, who encountered the Consult Legion whilst foraging for food to the south of the host.

Battle of Isal'imial—Also known as the Abandon, the final open battle of the Cûno-Inchoroi Wars, where Nil'giccas, leading the Ishroi of Siol and Injor, threw the last of the Inchoroi back into the Incû-Holoinas.

Battle of Kiyuth—An important engagement between the Imperial Army of Nansur and the Scylvendi, fought in 4110 on the banks of the River Kiyuth, a tributary of the Sempis river system. The overconfident Scylvendi King-of-Tribes led his people into a trap laid by Ikurei Conphas, the Nansur Exalt-General. The resulting defeat was unprecedented, given that it occurred on the Jiünati Steppe.

Battle of Maän—A minor battle fought between Conriya and Ce Tydonn in 4092.

Battle of Mehsarunath—The first great battle fought between the gathered might of Kyraneas and the host of the No-God on the Attong Plateau in 2154. Though Aurang, the No-God's Horde-General, won the battle, the Kyranean High King, Anaxophus V, was able to escape with much of his host intact, setting the stage for the far more decisive Battle of Mengedda the following year.

Battle of Mengedda, the Second—The desperate battle where Anaxophus V and his southern tributaries and allies made their victorious stand against the Horde of the No-God in 2155. Widely regarded as the most important battle in history.

Battle of Mengedda, the Fourth—The battle where the so-called Vulgar Holy War under Nersei Calmemunis suffered utter destruction at the hands of the Kianene under Skauras ab Nalajan in 4110.

Battle of Mengedda, the Fifth—The first decisive battle fought between the First Holy War and the Kianene, in 4111. Plagued with organizational problems and dissension among its commanders, the First Holy War, under the nominal command of Prince Coithus Saubon, was caught by Skauras ab Nalajan and his Kianene host on the Plains of Mengedda with only half of its available strength. From morning to late afternoon, the Inrithi managed to beat back innumerable Kianene charges. When the remainder of the First Holy War arrived on the Fanim flank, the will of the Kianene broke and they were routed.

Battle of Paremti—A minor battle fought between Conriya and Ce Tydonn in 4109, and the first military victory of Prince Nersei Proyas. Historically significant because Proyas had his cousin, Calmemunis, whipped for impiety, an act that many historians claim precipitated Calmemunis's decision to prematurely march with the so-called Vulgar Holy War.

Battle of Pir Minginnial—Second Battle of the Ark, which ended in the dramatic defeat of the assembled Mansions after Nin-janjin struck down Cu'jara Cinmoi. Often referred to as simply "the Battle," Pir Minginnial is widely eulogized in Nonmen treatises and lays for the sheer number of legendary heroes butchered there, as well as for the five centuries of woe that followed.

Battle of Pir Pahal—First great contest on the Fields of Eleneöt between the Inchoroi, under Sil, King-After-the-Fall, and the Nonmen under Cu'jara Cinmoi, who would strike down Sil and seize the Heron Spear. The Inchoroi fled back to the Incû-Holoinas so complete was the Nonmen victory. Facing crises elsewhere in his empire, Cu'jara Cinmoi instituted what has come to be called the Second Watch.

Battle of the Slopes—Name given to the prolonged contest between the Kianene and the Ainoni at the Battle of Anwurat.

Battle of Tertae Fields—The improbable victory of the First Holy War over Kascamandri and his Fanim host outside of Caraskand in 4112 that sealed the power of Anasûrimbor Kellhus over the Inrithi.

Battle of Trantis Bay—The decisive sea battle where the Kianene fleet, using Cishaurim, was able to annihilate the Imperial Nansur fleet under General Sassotian in 4111, thereby denying the First Holy War its primary source of water for its march across Khemema.

Battle of Tywanrae Fords—One of three disastrous defeats suffered by Akksersia and its allies at the hands of the Horde of the No-God. Tywanrae is often evoked by

Mandate scholars as an example of the limitations of using Chorae alone to cope with enemy sorcerers in battle.

Battle of Zirkirta—A major battle fought between the Kianene host of Hasjinnet ab Skauras and the Scylvendi under Yursut urs Muknai on the Jiünati Steppe in 4103. Though their cavalry proved no match for the Scylvendi, and Hasjinnet himself was slain, the Kianene were quick in recovering, and most of the ill-fated expedition survived.

Battleplain—See *Mengedda Plains*.

Battles of Agongorea—See *Apocalypse*.

Bayal—A semi-mountainous fiefdom in northern Galeoth, widely thought accursed.

Believer-King—Epithet belonging to Zaudunyani Kings during the Kellic Empire.

Bengulla (4103–12)—Son of Aëngelas and Valrissa.

benjuka—A subtle and ancient game of strategy played by caste-nobility throughout the Three Seas. A derivative of the more esoteric *mirqu* played by Nonmen, the first extant references to benjuka date back to the so-called Nonmen Tutelage (555–825).

Betmulla Mountains—A minor mountain range forming the southwestern frontier of both Xerash and Amoteu. The traditional location of the lost Nonman Mansion of Illisserû.

Biaxi, House—One of the Houses of the Congregate, and traditional rival to House Ikurei.

billows—Name of the specialized robes worn by sorcerers and witches of all Schools throughout the Great Ordeal. Typical robes possessed dozens of silk bolts as long as ten cubits or more, which, with the assistance of a specialized Cant, would writhe about the wearer when unfurled, providing some measure of protection from any thrown or fired Chorae.

Bios—The principle of living things independent of the soul.

Black Heaven—Sranc name for the No-God, translated from *Iruturu-ka* (Agurzhoi).

Black Iron Seat—The throne of the Nonman King of Ishterebinth, hewn from the spot where, during the Siege of Ishterebinth (2147-9), Aurang struck the ensorcelled Mirinotic Gates with the Sun Lance (sister of the Heron Spear) before it exploded. The impact crater forms the seat of the throne, with the slag thrown by the strike constituting the back and sides, and the remaining thickness of the Gate making the base.

blood-of-the-onta—A common term for what Zarathinius called the "ink" of the Mark.

Bloodthirsty Excuse—Memgowa's term for the use of atrocity suffered to justify the commission of atrocity.

Boatman—The Nonman charged with feeding the Erratics dwelling in the Holy

Deep of Ishterebinth, once known as Morimhira, the Father-of-Orphans, Most Ancient Warrior, and uncle of Cu'jara Cinmoi. As the only *aged* Nonman to be rendered immortal by the Inoculation, he is a perpetual reminder of the mortality and decrepitude his nephew exchanged for the Womb-plague.

Bogras, Praxum (4059–4111)—Man-of-the-Tusk, general of the Selial Column, slain at Anwurat.

Bogyar, Thurhig (4000–4132)—Holca Ordealman, descendant of the famed Thurror Eryelk, and Spearbearer to Coithus Saubon during the Great Ordeal.

Bokae—An old Ceneian fort on the western frontier of Enathpaneah.

Boksarias, Pirras (2395–2437)—The Ceneian Emperor who standardized trading protocols within the empire and established a thriving system of markets in its major cities.

Book of Circles and Spirals, The—The magnum opus of Sorainas, providing an entertaining blend of philosophical commentary and religious aphorism.

Book of Devices, The—An oft-revised Nansur military manual depicting the banner devices of their ancestral foes.

Book of Divine Acts, The—The magnum opus of Memgowa, the famed Zeümi sage and philosopher. Though not as commonly read or copied as his *Celestial Aphorisms*, most scholars consider it a vastly superior work.

"Bowing into the fire"—Zaudunyani metaphor for divine revelation.

Bowl—Caraskand's central quarter, which is surrounded by five of the city's nine heights.

Branch of Umiaki—The name given to the switches used in Penance.

Breacher—Mysunsai term used to describe members who renege on their contracts.

Breaking of the Gates—Legendary assault on the Gates of Eärwa, a series of fortified passes through the Great Kayarsus, by the Men of Eänna. Since *The Chronicle of the Tusk* ends with the determination to invade Eärwa, or the Land of the "Uplifted Sun," and since the Nonmen Mansions most involved in resisting the Tribes of Men were all destroyed, very little is known either of the Breaking of the Gates or of the subsequent migratory invasions.

Bukris—The God of famine. As one of the so-called Punitive Gods, who command sacrifices through threat and the imposition of suffering, Bukris has no real Cult or priesthood. According to Kiünnat tradition, Bukris is the older brother of Anagkë, which is why Anagkean Cultic Priests typically administer the rites of propitiation during times of hunger.

Burning of the White Ships—One of the more famous acts of treachery during the Apocalypse. Falling back before the Consult legions, Anasûrimbor Nimeric dispatched the Aörsic fleet in 2134 to shelter in the Kûniüri port of Aesorea, where it was burned by agents unknown mere days after its arrival, deepening the feud between the two peoples, with tragic consequences. See *Apocalypse*.

Burulan (4084–)–One of Esmenet's Kianene body-slaves.

Byantas (2463-2515)–A near antique writer of the Ceneian Empire. His *Translations*, an account of all the varied customs of the peoples making up the Empire, would render him famous to later generations. The precision of his observations remain unparalleled. The death of those customs in the intervening centuries has had a profound impact on Three Seas thought, embuing it with a historical self-awareness it had not possessed before. Before Byantas, Men were blind to the fundamental transformations wrought by the passage of time. A far smaller fraction of the soul belonged to the realm of the Immutable after him.

Byantas was Excised by Imperial Authorities in 4121 for perhaps this very reason.

C

Calasthenes (4055–4111)–Man-of-the-Tusk, a sorcerer of rank in the Scarlet Spires, slain by a Chorae at Anwurat.

Calmemunis, Nersei (4069–4110)–Man-of-the-Tusk, the Palatine of the Conriyan province of Kanampurea, and nominal leader of the Vulgar Holy War.

Canons of Imimorûl–Nonman regulative scriptures outlining a wide variety of largely anachronistic codes of personal and social conduct.

Canons of the Dead–One of six so-called Canons of Imimorûl.

Canted Horn–See *Horns of Golgotterath*.

Cants–The name given to offensive sorcerous incantations. See *sorcery*.

Cants of Calling–The family of incantations that enable communications over distance. Though the metaphysics of these Cants is only loosely understood, all long-distance Cants of Calling seem to turn on the so-called Here Hypothesis. One can call only to slumbering souls (because they remain open to the Outside) and only to those residing someplace where the Caller has physically been. The idea is that the "Here" of the Caller can only reach a "There," or other location, that has been a "Here" sometime in the past. The degree of similarity between Anagogic and Gnostic Cants of Calling has led many to suspect that they hold the key to unravelling the Gnosis.

Cants of Compulsion–The family of incantations that control the movements of an individual's soul. Typically these include the so-called Cants of Torment, though not always. An insidious aspect of these Cants is that their subject often has no way of distinguishing sorcerously compelled thoughts from his own thoughts. This has spawned a whole literature on the very notion of "will." If the compelled soul feels every bit as uncompelled as the free soul, then how can anyone truly know himself to be free?

Cants of Scrying–The family of incantations that enable observation from long distances or obstructed vantages.

Canute–A Province of Ce Tydonn, one of the so-called Deep Marches of the Upper Swa.

Caphrianus I (3722–85)–Commonly called "the Younger" to distinguish him from his Ceneian namesake. The Nansur Surmante emperor famed for his wily diplomacy and far-reaching reforms of the Nansur legal code.

Cara-Sincurimoi–"Angel of Endless Hunger" (Ihrimsû). Ancient Nonman name for the No-God. See *No-God*.

Caraskand–A major city and great caravan entrepot of the southwestern Three Seas. The administrative and commercial capital of Enathpaneah.

Carathay Desert–Vast arid region of dunes and gravel flats occupying southwestern Eärwa. Large oases are primarily found along the eastern regions of the desert, but there are skeletal river systems throughout.

Caravaneeri–Name for the route connecting the Three Seas to Kûniüri in Far Antiquity.

Carindûsû (4081–4132)–Ordealman, Grandmaster of the Vokalati in the Great Ordeal of Anasûrimbor Kellhus. Known for his pride and mercurial temper, Carindûsû is widely regarded as the soul most responsible for the disaster of Irsulor, where he met his end at the hands of Apperens Saccarees in 4132.

Caro-Shemic–The language of the scriptural pastoralists of the Carathay Desert.

Carû-Ongonean (524–588)–The third God-King of Ûmerau who, among many things, raised the original Library of Sauglish.

Carythusal–Also known as "the City of Flies." The most populous city in the Three Seas, and the administrative and commercial capital of High Ainon.

Casidas (3081–3142)–A famed philosopher and historian of Near Antiquity, best known for his magisterial *The Annals of Cenei*, and famed for his youthful tenure as a galley slave.

caste-apparati–A term for hereditary officials in Three Seas bureaucracies.

caste-menial–A term for the suthenti, or the hereditary labourer caste.

caste-noble–A term for the kjineta, or the hereditary warrior caste.

caste-priest–A term for the nahat, or the hereditary priest caste.

castes–Inherited social statuses. Though weaker in the so-called Middle-North, the Inrithi caste system is one of the central institutions of Three Seas society. In a technical sense, there are almost as many castes as there are occupations, but in practice they fall into roughly four different groups: the suthenti or labouring castes, the momurai or transactional castes, the nahat or priestly castes, and the kjineta or warrior castes. Elaborate protocols supposedly govern all interactions within and between castes to ensure the observances of various privileges and obligations, as well as to minimize ritual pollution, but in practical terms they are rarely adhered to unless in the pursuit of advantage.

caünnu–The Scylvendi name for the hot southwestern winds that cross the Jiünati Steppe during the height of summer.

Celestial Aphorisms–One of Memgowa's most celebrated texts.

Celmomas II, Anasûrimbor (2089–2146)–The implacable foe of Golgotterath in the early days of the Apocalypse, and last of the Kûniüric High Kings. See *Apocalypse*.

Celmomian Prophecy–The dying words of Anasûrimbor Celmomas II to Seswatha on the Fields of Eleneöt in 2146 to the effect that an Anasûrimbor would return at "the end of the world." Given that the prevention of the so-called Second Apocalypse is the Mandate's entire reason for existence, it is perhaps no surprise that most Mandate scholars think the Celmomian Prophecy authentic. Few others in the Three Seas credit their claims, however.

Cememketri (4046–)–The Grandmaster of the Imperial Saik.

Cenei–A city of the Kyranae Plain that arose from the Age of Warring Cities to conquer the entire Three Seas. Cenei was destroyed by the Scylvendi under Horiötha in 3351.

Ceneian Empire–The greatest Ketyai empire in history, embracing the entirety of the Three Seas at its greatest extent, from the Atkondras Mountains in the southwest, to Lake Huösi in the north, to the Kayarsus Mountains in the southeast. The primary agent in the creation and maintenance of this empire was the Ceneian Imperial Army, which was perhaps the best trained and organized in history.

No more than a minor river trading town in the days of Kyraneas, Cenei emerged from the Age of Warring Cities as the pre-eminent city of the Kyranae Plain. The conquest of Gielgath in 2349 sealed the city's regional dominance, and in the ensuing decades the Ceneians under Xercallas II would secure the remnants of what had once been Kyraneas. Xercallas's successors continued his aggressive, expansionist policies, first pacifying the Norsirai tribes of Cepalor, then waging three consecutive wars against Shigek, which fell in 2397. Then, in 2414, after conquering Enathpaneah, Xerash, and Amoteu, General Naxentas staged a successful coup and declared himself Emperor of Cenei. Though he would be assassinated the following year, all his successors would avail themselves of the Imperial institutions he created.

Triamis I became Emperor in 2478, beginning what most scholars consider the Ceneian Golden Age. In 2483 he conquered Nilnamesh, and then Cingulat the following year. In 2485 he defeated a great Zeümi host at Amarah, and would have invaded the Satyothi nation had not mutinies among his homesick troops prevented him. He spent the next decade consolidating his gains, and striving against the internecine religious violence between followers of the traditional Kiünnat sects and the growing numbers of "Inrithi." It was in the course of negotiating settlements that he became friends with the then Shriah of the Thousand Temples, Ekyannus III, and in 2505 he himself converted to Inrithism, declaring it the official state religion of the Ceneian Empire. He spent the next ten years putting down religious rebellions, while at the same time invading and occupying both Cironj (2508) and Nron (2511). He then spent ten years campaigning across the eastern Three Seas against the successor nations of the old Shiradi Empire, first conquering Ainon (2518), then Cengemis (2519), and finally Annand (2525).

Ensuing Aspect-Emperors would marginally add to the extent of the empire, but its boundaries remained fairly stable for nearly eight hundred years, during which time the language and institutions of Imperial Cenei and the Thousand Temples would be stitched into the very fabric of Three Seas society. Aside from periodic wars with Zeüm, and the interminable wars against the Scylvendi and Norsirai tribes across the empire's northern frontier, this would be an age of unprecedented peace, prosperity, and commerce. Only the periodic civil wars, usually fought over succession, posed any real threat to the empire, and in writings from the time the assumption is that the empire was eternal.

Though Cenei itself was destroyed by the Scylvendi under Horiötha in 3351, historians traditionally date the collapse of the Ceneian Empire in 3372, when General Maurelta surrendered to Sarothesser I in Ainon.

Cengemic—The language of Cengemis, a derivative of Sheyo-Kheremic.

Cengemis—The province that once marked the northern limit of the Eastern Ceneian Empire. After the collapse of the Eastern Empire in 3372, it enjoyed independence until overrun by Tydonni tribes in 3742.

Cepalor—A region of temperate, semi-forested plains extending east of the Hethantas from the Nansur frontier to the southwestern marches of Galeoth. Since the fall of Kyraneas, Cepalor has been inhabited by Norsirai pastoralists known as the Cepalorae, who have long been tributaries of the Nansurium.

Cepaloran—The language group of Norsirai pastoralists of the Cepaloran Plains.

Cerish Sea—The largest of Eärwa's inland seas.

Cerjulla, Sheorog (4069–4111)—Man-of-the-Tusk, Tydonni Earl of Warnute, claimed by disease at Caraskand.

Cern Auglai—Fortress and pirate entrepot located on the coast of Thunyerus.

Cet'ingira (?–)—See *Mekeritrig*.

Ce Tydonn—A Norsirai nation of the Three Seas, located north of Conriya on the eastern shoreline of the Meneanor, founded in 3742 in the wake of Cengemis's collapse. The first mention of the Tydonni is found in Casidas's *Annals of Cenei*, where he mentions their raids across the River Swa. Descendants of White Norsirai refugees from the Apocalypse, the Tydonni are thought to have occupied the southern regions of the Dameori Wilderness for centuries, prevented by their native fractiousness from causing much difficulty for their southern Ketyai neighbours. At some point in the thirty-eighth century, however, they united, and with little difficulty overwhelmed the Men of Cengemis at the Battle of Marswa in 3722. It wasn't until King Haul-Namyelk finally succeeded in unifying the various tribes under his absolute authority in 3741 that Ce Tydonn proper came into existence.

Perhaps the most peculiar and distinctive predilection of the Tydonni is found in their racial beliefs. *Ti dunn* literally means "struck iron" in their tongue, reflecting their belief that their people have been purified by the crucible of their long wandering through the Dameori wildernesses. They hold that this gives them "privileged blood," rendering them morally, intellectually, and physically superior to other races. This has made the Tydonni cruel overlords of the Cengemi, who have often rebelled against them.

Chalahall—Most famed of the Hundred Heavens named in *The Chronicle of the Tusk*. In the *Book of Songs*, it is "Where the soil sings and Men breathe most deep,/ where heartbreak melts into slow smiling joy,/ and pain dwells as a wise old friend in memory." It is sometimes named as the province of Onkhis, and sometimes Yatwer.

chanv—An addictive narcotic popular among the Ainoni aristocracy, although many eschew it because of its uncertain origins. Chanv reputedly sharpens the intellect, extends one's lifespan, and drains the body of all its pigment.

Charamemas (4036–4108)—The famed Shrial commentator and author of *The Ten Holies*. Achamian's replacement as Proyas's tutor in exoterics in 4093,

Charapatha, Sasal (4100–)—Ordealman, Believer-Prince of Nilnamesh, general of the Nilnameshi contingent in the Great Ordeal of Anasûrimbor Kellhus. Named the "Prince of One Hundred Songs" for his exploits during the Unification Wars, Charapatha was one of the few survivors of the Battle of Irsulor and the destruction of the Ketyai-of-the-South in 4132.

Charcharius, Trimus (4052–4114)—Patridomos of the House Trimus.

Chargiddo—A large fortress located on the frontier of Xerash and Amoteu beneath the Betmulla Mountains.

Chemerat—An ancient Kyranean name for Shigek, meaning "Red Land."

Chepheramunni (4068–4111)—Man-of-the-Tusk, King-Regent of High Ainon, nominal leader of the Ainoni during much of the First Holy War, claimed by disease at Caraskand.

Chiama—Walled town on the River Sempis, destroyed by the First Holy War in 4111.

Chianadyni—A governorate of Kian and one-time tributary of the Nansur Empire. Located to the west of Eumarna and east of Nilnamesh, Chianadyni is the traditional homeland of the Kianene and, after Eumarna, the wealthiest and most populous governorate in Kian.

Chigra—"Slaying Light" (Arghurzoi). An ancient Sranc name for Seswatha.

Children of Eänna—An epithet for Men in *The Chronicle of the Tusk*.

Children of the Ark—An epithet for the Inchoroi.

Chinjosa, Musammu (4078–)—Man-of-the-Tusk, Count-Palatine of the Ainoni province of Antanamera, appointed King-Regent of High Ainon shortly after Chepheramunni's death in the winter of 4111.

chirong—Traditional Ainoni form of combat.

Chogiaz—Aghurzoi name for the River Sursa. See *Sursa River*.

Chorae—Artifacts of the Ancient North, also known as "Trinkets" (to the Schools) and "The Tears of God" (to the Inrithi). In appearance, Chorae are small iron spheres, one inch in diameter, that are banded by runes written in Gilcûnya, the holy tongue of the Nonmen Quya. Chorae are extraordinary in that they render their bearer immune to all sorcerous Cants and instantly kill any sorcerer who comes into contact with them. Although the principles behind their creation (they belong to a lost branch of sorcery called the Aporos) are no longer understood, thousands are believed to circulate in the Three Seas alone. The Chorae play a pivotal role in the political balance of power in the Three Seas, insofar as they allow the non-scholastic Great Factions to check the power of the Schools.

Chorae bowmen—Specialized units that use Chorae affixed to the end of arrow shafts or crossbow bolts to kill enemy sorcerers. Chorae archers are a staple of almost every military organization in Eärwa.

Chorae Hail—Name given to the infamous barrage that killed the Sixty-One—more than a third of the Sohonc—attempting to overthrow Ûbil Maw, the Extrinsic Gate of Golgotterath, during the Second Great Investiture in 2142. Though following the command of Anasûrimbor Celmomas, the incident is widely cited as *Seswatha's* greatest blunder during the Apocalypse.

Chorgah, Namogritti (4098–)—Ordealman, and the of Lord Palatine of Eshganax.

Chronicle of the Tusk, The—The most ancient extant human text in Eärwa, and the scriptural foundation for all mannish faiths save Fanimry. As the oldest literate work, its provenance is almost entirely unknown. Even its language, Thoti-Eännorean, has become an ancient relic, rendering the Tusk the subject of endless interpretative dispute. Many Inrithi commentators have pointed out that it must have been a collective work, cobbled together from many (likely oral) sources over a period of many years. According to a handful of sources, the Nonmen believe it to be corrupted by the Inchoroi, an arguably successful means to effect their extinction. Like most scriptures, its popular interpretation is highly selective and idealized. It consists of the following six books:

Book of Canticles—The old "Tusk Laws" regarding every aspect of personal and public life, which were superseded in the Inrithi tradition by the revised strictures of *The Tractate*, and then amended once again by the Zaudunyani. It famously opens:

And lo, the Chieftains of Men gathered in the tent of meeting that hath been struck below the mountain where the bull bellows, and thus spake Angeshrael, saying, these are the words of the Hunter, who comes as pounding upon the horizon, declaring the pact binding God to God according to Man, and how souls shall reap as they had sown. And these were the laws of purity and offering and diet and conduct between all the walks that move us through life. And these were the laws of what may or may not be lawfully thought.

Book of Gods—The primary basis of individual Cultic scriptures, enumerating the various gods, and explaining the rites of purification and propitiation basic to each.

Book of Hintarates—The story of Hintarates, an upright man plagued with apparently undeserved adversity. "The life of Gods is the life after the hard passing of life," the nameless psalmist begins. "The Gods know no weal." The following fable explains how the suffering of Hintarates in this life was actually *commensurate* to his reward in the next, thereby encoding a deep instability into all "Faiths of the Tusk," the assumption that the successful, the powerful, were almost certainly damned. "Temporal fortune," we are assured, "is naught but the shadow of eternal damnation ..." In his *Annals*, Casidas contends that Hintarates was what drove the powerful to incessant war, "to leap to Gilgaöl lest falling deeper still." Later in the *Annals*, he writes that "contention is the greatest curse of our religion. If the powerful are not waging war to save their souls, their people are waging war against them for being damned," a passage that has been, not surprisingly, redacted in a great many copies.

Book of Songs—A collection of verse prayers and parables extolling the virtues of piety, manliness, courage, and tribal loyalty.

Book of Tribes—The extended narrative of the first Prophets and Chieftain-Kings of the Five Tribes of Men before the invasion of Eärwa.

Book of Warrants—The account of the observances governing the interactions between castes.

Chthonic Manse—Greatest manse of Ishterebinth, located below the Hanging Citadels, above the Qûlnimil, the nimil mines, and arrayed about the Ingressus.

Cil-Aujas—One the Nine Mansions of Eärwa, located in the Osthwai Mountains.

Cilcûliccas (?—)—Injori Quya, perhaps the most celebrated in the final days of Ishterebinth, often called Lord of Swans for his famed luck. During the Investiture, he gained renown by slaying Murathaur the Silver, the much-feared Dragon of Knives.

Cincûlic—The undeciphered tongue of the Inchoroi, which the Nonmen call *Cincûl'hisa*, or "the Gasp of Many Reeds." According to the *Isûphiryas*, communication between the Cûnuroi and the Inchoroi was impossible until the latter "birthed mouths" and began speaking Cûnuroi tongues.

Cinganjehoi ab Sakjal (4076—)—Famed Kianene Saptishah-Governor of Eumarna, known among his people as "the Tiger of Eumarna."

Cingulat—A Ketyai nation of the Three Seas, located on the northwestern coast of Kutnarmu, just south of Nilnamesh.

Cinguli—The language of Cingulat, a derivative of Sapmatari.

Ciogli (?—?)—Legendary Siolan Hero of the Nonman, perhaps the most famous of the Tall, slain at Pir Minginnial.

Cironj—A Ketyai island nation located at the juncture of all three of the Three Seas, and possessing a strong mercantile and maritime tradition.

Circumfix, The—symbol of Anasûrimbor Kellhus, the Holy Warrior-Prophet. The innumerable versions of the sacred image that proliferated across the Three Seas generally fall into three forms: abstract, typically consisting of a circle about an X; realistic, generally following the representational customs pertaining to idols in various nations; and baroque, where some feature is exaggerated to some degree, such as the "Phallic Circumfixes" outlawed by the Thousand Temples in 4119. For some reason, all forms consistently omit Serwë.

Circumfixion, The—The famed attempt to publicly execute Anasûrimbor Kellhus during the legendary 4112 Siege of Caraskand. An ancient practice of the Kunniat, the Inrithi generally reserved circumfixion for the most severe crimes of heresy, such as false prophecy. The practice involved binding the condemned first to the corpse of a loved one (typically a daughter or a wife), and then upside down upon an iron ring, which would then be displayed where the populace could watch their agonizing death (usually by asphyxiation) over the course of several hours.

The Circumfixion of Anasûrimbor Kellhus was remarkable in a number of respects. With the First Holy War trapped and starving within Caraskand, the so-called Great and Lesser Names hoped his execution would reunite and rekindle the resolve of the ailing host. Rather than dying quickly, however, Kellhus lived for more than two days, during which time the strife between the Orthodox and the so-called Zaudunyani intensified. Accounts vary, but somehow the return of Drusas Achamian brought about the conversion of Nersei Proyas, one of the most influential of the Great Names. This in turn inspired a Consult skin-spy masquerading as Cutias Sarcellus of the Shrial Knights to murder Kellhus, an attempt foiled by the Scylvendi Cnaiür urs Skiötha. Once Sarcellus was revealed, the Men-of-the-Tusk cut down Anasûrimbor Kellhus, who, before the assembled masses, miraculously pulled his heart from his chest as a final proof of his divinity.

Circumfix Throne—Primary throne of the Aspect-Emperor located in the Imperial Audience Hall upon the Andiamine Heights. The popular lore holds that the iron ring built into the back of the throne is the actual Circumfix, but such is not the case.

Cironjic—The language of Cironj, a derivative of Sheyo-Kheremic.

Cirrû-nol—"High Floor" (Ihrimsû). The great mall before Ishterebinth's gates.

Cishaurim—The notorious priest-sorcerers of the Fanim based in Shimeh. According to Fanim religious tradition, the Prophet Fane became the first of the Cishaurim after he went blind in the desert. Given Fane's claim that the true power of the Solitary God cannot be exercised so long as one sees the profane world, Cishaurim initiates voluntarily blind themselves at a certain point in their study, enabling them to dispense the "divine water" of the "Psûkhe," as the Cishaurim refer to it. Little is known about the metaphysics of the Psûkhe beyond the fact that it cannot be perceived by the Few and that it is in many ways almost as formidable as the Anagogic practice of the Schools.

Prior to the First Holy War, the Scarlet Spires categorized individual Cishaurim according to their power: Tertiaries, or those with only the most rudimentary strength; Secondaries, or those with strength comparable to sorcerous initiates; and Primaries, those with strength exceeding that of initiates (but still, according to the Scarlet Magi, short of strength possessed by true Anagogic sorcerers of rank).

Citadel of the Dog–The great redoubt of Caraskand as named by the Men of the Tusk. Raised by Xatantius in 3684, it was originally called Insarum, until it fell to the Fanim in 3839, who called it Il'huda, "the Bulwark."

Citadel of Citadels–One of many epithets given to the Library of Sauglish in Far Antiquity.

City of Robes–One of many epithets given to ancient Sauglish.

Ciworal–The famed redoubt of Dagliash.

Cleansed Lands–A Kianene epithet for nations where Fanimry is predominant.

Cleric–See, *Incariol*.

Cmiral–The great temple complex of Momemn, located near the heart of the city, adjacent to the Kamposea Agora.

Coffers–The legendary treasury of the ancient Library of Sauglish.

Coithus, House–The ruling dynasty of Galeoth.

Cojirani ab Houk (4078–4112)–The Grandee of Mizrai, famed for his enormous strength and size, slain by Prince Nersei Proyas at the Battle of Caraskand.

College of Luthymae–The College of the Thousand Temples responsible for spying and intelligence, unique in that it answers directly to the Shriah, and notorious for recruiting those of the Few who do not practice sorcery. Not surprisingly, no Collegians are more despised or feared by Schoolmen.

College of Marucee–A College of the Thousand Temples destroyed in the Sack of Shimeh in 3845.

College of Sareöt–A College of the Thousand Temples dedicated to the preservation of knowledge, destroyed in the Fall of Shigek in 3933.

Colleges–Organizations of priests directly subordinate to the Thousand Temples, with mandates ranging from caring for the poor and sick to the collection of intelligence.

come after, to–For the Dûnyain, "to come after" means to be victimized by events over which one has no control. See *Dûnyain*.

come before, to–For the Dûnyain, "to come before" means to master the passage of events. See *Dûnyain*.

Commerce of Souls, The–Ajencis's classic treatise on politics. For Ajencis, famously, market vendors are the best exemplars of politics, which he famously called "the obscure art of deriving two favours for one." More alarmingly, he extols *slavery* as the truest expression of political governance–a provocation that many have used to dismiss him over the centuries. These critics entirely overlook the satirical nature of the text, which argues, in sooth, that exploitation and coercion belong to the very *logic* of the political. As he famously puts it, "the coin stands as close to the lash as to the bread," revealing the "commerce of souls" as a network of substitutions, all mediated by currency, all bound into a single system. This is why, "there is always bounty, be it bread or lash." Where harvests fail, wars succeed.

This argument remains a perilous one. Even granted the ancient rite of "Protection," Ajencis had to fear for the well-being of his (apparently large) extended family, and like so many great intellects, took care to disguise his words with subtlety.

Compendium, The–Heretical treatise written by Drusas Achamian, one-time Holy Tutor of Anasûrimbor Kellhus, following his exile from the Three Seas in 4112. Much has been made of the fact that Anasûrimbor Kellhus exempted Drusas Achamian from Excision (removal from all records), especially following the appearance of *The Compendium* in 4119. The book itself was criminalized, but since Drusas Achamian yet retained the status of Holy Tutor in the scriptural canon, it amounted to a perpetual scandal, and so was doomed to be shared and copied across the Three Seas (and beyond). Some argue that the Blessed Empress, a former lover of the apostate Schoolman, was responsible, but such accounts merely explain Drusas Achamian's exemption from execution, not his exemption from Excision. This has led others to suspect that Anasûrimbor Kellhus I saw some advantage in the covert dissemination of *The Compendium*. The apparent absurdity of the charges leveled by the former Mandate Schoolman, coupled with the repudiation of the standard demonizations of the Aspect-Emperor, the argument contends, likely had the effect of confusing the Fanim and Orthodox Inrithi opposition.

Concavity–The immense, spherical throne-room of the Nonman King of Ishterebinth excavated by Nil'giccas, who had the history of his Race and Mansion engraved upon the walls to compensate for the Dolour.

Cond–Ancient High Norsirai pastoralists inhabiting the Istyuli Plains. The Cond first enter recorded history in c. 350, as the antagonist in a series of wars (the First Cond Wars) fought by all the greater cities of the Aumris against their barbaric cousins to the east. The destruction of Sauglish would galvanize the remaining cities under the leadership of Ûmerau, as opposed to Trysë, thus laying the groundwork for the eventual rise of the Ûmeri Empire. The Second Cond Wars would see the Ûmeri humiliated, forced to pay tribute for an entire generation. Finally, in 917, under the leadership of Aulyanau the Conqueror, the Cond sacked Ûmerau and became masters of the River Aumris and the age often referred to as Pseudo-Ûmeri, given the degree to which the Cond were assimilated.

Condic–The language group of ancient pastoralists of the Near Istyuli Plains.

Conditioned, the–A term used to refer to the Dûnyain.

Conditioning, the–Specifically, the arduous physical, emotional, and intellectual training undergone by Dûnyain monks, though the term has more general and far-reaching connotations as well. The Dûnyain believe that everything is conditioned in some way, but they draw a principled distinction between the arbitrary conditioning of the world and the rational conditioning of Men. Conditioning in the light of the Logos, they believe, allows *more* such conditioning, which in turn leverages more such conditioning, and so on. This virtuous circle, they believe, finds its apotheosis in the Absolute: the Dûnyain believe that, using reason, they can condition themselves to the point of becoming *unconditioned*, a perfect, self-moving soul. See *Dûnyain*.

Cond Yoke—Name given to the age following the Condic overthrow of ancient Ûmerau.

Confluence—In Neuropuncture, the structures of the brain most closely bound to the soul.

Congregate—In the Nansurium, the body of government expressing the legislative will of the great families of Nansur. In its New Imperial incarnation, the body of government tasked with informing and advising the Holy Aspect-Emperor.

Conphas, Ikurei (4084–)—Man-of-the-Tusk, nephew of Emperor Ikurei Xerius III and heir apparent to the Imperial Mantle.

Conriya—A pre-eminent Ketyai nation of the eastern Three Seas, located south of Ce Tydonn and north of High Ainon, founded in 3374 (after the collapse of the Eastern Ceneian Empire) around Aöknyssus, the ancient capital of Shir. Of the four successor nations to the Shiradi Empire (Cengemis, Conriya, Ainon, and Sansor), none has worked so hard to reclaim and preserve its ancient traditions. Nowhere are the caste divisions more rigidly observed, and nowhere are the codes governing caste-noble behaviour more strict. Though many, particularly the Ainoni, scoff at what they consider the affectation of antique ways, there can be little doubt that the resulting social discipline has served the Conriyans well. Since gaining independence, Conriya has successfully weathered innumerable incursions, invasions, blockades, and embargoes, almost all of them due to the machinations of High Ainon.

Conriyan—The language of Conriya, a derivative of Sheyo-Kheremic.

Consult—Name given to the Unholy Triumvirate of Men, Nonmen, and Inchoroi intent upon exterminating all souls in a bid to save their own souls from eternal damnation. The sheer age of the cabal, let alone its devotion to secrecy, renders its origins murky. Though the Gnostic Schools of Sohonc and Mangaecca are referenced as Far Antique contemporaries, the Mangaecca is the older of the two schools, as well as the one possessing the deepest Nonman affiliations—affiliations which would prove instrumental to the School's transformation into the Consult. Mandate scholars agree that Cet'ingira (Mekeritrig) revealed the location of the Ark to the Mangaecca at some point in the eighth century, seeking Mannish assistance in his mad attempt to gain entry into of the Incû-Holoinas. Nil'giccas had sealed the High (or Upright) Horn the age previous, first by heaping titanic amounts of debris upon impregnable soggomant from the inside, and then by commanding Emilidis to raise the Barricades across the only remaining portal high upon the heights. For centuries, the cunning of these impediments had denied every attempt to surmount them, until the year 1111, when Shaeönanra finally managed to bring down the Barricades.

The Mangaecca raised Nogaral upon Viri soon after, pretending to plumb the destroyed Nonman Mansion while in fact plumbing the Upright Horn—the intact heart of the Incû-Holoinas. At some point in their exploration they discovered and awakened the Last Inchoroi, Aurax and Aurang, at which point Cet'ingira ceased being Siqu and Shaeönanra ceased being Grandmaster of the Mangaecca, and the Unholy Consult of the Halaroi, Cûnuroi, and Inchoroi was born, a pact between the most brilliant and fearsome souls of all three races, an oath to destroy the World.

Though most Mandate scholars suspect Consult involvement in the death of the celebrated Sohonc Grandmaster Titirga some time around 1119, one hundred and fifty years would pass before the nations of Men began to suffer their efforts. The calamity of the First Great Sranc War, for instance, was almost certainly due to their efforts to breed and control Sranc. But it was not until the Apocalypse that the Far Antique World would learn of the true danger they represented.

Corrunc—Infamous northern "Tower of Ûgorrior," a great bastion of Golgotterath, cursed as the Eater-of-Sons in *The Book of Generals*.

"courage casts the longest shadow ..."—Zeumi saying signifying how the courage of one man is also the shame of another.

Coyauri—The famed elite heavy cavalry of the Kianene Padirajah, first organized by Habal ab Sarouk in 3892 as a response to the Nansur Kidruhil. The White Horse on Yellow is their standard.

Croimas, Sristai (4082–)—Ordealman and Lord Palatine of Kethantei, the second born son of Sristai Ingiaban, Holy Veteran of the First Holy War.

Csokis—A derelict Inrithi temple complex located in Caraskand.

Cuärweth—A province of interior Ce Tydonn, located to the north of Meigeiri.

Cuäxaji (4069–4112)—The Sapatishah-Governor of Khemema, thought lost at Shimeh.

Cubit—Catch-all phrase for the myriad units of measure used throughout Eärwa, generally indicating a length from the tip of the finger to the elbow, but also notoriously problematic, as with the Near Antique translation of Nonman *utils* (literally translated, "ten") into "cubits." Even the Nonman "cubit proper," or *priror*, is more than twice the length of a Mannish cubit, consisting, as it does, of the height of the waist from the floor.

Cu'huriol (?–?)—"White Burning" (Ihrimsû). King of Siol prior Arkfall, and grandfather of Cu'jara Cinmoi.

Cu'jara Cinmoi (?–?)—"White Shining Spear" (Ihrimsû). Issue of Cet'moyol and Linqirû, the scandalous son and daughter of Cu'huriol, King of Siol, who would raise the boy as his heir following the execution of his own children. Even as a young boy his beauty and charisma were legendary: "Perfection breathes," a nameless scribe writes of him in the Isûphiryas, "and we must assure it never bleeds." Ferocious in war, his renown only grew, reaching even those Mansions possessing little or no congress with Siol. The scandalous circumstances of his birth had merely anointed his legend, resonating, as it did, with the scriptural coupling of Tsonos and Olissis.

The death of Cu'huriol signalled the death of his popularity, and not simply because of the general hatred of Siol. As King of the House Primordial, Cu'jara Cinmoi quickly revealed an arrogance and ambition more characteristic of Men than Nonmen. The tenor of the Isûphiryas changes in the span of three cantos: "In him," one entry reads, "verily, purity hath become perversion." Across those Mansion Reaches bounding that of Siol, the blood of Ishroi began to flow. The King of Siol became the Tyrant. His name dominates the lays and records surviving from that period, such was his celebrity. Arkfall, and the catastrophes that ensued, would merely serve to make him tragic, if not reviled. (For an account of his role subsequent to Arkfall, see Cûno-Inchoroi Wars). He possessed, as one contemporary muses, "all Ishroi prized, all they called glory, only in proportions that cracked hearts and mountains."

Cu'jara Cinmoi was doomed to be the darling of myth and legend, by his nature as much as by his circumstances. Though the wont of Mannish poets is to see him as the cipher for the Nonman more generally, it serves to remember that he is extraordinary precisely because he is unlike any other Nonmen (more recognizably human) living in the age of his Race's destruction.

"Cû'jara Cinmoi is dead ..."—Ancient Siqu saying roughly meaning, "Seize the day."

Culling—Epithet given to the slaughter of Sranc worked daily by the Schools as the Horde retreated before the advance of the Great Ordeal.

Cultic Deities—See Hundred Gods, the.

Cultic Priests—Those priests, usually hereditary, devoted to the service and worship of one of the Hundred Gods.

Cults—The collective name of all the various sects devoted to the individual Gods of the so-called Kiünnat. In the Three Seas, the Cults have been administratively and spiritually subordinate to the Thousand Temples since Triamis I, the first Aspect-Emperor of Cenei, declared Inrithism the official state religion of the Ceneian Empire in 2505. See Kiünnat.

Cu'mimiral (?–4132)—Injori Ishroi called Dragon-gored and Lord Limper who stood among the last of the Intact in Ishterebinth.

Cumor, Haarnan (4043–4111)—Man-of-the-Tusk, High Cultist of Gilgaöl in the Holy War, claimed by disease at Caraskand.

Cûno-Halaroi Wars—The wars between Nonmen and Men following the Breaking of the Gates, of which very few accounts exist. See Breaking of the Gates.

Cûno-Inchoroi Wars—The protracted series of wars between the Nonmen and the Inchoroi following the ancient arrival of the latter.

According to the *Isûphiryas*, the Incû-Holoinas, the "Ark-of-the-Skies," plunged to earth to the west of the Sea of Neleost in land ruled by Nin'janjin, the Nonman King of Viri. The letter sent by Nin'janjin to Cû'jara Cinmoi, the King of Siöl, is recorded as follows:

The Sky has cracked into potter's shards,
Fire sweeps the compass of Heaven,
The beasts flee, their hearts maddened,
The trees fall, their backs broken.

Ash has shrouded all sun, choked all seed,
The Halaroi howl piteously at the Gates,
Dread Famine stalks my Mansion.
Brother Siöl, Viri begs your pardon.

Rather than send aid to Nin'janjin, Cû'jara Cinmoi assembled an army and invaded the lands of Viri. Nin'janjin and his Ishroi capitulated without battle; Viri became a bloodless tributary of Siöl. The western lands of Viri, however, remained shrouded in cloud and ash. Survivors from the region spoke of a fiery vessel streaking across the skies. So Cû'jara-Cinmoi commanded Ingalira, a hero of Siöl, to lead an expedition to find this Ark. What happened to Ingalira on this expedition is not recorded, but he returned to Siöl some three months later and presented two inhuman captives to Cû'jara Cinmoi. Ingalira called these captives *Inchoroi*, or "People of Emptiness," both because the sounds they made were empty of meaning and because they fell from the emptiness of the sky. He spoke of flattened forests and gouged plains, of mountains thrown into a ring, and of two golden horns rearing from a molten sea, so mighty they brushed the clouds.

Repelled by the obscene aspect of the Inchoroi, Cû'jara Cinmoi had them put to death, and set a Watch upon the Incû-Holoinas, the Ark-of-the-Skies. Years passed, and the power of Cû'jara Cinmoi and the High Mansion of Siöl waxed. The Mansion of Nihrimsul was subdued, and her King, Sin'niroiha, "First Among Peoples," was forced to wash the sword of Cû'jara Cinmoi. With the subsequent conquest of Cil-Aujas to the south, Siöl and her High King commanded an empire that ranged from the Yimaleti Mountains to the Sea of Meneanor.

During this time, the Watch was kept on the Ark. The land cooled. The skies cleared.

Either because of original inconsistencies or because of subsequent corruptions, extant versions of the *Isûphiryas* are unclear as to the subsequent order of events. At some point a secret embassy of Inchoroi reached Nin'janjin at Viri. Unlike the Inchoroi brought to Cû'jara Cinmoi by Ingalira, these possessed the ability to speak Ihrimsû. They reminded Nin'janjin of Cû'jara Cinmoi's treachery in his time of need, and offered an alliance to break the yoke of Siöl over Viri. They would undo, the Inchoroi said, the misfortune their coming had wrought upon the Cûnuroi of Viri.

Despite the warnings of his Ishroi, Nin'janjin accepted the Inchoroi terms. Viri revolted. The Siölan Ishroi within its halls were slain; the rest were enslaved. At the same time, the Inchoroi swarmed from the Ark, overwhelming the Watch. Only Oirinas and his twin, Oirûnas, survived, riding hard to warn Cû'jara Cinmoi.

Sil, the Inchoroi King, and Nin'janjin assembled their hosts to meet Cû'jara Cinmoi on the fields of Pir-Pahal, which Men would call Eleneöt in a later age. According to the *Isûphiryas*, the Nonmen of Viri were dismayed by the sight of their allies, who wore fierce and festering bodies as garments of war. Gin'gûrima, the greatest hero among them, pointed to Nin'janjin and declared, "Hate has blinded him." This treason within a treason was repeated by others, until it became a thundering chorus. Nin'janjin fled, seeking protection from Sil. The Inchoroi then turned upon their allies, hoping to destroy the host of Viri before Cû'jara Cinmoi and the great host of Siöl could close with them.

Overmatched by the Inchoroi and their weapons of light, the Nonmen of Viri were driven back, with horrendous losses. Only Cû'jara Cinmoi and his Ishroi Chariots saved them from utter destruction. The chroniclers of the *Isûphiryas* claim the battle raged through the night and into the following morning. Eventually, all but the most powerful of the Inchoroi were overwhelmed by the valour, sorceries, and numbers of the host of Siöl. Cû'jara-Cinmoi himself struck down Sil, and wrested from him his great weapon, Suörgil, "Shining Death," which Men in a latter age would call the Heron Spear.

Much reduced, the Inchoroi fled back to their Ark, taking Nin'janjin with them. Cû'jara Cinmoi hunted them within sight of the Ring Mountains, but was forced to abandon his pursuit when word of further disasters reached him. Emboldened by Siöl's distraction, Nihrimsul and Cil-Aujas had revolted.

Weakened by the Battle of Pir-Pahal, Cû'jara Cinmoi was hard pressed to recover his empire. A Second Watch was put upon the Holoinas, but no attempt was made to breach the gold-grooved faces of the Ark. After years of hard campaigning, Cû'jara Cinmoi finally brought the Ishroi of Cil-Aujas to heel, but King Sin'niroiha and the Ishroi of Nihrimsul continued to resist him. The *Isûphiryas* chronicles dozens of bloody yet indecisive confrontations between the two Kings: the Battle of Ciphara, the Battle of Hilcyri, the Siege of Asargoi. Proud beyond reason, Cû'jara Cinmoi refused to relent, and put to death every embassy Sin'niroiha sent to him. Only when Sin'niroiha became King of Ishoriöl through marriage did the High King of Siöl concede. "A King of Three Mansions," he is said to have declared, "may be Brother to a King of Two."

The *Isûphiryas* mentions the Inchoroi only once during this time. Unwilling to assign desperately needed Ishroi to the Second Watch, Cû'jara Cinmoi had charged

Oirinas and Oirûnas, the sole survivors of the First Watch, with recruiting Men for the duty. Among these Halaroi was a "criminal" named Sirwitta. Apparently Sirwitta had seduced the wife of a high-ranking Ishroi and conceived by her a daughter named Cimoira. The Judges of the Ishroi were perplexed: such a thing had never happened before. The truth of Cimoira was suppressed, and despite her mannish blood she was accepted as Cûnuroi. Sirwitta himself was banished to the Second Watch.

Somehow (the *Isûphiryas* does not go into detail) Sirwitta managed to enter the Incû-Holoinas. A month passed, and all thought him lost. Then he reappeared, deranged, screeching claims so alarming that Oirinas and Oirûnas brought him directly to Cû'jara Cinmoi. What was said between Sirwitta and the High King of Siöl is not recorded. The chroniclers say only that Cû'jara Cinmoi, after hearing Sirwitta speak, ordered him put to death. A later entry, however, describes Sirwitta as "tongueless and imprisoned." It appears the High King, for some unknown reason, had rescinded his warrant.

Many years of peace followed. From their fortresses in the Ring Mountains, the Ishroi of Siöl guarded the Ark. Whether the Inchoroi lived still or had perished, no one knew. Cû'jara Cinmoi grew old, for the Nonmen of those days were still mortal. His eyesight dimmed, and his once-mighty limbs began to fail him. Death whispered to him.

Then Nin'janjin returned. Invoking the ancient codes, he appeared before Cû'jara Cinmoi begging Mercy and Penance. When the High King of Siöl bid Nin'janjin come near so he might see him, he was astonished to discover his old adversary had not aged. Then Nin'janjin revealed his true reason for coming to Siöl. The Inchoroi, he said, were too terrified of Cû'jara Cinmoi's might to leave their Ark, so they dwelt in confinement and misery. They had sent him, he claimed, to sue for peace. They wished to know what tribute might temper the High King's fury.

To which Cû'jara Cinmoi replied: "I would be young of heart, face, and limb. I would banish Death from the halls of my people."

The Second Watch was disbanded and the Inchoroi moved freely among the Cûnuroi of Siöl, becoming their physicians. They ministered to all, dispensing the remedies that would at once make the Nonmen immortal and doom them. Soon all the Cûnuroi of Eärwa, even those who had initially questioned Cû'jara Cinmoi's wisdom, had succumbed to the Inchoroi and their nostrums.

According to the *Isûphiryas*, the first victim of the Womb-Plague was Hanalinqû, Cû'jara Cinmoi's legendary wife. The chronicler actually praises the diligence and skill of the High King's Inchoroi physicians. But as the Womb-Plague killed more and more Cûnuroi women, this praise becomes condemnation. Soon all the women of the Cûnuroi, wives and maidens both, were dying. The Inchoroi fled the Mansions, returning to their ruined vessel.

Ishroi from across Eärwa answered Cû'jara Cinmoi's call to war, even though many held the High King responsible for the deaths of their beloved. Grieved almost to madness, the High King led them through the Ring Mountains and arrayed them across the Inniür-Shigogli, the "Black Furnace Plain." Then he laid Hanalinqû's corpse before the unholy Ark and demanded the Inchoroi answer his fury.

But the Inchoroi had not been idle over the long years since the Battle of Pir Pahal. They had delved deep into the earth, beneath the Inniür-Shigogli and out into the Ring Mountains. Within these galleries they had massed hordes of twisted creatures unlike any the Cûnuroi had ever seen: Sranc, Bashrags, and mighty Dragons. The Ishroi of the Nine High Mansions of Eärwa, who had come to destroy the diminished survivors of Pir Pahal, found themselves beset on all sides.

The Sranc withered before the sinew and sorcery of the Ishroi, but their numbers seemed inexhaustible. The Bashrags and the Dragons exacted a horrifying toll. More terrible still were those few Inchoroi who ventured out into battle, hanging above the tumult, sweeping the earth with their weapons of light, apparently unaffected by the sorceries of the Ishroi. After the disaster of Pir Pahal, the Inchoroi had seduced the practitioners of the Aporos, who had been forbidden from pursuing their art. Poisoned by knowledge, they devised the first of the Chorae to render their masters immune to Cûnuroi magic.

But all the heroes of Eärwa stood upon the Black Furnace Plain. With his bare hands, Ciögli the Mountain, the strongest of the Ishroi, broke the neck of Wutteät the Black, the Father of Dragons. Oirinas and Oirûnas fought side by side, working great carnage among the Sranc and Bashrag. Ingalira, the hero of Siöl, strangled Vshikcrû, mighty among the Inchoroi, and cast his burning body into the Sranc.

The mighty closed with the mighty, and innumerable battles were fought. But no matter how hard the Inchoroi pressed, the Cûnuroi would yield no ground. Their fury was that of those who have lost wives and daughters.

Then Nin'janjin struck down Cû'jara Cinmoi.

The Copper Tree of Siöl fell into pitching masses of Sranc, and the Cûnuroi were dismayed. Sin'niroiha, the High King of Nihrimsul and Ishoriöl, fought his way to Cû'-jara Cinmoi's position, but found only his headless body. Then the hero Gin'gûrima fell, gored by a Dragon. And after him Ingalira, who had been the first to lay eyes upon the Inchoroi. Then Oirinas, his body sundered by an Inchoroi spear of light.

Realizing their plight, Sin'niroiha rallied his people and began fighting his way into the Ring Mountains. A greater part of the surviving Cûnuroi followed him. Once clear of their foe, the glorious Ishroi of Eärwa fled, gripped by a mad fear. Either too weakened or suspecting a trap, the Inchoroi did not pursue.

For five hundred years the Cûnuroi and the Inchoroi waged a war of extermination, the Cûnoroi to avenge their murdered wives and the eventual death of their race, and the Inchoroi for reasons they alone could fathom. No longer did the Cûnuroi speak of the Incû-Holoinas, the Ark-of-the-Skies. Instead they spoke of Min-Uroikas, "the Pit of Obscenities"—what would later be called Golgotterath by Men.

For centuries it seemed the abominations had the upper hand, and the poets of the *Isûphiryas* record defeat after defeat. But slowly, as the Inchoroi exhausted their fell weapons and relied more and more on their vile slaves, the Cûnuroi and their Halaroi servants gained the advantage. Then at long last the surviving Ishroi of Eärwa trapped the last of their diminished foe within the Incû-Holoinas. For twenty years they warred through the Ark's labyrinthine halls, finally hunting the last of the Inchoroi into the deep places of the earth. Unable to destroy the vessel, Nil'giccas instructed the remaining Quya to raise a powerful glamour about the hated place. He and the surviving kings of the Nine Mansions forbade their peoples from mentioning the Inchoroi or their nightmarish legacy. The last Cûnuroi of Eärwa withdrew to their Mansions to await their inevitable doom.

Cûnuroi—See *Nonmen*.

Cûnwerishau (*c.* 290–*c.* 390)—First God-King of Trysë, famed for conquering all the cities of the Aumris as well as forging the first treaty between Men and Nonmen.

"Cut from them their tongues ..."—The famous phrase from *The Chronicle of the Tusk* condemning sorcery and sorcerers.

Cynnea, Braelwan (4059–4111)—Man-of-the-Tusk, Galeoth Earl of Agmundr, claimed by disease at Caraskand.

D

Dagliash—"Shieldhold" (Ûmeri). The ancient Aörsic fortress overlooking the River Sursa and the Plains of Agongorea, raised in 1601 by Nanor-Mikhus, High-King of Aörsi, upon the ruins of Viri. It changed hands several times in the wars preceding the Apocalypse. During the Great Ordeal, it would be the site of the Scalding.

Dag'mersor—"Westhold" (Ûmeri). Ancient Kûniüric fortress raised to protect roads joining Anûnuarcû to Ûmer proper.

Daimos—Also known as noömancy. The sorcery of summoning and enslaving agencies from the Outside. Daimotic Cants involve exploitation of the extensionless nature of the soul, the fact that all souls occupy the identical space, one orthogonal to the space of Bios, yet still belonging to the space of speech. For both political and pragmatic reasons, many Schools forbid their utterance, condemning the Daimos as irresponsible, if not reprehensible. The Tusk condemns the practice as wicked, and lists three different ways to execute its practitioners. Some esoteric scholars claim that Daimotic sorcerers condemn themselves to eternal torment at the hands of their erstwhile slaves when they die. But then all sorcerers arrive where monsters have come before them.

Dakyas—A semi-mountainous district of Nilnamesh.

Dameöri Wilderness—A vast tract of forested, Sranc-infested wilderness extending from the Tydonni frontier in the south and running northeast of the Osthwai Mountains to the Sea of Cerish.

Dark Hunter, the—A common epithet for Husyelt, the God of the Hunt.

"[the] darkness which comes before"—A phrase used by the Dûnyain to refer to the congenital blindness of individuals to the worldly causes that drive them, both historical and appetitive. See *Dûnyain*.

Daskas, House—One of the Houses of the Congregate.

Day Lantern—See *Diurnal*.

Dayrut—A small fortress in the Gedean interior, built by the Nansur after the fall of Shigek to the Fanim in 3933.

Dead-God, the—See *Lokung*.

Decapitants—Name given to the two severed demon heads slung from the waist of Anasûrimbor Kellhus I. In 4121, following the installation of Nurbanu Soter as King-Regent of High Ainon, the Holy Aspect-Emperor famously stayed in Kiz as a guest of Heramari Iyokus, the famed Blind Necromancer, learning the most forbidden of the forbidden arts, the Daimos. He reappeared four months later with the heads of two demons bound to his waist by their hair. Whenever he was asked about them, he would demure, often, as Hilu Akamis, a one-time Mandate Court Advisor, reports in his journals, ignoring the question altogether.

Akamis recounts a tale told him by a Shigeki drover, Pim, pressed into Imperial service working the Aspect-Emperor's baggage train. According to Akamis, Pim told of a trip across Gedea that took the Aspect-Emperor and his travel court across the legendary Plains of Mengedda. In the deep of the night, near the end of his watch, Pim found Anasûrimbor Kellhus alone and raving on the haunted plain, *alternately removing his head and replacing it with one of the Decapitants*. Akamis is rightly dismissive of the man's lurid account, though the Schoolman readily admits being frightened by his sincerity. "He had the look of a Sempic simpleton to him, one who had left his brain with the fish to dry."

As might be imagined, the Decapitants were a matter of some delicacy among Zaudunyani writers, since focusing upon them exclusively (as the Fanim and Inrithi Orthodox opponents of the Kellian regime certainly did) easily led to questions regarding what kind of man would bear such horrific trophies. So even though regularly extolled as "a verifying contradiction" (a phrase attributed to Werjau) by the Thousand Temples, Zaudunyani were as a rule loathe to discuss them.

Defence of the Arcane Arts, A—The famed sorcerous apologia of Zarathinius, which is as widely cited by philosophers as by sorcerers because of its pithy critiques not only of the Inrithi prohibition of sorcery but of Inrithism itself. The work has long been banned by the Thousand Temples.

Demua Mountains—An extensive range located in northwestern Eärwa, forming the frontier between Injor-Niyas and what was once Kûniüri.

denotaries—In Gnostic sorcery, the "primer" Cants given to students to practice "dividing their voice," which is to say, saying and thinking two separate things.

Derived—See Sranc.

Detnammi, Hirul (4081–4111)—Man-of-the-Tusk, Palatine of the Ainoni province of Eshkalas, slain at Subis under dishonourable circumstances.

Dialogues of Inceruti, The—One of the most famous "missing works" of Far Antiquity, frequently referenced by Ajencis.

Dinchases (4074–4111)—Man-of-the-Tusk, Captain of Attrempus and lifelong comrade-in-arms to Krijates Xinemus, slain at Iothiah. Also known as "Bloody Dinch."

Displacement—The immense crack resulting from the Arkfall that cleaves Ishterebinth.

Dispossessed Sons of Siol—Epithet given to the Siolan survivors who made their home in Ishterebinth after the destruction of their Mansion following the Breaking of the Gates.

Diurnal—One of the Sublime Contrivances of the Artisan, Emilidis, the Diurnal was a sorcerous lantern reputed to transform night into day (and so was also called the Day Lantern), thus denying the advantage darkness conferred on their foes during the Cûno-Inchoroi Wars.

"Doff your sandals and shod the earth ..."—Common saying meant to remind listeners not to project their failings onto others.

Dolour—The complex of afflictions that eventually overcome all Nonmen, who are then called Erratic (as opposed to Intact). The Dolour is often called the Second Curse of the Inoculation (the first being, of course, the Wombplague) insofar as it follows as a direct consequence of the immortality the Nonmen gained via the Inoculation. The problem is that souls simply cannot remember indefinitely, there is a limit, necessitating that something be forgotten to remember as a certain point. What renders this problem tragic is the way memories of trauma and shame find themselves chiseled, as opposed to simply inked, into the Nonman soul. This mean that the longer a Nonman lives, the more their soul becomes a repository of anguish and pain. The Dolour proper is thought to happen when *only painful experiences remain*, robbing the sufferer of the ability to remember anything beyond several heartbeats (lest that memory be tragic). This has the effect of rendering them incompetent, *Erratic*, though in surprisingly diverse set of ways. Far and away the bulk of the Erratic become progressively more loathe to depart places familiar (or once familiar). The Nonman madness for graven image and statuary is often attributed to the Dolour, the hope that externalizing memory would preserve them. But a substantial proportion have been known to "forget home," to travel far and wide seeking out the kinds of tragic encounters that will reactivate their memory, render them nearly whole, if for only a brief span. These are the souls that populate Mannish history, mad and tragic figures such as Sujara'nin, Incariol, Cinial'jin, and many others. Many think these Wayward Erratics are in sooth suicides, souls that have found a means around the inborn inability to take their own lives.

The final stage of the Dolour is called the Gloom, the point where anguish has been worn into animal misery by the endless years. Sufferers lose the ability to speak or care about anything but the most instinctive necessities. As far as anyone knows, a Nonman may live in this state indefinitely.

Amongst human scholars there has been a long tradition of theorizing the Dolour, interrogating the metaphysical implications of the condition. How could a soul, which has no extension, become full? What would it be like to be such a soul? What does it say about the dependency of the present on the past? Is the *now* but, as Ajencis asks, "an excretion of the past"? These comprise a small fraction of the impious questions Men have pursued under the auspices of the Dolour.

Domyot–(Sheyic version of "Torumyan") Also known as the Black Iron City. The administrative capital of Zeüm, famed for the cruelty of its rulers and for its iron-skirted walls. For most in the Three Seas, Domyot is as much a place of legend as Golgotterath.

Dragons–See *Wracu*.

Dreams, the–The nightmares experienced by Mandate Schoolmen of the Apocalypse as witnessed through Seswatha's eyes.

Dunjoksha (4055–)–The Sapatishah-Governor of Holy Amoteu.

Dûnyain–A severe monastic sect that has repudiated history and animal appetite in the name of finding enlightenment through the control of all desire and all circumstance. Though the origins of the Dûnyain are obscure (many think them the descendants of the ecstatic sects that arose across the Ancient North in the days preceding the Apocalypse), their belief system is utterly unique, leading some to conclude their original inspiration had to be philosophical rather than religious in any traditional sense.

Much of Dûnyain belief follows from their interpretation of what they consider their founding principles. The Empirical Priority Principle (sometimes referred to as the Principle of Before and After) asserts that within the circle of the world, what comes before determines what comes after without exception. The Rational Priority Principle asserts that Logos, or Reason, lies outside the circle of the world (though only in a formal and not an ontological sense). The Epistemological Principle asserts that knowing what comes before (via the Logos) yields "control" of what comes after.

Given the Priority Principle, it follows that thought, which falls within the circuit of the before and after, is also determined by what comes before. The Dûnyain therefore believe the will to be illusory, an artifact of the soul's inability to perceive what comes before it. The soul, in the Dûnyain worldview, *is part of the world*, and therefore as much driven by prior events as anything else. (This stands in stark contrast to the dominant stream of Three Seas and Ancient North thought, where the soul is taken to be, in Ajencis's words, "that which precedes everything.")

In other words, Men do not possess "self-moving souls." Far from a given, such a soul is an *accomplishment* for the Dûnyain. All souls, they claim, possess *conatus*, the natural striving to be self-moving, to escape the circle of before and after. They naturally seek to *know* the world about them and so climb out of the circle. But a host of factors make outright escape impossible. The soul men are born with is too obtuse and clouded by animal passions to be anything other than a slave of what comes before. The whole point of the Dûnyain ethos is to overcome these limitations and so become a self-moving soul—to attain what they call the Absolute, or the Unconditioned Soul.

But unlike those exotic Nilnameshi sects devoted to various other forms of "enlightenment," the Dûnyain are not so naive as to think this can be attained within the course of a single lifetime. They think of this, rather, as a multi-generational process. Quite early on they recognized that the instrument itself, the soul, was flawed, so they instituted a program of selective breeding for intellect and dispassion. In a sense the entire sect became a kind of experiment, isolated from the world to maintain control, with each prior generation training the next to the limit of their capabilities, the idea being that over the millennia they would produce souls that could climb further and further from the circle of before and after. The hope was that eventually they would produce a soul utterly transparent to Logos, a soul capable of apprehending all the darknesses that come before.

Dûnyanic—The language of the Dûnyain, which remains very close to the original Kûniüri from which it is derived.

E

Eämnor—A lost White Norsirai nation of the Ancient North. The roots of Eämnor reach back to the days of Aulyanau the Conqueror and the Cond Yoke. In 927, Aulyanau conquered the fortress of Ara-Etrith ("New Etrith") and, struck by the anarcane characteristics of Mount Ankulakai, settled several Cond tribes in the vicinity. These tribes flourished, and under the influence of the nearby cities of the Aumris they quickly abandoned their pastoral ways. In fact the Cond were so effectively assimilated into Aumris culture that their White Norsirai cousins, the Scintya, took them for High Norsirai during the time of the Scintya Yoke (1228–1381).

Eämnor proper emerged from the Scintya Yoke as one of the pre-eminent nations of the Ancient North. Though laid waste in 2148, Eämnor could be considered the sole surviving nation of the Apocalypse, insofar as Atrithau survived. Due to the concentrations of Sranc, however, Atrithau has never been able to recover more than a fraction of the lands constituting historical Eämnor.

Eämnoric—The lost language of ancient Eämnor, a derivative of Condic.

Eänna—"[Land of the] Uplifted Sun" (Thoti-Eännorean). The traditional name of all the lands to the east of the Great Kayarsus.

Eärwa—"[Land of the] Felled Sun" (Thoti-Eännorean). The traditional name of all the lands to the west of the Great Kayarsus.

Ebara—A small fortress in the Gedean interior, built by the Nansur after the fall of Shigek to the Fanim in 3933.

Ecosium Market—The main "wares market" of Sumna, located just south of the Hagerna.

Escalumis (2299–2389)—Ceneian historian (of Antanameran descent) and famed author of *On the Arrangement of Souls in Battle and War*.

Ecstasis—Nonman expression for revelatory experiences obtained in contemplation of beauty.

Ej'ulkiyah—A Khirgwi name for the Carathay Desert meaning "Great Thirst."

Ekirick, Goettal (4089–)—Ordealman, Shield-Thane of King Hogrim, known as the Bald.

Ekkinû—Sorcerous arras behind Kellhus's bench in the Eleven-Pole Chamber. Sorcerous artifact of unknown provenance or function, first reported in the possession of Anasûrimbor Kellhus in 4122 (thus earning a place among the Orthodox "Articles of Damnation"). Several theories regarding its origins and uses have circulated through various literate entrepots around the Three Seas, among them the suggestion that the undulating displays constitute some kind of language, but consensus considers them decorative merely.

Ekyannus I (2304–72)—The first "institutional" Shriah of the Thousand Temples, and the author of the widely admired *44 Epistles*.

Ekyannus III, "the Golden" (2432–2516)—The Shriah of the Thousand Temples who converted Triamis the Great in 2505 and thus assured the predominance of Inrithism in the Three Seas.

Eleäzaras, Hanamanu (4060–)—Man-of-the-Tusk, Grandmaster of the Scarlet Spires.

Eleneöt, Fields of—See *Battle of Eleneöt Fields*.

elhusioli—The daimos of excess. As per standard Kiünnat metaphysics, souls directly move other souls, impart the imprint of daimos upon another daimos. Some, such as terror or enthusiasm, are set apart for the dramatic nature of their effects.

Eliriqû (?–?)—Legendary Siolan progenitor of the Quya (whom are often referred to as the "Sons of Eliriqû"), who established the "Lore-Kinning" to parallel the "War-Kinning" structure of the Ishroi found in all great Mansions (save Viri), laying the groundwork for what became the Quya.

elju—The Ihrimsû word for "book," referring to someone, either Man or Sranc, who accompanies a Nonman to aid with his failing memory.

elking—Sakarpan rite of passage conferring the rights and obligations of manhood upon adolescent boys.

Emilidis (?–?)—The Artisan, the famed "kinningless" Nonman Siqu who founded the Gnostic School of Contrivers, the Mihtrûlic, in Far Antiquity, and is credited with the manufacture of a wide number of sorcerous artifacts. A great deal of controversy and confusion surrounds the Artisan and his creations, the latter because the

School of Mihtrûlic insisted on crediting Emilidis with the manufacture of everything save the humblest sorcerous artifacts long after his disappearance, and the former because Emilidis was a foundling, and as such, possessed no family historian. The first mention of him in the *Isûphiryas* involves his gift of the Sky Lantern to King Sin'niroiha of Nihrimsûl, an artifact that not only secured his fame among the Mansions, but led to Sin'niroiha's marriage to Tsinirû, and thence the birth of Nil'giccas, and the end of the long war between Nihrimsûl and the Houses of Tsonos. He first enters human history during the Nonman Tutelage, founding the Mihtrûlic sometime late in the rule of God-King Nincama-Telesser (Mandate scholars give the date of 661, but this is disputed).

As kinningless, Emilidis grew up in the deep Qûlnimil, the famed nimil mines of Ishoriöl, a fact which perhaps explains his lifelong obsession with the sorcery of *materiality* when he could have been the greatest Quya the Nonmen had ever known. According to legend, the great Hero-Mage, Titirga once confessed that Emilidis "swam deep where he could only watch from the shallows." His greatest works, or Sublime Contrivances, exhibit miraculous reworkings of *nature itself*, be it the twisting of *down sideways* with the Immaculate Rim (*Orimuril*), or the spawning of *day* (as opposed to merely light) with the Diurnal, or the *recombination of souls* with the Amiolas. Though other Contrivers have managed to create artifacts immune to Chorae, Emilidis is unparalleled in that *all* his creations, from the merest dagger to the famed Day Lantern, exhibit such immunity. Mandate scholars cite this as why Nil'giccas charged him with raising the Barricades high upon the Upright Horn—what would prove to be his final, and most tragically flawed, work. The Legendary Artisan retreated from both the World and the historical record after this, admitting only private petitioners to his Foundry in the Qûlnimil.

Emiorali—The name of the mythical inhabitants of the Yimaleti in Far Antiquity, referenced several times in the *Holy Sagas* (typically as Men possessing unnatural ferocity and prowess in battle), but dismissed as a "wives fancy" by Ajencis.

Empharas, Krijates (4103–)—Ordealman, Palatine-Marshal of Attrempus, general of the Conriyans in the Great Ordeal of Anasûrimbor Kellhus.

Empire-behind-the-Mountains—A Scylvendi name for the Nansurium.

Emwama—The indigenous Men of Eärwa, who, as slaves of the Nonmen, were massacred by the Five Tribes following the Breaking of the Gates. Very little is known of them.

Enathpaneah—A governorate of Kian and former province of the Nansur Empire. Located at the hinge of Khemema and Xerash, Enathpaneah is a semi-mountainous, semi-arid land whose wealth is predominantly derived from the caravans that pass through Caraskand, its administrative and commercial capital.

Engûs (c. 1236–c. 1255)—The fifth son of Borswelka IV (1198–1249) famed for the loss of Swur Fords (to his eldest brother) in 1251, and his subsequent flight into the Demua mountains, where he and his remaining household would live a life of murderous outlawry before finally being hunted down and killed. According to the Yolkbook (the traditional verse chronicle of the Meöri Kings), the victors—the last two surviving brothers—found numerous Sranc bones and skulls scattered about Engûs's camp. According to Sakarpi legend, the vale that had hidden their encampment remains cursed to the present day.

Enhorû, Temus (4066–)—Ordealman, Grandmaster of the Imperial Saik in the Great Ordeal of Anasûrimbor Kellhus.

Ennutil—A Scylvendi tribe of the northwestern Steppe.

Enshoiya—Sheyic for "certainty." Zaudunyani name for the Warrior-Prophet's sword.

ensolarii—The base monetary unit of High Ainon.

Eöthic Garrison—The primary fortress and barracks of the Emperor's personal guard, dominating Momemn's northern quarter.

Eöthic Guard—The personal heavy infantry guard of the Nansur Emperors, consisting primarily of Norsirai mercenaries from Cepalor.

Epistemologies, The—A work oft attributed to Ajencis but more likely a redacted compilation drawn from his other works. Many consider it his definitive philosophical statement on the nature of knowledge, but some argue that it distorts his position since it presents a unitary vision of views that actually evolved quite dramatically over the course of his life.

Erengaw Plain—Tablelands located to the north of the Urokkas and to the east of the River Sursa.

Eritga (4092–4111)—A Galeoth slave-girl belonging to Cutias Sarcellus, slain in the deserts of Khemema.

Erratic—Name given to those Nonmen overcome by the Dolour. From the Ihrimsû, "*Mi,*" a term sometimes translated as "Wayward."

Eryeat, Coithus (4038–4116)—The King of Galeoth, and father of Coithus Saubon.

Eryelk, Thurror (3771–*c.* 3830)—Holca freebooter who earned fame as both a hero and a criminal during the Scholastic Wars (3796–3818).

Erzû—Iswazi gown stitched with one hundred and thirteen pockets for the one hundred and thirteen fetishes traditionally used by the Mbimayû.

Eshganax—A Palatinate of High Ainon, located across the north Secharib Plains.

Eshkalas—A Palatinate of High Ainon, famed for the quality of its cotton, located on the western edge of the Secharib Plains.

Eswarlû, Embas (4102–)—Ordealman, Angle-Thane of Scolow, a frontier march of Agmundr, Galeoth.

Etrithatta—Original city of the Aumris, ancient rival of Ûmerau, destroyed by the Scintya in 1228.

Eumarna—Populous province of the New Empire and former governorate of Kian. Located to the south of the Betmulla Mountains, Eumarna is a large, fertile land that is primarily known for its exports of wine and horses. Though once comprising the commercial heart of the Kianene Empire, its capitulation and subsequent conversion to Zaudûnyani proved remarkably swift. See *Unification Wars, the*.

Eumarni—The language of Eumarna, a derivative of ancient Mamati.

eunuchs—Men castrated either before or after the onset of puberty, but usually before. Eunuchs have become something of an informal caste in the Three Seas, both in the management of harems and also in high administrative posts, where their lack of progeny, the belief is, renders them more immune to influence and less likely to harbour dynastic ambitions.

Exalted Bark—"*Ishivaril*" (Ihrimsû). The levitating platform housing the urtotem of Ishterebinth, the Aeviternal Seal, and the throne of its king, the Black Iron Seat.

Exalt-General—The traditional title of the Imperial Army's supreme commander.

Excuciata—Famed fresco of the One Hundred and Eleven Hells in the Holy Junriüma, and perhaps the most well-known of the countless artistic renditions of perdition. Apparently inspired by ancient, pre-Arkfall Nonman statuary, the grand image—the product of the legendary "Ten Simpletons" to commemorate the Scholastic Wars in 3800—is the first depiction of the hells that defects from spatial and associative norms, bringing the chaos of damnation to the fore. As a ceiling fresco, it is sometimes referred to as the Hanging Hells or the Inverse Fire.

Excursi—Sranc bred to escort Mannish allies of the Consult through regions populated with wild Sranc. Their origins are obscure, though several references to Sranc fitting their description can be found in the Pit-of-Years, suggesting they were a creation of the Inchoroi, and thus fashioned via the Tekne proper, rather than being the product of some later Consult breeding regime.

Exhortations—The sole surviving work of Hatatian. See *Hatatian*.

"Expect not, and you shall find glory everlasting ..."—*The Tractate*, Book of Priests, 8:31. The famed "Expect Not Admonition" of Inri Sejenus, where he urges his followers to give without hope of exchange. The paradox, of course, is that by doing this, they hope for eternal paradise in exchange.

Extrinsic Gate—Epithet given to Ûbil Maw, the great outer gate of Golgotterath, in distinction to Ûbil Noscisor, the Intrinsic Gate.

F

Fallow Gate—The northernmost gate of Ishuäl.

Fama Palace—The residence and administrative seat of the Warrior-Prophet while the First Holy War remained in Caraskand, located on the Heights of the Bull.

Fanashila (4092–4112)—One of Esmenet's Kianene body-slaves during the First Holy War.

Fanayal ab Kascamandri (4075–4132)—The first-born son of the Padirajah, and leader of the Coyauri, his famed elite heavy cavalry.

Fane (3669–3742)—The Prophet of the Solitary God and founder of Fanimry. Initially a Shrial Priest in the Nansur province of Eumarna, Fane was declared a heretic by the ecclesiastical courts of the Thousand Temples in 3703 and banished to certain death in the Carathay Desert. According to Fanim tradition, rather than dying in the desert, Fane went blind, experienced the series of revelations narrated in the *kipfa'aifan*, the "Witness of Fane," and was granted miraculous powers (the same powers attributed to the Cishaurim) he called the Water of Indara. He spent the remainder of his life preaching to and consolidating the desert tribes of the Kianene, who after his death would launch the White Jihad under the leadership of Fane's son, Fan'oukarji I.

Fanim—The name used by the Inrithi to refer to the followers of Fanimry.

Fanimry—A monotheistic faith founded upon the revelations of the Prophet Fane. The central tenets of Fanimry deal with the solitary nature and transcendence of the God, the falseness of the Gods (who are considered demons by the Fanim), the repudiation of the Tusk as unholy, and the prohibition of all representations of the God. Despite the many sects within the religion, all are founded upon variant interpretations of the *kipfa'aifan*, the "Witness of Fane," which contains the narration of the Prophet's experiences following his apostasy as a priest in the Thousand Temples and subsequent banishment into the wilds of the Carathay Desert.

All Fanim, regardless of their sect, are enjoined to practice Dwiva, the Twelve Disciplines, the rigours which the desert forces upon those who would survive it (thus transforming, as Farjanjua, the great Invitic Inrithi critic of the upstart religion would declare, the deprivations suffered by all desert pastoralists into sacred rules of conduct). Almost every variant of the faith finds its distinction in its interpretation of the meaning and importance of various strictures named in the Dwiva. Either because of Fane's training as an Inrithi priest or his keen understanding of his spiritual competitors, the new faith almost immediately developed its own tradition of rational theology. The greatest sectarian divide predates the White Jihad in 3743, the product of a legendary dispute between the two most prominent and strong-willed disciples of Fane, Masurkur and Narunshinde. As the senior spiritual and military advisors of Fan'oukarji I (who always called them his "Bickering Crows"), both actively advocated drastically different interpretations of Dwiva, and so, starkly different visions of the future of Fanimry. For Masurkur, only a strict and violent interpretation of the Twelve Disciplines assured passage to paradise. He advocated the "Pok Harit" the One Direction, giving birth to the Pokariti, the first ascetic, militant strand of Fanimry. For Narunshinde, on the other hand, *belief in the Prophet alone* was enough to gain entrance, with the Dwiva acting primarily as an aspirational ideal. He advocated the Somha Jil, or the Clasped Hand, a far more inclusive—and from the standpoint of conversion—a far more marketable version of the faith. His followers, which came to form the decided majority, were known as the Sumajil. Fan'oukarji I would become notorious for using Pokariti or Sumajil justifications opportunistically, either to rationalize his many cruelties, or his just as numerous acts of generosity. He actively encouraged the institutionalization of both schools of interpretation after the deaths of both disciples, apparently assuming they would prove as useful to his successors as they had to him, rather than forming the chasm that would claim countless lives in the centuries that followed.

Fan'oukarji I (3716–71)–"Peerless son of Fane" (Kianni). The son of the Prophet Fane and the first Padirajah of Kian. Fan'oukarji is credited with the fantastic success of the White Jihad against the Nansur Empire.

Far Antiquity—The historical period beginning with the Breaking of the Gates and ending with the Apocalypse in 2155. See *Near Antiquity*.

Far Wuor—Name given to those portions of Wuor, the northwesternmost province of Kûniüri, gradually abandoned between 1440 and 1680 due to Sranc incursions across the Leash.

Fathoming—A pilgrimage to the Holy Deep of Ishterebinth, sometimes called the *Riminaloikas*, or "Journey to the Underworld [Pit]." Even though Avoidance (or Ascetic) Faiths such as those characterizing Nonmen belief often defy human understanding, a number of ritualistic parallels can be identified, such as pilgrimages and various analogous rites of passage. The Fathoming constitutes a symbolic re-enactment of Imimorûl's flight from the Heavens (or "Starving") into the depths beneath what became Siol, the House Primordial, the idea being that souls so deep can slip the notice of the Gods and find oblivion. Fathomings were most common undertaken by those upon the threshold of death, the thought being that the Deepest Deep lay on the edge of Oblivion.

Fatwall—Scalper name for the Imperial outpost located on the ruins of Maimor beneath the eastern Osthwai Mountains.

Feast of Kussapokari—A traditional Inrithi holiday marking the summer solstice.

fevers—A generic name for various forms of malaria.

Few, the—Those born with the innate ability to sense the onta and work sorcery. Perhaps few aspects of sorcery have been more debated than the so-called "Arcane Eye": what it consists in, how it enables sorcerous interventions, and why such a small proportion of Men (as compared, say, to Nonmen) are so unfortunate as to possess it. See *sorcery*.

Finaöl, Weofota (4066–4111)—Man-of-the-Tusk, Earl of the Tydonni province of Canute, slain at Anwurat.

Fingers—Name given to the summit of Irsûlor by the Men of the Ordeal during the Battle of Irsûlor, because of the five headless pillars jutting there.

First and Final Word—A common epithet for the words of Inri Sejenus.

First Holy War—The Inrithi host summoned by Maithanet that invaded Kian in 4111 bent upon the reconquest of Shimeh. Called by Hem Shibbo, quite without hyperbole, "The loins of all history to follow."

Characterized by strife and jealousy from the outset, the First Holy War was not in fact the first pilgrim host to answer Maithanet's call and march against the Fanim. It followed rather, upon the heels of the so-called "Vulgar Holy War," which was utterly annihilated by the Fanim of Skauras ab Nalajan, the Sapatishah of Shigek, on the Plains of Mengedda in 4110. Where the Vulgar Holy War had failed, the host that has come to be called the First Holy War prevailed, despite the superior tactics of their Fanim adversaries. The Men-of-the-Tusk, as the Inrithi were called, seized the north bank of the River Sempis, and committed innumerable barbarities in the name of all they held sacred. The first recorded mention of Anasûrimbor Kellhus dates to this time.

In Late Summer of 4111, the Inrithi crossed the Sempis and met the Fanim in full array beneath the fortress of Anwurat. Rattled by the numbers the Fanim had amassed, as well as by the nearness of the match on Mengedda, the Great Names, the Princes and Generals of the various nationalities and factions ceded command of the host to a Scylvendi freebooter named Cnaiür urs Skiötha, an extraordinary decision that would see Skauras killed and the Fanim routed.

On the Nansur Emperor's assurance that his fleet could keep the host supplied with fresh water, the Great Names made the fateful decision to immediately strike south along the coast of the Carathay Desert. The Fanim, however, managed to surprise and destroy the Nansur Fleet at the Battle of Trantis, stranding the First Holy War deep in the Carathay with nothing but a few poisoned wells and fouled oases. The legendary suffering of the host likely played no small role in the transformation of Anasûrimbor Kellhus from mere sage to a prophetic figure.

By the time the survivors reached Enathpaneah and laid siege to Caraskand that autumn, several Great Names were already arguing for his destruction. Some, perhaps sensing future advantage, advocated for him. Others simply found the idea of a holy war being conquered from within preposterous.

Caraskand fell to the Inrithi invaders even as the skirmishers belonging to Kascamandri, the Padirajah of the Kianene Empire, rode within sight of the city's great curtain walls. In another extraordinary twist, the First Holy War now found itself besieged within the very city it had spent weeks starving. Disease and deprivation wracked the host as violently as it had on the Carathay. The matter of Anasûrimbor Kellhus and his Zaudunyani finally came to a head; the Great Names condemned him and sentenced him according to Tusk Law. He was bound to the corpse of his wife, then hung upside down from an iron circumfix. Riots broke out between the Orthodox and the Zaudunyani.

According to various books in the *Novum*, it was the Scylvendi freebooter, Cnaiür urs Skiötha, who revealed the first of the Consult skin-spies in the host's midst. Vindicated, Anasûrimbor Kellhus was released and exalted in the eyes the entire host—all save a handful were subsequently whelmed into the Zaudunyani faith. The skin-spies were purged from the ranks, and then, in the early spring of 4112, the once fractious host marched out under the leadership of a *new prophet* to meet Kascamandri and his Fanim Grandees in battle. Despite their dreadful condition, their fanaticism and superior armaments proved invincible on the field, and the Kianene were once again put to route with grievous losses.

A far different First Holy War undertook the remainder of the epochal campaign. Called in the name of a long-dead prophet, Inri Sejenus, it now marched under the command of a *living prophet*, Anasûrimbor Kellhus. Once massive and inchoate, prone to fumble tactically, it was now compact and articulated, more liable to surprise than be surprised. The host swept into the Governorate of Xerash, and thence into Holy Amoteu itself, swatting aside what resistance the Fanim, now under the leadership of Fanayal ab Kascamandri, could rally to slow their advance.

Two factors prevented the final battle for Holy Shimeh from being the rote conclusion of three successive victories over a single foe. The first was the Cishaurim decision to finally take the field against the Scarlet Spires, and the second was the betrayal of the Nansur. The Cishaurim Primaries, in particular, proved far more powerful than any had imagined, leading to what is now widely referred to as the Scarlet Letting, the reduction of the Scarlet Spires to no more than fourteen sorcerers-of-rank. According the Novum, only the reappearance of Anasûrimbor Kellhus prevented this calamity from becoming an abject catastrophe.

The second was the treachery of the Nansur contingent of the Holy War under the stewardship of Ikurei Conphas, which, were it not for the actions of the Holy Tutor, would have sealed the doom of the First Holy War. Even though the Inrithi host ultimately achieved all of its primary objectives, a number of scholars (Hem Shibbo among them) have dared note that its ultimate consequence, the rise of Anasûrimbor Kellhus, precipitated the end of Inrithism almost as completely as the end of Fanimry.

Five Hosts of Nilnû—Collective name referring to the five (in truth six) tribal confederacies, the Eshdutt, the Harû (or sometimes, "Harataka"), the Midarû, the Invoira, and the Sombatti (which is in fact divided into the Rappol and the Sombatt) that have historically contended for power over the whole of Nilnamesh.

Five Tribes of Men—The five rough cultural and racial groups that migrated into the Eärwic subcontinent at the beginning of the Second Age; respectively, the Norsirai, the Ketyai, the Satyothi, the Scylvendi, and the Xiuhianni.

Flail, the—A constellation in the northern sky.

flat-place, the—According to Scylvendi custom, the ideal spiritual state wherein the Scylvendi warrior, freed of all passion and desire, becomes the very expression of the land.

Forbidden Road—A secret military road connecting the Scylvendi and Kianene frontiers of the Nansur Empire.

44 Epistles—The magnum opus of Ekyannus I, consisting of forty-four "letters" written to the God, including commentary and confession as well as philosophical inquiry and critique.

Four Armies, the—Name given to the division of the Great Ordeal (for the purposes of foraging) into four separate columns, each with their own command: the Army of the Middle North, the Army of the Ketyai-of-the-East, the Army of the Ketyai-of-the-West, and the Army of the Ketyai-of-the-South.

Four-Horned Brother—Common epithet for Ajokli in the Three Seas.

Fourth Analytic of Men, The—Also known as *The Book of Maxims*. One of the more famous works of Ajencis, containing several hundred not so flattering "Observations of Men" and the corresponding maxims outlining the practical way to deal with each of the Men so observed.

Fourth Dialogue of the Movements of the Planets as They Pertain to Astrology, The—One of the famed "lost works" of Ajencis.

Fustaras (4061–4111)—An Orthodox agitator and proadjunct from the Selial Column.

G

Gaenkelti (4068–4111)—The Exalt-Captain of the Palatial Eöthic Guard.

Gaenri—A fiefdom of Galeoth, located to the northwest near the Hethantas.

Gaeterius (2981–3045)—The Ceneian slave-scholar celebrated for his commentaries on *The Chronicle of the Tusk* collected under the title *Contemplations on the Indentured Soul*.

Gaethuni—A fiefdom of Ce Tydonn, located on the southwestern coasts.

Gaidekki, Shressa (4062–)—Man-of-the-Tusk, Palatine of the Conriyan district of Anplei.

Gâl, Plains of—A great expanse of grasslands to the north of the Cerish Sea.

Galeoth—A Norsirai nation of the Three Seas. Following the Apocalypse, countless thousands of Meöri refugees settled the environs north of Lake Huösi. Though nominally tributary to the Ceneian Empire, surviving records indicate that the "Galoti," as the Ceneians called them, were a fractious and warlike people. At some point in the thirty-fifth century, sedentary kingdoms began to displace the pastoral tribes along the Vindauga and Sculpa rivers. Galeoth proper did not arise until *c.* 3683, when King Norwain I reputedly concluded twenty years of campaigning and conquest by having his captive foes butchered en masse in the reception hall of Moraör, the great palace complex of the Galeoth Kings.

Galeoth Wars—The wars fought between Galeoth and the Nansur Empire, first in 4103–4, then again in 4106. In each case the Galeoth, under the generalship of

Coithus Saubon, enjoyed early successes, only to be subsequently defeated in more decisive engagements, the last of which was the Battle of Procorus, where Ikurei Conphas commanded the Imperial Army.

Galgota, Nisht (4062–)—Man-of-the-Tusk, Palatine of the Ainoni palatinate of Eshganax.

Gallish—The language of Galeoth, derived from Old Meoric.

Gam—Legendary Shiradi King featured in the Fable of Gam, the story of how he faked his own death to test the character of his sons, only to be murdered by them.

Ganbrota, Murworg (4064–)—Man-of-the-Tusk, Earl of the Thunyeri fiefdom of Ingraul.

gandoki—Gallish for "shadows." A traditional Galeoth sport where two men, their wrists bound to either end of two poles, attempt to knock each other off their footing.

Gangan-naru—"Parching Wind" (Sakarpic). Name for the periodic shift in prevailing summer winds on the Istyuli Plains. Typically seen as a harbinger of drought.

Ganrelka II, Anasûrimbor (2104–47)—The successor of Celmomas II and the last reigning High King of Kûniüri.

Ganrikka, Warthût (4070–4132)—Man-of-the-Tusk, client thane of Gothyelk during the First Holy War, and Ordealman in the Great Ordeal of Anasûrimbor Kellhus, slain at the Battle of Imweor.

Ganuiral—"Way of Sages" (Ûmeri). The grand avenue leading to the Library in ancient Sauglish, famously called the Mawagiral, or "Way of Ranters," for the heretics and visionaries who assembled along its length, arguing all manner of madnesses.

Ganyatti, Amurrei (4064–)—Man-of-the-Tusk, Conriyan Palatine of the district of Ankirioth.

Gaörtha—The true name of the second skin-spy to pose as Cutias Sarcellus.

Gara'gûl—A small yet strategic fortress located in Mongilea.

Garsahadutha, Ram-Sassor (4076–4111)—Man-of-the-Tusk, tributary Prince of Sansor, leader of the Sansori in the Ainoni contingent of the Holy War, slain at the Battle of Anwurat.

Gaspers—Nonman pejorative for the Inchoroi.

Gate of Horns—One of Caraskand's main gates.

Gate of Pelts—One of Sumna's famed Nine Great Gates, opening onto the Karian Way.

Gate of Wheels—See *Great Gate of Wheels*.

Gaumum, House—A Nansur House of the Congregate, with holdings scattered across the western Kyranae Plain.

Gayamakri, Sattushal (4070–)—One of the Nascenti, formerly an Ainoni baron.

Gedea—A governorate of Kian, and former province of the Nansur Empire. Located between Shigek and the Anaras Spur, Gedea is a semi-arid land with interior plateaus and semi-mountainous coasts. Historically, Gedea is primarily known as the battleground between ancient Shigek and Kyraneas.

Gekas—A palatinate of High Ainon, located on the upper River Sayut.

Gerotha—The administrative and commercial capital of Xerash.

Geshrunni (4069–4110)—Man-of-the-Tusk, Shield-Captain of the Javreh, slain in Carythusal.

Gesindal—A fiefdom of Galeoth located to the immediate northwest of Oswenta. A disproportionate number of Gesindalmen belong to the so-called Tattoo Cult of Gilgaöl—a subsect common among the Galeoth and Cepalorans—believing that skin tattooed with the sacred signs of War is immune to injury.

Ghoset—An ancient Wracu spawned during the Cûno-Inchoroi Wars.

Gielgath—An important Nansur city located on the Meneanor coast.

Gierra—The God of carnal passion. One of the so-called Compensatory Gods, who reward devotion in life with paradise in the afterlife, Gierra is very popular throughout the Three Seas, particularly among aging men drawn to the "aphrodisica," Cultic nostrums reputed to enhance virility. In the *Higarata*, the collection of subsidiary writings that form the scriptural core of the Cults, Gierra is rarely depicted with any consistency, and is often cast as a malign temptress, luring men to the luxury of her couch, often with fatal consequences.

Gift-of-Yatwer—Epithet for the White-Luck Warrior.

Gilcûnya—The tongue of the Nonmen Quya and the Gnostic Schools, thought to be a debased version of Auja-Gilcûnni, the so-called "ground" (or first) tongue of the Cûnuroi.

Gilgallic Gate—An immense gate located at the westernmost point of Momemn's walls.

Gilgaöl—The God of war and conflict. One of the so-called Compensatory Gods, who reward devotion in life with paradise in the afterlife, Gilgaöl is perhaps the most popular of the Hundred Gods. In the *Higarata*, the collection of subsidiary writings that form the scriptural core of the Cults, Gilgaöl is depicted as harsh and skeptical of Men, continually demanding proof of worth from those who would follow him. Though subordinate to the Thousand Temples, the Gilgallic Cult boasts nearly as many priests, and perhaps receives more in the way of sacrificial donations. Also known as the Dread Father of Death, the All-Taker, the Wielder, the Breaker-of-Heroes, among many other epithets.

Ginsil (2115–c. 2147)—The wife of General En-Kaujalau in *The Sagas*, who pretended to be her husband to fool the assassins coming to kill him.

Gin'yursis (?–2152)—Nonman King of Cil-Aujas, famously slain by the very Meori refugees (under the leadership of Nosol) he sheltered from the No-God during the Apocalypse.

Giolal—Name of the forests to the east of Ishterebinth reserved since ancient days for hunting.

Girgalla (1798–1841)—An ancient Kûniüric poet famed for his *Epic of Sauglish*.

Girgash—A nation of the Three Seas, located on the mountainous northern frontier of Nilnamesh, and the only Fanim nation aside from Kian.

Girgashi—The language of Fanic-Girgash, a derivative of Sapmatari.

Girgilioth—A ruined city on the south bank of the River Sempis, which was once the capital of Kyranean-occupied Shigek but was destroyed following Kyraneas's demise in the Apocalypse.

gishrut—A traditional Scylvendi drink made from fermented mare's milk.

Gloom—Final stage of the Dolour, suffered by the Reduced. See *Dolour*.

Gnosis—The branch of sorcery once practiced by the Gnostic Schools of the Ancient North but now known only to the Schools of Mandate and Mangaecca. Unlike Anagogic sorcery, Gnostic sorcery is leveraged through the use of the Abstractions, which is why Gnostic sorcerers are often referred to as Philosopher Magi. The Gnosis was first developed by the Nonmen Quya, who imparted it to the early Norsirai Anagogic sorcerers during the Nonman Tutelage, 555–825.

Gnostic Cants include: the Bar of Heaven, the Bisecting Planes of Mirseor, the Cirroi Loom, the Compass of Noshainrau, the Cross of Arches, the Ellipses of Thosolankis, the Entelechy Theorems, the First Quyan Fold, the Mathesis Pin, the Noviratic Warspike, the Odaini Concussion Cant, the Ribs of Gottagga, the Seventh Quyan Theorem, the Third Concentric, the Weära Comb, and the High Titirgic Axiom.

See *sorcery*.

Gnostic Schools—Those Schools that practice the Gnosis. Only two such Schools, the Mangaecca and the Mandate, survive, though prior to the Apocalypse some dozen or so Gnostic Schools were in existence, the Sohonc foremost among them.

Goat's Heart, The—The famed book of fables by Protathis.

God, the—In Inrithi tradition, the unitary, omniscient, omnipotent, and immanent being responsible for existence, of which Gods (and in some strains Men) are but "aspects." In the Kiünnat tradition, the God is more an abstract placeholder than anything else. In the Fanim tradition, the God is the unitary, omniscient, omnipotent, and *transcendent* being responsible for existence (thus the "Solitary God"), against which the Gods war for the hearts of men.

Gods, the—Supernatural inhabitants of the Outside possessing human characteristics and figuring as objects of ritual and worship. See *Hundred Gods, the*.

Goken the Red (4058–4117)—Man-of-the-Tusk, notorious pirate and Thunyeri Earl of Cern Auglai.

Golgotterath—The nigh impregnable stronghold of the so-called Consult, located to the north of Neleöst Sea in the shadow of the Yimaleti Mountains. Called Min-

Uroikas by the Nonmen during the Cûno-Inchoroi Wars, Golgotterath did not become significant to human history until its occupation by the Mangaecca School in 777, who excavated the Incû-Holoinas and raised vast fortifications about it.

The greater complex is utterly dominated by the twin Horns of the Incû-Holoinas, but the vast mound of black basalt comprising their foundation approaches their mass. The Nonmen called it Ûriqû, or the "Scab," (the name later adopted by the Kûniüri) because they believed as much *literally*: that the Wicked Ark had struck the World to its fiery blood. The network of monumental fortifications securing the base of the Horns follows the cliffs comprising the Scab's perimeter. These cliffs encircle the whole of the Scab, rendering the curtain walls upon them all but impossible to overcome—save, famously, for a great ramp running from the foot of the Upright Horn (the one inhabited) to the plains of Ûgorrior to the southeast. This was where history would shed the most blood.

The *Isûphiryas* relates that during the Cûno-Inchoroi Wars, the Inchoroi raised what the Nonmen called Ûlil'uroikar, or the "Portal-obscene," to guard the Ûgorrior, an apparently metal-skinned structure razed by the Nonmen upon their conquest of the Ark. Following their reoccupation of Min-Uroikas, the Consult raised Gwergiruh, the hated gatehouse of what would come to be called Ûbil Maw, the Extrinsic Gate of Golgotterath, along with two vast towers, Corrunc and Domathuz, to guard the self-same stretch of barren earth. Where the Inchoroi had used the ramping slopes beyond to house their slaves, the Consult blasted them into a series of nine terraces, or "Risers" as the Kûniüri called them, each rimmed in more fortifications, a climbing succession of walls that would be called the Oblitus. Upon the Ninth Riser they constructed the High Cwol, a citadel that would have boggled for its dimension, had it not served as porch to the golden immensity of the Upright (or High) Horn. Within the High Cwol lay the dread Ûbil Noscisor, the Intrinsic Gate.

Unlike the Nonmen, the Sons of Men never succeeded in avenging the countless souls lost attempting to overcome these foul constructions.

Gonrain, Hoga (4088–)—Man-of-the-Tusk, second-eldest son of Earl Gothyelk.

gopa—A red-throated gull common to the southern Three Seas, and notoriously ill-mannered.

Gotagga (c. 687–735)—Great Umeri sorcerer credited with the birth of philosophy apart from what had been purely theological speculation. According to Ajencis, Men explained the world with characters and stories before Gotagga and with principles and observations after.

Gotheras, Hoga (4081–4125)—Man-of-the-Tusk, eldest son of Earl Gothyelk.

Gothyelk, Hoga (4052–4112)—Man-of-the-Tusk, Earl of Agansanor, and leader of the Tydonni contingent of the Holy War, slain by Fanayal ab Kascamandri at the Battle of Shimeh.

Gotian, Incheiri (4065–4112)—Man-of-the-Tusk, Grandmaster of the Shrial

Knights and Maithanet's representative in the Holy War, slain by an arrow to the armpit in the Battle of Shimeh.

Gow-gow seeds—From the gow-gow fruit, chewed throughout Ainon and Sansor as a mild stimulant.

Grandmaster—The title bestowed upon the administrative rulers of the Schools.

Great Desert—See *Carathay*.

Great Entresol—The massive chamber formed by the juncture of the Vast Ingressus and the Chthonic Manse in the heart of Ishterebinth, once the hub for all the Mansion's commercial activity, but since reduced to the primary point of congregation for Erratics.

Great Factions—The general term used to refer to the most powerful military and political institutions of the Three Seas.

Great Gate of Wheels—The sorcerous portal of the Coffers, notorious for using trapped souls, "proxies," to proof the gate against Chorae. According to legend, the doors did not so much *host* sorceries, as continually *cast and recast them*.

Great Kayarsus—The vast system of mountain ranges that forms the eastern frontier of Eärwa.

Great Library of Sauglish—The archive founded by Carû-Ongonean, the third Umeri God-King, *c.* 560, and transformed by Nincaerû-Telesser II (574–668) into the cultural heart of the Ancient North. At the time of its destruction in 2147, it was rumoured to be as large as some small cities.

Great Names—The epithet for the ranking caste-nobles leading the various contingents of the First Holy War.

Great Ocean—The ocean to the west of Eärwa, largely uncharted beyond the coastline, though some claim the Zeümi have mapped its extent.

Great Ordeal—Immense military expedition dedicated to the destruction of Golgotterath and the Unholy Consult undertaken by Anasûrimbor Kellhus I in 4132.

Great Pestilence—Also known as the Indigo Plague. The devastating pandemic that swept Eärwa following the death of the No-God in 2157.

Great Ruiner—A folkloric name of the No-God among the surviving tribes of Men in the Ancient North.

Great Salt—A particularly harsh region of the Carathay Desert bordering traditional Chianadyni.

Great Teacher—Epithet for Ajencis.

Great Ziggurat of Xijoser—The largest of the Shigeki Ziggurats, raised by the Old Dynasty God-King Xijoser *circa* 670.

Griasa (4049–4111)—A slave belonging to House Gaunum, and a friend of Serwë's.

Grojehald—Horselord Tower on the Sakarpic Pale, overrun by Sranc in the winter of 4129.

Grooming Laws—Traditional edicts governing the appearance of Zeumi caste-nobles, typically invoked in times of cultural paranoia, often as a way to imprison or execute malcontents.

Gropers—Pejorative referring to the thousands of Numaineiri Orthodox blinded at the command of Anasûrimbor Kellhus during the Unification Wars.

Gunsae—A long-abandoned Ceneian fortress located on the Gedean coast.

Gurnyau, Hoga (4091–4111)—Man-of-the-Tusk, youngest son of Earl Gothyelk, slain in Caraskand.

Gûswuran, Obwë (4178–)—Ordealman, Grandmaster of the Mysunsai in the Great Ordeal of Anasûrimbor Kellhus, renowned for his religious zealotry, a character trait never before seen in the so-called "Mercenary School."

Gwergiruh—The accursed Gatehouse of Ûbil Maw, the Extrinsic Gate of Golgot-terath. First raised *c*. 800, the subsequently expanded and rebuilt over the ensuing centuries, now some seventy cubits high, shaped as a cleft pentagon, with Ûbil Maw at its centre.

H

haeturi—The Nansur name for the bodyguards assigned to high-ranking officers in the Imperial Army.

Hagarond, Raeharth (4059–4111)—Man-of-the-Tusk, Galeoth Earl of Usgald, slain at Mengedda.

Hagerna—The vast temple complex located in Sumna, housing the Junriüma, the many Colleges, and the administrative machinery of the Thousand Temples.

Halarinis—"Summer Stair" (Ihrimsû). The road leading to Cirrû-nol, the mall before the Soggomantic Gate.

Halikimmû, Grinar (4103–)—Ordealmen, famed for being a one-time champion of the Sranc Pit in Carythusal.

Hamishaza (3711–83)—A renowned Ainoni dramatist, remembered for his *Tempiras the King* and his jnanic wit, which was rumoured to be unparalleled.

Ham-Kheremic—The lost language of ancient Shir.

Hamoric—The language group of the ancient Ketyai pastoralists of the eastern Three Seas.

Hanalinqû (?–?)—The legendary wife of Cu'jara Cinmoi, whose death symbolizes the beginning of the Cûno-Inchoroi Wars.

"[the] hand of Triamis, the heart of Sejenus, and the intellect of Ajencis"—The famous saying attributed to the poet Protathis, referring to the qualities all men should strive for.

Hanging Citadels—The manse of Ishterebinth chambering the downward faces of the Ilculcû Rift, housing the Ishroi of Ishterebinth, and famed in Far Antiquity for the assemblage of suspended iron platforms flooring the plummet of the Rift, the Sky-Beneath-the-Mountain.

Hansa—A slave-girl belonging to Cutias Sarcellus.

Hapetine Gardens—One of many architectural idylls on the Andiamine Heights.

Harapior (?–4132)—Lord Torturer of Ishterebinth under Nin'ciljiras.

Harnilas, Xarotas (4187–4132)—Ordealman, Kidruhil Captain of the Scions, a unit consisting of treaty hostages.

Harsunc—"Fish Knife" (Aörsic). Name given to the River Sursa, both for its appearance from the ramparts of Dagliash, and for the slaughters it occasioned.

Hasjinnet ab Skauras (4067–4103)—The eldest son of Skauras ab Nalajan, slain by Cnaiür urs Skiötha at the Battle of Zirkirta in 4103.

Hatatian (3174–3211)—The infamous author of the *Exhortations*, a work that eschews traditional Inrithi values and espouses an ethos of unprincipled self-promotion. Though long censured by the Thousand Temples, Hatatian remains popular among the caste-nobility of the Three Seas.

Haurut urs Mab (4000–4082)—An Utemot memorialist when Cnaiür was a child.

Heights of the Bull—One of the nine heights of Caraskand.

Heilor—The acropolis of ancient Kelmeol, and the famed home of the Three Auguries.

hemoplexy—A common disease of war characterized by intense fevers, vomiting, skin irritation, severe diarrhea, and, in the most extreme cases, coma and death. Also known as "the hollows" or "the hemoplectic hand."

Hemrût ab Urmakthi (4089–4132)—Ordealman, Prince of Girgash, killed in the days preceding the Battle of Irsulor.

Heörsa, Dun (4078–4112)—Man-of-the-Tusk, Shield-Captain of the Hundred Pillars, formerly a Galeoth thane.

Herder's Gate—The main gate of Sakarpus, so called for being the city entrance designated for leading animals to slaughter.

Heresiarch—The title of the leader of the Cishaurim.

Heron Spear—A powerful artifact of the Inchoroi Tekne, so named because of its unique shape. The Heron Spear first appears in the *Isûphiryas* as Suörgil (Ihrimsû, "Shining Death"), the great "spear of light" taken by Cu'jara Cinmoi from the corpse of Sil, the Inchoroi King, at the battle of Pir Pahal. For millennia the Heron Spear lay in the possession of the Nonmen of Ishoriol, until it was stolen by Cet'ingira (see *Mekertrig*) and delivered to Golgotterath *c.* 750. Then in 2140 it was stolen again by Seswatha (see *Apocalypse*), who believed it to be the only weapon capable of destroying the No-God. For a brief time it was thought destroyed at the catastrophic Battle of Eleneöt Fields, but it reappeared in 2154 in the possession of Anaxophus V, High King of Kyraneas, who used it to slay the No-God at the Battle of Mengedda. For centuries it resided in Cenei, a treasured possession of the Aspect-Emperors, only to be lost once again when the Scylvendi sacked Cenei in 3351. Its whereabouts are presently unknown.

Heteshiras—The famed night-long bacchanals of the Ainoni caste-nobility.

Hethanta Mountains—A large mountain range located in central Eärwa.

Hifanat ab Tunukri (4084–4111)—A Cishaurim sorcerer-priest and servant of Anasûrimbor Moënghus, slain at Caraskand.

High Ainon—A Ketyai nation of the eastern Three Seas, and the only nation to be ruled by one of the Schools, the Scarlet Spires. Founded in 3372 after Sarothesser I defeated General Maurelta at the Battle of Charajat, High Ainon has long been one of the most populous and powerful nations of the Three Seas. The agricultural production of the Secharib Plains combined with that of the Sayut Delta and River Valley supports both an extensive caste-nobility (noted for their wealth and their obsession with jnan) and an aggressive mercantilism. Ainoni ships can be found berthed in every port in the Three Seas. During the Scholastic Wars (3796–3818), the School of the Scarlet Spires, which is based in the capital, Carythusal, managed to destroy the army of King Horziah III and assumed indirect control of the nation's primary institutions. The nominal head of state, the King-Regent, answers directly to the Grand-master.

High Keeper of the Hoard—Honorific belonging to the King of Sakarpus.

High Kunna—The debased version of Gilcûnya used by the Anagogic Schools of the Three Seas.

High Sakarpean—The language of ancient Sakarpus, a derivative of ancient Skettic.

High Sheyic—The language of the Ceneian Empire, a derivative of ancient Kyranean.

High Vurumandic—The language of the Nilnameshi ruling castes, a derivative of Vaparsi.

Hilderath, Solm (4072–)—Man-of-the-Tusk, one of the Nascenti, formerly a Tydonni thane.

Himonirsil—"The Accusatory" (Ihrimsû). Nonman name given to promontory of stone jutting like a pointing finger toward Golgotterath. During the Cûno-Inchoroi Wars it famously lay at the heart of the Arobindant.

Hinayati Mountains—A large system of mountain ranges located in southwestern Eärwa, sometimes called "the spine of Nilnamesh."

Hingeath, Sucoithus (4088–4132)—Ordealman, Earl of Gaenri, and commander of the Gaenrish contingent in the Great Ordeal of Anasûrimbor Kellhus, slain at the Battle of Imweor.

Hinnant—A palatinate of High Ainon, located in the heart of the Secharib Plains.

Hinnereth—The administrative and commercial capital of Gedea, located on the Meneanor coast.

Hinsursa, River—Kûniüric name for the river draining the high Aorsic plains into the Sea of Neleost, forming the natural frontier between Illawor and Yinwaul. Known as the Migmarsa ("Bone-tumbler") in Aörsic sources.

Hipinna—Book of Nonman hymns dedicated to love, among them the celebrated

"Fear Flee You," one of a mere handful of songs to be adopted by Men:

> *Fear flee you.*
> *Sun and Starving glare not down upon thy brow,*
> *thy breath.*
> *Fear flee you.*
> *Hunger and Dolour clutch not at thy ankles,*
> *thy hope.*
> *Fear flee you.*
> *Let Love climb high upon thy arch,*
> *Let Passion delve deep.*
> *Fear flee you,*
> *my slave.*

Hiril—Ancient Ûmeri road pacing the River Aumris across the highland interior of Kûniüri.

History (Dûnyain)—The movement of human events through time. The significance of History for the Dûnyain is found in the fact that past circumstances dominate and determine present actions, such that individuals continually find themselves "coming after," which is to say, at the mercy of events over which they have no control. The Dûnyain believe that utter detachment from history is a necessary precondition for absolute awareness.

History (Inrithism)—The movement of human events through time. The significance of History for the Inrithi is that the God is manifested within it. The Inrithi believe that certain configurations of events express the truth of the God while certain other configurations are inimical to such expression.

Hoar-Pelt—White bear-skin mantle that the Kings of Viri wore instead of a crown, rumoured to be a gift of Hûsyelt, Dark Hunter.

Hoga, House—The ruling dynasty of Agansanor. The Black Stag on Green is their traditional device.

Hoga Brood—The name given in the Conriyan court to Hoga Gothyelk's sons.

Hogrim, Hoga (4093–)—Ordealman, Believer-King of Ce Tydonn, nephew of Earl Hoga Gothyelk.

Hoilirsi—Province of Sheneor in Far Antiquity, noted for the violent River Irshi, which once formed its northern frontier, and for the cultivation of grains.

hollows—See *hemoplexy*.

Holol—"Breathtaker" (Ihrimsû). Famed sorcerous blade forged by Iblil'accullil during the Cûno-Inchoroi Wars.

Holy Bounty—Fee dispensed by the Imperial treasury in exchange for Sranc Scalps. Originally two scalps per silver empress when Anasûrimbor Kellhus first announced the Bounty in 4119, this payout would be more than halved when the

Scalper companies began perfecting their tactics. Corruption involving both tallies and payouts was initially rampant, leading to the execution of hundreds of scalpers and imperial officers alike in the first of the Scalper Purges of 4125.

Holy Deep—The ultimate depth of Ishterebinth, and for ages a place of pilgrimage and worship for the Nonmen of Injor-Niyas, given the absolute silence and blackness.

Holy Precincts—See *Hagerna*.

Holy Sagas, The—A collection of epic lays that recount the Apocalypse. The opening invocation runs:

> *Rage—Goddess! Sing of your flight!*
> *From our fathers and our sons.*
> *Away Goddess! Secret your divinity!*
> *From the conceit that makes kings of fools,*
> *From the scrutiny that makes corpses of souls.*
> *Mouths open, arms thrown wide, we beseech thee:*
> *Sing us the end of your song.*

Raised to the status of scripture following the Zaudunyani conquest of the Three Seas, the *Holy Sagas* primarily consists of "The Kelmariad," the story of Anasûrimbor Celmomas and his tragic Ordeal; "The Kayûtiad," the account of Celmomas's son, Nau-Cayûti, and his heroic exploits; "The Book of Generals," the story of the deceptive events following Nau-Cayûti's murder; "The Trisiad," which recounts the great city's destruction; "The Eämnoriad," the story of ancient Atrithau's expulsion of Seswatha and subsequent survival; "The Annal Akksersa," which recounts the Fall of Akksersia; and lastly, "The Annal Sakarpa," or "The Refugee's Song" as it is sometimes called, the strange account of the city of Sakarpus during the Apocalypse.

Home City—A common Nansur epithet for Momemn.

Homirras, Ersa (3972–4025)—Author of *The Ten Thousand Day Dynasty*, a history of the short-lived ascendency of House Sorgis in Nansur, banned both by the Ikurei and the Anasûrimbor, allegedly for arguing that power corrupts rather than purifies souls. He would die in the Tower of Ziek in 4025.

Hording—The instinctive tendency of Sranc to muster in numbers far surpassing those of their foes, only on the scale of tens of thousands or more.

Horns of Golgotterath—One of many epithets given to the two Oars of Ark, the portions of the Incû-Holoinas remaining exposed. The Isûphiryas gives the height of the Upright Horn as one thousand tens, or ten thousand Nonman cubits, which is almost certainly an exaggeration. Sohonc accounts, which rely on mathematics and the measurement of shadows, put the height at some nine thousand seven-hundred and twenty-four Umeritic cubits, or a little less than half the height reported by the Nonmen. Needless to say, this remains a stupendous number.

Hortha, Sonhail (4064–4121)—Man-of-the-Tusk, Galeoth knight, client to Prince

Coithus Saubon, whelmed as a Judge following the conquest of Shimeh, only to be found murdered in Aöknyssus under suspicious circumstances some six months afterward.

Hoshrut—One of Carythusal's great agoras, noted for its view of the Scarlet Spires.

Hoshrut Pole—Traditional post, located in the heart of the Hoshrut Agora, used for the public flogging of notorious criminals. Torn to the ground with oxen and chains during the Great Yatwerian Sedition of 4132.

House Primordial—See *Siol*.

Houses of the Congregate—A quasi-legislative assembly consisting of the primary landholding families of the Nansur Empire.

Hull—Name given to the walls and fortifications of Kelmeol.

Hulwarga, Hringa (4086–4121)—Man-of-the-Tusk, second son of King Hringa Rauschang of Thunyerus, and leader of the Thunyeri contingent of the First Holy War after the death of his older brother, Prince Hringa Skaiyelt, in Caraskand. Called the Limper because of his uneven gait. Found murdered in 4121, apparently at the hand of a jealous mistress, though rumours of sorcerous assassination persist.

Hundred Gods—The collective name of the Gods enumerated in *The Chronicle of the Tusk* and worshipped either under the auspices of the Cults (which is to say, subordinate to the Thousand Temples), or in the traditional versions of the Kiünnat. In the Inrithi tradition, the Hundred Gods are thought to be aspects of the God (whom Inri Sejenus famously called "the Million Souled"), much the way various personality traits could be said to inhabit an individual. In the far more variegated Kiünnat tradition, the Hundred Gods are thought to be independent spiritual agencies, prone to indirectly intervene in the lives of their worshippers. Both traditions recognize the differences between the Compensatory Gods, who promise direct reward for worship and devotion, the Punitive Gods, who secure sacrifices through the threat of suffering, and the more rare Bellicose Gods, who despise worship as sycophancy and favour those who strive against them. Both the Inrithi and Kiünnat traditions see the Gods as indispensable to eternal life in the Outside.

The esoteric apologist Zarathinius is infamous for arguing (in *A Defence of the Arcane Arts*) the absurdity of worshipping deities as imperfect and capricious as mere Men. The Fanim, of course, believe the Hundred Gods are renegade slaves of the Solitary God—demons.

Hundred Pillars—The Warrior-Prophet's personal bodyguard, named after the one hundred men rumoured to have surrendered their water—and their lives—to him on the Trail of Skulls. The coronation of Anasûrimbor Kellhus as Aspect-Emperor led to the institutionalization of the bodyguard as a military subministry charged with the protection of the Imperial Family.

Huösi, Lake—A large freshwater lake draining the Vindauga and Sculpa river systems, and emptying into the Wutmouth.

Hurminda, Possû (4101–4132)—Ordealman, Satrap of Sranayati, killed in the days leading up to the disaster at Irsûlor.

Hûrochur—"Jutting Nail" (Kûniûric). See *Dagliash*.

hustwarra—The Galeoth name for camp wives.

Husyelt—The God of the hunt. One of the so-called Compensatory Gods, who reward devotion in life with paradise in the afterlife, Husyelt comes after only Yatwer and Gilgaöl in Cultic popularity, particularly in the Middle-North. In the *Higarata*, the collection of subsidiary writings that form the scriptural core of the Cults, Husyelt is depicted as the most anthropocentric of the Hundred Gods, as intent upon enabling his worshippers as he is upon securing their obedience and devotion. The Cult of Husyelt is rumoured to be extraordinarily wealthy, and high-ranking members of the Husyeltic priesthood often possess as much political clout as Shrial apparati.

Huterat—A town on the Sempis Delta, destroyed by the First Holy War in 4111.

I

idolaters—A term commonly used by Fanim to refer to Inrithi.

Iëva (2112–2140)—Legendary wife of Anasûrimbor Nau-Cayuti, tried and executed for his murder in 2140.

Ihrimsû—The tongue of Injor-Niyas.

Ikurei, House—A Nansur House of the Congregate, with holdings concentrated in and about Momemn. The Imperial House since 3941.

Ikurei Anphairas I (4022–4081)—The Emperor of Nansur from 4066 until his death in 4081, and grandfather of Ikurei Xerius III. Assassinated by persons unknown.

Ikurei Dynasty—Always one of the more powerful Houses of the Congregate, the Ikurei seized the Imperial Mantle in 3941, capitalizing on the turmoil following the loss of Shigek and then Gedea to Kian in the Dagger Jihad. Ikurei Sorius I became the first of a line of shrewd yet defensive Ikurei Emperors. See *Nansur Empire*.

Ikurei Xerius III (4059–)—The Emperor of the Nansur Empire.

Ilculcû Rift—"Sky of Ulcû" (Ihrimsû). Vast fracture cavern, sometimes referred to as the Sky-Beneath-the-Mountain, located in the heart of Ishterebinth, and forming the abyssal heights that are the fame of the Hanging Citadels.

Illawor—Coastal province of ancient Aörsi.

Illisserû—"The Lighthouse" (Aujic). One of the great Nonman Mansions before the Breaking of the Gates, located in what Men now call the Betmulla Mountains. "*Sepil himi loi'nu muomi,*" the nameless poet of *Six-Skins-Folded* writes of the Illisserû: "The Sea is their Deepest Deep." The Illisseri love of the sea is the primary reason they remain at the margins of Nonman lore as inherited by the Three Seas.

Imbeyan ab Imbaran (4067–4111)—Sapatishah-Governor of Enathpaneah and son-in-law of the Padirajah, slain at Caraskand.

Imburil—"Newborn" (Aujic). Nonman name for the Nail of Heaven.

Imimorûl–The central figure of Nonman scriptures, named "Father of the False" in *The Chronicle of the Tusk*, and in Mannish traditions, a once-glorious God imprisoned deep in the earth as punishment for teaching sorcery to the Nonmen. According to Cûnuroi traditions, Imimorûl was not imprisoned within the earth, but sought refuge in the "Deepest Deep," those places the gods could not judge because they could not see. Though Ajencis famously attributes the Nonman aversion to open sky to his theory of "vital accommodations," the Nonmen themselves see this predilection as a sacred observance of Imimorûl's ancient straits–as well as the best way to find oblivion upon their deaths.

Im'inaral Lightbringer (?–?)–Hero of Siol struck down beneath the original gatehouse of Min-Uroikas by Sil, the Inchoroi King.

Imirsiol–"Hammer of Siol" (Gilcûnya). Legendary blade forged for Oirûnas by the arcane smith Virimlû once the Hero grew Tall.

Imhailas, Gawol (4093–4132)–Exalt-Captain of the Eöthic Guard, rumoured to be the lover of Anasûrimbor Esmenet, summarily executed by the Inchausti in 4132 for harbouring the fugitive Empress during the Shrial Insurrection.

Immiriccas (?–?)–Son of Cinial'jin, called the Goad, the Malcontent, the Despiser. Sentenced to death in the month preceding the Second Battle of the Ark, his sentence was committed to his Kinning, who sold him to Ishoriol as a battle slave, a role which saw him heaped with glory, for none bore the Vile more hatred. His notoriety allegedly secured the affections of Mu'miorn, the most coveted lover in the Citadels, and long-time paramour of Nil'giccas. Claiming the Seal of the House Primordial, the Nonman King assumed the claims-of-grievance belonging to Cu'jara Cinmoi, and commanded the execution of Immiriccas. Strife between Injori Ishroi and the Dispossessed Sons of Siol followed, a rift that was only partially healed when Nil'giccas commended Immiriccas to Emilidis, who asked the condemned Ishroi to choose between execution and sorcerous transmogrification–eternal life bound to the Amiolas.

Imperial Army–A common name for the standing Nansur army.

Imperial Precincts–The name given to the grounds of the Andiamine Heights.

Imperial Saik–The School indentured to the Nansur Emperor.

Imperial Sun–The primary symbol of the Nansur Empire.

Imperial Synod–The highest council of the Greater Congregate, held in the Synodine on the Andiamine Heights, tasked with advising the Aspect-Emperor.

Impromta, The–The anonymously written collection of the Warrior-Prophet's earliest sermons and aphorisms.

Imrothas, Sarshressa (4054–4111)–Man-of-the-Tusk, Palatine of the Conriyan province of Aderot, claimed by disease at Caraskand.

Incariol–"Lord Wanderer" (Ihrimsû). Enigmatic Nonman Erratic companion of Lord Kosoter. Also known as Cleric.

Incarnal—Name given to the battle-madness suffered to varying degrees by the Holca.

Incest Song of Linqiru—Famous Nonman lay recounting the scandalous love affair that produced Cu'jara Cinmoi.

> And hidden from the sky,
> in the deepest of the Holy Deep,
> they conceived the very point of the spear,
> Cu'jara Cinmoi, cast upon
> godhead, arrogance-that-is-joy,
> conjoining the very blood their birth had torn asunder,
> as holy Tsonos and Olissis ...

Inchausti—The personal bodyguard of the Holy Shriah following the institutional reforms of Anasûrimbor Maithanet, selected from the most faithful and formidable of the Shrial Knights.

Inchoroi—"People of Emptiness" (Ihrimsû). A mysterious and obscene race that, according to legend, descended from the void in the Incû-Holoinas. Calling themselves the Iyiskû, the Inchoroi have always claimed (during brief truces with the Cûnuroi) to be shipwrecked upon the World, the victims of a cataclysm that brought them flaming down from the Void. In truth, however, they have come to extinguish all life, believing that destroying all souls upon our World will shut it against the Outside, thus saving their souls from damnation should they die.

Incû-Holoinas—"Ark-of-the-Skies" (Ihrimsû). The great vessel that brought the Inchoroi from the heavens and became the golden heart of Golgotterath. All scholars agree that the Incû-Holoinas was some kind of ship built to sail the sky, that it crashed some time prior to the inscription of the Tusk, but only a rare handful concede the claim that it sailed the Void proper, which is to say, *between stars*. The most compelling rebuttal of this fanciful notion comes from Ajencis himself, who pointed out that the stars would move relative one another were they not uniformly embedded in a sphere hanging a fixed distance about the sky. Since the relative positioning of the stars is identical in star charts inked from different corners of the World, we can be assured that the Incû-Holoinas "came from someplace distant, but not far away." This, the Great Kyranean concludes, means the Incû-Holoinas must hail from the Outside and not the stars.

This disagreement in origins forms the basis of the two different families of speculation on the Incû-Holoinas, with Nonmen and Far Antique Mannish accounts generally insisting it's a vessel constructed to cross the Void, and with more recent Mannish accounts agreeing that it's a vessel constructed to escape damnation in the Outside. Where the former accounts hold the occupants to be "aliens," monstrosities from another World, the latter accounts claim the Inchoroi were in fact ciphrangi—demons, in effect.

The tremendous advantage of the latter theories turns on their *economy*, on the fact that they need posit nothing new to explain either the Incû-Holoinas or the Inchoroi. If the Ark were a vessel from another planet, then it had to be constructed by the Inchoroi themselves, when plainly, given its boggling dimensions, only a God could have forged it. Given the evil, rapacious nature of the Inchoroi, the construction is typically attributed to Ajokli. Some even think the Incû-Holoinas comprises two of the fabled Four Horns attributed to the trickster God in the Tusk and elsewhere. Indeed, some Near Antique lays refer to the conspicuously golden vessel as the Halved Crown of Hate.

Though the question of the origin of the Incû-Holoinas can be assumed to be safely settled, vexing questions abide, not the least of which concerns the actual size of the unholy vessel, and, most notoriously, whether the Consult still inhabits it. Though some promise is to be had in the resolution of the former controversy, Mandate arrogance and delusion promises to render the latter debate an endless mire.

Indara-Kishauri—The "tribe" of the Cishaurim. The "Indara" refer, in Kianene tradition, to the "tribe of water-bearers," a legendary band that supposedly wandered the dunes dispensing water and mercy to the faithful. The designation is critical (according to the *kipfa'aifan*, it saved Fane's life), given the importance of tribal affiliation in desert Kianene society.

The pastoralists of the Carathay desert are unique in possessing a grammatical distinction between us and them, self and other, one which can only be captured in Sheyic as "us-them." The stories of the Indara-Kishauri ranging from their mythical home of Udavant hidden somewhere in the lifeless heart of the Great Salt personify this distinction for the Kianene in particular, who referred to their shamanistic Kiunnat priests as such. These formed the trans-tribal basis for the spread of Fanimry, as well as the sudden transformation of a fractious, internecine tribal people into a cohesive, empire-building nation. By characterizing his miraculous powers as "water" and himself as a divine "water-bearer," Fane managed to seize high ground built into the very structure of Kianene language.

Indenture, the—The infamous document used by Ikurei Xerius III in his attempt to secure the lands conquered by the First Holy War.

Indigo Plague—According to legend, the pestilence swept up from the No-God's ashes after his destruction at the hands of Anaxophus V in 2155. Mandate scholars dispute this, claiming that the No-God's body was recovered by the Consult and interred in Golgotterath. Whatever the cause, the Indigo Plague ranks as among the worst in recorded history.

Indurum Barracks—A lodging for soldiers located in Caraskand and dating back to the Nansur occupation of the city.

Ingiaban, Sristai (4059–4121)—Man-of-the-Tusk, Palatine of the Conriyan province of Kethantei. Murdered by thieves while visiting family in Aoknyssus.

Ingol—Mountain in the Urokkas.

Ingoswitu (1966–2050)—A far antique Kûniüric philosopher, famed in his own day for *Dialogia* but primarily known in the Three Seas through Ajencis and his famed critique of Ingoswitu's *Theosis* in *The Third Analytic of Men*.

Ingraul—A fiefdom of the Thunyeri Sranc Marches.

Ingressus—The great well of Ishterebinth, often referred to as the Vast Ingressus given its boggling dimensions.

Ingusharotep II (c. 1000–c. 1080)—The Old Dynasty Shigeki King who conquered the Kyranae Plains.

Injor-Niyas—The last remaining Nonman nation, located beyond the Demua Mountains. See *Ishterebinth*.

Inner Luminal—Hall of Ishterebinth connecting the Concavity (the "Mnemonic") to the greater mansion, eventually becoming a sobriquet for Nil'giccas.

Inoculation—According to the *Isûphiryas*, the infamous "cure for mortality" first given to Cû'jara Cinmoi, King of Siol, by Sarpanur of the Inchoroi, and thence to nearly every Cûnuroi living. The term 'inoculation' specifically refers to the most agonizing stage of the therapy, whereby hollow pins are inserted into every tissue in the body, steeping them in the age-killing nostrum. The Nonmen were by no means foolish enough to embrace the Inoculation all at once—nearly a century passed before the last dissenters relented, and allowed the servile (appearing) Inchoroi to minister to them. The first problems did not appear until those already advanced in age began to die, universally (with the notable exception of Morimhira). But since those lost were so near the Deepest Deep already, very little suspicion was aroused. Queen Hanalinqû was the first to fall to what would come to be called the "Womb-Plague," a lethal malady that seemed to spread as contagion, but was in fact manifesting according to when womenfolk were first Inoculated. Even still, suspicions were not aroused until it became apparent the Inchoroi were evacuating Eärwa. Thus began the disaster that would be the doom of the Nonmen, and the woe that would drive so many Ishroi mad for grief and loss. The "death of death" promised by Nin-janjin, Sil, and Sarpanur, became the *death of birth* (*Nasamorgas*) as well.

Inrau, Paro (4088–4110)—A former student of Drusas Achamian, slain in Sumna.

Inri Sejenus (c. 2159–2202)—The Latter Prophet and spiritual (although not historical) founder of the Thousand Temples, who claimed to be the pure incarnation of Absolute Spirit ("the very proportion of the God"), sent to emend the teachings of the Tusk. After his death and supposed ascension to the Nail of Heaven, his disciples recounted his life and teachings in *The Tractate*, the text that is now considered by the Inrithi to be as holy as *The Chronicle of the Tusk*.

Inrilil ab Cinganjehoi (4099–)—Ordealman, Believer-Prince of Eumarna, general of the Eumarnan contingent in the Great Ordeal of Anasûrimbor Kellhus.

Inrithi—The followers of Inri Sejenus, the Latter Prophet, and his amendments to the Tusk.

Inrithism—The faith founded upon the revelations of Inri Sejenus, the Latter Prophet, which synthesizes elements of both monotheism and polytheism. The central tenets of Inrithism deal with the immanence of the God in historical events, the unity of the individual deities of the Cults as Aspects of the God, and the role of the Thousand Temples as the very expression of the God in the world.

Following the alleged ascension of Inri Sejenus, Inrithism slowly established itself throughout the Ceneian Empire as an organized hierarchy independent of the state—what came to be called the Thousand Temples. Initially, the existing traditionalist Kiünnat sects simply dismissed the new religion, but as it continued to grow, a number of attempts were made to circumscribe its powers and prevent its further spread, none of them particularly effective. Escalating tensions eventually culminated in the Zealot Wars (c. 2390–2478), which, although technically a civil war, saw battles fought far outside the boundaries of what then constituted the Ceneian Empire.

In 2469, Sumna capitulated to Shrial forces, but hostilities continued until Triamis was anointed Emperor in 2478. Though himself Inrithi (converted by Ekyannus III), and despite enacting the constitution governing the division of powers between the Imperium and the Thousand Temples, he refrained from declaring Inrithism the official state religion until 2505. From that point the ascendancy of the Thousand Temples was assured, and over the ensuing centuries the remaining Kiünnat "heresies" of the Three Seas would either wither away or be forcibly stamped out.

The rise of Fanimry and the Kianene Empire from the 38th century onward posed the first great challenge to the dominance of Inrithism—a threat so severe as to induce many in the Thousand Temples to advocate the removal of the Holy Tusk in Sumna to Aöknyssus. If anything, however, the existential challenge led to a revival of enthusiasm and militancy both among Inrithi faithful of all castes, culminating in the election of Anasûrimbor Maithanet as Shriah and the calling of the First Holy War in 4111.

The success of the expedition either destroyed Inrithism (the Orthodox position) or actualized it (as the Zaudunyani claim). Either way, the bulk of Inrithi institutions and dogma survived intact under the otherwise bloody rule of Anasûrimbor Kellhus, unlike Fanimry, which was all but destroyed.

Inrûmmi (4058–4112)—Man-of-the-Tusk, ranking member of the Scarlet Spires, assumed lost at the Battle of Shimeh.

Inshull (?–?)—One of the Chieftain-Kings named in the Tusk.

Insinger—Archaic term for sorcerer.

Inskarra, Saweor (4061–4111)—Man-of-the-Tusk, Earl of the Thunyeri province of Skagwa, slain at Anwurat.

Interdiction—The embargo on communication between the Great Ordeal and the New Empire declared by Anasûrimbor Kellhus.

Interval—Name of the man-sized tubular bell used by the Great Ordeal to communicate time and orders. Originally cast in Seleukara, the bell was transported to Holy Sumna, where priests belonging to various Colleges and Cults were charged with inscribing its exterior with their holiest benedictions. The bell was subsequently mounted on a great, oaken wain drawn by a team of four oxen, and manned by four priests (including one eunuch) and six Shrial slaves (all of whom would be executed en route to Golgotterath).

Intrinsic Gate—The ensorcelled gate raised by Nil'giccas, sealing the rent portion the High Horn upon the summit of the Scab. Known to the Nonmen by the same name they had given its Inchoroi predecessor, *Ûbil Noscisor*, 'Shut Teeth' (Ihrimsû). Now located within the citadel of the High Cwol.

Inûnara Highlands—A region of foothills to the northeast of the Unaras Spur of the Hethanta Mountains.

The Inverse Fire—Xir'kirimakra (Cûno-Cincûlic). Subparticular intentional field machine linking individual observational frames of reference to their eternal fate in the Outside. Given that the Gods are both jealous and connoisseurs, most souls peering into the Inverse Fire discover the fact of their eternal damnation, an experience so profound as to drive all who witness it into the horrifying embrace of the Consult. This was what rendered Mekeritrig an inevitable consequence of Cet'ingira's survival, and why Apocalypse has always clustered as bees about this perpetually disastrous device.

Inversi—Ursranc specifically bred to guard the Upright Horn, and thus the Inverse Fire. More heavily armoured and armed, they are also more disciplined and cunning. An upside-down flame traced in gold is their emblem.

Inversions—Daimotic Cants of Dispossession, or more generally, sorcery allowing the souls of the living to wander the ways of the dead. Outlawed by the Thousand Temples, eschewed by the Mandate, Inversions are the most feared discipline of the Daimos, especially within the Scarlet Spires.

Invishi—The commercial and spiritual capital of Nilnamesh, and one of the most ancient cities of the Three Seas.

Inward Stair—The great stair running from the Pith of Ishterebinth, across the upward face of the Ilculcû Rift beneath the Hanging Citadels, down to the Chthonic Manse.

Iothiah—A great Old Dynasty city located on the Sempis Delta.

Irreüma—A so-called "all-Gods temple" located in the administrative quarter of the Hagerna. Though its architecture belongs to the classical Kyranean period, its provenance is unknown.

Irsalfus, Hiappus (4068–4132)—The first Schoolman to be killed in the Culling.

Iros—Viritic name for Antareg. See *Antareg*.

Iryssas, Krijates (4089–4121)—Man-of-the-Tusk, young and impetuous majordomo of House Krijates, and cousin to Krijates Xinemus. Lost in calm seas off the coast of southern Conriya.

Ishoiya—Sheyic for "uncertainty." The so-called Day of Doubt, an Inrithi holy day celebrated in late summer, commemorating the spiritual turmoil and renewal undergone by Inri Sejenus during his imprisonment in Xerash. Among the less pious, Ishoiya is renowned as a day of copious drinking.

Ishoriöl—"Exalted Hall" (Ihrimsû). See *Ishterebinth.*

Ishroi—"Exalted Ones" (Ihrimsû). The name given to the Nonmen warrior castes.

Ishterebinth—"Exalted Stronghold" (Ûmeri derivation of the Ihrimsû, *Ishûr'îi*). Mansion of Eärwa located to the west of the Demua Mountains, and the last surviving (and so often referred to as the House Charnel). Known as Ishoriöl ("Exalted Hall") in the *Isûphiryas*, Ishterebinth was considered one of the premier cities of the Cûnuroi after Siöl and Cil-Aujas. One of the Nine, those Mansions older than the *Isûphiryas*, the founding of Ishoriöl is lost to the mists of prehistory. Tradition attributes the founding to the third Ladling (third generation following Tsonos), claiming the Hero Ûlkû'kolil as their founder, the problem being that the great southern Mansion of Incissal also claims Ûlkû'kolil as their founder (thus the ironic connotations of any reference to "the Sons of Ûlkû'kolil" in Nonman literary traditions, and Kû'jara-Kinmoi's famous disparagement of his age-old competitor as the *isullû'imiroi*, or "Sons of Someone"). The tradition holds that Ûlkû'kolil, fleeing the House Primordial after seducing his stepmother (while wearing his father's armour), traveled west chasing visions sent by Imimorûl, promising a new home bloody with Nonman silver, a "House Eschatological" to match and ultimately surpass the glory of Holy Siol.

This (likely apocryphal) prophecy of competition between Ishoriöl and Siol did not come to pass until the famed marriage of Queen Tsinirû (one of the most gifted of the Quyil) with Sin'niroiha, the Nonman King of Nihrimsûl, the ancient rival of Ku'jara-Kinmoi. Whether due to the wealth of her nimil mines, or the engineering marvel of the Vast Ingressus, or the formidable will of his sorceress wife, Sin'niroiha's decision to relocate his court to Ishoriöl would have the effect of radically rewriting the politics of Eärwa. Almost overnight, ancient Nihrimsûl, the ageless rival to Siolan hegemony, became an outpost projecting a far different power. The subsequent birth of their son, Nil'giccas, would bring the Sons of Nihrimsûl into the House of Tsonos, and so removed illegitimacy as a perpetual pretext for Siolan aggression. The fusion of the more ancient mansion's martial vigour with the commercial might and artistic sensibilities of Ishoriöl resulted in one of the most glorious periods of cultural efflorescence in Nonman history—ultimately to become the very House Eschatological prophesied, the one Mansion to survive both the apocalypse occasioning the arrival of Men and the apocalypse occasioning their departure.

Following the disaster of Pir-Minginnial, the remnants rallied about Sin'niroiha, and Ishoriöl, given its proximity to the Incû-Holoinas, found itself perpetually embattled, besieged no less than five times for spans exceeding ten years. Sin'niroiha, who had never been inoculated, became the last Nonman to die of old age during the Siege of the Second Delve, leaving his gifted son, Nil'giccas, the Seals of Nihrimsûl and Ishoriöl. As a Son of Tsonos, Nil'giccas was able to lead the other Mansions in a way his father could not.

See *Cûno-Inchoroi Wars.*

Ishuäl–"Exalted Grotto" (Ihrimsû). The secret fastness of the Kûniüric High Kings, located in the Demua Mountains, and subsequently inhabited by the Dûnyain.

Isiramûlis–"Hearth-cracker" (Ihrimsû). First of six Cinderswords forged by Emilidis, coveted in ancient times for the immunity it provided to Dragon fire.

Iskaul, Powtha (4094–)–General of the Twenty-ninth Imperial Column, stationed in Oswenta.

Israti–One of the Houses of the Congregate.

Israzi'horul–"Shining Men" (Aghurzoi). Sranc term for the Great Ordeal of Anasûrimbor Kellhus.

Issiral–"Fortune" (Shigeki). The name the White-Luck Warrior gives to Anasûrimbor Esmenet after she contracts him to murder Maithanet.

Istriya, Ikurei (4045–?)–The mother of Emperor Xerius III, once famed for her legendary beauty.

Istyuli Plains–A vast and largely semi-arid tableland running from the Yimelati Mountains in the north to the Hethanta Mountains in the south.

Isûphiryas–"Great Pit of Years" (Ihrimsû). The great work chronicling the history of the Nonmen prior to the Breaking of the Gates. In all likelihood it is the most ancient text in existence. Sometime in the fourth century, a copy of the *Isûphiryas* was given to Cûnwerishau by Nil'giccas, the Nonman King of Ishoriöl (Ishterebinth), as part of the ancient treaty between their two peoples—the first between Nonmen and Men. During the reign of the God-King Carû-Ongonean, five Ûmeri translations of the *Isûphiryas* were bequeathed to the Library of Sauglish. Four of these were destroyed in the Apocalypse. The fifth was saved by Seswatha, who delivered it to the scribes of the Three Seas.

As a historical chronicle, the *Isûphiryas* exhibits a number of peculiarities beyond its inhuman provenance and enormous length (Seswatha famously referred to it as the "great pyre of eyes"). For one, it relies on a *place* dating system: the year chronicled can only be determined by *where* the entry stands in relation to all other entries. As legend has it, this was why the Nonmen refer to it as a "pit": the earlier the entry, the *deeper* the reader stands in the pit of history (recalling that for the Nonmen, the connotation of the term "pit" is general opposite that typically found in Mannish languages). The absence of any numerical dating system means, crucially, that the *Isûphiryas* is a perpetually *living* document, one that can only place events in historical context via the continuous inscription of *present* events. Although human historians generally find this vexing in the extreme, Nonmen scholars seem entirely unconcerned.

The second glaring peculiarity lies in the scriptural status the *Isûphiryas* enjoys among the Nonmen, who, seeing a holy analogue between the chronicle and their subterranean pilgrimages, believed it *could only be read backward*. The reader of the *Isûphiryas*, according to the Nonmen, had *to descend into it*, laying eye upon entry after entry, until arriving at the depth they had sought. The *Isûphiryas* itself recounts the execution of three different scholars for "despoiling the Holy Deep" whilst reading the chronicle. This so struck the Men of ancient Ûmeri that "consulting the pit" became a common idiom for delaying tactics during the Nonman Tutelage.

Iswa (c. 1450–c. 1530)—Legendary creator of the Iswazi. A despised Hapwee (the child of a Satiothi women raped by Nilnameshi soldiers), Iswa famously grew up as a prostitute in Domyot, and in this way secured the patronage of Xarah Wab-wabi, the feared and maligned Satta Warlock, who took him as a student and comfort-slave. A prodigy, Iswa very quickly outstripped his master. As a child of the street he knew well enough to conceal his burgeoning ability. According to legend, a dozen bronze and wooden figurines—little idols and fetishes he had filched for toys during his years on the street—were his sole possessions. These became the raw materials of an entirely new way to conceive sorcery, one which he would use to wreak vengeance upon Xarah Wab-wabi when he was scarcely twelve years old.

Iswazi—"Way of Iswa" (Ankmuri). A branch of sorcery that turns on the resonance between meanings and concrete things, via the medium of physical fetishes. The result is a sorcery in some ways more powerful yet generally less flexible than the Anagogis. Arcane legend offers several accounts of battles fought between Anagogic and Iswazi Magi, with the outcome favouring the former in group combat, and the latter in individual contests.

Ivory Gate—The northernmost gate of Caraskand, so named because of the pale sandstone used to construct it (as well as the Gate of Horns).

Iyengar, Nûkulk (4070–4112)—Man-of-the-Tusk and Earl of Nangaelsa, slain at the Battle of Shimeh.

Iyiskû—The Inchoroi term for themselves.

Iyokus, Heramari (4014–)—Ordealman (and one-time Man-of-the-Tusk), chanv addict, and Grandmaster of the Scarlet Spires in the Great Ordeal of Anasûrimbor Kellhus, often called the "Blind Necromancer." Master of Spies to Hanamanu Eleäzaras during the time of the First Holy War, he was made Grandmaster immediately after the fall of Shimeh in 4112. Also called "Second Tutor" (Drusas Achamian being the first) of Anasûrimbor Kellhus, who was rumoured to have spent months with Iyokus in the fortress of Kiz (the "Scarlet Spires") plumbing the depths of the Daimos in 4121.

J

Jahan Plains—The large, arid tableland that makes up the western frontier of Eumarna.

Jarutha—A small agricultural town some twenty miles southwest of Momemn.

Javreh—The slave-soldiers of the Scarlet Spires, famed for their ferocity in battle. The first unit was created in 3801 by Grandmaster Shinurta at the height of the Scholastic Wars.

Jekhia—A tributary nation of High Ainon, famed as the mysterious source of chanv, located at the headwaters of the River Sayut in the Great Kayarsus. The Men of Jekhia are unique in that they exhibit Xiuhianni racial characteristics.

Jeshimal River—The primary river system of Amoteu, draining the Betmulla Mountains and emptying into the Meneanor Sea at Shimeh.

Jihads—Fanim holy wars. Since the inception of Fanimry, the Kianene have waged no fewer than seven jihads, all of them against the Nansur Empire.

Jirux—A great Kianene fortress on the north bank of the River Sempis.

Jiünati Steppe—A vast region of semi-arid plains extending northward from the Carathay Desert to the Istyuli Plains, and inhabited by Scylvendi pastoralists since the early years of the Second Age.

jnan—An informal code of manner and speech understood by many to be a "war of word and sentiment." Adeptness at jnan is understood, particularly by the more refined subcultures of the Three Seas, to be the key determinant of status among individuals who are otherwise of equal caste or station. Given that the God is believed to be manifested in the movement of history, and history is determined primarily by the disparate statuses of men, for many jnan is understood as a sacred and not simply an instrumental enterprise. Many others, however, especially the Norsirai of the Three Seas, regard jnan with contempt, as a "mere game." Jnanic exchanges are typically characterized by concealed antagonism, the appreciation of irony and intellect, and the semblance of detached interest.

Joktha—A port city on the Enathpanean coast.

Jorua Sea—A great inland sea located in mid-western Eärwa.

Journals and Dialogues—The collected writings of Triamis I, greatest of the Ceneian Aspect-Emperors.

Judges—The name given to Zaudunyani missionaries.

Jukan—The God of sky and season. One of the so-called Compensatory Gods, who reward devotion in life with paradise in the afterlife, Jukan rivals Yatwer in popularity among subsistence farmers yet is scarcely represented in major urban centres. The priests of Jukan are readily recognizable by their blue-dyed skin. The Marjukari, an extreme ascetic branch of the Jukanic Cult, are notorious for living as hermits in the mountains.

Junriüma—Also known as the Vault-of-the-Tusk, the ancient fortress-temple that houses the Tusk, located in the heart of the Hagerna in Sumna.

Jurisada—A governorate of Kian and former province of the Nansur Empire. Located on the southeastern end of the Eumarnan Peninsula, Jurisada is an intensively agricultural region, densely populated, and thought to be a land of "spiritual sloth" by many Kianene.

Juru—God of virility and fertility. One of the so-called Compensatory Gods, who reward devotion in life with paradise in the afterlife, Juru is popular among aging caste-noble men, and possesses only a handful of temples, most of them found in major cities. It is often mocked as the Mistress Cult.

Juterum, the—The so-called Sacred Heights in Shimeh, where, according to scripture, Inri Sejenus ascended to the Nail of Heaven.

Juürl, Holy—A founding scripture of the Nonmen, relating the story of Imimorûl, and the divine origins of their race. Very little of the text has been translated into Mannish tongues, though the opening verses, "The Invocation to Imimorûl," are well known to Three Seas scholars:

> *Run, and breath becomes a blade.*
> *Weep, and eyes become coals.*
> *Live, and skin grows old.*
> *Shout, and heart becomes sound.*
> *Dance, and limbs become twirling gowns.*
> *Love, Imimorûl! Leap, Deep Father!*
> *Live, lest this skin grow old!*
>
> *We are the beast that ponders what he prowls.*
> *Dance for us, Deep Father!*
> *Shout so that we might weep and know.*

K

Kahiht—The name given to so-called World-Souls in the Inrithi tradition. Since the God manifests himself in the movement of historical events in Inrithism, to be Kahiht, or a world historical individual, is considered sacred.

Kairil—Ancient Ûmeri road that traverses the once-fertile plains of the lower River Aumris.

Kalaul—The great campus of the Csokis temple complex in Caraskand.

Kamposea Agora—A great bazaar adjacent to the temple complex of Cmiral in Momemn.

Kanampurea—A palatinate in the Conriyan interior, famed for its agricultural productivity, traditionally held by the brother of the Conriyan King.

Kanshaïva—A district of Nilnamesh.

kanti—A kind of antelope common to the Famiri grasslands.

Karian Way—An old Ceneian road running through the province of Massentia that once linked Sumna to Cenei during the reign of the Aspect-Emperors.

Karyot—A palatinate of High Ainon, located on the upper Sayut and forming the Jekhian frontier.

Kasalla, Porsentius (4062–4112)—Man-of-the-Tusk, one of the Nascenti, formerly a Captain in the Imperial Army. Killed at the Battle of Shimeh.

Kasaumki, Memshressa (4072–4121)—Man-of-the-Tusk, one of the Nascenti, formerly a Conriyan knight.

Kascamandri ab Tepherokar (4062–4112)—The Padirajah of Kian, slain by the Warrior-Prophet at the Battle of Tertae Fields.

Kayarsus Mountains—See *Great Kayarsus*.

Ke—The wooded reserve of the Conriyan King in Aoknyssus.

Kellian Reconstitution—The reformation of the School of Mandate into the "Imperial School" in 4124 by Anasûrimbor Kellhus.

Kelmeöl—The ancient capital of the Meöri Empire, destroyed in the Apocalypse in 2150.

Kemkaric—The language group of the ancient Ketyai pastoralists of the northwestern Three Seas.

Kengetic—The language group of the Ketyai peoples.

Kensooras—"between dogs" (Sakarpic). Sakarpi name for suicidal melancholy.

Keopsis, Sut (4089–)—Imperial Exalt-Counter under Anasûrimbor Esmenet.

Kepfet ab Tanaj (4061–4112)—The Kianene officer who betrayed Caraskand to Coithus Saubon and the First Holy War in 4111.

Kerathotics—The native Inrithi minority of Shigek prior to the First Holy War.

Kerioth—A major port city on the south coast of Eumarna.

Kethantei—A palatinate located in south central Conriya, noted for its wine and fruit production.

Ketyai—The typically black-haired, brown-eyed, dark-skinned race predominantly concentrated about the Three Seas. One of the Five Tribes of Men.

Khemema—A region of Kian and former province of the Nansur Empire. Located to the south of Shigek, Khemema marks the point where the great Carathay Desert reaches the Meneanor Sea. Sparsely inhabited by desert tribesmen (see *Khirgwi*), Khemema's only source of wealth derives from the regular trade caravans that travel between Shigek and Caraskand.

Khirgwi—The tribesmen of the eastern Carathay Desert, often tributary to the Kianene but ethnically distinct.

Kian—The most powerful nation of the Three Seas before the rise of the New Emprire, extending from the southern frontier of the Nansur Empire to Nilnamesh. The

Kianene were originally a desert people from the fringes of the Great Salt. Various Ceneian and Nilnameshi sources refer to them as cunning and audacious raiders, the target of several different campaigns and punitive expeditions. In his monumental *The Annals of Cenei*, Casidas describes them as "courtly savages, at once disarmingly gracious, and murderous in the extreme." Despite their reputation and apparent numbers (Nansur records indicate several attempts to gauge their numbers by concerned provincial governors), the Kianene spent most of their time battling amongst themselves over scarce desert resources. Their conversion to Fanimry (c. 3704–24) would change this, and with drastic consequences.

Following the unification of the Kianene tribes under Fane, Fan'oukarji I, Fane's eldest son and the first of Kian's Padirajahs, led his countrymen in the so-called White Jihad, winning a series of spectacular victories over the Nansur Imperial Army. By the time of his death in 3771, Fan'oukarji I had conquered all of Mongilea and had made serious inroads into Eumarna. He had also founded his capital, Nenciphon, on the banks of the River Sweki.

Successive Jihads would see Eumarna (3801), Enathpaneah (3842), Xerash and Amoteu (3845), then finally Shigek and Gedea (3933) all fall to Kian. Though the Nilnameshi would successfully thwart several different Kianene invasions, Fanic missionaries would succeed in converting the Girgashi to Fanimry in the thirty-eighth century. By the end of the fourth millennium Kian was easily the pre-eminent military and commercial power of the Three Seas, and a source of endless consternation not only for the much-diminished Nansur Empire but for Inrithi Princes in every nation.

Kianni—The language of Kian, a derivative of Caro-Shemic.

Kidruhil—The most celebrated cohort of heavy cavalry in the Three Seas, primarily constituted by Nansur caste-nobles from the Houses of the Congregate. Reorganized in 4125 under the auspices of Anasûrimbor Kellhus, it was expanded to include Zaudunyani from across the Three Seas. Riding under the Golden Horse and Black Circumfix, the Kidruhil were used extensively throughout the so-called Unification Wars.

Kig'krinaki—A Sranc tribe from the Plains of Gâl.

Kimish (4058–4121)—The Prime Interrogator to Ikurei Xerius III. Found dead in a ditch south of the Famiri frontier in 4121.

King-Fires—The ritual bonfires signifying kingship among the Galeoth.

King-of-Tribes—The title given to the individual elected by the Scylvendi chieftains to lead the gathered tribes in war.

King-Temple—Legendary palace of the Kûniüric High-Kings in Trysë, home of the Ur-Throne, destroyed in 2147.

Kinning—Name for the various Ishroi bloodlines, many of which transcended the Mansions, and so considerably complicated the politics of the day.

Kinnings-of-the-Sworn—The lowest status and most numerous of the Nonmen Kinnings, largely consisting of individuals sworn to various Ishroi or Quya.

Kinning Most-High-and-Deep—Honorific accorded the House of Tsonos.

kipfa'aifan—"Witness of Fane" (Kianni). The holiest scripture of Fanimry, chronicling the life and revelations of the Prophet Fane from his blinding and exile into the Great Salt in 3703 to his death in 3742. See *Fane*.

Kishyat—A palatinate of High Ainon, located on the south bank of the River Sayut on the Sansori frontier.

Kiskei, House—A Nansur House of the Congregate.

Kisma—The adoptive "father" of Mallahet.

Kites—Euphemism for Schoolmen in the argot of the Great Ordeal, especially when engaged in Culling.

Kiz—Original name of the river fortress that would become the Scarlet Spires.

Kiyuth River—A tributary of the River Sempis, running deep into the Jiünati Steppe.

Kizzi Bones—Divination fetishes popular among the Zeumi.

kjineta—See *castes*.

Kneeling Heights—One of the nine heights of Caraskand and the location of the Sapatishah's Palace.

knight-commander—The rank directly subordinate to the Grandmaster in the Shrial Knights.

Knights of the Tusk—See *Shrial Knights*.

Knights of Trysë—Also known as the Knights of the Ur-Throne. An ancient order of knights sworn to defend the Anasûrimbor Dynasty, thought destroyed in 2147 with the Sack of Trysë.

Koll (4098–?)—The last of the Stone Hags to survive the Skin-Eaters.

Koraphea—The most populous city of High Ainon after Carythusal, located on the coast north of the Sayut Delta.

Korasha—Also known as the White-Sun Palace. An extensive palace complex in Nenciphon, and traditional residence and administrative seat of the Kianene Padirajahs.

Kothwa, Hargraum (4070–4111)—Man-of-the-Tusk, Tydonni Earl of Gaethuni, slain at Mengedda.

Kûburû—The canonical compilation of the heroic lays of ancient Zeum.

Kucifra—"Blinding Light" (Caro-Shemic). Fanim epithet for Anasûrimbor Kellhus.

Kumeleus, Sirassas (4045–)—A staunch supporter of House Ikurei, and Exalt-General prior to Ikurei Conphas.

Kumrezzar, Akori (4071–4110)—Man-of-the-Tusk, Palatine of the Ainoni district of Kutapileth, and one of the leaders of the Vulgar Holy War.

Kûniüri—A lost nation of the Ancient North and the last of the ancient Aumris empires. High Norsirai city-states developed along the River Aumris and from *c.* 300

were united under Cûnwerishau, the God-King of Trysë. From *c.* 500 the city of Ûmerau gained ascendancy, leading to the Ûmerau Empire and the cultural efflorescence of the Nonman Tutelage under Carû-Ongonean. Ancient Umeria thrived until defeated by the Cond tribesmen of Aulyanau the Conqueror in 917. The rapid collapse of the so-called Cond Yoke led to a second period of Trysean dominance of the Aumris, this one lasting until 1228, when another series of White Norsirai migratory invasions resulted in the so-called Scintya Yoke.

The Kûniüric period proper did not begin until 1408, when Anasûrimbor Nanor-Ukkerja I, exploiting the confusion surrounding the collapse of the Scintya Empire, seized the Ur-Throne in Trysë, declaring himself the first High King of Kûniüri. Over the course of his long life (he lived to the age of 178, the reputed result of the Nonman blood in his veins), Nanor-Ukkerja I extended Kûniüri to the Yimelati Mountains in the north, to the westernmost coasts of the Cerish Sea in the east, to Sakarpus in the south, and to the Demua Mountains in the west. At his death, he divided this empire between his sons, creating Aörsi and Sheneor in addition to Kûniüri proper.

Kûniüri became, largely by virtue of its cultural inheritance, the centre of learning and craft for all Eärwa. The Trysean court hosted what were called the Thousand Sons, the scions of Kings from lands as far away as ancient Shigek and Shir. The holy city of Sauglish hosted pilgrim scholars from as far away as Angka and Nilnamesh. High Norsirai fashions were emulated throughout Eärwa.

This golden age came to an end with the Apocalypse and the defeat of Anasûrimbor Celmomas II on the Fields of Eleneöt in 2146. All the ancient cities of the Aumris would be destroyed the following year. The surviving Kûniüri were either enslaved or scattered. See *Apocalypse.*

Kûniüric—The lost language of ancient Kûniüri, derived from Ûmeritic.

Kunniat—Name for the collection of religious practices and observances centred upon *The Chronicle of the Holy Tusk* and the deities named therein. Apart from sharing a common scriptural foundation, Kunniat practices and mores differ radically— as much between Cults as between nations. They do all share, however, the belief that the *function* of religious belief is to commend souls to the Afterlife as well as to maintain the connection between the present and the ancestral past.

Kuöti—A Scylvendi tribe of the northwestern Steppe.

Kurigald—A fiefdom of Galeoth, located on the eastern shores of Lake Huösi.

Kurrut—A small fortress in the Gedean interior, built by the Nansur after the fall of Shigek to the Fanim in 3933.

Kurwachal—"Altar" (Aörsic). One of the most fortified towers of Dagliash.

Kushigas, Ersa (4070–4111)—Man-of-the-Tusk, Palatine of the Conriyan province of Annand, slain at Anwurat.

Kusjeter (4077–4111)—Man-of-the-Tusk, Count-Palatine of the Ainoni province of Gekas, slain at Anwurat.

Kussalt (4054–4111)–Man-of-the-Tusk, groom to Prince Coithus Saubon, slain at Mengedda.

Kutapileth–An administrative district of eastern High Ainon, noted for its iron and silver mines.

Kutigha (4063–4111)–A Thousand Temples informant for the Scarlet Spires.

kut'ma–In benjuka, the "hidden move" that seems insignificant but actually determines the outcome of the game.

Kutnarmu–The generic name for the unexplored continent south of Eärwa.

Kyranae Plains–A fertile region drained by the River Phayus and extending from the southern Hethanta Mountains to the Meneanor Sea. Its peoples have given birth to three great empires: ancient Kyraneas, the Ceneian Empire, and most recently the Nansur Empire.

Kyranean–The lost language of ancient Kyraneas, derived from ancient Kemkaric.

Kyraneas–A lost nation of the ancient Three Seas, located on the River Phayus, with a capital first at Parninas then at Mehtsonc. Culturally linked and long tributary to Shigek, Kyraneas expanded to include much of her erstwhile ruler's empire, and was at the height of her power at the time of the Apocalypse. With the loss at Mehsarunath in 2154 and the destruction of Mehtsonc shortly after, the fate of the ancient kingdom was sealed, even though the Kyranean High King, Anaxophus V, managed to defeat the No-God the following year. See *Apocalypse*.

L

Labyrinth–See *Thousand Thousand Halls*.

Lance, the–A Scylvendi constellation in the northern sky.

Languages of Men–Until the Breaking of the Gates and the migration of the Four Nations from Eänna, the Men of Eärwa–called the Emwama in *The Chronicle of the Tusk*–were enslaved by the Nonmen and spoke debased versions of their masters' tongues. No trace of these languages remains, nor does any trace of their original, pre-bondage language. The great Nonman history, the *Isûphiryas*, or the "Great Pit of Years," suggests the Emwama originally spoke the same tongue as their kin across the Great Kayarsus. This has led many to believe that Thoti-Eännorean is indeed the primeval language of all men.

THOTI-EÄNNOREAN–the mother tongue of all Men, and the language of the *Chronicle of the Tusk*.
↘

VASNOSRI - language group of the Norsirai peoples.
↘

AUMRI-SAUGLA - language group of the ancient Norsirai peoples of the Aumris Valley.

UMERITIC - lost language of ancient Ûmerau.

KÛNIÜRIC - lost language of ancient Kuniüri.

DÛNYANIC - language of the Dûnyain.

NIRSODIC - language group of ancient Norsirai pastoralists ranging from the Sea of Cerish to the Sea of Jorua.

AKKSERSIAN - lost language of ancient Akksersia, and "purest" of the Nirsodic Tongues.

CONDIC - language group of ancient pastoralists of the Near Istyuli Plains.

EÄMNORIC - lost language of ancient Eämnor.

ATRITHI - language of Atrithau.

SKETTIC - language group of ancient pastoralists of the Far Istyuli Plains.

HIGH SAKARPEAN - language of ancient Sakarpus.

SAKARPIC - language of Sakarpus.

OLD MEORIC - lost language of the early Meorn Empire.

MEORIC - lost language of the late Meorn Empire.

GALLISH - language of Galeoth.

THUNYERIC - language of Thunyerus.

TYDONNI - language of Ce Tydonn.

CEPALORAN - language group of pastoralists of the Cepaloran Plains.

NYMBRICANI - language of the Nymbricani clans.

KENGETIC - language group of the Ketyai peoples.

KEMKARIC - language group of the ancient Ketyai pastoralists of the Northwestern Three Seas.

⬎

KYRANEAN - lost language of ancient Kyraneas.

⬎

HIGH SHEYIC - language of Ceneian Empire.

⬎

LOW SHEYIC - language of the Nansur Empire and *lingua franca* of the Three Seas.

⬎

SOROPTIC - lost language of ancient Shigek.

⬎

HAMORIC - language group of the ancient Ketyai pastoralists of the Eastern Three Seas.

⬎

HAM-KHEREMIC - lost language of ancient Shir.

⬎

SHEYO-KHEREMIC - lost language of the lower castes of the Eastern Ceneian Empire.

⬎

CONRIYAN - language of Conriya.

⬎

NRONI - language of Nron.

⬎

CIRONJIC - language of Cironj.

⬎

CENGEMIC - language of Cengemis.

⬎

SANSORI - language of Sansor.

⬎

OLD AINONI - language of Ceneian occupied Ainon.

⬎

AINONI - language of High Ainon.

⬎

SHEM-VARSI - language group of the ancient pastoralists of the Southwestern Three Seas.

⬎

VAPARSI - lost language of ancient Nilnamesh.

⬎

HIGH VURUMANDIC - language of Nilnameshi ruling castes.

⬎

SAPMATARI - lost language of Nilnameshi labouring castes.

⬎

SHEYO-BUSKRIT - language of Nilnameshi labouring castes.

⬎

GIRGASHI - language of Fanic-Girgash.

CINGULI - language of Cingulat.

XERASHI - lost language of scriptural Xerash.

SHEYO-XERASHI - language of Xerash.

SHEMIC - language group of the ancient non-Nilnameshi pastoralists of the Southwestern Three Seas.

PROTO-CARO-SHEMIC - language group of the ancient pastoralists of the Eastern Carathay Desert.

CARO-SHEMIC - language of the scriptural pastoralists of the Carathay Desert.

KIANNI - language of Kian.

MAMATI - language of scriptural Amoteu.

AMOTI - language of Amoteu.

EUMARNI - language of Eumarna.

SATIOTHI - language group of the Satyothi peoples.

ANKMURI - lost language of ancient Angka.

OLD ZEÜMI - language of ancient Zeüm.

ZEÜMI - language of the Empire of Zeüm.

ATKONDO-ATYOKI - language group of the Satyothi pastoralists of the Atkondras Mountains and surrounding regions.

SKAARIC - language group of the Scylvendi peoples.

OLD SCYLVENDI - language of ancient Scylvendi pastoralists.

SCYLVENDI - language of the Scylvendi.

XIANGIC - language group of the xiuhianni peoples (the Lost Nation).

Languages of Nonmen—Without doubt, the Nonmen, or Cûnuroi, tongues are among the oldest in Eärwa. Some Aujic inscriptions predate the first extant example of Thoti-Eännorean, *The Chronicle of the Tusk*, by more than five thousand years. Auja-Gilcûnni, which has yet to be deciphered, is far older still.

AUJA-GILCÛNNI– the lost "ground tongue" of the Nonmen.

AUJIC–lost tongue of the Aujan Mansions.

IHRIMSÛ–tongue of Injor-Niyas.

GILCÛNYA–tongue of the Nonmen Qûya and the Gnostic Schools.

HIGH KUNNA–debased version of Gilcûnya, used by the Anagogic Schools of the Three Seas.

Larsippas, Memplei (4086–)–A physician-priest assigned to the Andiamine Heights.

Latter Prophet–See *Inri Sejenus*.

"[to] laugh with Sarothesser"–An Ainoni phrase expressing their belief that laughter at the moment of death signifies triumph. This tradition stems from the legend that Sarothesser I, the founder of High Ainon, laughed at death the moment before it claimed him.

Law of the Tusk–The traditional law as laid out in the Book of Canticles in *The Chronicle of the Tusk*. Though largely superseded by *The Tractate*, it is still referred to in cases on which Inri Sejenus has nothing to say.

"Lay of Little Teeth"–Famous epic verse cycle recounting the Fall of Siol following the Breaking of the Gates.

Legion–A Dûnyain term referring to the preconscious sources of the conscious thought.

Letting–Also known as the Great Letting. The final act of self-mutilation committed by the Great Ordeal before assailing Golgotterath.

Leweth (4061–4109)–A trapper in the abandoned Atrithan province of Sobel.

Library of Sauglish–The famed temple complex and text repository found in ancient Sauglish. According to legend, the Library had grown to the size of a city within the city by the time of Sauglish's destruction in 2147.

Library of the Sareöts–See *Sareötic Library*.

Ligesseras, House–One of the Houses of the Congregate.

Lioning–Sakarpi rite, involving the ritual hunt of mountain lions in the Osthwai Mountains, whose carcasses are given in burnt offering to Yatwer, Goddess of Fertility.

Lists, The–A registry of names of suspected skin-spies in the First Holy War.

Logos–The name used by Dûnyain to refer to instrumental reason. The Logos describes the course of action that allows for the most efficient exploitation of one's circumstances in order "to come before," that is, to precede and master the passage of events.

"[The] Logos is without beginning or end."—A Dûnyain phrase referring to the so-called Rational Priority Principle. See *Dûnyain*.

Lokor—An early city of the Aumris, and ancient rival of Ûmerau, destroyed by the Ûmeri c. 440.

Lokung—The "Dead-God" of the Scylvendi. See *No-God*.

Long Side—Scalper name for the lands to the northeast of the Ostwai Mountains.

Lonely City—Common epithet for Sakarpus among the Sakarpi.

Low Sheyic—The language of the Nansur Empire and lingua franca of the Three Seas.

M

Maëngi—The true name of the first skin-spy to pose as Cutias Sarcellus.

Magga, Hringa (4080–4111)—Man-of-the-Tusk, cousin of Prince Hringa Skaiyelt of Thunyerus.

Maimor—See Aenkû Maimor. Ancient Meöri fortress that once guarded Telmeol.

Maithanet—The Shriah of the Thousand Temples, and primary instigator of the First Holy War.

Mallahet—A notorious member of the Cishaurim.

Mamaradda (4071–4111)—Man-of-the-Tusk, Javreh Shield-Captain assigned to execute Drusas Achamian.

Mamati—The language of scriptural Amoteu, a derivative of Caro-Shemic.

Mamayma (?–?)—One of the Chieftain-Kings named in *The Chronicle of the Tusk*.

Mamot—A ruined Ceneian city located near the mouth of the River Sweki.

Mandate, School of—The Gnostic School founded by Seswatha in 2156 to continue the war against the Consult and to protect the Three Seas from the return of the No-God. Based in Atyersus, the Mandate maintains missions in several different cities about the Three Seas and embassies in the courts of all the Great Factions. Aside from its apocalyptic calling, the Mandate is distinct from the other sorcerous Schools in several respects, not the least of which is its possession of the Gnosis, a monopoly it has been able to protect for almost two thousand years. The Mandate also differs in the fanaticism of its members: apparently, all sorcerers of rank continuously dream Seswatha's experiences of the Apocalypse every night, the effect of a sorcerous rite called the Grasping, where initiates reputedly submit to incantations while holding Seswatha's mummified heart. Also, the members of the Mandate elect an executive council (called the Quorum) rather than an individual Grandmaster to further guard against deviations from their core mission.

Prior to accession of Anasûrimbor Kellhus, the Mandate could boast between fifty and sixty sorcerers of rank, and perhaps twice that number of initiates. These numbers, typical of minor Anagogic Schools, are deceptive, however, since the power of the Gnosis makes the Mandate more than a match for Schools as large as, say, the

Scarlet Spires. Because of this power, the School has long been courted by the Kings of Conriya.

One cannot overestimate the impact of Anasûrimbor Kellhus—who in effect managed to graft Mandate doctrine into the heart of Inrithi dogma—on the fortunes of the School. Once the laughingstock of the Three Seas, the Mandate found itself the counterpart of the Thousand Temples in the New Empire, and its Grandmaster the right hand of the Holy Aspect-Emperor.

Mandate Catechism—The ritual set of questions and answers on Mandate doctrine, recited by teacher and student at the beginning of each day of study. The first thing learned by all Mandate Schoolmen.

Mangaecca—The ancient rival to the School of Sohonc, and last of the four original Gnostic Schools. From its founding in 684 by Sos-Praniura (the greatest student of Gin'yursis), the School of Mangaecca had pursued a predatory ethos, regarding knowledge as the embodiment of power. Though this earned the School an ambiguous reputation, the Mangaecca managed to avoid running afoul of the High Gnostic Writ, the edict of Nincama-Telesser circumscribing sorcerous conduct. Then, in 777, at the behest of a Nonman Erratic named Cet'ingira, they discovered the Incû-Holoinas, the dread Ark of the Inchoroi. Over the following centuries they continued their excavations of the Ark and their investigations of the Tekne. In 1123 rumours began spreading that Shaeönanra, then Grandmaster of the Mangaecca, had discovered a catastrophic means to undo the scriptural damnation of sorcerers. The School was promptly outlawed, and the remainder of its members fled to Golgotterath, abandoning Sauglish forever. By the time of the Apocalypse, they had transformed into what would be called the Consult. See *Apocalypse*.

Manghaput—A major port city in Nilnamesh.

Mansions—The Mannish name for the great subterranean cities of the Nonmen.

Mantigol—Highest mountain in the Urokkas.

Mantraitor—See *Mekeritrig*.

Marakiz—The tallest of the Scarlet Spires.

Mark, the—The name for what is otherwise known as the "bruising of the onta." Aside from the Psûkhe, which may or may not be a true sorcery, all sorcerous manifestations and practitioners exhibit what is called the Mark. Various descriptions of the Mark have come down through history, but there seems to be little consistency in the accounts, apart from the experience's ephemeral nature. According to religious accounts, the Mark is akin to the disfiguring of criminals, the way the God reveals the blasphemers in the presence of the righteous. But apologists such as Zarathinius point out that if this is indeed the case, then it is more than a little ironic that only the *blasphemers* can see the Mark. In secular accounts, textual analogies are typically resorted to: seeing the Mark is akin to seeing where text has been scratched away and overwritten in ancient documents. In the case of sorcery, since the amendments to reality are as flawed as the Men who do the amending, it stands to reason that some essential difference would be visible.

Marsadda—The former capital of Cengemis, located on the coast of Ce Tydonn.

Marsalees, Urdrûsû (4094–)—Ordealman, Palatine of Kûtapileth.

Martemus (4061–4111)—Man-of-the-Tusk, Nansur General, and aide to Ikurei Conphas.

Martial Prohibitions—Collection of edicts determining the conduct of Ordealmen when engaged in pitched battle.

Massar ab Kascamandri (4089–4132)—Ordealman, Believer-King of Kian, leader of the Kianene contingent in the Great Ordeal of Anasûrimbor Kellhus, the younger brother of Fanayal ab Kascamandri. He was often called the "Kneeler," both in praise (by the Zaudunyani) and in condemnation (by the Fanim). Famed for severing his own ear to demonstrate his devotion to Anasûrimbor Kellhus, he would be killed by Sranc at the Battle of Irsûlor in the autumn of 4132.

Massentia—A province of the central Nansurium, called "the Golden" because of the bounty of her wheat fields. Given the profound cultural impact of the Ceneian Empire, the name has long been a byword for bucolic prosperity across the Three Seas.

Maumurine Gate—An immense gate located at the southernmost point of Momemn's walls.

Mbimayu—The Major sorcerous School of Zeum based in High Domyot, functioning under the auspices of the Satakhan, much as the Imperial Saik once served the Emperors of Nansur.

Mbotetulu (c. 1340–1426)—Ojogi-Dynasty Satakhan credited with the first true unification of Zeum.

Meärji (4074–)—Man-of-the-Tusk, Galeoth thane, client to Prince Coithus Saubon.

Medial Screw—Great stair that plumbs the entirety of Cil-Aujas.

Medicine-wig—Traditional headdress worn by members of Zeumi royal bloodlines, denoting their status as "Healers of the Many."

Meerskatu, Sholis (4092–)—Ordealmen and Exalt-Captain of the Pillarians.

Mehtsonc—The ancient administrative and commercial capital of Kyraneas, destroyed in the Apocalypse in 2154.

Meigeiri—The administrative and spiritual capital of Ce Tydonn, founded in 3739 about the Ceneian fortress of Meigara.

Meigon (4002–)—A member of the Dûnyain Pragma.

Mekeritrig (?–)—"Traitor of Men" (Kûniüric). The mannish name for Cet'ingira, the Nonman Siqu who revealed the location of Min-Uroikas to the School of Mangaecca in 777, and who would become a ranking member of the Consult during the Apocalypse. See *Mangaecca* and *Apocalypse*.

Memgowa (2466–2506)–The famed near antique Zeümi sage and philosopher, primarily known in the Three Seas for his *Celestial Aphorisms* and *The Book of Divine Acts*.

Memkuri, Apsa (4080-4112)–Man-of-the-Tusk, Ainoni client of Lord Uranyanka rumoured to have been murdered by the Scarlet Spires.

memorialists–Those members of a Scylvendi tribe, typically the old and infirm, entrusted with the memorization and recitation of the Scylvendi oral tradition.

memponti–A Sheyic term meaning "fortuitous turn." In jnan, the most auspicious moment to make one's purposes clear.

Men–With the possible exception of the Sranc, the dominant race of Eärwa.

Meneanor, Sea of–The northernmost of the Three Seas.

Mengedda–A ruined city in the heart of the Mengedda Plains, famed as the battleground where Anaxophus V struck down the No-God with the Heron Spear in 2155.

Mengedda Plains–The natural geographical frontier between Shigek and Nansur, just south of the Unaras Spur and north of the Gedea Highlands. As the site of innumerable battles, the fields are widely reputed to be haunted.

Men of the Tusk–The warriors of the First Holy War.

Meöri Empire–A lost nation of the Ancient North. Founded as a trading stronghold by Akksersian colonists c. 850, the city of Kelmeöl grew rapidly, and its people, the Meöri, progressively asserted more and more authority over the neighbouring White Norsirai tribes. By the time Borswelka I was declared King in 1021, it had become an aggressive, militaristic city-state. By the time his grandson Borswelka II died in 1104, it had conquered most of the Vosa River Basin and had established trading contacts with Shir to the south through a series of forts along the River Wernma. Strategically situated, and without any regional competitors, the Meöri Empire, as it came to be called, flourished as a mercantile nation. It collapsed with the destruction of Kelmeöl in 2150 during the Apocalypse.

Mepmerat (4084–)–Imperial Mathematician belonging to the court of Anasûrimbor Kellhus I.

Mere–Sacred lake that forms the floor of the Holy Deep at the very foundation of Ishterebinth, once renowned for its purity, now choked with putrefaction.

Metagnosis–Complication of the Gnosis discovered and elaborated by Anasûrimbor Kellhus over the course of his tenure as Aspect-Emperor. A great deal of speculation regarding the metaphysics and the capacities of the Metagnosis have arisen since Our Lord and Prophet first used it to strike down the Cishaurim at Shimeh. Aside from descriptions of its exercise, the sum of our knowledge of the discipline turns upon a single passage in the *Novum Arcanum*:

> *All sorcery proceeds on the basis of two inner voices, because the soul, as subject, remains inside its meaning, and so blind to that meaning. Only by speaking to our*

speech do we create something absolute, an overlap of contingencies. This becomes the godlike spark, the manifestation of human will upon obdurate matter. But as a mole can only see tunnels, so are sorcerers cursed to remain blind to the Metagnosis, for it exceeds their craft as I exceed them. To speak a third is to distill the all-solving binary, to seize the voices of the two, and so fix, not only the meaning, but the relation between those meanings, to render Absolute our fleeting acquaintance with the Absolute, and to work miracles.

metaphysics—Generally, the study of the ultimate nature of existence. More specifically, the study of the operative principles behind the various branches of sorcery (see, *Sorcery*). Perhaps no topic has been more fiercely debated among Nonmen or Men, since metaphysics bears directly upon death and Nonmen and Men fear death above all other things.

Meümaras (4058–)—The Captain of the *Amortanea*.

mibu—Small jackal native to Zeum.

Middle North—A term sometimes used to refer to the Norsirai nations of the Three Seas.

Migmarsa—See Hinsursa, River.

Mihtrûlic—The Far Antique School of Contrivers founded by the Artisan *c.* 660. Though no Mannish smith ever achieved the near miraculous abilities of Emilidis, the Mihtrûlic managed to create a vast number of sorcerous artifacts, some possessing awesome power. Among Men, the most gifted sorcerous artificer was Davdûl, the long-lived Grandmaster who forged the battleaxe Tharmondal, the dreaded Sky-cleaver, among many other artifacts, once famed, but now lost to the mists of time. Given the absence of any artificing traditions in the Three Seas, fairly all sorcerous artifacts in the South trace their origins back to Mihtrûlic.

Mimaripal (4067–)—Man-of-the-Tusk, client baron of Chinjosa.

Mim-Paresh Quarter—Affluent, south bank section of Carythusal, adjacent to the famed Pruvineh Agora, the largest spice market in the World.

Ministrate—The Zaudunyani organization dedicated to the conversion of the Orthodox, but effectively a form of religious police.

Minror—"Heap" (Ihrimsû). The famed Soggomantic Gate of Ishterebinth, so-called because constructed of debris carted from Min-Uroikas. The conception of Nil'giccas, Minror remained a topic of furor among the High Kinnings until it repelled the No-God during the Apocalypse.

Min-Uroikas—"Pit of Obscenities" (Ihrimsû). The Nonman name for Golgotterath. See *Cûno-Inchoroi Wars*.

Mi'punial (?–?)—One of the great Hûlya poets of Siol.

Miracle of the Circumfixion—The second of the Warrior-Prophet's three so-called "Miracles," referring to his survival of the Circumfix in Caraskand.

Miracle of Water—The first of the Warrior-Prophet's three so-called "Miracles," referring to his discovery of water in the wastes of Khemema.

Miramis, Nersei (4090–)—Wife of Nersei Proyas, Believer-King of Conriya, mother of Xinemus and Thaila.

Mirawsul—"Cracked Shield" (Ûmeri). Central highland region of ancient Kûniüri.

Misarat—An immense Kianene fortress located on the northwestern frontier of Eumarna.

Misty Sea—See *Neleost Sea*.

Mobbing—The instinctive tendency of Sranc to muster in numbers far surpassing those of their foes, only on the scale of hundreds, even thousands.

Mog-Pharau—The ancient Kûniüric name for "No-God." See *No-God*.

Mohaïva—A district of Nilnamesh.

Moimoriccas (?–?)—Son of Ishoriol, called Earth-eater as wielder of the famed cudgel, Gimimra.

Momas—The God of storms, seas, earthquakes and luck. One of the so-called Compensatory Gods, who reward devotion in life with paradise in the afterlife, Momas is the primary deity worshipped by seamen and merchants, and is the patron divinity of Cironj (and to a lesser extent Nron). In the *Higarata*, he is depicted as cruel, even malicious, and obsessed with minute matters of propriety—leading some commentators to suggest he is in fact a Bellicose, as opposed to a Compensatory, God. His primary device is the White Triangle on Black (representing the Shark's Tooth worn by all devotees of Momas).

Momemn—"Praise Momas" (Kyranean). The administrative and commercial capital of the Nansurium. Heavily fortified, Momemn houses the residence of the Nansur Emperor, as well as one of the busiest harbours on the Three Seas. Historians have oft noted how each of the three capitals (Mehtsonc, Cenei, and Momemn) of the three great empires to arise from the Kyranae Plain have stood along the River Phayus, each closer than the last to the Meneanor. Some claim that Momemn, which stands at the river's mouth, will be the last, thus leading to the common phrase "running out of river" to indicate changing fortunes.

Mongilea—A governorate of Kian and former province of the Nansur Empire, located along the coasts adjacent to the River Sweki. Long a tributary land, Mongilea has exchanged masters many times. As the original conquest of Fan'oukarji I (3759), it has become the "Green Homeland" of the Kianene, and a famed producer of horses.

Mop—Name for the Sranc-infested, forest wilds of what was once the ancient Meöri Empire.

Mopuraul, Hapama (4094–4132)—Ordealman, Satrap of Tendant'heras, killed in the days leading up to the disaster at Irsulor.

Moraör–"Hall of Kings" (Old Meoric). The famed palace complex of Galeoth's rulers, located in Oswenta.

Morghund, House–The ruling dynasty of Atrithau since 3817.

Morimhira (?–)–The oldest of the Nonmen to be rendered immortal by the Inoculation. The elder brother of Cu'huriol, Morimhira gained fame for refusing to accept the Seal of the House Primordial, dooming his younger brother to be King instead, and so delivering his race to the folly of Cu'jara Cinmoi. According to legend, he believed himself too bloodthirsty–and true to this appraisal, lived a life of near continuous war and slaughter. His age relative to his appearance was already a marvel ere he received the Inoculation. When he alone, out of all the elders, survived, he became known as the Most Ancient Warrior–for he was indeed the oldest Nonman living.

Moserothu–An Ainoni city located in the heart of the populous Secharib Plains.

Mother-of-Cities–See *Trysë*.

Mother of Birth–See *Yatwer*.

Mount Eshki–The legendary "Mountain of Revelation" where, according to *The Chronicle of the Tusk*, the Prophet Angeshraël received the call to lead the Tribes of Men into Eärwa.

Mount Kinsureah–The legendary "Mountain of Summoning" where, according to *The Chronicle of the Tusk*, the Prophet Angeshraël sacrificed Oresh, the youngest of his sons by Esmenet, to demonstrate his conviction to the Tribes of Men. The so-called Oreshalat (Issue-of-Oresh) constitutes one of the most important crossroads of theology, or religious speculation, with philosophy, rational or sorcerous speculation. Of particular interest is the strand called the Imboreshalat (Issue-of-Oresh-if), which asks what follows from Angeshraël's resolution by exploring what follows from a possible failure of resolve, where Angeshraël tells his tribe that the Gods staid his hand.

Mouth-of-the-Worm–A Yatwerian temple in Carythusal, so named because of its proximity to the slums commonly called the Worm.

Mu'miorn (?–4132)–Dispossessed Son of Nihrimsûl, longtime favourite of Nil'giccas, famed for his promiscuity.

Munuäti–A powerful Scylvendi tribe from the interior of the Jiünati Steppe.

Murathaur–Wracu of Far Antiquity, called *Ilnimili*, or "the Silver," for his crest, a feature that was likely responsible for his other common cognomen, "the Dragon of Knives." Famously slain by Cilcûliccas, who thenceforth was known as the Lord of Swans.

Muretetis (2789–2864)–An ancient Ceneian scholar-slave famed for his *Axioms and Theorems*, the founding text of Three Seas geometry.

Mûrminil Halls–The great subterranean plaza of Cil-Aujas.

Mursiris–"Wicked North" (Ham-Kheremic). The ancient Shiradi name for the

No-God, so named because his presence was for so long sensed only as an intimation of doom on the northern horizon.

Mursidides, Eselos (4081–4132)—Ordealman, Believer-King of Cironj, leader of the Cironji contingent in the Great Ordeal of Anasûrimbor Kellhus, called "the Cunning" for his near bloodless conquest of Cironj during the Unification Wars, and killed in the Battle of Irsûlor in 4132.

Muraw—"Gate of the Word" (Ûmeri). The bastion protecting the main entrance to the Library of Sauglish.

Murussar—"Gate of the Cage" (Ûmeri). The ceremonial bastion marking the entrance to the "Cage," or Issarau, the outland quarter of Sauglish.

Musyerius, Keles (4072–)—Ordealman and Mysunsai sorcerer-of-rank.

Myclai—The ancient administrative and commercial capital of Akksersia, destroyed in 2149 during the Apocalypse.

Mygella, Anasûrimbor (2065–2111)—The famed Hero-King of Aörsi, whose deeds are recounted in *The Sagas*.

Mysunsai—"The Bond of Three" (Vaparsi). The self-proclaimed "mercenary School," which sells its sorcerous services across the Three Seas. Perhaps the largest of the Anagogic Schools, though far from the most powerful, the Mysunsai are a commercial result of the 3804 defensive amalgamation of three minor Schools during the Scholastic Wars: the Mikka Council from Cironji, the Oaranat from Nilnamesh, and the (Cengemic) Nilitar Compact from Ce Tydonn. Under the terms of the infamous Psailian Concession during the Scholastic Wars, the Mysunsai assisted the Inrithi in their Ainoni campaigns, an act for which the School was never forgiven, though it did much to confirm the School's exclusive commercial interests to its customers.

N

Nabathra—A mid-sized town in the province of Anserca, whose markets control the regional distribution of wool, the province's primary commodity.

Nagogris—A large New Dynasty city on the upper River Sempis, famed for her red sandstone fortifications.

nahat—See *castes*.

Nail of Heaven—The northern star that, aside from being the brightest in the night sky (it is sometimes visible in daylight), provides the axis from which all other stars revolve. The Nail is universally extolled by Men as a "guiding light," a means of navigation and calendrical time keeping, the Nonman, who call it Imburil (or "Newborn" in Aujic), view it as a sinister harbinger of doom, as the star that occasioned the Arkfall.

Naïn (4071–4111)—Man-of-the-Tusk, sorcerer of rank in the Scarlet Spires, slain by Chorae at Anwurat.

Nangael—A fiefdom of Ce Tydonn, located along the Swa Marches. Nangael warriors can be readily identified by their tattooed cheeks.

Nanor-Ukkerja I (1378–1556)—"Hammer of Heaven" (Kûniüric from Umeritic *nanar hukisha*) The first Anasûrimbor High King, whose defeat of the Scintya in 1408 would lead to the founding of Kûniüri and begin what most scholars regard as the longest-reigning dynasty in recorded history.

Nansur—See *Nansur Empire*.

Nansur Empire—A nation of the Three Seas and self-proclaimed inheritor to the Ceneian Empire. At the height of its power the Nansur Empire extended from Galeoth to Nilnamesh, but it has been much reduced by centuries of warfare against the Fanim Kianene.

Though the Nansur Empire has witnessed its fair share of usurpers, palace revolts, and short-lived military dictatorships, it has enjoyed a remarkable degree of dynastic stability. It was under the Trimus Emperors (3411–3508) that the "Nansur" (the traditional name for the district surrounding Momemn) emerged from the chaos following Cenei's destruction to unify the Kyranae plains. But true Imperial expansion did not occur until the Zerxei Dynasty (3511–3619), which, under the rule of successive and short-lived Emperors, managed to conquer Shigek (3539), Enathpaneah (3569), and the Sacred Lands (3574).

Under the Surmante Emperors (3619–3941), the Nansurium enjoyed its greatest period of growth and military ascendancy, culminating in the rule of Surmante Xatantius I (3644–93), who subdued the Cepaloran tribes as far north as the Vindauga River, and who even managed to capture the ancient Nilnameshi capital of Invishi, thus very nearly restoring all the so-called Western Empire that had once belonged to Cenei. But his practice of debasing the talent in order to finance his endless wars fairly wrecked the empire's economy. By the time Fan'oukarji I embarked on his White Jihad in 3743, the empire still had not recovered from Xatantius's excesses. His Surmante descendants found themselves embroiled in never-ending wars they could ill afford, let alone win. Scarce resources and an intransigent commitment to the Ceneian model of warfare, which seemed incapable of coping with Kianene tactics, conspired to render the empire's decline an inevitability.

The dynasty of the most recent claimants to the Imperial Mantle, the Ikurei, arose as the result of a coup brought about by the turmoil following the loss of Shigek to the Kianene in 3933 (in the so-called Dagger Jihad of Fan'oukarji III). A former Exalt-General, Ikurei Sorius I reorganized both the Imperial Army and the empire, changes that allowed him and his descendants to defeat no fewer than three full-scale Fanim invasions.

Though the First Holy War ended the threat of Fanimry once and for all, it also led to the demise of the Nansur Empire—or at least its relegation to something possessing diminished significance. Momemn remained an Imperial Capital, but one serving the interests of a far different Empire.

nansuri—Name of the short, thrusting swords used by Ordealmen for close-quarter melee, so-called for its resemblance to the Columnary shortsword upon which it was based.

Nansurium—See *Nansur Empire*.

Nantilla, Couras (4089–)—Ordealman, Earl of Pikka, General of the Cengemi in the Great Ordeal of Anasûrimbor Kellhus.

Narindar—In Kunniat and Inrithi lore, the Gods own assassins. A number of assassination cults have arisen across the Three Seas over the ages, but none could approach the dread commanded by the Narindar. In one sense, the term is a catch-all for those souls, sometimes hapless, who find themselves the instrument of some divinity's retribution. The only thing conjoining these "Anointed Narindar" with the Narindarjû, the clerics of Ajokli who worship the Trickster with contracted murders, is the Unerring Grace, the degree to which eternal necessity, or Fate, guides their actions. For some Narindar—such as the Yatwerian "White-Luck Warrior"—the Unerring Grace is absolute, and the assassin acts in utter accord with what has already happened. For others, the Grace resolves and fades much as inspiration.

Narnol, Coithus (4065–)—Ordealman, Believer-King of Galeoth, and elder brother of Coithus Saubon.

Narradha, Hringa (4093–4111)—Man-of-the-Tusk, youngest brother of Prince Hringa Skaiyelt, slain at Mengedda.

Nascenti—The nine primary disciples of Anasûrimbor Kellhus, the so-called "Thanes of the Warrior-Prophet."

Nasueret Column—Also known as the "Ninth Column." A Column of the Nansur Imperial Army, traditionally stationed on the Kianene frontier. Their device is the Black Imperial Sun halved by an eagle's wing.

Nasurius—One of many rumour-skewed names attributed to Anasûrimbor Kellhus during his rise to power.

Nau-Cayûti (2119–2140)—"Blessed Son" (Umeritic). The youngest son of Celmomas II and the famed "scourge of Golgotterath." Nau-Cayûti is famed for his heroism and martial brilliance during the dark days after the fall of Aörsi (2136), when Kûniüri stood alone against Golgotterath. Many of his exploits, such as the Slaying of Tanhafut the Red and the Theft of the Heron Spear, are recounted in *The Sagas*.

Naures River—An important river system in eastern Nilnamesh.

Nausk Mausoleum—The Far-Antique temple in Kelmeol where, according to legend, the bones of the Meori High-King Aratrula the Mad are interred. Convinced of his own damnation, Aratrula fairly enslaved his nation attempting to build a Mausoleum, allegedly lined in plates of lead, that might keep his souls safe from the Outside.

Nautzera, Seidru (4038–)—A senior member of the Mandate Quorum. See *Mandate*.

Near Antiquity—Sometimes called the Ceneian Age. The historical period beginning in 2155 (the end of the Apocalypse) and ending with the Sack of Cenei in 3351. See *Far Antiquity*.

Neberenes (4067–4124)—An Ainoni Zaudunyani informant.

Neleöst Sea—A large inland sea located in northwestern Eärwa that formed the traditional northern frontier for those nations arising from the Aumris River Valley.

Nenciphon—The administrative capital of Kian, and one of the great cities of the Three Seas, founded by Fan'oukarji I in 3752.

Nergaöta—A semi-mountainous fiefdom in northwestern Galeoth, renowned for the quality of its wool.

Nersei, House—The ruling House of Conriya since the Aöknyssian Uprisings of 3742, which saw the entire line of King Nejata Medekki murdered. The Black Eagle on White is their device.

Nerum—A minor port city and the administrative capital of Jurisada, located on the coast just south of Amoteu.

nesh—Sheyic term meaning "chattel of."

Neuropuncture—The Dûnyain art of producing various behaviours by probing the exposed brain with fine needles.

New Covenant—The revision of religious law, canonized in 4114, occasioned by the revelations of Anasûrimbor Kellhus, the Rehabilitation of Sorcery, and the Manumission of the Feminine being among the most remarkable.

Nganka'kull ut Imbaroon (4087–)—Satakhan of High Holy Zeum.

Ngarau (4062–)—The Grand Seneschal to Ikurei Xerius III.

Niehirren Halfhand (c. 3450–c. 3500)—Legendary Lord of the Sakarpi Pale famed for actually surviving five years on the open Istyuli (after being exiled).

Nihrimsûl—One the Nine Mansions of Eärwa and the only Mansion not derived from Siol, located on the southernmost spur of the East Yimaleti, lost shortly after the Breaking of the Gates of Thayant—following the destruction of its ancient rival, Siol. What little is known regarding Nihrimsûl comes refracted through the lens of Ishoriöl, which though unified with Nihrimsûl through the marriage of Sin'niroiha and Tsinirû, remained thoroughly Tsonic in custom and outlook. Though all sources agree that Nihrimsûl alone was not founded by Siol, they universally deride its claim to be the *true* House Primordial, and the alternate mythology wherein Tsonos and Olissis murder Imimorûl while he slumbered, before fleeing the wrath of their siblings to found Siol.

Nikussis, Gamag (4090–)—The Imperial Scrollmaster of the Andiamine Heights.

Nil'giccas (?–4132)—The Nonman King of Ishterebinth and Nihrimsûl, eldest son of Sin'niroiha and Tsinirû. Known as King-upon-the-Summit, Lightbearer, Mantutor and many other names in the legends and histories of Men and Nonmen. Following the death first of Cu'jara Cinmoi and then Sin'niroiha, Nil'giccas would become the de facto leader of the war against the Vile following the disasters of the Womb-Plague and Pir-Minningial.

Nilnamesh—A populous Ketyai nation on the extreme southwest edge of the Three Seas, famed for its ceramics, spices, and stubborn refusal to relinquish its exotic versions of Kiünnat either to Inrithism or to Fanimry. Primarily for geographical reasons, the fertile plains to the south of the Hinayati Mountains have long enjoyed cultural and political independence from the Three Seas. Casidas was the first to remark that the Nilnameshi were an "inward people," both in the sense of their obsession with the plight of their souls and in their utter disdain for outland Princes. Only two periods in their history cut against this tendency. The first is the Old Invishi period (1023–1572), when Nilnamesh was united under a series of aggressively expansionist Kings based in Invishi, which is now the traditional spiritual capital of Nilnamesh. In 1322 and then again in 1326, Anzumarapata II inflicted crushing defeats on the Shigeki, and for some thirty years compelled tribute from the proud river kingdom. Then, in 2483, Sarnagiri V, leading a coalition of Princes, was routed by Triamis the Great, and Nilnamesh found itself a province (albeit an unruly one) for more than a thousand years.

The era following the collapse of the Ceneian Empire is commonly called the New Invishi period, though none of the ancient city's Kings has been able to hold more than a fraction of Nilnamesh for more than a generation. During the Unification Wars, Nilnamesh would prove one of the most difficult nations for the Zaudunyani to conquer and pacify.

Nimeric, Anasûrimbor (2098–2135)—The son of the hero Mygella and King of Aörsi until its destruction in the Apocalypse. See *Apocalypse*.

nimil—The Nonmen steel forged in the sorcerous furnaces of Ishterebinth.

Nincaerû-Telesser (c. 549–642)—The fourth God-King of the Umeri Empire, and famed patron of the ancient Gnostic Schools.

Nin'ciljiras (?–4132)—Son of Ninar, Son of Nin'janjin, and the last known Nonman King.

Nin'sariccas (?–)—Dispossessed Son of Siol sent as a false emissary to treat with Anasûrimbor Kellhus.

Nin'janjin (?–?)—Nonman King of Viri, widely regarded as a tragic figure in Mannish commentary, though seen as epitomizing villainy in Nonman myth and legend. See *Cûno-Inchoroi War*.

Nine Great Gates—The epithet given to the main gates of Sumna.

Nine Mansions—Name of the nine greatest subterranean cities of the Nonmen, consisting of Siöl, Nihrimsûl, Ishoriöl, Viri, Cil-Aujas, Illisserû, Curunq, Incissal, and Cil-Aumûl. Siol claims to be the first, but then so does Nihrimsûl. What seems clear is that some time in Nonmen prehistory Siol founded Ishoriöl, Viri, Illisserû, and Cil-Aujas, which in turn founded Curunq, Incissal, and Cil-Aumûl. Of the Nine, the Blood of Tsonos ruled all but Nihrimsûl.

Niom—"Three Souls" (Ihrimsû). Given the treacherous nature of Men, the Nonmen typically demanded three hostages to secure all their treaties with them: a son and a daughter to vouchsafe cooperation, and a captive human *enemy* to assure honesty. Also known as the "Law of Niom."

Nirimenes (4078–)—Ordealman and sorcerer-of-rank in the School of Mandate.

Nirsodic—The language group of ancient Norsirai pastoralists ranging from the Sea of Cerish to the Sea of Jorua.

Nirsi shal'tatra—"Honey and goad" (Kianni). Traditional Kianene phrase referring to the need to balance punishments with rewards to rule.

Niz-Hû (*c*. 1890–*c*. 1935)—Legendary Chieftain-King of Famiri, famed for his military humiliation of Shir.

Nogaral—"High Round" (Ûmeri). Ancient fortress the School of Mangaecca raised upon Mount Iros to better plumb the ruins of Viri in the days of the Cond Yoke, mysteriously destroyed in 1119.

No-God—Also known as Mog-Pharau, Tsurumah, and Mursiris. The entity summoned by the Consult to bring about the Apocalypse. Very little is known about the No-God, save that he utterly lacks remorse or compassion and possesses terrible power, including the ability to control Sranc, Bashrag, and Wracu as extensions of his own will. Because of his armour (the so-called Carapace), which eyewitnesses describe as an iron sarcophagus suspended in the heart of a mountainous whirlwind, it is not even known whether he is a creature of flesh or of spirit. According to Mandate scholars, the Inchoroi worship him as their saviour, as do—according to some—the Scylvendi.

Somehow, his mere existence is antithetical to human life: during the entirety of the Apocalypse, not one infant drew breath—all were stillborn. He is apparently immune to sorcery (according to legend, eleven Chorae are embedded in the Carapace). The Heron Spear is the only known weapon that can harm him.

See *Apocalypse*.

Nomur (?–?)—One of the Chieftain-Kings named in the Tusk.

Nonman King—The poetic name of Cu'jara Cinmoi in the High Norsirai bardic tradition.

Nonmen—At one time the pre-eminent race of Eärwa, but now much reduced. The Nonmen call themselves *ji'cûnû roi*, "the People of Dawn," for reasons they can no longer remember. (They call Men *j'ala roi*, "the People of Summer," because they burn so hot and pass so quickly.) *The Chronicle of the Tusk*, which records the coming of Men to Eärwa, generally refers to Nonmen as Oserukki, the "Not Us." In the Book of Tribes, the Prophet Angeshraël alternately refers to them as "the Accursed Ones" and "the sodomite Kings of Eärwa," and he incites the Four Nations of Men to embark on a holy war of extermination. Even after four millennia, this xenocidal mission remains part of the Inrithi canon. According to the Tusk, the Nonmen are anathema:

Hearken, for this the God has said,
"These False Men offend Me;
blot out all mark of their Passing."

But Cûnuroi civilization was ancient even before these words were carved into the Tusk. While the Halaroi, Men, wandered the world dressed in skins and wielding weapons of stone, the Cûnuroi had invented writing and mathematics, astrology and geometry, sorcery and philosophy. They dredged mountains hollow for the galleries of their High Mansions. They traded and warred with one another. They subdued all Eärwa, enslaving the Emwama, the soft-hearted Men who dwelt in Eärwa in those early days.

Their decline is the result of three different catastrophic events. The first, and most significant, was the so-called Womb-Plague. In the hope of achieving immortality, the Nonmen (specifically, the great Cu'jara Cinmoi) allowed the Inchoroi to live among them as their physicians. The Nonmen did in fact attain immortality, and the Inchoroi, claiming their work done, retired back to the Incû-Holoinas. The plague struck shortly after, almost killing males and uniformly killing all females. The Nonmen call this tragic event the Nasamorgas, the "Death of Birth."

The following Cûno-Inchoroi Wars further sapped their strength, so that by the time the first Tribes of Men invaded, the Nonmen had not the numbers or, some say, the will to resist their advance. Within the course of a few generations they were nearly exterminated. Only the Mansions of Ishoriol and Cil-Aujas survived.

See *Cûno-Inchoroi Wars*.

Nonmen Tutelage—The great period of Norsirai-Cûnuroi trade, education, and strategic alliances, beginning in 555 and ending with the Expulsion in 825 (following the famed Rape of Omindalea).

Norsirai—The typically blond-haired, blue-eyed, fair-skinned race predominantly concentrated along the northern fringe of the Three Seas, although they once ruled all the lands north to the Yimaleti Mountains. One of the Five Tribes of Men.

noschi—A Kûniüric term meaning "source of light," but used in the sense of "genius" as well.

Noshainrau the White (c. 1005–72)—The founding Grandmaster of the Sohonc and author of the *Interrogations*, the first elaboration of the Gnosis by Men.

Nosol (c. 2111–2152)—The Meori Prince famed for securing refuge for his people in Cil-Aujas, fighting with Gin'yursis in the victory at Kathol Pass, then ultimately betraying him, and sacking the famed Nonman Mansion.

Novum Arcanum—Esoteric metaphysical treatise written by Anasûrimbor Kellhus instrumental in recruiting the Major Three Seas Schools during the Unification Wars.

Nron—A minor island nation of the Three Seas, nominally independent but in fact dominated by the School of Mandate in Atyersus.

Nroni—The language of Nron, a derivative of Sheyo-Kheremic.

nukbaru—"stone-hewer" (Zeumi). Zeumi euphemism for souls hardened by perpetual war.

Nûlrainwi—Watchtowers raised in early Far Antiquity by Cûnwerishau, allowing the cities of the River Aumris to communicate via beacons of fire.

Numaineiri—A populous and fertile fiefdom of interior Ce Tydonn, located to the west of Meigeiri. Numaineiri warriors are known to paint their faces red whenever they believe themselves doomed in battle.

number-sticks—A means of generating random numerical results for the purposes of gambling. The first references to number-sticks reach as far back as ancient Shigek. The most common variations consist of two sticks typically referred to as the Fat and the Skinny. A groove is carved all the way through the Fat so that the Skinny can drop up and down its interior length. The Skinny is then capped on either end to prevent it from falling out. Numerical values are marked along the length of the Fat, so that when the sticks are thrown, the Skinny can indicate a result.

Numemarius, Thallei (4069–4111)—Man-of-the-Tusk, Patridomos of House Thallei, and General of the Kidruhil until his death in Nagogris.

Nuns—Epithet given to the Swayali witches during the Great Ordeal for the way they resembled Jokian nuns when wearing their billows bound.

Nymbricani—A tribe of Norsirai pastoralists who range southern Cepalor.

Nyranisas Sea—The easternmost of the Three Seas.

O

Obligate—Individual indentured to mentor some member of the Satakhanic family in Zeum.

Obotegwa (4069–4132)—Obligate to Prince Zsoronga.

Observances—The manse between the Apiary and the Pith, once reserved for Hûlya ritualists.

Occlusion, The—The name given to the mountainous crater rim surrounding the Incû-Holoinas, derived from the Cûnûroi name, *Vilursis*, or "obscurity."

Oinaral Lastborn (?–4132)—The last Nonman born during the Womb-Plague. Son of the hero Oirûnas, and Siqu (something rare for Dispossessed Sons of Siol).

Oirûnas (?–4132)—Eldest son of Oirasis, legendary Ishroi Hero of the Nonmen, Dispossessed Son of Siol, twin brother of Oirinas, survivor of the First Watch, and Lord of the Second Watch.

Oirinas (?–?)—Ishroi Hero, twin brother of Oirûnas, slain at the Battle of Pir Minginnial.

Oknai One-Eye (4053–4110)—The inveterate chieftain of the Munuäti, a powerful federation of Scylvendi tribes.

Okyati urs Okkiür (4038–4082)—The cousin of Cnaiür urs Skiötha, who first brought Anasûrimbor Moënghus as a captive to the Utemot camp in 4080.

Old Ainoni—The language of Ceneian Ainon, a derivative of Ham-Kheremic.

Old Father—An epithet used by skin-spies to describe their Consult makers.

Old Meöric—The lost language of the early Meöri Empire, a derivative of Nirsodic.

Old Name—A term referring to the original members of the Consult.

Old Science—See *Tekne*.

Old Scylvendi—The language of ancient Scylvendi pastoralists, a derivative of Skaaric.

Old Zeümi—The language of Angka (ancient Zeüm), a derivative of Ankmuri.

Olekaros (2881–2956)—A Ceneian slave-scholar of Cironji descent, famed for his *Avowals*, and the five *Economies*, his treatises on machines, from the base and terrestrial, to the celestial and superluminary.

Oloreg—Mountain in the Urokkas.

omba—Face mask of black gauze worn by Mbimayu to better cope with the glare of sorcery.

omen-texts—The traditional indexes, usually specific to each of the Cults, detailing the various omens and their meaning.

Omiri urs Xunnurit (4089–4111)—The lame daughter of Xunnurit and wife of Yursalka.

Omrain—The first woman according to *The Chronicle of the Tusk*:

> *And the Mother did blow upon the dust, raising forth Omrain from a smoking column. And the Sky blessed her, and she had skin and bone and blood and was alive. And the Mother sayeth unto her, "As he doth take, so shall ye give."*

Oncis Sea—The westernmost of the Three Seas.

111 *Aphorisms*—A minor work of Ekyannus VIII, consisting of 111 aphorisms that primarily deal with matters of faith and integrity.

"one lamb for ten bulls"—A saying that refers to the relative difference in value between a witting and an unwitting sacrificial victim.

One-Thousand-Gift-Shields—The collected treaty-tokens that lined the Ursilaral in the Library of Sauglish in Far Antiquity, signifying the peace between the School of Sohonc and all the Norsirai tribes, which is to say, the neutrality of the Schoolmen and Sauglish.

Onkis—The Goddess of hope and aspiration. One of the so-called Compensatory Gods, who reward devotion in life with paradise in the afterlife, Onkis draws followers from all walks of life, though rarely in great numbers. She is only mentioned twice in the *Higarata*, and in the (likely apocryphal) *Parnishtas* she is portrayed as a prophetess, not of the future, but of the motivations of Men. The so-called "shakers" belong to an extreme branch of the Cult, where the devotees ritually strive to be "possessed" by the Goddess. Her symbol is the Copper Tree (which also happens to be the device of the legendary Nonman Mansion of Siol, though no link has been established).

"Only the Few can see the Few"—The traditional expression used to refer to the unique ability of sorcerers to "see" both the practitioners and the products of sorcery.

Onoyas II, Nersei (3823–78)—The King of Conriya who first forged the alliance between the School of Mandate and House Nersei.

onta—The name given by the Schools to the very fabric of what is.

On the Carnal—The most famous of Opparitha's exhortatory works, popular among lay readers though widely derided by Three Seas intellectuals.

On the Folly of Men—The magnum opus of the famed satirist Ontillas.

On the Temples and Their Iniquities—A quasi-heretical Sareot text.

Ontillas (2875–2933)—The near antique Ceneian satirist most famous for his *On the Folly of Men*.

Opparitha (3211–3299)—The near antique Cengemian moralist most famous for his *On the Carnal*.

Opsara (4074–)—A Kianene slave who serves as the infant Moënghus's wet nurse.

Oratorium—Wrought iron platform set within the Concavity where petitioners assemble for audiences with the Nonman King of Ishterebinth.

Ordeal, the—Sometimes referred to as the Great Ordeal. The tragic holy war Anasûrimbor Celmomas called against Golgotterath in 2123. See *Apocalypse*.

Orimuril—"Immaculate Rim" (Ihrimsû). Ensorcelled armour (known as "the Scarp" by Men), one of the Sublime Contrivances of Emilidis, belonging to Sûjara-nin.

Orovelai—Stronghold of the Swayali, located upon (and within) the extinct Nonman Mansion of Illisserû.

Orsuleese (c. 3780–c. 3820)—Sakarpic Hero famed for racing on foot from the Pale to the Lonely City—outrunning Sranc—to warn of a vast mobbing.

Orthodox—The name first taken by the Inrithi opponents of the Zaudunyani during the siege of Caraskand, before becoming the general term referring to all those who vied against Anasûrimbor Kellhus during the Unification Wars. The term is deceptive insofar as it suggests that all opponents of the Zaudunyani hewed to some common doctrine or dogma—an "orthodoxy"—when such was not the case. See *Unification Wars*.

Orthogonal—Quyan receptacle (typically a pouch or purse of some kind) capable of concealing the arcane (or anarcane) nature of its contents. Though prized in Far Antiquity, not one of the five Orthogonals originally fashioned by Emilidis has survived the ages. Legend claims that the Artisan fashioned them in the course of researching the "Uncreated Creation," the artifact so perfectly wrought as to be indistinguishable from the issue of God.

Osbeus—A basalt quarry used in Near and Far Antiquity, located near the ruins of Mehtsonc.

Osfringa, Nûkulk (4083–4118)—Orthodox Earl of Nangaelsa, famously blinded and chained by Anasûrimbor Kellhus for display beneath Meigeiri's walls.

Osseoratha (c. 960–1021)—Far-Antique King of Trysë responsible for destroying the Cond capital of Saulya and overthrowing the Yoke. His liberation of Sauglish in 1004 is generally taken as the beginning of the so-called Gnostic Renaissance.

Osthwai Mountains—A major mountain range located in central Eärwa.

Oswenta—The administrative and commercial capital of Galeoth, located on the north coast of Lake Huösi.

Other Voice—The name given to the "voice" used to communicate in all Cants of Calling.

Othrain, Eorcu (4060–4111)—Man-of-the-Tusk and the Tydonni Earl of Numaineiri, slain at Mengedda.

Ottma, Cwithar (4073–4121)—Man-of-the-Tusk, one of the Nascenti, formerly a Tydonni thane.

Outhrata (c. 1060–c. 1115)—Famed Sohonc metaphysician (and eventual Grandmaster) who became a central figure in the so-called Gnostic Renaissance.

Outside—That which lies beyond the World. Most commentators follow Ajencis's so-called Dyadic Theory when characterizing the World and its relation to the Outside. In *Meta-Analytics*, Ajencis argues that it is the relation between subject and object, desire and reality, that underwrites the structure of existence. The World, he argues, is simply the point of maximal objectivity, the plane where the desires of individual souls are helpless before circumstance (because it is fixed by the desire of the God of Gods). The many regions of the Outside then represent diminishing levels of objectivity, where circumstances yield more and more to desire. This, he claims, is what defines the "spheres of dominance" of Gods and demons. As he writes, "the greater will commands." The more powerful entities of the Outside dwell in "sub-realities" that conform to their desires. This is what makes piety and devotion so important: the more favour an individual can secure in the Outside (primarily through the worship of Gods and the honouring of ancestors), the greater the chance of finding bliss rather than torment in the afterlife.

Over-Standard—The sacred military standard of the Nansur Exalt-General, decorated with the disc-shaped breastplate of Kuxophus II, the last of the ancient Kyranean High Kings. Imperial Columnaries often refer to it as "the Concubine."

P

Paäta (4062–4111)—A body-slave belonging to Krijates Xinemus, slain in Khemema.

Pa'bikru—"Warring Glimpse" (Invitic). Known as "Cage-carvings" in the Eastern Three Seas, Pa'bikru are the product of the peculiar spiritual sensibilities of Nilnamesh. In the twilight preceding the ruin of the Ceneian Empire, a nameless monk translated Memgowa's *Celestial Aphorisms* into the Invitic dialect of Sheyic, thus inspiring the famed "screen sculpture" of Nilnamesh. The techniques evolved wildly over the centuries, but the premise was always the same: the sculptor would carve miniature scenes, many of them drawn from the Tusk that they then placed in a so-called "peering box" or behind some other obstruction. The original idea was to recreate Memgowa's conception of the "Blind Beggar Soul." Like Ajencis, the famed Zeumi sage was forever arguing the folly of Men, but unlike the famed Kyranean philosopher, he argued that it was the *inability of the soul to know itself*, and not the inability of intellect to grasp the World, that was the origin of the problem.

In *Celestial Aphorisms*, the Sage continually returned to the Rebuke of Angeshraël in *The Chronicle of the Tusk*, the famed story where War, dread Gilgaöl, upbraids the Prophet for "peering through cracks and describing skies." He also uses the legend of Ilbaru, a Zeumi folk tale about a man who spies his wife through a cracked shutter, and confusing her attempt to save his wounded brother for an act of passion, murders her, and then must watch his brother die. His argument, refracted through the smoked glass of his aphoristic style, is that the soul is *that which sees*, and therefore can scarcely be seen.

Thus the aesthetic of screen sculpture: the creation of scenes that utterly contradicted the way they appeared when seen through some fixed aperture.

Historically, the most famous of these was Modhoraparta's "Dance of the Demons," where the face of the God of Gods viewed through the aperture became a group of demonic monstrosities viewed from all other angles. The rumour of the work so incensed Shriah Ekyannus IX that in 3682 he outlawed all art works that "blaspheme the Simple, the Pure, and the True with foul Complication." At his trial in Invishi, Modhoraparta claimed that he wanted to show the how the myriad evils suffered by Men find themselves redeemed in the God of Gods. Indeed, all the sculptor's acts, let alone his work and his claims, argued that he was as devout as any who would presume to judge him. He would be burned for impiety nonetheless: reason counts for naught in matters of outrage—truth even less so. In those days, the Thousand Temples was always eager to display its authority in Nilnamesh, where the scalding sun and indolent air seemed to engender heresy as regularly as harvests.

Padirajah—The traditional title of the ruler of Kian.

Painted Cities—Bardic epithet for the cities of the River Aumris.

Palaparrais—The massive palace of Sarothesser I (3317–3402) in Carythusal.

Palpothis—One of the famed Ziggurats of Shigek, named after Palpothis III (622–78), the Old Dynasty God-King who raised her.

Pansulla, Cutias (4088–4132)—The New Imperial Consul of Nansur, and political rival of Anasûrimbor Esmenet, imprisoned on the charge of treason in 4132.

Panteruth urs Mutkius (4075–4111)—A Scylvendi of the Munuäti tribe.

Parrhae Plains—A region of fertile tablelands located in northwestern Galeoth.

Pasna—A town on the River Phayus, known for the quality of its olive oil.

Pausal—Antechamber to the Coffers beneath the Library of Sauglish.

peering—Sorcerous lanterns used by the Nonmen to illuminate their Mansions.

Pier Floor—The floor of the Great Entresol.

pembeditari—A common pejorative used for camp prostitutes, meaning "scratchers."

pemembis—A wild bush prized for its fragrant blue blooms.

Penance—Zaudunyani purificatory rite where gathered penitents strip to the waist to be lashed by Judges three times for their complicity in the Sin of the Circumfixion.

peneditari—A common name given to camp prostitutes, meaning "long-walkers."

perrapta—A traditional Conriyan liquor, often used to inaugurate meals.

Persommas, Hagum (4078–)—Man-of-the-Tusk, one of the Nascenti, formerly a Nansur blacksmith.

Pharixas—A disputed island stronghold in the Meneanor Sea.

Pharroika—Name, meaning "The Wayward" in Ihrimsû, given to Erratics.

Phayus River—The primary river system of the Kyranae Plains, draining the south central Hethanta Mountains and emptying into the Meneanor Sea.

Pherokar I (3666–3821)—One of Kian's earliest and fiercest Padirajahs.

Phiolos—Famed mount ridden by Halas Siroyon in the Great Ordeal of Anasûrimbor Kellhus.

pick—A derogatory term often used by Norsirai when referring to Ketyai. The word comes from the Tydonni *pikka*, or "slave," but has come to have broader, racial connotations.

Pilaskanda (4060–4112)—The King of Girgash and a tributary ally of the Kianene Padirajah, killed at the Battle of Shimeh.

Pillarian—A member of the Hundred Pillars.

Pirasha—An old Sumni whore befriended by Esmenet.

Pir Minginnial—See *Battle of Pir Minginnial*.

Pir Pahal—See *Battle of Pir Pahal*.

Pisathulas—The personal eunuch attendant of Ikurei Istriya.

Pith—The most ancient and sacred manse of Ishterebinth, located below the Observances, and above the Hanging Citadels. Also called the Radial Pith.

Pitiril–Divider (Ihrimsû). Ensorcelled blade belonging to the Ishroi Hero Oirinas, lost at the Battle of Pir-Minginnial.

Plaideöl–A fiefdom of Ce Tydonn, one of the "Deep Marches" above the eastern headwaters of the River Swa. Plaideölmen are famed for their ferocity in battle, and are easily distinguished by their great beards, which they never trim.

Pon Way–An old Ceneian road that runs northwest from Momemn parallel to the River Phayus and serves as one of the Nansurium's primary commercial arteries.

Poripharus–An ancient Ceneian philosopher and advisor to Triamis the Great, famed for drafting the Triamic Code, the body of laws that forms the basis of legal practice in most Three Seas nations (with the notable exception of Kian).

Porsparian (4071–4132)–Ordealman, Shigeki slave (and secret Yatwerian priest) assigned to Sorweel upon his arrival in the Great Ordeal.

Possessors of the Third Sight–An alternate name for the Cishaurim, so called because of their reputed ability to see without their eyes.

Postern Terrace–The verandah immediately behind the Mantle on the Andiamine Heights.

Pow–The slum district of ancient Kelmeol.

Pragma–The title given to the most senior of the Dûnyain.

Premparian Barracks–Fortress housing the Conriyan King's Reserve Guard in Aöknyssus.

Prima Arcanata, The–The magnum opus of Gotagga, representing the first sustained examination of sorcerous metaphysics by Men.

Prince of God–One of several names given to the Warrior-Prophet by the Men of the Tusk.

Principle of Before and After–Also known as the Priority Principle. See *Dûnyain*.

Proadjunct–The highest non-commissioned rank in the Imperial Nansur Army.

Probability Trance–A meditation technique used by the Dûnyain to assess consequences of hypothetical acts in order to determine the course of action that will most effectively allow them to master their circumstances.

Promised World–Inchoroi epithet for the world of Eärwa.

Prophet of the Tusk–The name given to the prophets depicted in *The Chronicle of the Tusk*.

Prophilas, Harus (4064–)–The commander of Asgilioch during the First Holy War.

Protathis (2870–2922)–A famed near antique poet of Ceneian descent, celebrated for many works, including *The Goat's Heart*, *One Hundred Heavens*, and the magisterial *Aspirations*. Protathis is regarded by many as the greatest Ketyai poet.

Proto-Caro-Shemic–The language group of the ancient pastoralists of the Eastern Carathay Desert, a derivative of Shemic.

Psailas II (4009–4086)–The Shriah of the Thousand Temples from 4072 to 4086.

Psalm of Imimorûl—Verse passages beginning the *Juürl*, the primary scripture of the Nonmen.

The World to him, who sings my song,
for I am the Font, the Spirit of the Deepest Deep,
and mine is the first heart to beat your blood.

The World to him, who sings my song.
I, Imimorul, fled the Heavens,
so much did I love
the brooks that chirrup,
the high mountains that hiss,
the myriads that bolt through this blessed hair,

The World to him, who raises up
rooves in the Deep.

I, Imimorul, did flee the Starving [sky],
so much did I fear the Heavens,
the wrath of those who were wroth,
who would forbid my love,
of the myriads of the World.

The World to her, who kindles
her fire in the Deep.

I, Imimorul, did cut from my hand my fingers,
and from my arm, my hand,
and from my body, my arm,
and these pieces of me I did place
in the wombs of Lions, so that I might
dwell content in my own company.
And I became One-Armed,
Imimorul, the Unshielded.

And you were as children to me,
the form of Gods as the issue of Lions,
sons who would father nations, and
daughters who would mother the
myriads of the World.

And I sang to you such songs
as are only heard in the highest of Heavens,
and nowhere in the Hells.

We did weep together, as we sang,
for woe cares not for names or glory
only that skin blackens for bruising,
breaks for blood.

The World to him, who sings my song.
The World to him, who finds me in the Deep.
The World to him, and woe.

Psammatus, Nentepi (4059–?)–A Sumni Shrial priest of Shigeki descent, and regular customer of Esmenet's.

Psûkalogues, The–The magnum opus of Imparrhas, sorcerer of the Imperial Saik and esoteric metaphysician primarily interested in the Psûkhe of the Cishaurim.

psûkari–Practitioners of the Psûkhe.

Psûkhe–The arcane practice of the Cishaurim, much like sorcery, though cruder in its exercise, and distinguished by its invisibility to the Few. See *sorcery*.

Pulit–A tribe of Scylvendi from the southern desert fringes of the Jiünati Steppe.

Q

Qirri–"Essence" (Auja-Gilcûnni (?)). Drug made of the ashes of some great soul–at once well known and profoundly taboo among the Nonmen. Much as a furnace burns away impurities from iron, the pyre burns great souls down to the raw kernel of their *vitality*, which, when ingested by another, obeys the Principle of Superordinate Identities, providing them with a vitality they could have never possessed otherwise.

Quandary of Man–The classic Dûnyain problem referring to the fact that Men, though beasts like other beasts, can apprehend the Logos.

Quorum–The ruling council of the Mandate.

Qûlnimil–The legendary nimil mines of Ishterebinth, source of most nimil found in Eärwa.

Quya–"Miners" (Ihrimsû). The generic name for Nonmen Magi.

R

Rank-Principal–The title given to fully invested members of the Scarlet Spires.

Rash (4073–4112)–The nickname of Houlta, Man-of-the-Tusk, and a caste-menial Zaudunyani agitator, slain in the Battle of Caraskand.

Rauschang, Hringa (4054–4014)–The King of Thunyerus and father of Skaiyelt and Hulwarga.

Reduced–Name given those who have entered the Gloom, the final stage of the Dolour, when the sheer repetition of anguish has burned away the behaviour of anguish, leaving the soul with only the most fundamental routines of survival.

Remonstrata–The name of the complex comprising the Imperial Court in the Andiamine Heights.

Restored Empire–For some in Nansur, the cherished goal of restoring all the "lost provinces" (the territories seized by the Kianene) to the Nansur Empire.

Revenging–Name given to the wars following the Womb-Plague. See *Cûno-Inchoroi Wars*.

Ribbaral—Section of Dagliash once housing smithies and other workshops.

Ring Mountains—The range that encircles Golgotterath, typically called "the Occlusion" in Mandate scholarship.

Rite-of-the-Spring-Wolves—A rite of passage marking the transition of Scylvendi adolescent boys to manhood.

Rohil River—The easternmost of the three major river systems draining into Lake Huösi.

Round of Horns—Famed constellation visible in the skies of the Ancient North.

Ruminations—The magnum opus of Stajanus II, the so-called Philosopher-Emperor who ruled Cenei from 2412 to 2431.

Ruöm—The innermost citadel of Asgilioch, often called the High Bull of Asgilioch, destroyed by an earthquake in 4111.

rushru—Zeumi term for the moral significance of concrete circumstances.

S

Saccarees, Apperens (4092–)—Ordealman, Grandmaster of the Mandate in the Great Ordeal of Anasûrimbor Kellhus. The so-called Kellian Reconstitution of the Mandate in 4123 led to the dissolution of the Quorum and the adoption of the more autocratic, "magisterial form" of governance characteristic of the other Major Schools. A prodigy as a child, Saccarees was selected by the Aspect-Emperor to become the first Grandmaster of the Mandate. In arcane circles, he is widely rumoured to be the only soul lacking Anasûrimbor blood able to perform Metagnostic Cants.

Sack of Sarneveh—One of several Orthodox Ainoni cities plundered by the Zaudunyani during the Unification Wars, noteworthy for the subsequent dissemination of the Toll, and the knowledge that some five thousand children had been butchered. The historian Hem-Maristat notes that following the infamous pamphlet, Kellhus ceased his meticulous account of lives lost.

Sacral Enclosure—Name of the private, octagonally shaped Imperial gardens following the Kellian renovation of the Andiamine Heights.

Sacred Hewer—*Inris Hishid* (Ham-Kheremic). Title awarded to champions of the Sranc Pits.

Sacred Lands—A name for Xerash and Amoteu, the two lands that figure directly in *The Tractate*.

Sadu'waralla ab Daza (4084–)—Ordealman, Chieftain of the Low Imit, General of the Khirgwi contingent in the Great Ordeal of Anasûrimbor Kellhus. A sufferer of the apoplexy, he is famed across the Three Seas for visions confirming the identity of the Aspect-Emperor, even though the Khirgwi are renowned for refusing to relinquish their ancient forms of devil worship.

Sagland—Southernmost province of Sakarpus, whose inhabitants ("Saglanders") are thought simple and weak for being spared the rigours of the Pale.

Sag-Marmau (*c*. 2094–2143)—Husband of the legendary Ysilka, prominent in the *Book of Generals* (in *The Holy Sagas*) first as the General who saves the Ordeal from the disarray and dismay following the murder of General En-Kaujalau, and then as the General who witnesses Initiation, the birth of the No-God and the beginning of the Apocalypse.

Saik—The Anagogic School based in Momemn and indentured to the Nansur Emperor. The Saik, or the Imperial Saik as they are often called, are the institutional descendants of the Saka, the notorious state-sanctioned School of Imperial Cenei, who for a thousand years dominated the Three Seas under the aegis of the Aspect-Emperors. For centuries they existed as an organ of the Nansurium, and at war with the Cishaurim on an almost perpetual basis. The Accession of Anasûrimbor Kellhus as Aspect-Emperor of the Three Seas saw them largely divested of their state affiliations, simply because the new ruler already possessed his Saka: the School of Mandate.

saka'ilrait—"Trail of Skulls" (Khirgwi). The Khirgwi name for the route taken by the Holy War across Khemema.

Sakarpic—The language of Sakarpus, a derivative of Skettic.

Sakarpus—A city of the Ancient North located in the heart of the Istyuli Plains, and, aside from Atrithau, the only city to survive the Apocalypse. Originally a trade outpost on the caravan route delivering Ûmeri wares in exchange for Shigeki spices, the fortunes of Sakarpus long depended on the fortunes of trade in Eärwa. The "Lonely City," as it was called even in Far Antique days, grew as the civilization developing around the Three Seas came to covet the status conveyed by Norsirai textiles and manufactured goods. As Kyraneas and Shir waxed as markets, so did Sakarpus wax as a regional power. The most shrewd of its many decrees in those days, was the Chorae Toll, the demand that merchant families donate Chorae as the price of purchase for (generally lifelong) trade indulgences, a practice which lead to the accumulation of the famed Chorae Hoard—which, legend insists, induced the No-God to bypass the city during the Apocalypse.

Post-apocalypse, the collapse in trade and the Sranc domination of the Istyuli transformed the enterprising character of the Sakarpi into a defensive one. The Pale was organized, consisting of a network of fortified towers scattered across the plains to the north of Sakarpus and on the headwaters of the River Vindauga, or "Sagland," the breadbasket of the city.

Sakthuta—A mountain in the Hethantas overlooking the River Kiyuth.

Sampileth Fire-singer (1658–1712)—Legendary Far Antique Magi credited with inventing the famed Dragonhead Cant, as well as founding the Surartu, the precursor to the Scarlet Spires.

Sanathi (4100–?)—The daughter of Cnaiür and Anissi.

Sancla (4064–4083)—Achamian's cellmate and lover during his adolescence in Atyersus.

Sankas, Biaxi (4066–4132)–The Patridomos of House Biaxi, and confidant of Anasûrimbor Esmenet. Granted Consulship of Nansur after the arrest of Cutias Pansulla in 4132. Found murdered in the Andiamine Heights the autumn of that same year.

Sansor–A nation of the Three Seas and tributary of High Ainon.

Sansori–The language of Sansor, a derivative of Sheyo-Kheremic.

Sapatishah-Governor–The title of the regional, semi-autonomous rulers of the various provinces of Kian during the time of the Kianene Empire.

Sapatishah's Palace–The name given by the Men of the Tusk to Imbeyan's palace in Caraskand, located on the Kneeling Heights.

Sapmatari–The lost language of Nilnameshi labouring castes, a derivative of Vaparsi.

Sappathurai–A powerful mercantile city in Nilnamesh.

Sarcellus, Cutias (4072–99)–A Knight-Commander of the Shrial Knights, murdered and replaced by Consult skin-spies.

Sareötic Library–In the time of the Ceneian Empire, one of the greatest libraries in the known world. The so-called "script law" of Iothiah forced, on punishment of death, all visitors bearing books to surrender them for copying and inclusion in the Library. Though the Sareots were massacred when Shigek fell to the Fanim in 3933, Padirajah Fan'oukarji III spared the Library, thinking it the will of the Solitary God.

Sarosthenes (4064–4112)–Man-of-the-Tusk, ranking member of the Scarlet Spires, killed at Shimeh.

Sarothesser I (3317–3402)–The founder of High Ainon, who overthrew the yoke of the Ceneian Empire in 3372 and ascended the Assurkamp Throne as the first Ainoni King.

Sasheoka (4049–4100)–The Grandmaster of the Scarlet Spires, assassinated in 4100 by the Cishaurim for reasons unknown, and predecessor to Eleäzaras.

Saskri River–A major river system in Eumarna, with headwaters in Eshgarnea and draining the Jahan Plains.

Sassotian (4058–4111)–The General of the Imperial Fleet during the First Holy War, slain at the Battle of Trantis Bay.

Sathgai (c. 2100–c. 2170)–The Norsirai name for Uthgai, Chieftain of the Utemot and legendary Scylvendi King-of-Tribes, who led the People under the No-God during the Apocalypse.

Satiothi–The language group of the Satyothi peoples.

Satyothi–The black-haired, green-eyed, black-skinned race predominantly concentrated in the nation of Zeüm and the southern extremities of the Three Seas. One of the Five Tribes of Men.

Saubon, Coithus (4069–4132)–Man-of-the-Tusk, seventh son of King Coithus Eryeat of Galeoth and titular leader of the Galeoth contingent during the First Holy

War. Ordealman, Believer-King of Caraskand, and Exalt-General of the Great Ordeal of Anasûrimbor Kellhus.

Sauglish—One of the four great ancient cities of the Aumris Valley, destroyed in the Apocalypse in 2147. From the early days of the Nonmen Tutelage, Sauglish was established as the intellectual capital of the Ancient North, home to the first Gnostic Schools and to the Great Library of Sauglish. Commonly referred to as the "City of Robes," for the way Sauglishmen eschewed trousers in imitation of the Siqu. See *Library of Sauglish* and *Apocalypse*.

Saxillas, Clia (4089–)—Captain of the Inchausti, the private bodyguard of the Holy Shriah.

Sayut River—One of the great rivers of Eärwa, originating in the Southern Great Kayarsus and draining into the Nyranisas.

Scald, The—Name given to the vast explosion responsible for destroying Dagliash.

Scaralla, Hepma (4056–4111)—Man-of-the-Tusk, ranking high priest of Akkeägni during the First Holy War, taken by disease at Caraskand.

Scarlet Magi—A name for Schoolmen belonging to the Scarlet Spires.

Scarlet Spires—The most powerful School of the Three Seas and de facto ruler of High Ainon. The roots of the Scarlet Spires reach as far back as ancient Shir (to this day traditionalists within the School refer to themselves as the "shiradi"). In many ways the development of the Scarlet Spires exemplifies the development of every Three Seas School, that of loose networks of sorcerous practitioners becoming progressively more organized and insular in the face of chronic, religiously motivated persecution. Originally called the Surartu—"Hooded Singers" (Ham-Kheremic)—the Scarlet Spires secured the river fortress of Kiz in Carythusal c. 1800, and emerged from the chaos surrounding the Apocalypse, the collapse of Shir, and the Great Pestilence as one of the most powerful factions in ancient Ainon. Sometime around 2350, Kiz was severely damaged in an earthquake and subsequently covered with red enamel tiles in the reconstruction, thus leading to the School's now-famous moniker.

Scholastic Wars—A series of holy wars waged against the Schools from 3796 to 3818. Called by Ekyannus XIV, the Scholastic Wars saw the near-destruction of several Schools and the beginning of the Scarlet Spires' hegemony over High Ainon.

Schoolmen—Sorcerers belonging to the Schools.

Schools—Given the Tusk's condemnation of sorcery, the first Schools, in both the Ancient North and the Three Seas, arose out of the need for protection. The so-called "Major Schools" of the Three Seas are the Circle of Nibel, the Imperial Saik, the School of Mandate, the Mysunsai, and the Scarlet Spires. The Schools are among the oldest institutions in the Three Seas, surviving, by and large, both because of the terror they inspire and by their detachment from the secular and religious powers of the Three Seas. With the exception of the Mysunsai, for instance, all the Major Schools predate the fall of the Ceneian Empire.

Scindia—The Scylvendi-dominated land to the immediate west of the Hethanta Mountains. The name itself is a relic of early Kyranean times, when the Scylvendi yet shared the Jiünati Steppe with the White Norsirai.

Scintya—Ancient White Norsirai pastoralists who, driven from their own lands by the Scylvendi, plagued the High Norsirai cities of the River Aumris for generations.

Scions—Kidruhil company belonging to the Great Ordeal consisting entirely of treaty hostages, the male heirs of nations obligated to the Kellian (or "New") Empire.

Scorpion Braid—A mummer's trick, consisting of a rope soaked in a poison that makes the jaws and claws of scorpions seize when they grasp it.

Scoulas, Biaxi (4075–4111)—Man-of-the-Tusk, second Knight-Commander of the Shrial Knights, slain at Mengedda.

Scuäri Campus—The main parade ground of the Imperial Precincts in Momemn.

Sculpa River—The northernmost of the three major river systems draining into Lake Huösi.

Skûlsirai—"Shield-people" (Aörsic). Name the ancient Aorsi used to refer to themselves.

Scylvendi—The dark-haired, pale-blue-eyed, and fair-skinned race predominantly concentrated in and around the Jiünati Steppe. One of the Five Tribes of Men.

Seat, the—A symbolic name for the station of Shriah.

Secharib Plains—The vast alluvial tablelands that sweep north from the River Sayut in High Ainon, noted for their fertility (sixty- to seventy-fold crop yields) and dense population.

Second Apocalypse—System Resumption. The hypothetical catastrophe that will inevitably befall Eärwa should the No-God ever walk again. According to the Mandate tradition, Anasûrimbor Celmomas, the High King of Kûniüri during the Apocalypse, prophesied that the No-God will in fact return. The prevention of the Second Apocalypse is the Mandate's ultimate goal.

Seeing-Flame (or "Seeing Hearth")—Sorcerous hearth cast from iron in the shape of an octagon. Arcane scholars dispute its origins (it is neither a Quyan nor a Mihtrûlic artifact), though several extant sources claim that it was presented as a gift to Anzumarapata II in 1331, and subsequently fell into the hands of none other than Triamis the Great in 2483. At some point it passed to the Fanim (likely in one of their many victories over the Nansur), and thence to Anasûrimbor Kellhus following the fall of Nenciphon in 4113.

Seleukara—The commercial capital of Kian, and one of the great cities of the Three Seas.

Selial Column—A division of the Imperial Nansur Army traditionally stationed on the Kianene frontier.

"selling peaches ..."—A common Three Seas euphemism for selling sex.

Sempis River—One of the great river systems of Eärwa, draining vast tracts of the Jiünati Steppe and emptying into the Meneanor Sea.

Semper, Midru (4078–4121)—Man-of-the-Tusk, Ainoni Baron in the First Holy War, murdered by unknown assassins while sleeping in 4121.

Seökti (4051–4112)—The Heresiarch of the Cishaurim, one of the most powerful Cishaurim ever known, killed at Shimeh by Anasûrimbor Kellhus.

Sepherathindor (4065–4111)—Man-of-the-Tusk, Count-Palatine of the Ainoni palatinate of Hinnant, claimed by disease at Caraskand.

Seswatha (2089–2168)—The founder of the School of Mandate and implacable enemy of the Consult throughout the Apocalypse. Born the caste-menial son of a Trysean bronzesmith, Seswatha was identified as one of the Few at a very young age and brought to Sauglish to study with the Gnostic School of Sohonc. A prodigy, he became the youngest sorcerer of rank in the history of the Sohonc at the age of fifteen. During this time he became fast friends with Anasûrimbor Celmomas, a so-called "Hostage of the Sohonc," as the School referred to its resident exoteric students. As this strategic friendship might suggest, Seswatha proved an adroit political operator, both before becoming Grandmaster and after, forging relationships with important personages across the Three Seas, including Nil'giccas, the Nonman King of Ishterebinth, and Anaxophus, who would become the High King of Kyraneas. These skills, in addition to his peerless command of the Gnosis, would make him the natural, if not the titular, leader of the various wars waged against the Consult before the Apocalypse. He and Celmomas would become estranged during this time, apparently because Celmomas resented Seswatha's influence over his youngest son, Nau-Cayûti, but legends have long circulated that Nau-Cayûti was in fact Seswatha's son, the product of an illicit union between him and Sharal, the most prized of Celmomas's wives. They would not be reconciled until the eve of the Apocalypse—after it was far too late. See *Apocalypse.*

Seswatha's Dreams—See *Dreams, the.*

Seswatha's Heart—The mummified heart of Seswatha, which is the key artifact in the so-called Grasping, the sorcerous rites that transfer Seswatha's memories of the Apocalypse to Mandate Schoolmen. See *Mandate, the.*

Setpanares (4059–4111)—Man-of-the-Tusk, general of the Ainoni contingent of the First Holy War, slain by Cinganjehoi at Anwurat.

Seven Wolf Shield—Crest of the ancient Meöri Empire, consisting of seven wolves arrayed like flower petals.

Shaeönanra (c. 1086–)—"Gift of Light" (Ümeritic). The Grandvizier of the Mangaecca who, according to legend, went mad studying the Incû-Holoinas, and whose subsequent acts would eventually see him convicted of impiety and his School outlawed in 1123. The greatest prodigy of his age, Shaeönanra claimed to have rediscovered a means of saving the souls of those damned by sorcery. He reputedly spent his life investigating various soul-trapping sorceries in the hope of avoiding passage to the Outside—and to great effect, given that he allegedly continues to live some three thousand years afterward, though in an obscene and unnatural manner. By the fourteenth century the Trysean annals began referring to him as Shauriatas, the "Cheater of Gods."

Shaita'anairull—"The Grave-that-is-Golden" (Skaaric). Name given to the resting place of Lokung, the Dead God of Scylvendi religious tradition.

Shakers—The name given to extreme devotees of Onkis who claim that their fits are the result of divine possession.

Shaman—Sorcerer-prophets periodically condemned by the Old Prophets in the Chronicle of the Tusk, but redeemed via the New Covenant of Anasûrimbor Kellhus, Holy Aspect-Emperor of the Three Seas.

Shanipal, Kemrates (4066–)—Man-of-the-Tusk, Baron of Hirhamet, a district in south central Conriya.

Shaugiriol—"Eaglehorn" (Ûmeritic). The northernmost peak of the Demua.

Shaul River—The second most important river system in the Nansur Empire, after the Phayus.

Shauriatas (c. 1086–)—"Cheater of Gods" (Umeritic). See *Shaeönanra*.

Sheära—"Sunskin" (Ûmeritic). Sorcerous golden armour crafted in Far Antiquity by the School of Mihtrûlic.

Shelgal (?–?)—One of the Chieftain-Kings named in the Tusk.

Shemic—The language group of the ancient non-Nilnameshi pastoralists of the southwestern Three Seas.

Shem-Varsi—The language group of the proto-Nilnameshi pastoralists of the southwestern Three Seas.

Sheneor—Far Antique High Norsirai nation, the least of three nations created by Nanor-Ukkerja I to divide between his sons in 1556.

Sheyic—The language of the Ceneian Empire, which still serves, in debased form, as the liturgical language of the Thousand Temples and as the "common tongue" of the Three Seas.

Sheyo-Buskrit—The language of Nilnameshi labouring castes, a derivative of High Sheyic and Sapmatari.

Sheyo-Kheremic—The lost language of the lower castes of the Eastern Ceneian Empire.

Sheyo-Xerashi—The language of Xerash, a derivative of Xerashi and High Sheyic.

Shield-Breaker, the—A common name for Gilgaöl, God of War.

Shield of Sil—The soggomantic great shield belonging to the King-After-the-Fall, which Shauriatas took as a platform for the decrepit amputees bearing his soul.

Shigek—A governorate of Kian and former province of the Nansur Empire. Located on the fertile delta and alluvial plains of the River Sempis, Shigek was the ancient competitor of Kyraneas and the first civilized nation of the Three Seas.

Shigek reached the height of her power during the so-called Old Dynasty period, when a succession of Shigeki God-Kings extended their dominion to the limits of the Kyranae Plains in the north and to ancient Eumarna to the south. Great cities (of which only Iothiah survives) and monumental works, including the famed Ziggurats, were raised along the River Sempis. At some point in the twelfth century various Ketyai tribes began asserting their independence on the Kyranae Plains, and the God-Kings found themselves waging incessant war. Then, in 1591, the God-King Mithoser II was decisively defeated by the Kyraneans at Narakit, and Shigek began its long tenure as a tributary to greater powers. It was most recently conquered in 3933 by the Fanim hosts of Fan'oukarji III. Much to the dismay of the Thousand Temples, the Kianene method of simply taxing non-believers—as opposed to out-and-out persecuting them—led to the wholesale conversion of the populace to Fanimry within a few short generations. The Inrithi revival following the reconquest of Shigek by the First Holy War, of course, either revealed the brittleness of this conversion or the fickle nature of the Shigeki soul.

Shigogli—Desolate plain encircled by the Ring Mountains and encircling Golgotterath. Arguably no place in the World has witnessed so much butchery. After his victory at Pir Pahal, Cu'jara Cinmoi squandered the lives of thousands attempting to overcome the crude breastworks the Inchoroi had raised before rebuilding Arobindant and resuming the Watch. The day of Pir Minginnial, the Second Battle of the Ark, saw more Ishroi and Quya die on Shigogli than on any other. Though the toll at the Battle of Imogirion was smaller, the fact that Illisserû alone bore its brunt made its impact every bit as profound. Some suspect the toll exacted at the Battle of Isal'imial approaches that of Pir Minginnial, but is never reported given the totality of Nil'giccas's triumph. In terms of numbers, the toll exacted upon Men was every bit as high, with the losses of the First Great Investiture (2125–2131) matched by those of the Second in 2143, which, of course, ended with the disaster of Initiation—Apocalypse. Also known as Innuir-Shigogli, or "Black Furnace Plain."

Shikol (2118–2202)—The King of ancient Xerash, famed for sentencing Inri Sejenus to death in 2198, as recounted in *The Tractate*. For obvious reasons, his name has become synonymous with moral corruption among the Inrithi.

Shilla Amphitheatre—Primary locus for religious festivals, drama, and official speeches in Aöknyssus. Carved from the hip of Mount Omprempa, the Shilla is famed for the view it affords the entire city.

Shimeh—The second-holiest city of Inrithism, located in Amoteu, and the site of Inri Sejenus's ascension to the Nail of Heaven.

Shinoth—The legendary main gate of ancient Trysë.

Shinurta, Khui (3741–3828)—Renowned Grandmaster of the Scarlet Spires credited with using the Scholastic Wars (3796 to 3818) as a means of conquering High Ainon. Famously slain by the legendary Holca freebooter, Eryelk, while investigating the Daimos.

Shir—An ancient city-state on the River Maurat that eventually became the Shiradi Empire. See *Shiradi Empire*.

Shiradi Empire—The first great nation to arise in the eastern Three Seas, where it ruled much of what is now Cengemis, Conriya, and High Ainon for much of Far Antiquity. By c. 500 a number of Hamori Ketyai tribes had settled the length of the River Sayut and the Secharib Plains, becoming more sedentary and socially stratified as they exploited the rich cereal yields afforded by the fertile soils of the region. But unlike Shigek, where the first God-Kings were able to unify the Sempis River Valley quite early, Seto-Annaria, as it came to be called (after the two most dominant tribes), remained a collection of warring city-states. Eventually the balance of power shifted to the north, to the city-state of Shir on the River Maurat, and sometime in the thirteenth century it managed to subdue all the cities of Seto-Annaria, though its rulers would spend generations putting down rebellions (the Seto-Annarians apparently thought themselves superior to their uncouth cousins from the north). Then, sometime in the fifteenth century, Xiuhianni invaders from Jekk ravaged the empire and Shir was razed to the ground. The survivors moved the capital to ancient Aöknyssus (the present administrative capital of Conriya), and after some twenty years managed to oust the Eänneans. Centuries of stability followed, until 2153, when the forces of the No-God inflicted a disastrous defeat on the Shiradi at the Battle of Nurubal. The following two hundred years of chaos and internecine warfare effectively destroyed what remained of the empire and its central institutions.

The influence of ancient Shir is evident in many respects in the eastern Ketyai nations of the Three Seas, from the revering of beards (first cultivated by caste-nobles to distinguish themselves from the Xiuhianni, who were reputed to be unable to grow beards) to the continued use of a Shiradi-derived pictographic script in High Ainon.

Shorathises, Matmuth (4088–)—Ordealman, Ainoni Palatine of Karyoti, eldest son of Ramgath.

Shortest Way—See *Logos*.

Shriah—The title of the Apostle of the Latter Prophet, the administrative ruler of the Thousand Temples, and the spiritual leader of the Inrithi.

Shrial Apparati—The generic term for career and hereditary functionaries in the Thousand Temples.

Shrial Censure—The excommunication of Inrithi from the Thousand Temples. Since it rescinds all rights to property and vassalage as well as to worship, the worldly consequences of Shrial Censure are often as extreme as the spiritual. When King Sareat II of Galeoth was censured by Psailas II in 4072, for instance, fairly half of his client nobles rebelled, and Sareat was forced to walk barefoot from Oswenta to Sumna in contrition.

Shrial Insurrection—The successful coup initiated by Anasûrimbor Maithanet against his sister-in-law, Anasûrimbor Esmenet, in 4132.

Shrial Knights—Also known as Knights of the Tusk. The monastic military order founded by Shriah Ekyannus the Golden in 2511, charged with prosecuting the will of the Shriah.

Shrial Law—The ecclesiastical law of the Thousand Temples, which in a labyrinthine variety of forms serves as the common law for much of the Three Seas, particularly for those areas lacking any strong secular authority.

Shrial Priests—Inrithi clerics who, as opposed to Cultic Priests, are part of the hierarchies of the Thousand Temples, and perform the liturgies of the Latter Prophet and the God rather than those of the Gods.

Shrial Remission—A writ issued by the Thousand Temples absolving an individual of sin. Remissions are commonly awarded to those who accomplish some act of penance, such as joining a pilgrimage or a sanctioned war against unbelievers. Historically, however, they are primarily sold.

Shrial Warrant—A writ issued by the Thousand Temples authorizing the arrest of an individual for the purpose of trial in the ecclesiastical courts.

Sibawûl te Nurwul (4092–)—Ordealmen, Believer-Prince of Nymbrica, leader of the Cepaloran contingent in the Great Ordeal.

Sign of Gierra—The twin serpents that Sumni harlots must have tattooed on the back of their left hand, apparently in imitation of the Priestesses of Gierra.

Siklar, Gaes (4101–4132)—Tydonni Ordealman, cousin to King Hogrim, slain at the Battle of Imweor.

Simas, Polchias (4052–)—Achamian's old teacher and a member of the Quorum, the ruling council of the School of Mandate.

Sinerses (4076–)—Man-of-the-Tusk, Shield-Captain of the Javreh and favourite of Hanamanu Eleäzaras.

Singer-in-the-Dark—See *Onkis*.

Sin'niroiha (?–?)—"First Among Peoples" (Ihrimsû). Nonman King of Nihrimsûl, initially, and thence Ishoriol through his marriage to the sorceress Tsinirû, who would bear him Nil'giccas, his only son, and at long last unite all Mansions under the Blood of Tsonos. He is also famed as the longtime foe of Cu'jara Cinmoi, for refusing the Inoculation, and for rallying the Cûnuroi after the Breaking of the Second Watch and the disaster of Pir Minginnial.

Sin-Pharion—"Angel of Deceit" (Ihrimsû). Nonman epithet for Aurang following the Womb-Plague.

Siol—The Nonman Mansion from which, according to tradition, all other Mansions save Nihrimsûl are derived, and thus called the "House Primordial." Located deep in the northeastern Kayarsus, Siol was the perpetual bulwark against the Mannish hordes to the east, heir to a ruthless martial ethos that would see its Sons conquer all Eärwa save Nihrimsûl (which famously endured the One-Thousand-Year-Siege). Even as Nonmen are more profound in their commitment to authority, so are they more savage in rebellion. The *Isûphiryas* chronicles the slow fracture of the Tsonos Dynasty as the interests of each diverged, eventually becoming as distinct as the Nihrimsûli (or "Dark Nonmen"). Thus the Sons of Tsonos ceased to recognize their common Kinning, and begin to wage war one against the other.

Siol remained pre-eminent, but more as a provender of human slaves and a perpetual aggressor than as a font of wealth and wisdom. Commercially, the Mansion would be eclipsed by Cil-Aujas, Illiserû, and Ishoriol, the "House Eschatological," which would culturally eclipse Siol as well. If one believes, as many scholars do, that Siol is the "Gate of Thayant" referred to in the Tusk, then its "Breaking" literally marks the beginning of human civilization in Eärwa.

Siqu—Generally, the term referring to Nonmen who find themselves in the service of Men, usually as mercenaries or in some advisory capacity. Specifically, those Nonmen who participated in the so-called Nonman Tutelage from 555 to 825. See *Nonman Tutelage*.

Sirol ab Kascamandri (4004–)—The youngest daughter of Kascamandri ab Tepherokar.

Siroyon, Halas (4098–)—Ordealman, Prince of Erras, General of the Famiri in the Great Ordeal of Anasûrimbor Kellhus.

Sirro (2367–2415)—Female Seleukaran poet, naturalist, and philosopher, famed author of *The Holy Crone*, burned by the Thousand Temples on suspicion of practicing witchcraft in 2415.

Skafadi—A Kianene name for the Scylvendi.

Skafra—One of the principal Wracu, or Dragons, of the Apocalypse, finally slain by Seswatha at Mengedda in 2155.

Skagwa—A fiefdom on the Thunyeri Sranc Marches.

Skaiyelt, Hringa (4073–4111)—Man-of-the-Tusk, eldest son of King Rauschang of Thunyerus and leader of the Thunyeri contingent of the Holy War. Claimed by disease at Caraskand.

Skala (4069-4132)—Cepaloran named Exalt-Captain of the Palatial Eöthic Guard by Xerius III following the death of Gaenkelti.

Skalateas (4069–4111)—A member of the Mysunsai School, murdered in the Ansercan countryside by the Scarlet Spires.

Skauras ab Nalajan (4052–4111)—The Sapatishah-Governor of Shigek and the first principal antagonist of the First Holy War, slain at Anwurat. A veteran of many wars, he was deeply respected by both his allies and his enemies. The Nansur called him Sutis Sutadra, the "Southern Jackal," because of his Black Jackal standard.

Skavric—The language group of the Scylvendi peoples.

Skettic—The language group of ancient pastoralists of the Far Istyuli Plains, a derivative of Nirsodic.

Sketti Empire—Norsirai empire arising from the collapse of the White Cond in Myclai in 1097, extending along the northern coasts of the Cerish Sea.

Skilura II (3619–68)—Also called "the Mad." The most cruel of the Surmante Emperors of Nansur, whose deranged antics led to the Granary Revolts of 3668 and the accession of Surmante Xatantius I to the Mantle.

Skin Eaters—Famed company of Scalpers.

Skinny—Scalper argot for Sranc.

Skiötha urs Hannut (4038–79)—The father of Cnaiür urs Skiötha, and former Chieftain of the Utemot.

Skogma—An ancient Wracu thought destroyed during the Cûno-Inchoroi Wars.

Skûlsirai—"Shield-People" (Aorsic). Common epithet used by the Aorsi to describe themselves.

Skuthula the Black—An ancient Wracu spawned during the Cûno-Inchoroi Wars, one of the few Dragons known to have survived the Apocalypse, though his present whereabouts are unknown. Widely thought to have inspired the Nonman use of "Snakes" to refer to the species given his elongated form and serpentine movement.

Skûtiri—Name of the nine-hundred and ninety-nine ensorcelled plates of bronze girding the stoneworks of the Turret, the great citadel of the Library of Sauglish, in Far Antiquity.

Skûtsa the Elder (4053–4129)—Girgallic Priest from Sorweel's childhood.

Sky-Beneath-the-Mountain—Name of the iron platforms that famously gird the downward face of the Ilculcû Rift in Ishterebinth. See *Hanging Citadels*. Also referred to as the "Sky-Beneath."

Slave Laws—Canon of Imperial decrees laid out by Anasûrimbor Kellhus in 4124 extending a variety of legal and religious protections to slaves. Subsequently repealed by Anasûrimbor Esmenet in 4132 in an attempt to control the Great Yatwerian Sedition.

Slog—Scalper slang for expeditions against the Sranc.

Slough, the—Sickness suffered by those too near the Scalding of Dagliash, characterized by convulsions, hair loss, anal or oral expulsion of blood, severe ulceration, and blindness—all symptoms suffered by the Nonmen at the beginning of their ancient wars with the Inchoroi, according to some deepest verses in the *Isûphiryas*:

> The Vile hath called the very Starving down upon the Bone of the Land, mountains
> of fire cast upon our Eight Holy Mountains, breaking into black vapour that delivers
> woe unto our Slaves, who clutch themselves wailing, breaking red blood, holding fast
> their falling skin.

Snakeheads—An Inrithi epithet for the Cishaurim.

Sobel—An abandoned province north of Atrithau.

Sodhoras, Nersei (4072–4111)–Man-of-the-Tusk, Conriyan Baron and cousin of Prince Nersei Proyas.

soggomant–Name (possessing no known origin) of the gold-hued, but otherwise impenetrable, metal used to construct the Incû-Holoinas.

Soggomantic Gate–See *Minror*.

Sogian Way–A Nansur coastal road first constructed in the age of Kyraneas.

Soholn–Ancient road constructed by Nanor-Ukkerja I that once ran from Trysë to the province of Ûnosiri.

Sohonc–Premier ancient Gnostic Schools, proprietor of the Library of Sauglish.

Solitary God–"Allonara Yulah" (Kianni). The name used by Fanim to denote the *transcendent* singularity of their supreme deity. According to Fanim tradition, the God is not, as the Inrithi claim, immanent in existence, nor is He manifold in the way described by the Latter Prophet. The transcendental nature of Yulah is the primary reason Inrithi theologians dismiss Fanim apologia as mere hokum. If God is set apart from Creation, they argue, then God is merely a moment in a larger, unexplained system. Pokariti mystical traditions, however, hold that Yulah is an infinite *function*, that transcendental divinity possesses no being, and thus moots the "Mereology Problem." Yulah is the force that makes all things happen. Inrithi critics reply by simply asking how functions are not parts of a greater whole. The problem with Fanimry, they contend, is the inability to countenance the fact that the God of Gods *can be unconscious*. This perpetually strands them with a partial concept of deity, and therefore countless questions they have no means of answering. The Pokariti mystical tradition generally responds by demonstrating the way various Inrithi critiques actually presuppose the transcendental functions of Yulah, which they require as necessary conditions of coherence.

Somarae–Archive containing the accumulated accounts and studies of Seswatha's Dreams in Atyersus.

Sompas, Biaxi (4068–)–Man-of-the-Tusk, general of the Kidruhil following the death of General Numemarius in Nagogris. Sompas is the eldest son of Biaxi Coronsas, Patridomos of House Biaxi.

Song-cage–Legendary Iswazi artifact able to imprison souls.

Song-of-Iswa–Iswazi counterpart of an Anagogic Cant.

Song of the Violet Ishroi–Also known as "Song of the Bloody Ishroi." A Cûnûroi epic verse work (in the Illessa tradition, no less) of unknown origin, purporting to relate the life of Cu'jara Cinmoi in his voice.

Soptet, Rash (4088–)–Ordealman, Palatine-Governor of Shigek, General of the Shigeki contingent of the Great Ordeal of Anasûrimbor Kellhus, referred to as "Lord of the Sempis," for his successes against the Fanim during the Unification Wars.

Sorainas (3808–95)–A celebrated Nansur scriptural commentator, and author of *The Book of Circles and Spirals*.

Soramipur—One the greater cities of western Nilnamesh.

sorcerer of rank—Though practices differ extensively between Schools, generally the title given to a sorcerer who is qualified to teach sorcery to another.

Sorcerers of the Sun—A common epithet for the Imperial Saik. See *Saik*.

sorcery—The practice of making the world conform to language, as opposed to philosophy, the practice of making language conform to the world. Despite the tremendous amount of apparently unresolvable controversy surrounding sorcery, there are several salient features that seem universal to its practice. First, practitioners must be able to apprehend the "onta," which is to say, they must possess the innate ability to see, as Protathis puts it, "Creation *as created*." Second, sorcery also seems to involve a universal commitment to what Gotagga calls "semantic hygiene." Sorcery requires precise meanings. This is why incantations are always spoken in a non-native tongue: to prevent the semantic transformation of crucial terms due to the vagaries of daily usage. This also explains the extraordinary "double-think" structure of sorcery, the fact that all incantations require the sorcerer to say and think two separate things *simultaneously*. The spoken segment of an incantation (what is often called the "utteral string") must have its meaning "fixed" or focussed with a silent segment (what is often called the "inutteral string") that is simultaneously thought. Apparently the thought incantation sharpens the meaning of the spoken incantation the way the words of one man may be used to clarify the words of another. (This gives rise to the famous "semantic regress problem": how can the inutteral string, which admits different interpretations, serve to fix the proper interpretation of the utteral string?) Though there are as many metaphysical interpretations of this structure as there are sorcerous Schools, the result in each case is the same: the world, which is otherwise utterly indifferent to the words of Men, *listens*, and sorcerous transformations of reality result.

With great power, however, comes grave consequences. Given these perspectival revisions of being are necessarily incomplete, they constitute desecrations of being, and so appear as the aesthetic violation called the Mark, while heaping damnation on the sorcerer responsible. In this sense, sorcery could be said to be, in the immortal words of Zarathinius, "Hell's most toilsome and tedious route."

Soroptic—The lost language of ancient Shigek, a derivative of Kemkaric.

Soter, Nurbanu (4069–)—Ordealman, Believer-King of High Ainon, leader of the Ainoni contingent in the Great Ordeal of Anasûrimbor Kellhus. Originally Palatine of the Ainoni district of Kishyat when he joined the First Holy War, but made "King-Regent" of High Ainon as reward for his role in the Unification Wars. Renowned for his pragmatic brutality.

"[The] soul that encounters Him passes no further."—A line from *The Sagas* referring to the Battleplain and the belief that all those who perish there remain trapped.

Southern Columns—Those divisions of the Imperial Nansur Army stationed on the Kianene frontier.

Southron Gates—The series of passes through the Unaras Spur guarded by Asgilioch.

Spiderface—Scalper argot for skin-spies.

Sranc—The violent, inhuman creatures first created by the Inchoroi as instruments of war against the Nonmen. They are the weakest, yet most numerous of the accursed Weapon Races. The chroniclers of the *Isûphiryas* write:

> And they forged counterfeits from our frame, creatures vile and obscene who hungered only for violent congress. These beasts they loosed upon the land, where they multiplied, no matter how fierce the Ishroi who hunted them. And soon Men clamoured at our gates, begging sanctuary, for they could not contend with the creatures. 'They wear your face,' the penitents cried. 'This calamity is your issue.' But we were wroth, and turned them away, saying, 'These are not our Sons. And you are not our Brothers.'

The motivations of the Sranc seem to be as base as possible, in that they seem to find sexual gratification in acts of violence. There are innumerable accounts of the indiscriminate rape of men, women, children, and even corpses. They seem to know nothing of mercy or honour, and though they do take prisoners, very few are known to have survived captivity, which is said to be savage beyond imagining.

They reproduce rapidly. Though no outward physical differences are readily visible, female Sranc seem to have roles identical to those of male Sranc. Apparently, a great number of Sranc in various stages of pregnancy were observed in battle over the course of the Apocalypse. Though generally inferior to Men in individual combat, they are ideal logistically, as they are able to live for sustained periods on little more than grubs and insects. Survivors recount tales of vast tracts of ground overturned and rooted by passing Sranc hordes. Under the command of the No-God they are utterly fearless, and seem to strike with unerring control and coordination.

Typically, Sranc stand no higher than the average caste-menial's shoulder. Their skin is devoid of pigment, and despite the refined—to the point of repulsiveness—beauty of their faces, their physiognomy is bestial (though hairless), with pinched shoulders and deep, almond-shaped breasts. They are exceedingly fast across both open and broken terrain, and their sheer viciousness is said to compensate for their slight stature.

Mandate scholars are prone to make dire warnings about the present numbers of Sranc in Eärwa. Apparently the ancient Norsirai had reduced the Sranc, pressing them to the margins of Eärwa, and the No-God was still able to summon hosts that reportedly blackened the horizon. Now Sranc dominate half the continent.

Sranc Pits—The famed gladiatorial arena of Carythusal, where human slaves are typically pitted against Sranc. Though often likened to an inverted ziggurat, the tiers of the pit are so precariously arranged that spectators must rope and hook themselves to avoid tumbling to the killing floor. The spectacle of thousands *hanging* out over the carnage of the killing floor (or the "Purple Coin"), combined with several other curious customs (such as urinating in zurigants to cast upon the combatants below), has rendered the Sranc-Pits famous throughout the Three Seas, as well as a common literary figure.

Stajanas II (2338–2395)—The famed "Philosopher-Emperor" of Cenei, whose *Ruminations* has remained an important work in the Three Seas literary canon.

Stalker, the—A common epithet for Husyelt.

Starving—Alternate translation of the Nonman (Ihrimsû) *"tilis,"* or "sky."

Steppe, the—See *Jiünati Steppe.*

Stone Hags—Renegade scalper company notorious for attacking other companies.

Stump—Campsite frequented by scalpers passing through the Mop, consisting of a series of platforms raised across an enormous felled tree.

Subis—A once-fortified oasis in Khemema, frequented by caravans passing between Shigek and Eumarna.

Sudica—A province of the Nansur Empire, largely depopulated by 4111 but among the wealthiest districts of the Kyranae Plain during the ages of Kyraneas and the Ceneian Empire.

"suffer not a whore to live ..."—The passage from Canticles 19:9, *The Chronicle of the Tusk*, condemning prostitution.

Sûjara-nin (?–)—Injori Ishroi, a Dispossessed Son of Siol, famed for his exploits in the Three Seas, where he was known as the "Red Ghoul" given the crimson of his famous, ensorcelled armour, the Immaculate Rim.

Sumajil ut Hest (4093–)—Ordealman, Kianene Grandee of Mitirabis.

Summer Stair—See Insirinis.

summoning horns—The great horns of bronze used to signal the "prayer watches" to the Inrithi faithful.

Sumna—The site of the Tusk and the holiest city of Inrithism, located in Nansur.

Suönirsi—Trading entrepot on the frontier of ancient Sheneor.

Suortagal (c. 1300–c. 1360)—Sauglian author of the *Epimeditations.*

Surmante, House—A former Nansur House of the Congregate, and the Empire's ruling dynasty from 3619 to 3941.

Surmantic Gates—The great northern gate of Carythusal, whose construction was financed in 3639 by Surmante Xatantius I to commemorate the ill-fated Treaty of Kutapileth, a short-lived military pact between Nansur and High Ainon.

Sursa River—The river system that once formed the crucial frontier between Agongorea and Aörsi before the Apocalypse, and often referred to as the Harsunc, or "Fish Knife," in Bardic literature.

Suskara—A vast region of broken plains and highlands between Atrithau and the Jiünati Steppe, inhabited by numerous tribes of Sranc, some of which are tributary to the so-called Sranc King of Urskugog.

Sûthaugi—"Earthsnake" (Ûmeri). Ancient Kûniüric epithet for Dragons.

suthenti—The menial castes. See *castes*.

Sutis Sutadra—See *Skauras ab Nalajan*.

Swa River—The river that forms the northern frontier of Ce Tydonn.

Swaranûl—"Oath Tower" (Ûmeri). Isolated hill in the ancient Kûniüri province of Akirsuäl, crowned by the ruins of the Hiolis, a shrine commemorating the legendary and likely mythical Alotting, where the Gods allegedly apportioned lands to the different Chieftains of the High Norsirai tribes.

Swarjuka (4061–4112)—The Sapatishah-Governor of Jurisada.

Swayal Sisterhood—The first School of Witches, based in the fortress-complex of Orovelai in Holy Amoteu. Named after Swayal, the famed maiden who rebuked the amorous advances of Gilgaöl and was condemned to live all eternity as a Golden Swan. The New Covenant declared by Anasûrimbor Kellhus in 4114 was widely thought to include two major revisions to traditional Inrithi dogma, the Rehabilitation of Sorcery, rescinding all Shrial and Tusk condemnations of sorcerous activity, and the Manumission of the Feminine, rescinding all traditional restrictions of female conduct. Several scholars have noted (with approval, in some cases) that for all the fundamental transformations wrought by the first, the latter possessed only a nominal effect on the lives of women in the New Empire—with the notable exception of the caste-nobility (because of the expansion of property rights) and most famously, witches. According to rumour, agents of the Aspect-Emperor had already begun recruiting witches in anticipation of the New Covenant. Their successes were only marginal at first: the horror of every mother was to discover her daughter possessed the Gift of the Few, and the practice of concealing the identities of those engaging in witchcraft was arguably as old as the Tusk's condemnation of sorcery. Only when the first of the Swayali *themselves* began recruiting that their numbers began to swell. Within ten years, the last of the male Mandati teachers at Orovelai were sent back to Atyersus, and the Sisterhood became independent of all save Imperial concerns. By the time of the Great Ordeal, the Swayali Sisterhood was easily the match of any other Major School in the Three Seas, including the Mandate, whom they outnumbered almost two to one.

Though officially dedicated to teaching and researching the Gnosis, the Sisterhood is also committed to the preservation of the myriad "folk sorceries" developed by generations of witches across the Three Seas.

swazond—The ceremonial scars used by Scylvendi warriors to denote foes slain in battle, believed by some to be markers of stolen strength.

Swazond Standard—The name given to Cnaiür's banner at the Battle of Anwurat.

Sweki River—"The Sacred" (Kianni). The so-called "miracle river," revered as holy by the Kianene, who claim that its waters arise from nothing by the will of the Solitary

God. Before the first Jihads, Nansur cartographers made several attempts to locate its headwaters in the Great Salt, none of them successful.

Synodine—Chamber on the Andiamine Heights housing the Imperial Synod.

Synthese—Artifacts of the Inchoroi Tekne, thought to be living "shells" specifically designed to house the souls of senior Consult figures.

syurtpiütha—A Scylvendi euphemism for life, meaning "the smoke-that-moves."

T

talent—The base monetary unit of the Nansur Empire prior to the Zaudunyani conquest.

Tamiznai—A fortified oasis two days south of the River Sempis, frequented by caravans.

Tarpellas, Biaxi (4101–)—Ordealman, Patridomos of House Biaxi, General of the Nansur contingent of the Great Ordeal of Anasûrimbor Kellhus.

Tears of God—See *Chorae*.

Tekne—Also known as the Old Science. The non-sorcerous craft of the Inchoroi, used to mold abominations out of living flesh. According to various Nonman sources, the Tekne proceeds on the presumption that everything in nature, including life, is fundamentally mechanical. Despite the absurdity of this claim, few dispute the efficacy of the Tekne, as the Inchoroi and the Consult after them have time and again demonstrated the ability to "manufacture flesh." Mandate scholars claim that the fundamental principles of the Tekne have been long lost, and that the Consult can only proceed in a trial-and-error fashion, on the basis of an incomplete understanding, and using ancient and ill-understood instruments. This ignorance, they claim, is all that preserves the world from the No-God's return.

Teleol—Ancient Meöri town located on the foot of the Osthwai Mountains.

Tempiras the King—A work widely thought the greatest of Hamishaza's satiric tragedies.

Temple of Exorietta—A notorious temple in Carythusal.

Temple Prayer—Also referred to as the High Temple Prayer. Prayer Inri Sejenus taught to his disciples in *The Tractate* that was later adopted as the canonical institutional prayer of the Thousand Temples in both its Inrithi and Zaudunyani incarnations. Several versions of the prayer, or "Comprehensions," have always circulated throughout the Three Seas, despite the traditional importance accorded to it.

The text of the most common version runs:

Sweet God of Gods,
who walk among us,
innumerable are your holy names.
May your bread silence our daily hunger,
may your rains quicken our undying land,

may our submission be answered with dominion,
so we may prosper in your name.
Judge us not by our trespasses
but according to our temptations,
and deliver unto others
what others have delivered unto us,
for your name is Power,
and your name is Glory,
for your name is Truth,
which endures and endures,
for ever and ever.

Ten, the—Epithet for the ten most powerful and widely worshipped of the Hundred, consisting of Yatwer, Gilgaöl, Husyelt, Gierra, Jukan, Anagke, Onkhis, Akkeägni, Bûkris, and Ajokli.

Tendant'heras—An extensive fortress located on Nilnamesh's frontier with Girgash and Kianene.

Tertae Plains—The heavily cultivated alluvial plain bordering northeast Caraskand.

tesperari—A Nansur term for naval captains who retire to command merchant ships.

Thaila, Nersei (4123–)—The only daughter of Nersei Proyas.

Thampis, Kemetti (4076–4118)—Man-of-the-Tusk, Conriyan Baron from the Anpleian frontier, killed during the Unification Wars.

Tharschilka, Heänar (4068–4110)—Man-of-the-Tusk, Galeoth Earl of Nergaöta, and one of the three leaders of the Vulgar Holy War.

Thassius (4054-4115)—A ranking member of the Imperial Saik.

Thawa Ligatures—Gnostic Torture Cant.

Therishut, Gishtari (4067–4111)—Man-of-the-Tusk, Conriyan Baron from the Ainoni frontier, murdered by persons unknown.

Thesji Bowmen—An elite Kianene unit of Chorae bowmen.

thil—"Salt" (Sakarpi). Sakarpic euphemism for wisdom.

Third Analytic of Men, The—Regarded by many as Ajencis's magnum opus, the *Third Analytic* interrogates the aspects of human nature that make knowledge possible, as well as the human weaknesses that make knowledge so difficult to attain. As Ajencis notes, "if all Men disagree on all matters, then most Men confuse deception for truth." He investigates the reasons, not only for deception in general, but for the erroneous sense of conviction that sustains it, giving what has come to be called the "selfish knower" thesis, the idea that convenience, conditioning, and appeal (as opposed to evidence and rational argumentation) are the primary motivation for the beliefs of the vast majority.

Thoti-Eännorean—The alleged mother tongue of all Men, and the language of *The Chronicle of the Tusk.*

"Though you lose your soul, you shall gain the world."—The penultimate answer in the Mandate Catechism, referring to the fact that Mandate Schoolmen, unlike other Schoolmen, damn themselves for a purpose.

Thousand Temples—The ecclesiastical and administrative framework of Inrithism, based in Sumna but omnipresent throughout most of the Three Seas. The Thousand Temples first became a dominant social and political institution during the reign of the first Aspect-Emperor, Triamis the Great, who declared Inrithism the official faith of the Ceneian Empire in 2505. Authority is nominally centralized in the person of the Shriah, who is regarded as the Latter Prophet's living representative, but the sheer size and complexity of the Thousand Temples often renders that authority ceremonial. Aside from the management of the temples proper, there are the ecclesiastical courts, the political missions, the various Colleges, and the labyrinthine interconnections with the Cults to administer. As a result, the Thousand Temples often suffers from weak leadership, and is regarded with cynicism by many in the Three Seas.

This situation would radically change once Anasûrimbor Maithanet was elected Shriah, even moreso when Anasûrimbor Kellhus was declared Holy Aspect-Emperor in Shimeh in 4112, an event that effectively sundered the Thousand Temples into warring camps. An oft overlooked fact of the Unification Wars was the degree to which it involved the reunification of the Thousand Temples beneath the hegemony of Anasûrimbor Maithanet. A relic of the Ceneian Empire, the Thousand Temples have long been the institutional skeleton connecting the Three Seas, even so far as functioning as a moneyhouse for transnational commerce.

Thousand Thousand Halls—The labyrinth constructed by the Dûnyain beneath Ishuäl and used by them to test their initiates. Those who become lost in the Thousand Thousand Halls invariably die, ensuring that only the most intelligent survive.

Three Flutes—Name of the three enclosed waterfalls that track the length of the Vast Ingressus in Ishterebinth.

Three-Headed Serpent—The symbol of the Scarlet Spires.

Three Hearts of God—A term referring to Sumna, the Thousand Temples, and the Tusk.

Three Kingdoms—Collective name for Kûniüri, Aörsi, and Sheneor, the nations that Nanor-Ukkerja I created for his sons in 1556.

Three Seas—Specifically, the seas of Meneanor, Oncis, and Nyranisas, located in south central Eärwa. More generally, the (primarily Ketyai) civilization that has thrived in this region since the end of the Apocalypse.

Three Sickles—The famed symbol of Triamis the Great, and by extension, the Ceneian Empire.

Threesie—The name given to Nansur who sign on for a third fourteen-year term of service in the Imperial Army.

Thresholds—The torture chamber of Ishterebinth, designed so as to be invisible to the Gods, and so to spare Nonmen interrogators the burden of their sins.

Throseanis (3256–3317)—A late Ceneian dramatist, famed for his *Triamis Imperator*, a dramatic account of the life of Triamis I, the greatest of the Ceneian Aspect-Emperors.

Thunyeric—The language of Thunyerus, a derivative of Meoric.

Thunyerus—A Norsirai nation of the Three Seas located on the northeastern coasts of the Meneanor Sea. According to Thunyeri legend, their peoples migrated down the length of the Wernma River, continually pressured by the Sranc tribes that largely rule the great forests of the Dameori Wilderness. For two hundred years the Thunyeri plied the Three Seas as pirates and raiders. Then, in 3987, after three generations of Inrithi missionaries had largely converted them from their traditional Kiünnat beliefs, the tribes elected their first King, Hringa Hurrausch, and began adopting the institutions of their Three Seas neighbours.

Tikirgal ab Ramitju (4101–4132)—Ordealman, Grandee of Makreb'at-Akii, killed in the days leading up to the disaster at Irsulor.

Tirummas, Nersei (4075–4100)—The eldest brother of Nersei Proyas, and Crown Prince of Conriya until his death at sea in 4100.

Titirga (c. 1055–c. 1119)—The second Grandmaster of the Sohonc, childhood pupil of Noshainrau the White, and the famed Hero-Mage of Ûmerau, reputed to be the most powerful sorcerer, Man or Nonman, to have drawn breath. He is rumoured to have been murdered by his great rival, Shaeönanra, and buried in the ancient ruins of Viri.

Tokush (4068–4111)—The Master of Spies to Ikurei Xerius III.

Toll—Orthodox pamphlet circulated during the Unification Wars, containing the Imperial Appraisal detailing the numbers of dead woman and children counted following the Sack of Sarneveh in 4120.

topoi—Locations where the accumulation of trauma and suffering has frayed the boundaries between the World and the Outside.

Tracery—Dûnyain ritual practiced at Ishuäl used to determine who among the Brethren would sire children.

Tractate, The—The writings of Inri Sejenus and his disciples, forming the second part of the Inrithi scriptural canon. The Inrithi believe *The Tractate* to be the prophesied culmination of *The Chronicle of the Tusk*, an amendment of the Covenant of Gods and Men for the realities of a new age. Among its seventeen books are various accounts of the life of the Latter Prophet, many parables for the purposes of moral instruction, and Inri Sejenus's own explanation of the "Intervention" he himself represents: that mankind, as it matures, will become more and more able to worship the God in His "singular multiplicity." Given that *The Tractate* was written more as a testament to the divinity of Inri Sejenus's vision than out of any real commitment to historical rigour, it is impossible to assess the veracity of the text. Zarathinius and, more recently, Fanim commentators have pointed out several glaring inconsistencies in the text, but nothing that Inrithi apologists have not been able to explain away.

Trail of Skulls—See *saka'ilrait*.

Triamarius I (3470–3517)—The first of the Zerxei Emperors, acclaimed by the Imperial Army following the assassination of Trimus Meniphas I in 3508. See *Nansur Empire*.

Triamarius III (3588–3619)—The last of the Zerxei Emperors of Nansur, murdered by palace eunuchs. See *Nansur Empire*.

Triamic Walls—Caraskand's outermost fortifications, raised by Triamis the Great in 2568.

Triamis Imperator—The famed drama by Throseanis, based on events in the life of Triamis the Great.

Triamis the Great (2456–2577)—The first Aspect-Emperor of the Ceneian Empire, famed for his conquests and for declaring Inrithism the official state religion in 2505. See *Ceneian Empire*.

Triaxeras, Hampei (4072–)—The Captain of Ikurei Conphas's bodyguard.

Trimus, House—A Nansur House of the Congregate.

Trinkets—See *Chorae*.

Triple-Crescent—The symbol of the Anasûrimbor of Trysë in Far Antiquity.

Troinim—Name of the three low hills upon which the Library of Sauglish was raised.

Trondha, Safirig (4076–4117)—Man-of-the-Tusk, Galeoth thane, client to Earl Anfirig of Gesindal.

Trucian Dramas, The—The magnum opus of Xius, a near antique poet and playwright.

Truth Room—An interrogation chamber located deep in the catacombs beneath the Andiamine Heights.

Trysë—The ancient administrative capital of Kûniüri, destroyed in the Apocalypse in 2147. Arguably the greatest city of the Ancient North and, with the exception of Sauglish, Ûmerau, and Etrith, also the oldest.

Tshuma (4073–?)—Man-of-the-Tusk, one of the Nascenti, formerly a Kutnarmu mercenary. He returned to his homeland in 4118 declaring his intention to convert his nation, but was never heard from again.

Tsonos (?–?)—Son of Imimorûl, legendary Ur-King of Siol, and the name given to the Kinning-most-High-and-Deep, the bloodline of so many Nonman Kings that it has become a necessary condition of any claim of royal authority.

Tsuramah—"Hated One" (Kyranean). The ancient Kyranean name for the No-God. See *No-God*.

Turret, the—The primary citadel of the Library of Sauglish, raised by Noshainrau in 1058.

Tusam—A village in the Inûnara Highlands destroyed by Fanim raiders in 4111.

Tusk, the—The premier holy artifact of both the Inrithi and Kiünnat traditions, and the most unholy in the Fanim tradition (where it is referred to as Rouk Spara, or "Cursed Thorn"). Since the Tusk bears the oldest extant version of *The Chronicle of the Tusk*, which in turn is the oldest human text, its provenance remains an utter mystery, though most scholars agree that it predates the coming of the Tribes to Eärwa. It has been installed in the holy city of Sumna throughout most of recorded history.

Tusking—Legendary event following the mass execution of Fanim captives on the Holy Kalaul of Caraskand, where Anasûrimbor Kellhus marked Tusks in blood upon the foreheads of the faithful.

Tûtmor, Beotha (4071–)—The New Imperial Consul of Ce Tydonn.

Tûthorsa, Beotha (4089–4121)—Man-of-the-Tusk, Tydonni Thane in the First Holy War.

Tutseme—The pigeon dialect of slaves and caste-menials in Carythusal.

Twelve Germs—The twelve bloodlines of the Dûnyain.

Twin Scimitars—The primary holy device of Fanimry, symbolizing the "Cutting Eyes" of the Solitary God.

Tydonni—The language of Ce Tydonn, a derivative of Meoric.

Tyrûmmas (4075-4100)—See Tirummas.

Tywanrae River—A major river system in north central Eärwa, draining the Gâl basin and emptying into the Cerish Sea.

U

Uän, Samarmau (4001–)—One of the Dûnyain Pragma.

Ûgorrior, Plain of—Name of the flat tracts immediately before Gwergirah, Corrunc, and Domathuz, demarcated not so much by virtue of geography as history. Called Mirsurqûl by the Nonmen (the "Final Dust"), countless Men and Nonmen have perished upon it.

Ukrummu, Madarezer (4045–4111)—Man-of-the-Tusk, sorcerer of rank in the Scarlet Spires, slain by Chorae at Anwurat.

Ûliqara (?–?)—Wife of Oirûnas, Lord of the Watch, and mother of Oinaral Lastborn.

Ulnarta, Shaugar (4071–)—Man-of-the-Tusk, one of the Nascenti, formerly a Tydonni thane.

Umbilicus—The residential and command pavilion used by Anasûrimbor Kellhus throughout the Great Ordeal.

Ûmerau—See Ûmeri Empire.

Ûmeri Empire—The first great nation of Men, encompassing the length of the River Aumris, founded after the overthrow of the Trysean God-Kings, *c.* 430. See *Kûniüri.*

Ûmeritic—The lost language of ancient Ûmerau, a derivative of Aumri-Saugla.

Umiaki—The name of the ancient eucalyptus tree located in the heart of the Kalaul in Caraskand, famed as the tree from which the Warrior-Prophet was hung on the Circumfix.

Umrapathur, Sasal (4078–4132)—Ordealman, Believer-King of Nilnamesh, Marshal of the Ketyai-of-the-South in the Great Ordeal of Anasûrimbor Kellhus, among the last souls killed at the disastrous Battle of Ursulor.

"umresthei om aumreton"—Kyranean for "possessing in dispossession." Ajencis's term for those moments where the soul comprehends itself in the act of comprehending other things, and so experiences the "wonder of existence."

Unaras Spur—The low mountain range that extends from the southern terminus of the Hethantas to the Meneanor coast, marking the geographical frontier between the Kyranae Plain and Gedea.

Unclean, the—A name, derived from *The Chronicle of the Tusk,* commonly used by Inrithi as a pejorative for sorcerers.

Unerring Grace—The capacity to act and desire in perfect coincidence with one's Fate, attributed especially to the Narindar. See *Narindar.*

Unification Wars—The Fall of Shimeh to Anasûrimbor Kellhus in 4112 did not so much occasion the end of his Holy War as lend it the legitimacy required to take on new, even larger quarry. What had begun as an Inrithi war against the Fanim had quickly become a Zaudunyani war against all. Conriya, of course, came to the Aspect-Emperor by virtue of Nersei Proyas. With the death of Ikurei Xerius and his heir, Ikurei Conphas, Maithanet need only proclaim Kellhus Aspect-Emperor to make Momemn the capital of his nascent empire. The successive defeats suffered at Mengedda, Anwurat, Caraskand, and Shimeh had so severely depleted the ranks of the Kianene nobility as to assure that Kellhus would install his Empress in the White-Sun Palace in Nenciphon in the winter of 4113. That year, the year that apocalypse was visited upon Fanimry, would become known as the Year of the Child Grandees.

Some among the wise contend that this first series of conquests belongs to the First Holy War proper, since the newly minted Aspect-Emperor spent three years consolidating his martial and spiritual conquests following the capitulation of the main Chianadyni tribes (decisively influenced by the Whelming of Massar ab Kascamandri in 4113). On this view, the Unification Wars proper begin with the Battle of Pinropis, in 4115. A substantial shortcoming of this view, however, is that it takes a shallow view of "Unification," assuming it pertains only to the annexation of once sovereign nations.

By no means did even a fraction of the Three Seas consider Anasûrimbor Kellhus anything but an imposter of some mundane or arcane variety—this despite the declarations Maithanet, the Holy Shriah of the Thousand Temples. Even within the Nansurium and the provinces of the former Kianene Empire, the Orthodox, as those defending their rights and privileges against the Aspect-Emperor came to be called, vastly outnumbered the Zaudunyani. The war waged by the so-called Aspect-Emperor was not a war for power over (this was simply the first step toward Unification) *but war for consent*. Ils Hidarei calls the zealots, "an army of mathematicians, scribes, and merchants," and comes to see them as all the more deadly for it:

> "And they murder us, more surely than if they chased us into the wilds. They fat us upon our own fears, our own weaknesses and greed. All the pomegranate seeds they leave lead to them, to their mercy, their employ, their milder taxes. Even their *daughters*, affluent and poor, are encouraged to take us as lovers. The proof of their God, they say, is plainer to see!"

Rumours of skin-spies, declarations made by famously pious men. The stories of miracles. What had happened in Shimeh had united the *attention* of the Three Seas in a way not seen since the days of Cenei. Wonder had opened every soul before suspicion had a chance to winch them shut. And always the bottomless *ghus* of the End, the Second Apocalypse. The Mandate, who all had thought mad, had all along spoke true. And simple, catastrophic claim that the God of Gods had sent Anasûrimbor Kellhus to assure that the World at last *listened*.

The Three Seas must act of one will. God's.

Unification for the Aspect-Emperor was Unification of *will*, the remaking of the Three Seas into a vast engine, for as the close of the Unification Wars would make amply clear, the Second Apocalypse was indeed his sole concern. "As you fear me," he famously declared at the Paremti Massing, "your children will praise my name. And through me, shall you become the most revered name on their Lists, the most proud and hallow on the Lists of their children." The strategies employed were ingenious, and became more so as time went on. Whole districts, cities, tribes, converted *en masse*, such that the first nations overthrown militarily (those comprising Nansur and Kian) were entirely subdued ere the last nations fell, their peoples Inrithi first, certainly, but in a manner corrupted by Zaudunyani concessions. Ere the departure of the Great Ordeal, more than half the population of every province in the Empire had been Whelmed, more than three quarters in a few (such as Nansur and Conriya).

Again, Ils Hidarei writes to his cousin (who was already, quite famously, a Zaudunyani convert by this time):

> "He creeps through us like a contagion, everyday stronger for our own courage, our own skill, stealing, forever stealing our hopes and our thoughts, until now

our very brothers slay us, greet us with a derision and hate that makes a paste of that demonstrated by their slavers."

Of the Great Names of the First Holy War, only Nersei Proyas possessed the charisma required to deliver his nation to his Warrior-Prophet entire. Anasûrimbor Kellhus bid the others to return to their homes as soon as he could dispense with their resources in the field, thus assuring that all nations participating in the First Holy War possessed some powerful faction fanatically loyal to him. Within a year of Nenciphon's fall, the first missionaries began graduating from the famed Zaudûn Angnaya, the "floating college" of young aspirants that followed Anasûrimbor Kellhus about the Three Seas, imbibing his wisdom whenever his martial duties permitted. At least initially, the "suicide sermons," as they came to be called, had the effect of galvanizing *opposition* around the Three Seas. The Edict of the first Orthodox council in 4114 (the Numaineiric Council), even refers to these embassies by name, claiming them "proof of madness." But there can be little doubt that the ferocity of the message—men cutting their own throats in demonstration—had the long-term effect of softening Orthodox resolve, or, what amounted to the same, undermining their religious certitude.

Throughout the Unification Wars, in fact, the Orthodox could do no more than aspire to the conviction of their foe. No matter what the nation, they found themselves on the defensive, rhetorically if not spiritually, before the first blades were drawn. Though apparently chaotic, fraught with lulls and desperate contingencies, careful study reveals that the Unification Wars were as much a matter of calculation as contingency. Anasûrimbor Kellhus, understanding that the Three Seas were as much a spiritual amphitheatre as a military arena, proved himself a master of provocation, acting to "redress" the very atrocities he compelled his foes to commit.

The chronology of significant events runs as follows:

4112 - Shimeh falls.

4113 - The Year of the Child Grandees; Nenciphon falls.

4114 - The *Novum Arcanum* is circulated throughout the Three Seas; Rash Soptet (4088–) is hailed as "Lord of the Sempis" after quelling Fanim uprisings. Schismatics denounce Maithanet; the War-between-Temples begins.

4115 - Prince Shoddû Akirapita (4099–4123) routes the first Zaudunyani invasion of Nilnamesh at the Battle of Pinropis.

4116 - The death of King Eryeat, combined with the secret conversion of his eldest surviving son, Coithus Narnol, delivers Galeoth to the Empire nearly intact. King Hringa Vûkyelt expels Schismatics from Thunyerus.

4117 - The first songs extolling the exploits of Sasal Charapatha against the Nilnameshi Orthodox begin circulating throughout the Three Seas; First Carythusali uprising; Earl Couras Nantilla is Whelmed, raises Cengemic provinces in revolt against Meigeiri; the Tydonni Orthodox begin massacring ketyai villages and towns along the Eleterine Coast.

4118 - Meigeiri falls; Anasûrimbor Kellhus orders the Orthodox of Numaineiri blinded; Eselos Mursidides (4081–4132) conquers Cironj for the Zaudunyani losing, miraculously, only one hundred and eighteen souls.

4119 - The Koraphean Uprising; Hoga Hogrim (4093–) is declared Zaudunyani Believer-King of Ce Tydonn; King Hringa Vûkyelt of Thunyerus declares himself a Believer-King as well; the Mandate takes up residence in Kiz.

4120 - Anasûrimbor Kellhus declares Imperial Bounty on Sranc scalps; Sack of Sarneveh; Circulation of the Toll pamphlet, and subsequent Toll uprisings.

4121 - Nurbanu Soter (4069–) declared King-Regent of High Ainon; Invishi falls after the famed Throwing-of-the-Hulls.

4122 - Nilnameshi Orthodox crushed at the Battle of Ushgarwal. Anasûrimbor Kellhus declares the Unification Wars concluded. The Shriah of the Thousand Temples, Maithanet, proclaims him Holy Aspect-Emperor of the Three Seas.

4123 - Prince Shoddû Akirapita (4099–4123) is found drowned in a well in Girgash. Only Fanayal ab Kascamandri remains of the Empire's notorious enemies.

4124 - Reconstruction of Auvangshei begins.

4125 - First of the Angnaya are sent to the Palace of Plumes in Zeum.

If Nilnamesh proved the most stubborn of the Empire's many conquests, and Ce Tydonn the most brutal, then High Ainon proved the most complicated. The hegemony exercised by the Scarlet Spires over that nation had not been a benevolent one. The Cishaurim decimation of the School in 4112 in Shimeh effectively robbed governing institutions of the coercive threat required to maintain authority. The unrest actually began as soon as word of the "Scarlet Letting," as it came to be known, spread beyond the walls of Carythusal. The infamous "Dread-of-Kiz" evaporated, and the general hatred began condensing into acts hard and visible. The fact is the Scarlet Spires' case for Anasûrimbor Kellhus's divinity would have been far better made had they claimed him diabolical. Over a period of months, what had been the Three Sea's most decadent believers became the most pious, to the point of calling themselves the Sons of Shir. A great many would die in sorcerous fire. In one of the great ironies of the Unification Wars, the bulk of the Mandate would occupy the Spires themselves, the very fastness of their greatest rival.

No other facet of the Unification Wars illustrates the political genius of Anasûrimbor Kellhus quite so dramatically as his handling of the Schools. As commentators are quick to point out, he began his campaign already possessing *three* of the so-called Major Schools: the Imperial Saik, the Scarlet Spires, and the Mandate. Even given the decimation of the former two (especially the Scarlet Spires, which was reduced to fourteen sorcerers of rank following Shimeh), the Gnostic sorcery of the Mandate rendered Kellhus the indisputable master of the arcane field.

And if this advantage were not enough, the wonder of the Metagnosis and his clarification of sorcerous metaphysics in the *Novum Arcanum* all but assured him the *attention* of his sorcerous peers (and as historians of the Aspect-Emperor know, this is typically all that he needed). The antipathy between the Schools and traditional Inrithism, meanwhile, assured that few sorcerers aligned themselves with Orthodox movements (Jishamurtë and Panarossa being, of course, the most notorious examples). 4115 marks the first of the Five Amassings, gatherings of sorcerers-of-rank from across the Three Seas, where Kellhus, in addition to astounding his guests with Metagnostic demonstrations, argued the imminent threat posed by the Second Apocalypse. The *sorcerous* conquest of the Three Seas would turn out to be very nearly bloodless. Although much has been made of the tactical genius of Anasûrimbor Kellhus, many argue this one strategic move in particular all but doomed the Orthodox.

Unmasking Room—A chamber located in the labyrinth below Ishuäl where Dûnyain children are taught the connections between facial musculature and passions.

Unnûrull—"Trackless Plain" (Ihrimsû). Cûnuroi name for Agongorea, given its desolation and the uncanny way it resists footprints.

Ûnosiri—Lost province of ancient Kûniüri, once the hunting preserve of the Ûmeri All-Kings.

Unterpa—River fortress to the south of Sakarpus.

Upper Pausal—First stage of the antechamber to the Coffers, buried deep beneath the Library of Sauglish.

Upright Horn—Also known as the High Horn. See *Horns of Golgotterath*.

Uranyanka, Sirpal (4062–)—The Palatine-Governor of the Ainoni city of Moserothu.

Urmakthi ab Makthi (4068–4132)—Ordealman, Believer-King of Girgash, leader of the Girgashi contingent in the Great Ordeal of Anasûrimbor Kellhus, called Ama'morit, or "Skullhammer," by his people for felling a mastodon with a single blow in the Battle of Chianadinara in 4120. Killed in the Battle of Irsulor.

Ur-Mother—One of many names for Yatwer.

Uroborian Circle—A so-called "artifactual Cant" used to prevent the utterance of sorcery and thought to turn on the same aporetic principles that make Chorae possible.

Urokkas—Low range of five mountains, consisting of Antareg (or Iros), Ingol, Oloreg, Mantigol, and Yawreg, located north northwest of the Neleost Sea, famed for once housing the Nonman mansion of Viri (who called them Virolotoi, or the "Wards-of-Viri") and for lying on the Agongorean frontier.

Uroris—A constellation in the northern sky.

Ursilaral—"Way of the Spine" (Ûmeri). Main avenue joining the fortified cells of the Library of Sauglish.

Ursranc—The Sranc of Golgotterath, a stock bred by the Consult over thousands of years for strength and obedience, primarily charged with defending the Ark, often used to manage their wilder cousins on the field of battle. They stand more erect (making them appear taller) and are broader through the shoulder—enough to resemble stunted Nonmen as much as Sranc. They are generally armoured in a uniform manner (with black-iron scale hauberks and conical, sometimes brimmed, helms). They are also commonly branded with the wedges symbolizing the Twin Horns.

Ussiliar, Sampë (4091–)—Ordealman, Grandmaster of the Shrial Knights in the Great Ordeal of Anasûrimbor Kellhus.

Usgald—A fiefdom in the Galeoth interior.

Uskelt Wolfheart (?–?)—One of the Chieftain-Kings named in the Tusk.

Utemot—A tribe of Scylvendi located in the northwest extremes of the Jiünati Steppe. Among the Scylvendi, the Utemot are noted as the tribe of both Uthgai and Horiötha, the two greatest conquerors in their history.

Utgarangi ab Hoularji (4059–)—The Sapatishah-Governor of Xerash.

Uthgai (c. 2100–c. 2170)—The folklore hero and Scylvendi King-of-Tribes during the Apocalypse, whose deeds are oft recited in the Scylvendi oral tradition.

V

Valrissa (4086–4112)—A daughter of the Werigda and wife of Aëngelas.

Vaparsi—The lost language of ancient Nilnamesh, a derivative of Shem-Varsi.

Vasnosri—The language group of the Norsirai peoples.

Vast Ingressus—See *Ingressus*.

Vastwhite—Akksersian name given to the unexplored northern wastes extending the length of the Great Kayarsus.

Vault-of-the-Tusk—See *Junriüma*.

Venicata—An Inrithi holy day celebrated in late spring, commemorating the so-called First Revelation of Inri Sejenus.

Vile—Nonman pejorative for Inchoroi. See *Inchoroi*.

Vindauga River—The westernmost of the three major river systems draining into Lake Huösi, and the primary geographical boundary between Galeoth and Cepalor.

virnol—The finger-locking hand shake that Sakarpi warriors reserve for their boonsmen.

Viri—One the Nine Mansions of Eärwa, and the first to be destroyed in the wars against the Inchoroi, located on the northern coasts of the Neleost Sea. Though populous, and though her sons were as widely traveled as those of any other Mansion, Viri was in many ways the most parochial of the Mansions, committed to the spare traditions of their fathers with zeal they saw only as wisdom. They were commonly derided as a result, and therefore more defensive of their characteristic identity than any other Mansion. ("Where the hearts are as callused as the hands, and the vision as crude as the cloth," one chronicler of the *Isûphiryas* notes). They were, for instance, reluctant slavers, and unlike any other Mansion, still possessed Kinnings devoted to agriculture and menial trades, until, that is, Arkfall lead to their ruin and treachery.

Vishrûnûl–"Field Appalling" (Ihrimsû). The Nonman name for Agongorea.

Viturnal Nesting–Grounds to the northeast of Sakarpus periodically frequented by thousands of mating storks.

Vokalati–"Sun-wailers" (Vaparsi). The Major sorcerous School of Nilnamesh, famed for its subtlety, secrecy, and insularity. The Vokalati trace their origins to the very beginning of the Old Invishi period (1023–1572), arising from an informal confederacy under Ogadûl the Great designed to control prices among Invitic magi. They were instrumental to the expansionist ambitions of Anzumarapata II, and even feature in several famed weaves commissioned to commemorate his Far Antique victories. Their first true crisis was none other than Triamis the Great, whose Saka proved their tactical betters on the field of war. The Aspect-Emperor's rout of Sarnagiri V in 2483 left them with no more than six sorcerers-of-rank. Faced with dissolution, the Six, as they would be called, agreed to acknowledge the rule of Imperial Cenei, as well as to perpetually limit their numbers to six. The Vokalati even changed the colours of their emblem–the Sundered Scroll–to the Triamic white and violet, so eager were they to appease Cenei and escape the fury of the Saka.

With the fall of Cenei in 3351, the Vokalati immediately began rebuilding, reestablishing themselves as one of the Great Factions of the Three Seas in three short generations.

Vûkyelt, Hringa (4097–)–Ordealman, Believer-King of Thunyerus, son of Hringa Skaiyelt.

Vulgar Holy War–The name given to the first contingent of the Holy War to march against the Fanim.

W

Wainhail, Swahon (4055–4111)–Man-of-the-Tusk, Galeoth Earl of Kurigald, slain at Mengedda.

Wair Chirsal–The "Fords of the Skull," several miles to the north of Antareg, famed for the Far Antique wars waged upon them (primarily between Golgotterath and Aörsi), and so named for the countless lives they have taken.

wairo–Zeumi folk term meaning "entangled" with the Gods, a somewhat more sophisticated way of thinking "accursed."

Wall of the Dead–Name given to the seaward fortifications of Dagliash following its fall to Golgotterath in 2133.

war, Scylvendi mode of–Despite their illiteracy, the Scylvendi possess an extensive war nomenclature that provides them with a thorough understanding of battle and its psychological dynamics. They call battle *otgai wutmaga*, a "great quarrel," wherein the point is to convince the foe of their defeat. The concepts central to the Scylvendi understanding of war are as follows:

unswaza—envelopment
malk unswaza—defensive envelopment
yetrut—penetration
gaiwut—shock
utmurzu—cohesion
fira—speed
angotma—heart
utgirkoy—attrition
cnamturu—vigilance
gobozkoy—moment of decision
mayutafiüri—ligaments of conflict
trutu garothut—flexible unit cohesion (literally, "men of the long chain")
trutu hirthut—inflexible unit cohesion (literally, "men of the short chain")

War-Cants—The Gnostic sorceries developed in Sauglish (primarily by Noshain-rau the White) for the express purpose of waging war and overcoming opposing sorcerers. See Gnosis.

Wards—The name given to defensive sorceries in contradistinction to offensive sorceries, or Cants. See *sorcery*. The most common types of Wards (found in both Anagogic and Gnostic sorceries) are: Wards of Exposure, which provide advance warning of intruders or imminent attacks; Shield-Wards, which provide direct protection against offensive sorceries; and Skin-Wards, which provide "protection of last resort" against all types of threat.

Warling—In traditional Kunniat faith and the Girgallic Cults of both Inrithism and Zaudunyani-Inrithism, the name given to those ritually committed (typically as children) to the aegis of Gilgaöl, God of War.

Warnute—A fiefdom of Ce Tydonn, one of the so-called Deep Marches of the Upper Swa.

"war of word and sentiment"—The explanation of jnan found in Byantas's *Translations*.

Water—Euphemism for displays of the Psûkhe. Versions include, "Accursed Water," and "Water-that-is-Light."

Wathi Doll—A sorcerous artifact common to Sansori witches, also known as a "murder doll," either because a human sacrifice is required for its manufacture (a soul is imprisoned as the artifact's animus) or because the Dolls are often used as remote assassins.

Wayward, the—See *Erratic*.

Weal—Name given to those suffering memories of the wars against the Inchoroi.

Weeping Mountain—Epithet for Ishterebinth.

Werigda—A Norsirai tribe from the Plains of Gâl.

Werijen Greatheart, Rilding (4063–)—Man-of-the-Tusk, Tydonni Earl of Plaideöl.

Werjau, Sainhail (4070–)—Man-of-the-Tusk, one of the Nascenti, formerly a Galeoth thane.

Wernma River—An extensive river system in east central Eärwa, draining vast tracts of the Dameori Wilderness and emptying into the Meneanor Sea.

Whelming—A hypnotic trance instrumental to Dûnyain Conditioning, and a purificatory rite of induction for the Zaudunyani.

"When sorcerers sing, men die"—The traditional expression used to refer to the fact that sorcery is destructive rather than constructive.

Wiglic—Legendary founder of the Holca, the first Man to possess the second heart that is reputedly the source of their physical strength.

White Jihad—The holy war waged against the Nansur Empire by Fan'oukarji I and the Kianene from 3743 to 3771. See *Kian.*

White Lord of Trysë—An honorific of the Kûniüric High King.

White-Sun Palace—See *Korasha.*

White Yaksh—The traditional tent of Scylvendi tribal chieftains.

Whore, the—A popular name for the Goddess Anagkë. See *Anagkë.*

Wight-in-the-Mountain—The accursed shade of Gin'yursis, the long dead Nonman King of Cil-Aujas.

witches—The name given to women who practice sorcery, despite their persecution by both the Thousand Temples and the Schools.

wizards—The name given to men who practice sorcery independent of any School, despite their persecution by both the Thousand Temples and the Schools.

World Between—The world as it exists "between" our perceptions of it, or "in itself."

World-Breaker—A name for the No-God. See *No-God.*

World-Curse—"*Urimculis*" (Ihrimsû). Name given to the etching upon the Incû-Holoinas.

Worldhorn—A ceremonial sorcerous artifact belonging to the Aörsic House of the Anasûrimbor and lost in the destruction of Shiarau in 2136.

Worm, the—A vernacular name for the great slums of Carythusal.

Wracu—"Serpent" (Ihrimsû, *wracu'jaroi*, or "firesnake"). Also known as Dragons. Immense, fire-spitting, winged reptilian monstrosities created by the Inchoroi during the ancient Cûno-Inchoroi Wars to destroy the Nonmen Quya, then subsequently wielded by the No-God during the Apocalypse. Very few are thought to have survived.

Wreoleth—The capital of the ancient Aorsi province of Illawor, and for a time, the commercial capital of the Far Antique nation. Overrun in the Fall of Aorsi in

2136, a good many refugees dared return to the city during the Investitures of Golgotterath in the time of the Generals. More than half the population had returned when System Initiation occurred in 2142. Most still believed Golgotterath was doomed when the No-God and His Horde engulfed them, trapping them in what would come to be called the Accursed Larder-of-Men, a tract where the Sranc could not go, allowing them to eke out a hard living on that hard land, so that they might be picked as ripened fruit, and fed to whomever—whatever—needed them.

Writ of Psata-Antyu—The proclamation issued by the high clergy of the Thousand Temples at the Council of Antyu (3386) that limits the power of the Shriah. The Writ was motivated by the cruel excesses of Shriah Diagol, who held the Seat from 3371 until his assassination in 3383.

Wutmouth River—The immense river joining Lake Huösi to the Meneanor Sea.

wutrim—A Scylvendi word meaning "shame."

Wutteät—The legendary Father of Dragons, the Unholy Archetype used by the Inchoroi to culture and brood all other Wracu. Also known as the Black-and-Golden, the Terrible.

X

Xatantian Arch—The triumphal arch marking the ceremonial entrance to the Scuäri Campus, which depicts the military exploits of Emperor Surmante Xatantius. See *Xatantius I*.

Xatantius I (3644–93)—The most warlike of the Surmante Emperors of Nansur, Xatantius enlarged the Nansur Empire to its greatest extent, pacifying the Norsirai tribes of the Cepalor and for a time even managing to hold the far southern city of Invishi (though he failed to entirely subdue the Nilnameshi countryside). Despite his military successes, his continual wars exhausted both the Nansur people and the Imperial Treasury, inadvertently laying the groundwork for the disastrous wars against the Kianene following his death. See *Nansur Empire*.

Xerash—A governorate of Kian and former province of the Nansur Empire. Located north of Eumarna on the Meneanor coast, Xerash is primarily known, through *The Tractate*, as the violent and debauched neighbour of Amoteu during the time of Inri Sejenus. See *Amoteu*.

Xerashi—The lost language of scriptural Xerash, a derivative of Vaparsi.

Xerius—See *Ikurei Xerius III*.

Xiangic—The language group of the Xiuhianni peoples.

Xijoser (c. 670–c. 720)—An Old Dynasty God-King of Shigek, known primarily for the Ziggurat bearing his name.

Xinemus, Krijates (4066–4112)—Man-of-the-Tusk, Conriyan Marshal of Attrempus.

Xinemus, Nersei (4121–)—Only son of Nersei Proyas, heir to the throne of Conriya.

Xinoyas, Shressa (4081–4119)—Orthodox Palatine of Etara-Anplei, famously butchered before his own children by the Aspect-Emperor.

Xir'kirimakra—Inchoroi name for the Inverse Fire, which, according to Nonmen sources, apparently translates into the nearly nonsensical, "immersive post-material interface."

Xiuhianni—The black-haired, brown-eyed, olive-skinned race that still dwells beyond the Great Kayarsus. One of the Five Tribes of Men, who, according to *The Chronicle of the Tusk*, refused to follow the other four tribes into Eärwa.

Xius (2847–2914)—The great Ceneian poet and playwright, famed for *The Trucian Dramas*.

Xoägi'i—A Sranc tribe from the Plains of Gâl.

Xothei, Temple of—The primary edifice of the Cmiral temple complex, famed for its three great domes. Built of black basalt.

Xunnurit (4068–)—The Scylvendi chieftain of the Akkunihor tribe.

Y

yaksh—The conical tents of the Scylvendi, made of greased leather and poplar branches.

Yalgrota Sranchammer (4071–4121)—Man-of-the-Tusk, Thunyeri groom of Prince Hringa Skaiyelt, famed for his giant stature and ferocity in war.

Yasellas—A prostitute acquaintance of Esmenet.

Yatwer—The Goddess of fertility. One of the so-called Compensatory Gods, who reward devotion in life with paradise in the afterlife, Yatwer is far and away the most popular Cultic deity among caste-menials (as Gilgaöl is among caste-nobles). In the *Higarata*, the collection of subsidiary writings that form the scriptural core of the Cults, Yatwer is depicted as a beneficent, all-forgiving matron, capable of seeding and furrowing the fields of nations with a single hand. Some commentators have noted that Yatwer is anything but revered in either the *Higarata* or *The Chronicle of the Tusk* (wherein "tillers of soil" are often referred to with contempt). Perhaps this is why Yatwerians tend to rely on their own scripture, the *Sinyatwa*, for their liturgical rites and ceremonies. Despite the vast numbers of adherents enjoyed by the Cult, it remains one of the more impoverished, and seems to generate a large number of zealous devotees as a result. Commonly referred to as the Mother-of-Birth or the Dread Mother in her more vengeful guises.

Yawreg—Easternmost mountain in the Urokkas.

Year-of-the-Tusk—The primary dating system for most mannish nations, which takes the legendary Breaking of the Gates to be year zero.

Years of the Crib—A common term for the eleven years of the No-God's manifestation during the First Apocalypse, wherein all infants were stillborn. See *Apocalypse*.

Yel (4079–)–One of Esmenet's Kianene body-slaves.

Yellow Sempis River–A tributary of the River Sempis.

Yimaleti Mountains–An extensive mountain range located in the extreme north-west of Eärwa. High Norsirai derivation of the Viritic Ihrimsû, "Im'valaral" ("Horizon-has-teeth").

Yinwaul–Land famed for bordering Agongorea and hosting Dagliash. The contested frontier of Aörsi in the centuries preceding the First Apocalypse.

Yoke–A Consult Sranc Legion, so called for the way the Sranc belonging must be chained one to the other to be deployed with anything resembling order. Yokes would be driven to strategic positions, then loosed once the creatures could smell their foes on the wind. Even Yoked, however, the creatures proved unruly, forcing Aurang to continually rely on feint and subterfuge. His Mannish foes responded with a combination of wariness and daring, transforming many of the battles into tests of cunning and patience as much as ferocity and will. At the Battle of Twenty-Yokes in 2142, Aurang managed to lure General Sag-Marmau into Agongorea by concealing his ambush *within a false ambush*, only to watch his Horde destroyed by the Kûniüric adoption of the Aörsic spear-barred shields (which allowed the Sohonc to wreak enormous damage).

Ysilka–The wife of General Sag-Marmau in *The Sagas*, whose name is often used as a euphemism for "adulteress" in the Three Seas.

yursa–A Galeoth liquor made from fermented potatoes.

Yursalka (c. 4065–4110)–A Scylvendi warrior of the Utemot tribe.

Yutirames–A sorcerer of rank in the Scarlet Spires, slain by Achamian in the Sareötic Library.

Z

Zabwiri (4025–4101)–Long time Grandmaster of the Mbimayu, scholar of Memgowa, and Malowebi's master early in his sorcerous training.

Zarathinius (3688–3745)–The famed author of *A Defence of the Arcane Arts*.

Zaudunyani–"Tribe of Truth" (Kûniüric). The name taken by Kellhus's followers during the First Holy War.

Ze, Nurbanu (4105–)–Ordealmen, Palatine of Jekk, adopted son of King Nurbanu Soter, general of the Jekki contingent of the Great Ordeal.

Zealot Wars–The prolonged religious conflict (c. 2390–2478) between the early Inrithi and the Kiünnat, which eventually led to the ascendancy of the Thousand Temples in the Three Seas.

Zenkappa (4068–4111)–Man-of-the-Tusk, Captain of Attrempus, formerly a Nilnameshi slave belonging to the household of Krijates Xinemus, slain at Iothiah.

Zerxei, House–A former Nansur House of the Congregate, and the empire's ruling dynasty from 3511 to 3619, when Zerxei Triamarius III was assassinated by his palace eunuchs.

Zeüm—A mysterious and powerful Satyothi nation beyond Nilnamesh, and the source of the finest silks and steel in the Three Seas.

Zeümi—The language of the Empire of Zeüm, a derivative of Old Zeümi.

Zeümi Sword-Dancers—The members of an exotic Zeümi Cult that worships the sword and has developed sword fighting to an almost supernatural level.

Ziek, Tower of—The prison, located in Momemn, used by the Nansur Emperors to incarcerate their political foes.

Ziggurats of Shigek—The immense stepped pyramids found to the north of the Sempis Delta and raised by the ancient God-Kings of Shigek to serve as their mortuary tombs.

Zikas—The women taken as secondary wives by Anasûrimbor Kellhus, all of whom, according to rumour at least, died in the course of childbirth. The name derives from the small libation bowls used on Ascension.

Zirkirta—See *Battle of Zirkirta.*

Zohurric—See *Aghurzoi.*

Zursodda, Sammu (4064—4111)—Man-of-the-Tusk, Palatine-Governor of the Ainoni city of Koraphea, claimed by disease at Caraskand.

APPENDIX TWO

The False Sun

Beasts only show the white of their eye in terror. Men show it always.
—GOTTAGGA, *The Book of Chalk*

For I have seen the virtuous in Hell and the wicked in Heaven. And I swear to you, brother, the scream you hear in the one and the sigh you hear in the other sound the same.
—Anonymous

1119, Year-of-the-Tusk, the North Shore of the Neleöst Sea.

Like many great and dangerous Men, Shaeönanra was despised for many things, his penchant for mongering spies not the least of them. The rules that bound the Norsirai were unforgiving in those days. Trysë, the Holy Mother of Cities, was little more than a village huddling behind ruined walls of stone. The God-Kings of Imperial Ûmerau stared blindly from overthrown stone, moss-covered and almost forgotten. The Cond ruled the cities of the River Aumris, an empire they called the Great All, and few people were so proud or so headstrong. They divided the Ground between the Feal and the Wirg—the weak and the glorious. They adhered to a simplicity that was at once a fanaticism. And they judged the way all Men were prone to judge in those Far Antique days, without patience or mercy.

Shaeönanra, for his part, celebrated the Cond hatred of spying. What did it matter if they declared him Feal, so long as he knew their secrets? He knew what stout the All-King drank, and what slave decanted it for him. He knew what was bellowed in counsel and whispered across pillows.

Most importantly, he knew what was *plotted*.

So he stood waiting before the gate of his cyclopean tower, Nogaral, staring southward across the heaving leagues of the Neleöst Sea, knowing that soon—very soon—a light would stride across the moonlit waters.

To the west lay the River Sursa, whose rusty waters bloomed far into the Sea during day. Beyond it, the wastes of Agongorea plaited the horizon, chapped and cracked like untanned leather. Low mountains knotted the north and east, domes of bald granite rising from forested slopes: the hunchbacked Urokkas.[1]

Nogaral stood upon the westernmost summit, Iros, a mountain that was a mass grave. Little more than a ramp of blunt granite, it climbed from the River toward the Sea, where it ended in scarped confusion. Ruins made gums and teeth of its heights, structures obliterated in an age that Men could not recollect for ignorance and savagery.[2] Nogaral was both squat and rotund, resembling a monstrous byre more than a proper tower. Only the grand, central chamber could boast any architectural splendour. Otherwise, it was cramped and labyrinthine, the lower levels pillared as densely as a forest, the upper levels celled like a hive.

The construction of the tower had caused an uproar in Sauglish two centuries previous. The Sohonc, in particular, had objected, seeing in it the designs of their old rival, Cet'ingira. Even then they had suspected. But suspicions were not enough to sway an All-King who had grown to prize the Mangaecca and their disdain of scruple.

Nogaral, they named it, the "High Round."

"They are called the Barricades," the Nonman says. "The Artisan himself fashioned them."

The Man gazes in wonder at the configurations of nimil and light. "So that none might enter ..." he murmurs.

Cet'ingira lowers his porcelain face in assent. "So that none might enter."

Shaeönanra almost stumbles, so dazzling is the sunlight across the immense curvatures of gold, so deep is the pitch of the surrounding fall. The Nonman steadies him with a firm hand.

"This was what my master sought? To tear down the Barricades?"

"And his masters before him," the Nonman replies. "For more than two hundred years."

He studies the mad Nonman. "And what lies within?"

The black eyes did not waver. "The truth my brothers could not bear."

At last he glimpsed it, a point like a failing star.

Shaeönanra stood immobile. The Wind came from the north, answering the Sea's long inhalation. It made lunacy of his hair and braids, slapped his robes with a snared thrush's fury. The distant light blinked through it, a white glitter from across the black back of the Sea, vanishing and reappearing as faraway rollers plucked the nocturnal line of the horizon.

The Wind howled about the tower, made moaning flutes of the surrounding ruin. And it comforted Shaeönanra even as its violence forced him to lean against his toes: always at his back, always rushing south, across the Sea and over the Painted Cities, into the eyes of his witless enemies.

The distant spark became more constant, gathered both luminosity and portent as it crept above the blind line of the Neleost. Clouds like scrapes formed a skein across the starry vault. The star the Nonmen called Imburil[3] cast his shadow over the cobble before him, and Shaeönanra considered the wildness of his windblown outline. The Wind and the Nail, Shaeönanra thought in elation. *Both* would be at his back.

This had been an old habit of his, identifying and assessing omens, born of days when he still walked paths that the Gods could reckon. Had he not known *who* was about to darken his threshold, he would have cursed himself for a fool for indulging it.

The light gathered brightness all out of proportion to its approach, and despite the Stain, Shaeönanra found himself wondering at its brilliance. Then finally he saw *him* ... Little more than a region of blackness at first, a shadowy glimpse behind the luminous corona. Then more substantial ... more human.

Titirga.

The Sohonc Archideme walked the low sky, holding high the Diurnal, the famed Day Lantern, a fan of mirrors that reflected the Sun even in the deepest night. The glare climbed as he neared, and Shaeönanra watched the great oblong of illumination—impossible daylight—slip across the stony expanses, reaching out toward Nogaral. It seemed miraculous, the weightlessness of light, the way whole fields of detail and swinging shadows could be dandled in the thin-fingered hands of a man. The Day Lantern scrolled over the rising slopes, then at last caught Nogaral's western curve, where it paused as though fixed. And from night, Shaeönanra found himself staring *into day*—the pitch and scrawl of ruin, the black mortices sketching the stones of the tower's ponderous wall, the knots of scrub and hanging weed. For the first time he saw how shadows were simply pieces of night.

And even though he knew as profoundly—as fanatically—as only a member of the Holy Consult could know, he found himself wondering how it had come to this ...

Shaeönanra could not but marvel. The Sun! The Sun itself raised in the hands of a Man.

Squinting, he could see him, Titirga, his outline gilded in the manner of those peering into the bright outside from the recesses of a dark room. The great Hero-Mage come to deliver his ultimatum. The legendary Archidemu Sohoncu, the Glorious Pupil, perhaps the most powerful sorcerer the Ground had ever known.

At last Titirga saw him below, and the Diurnal answered his sudden attention. Shaeönanra could no more look at the man than he could look into the sun. He raised his arms like a slave in summer fields, and for the first time he witnessed the magic of the Diurnal *from the inside*. Blue skies had been pulled across the void of night. His skin pricked with the promise of sunburn. It was a sight so miraculous as to almost blot the Stain, the premonition of deceit that marred all things sorcerous.

He watched the false sun set in the false sky, then stop, low and bloody as sunset, throwing shadows outward along lines the Nonmen could describe in arithmetic. Titirga had set the Day Lantern down, he realized. The Hero-Mage would deny the advantages that night bestows upon cunning ...

No matter.

The shadow of the walking Archideme reached Shaeönanra long before the man.

"The Diurnal," Titirga called, still a silhouette in the sun's cauldron. "Emilidis gave it to me."[4]

"Archideme," Shaeönanra said in numb greeting.

"Shaeönanra," Titirga replied, coming to a stop mere paces from him. He was tall, broad of shoulder. He wore a Pircondi cloak over his black woolen robes, two wolf-skins sewn together, so that the tailings of the face fluttered side-by-side below his groin. His hair was white, spun with the odd memory of gold. It matched his physique, holding something of its cascading form even in the Wind. But it was his high blunt face that commanded attention: shallow of nose, thick of brow and cheek.

And of course the bronzed skull of an infant child braided into his beard—his famed totem.

"*Archideme*," Shaeönanra repeated, offering the ritual repetition, at once a rebuke and reprieve: to refer to equals by name before formal greetings was an affront among the Umeri. Had the Archidemu Sohoncu at last adopted the crude ways of the Cond?

"You look pale" Titirga said. "It is good that I bring sunlight."

Shaeönanra snorted.

"You Mangaecca," the Hero-Mage continued, "always thinking that Wisdom is a mushroom. The Ground is so broad, and yet you and your brothers insist on *digging deep*."

A sour look.

"Nogaral greets you ... *Archideme*."

Titirga walked about him as if pacing the high corner of a circle. He carried himself as only a master of the Sohonc, the Learned School,[5] could: erect in the manner of nimble, sound-sleeping men, relaxed in the way of high clan-nobility. He gestured to the marmoreal wreckage about them, the stumps of pillars struck in arrested daylight.

"The ruins of Viri."

"The very same," Shaeönanra replied.

"A lesson," Titirga said, "to those who would dig *too* deep."

Shaeönanra sighed conspicuously. "To what do I owe the honour of this visit?" he asked, gesturing for Titirga to enter his vast abode.

"Whispers," Titirga responded, drawing his gaze about him before stepping into the shadow of Nogaral's gate. He was making an inventory, Shaeönanra knew, of all the Wards coiled within the stonework about him.

Nothing that could threaten *him*—certainly.

Casting a final glance at the impossible dusk, Shaeönanra strode forward, baring his back the way the laws of hospitality demanded. He fairly cracked his teeth for apprehension.

He passed beneath the enormous lintel, into the warmth of plastered walls. The Wind's roar was pinched into a chalky whistle. A step ahead of the Hero-Mage, Shaeönanra walked on a bolt of sunlight so bright that, for the first several paces, the braziers were filled with wavering invisibility for fire.

"*Whispers* brought you here?"

"Aye," the man said from behind. "They say that you have *found* something."

Had he not known Titirga, Shaeönanra would have thought him a rank fool, coming here like this, alone. But he knew Titirga's might, and more importantly, he knew the way the man used hectoring boldness to magnify that might. To come here like this was to say he could arrive at any time ...

And that he possessed no fear.

Shaeönanra paused and turned, regarded his old rival. The man had a warrior's face, chipped from fearless bone, everything blunt in the way of shields. "What does it matter what we find?" he said. "The Ark is a riddle without solution."

The first hard moment passed between them.

"Who," the Archidemu Sohoncu replied, "can say which riddles can or cannot be solved beforehand?"

He gazes past the mad Nonman, to the second Horn, vast and golden, its phallic curve canted over the mountainous ruin of the Occlusion.

"*None possessed my cunning.*"

Cet'ingira lowers his chin to his chest.

"*We shall see.*"

"Come," Shaeönanra said. "Loose your gaze. *See.* You will understand what I mean."

He resumed leading Titirga down the main reception hall, "winding the small," as the Nonmen put it, affecting careless questions about the affairs of the All. "Do they still riot in Sauglish?"[6]

"The Library is secure," the Sohonc Insinger[7] said in clipped dismissal. "And yet, I see Nogaral is all but abandoned ..." he added in an airy, peering-around-corners tone. "Just as they say."

The Archideme of the Mangaecca resisted looking back, knowing the Hero-Mage smiled.

"*Who* says?"

At last they outran the final vestiges of the Day Lantern. Their shadows now jumped in counterpoint, sweeping like spiders' legs as they approached and passed each of the corridor's flaming braziers.

"Your *spies*, Shaeönanra."

The Archidemu Mangaeccu managed to stifle his laughter. They walked the remainder of the corridor in silence. Despite his worry, Shaeönanra had occasion to feel shame for the mean and brutish nature of his abode, for in spite of everything, he had been raised an Umeri of the Long-bones, the same as Titirga. He knew the askance judgments, the summary ease of the man's condemnation: Only dogs dwelt in kennels.

But what did it matter, this false home, when their *true* abode would drop any mortal to his knees? The Ark. They could stack a hundred Libraries within it ... A thousand!

At last they entered the broad circle of the Asinna, the expansive hub of Nogaral. A great rug woven of brushed white grasses softened both the floor and the gloom. Bronze tripods glowered golden, casting yellow petals across the weave. Tablet racks fashioned of black ash loomed about the chamber's circumference. Shaeönanra stifled a grin of duping glee, knowing that a stylus had never touched any of them.

He walked toward the lone attendant—a near-naked Scintian slave—who awaited them with refreshment near the centre. He paused and turned when he realized that Titirga had failed to follow him.

"There is someone beneath me," the Hero-Mage said scowling. "Someone *deeply* Stained."

Shaeönanra paused ... nodded. "A precaution, nothing more. It is of no consequence."

Wrath flashed in Titirga's eyes. "Nevertheless, there remains someone *beneath me*. Someone hooded in our shared sin."

They gazed at each other with the flat hostility of lizards. Shaeönanra found himself shirking first, if only to hasten the pantomime—or so he reassured himself. Even still, he could feel the prickle of stink beneath his robes. The ache of expectation in his throat.

"Must I take precautions of my own?" Titirga asked, his voice as mild as blades in water.

The Archidemu Mangaeccu made as if his throat required clearing. "I apologize. He will withdraw."

This earned a heartbeat of avid scrutiny.

"No. I would like to hold him in my eye."

Again, Shaeönanra found himself wilting before the Hero-Mage's glare, exactly (it seemed to him) as he would have in the old days. Paramount among the many worries that had plagued this mad gambit was the fear that he could no longer be the Feal that Titirga would expect him to be, now that death had become his sole horror ...

Now that he had *seen*.

"Very well," Shaeönanra conceded, bowing in the shallow, cursive way of the

Umeri. He turned to the attendant. "Summon our ..." He paused as if at the humour of the word Onkhis had delivered to him. "Our *guest*."

His terror plain, the young slave scampered into the gloom of the nearest hallway. Shaeönanra resumed suffering Titirga's onerous regard ...

And contempt, as it turned out.

"They speak of you often in Ûmerau and Sauglish," Titirga said, his manner sinister for being so bland. "They *say* you have the eyes of a serpent ..."

Shaeönanra smiled. Vanity had been a well-known flaw of his, yes. He had preened in the days before ...

"No. Just a dog. No different than other Men."

What a child he had been.

They call it the Threshold, a narrow phalange of iron set high upon the Upright Horn, the hanging porch of the Barricades, which the Ishroi of old had raised about the uppermost sanctum of their wicked foe. You can see the Nonman there as much as not, sitting on the edge, where the air is too thin for fat men to breathe, waiting for souls more ordered than his own to tear down the Barricades.

"What the Artisan has wrought ..." Shaeönanra says to him.

"Does not seem possible."

The Archidemu Mangaeccu nods.

"Yes ... But only if you look at it as something to be forced."

Tears well in the Nonman's eyes. "What are you saying?"

"Some doors need not be broken."

The attendant reappeared, pale, eyes anxious unto rolling. A raggish shadow lurched beyond the threshold behind him, a movement that would have been limping were it not balanced leg for leg. At the last instant Shaeönanra turned to watch the mighty Titirga's face ...

He saw the famed eyes slacken, dull—even weary in the manner of wise men grasping the inevitability of horrific futures. How many years of concerned watching? How many months of labourious counsel, fretting *this very possibility* ...

An odour of sweat and fish insinuated the chamber.

They stood thus, motionless. Something fluid had entered the breathing silence of the room. A fluttering of mucous and membrane.

Even though nothing was said, Shaeönanra could see it plain in the Hero-Mage's look.

True. The dread rumours were true.

The Archidemu Mangaeccu turned to the newcomer as much to conceal his smile as to bask in the glory of his foul image. For he had literally wept upon finding him and his brother, wept for joy, knowing that the two could decipher the horror of what they had seen.

The creature stood naked, as was his wont, his wings folded into wicked hooks about either side of his great skull, which would have been cumbersome, had it not curved into a crest, narrow and deep, like an oyster set on end. A proportionate face hung from the fore, loutish with the absence of expression, nostrils drawn into shining gashes, sockets plugged with lobes of bare white meat. A second face filled the mouth, sheathing a second skull fused within the crocodilian jaws of the greater. Second eyes regarded the Hero-Mage with leering expectation. Second lips grinned about teeth like nails ...

The light cast by the tripods slicked the creature in lines of luminous white, yellow and crimson, but otherwise, the intestinal translucence of its skin rendered it devoid of colour—the pallor of things drawn from the depths. Though he stood no more than half again as tall as man, he seemed enormous: for the wings, for the fiendish stoop, for the webbing of stone-dense muscle ...

And Shaeönanra could feel the tugging glamour, the promise of surrender within irresistible limbs. He could feel his own ardour rise, an answering will to be taken ... ravished!

Aurang ... a fabled *Inchoroi* ... A creature out of legend and childhood terror.

His lover.

"He bears the Stain as deeply as any Quya ..." Shaeönanra heard Titirga say from behind him. The Mangaeccan Archideme turned from his infatuation to face his hated foe.

"Is this why you await me thus?" the Hero-Mage said. He bent his head in a curious, almost Cunuroi way, as if some rage to kill bent him from within. "Do you think that combined you could rival me?"

And Shaeönanra knew that this was no *ploy*, that Titirga *would*, without a breath of hesitation, deliver his impossible fury to his tower. He had heard the tales—the whole Ground had heard the tales. Titirga Mithalara, they called him—the Giver of Mercy!—ironic renown for his ruthless extermination of his foes. He was certainly the most powerful Insinger ever born. And if what Cet'ingira said was true, the most powerful, period. No living Quya had the purity of his Recitations. Even his Stain was different, somehow muted, as if he could cut the Inward without scarring it. Even now, simply regarding him, his distinction literally glared from his image, a strange, sideways rinsing of the Stain.

The vital difference. The threat.

They said he had been blind as a child, that Noshainrau himself had found him begging in the streets. They said he went mad while Canting. They said his words seized things that should not be seized.

Shaeönanra gestured to the attendant to dispense the *sere*.[8] The fool almost fumbled the vessels for terror.

"Rival you?" he replied under cover of this trivial distraction. "The Ground is at peace. The Scintya are pacified.[9] The All-King watches from Ûmerau." He turned with a bronze vessel that Titirga waved away.

"Aurang is my guest," he said, sipping the burning liquor.

The Hero-Mage did not shout or rave. He did not need to, so grating was the resolve of his voice.

"It is *Inchoroi*."

The man spat the name with its clipped, Nonman inflection, the hatred of his teachers cracking his voice. Inchoroi. For the first time, he let slip his Umeri face—the one that would claim all judgment for itself, such was the gulf that divided the Feal from the Wirg—and *beseeched* his rival Archideme.

"Shaeönanra ... *Think!*"

Think. No word was so raw with ancient assumption.

The Archidemu Mangaeccu simply regarded his Sohonc counterpart, the way one might regard a fool brother who has yet again spoken foolishly. Something scarcely perceptible hardened the man's stance and manner.

"I will not implore you a second time, old friend."

Finally. A genuine threat. Shaeönanra pursed his lips against the tickle of his thin mustache, sighed as if in profound resignation. He glanced at the black coin of *sere* swinging in the bottom of his appropriated cup, downed it with a gasp.

How could the man know? Even with his rumoured Grace. There was no going back, no undoing what had been done, no unseeing. Shaeönanra had committed unspeakable ... nay, *unthinkable* ... acts. They all had. Debaucheries. Desecrations of self and other. Shrieks for cries of passion. Blood for grease. Mere recollection set his skin afire, such was the orgiastic ecstasy. He had exalted in the trackless void, the hole where good and evil had once been.

And he had *resolved*. Resolved most of all, for *he had seen*.

⸙

He watches the true sun rise above the horizon's crown, low and bloody as sunset, throwing shadows outward along lines the Nonmen could describe in arithmetic. He can sense Cet'ingira's desperation, so he prolongs the reverie, pretending to wonder at the fragments of darkness scoring the broken landscape below.

Then he turns to the Barricades, examines its fractal complexities.

He begins to sing ...

His voice slips the point of vocalization, drops outward in every direction, until all of Creation sings with him. Between his hands, a needle of raw incandescence twists into existence, shines with a brilliance undimmed by the glare of dawn.

Shaeönanra turns to the great Nonman Quya. "Do you see, old friend?"

Cet'ingira stands gazing, parsed by the sun into silken light and dolphin shadow. A

vulture rides a great arc in the blue emptiness behind him, ragged and black. More and
more, the scavengers have taken to circling the Horns.

"The Barricades," he continues. "They fold ... intervals. Somehow Emilidis found a
*way to pinch emptiness into angles. This was why no dispensation of sheer force could
batter them down ... In a sense, everything you and my predecessors threw at it simply
... missed."*

The black eyes pierce him. "And what is this?"

"A Mathesis Pin ... A derivative of an ancient Entelechy Theorem. It whittles force
down to an arithmetical point—pricks where all else bludgeons ..."

Wonder dawns in the ancient gaze. "A force that does not occupy space ... cannot be
redirected in space."

"Yes," Shaeönanra says. "My gift to you."

He could feel it all the time, what he had seen, feel it like worms in his bones, rotting
him, making him less substantial than what he was, a tingling fog, a meaty flex. Horror
now thumbed the edges of his every sensation.

The image of his Damnation.

"Who are *you* to condemn?" Shaeönanra cried in the mock way of too-learned
Men. "The Schools have no stake in *Nonman* wars."

This much was true. The Siqu were loathe to speak of the War—even Cet'ingira,
who had led the Mangaecca to the Ark and the revelation of the Xir'kirimakra. Their
feud with the Inchoroi was theirs and theirs alone, so much so they denied their Mannish pupils all but the most elliptical knowledge of it.

But Titirga frowned as if at a tiresome juvenile. "Who are *you* to decide our stake?"

Shaeönanra stood blinking, cursing. "How?" he cried, holding an arm out to the
hoary majesty of Aurang. "How can you fools not see how *small* this makes us?"

"Plainly," Titirga replied, frowning at the creature's groin.

"Fool! The stakes of *everything* have been rewritten! Everything!"

At long last fury clenched Titirga's brow.

"What was sane before we knew of the Ark remains sane now! Shaeönanra! This
thing is ... is *obscene!*"

Why could they not see? They were every bit as damned as he—*damned!* What
overriding reason could there be? What possible logic could annul Eternity?

"The *sky*, Titirga! Think! The *sky is an endless void*. Each star is another Sun, like our
own, and *Grounds spin about them*—whole Grounds hanging like motes in the Great Void!"

He was not simply offering them salvation, he was showing them *sanity!*

"Other Grounds?" Titirga cried with a derisive bark, and why not? when the
Ground was by definition the basis of everything. It was just as Aurax had said. Truth
becomes ignorance when Men make gods of Deceit.

"I know how this sounds," Shaeönanra said. "But what of the Ark? The Inchoroi? They prove the existence of other Grounds, do they not? Grounds like our own!"

"*Noooo ...*" the glistening Inchoroi rasped, speaking an archaic intonation of Ihrimsu, his inhuman voice falling like a flake of ice upon sweaty skin. He had stepped into Shaeönanra's blind flank and now loomed over him, his frame a sleek motley, like fish skinned and sutured together. "*Not like your own.*"

The Hero-Mage fairly gaped at the creature.

"It speaks to me."

"*This Ground ...*" Aurang continued, oblivious to his transgression. "*This Ground is the one Promised. Salvation lies within your grasp. Salvation in* this *life ...*"

Insolence.

"Other Voices must *commend* yours before you speak," Shaeönanra said to the creature, trusting the savagery of his backward glance to serve as warning.

But Aurang continued his shining scrutiny of Titirga. A transgression that Shaeönanra found unnerving.

"*Do you not fear damnation?*"

A careful look from the Hero-Mage.

"The Nonmen ..." he said evenly. "They have taught us how to hide our Voices. How to bypass the Outside, find Oblivion."

Eyes like bladders of ink, each reflecting the tripods across their shining curve. The fluting of gill-tissues along the neck. "*You worship the spaces between the Gods ...*"

"Yes."

A rasp like the screams of faraway children tangled in the wind. Inchoroi laughter. "*You are already damned. All of you are already damned.*"

"So say you."

A deep chested rumble. Popping mucous. "*So says the Inverse Fire.*"

A flush of horror. Shaeönanra tensed against the sudden loosening in his bowel, not quite believing that the Inchoroi had dared name it aloud. *Xir'kirimakra.* The Inverse Fire. For a heartbeat he found his Voice divided between mere fear and what mattered. What? Did Aurang seek to *seduce* the Sohonc Archideme? Could he not see that Titirga was not one to suffer rivals, that *Shaeönanra himself* would be doomed were he to embrace their Holy Consult?

But these were vain questions. They fell away as quickly as Onkhis offered them up, so flimsy were the concerns that moved them. All that mattered, the Ground's only consequential thing, was *what he had seen ...*

Damnation.

Experience shredded into a thousand strings, each clawed and burned and burned, sucked like bottomless bones. Agony. Anguish. Horror. Lament. Shame ... Shrieking-thrashing-screaming through the throat of his every memory, innumerable and one, groaning-choking-vomiting, his every particle a unique agony, a bereavement,

a weeping-howling-scratching out eyes that grew and grew to witness anew, while
burning-blistering-breaking—

It defeated the tongue, the intellect, what he had seen. Nevertheless it was *in him*,
every moment in him, if not at the centre of his care then beneath, a hole that endlessly gnawed at his gut ...

A terror, so profound, so abiding—and, yes, *pure*—that all other fears guttered into
nothingness for lack of air. A terror *that was a gift* ... such was the peace and certainty
that followed upon it.

They had conjectured, the Mangaecca. They had experimented. They had taken
captives and inflicted every possible agony simultaneously all in the name of some
flimsy purchase, some scant knowledge of Hell. Drawing toenails, while crushing gen-
itals, while setting afire, while murdering children, raping wives, strangling mothers,
blinding fathers ... They had visited lunatic misery on innocents, and they had found
themselves utterly impervious, immune to the least remorse. Some of them had
even laughed.

What was earthly anguish compared to what awaited them? Singular. Ephemeral.
Little more than a bauble laid upon the monumental steps of the wretchedness to
come. They were deluded fools, the Schoolmen of the Sohonc. Every one of them
lived making belief—even more, making witless and numb—when it came to their
Voices. It was *sorcery* they coveted, the lure of the power—such potency! The Voice
had a way of walling off the future when power was at hand.

All Men wailed. All Men burned all the time. They need only die to realize it.

"So that is the source of your madness," Titirga said. "The Inverse Fire."

Shaeönanra closed his eyes against a shudder. "So you know of it ..." he said on a
long intake of breath.

"Nil'giccas told me. Yes."

"He told you of the Three? The Three who entered the Golden Court of Sil during
the Scourging of the Ark."

"Upon the Upright Horn ... Yes."

"So you know what happened."

A draft whisked through the chamber, the kind that washes over a floor of cloistered air in a flood. The golden infant skull braided into the Hero-Mage's beard
seemed to laugh for the to-and-fro sway of the fires potted upon the bronze tripods.
It struck Shaeönanra that Titirga had stood absolutely motionless ever since setting
foot in the Asinna. He seemed hewn of heavy oak as it was, but standing as he did,
glaring from Man to Inchoroi to Man again, he almost seemed a thing of stone. Indestructible.

"Min-Uroikas had fallen," the Hero-Mage replied. "The Ishroi laboured in vain
to destroy the Ark, as did the Quya. They knew of the Golden Court, the Inver—"

"From Nin-janjin," Shaeönanra found himself interrupting. Why? Why did they insist on repeating its name? A thing need not be named to be spoken of ...

"Yes ... From Nin-janjin," Titirga repeated, something not quite identifiable sparking in his eyes. "And because they knew, Nil'giccas chose the Three to enter it. Two Ishroi, renowned for their valour—Misariccas and Runidil—and one Quya ..." He paused as though to set his teeth against his hatred. "Cet'ingira."

Shaeönanra found himself turning to the Inchoroi, cackling, crying, "He knows!" in a voice too maniacal to be his own. "He *knows!*"

"I know only what Nil'giccas told me. That Misariccas and Runidil returned shrieking—"

Yes. Shaeönanra had also shrieked ... for a time. And wept.

"—and that Cet'ingira counselled his King to have them killed."

A barking laugh. "And did he tell you *why?*"

A moment of fierce scrutiny.

"Because they could not be trusted. Because they had been ensorcelled ... *Possessed.*"

"No!" Shaeönanra heard himself cry. "No!" Could this be him, wagging his head like a fly-maddened ox, gesticulating like an old hag at a funeral? "Because they had *seen the Truth!*"

Titirga gazed with undisguised distaste. "Such is the form of all possession. You know as mu—"

"Nooo!" Shaeönanra cried. "Nil'giccas *lied to you!* What else could he do? Think! Think of the war they had just won—think of the toll! The Nonmen had sacrificed *everything*, their wives, their daughters, to triumph over the Inchoroi. And now they discover that all along *the Truth belonged to their foe?*"

The Archidemu Mangaeccu began berating himself even before he finished, such was the unmanly violence of his expression. He had to recollect himself ... Recall! He had to own what happened here, not for the sake of Men—for none would ever know—but for the sake of his immortal Voice.

"Nil'giccas lied to his Ishroi," he continued, speaking on a long drawn breath, "just as he deceived you. He lied *because he had to!*"

Titirga stood watching him, his fulsome lips hanging open in hesitation. And Shaeönanra rejoiced, knowing even the mighty Hero-Mage had his doubts. That the Mangaecca could be seduced was no surprise, for they had always placed knowledge before honour. But Cet'ingira? The most famed of the Siqu? For that matter, how could *any* Nonman enter into a pact with *Inchoroi?*

Unless ...

Shaeönanra cackled, feeling a new deliberation sop the wildness from his bones.

"Horrifying, isn't it? Titirga. *Hero* of Ûmerau. Disciple of *Noshainrau.* To think that *everything* you have believed, you have believed for naught. A whole life expended, toiling, condemning, *murdering*, all in the name of misapprehension!"

The gaze of an old and undefeated chieftain.

"What has become of you, old friend."

Shaeönanra had expected many things from this visit, but never that it would become so *quaint.*

"Yes," he said on a sigh. "You *did* know me before. You knew many of us.[10] You knew how fractious we were, how given to mercenary pursuits, all the Mannish flaws that you Sohonc used to evidence your superiority. You remember when *gold* was all that you needed to induce treason ..."

He raised a hectoring fist, one Royal Umeri to another. "And now you hear the whispers ... the *rumours* ..." He drew his hand out to embellish the sarcasm. "Your torturers shake, so deep they must reach!"

He had stepped forward as he spoke, coming to a halt directly before the Hero-Mage and his legendary wrath. Something in the man's height and proportion made him think of the Nonmen heroes, and how they never ceased growing.

"Possessed, you tell yourselves. *Possessed!* We are different because we are no longer *ourselves.* You counsel the All-King to crack our Seal, destroy us and all we have toiled to achieve. Our Voices are polluted, unclean!" He threw his back in Feal laughter, cackled with spite and glee. "So tell me, if we are possessed, *who* is our new owner?"

"The Tekne," the Archidemu Sohoncu said with grim confidence. "The Mangaecca have been enslaved. *You* have been enslaved."

Shaeönanra blinked. Of course the fool was unmoved. Of course he had *his* reasons. No matter. This was indulgence, arguing like this, availing reason.

He warred with his expression—something between a grimace and a grin. "Yes ... But *who* is our new master?"

A peculiar weariness haunted Titirga as he shook his maned head: one not so much of as *for.*

Feal, something whispered from his gaze.

"A lunatic God ... perhaps. The Hells that you think you see. *Something* ... Something adulterate, foul. Something that craves feasting, that hungers with an intensity that can bend the very Ground."

Aurang had stood silent during this time, gazing down at the two bickering men. After the intimacies they had shared, it seemed Shaeönanra could sense the pulse of his passion. Lust in the lazy tumescence of his member. Impatience in the incline of his shield-long head. Hatred in the flicker of membranes ...

"Does that not trouble you?" the Hero-Mage pressed. "That you have but *one* eye!"

Tedious. Tedious. Tedious.

"*Why,* Titirga?" Shaeönanra implored. "Why have you come here?" He shook his head, arguing with the floor. "Did you hope to show me my folly?" And it all seemed a pantomime, this incontinence of voice and expression. For beneath, he knew exactly what he needed to do. He could feel it, the certainty of snakes coiled in the darkness, the confidence of things that neither run nor sleep. "There's no folly in what I do, I *assure* you. I know. *I have seen!*" He jerked his face back, squinting and scowling. "What are your reasons compared to this? Your guesses? Your rumours of a dead age?"

"But *what*, Shaeönanra? What is it you have seen? Your *damnation* or your *goad*?"

"Did you hope to strike a bargain?" Shaeönanra exclaimed, spinning to face the Hero-Mage. "Or did you come here to *cow* me, to strut and boast and discourse, thinking that the throat of my design might choke on the bone of your glorious presence?"

The Hero-Mage had stalked him in a curious, distanced way, careful to move at tangents that would keep him facing both of his antagonists, Mannish and Inchoroi. His manner, which had seemed lazy with arrogance but a moment earlier, had become wary, expectant.

"Titirga ... Did you come here to *kill*?"

For the first time the man surprised him.

"Of course I did."

Six days.

Six days Cet'ingira, the most-famed of the Siqu, the Most-feared-and-hated, stands upon the High Threshold, the arcane bass of his voice climbing from the pores of all that could be seen, his arms outstretched, a myriad of Mathesis Pins drawn into a circle of sparking white before him, a disc of needles, endlessly pricking the fractal intricacies of the Barricades.

And Shaeönanra, the Balancer's son who had risen to become Archidemu Mangaeccu, Master of the Cunning School, felt a different fear hiss through the anxious hum of his schemes. He retreated as if in disgust, took four steps, steeling himself against the impulse to cringe—because at any instant, any heartbeat, he could find himself cut or bludgeoned or blasted from this world and—

"Kill *me*?" he heard himself say, his tone far from manly.

The Hero-Mage laughed his famed laugh, the one that had inspired so many lays. With his beard and wolf-skin cloak, he looked both savage and indomitable, every bit as elemental as the legends painted him. With his Stain, drawn and tinctured in a manner no Man or Nonman had ever seen, he seemed outrageous with power.

"No, my friend," he said, letting his gaze stray to the Inchoroi, hulking and inhuman. "I have come to kill this ... *obscenity*."

A new Age was dawning. Since the First Father, Men had always *spoken* to command the Ground. Since the Shamans, they had called and Reality had answered, a brother, a deceiver, an assassin. But there *was another way*, one without the treacherous hooks of meaning, one built *up out of* the granules of existence, the way termites raise their multiform wattle. A power that could be crafted and shaped, that could be applied to its own proliferation, and so accelerate, radiating out across the span of need and desire. A power that could uproot cities and hurl them across the Void.

The Tekne.

Mechanism. Only mechanism could save their Voices.

"Perhaps it is fitting," Titirga said to the glistening Inchoroi, advancing a step. "Perhaps this is your Doom, to die here on the grave of Viri."[12]

Wheezing silence.

"*Shaeönanra*," Aurang finally said. "*I tire of this.*"

"Patience, my brother," the Mangaeccan Archideme replied, drawing the Inchoroi back by the forearm, pressing him to the perimeter of the grand room.

It would happen soon.

"Brother?" the Hero-Mage cried, his voice cracked with what seemed genuine dismay, pained incredulity. "You call this monstrosity *brother*?"

Only now was it dawning on the fool, the intimacy of their pact, the truth of their Holy Consult. Only now, Shaeönanra realized, could he see how profoundly Damnation had conjoined them.

Man. Nonman. Inchoroi.

Six days. Until his voice dwindled to a rasp. Until blood fell from his nose, tracing the branches of his grimace. Six days singing.

Titirga strode toward him, to the centre of the Asinna, the point where all the glittering fires overlapped. Shaeönanra resisted the urge to raise his arms in warding. He understood why the bards called him the Bull in their songs. The way he lowered his face to glare through his brows. How he puffed out his chest, huffed fury through his flared nose. How he trembled for rage ...

Titirga was the very embodiment of the Wirg, a true Long-boned Son of Ûmerau. He used all the tools the Gods had bequeathed him, including his famed stature. He always came close ... eventually ... always *loomed*, carrying the stink of the garlic they so prized in Sauglish.

Vanity. Nothing makes Men more predictable.

"You will *answer* for this, Shaeönanra!"

The Archidemu Mangaeccu turned his back on the Hero-Mage for a third and final time. He glanced at Aurang, who fairly hunched over his famished loins—an Inchoroi battle stance.

"You! Will! Face! Me! Feal!"

He nodded to the black shining eyes.

"*Face me!*" Titirga thundered, his voice booming so raw that spiders seemed to scuttle across Shaeönanra's spine and back. "Need I *show* you the fact of your Damnation!"

A sorcerous word sizzled across the corners of everything. Aurang's eyes flared crimson.

"Face me or di—!"

A crack of wood and stone, beam and joist. Shaeönanra whirled just in time to see it happen: the floor dropping, the brushed rug sucked down, folding into ravines about the falling Hero-Mage, the tripods tipping outward, fires bursting into sparks, the whole slipping into the plummet, a great white iris dropping into deeper stages of gloom—

Gone.

Shaeönanra finds the Nonman thus, sprawled unconscious before the Barricades—or what remains of them. He kneels at his side, lays fingers on his cheek. Warm. He looks to the shattered portal, to the hanging plates, the mangle of the Stain. His immobility shocks him as much as his terror shames. He has always been proud with power, Shaeönanra, knowing that even the Quya wonder at his subtlety. But now he is simply a Man, a lowly mortal, and he can smell his own stink taint the aura of burning.

The true sun is rising behind him.

The shadow of the Threshold arcs across the soaring cylinder of gold. He sees his frail silhouette hunched atop it. And he watches it descend, as inexorable as the rising dawn, sinking into the maw of the broken Barricades.

He shivers uncontrollably.

Only when the sun has drawn even to his height, when the first light draws his outline into the blackness within, does he stand upon the spine of his own shadow.

How? How could mere knowledge command such horror?

He will see for himself.

The whole centre of the chamber, gone.

It was not for nothing the Mangaecca had come here. It was not for nothing they had raised Nogaral upon the ruins of ancient Viri. Intent on plundering the dead Mansion, they took the vast pit they had discovered—the Viritic Well—as the axle of their construction. And so unknowingly created the one trap that could destroy the famed Titirga.

A great dank rose from the blackness, the stench of a mountain rotted with hollows. In ancient times the Well had sounded Viri, a city as magisterial as Ishterebinth, and *deep*, struck to the Ground's very root. Shaeönanra teetered for a moment, his senses unbalanced by the cavernous absence before and below. He steadied himself, then leaned to better cast his spit after his foe.

"*Tikhhus pir yelmor graum nihal!*"[13] he cried, the ancient curse of his forefathers.

He glimpsed a white twinkle sparking far below, a tube of surrounding stone. A sorcerous mutter climbed from the bottomless reek ...

He blinked in disbelief.

"*Quickly,*" the nude Inchoroi cried, a noise like a dog's cough.

He walks into the golden gloom, squinting, staring. Dust puffs about his feet, particles blooming in the intrusive brilliance of the sun, then vanishing into the flanking darkness. He peers ... notices a different luminance wavering across the interior, more fluid and sultry, webbed as though refracted through waters ...

Canto of Concussion. So the Man and the Inchoroi began, blasting the circular lip, striking great fractures into the grain of the rock, so that the Well's mouth sloughed into its throat, a rumbling, clacking torrent. They pulled down the rooves of the Asinna, baring the deceit that was high blue sky. They stepped into the sunlight ...

The Inchoroi beat his great scabbed wings, rising high upon the relentless Wind, spiralling like a vulture about a failing beast; the Man stood upon the earth's phantom, hanging. Their skulls were as chalices of arcane light.

Their disparate voices seemed thrown from the horizon's farthest corners, the mutter of petulant Gods. And the light of the Diurnal bathed them, so they seemed to glow in the way of things held high in the sun's declining light. Their own shadows halved them, so that from certain angles they seemed naught but the rims of who they once were.

Quyan sorceries inscribed the empty spaces. Structure collapsed into the afterimage of searing geometries. Aurang husked the tower from without as he sailed in broad circles, slowing into a climb when turning to the Wind, then swooping about in a descending arc. The Diurnal's arcane sun warmed cloth, pinched skin. Shaeönanra gouged the tower from within, hanging above the cratered Asinna, his hair and garment lashed into fins and ribbons. Sections of wall pitched into blackness, roared against the throat of the Well. Furnishings glittered like tossed torches, scraped and skidded, trailing clouds of orange sparks before blackness encompassed them.

Together they pulled down Nogaral, the High Round, raised it into a heap over the mouth of the Well.

He hears it, a faraway wind, the groan of impossible multitudes—the collective shriek. His lungs become as stone. Horror makes pins of his skin. And he feels it, the burning vaults above, the smoldering glimpses ...

Shaeönanra raises his eyes.

⸙

At last they paused to regard their labour, the Inchoroi alighting upon the same spectral floor that bore Shaeönanra. Crimson sunlight bathed the southern ramps, inking the numberless crevices across the wrack and ruin. And they rejoiced, Man and Inchoroi ...

They had no inkling of the greater violence their sorcery had unleashed.

The sky cracked. Iros shuddered. The impossible sun tipped and stumbled. Plumes of ejecta exploded from points along the mountain's perimeter, scarcely visible for the Diurnal's encompassing glare. The mound that had been Nogaral shrugged then slumped into its contradiction. It was as if a dome of cloth had been pressed into a dimple. Summit became basin. Illumination became shadow. The mountain had been rotten with Viri, its innumerable ways fractured by the cataclysmic impact of the Ark thousands of years before. The underworld mansion imploded, collapsed inward and downward, tier upon tier, hall upon hall, undone by this final indignity. This last outrage.

The Man and the Inchoroi toppled with it. Though suspended, they remained bound to the earth, and as with all drastic changes of circumstance, the meaning of their sorcery ceased to be. Only Aurang's wings saved them. The Inchoroi seized the Man from kicking emptiness, bore him up beyond the Diurnal blue into the truth that was cold and night.

They set foot upon the depression's edge. The Day Lantern painted a dishevelled landscape, drawing their shadows into the darkness of the great concavity below. The earth still shivered, resounded with hidden percussions, knocking dust into smoky halos about the debris.

Shaeönanra laughed in the crazed, marvelling way of children who find their destruction multiplied beyond belief. Once again, he succumbed to the sacrilege of Fate, he who walked ways invisible to the Gods. He exulted at this Sign, rejoiced that his hated foe would have a pit and not a barrow to memorialize his fall. And as the echoes trailed into cavernous thunder, he began singing, as a true Long-boned Son of Ûmerau should,

> *Your pride lies shattered with your shield,*
> *Your wrath curls bleeding upon the field,*
> *Now you linger in my shade weeping,*
> *Mourning an honour that is my keeping,*
> *Praying for children who are mine to enslave,*
> *Beseeching lovers who are mine to deprave.*

So the Archidemu Mangaeccu intoned: a paean for his vanquished enemy, a lament that was at once a psalm to his own glory—and the might of their Holy Consult.

For nothing mattered apart from what they had seen. Nothing.

They coupled on the smoking slopes, Man and Inchoroi, their silhouettes entangled, arching against a skewed, perpetually setting sun. They grunted for wonder, wheezed with ecstasy. They gazed in delirium, cried out across the great bowl of ruin, over flames arrayed in descending echelons, like teeth growing out a shark's throat.

And daylight Stained everything, a false pocket of sun in the night.

The infinite night.

ENDNOTES

[1] As the Norsirai called them. The Nonmen called them the Vir'holotoi, the "Wards-of-Viri."

[2] The Blessed Falling, when the Flesh-Angels first descended from the Void.

[3] "The Newborn." The star that Men call the Nail of Heaven.

[4] The Artisan. The Siqu founder of the School of Contrivers, the Mihtrûlic.

[5] Founded by Gin'yursis, Holy Siqu, in the time of Nincama-Telesser (574-668).

[6] This was a tumultuous time in the history of the Cond Empire, when Scintya depredations forced the All-King, the much maligned Aulyanau Cawa-Imvullar (c. 1091-1124), to levy punitive taxes upon the All.

[7] Derived from the Ancient Umeri term for "sorcerer," derived in turn from ancient shamanistic Hulwa Ilruga, "the Bottomless Inward."

[8] A kind of whiskey smoked in peat.

[9] Untrue, insofar as Aulyanau Cawa-Imvullar (c. 1091-1124) was forced to pay the White Norsirai tribes of the Scintya tribute, the amount of which was never disclosed, but was apparently substantial enough to cripple Cond Ûmerau over time.

[10] The Sohonc, which was by far the largest of the Tutelage Schools, could boast only some fifty sorcerers of rank (at this time). The Mangaecca, it could be assumed, possessed no more than thirty.

[11] Treasurer.

[12] An indirect reference to the fact that Viri was destroyed by the falling of the Ark, which is to say, by the Inchoroi.

[13] "So death denies you your lesson."

APPENDIX THREE

Four Revelations

You drink of the River and it is clear. You drink of the River and it is foul. You breathe of the Sky and it never empties. You weep, and the Sea stings your lips. Rejoice, and mourn, for you belong to this World.

Heaven does not know you.

—NIN'HILARJAL, Psalms to Oblivion

The World is a glare when you are helpless.

The Men had bound him, pierced his flesh with nails, but their terror so overmatched their hatred, they were gentle, and so left no memory of their indignity. They shout and laugh. *Papa ...* A walnut tree stands upon the rising pasture beyond them, great with age and solitude, dark with interior shadow. *Please, Papa ...*

Aisralu!

A woman who has outlived her teeth scourges him with thistles. Her arms are frantic with hatred and heartbreak, her knobbed knuckles shake, but her eyes remain slack with incredulity ... eyes that were once daring and mercurial, grown stagnant at the bottom of crinkled pockets. For the first time he realizes he has never understood Men, the way they toil against the yoke of dwindling years. The way they do not so much fail as are betrayed.

The Horns rear golden, so high as to hook the woolen sky. The Host of the Nine Mansions groans.

They raise him upon a pole, pile sheaves of bracken about his feet. He has wondered whether death would be beautiful. He has wondered how the end of memory would appear at memory's end. He has wondered what it means to so outrun glory as to become blind to disgrace. It seems proper that these screeching animals show him.

He watches them tip the amphorae, sees the oil pulse white in the sun. They are all there: Tinnirin, Rama, Par'sigiccas, sheeted in the blood of obscenities, their warcries cracked into gasps of effort, grunts of desperation. As the Men stand milling in the sun-

light, filthy, bestial for hair, their brows dark so their eyes seem fires in angry caves. Rama's
head tips back like a bust on an unbalanced pedestal, painting witless shoulders in blood,
as a plummeting shadow blots him, an Inchoroi monstrosity, decked in the corpse of
some luckier brother. And he sorts them with his gaze, his frail captors, glimpsing dog-
teeth, gloating for all the faces he will remember, for shame if not for torment. As Quya
Chariots soar like polished stones cast against the sky. *Rama! Rama!* And a torch is
brought forth, little more than a smoking blur in the open sunlight; a wave of exclamation peaks in a raw little cheer. As Ciogli makes a bastion of the Father of Dragons, his
shouts ringing from his cauldron helm, Bashrag slumping from the arc of his hammer.
A sobbing boy-child takes the torch. He and his brothers cry, *Lord Mountain!* Bullied
forward, he turns to him, sobbing, the torch held like a poisonous snake. The Horns
rise as golden haze through pitched skies, distant Quya drifting like sparks from the
evening fire, dragons like twirling soot, making deep a World crabbed with violence. So
like his dead sister in the dove-breasted beauty of his cheek (though she had hated fear
more) Great Ciogli teeters, and the hacking floor drops into watery insignificance ....

"Papa *hates* that he is my image," she says, laughing, squinting as if about to sneeze
at the sunlight.

How could ... How could ...

Great Ciogli teeters, his head turning as if to catch some uncommon sound from
a drowse, and they see it: the lone arrow pricking from the slot of his helm. The boy
is thrust forward, a push like a blow, so that his stride is caught on a thrown shoulder,
and he stumbles, flinches from kissing the unseen flame. "No." A flicker hooks his
gaze, and out of the thousand pockets of tumult, he is cursed with seeing ... seeing ...
The same mouth slung about indecision, the same tipping look (though she hated
fear more). Nin'janjin leaps crisp from the tumult, his spear poised high, his shield a
burnished coin. The boy grimaces, cries out to the rag-garbed women—

What is your name?

She crinkles her nose. "Are you dying?"

Can a moment be caught? clapped like a fly in the palm of the heart that needed
it, a *memory*, painting deep the illumination of life. Can a moment be caught *by a*
moment? a heart within a heart within a heart, versions receding, a pit that sound the
very fathom of oblivion, life drawn into a spear. And he realizes he has never understood Men, not even when he loved them. Cu'jara Cinmoi turns into the nimil point,
cramps about the rod of ash, so that he crouches, every bit as crisp, his hands hooked,
sinking to his knees on the chest of the Host of Nine Mansions. His chin against his
breast, the boy lowers the torch like something that might break of its own weight.
The Copper Tree of Siol staggers, then falls. He lets it slip into the heaped bracken,
the boy. He runs intent, shield raised against raining pots of fire, sprinting from the
roar of barking massacre behind him into dismay. *Dead!* And the flames take shallow
root, spinning outward across the oil-soaked regions, smokeless lines which beget in-

cendiary blooms, until all the fuel heaped about his bound feet is skinned in frantic orange and gold, the fire sinking in, sparking deeper and deeper, unlocking curlicues of smoke, threads that become ribbons that become streaming plumes, hanging like ink, misting like fog, raising a shroud across the hollow sky, smearing the sun into a blinding stain. *Our Beloved King is dead!* And a cool falls across his scalp and shoulders, the gift of rolling fronds of smoke-shadow, even as the heat begins chewing his feet, biting and biting with dog's teeth. Fire is the youngest thing, the most ancient. They draw up his youngest, sweet Enpiralas, on an Inchoroi shield, his face flattened where the skull was missing. He rolls his gaze across the world, peers through the hazy screens, to the huddled knots of Men, and sees the demented grins of mortals inflicting their horror of death upon another, hands outstretched in wild gesture, fists beating his image, and the horsemen in gleaming cuirasses beyond, banners tipping as they yank short their galloping rush. And she grows still in his arms, Aisarinqu, at once kindling light, and a stone, such a heavy stone, and he weeps for holding her so punishing is her weight, his life unwinding for her density, the gravity of her stationary heart, her mouth hung about emptiness. He shrieks for the finality, for the *relief*, the sobbing knowledge that her suffering has ended, that he cradles oblivion in his arms. He begins choking, coughing up the convulsions that wrack his bound flesh, flap him like a blanket, for the fire was upon him, and he *could see it*, laving the white lines of his feet, the searing, the blistering, the charring—*his feet*, which had been with him since ... since ... now writhing and kicking of their own volition, and he throws his eyes skyward and he screams and he laughs, knowing that *this* ... this he would *remember*, that his burning would not pass through him, would not fall away into the black-of-black, but would dwell forever as another horror, so welding him to *who he had been*. The boy throws his hands to his eyes, only to have his father wrench them aside, shake him, point at the place that shrieks, writhes, burns. And he stands in the blackness, the eternal dank that rules the guttural foundations of Siol, his hand upon the neck and shoulder of *his* daughter, Aisralu, who even now clutches her belly, her womb, groaning against her headstrong pride, whispering, *Please ... Father ... Please ... You ... Must ...* again and again, searching for his eyes, her face a summit, a beauty he worships, bent into a pageant of strangers by anguish. He screams and he laughs and through smoke and undulating air he sees worry unbalance the beasts that caper about his perimeter. Aisarinqu screams and Aisarinqu screams, again and again, not so much words as a storm of occasions, her delicate face crushed into instants and flayed across an age, for theirs had not been a happy union. And it seems he should be a thing of wax, that the roaring phosphor should melt and consume him, not cook. *That is the sole curse of the Ishroi*, she hisses. He is a sack, a net bound about furious, ice-cold fish, each part of him thrashing, fleeing, and he howls realizing, for the first time in ten thousand years comprehending, that he is *a thing of meat*, that he is of the self-same flesh, the very thing that nourishes him, boar-squealing, bloody and alive. *To only* hope *they had fathered their sons!* His eyes are pinched and pricked by the effluence of the encircling furnace—no longer his own. The blackness falls away from her sagging face, and for an instant he gazes upon her, beloved Aisarinqu. A second, shrieking revelation. The white spark of some faraway light refracts in her tears, so that her contrition seems holy, and his embittered and profane. Fire is a thing that eats. A wondering instant, before the wrath seizes his fists anew.

He slumps into his corporeal anguish; burning seems ... proper.

A wind laves him, drawn in from the smoke-wreathed world, the radial distances, and blown upward through glittering rags of flame. He understands he is the base of an invisible pillar, a roiling column of heat, fluted and fanning into the shrouded sky, and he wonders whether a falcon might ride the updraft, the heat of his burning. The fish are warm now—sluggish. He glimpses armoured Men raising scabbarded swords, dropping them like clubs.

Please ... Father ...

Aisralu!

A glimpse of water, like a silver coin wobbling beneath the lip of an upraised pail, and it seems the most beautiful thing he has ever seen, a trophy scalped from the very sun. The little human girl, the one who found him where he cannot remember, the girl who was whipped by her father for stealing food out of pity, who sings songs in her queer, manling language, laughing for the way the stream tickles her feet, her face purpling above his grip, kicking and flailing like a woodland beast, as he sobs and explains to her, professing his love, his adoration. *I must ... I must remember.* Even before the coming of the Flesh Angels, the Inchoroi, they live lives long enough for children to become strangers. The torment has been a peculiar, more like a casting of liquid than a form of retribution. He ponders the way life bloats upon the threshold of dying.

Thinks it proper.

What is this hunger? Lights diminish, sputtering before being kicked into smoke by shadows. What is this need to strike meaning into the heart of stones? A different kind of nudity, chill and wet and horrifically amphibian. This blindness to surface—*what is it?* Voices. Something too absurd to be agony. His limbs vague and distant, twitches sensed only at the sockets. Hazy black bubbles clot the sky. Heaven tipping. Something ... his body ... jerking—shivering. Darkness, a shadow looming out from every corner of his vision, bricking him in. A Man leans over him, elbows out, hands on his thighs, and he sees a face that could belong to a brother, such is its beauty—and eyes that see only a blessed reprieve from boredom. "You smell of lamb ..." he says, bent across the spiking corona of the sun. Parasols of smoke float behind his head, drifting ...

"My kind cooks like pig."

And he is not dead.

He lies unbound, sprawled naked beneath the sprawling canopy of a tree. Everything tingles, and he understands he has been stripped of his skin, or a good part of it. He experiences another revelation, *that agony is the root*, the very truth of sensation, for the blades of the grasses had become knives, and the clicking legs of the spider had become needles, and the wind burns with a perpetual fire. They stand there, at the blackest heart of their dying Mansion, the deepest, the mountain above and about them groaning with the chorus of ten thousand lamentations—all the heart-cracking losses. "I confess, I did not believe it." There they stand, the famed father and the cherished daughter, their names no longer remembered, their sandalled feet upon the abyssal lip, so that emptiness yawns like a slow-waking dragon. A single Man sits beside him, clotted with shining insignia he has never seen before, saying, "They claim you killed a man's daughter." And it sickens him, the obscenity of the vision, the faces of his brothers—his *race!*— nailed like pelts to the abominations that loped across the scourged plains, pale save for the clotting of blood and excrement, screaming like girlish beasts, their members curved across their abdomens, running, shrieking. The Man's black hair trembles in the breeze, as fine as hummingbird feathers. An old yearning comes upon him—or the memory of one—his Ishroi brothers wading into the mobs of Halaroi, starved mothers clutching starved babes. "No matter ..." the Man says. "One must be *criminal* to commit a crime." He witnesses the magic that is brutality, the way cries become piteous silence and a jerking mandala of crimson. "One must be something *small* ..." A cold look of satisfaction. "And *you*, my False friend, smack of *immensity*."

His cousin, Pil'kmiras, curls like a dog on the dust, coughing about some unseen catastrophe. *Show me! Where?*

The Man's gaze searches the encircling World, squints for the glare. "We are alike in this regard." He raises a thumb to pick at his teeth. "When I was a child, my grandmother would raise me on her knee and tell me that I was *indistinguishable* from justice." He snorts. "'The *Gods*,' she would drawl—Grandmother split her passion between drinking and oblivion, you see. 'The *Gods* say that the *goodness* of our *acts*, my darling *dear*, resides in our *rank*. Do you *know* what this *means*, hmm?' She always liked to lean her forehead against mine. 'It *means* you cannot *sin* against your *lessersssss!*'" The Man breaks into a winning grin, one that should be remembered for its resemblance to vertigo. "Can you believe it? What grandmother says such things to a child?" The Wracu fall like barks of iron upon them. Bodies stick-whipping. Geysers of brilliance crossing like swords. "She's mad, my grandmother ... Mad with cunning." Yes ... *This* was what they suffered, the ones they dragged clear the fiery vomit, the way shrieking had delivered them to someplace calm, where they could swallow without taste. "Is beauty a *sign*, do you know?" the Man asks. "A mark of who defines justice? *These* are the kinds of questions I need to ask you ..." Skafra uncoils his shining bulk and reveals Par'sigiccas, half of him white flesh, half of him black charcoal. *What grieves thee, Son of Siol?* "I used to think my grandmother was wise because she was *old*. Now I think she is simply ... savage, I guess. Savage with fear ..." The Man pauses to work his jaw about an involuntary snarl. "But *you* ... You have seen things ... *times* ... You have witnessed what Men can scarce *dream*, let alone imagine!" *All great things,* the saurian maw croaks, *are round, Cinial'jin.* "Enough to rot you from the inside, they say ... Like a *melon.*" Par'sigiccas gazes with one eye from a half-husked skull. "You see, I look at you, and *I see* ..." A sly, mortal wink. "Me."

The Wracu seems skinned in flame. *Someday thou shalt tip over the edge of thine world.*

"This is why I saved you ... You are *my map.* My chart." Cu'jara Cinmoi leaps upon the altar, gloating, displaying the mad extent of his arrogance, openly, outrageously, knowing that his own would celebrate his impiety as strength, and that his enemies would cry out for heartbreak and fury. "I'm curious ..." He smiles in the sad way of mothers seeing mediocrity in their children. "Do you *feel* it? Or is it a thoughtless assumption, the fact that Men shrink in your presence?" There is a breath that belongs to the first glimpse of madness in some beloved soul, a hook and a pang, a consciousness of the tunnels that branch into caverns within you—a place where breath *should* be. *What Siöl requests, Siöl compels! The Cûn is a code of tyrants. When I stretch forth my hand, you shall be its shadow.* "What is the *sensation* of immortality? I'm sure I ... know it ... But without any to-to *compare* ..." The Man leans over him, his knife unnatural for its gleaming proximity to his face, something monolithic tapering to a shining prick, the point where earthly edges intersect, then cross over into death.

The humour was peeled from his eyes, revealing the dead dark look beneath. "I fear that I *require* that you speak."

Cu'jara Cinmoi's glare somehow slips the uproar and picks him from the confusion. *Yes. You know.*

Is he shaking?

He dandles the knife with the mock clumsiness of an elder brother teasing a younger. "You *must* have something to tell me. Surely the Whore delivered you for a reason." And they approach the northern entrance, the Way of Upright Kings, where the peach trees forever bloom out of season, finding naught but a great black rope of smoke hanging heavenward from the Mansion's shattered maw, inking the clouds. "Shh ... Shh ... Just tell me ..." The knife pricks across his cheek. "Tell me ..." And Lord Mountain turns as if from between worries, and they see it, the black shaft jutting from their hearts. And he watches, his spirit cringing, flinching, warding, even though he cannot move; the point's lazy swing, the hanging heartbeat above his pupil, then the drop, as though everything seen were the skin of a grape. Someone grimaces and screams. *How does one love in such times?* Aisarinqu whispers, cupping his head against her, so that his tears make a cheek of her breast. A laugh with the reed timbre of mortality. His face clenched as if about some splintered outrage. A mouth hung about emptiness. Something. Something in the meat. And it dawns that he does not comprehend these beasts.

A man reclines in the grasses that wreath his head, stares down at him with uncommon familiarity. And he just ... pushes ... her ... *Aisralu* ... A motion too banal to be anything but murderous and insane, opening a door, perhaps, or closing one, and he feels it, the kiss of skin forming to skin, the hand of the father across the nape of the daughter, the *cherished* daughter; a push and nothing more, an effort slight enough to slip the nets of awareness, to be no effort at all, and still, miraculously, *impossibly*, violent with excess, savage, a crime unlike any other; the bare palm against the nape of her neck, her shoulders hunched about a ravaged womb, his arm extending, the gentle insistence of nudging a younger brother toward a maid, and an *entire life* tipping, a cherished life, an engulfing presence, *tipping*, how? how? the push floating into slipping, plummet ... The wind barges through the walnut tree, a groaning susurrus. Tipping, the beloved voice crimped high, a kicking intake of breath, a sound that should strike sparks. *No* ... And a life slips into the abyss, dropping like water, lines sprawling across the plummet, shrinking into something small enough to be swallowed ... Shrieking. *No* ...

"You make me ... curious ..."

A man dangles from the glare of blood and sun. There is even envy in his gaze.

Please, Papa ...

A final revelation. Sunlight cracking through spanning limbs. The whole mountain wheezes for the weeping of thousands, the wreckage of ... The breeze burning, eating. The world tipping.

No.

A bare palm against a cherished back—

APPENDIX FOUR

Maps

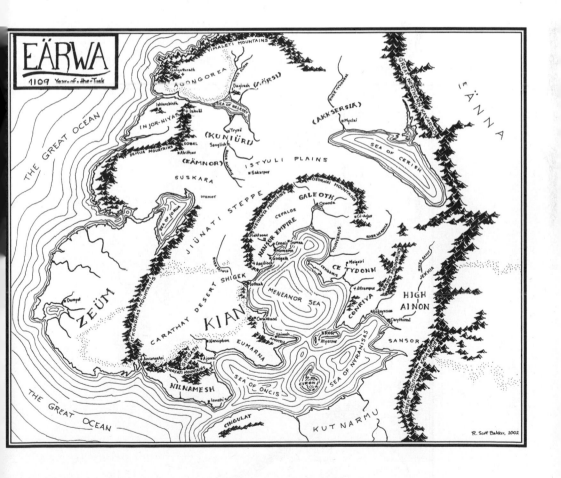

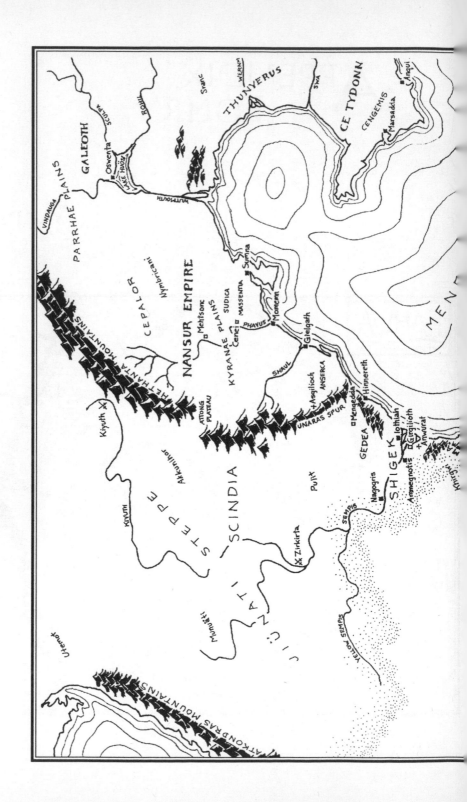

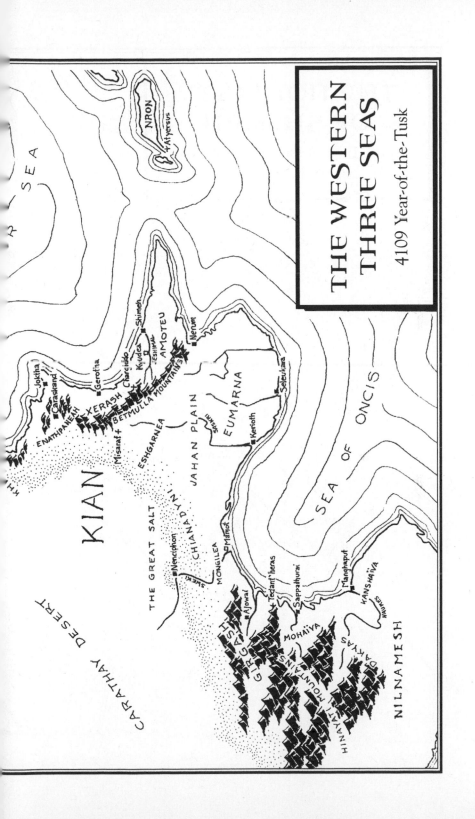

THE WESTERN THREE SEAS

4109 Year-of-the-Tusk

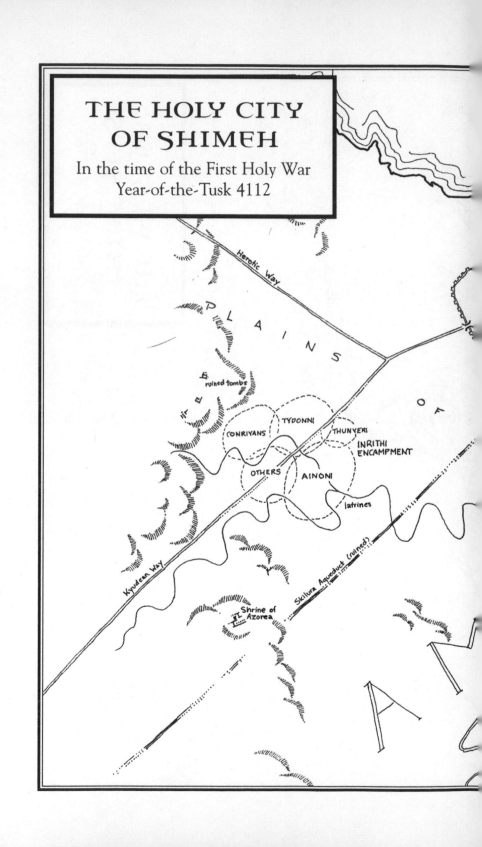

THE HOLY CITY
OF SHIMEH

In the time of the First Holy War
Year-of-the-Tusk 4112

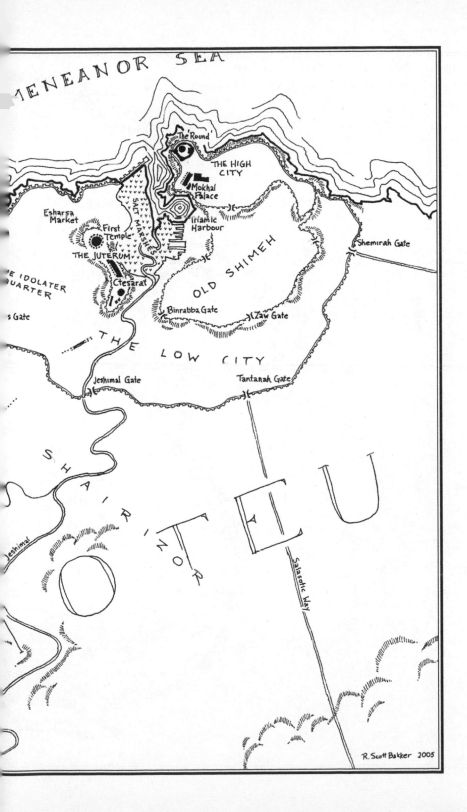

MENEANOR SEA

The Round

THE HIGH CITY

Mokhal Palace

Esharsa Market

First Temple

SALT MARSHES

Iriamic Harbour

THE JUTERUM

Shemirah Gate

THE IDOLATER QUARTER

Ctesarat

OLD SHIMEH

s Gate

THE LOW CITY

Binrabba Gate

Zaw Gate

Jeshimal Gate

Tantanah Gate

SHAIRIZOR

Jeshimal

EU

Salaschic Way

R. Scott Bakker 2005

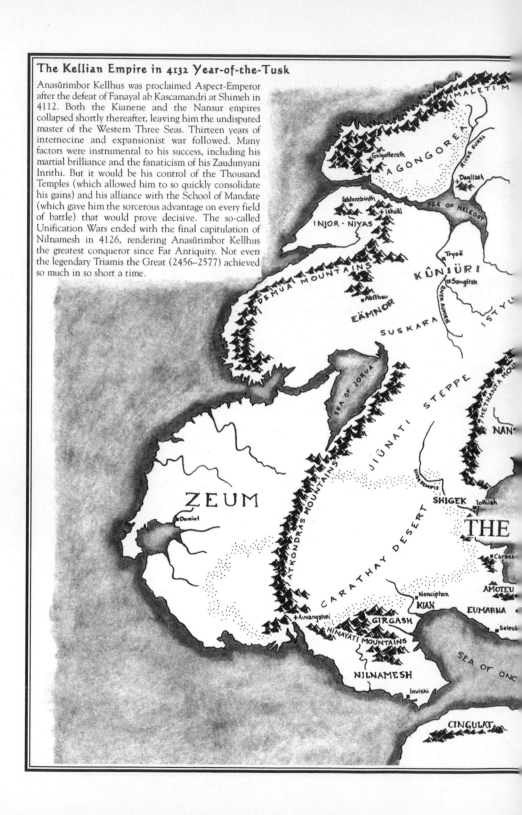

The Kellian Empire in 4132 Year-of-the-Tusk

Anasûrimbor Kellhus was proclaimed Aspect-Emperor after the defeat of Fanayal ab Kascamandri at Shimeh in 4112. Both the Kianene and the Nansur empires collapsed shortly thereafter, leaving him the undisputed master of the Western Three Seas. Thirteen years of internecine and expansionist war followed. Many factors were instrumental to his success, including his martial brilliance and the fanaticism of his Zaudunyani Inrithi. But it would be his control of the Thousand Temples (which allowed him to so quickly consolidate his gains) and his alliance with the School of Mandate (which gave him the sorcerous advantage on every field of battle) that would prove decisive. The so-called Unification Wars ended with the final capitulation of Nilnamesh in 4126, rendering Anasûrimbor Kellhus the greatest conqueror since Far Antiquity. Not even the legendary Triamis the Great (2456–2577) achieved so much in so short a time.

IMALETĪM

AGONGOREA

Golgotterath

RIVER SURTA

Dagliash

SEA OF NELEOST

Ishterebinth

Ishuäl

INJOR-NIYAS

Trysë

KÛNJÜRI

Sauglish

DEMUA MOUNTAINS

Aörsi

RIVER AUMRIS

Aörithau

EÄMNOR

SUSKARA

ISTYU

THE HĀNTA MOU

SEA OF JORUA

JIÜNATI STEPPE

NAN

ZEUM

ATKONDRAS MOUNTAINS

RIVER SEMPIS

SHIGEK

Iothiah

Domiot

CARATHAY DESERT

THE

Carask

Nenciphon

AMOTEU

KIAN

EUMARNA

Auvangshei

GIRGASH

Seleuk

HINAYATI MOUNTAINS

SEA OF ONC

NILNAMESH

Invishi

CINGULAT

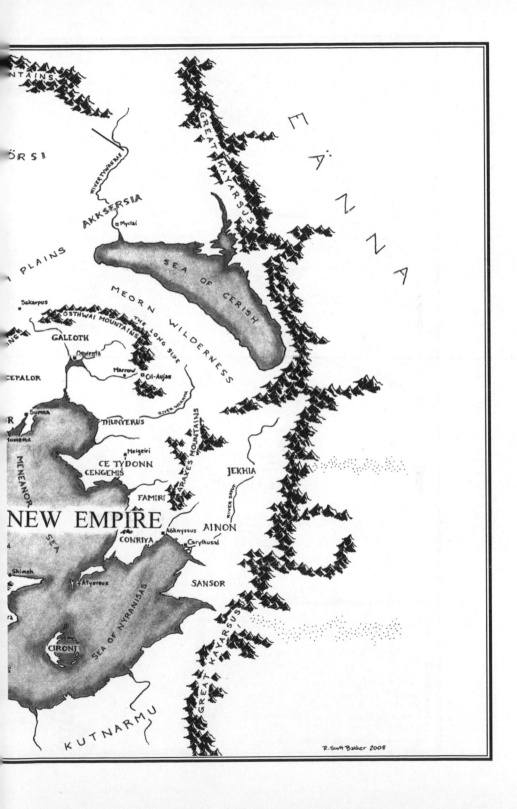

MOUNTAINS

ÖRSI

RIVER TYNHIRMU

AKKSERSIA

GREAT KAYARSUS

EÄ ZZA

Myclai

PLAINS

MEORN

Sakarpus

ÖSTHWAI MOUNTAINS

THE LONG SIDE

WILDERNESS

SEA OF CERISH

GALEOTH

Oswenta

CEPALOR

Marrow

Oil-Aujas

Sumna

RIVER WERNMA

THUNYERUS

Meigeiri

MENANOR

CE TYDONN

ARAXES MOUNTAINS

JEKHIA

CENGEMIS

FAMIRI

RIVER SAYUT

NEW EMPIRE

AINON

SEA

Aöknyssus

CONRIYA

Carythusal

Shimeh

SANSOR

Atyersus

SEA OF NYRANISAS

GREAT KAYARSUS

CIRONJ

KUTNARMU

GREAT KAYARSUS

R. Scott Bakker 2008

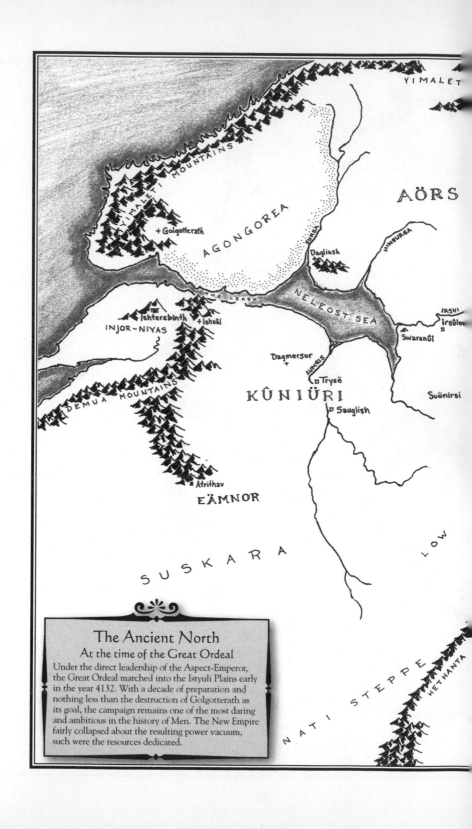

YIMALET

AÖRS

YIMALETI MOUNTAINS

+ Golgotterath

AGONGOREA

Dagliash

HINSURGA

THE LEASH

NELEOST SEA

IRSHI
Irsûlor

Swaranûl

INJOR~NIYAS

■ Ishterebinth
+ Ishuäl

Daqmersor
+

AUMRIS

□ Trysë

KÛNIÜRI

Suönirsi

DEMUA MOUNTAINS

□ Sauglish

■ Atrithau

EÄMNOR

S U S K A R A

L O W

The Ancient North
At the time of the Great Ordeal

Under the direct leadership of the Aspect-Emperor,
the Great Ordeal marched into the Istyuli Plains early
in the year 4132. With a decade of preparation and
nothing less than the destruction of Golgotterath as
its goal, the campaign remains one of the most daring
and ambitious in the history of Men. The New Empire
fairly collapsed about the resulting power vacuum,
such were the resources dedicated.

N A T I   S T E P P E

HETHANTA

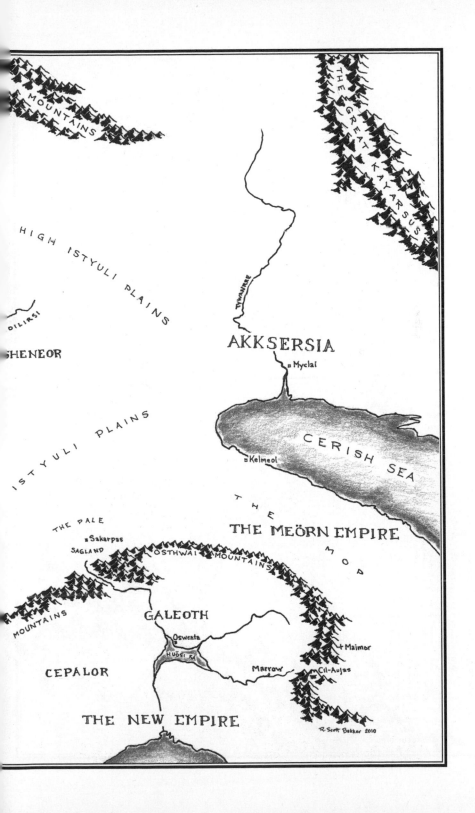

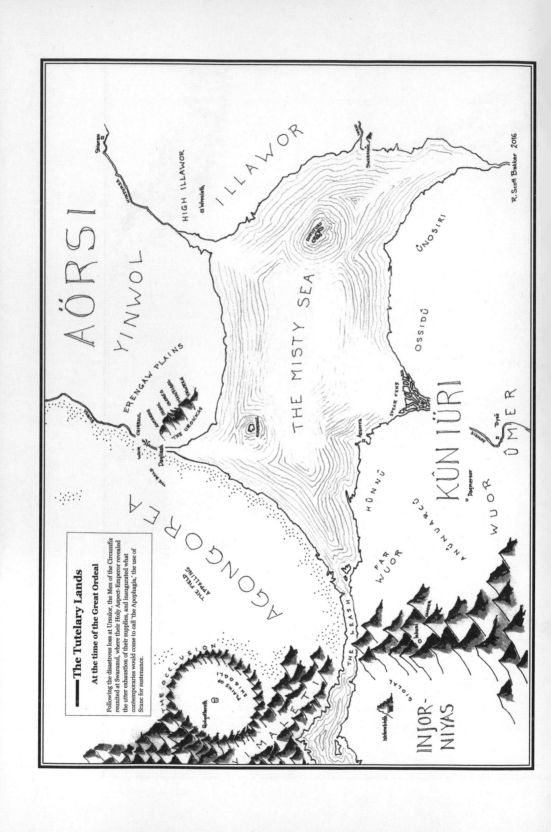

The Tutelary Lands

At the time of the Great Ordeal

Following the disastrous loss at Ursulor, the Men of the Circumfix reunited at Swaranul, where their Holy Aspect-Emperor revealed the utter exhaustion of their supplies, and inaugurated what contemporaries would come to call 'the Apophagia,' the use of Sranc for sustenance.

AÖRSI

YINWOL

HIGH ILLAWOR

ILLAWOR

ERENGAW PLAINS

THE UROKKAS

AGONGOREA

THE OCCLUSION

PLAINS OF MENGEDDA

YIMALETTI

THE MISTY SEA

SPEAR FENS

KÛNIÛRI

HÛNNÛ

FAR WUOR

WUOR

ÜMER

ANGUIRZISH

INJOR-NIYAS

THE LEASH

THE PELD APPALLING

R. Scott Bakker 2016

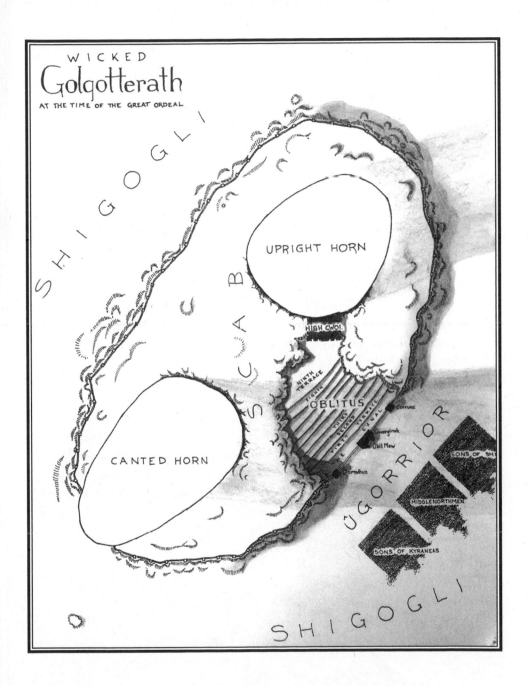

Acknowledgments

What a journey it has been. Each life is a caravan, and the same could be said of every book as well. Now, seven volumes in, the journey has become nothing if not *migratory*, a project turning on a great many people in countless ways. My family, of course, makes the whole thing possible. Sharron and Ruby are my binary star system—the reason for life on my planet. I need to thank my Agent, Chris Lotts, along with everyone who makes him possible. I need to thank Tracy Carns, Michael Mah, and the crews at Overlook and Orbit. My beta readers, Mike Hillcoat, Zach Rice, Andy Tressler, Jason Deem, Ken Thorpe, Bryan Bakker, and Roger Eichorn deserve special mention, as does Mike Roy. I want to thank everyone who participates at the Second Apocalypse forum and at Three Pound Brain.

I would also like to give a shout-out to all those who have joined this mad trek, all my fellow scalpers on the Slog. This series is unlikely in so many ways that only you, ultimately, could make it possible. An epic fantasy series with a companion piece in *The Journal of Consciousness Studies*! That would be some crazy shit, as the saying goes. I have to thank you, gentle reader, for suffering this old Schoolman for a span, and listening to his apocalyptic tales, both real and imagined.